BREAKING JADE

A COMPANION BOOK TO FALLOCAUST BOOK 1

QUIL CARTER

Breaking Jade Copyright © 2014 by Quil Carter

All rights reserved. No part of this book may be used or reproduced in any manner whatsoever without written permission except in the case of brief quotations embodied in critical articles or reviews.

www.quilcarter.com

Cover by Quil Carter with help from Giced photo

First Edition

1508414459

978-1508414452

This book is dedicated to AJ, who was a very special little cat.

Hug your kitty today.

BOOK 1

Imprisoned

CHAPTER 1

THE BLUE EMBER WAS LIKE A SMALL SAPPHIRE SUN, giving the room a pale ambience that was only intensified by billows of menthol-scented smoke seeping out of the cigarette.

It was Skyland made, the elite district hidden inside Skyfall. Though what Tiger of Nyx was doing with one of them the thief didn't know. Perhaps it was an attempt to show off his wealth, though if this was the case he was flaunting his feathers at the wrong guy. Throwing around expensive novelties only made Jade suspect this man felt he had something to prove. A novice mistake that usually ended up with betrayal or a robbery.

Tiger picked up a small music player, a Discman, and turned it on. The CD whirred in its plastic case and the high timbre of music through headphones broke the smoky silence in the room. The fence nodded and placed it onto an adjacent pile. The only things that remained in the pile were VHS tapes and a gold ring.

He regarded these last items with an uninterested expression. Blowing silvery smoke onto the pile, he made a disappointed clucking noise with his tongue.

That's it? That's what he does to try and drive down the price? Surely he doesn't think I'm that stupid. Jade resisted furrowing his brow; instead he took a puff of his own cigarette. It had a red ember like every other smoke that wasn't Skyland made.

Tiger opened the VHS tape of *Independence Day* and checked the ribbon. Jade knew it was perfect though, he had already checked. The fence tsked and slid it back into the faded cardboard case.

The fences were all cut from the same cloth. If it wasn't Tiger trying to screw him, it was Badger, and if it wasn't Badger it was Shark. They were all the same, and their dance got tiring after a while.

"Twenty dollars," Tiger said, stressing his obviously fake Russian accent; someone had been watching too many movies. Though it could have been worse: Shark liked talking like a mafia don. Jade found it hard to try and keep a straight face when he was doing business with that joke.

"Thirty, or just leave it," Jade said flatly. Though the other thieves liked bargaining, it annoyed Jade no end. The atmosphere around him made him tense, and he disliked being in such a dark room with people he didn't know. If they would meet on his turf, on his game board, sure - kick back, have a beer and shoot the shit. But this was Nyx, the middle class district of Skyfall. There were thiens around and, unlike the ones in Moros, they didn't turn a blind eye to the black market.

When the fence glanced up at him, the cigarette clenched between his teeth, Jade didn't even blink. Wavering was for rookies and he had been tempered to this since he left the orphanage.

Tiger stood up and took another inhale before offering the smouldering tailor-made to Jade.

Jade took it without hesitation, the blue flame turning his golden eyes green as he inhaled. Skyland cigarettes were smooth and sharp and didn't make you feel like you'd just inhaled drain cleaner like the Moros smokes. Inside, Jade felt his stress dissipate under the tangy nicotine.

"Your eyes, they freak me out." Tiger's face turned into a sneer. "So I cut you a deal just to get your face out of mine." With a flick of blond-streaked brown hair he turned around and motioned for a nearby woman to come closer. The woman was dressed in a skimpy outfit that looked more like a swimsuit and was obviously a slave. She walked towards Tiger and waited to be instructed.

Tiger handed her a bag before wheeling himself back to the counter that separated thief and fence.

Jade eyed the bag, but what its contents were was beyond him, though they had better be good.

"Twenty, no more bargaining. But just so you feel like you won, since I know how you Morosians are, I'll throw in some fruit to seal the deal."

He knows what I like... he must've talked to Shark before he started filling in for him.

Jade blew the smoke from his mouth and handed the cigarette back. "What are we talking about?"

Tiger gave him a smile, his steel teeth sparkling blue hues from the cigarette's reflection. The thick-necked Nyxian looked proud of himself, though why was anyone's guess. Fruit was worth more in Moros than money. When the diet in the slums was tact, ramen noodles, drugs, and alcohol it was hard to get the nutrients the body needed. No one sold fruit or vegetables in Moros; it all had to be stolen or bought for a huge mark-up in Nyx or the surrounding districts.

This resulted in most Morosians looking like thin, boney skeletons. Most were grey-faced and sunken-in like they were addicted to drugs, which in some cases they were, but even the straight shooters had a look to them that told you death was only a cold winter away.

At least in Edgeview Orphanage they had vitamin shots, so most of the kids grew up looking decent enough; not stunted like some family-raised kids. But once you hit thirteen you were out on your own. Because of that, most people peaked at about thirteen.

"You'll like this, Shadow." Tiger waved a hand and one of his pets came forward with a small plastic bag. The pet handed it to him before disappearing into the corner of the room.

Jade looked inside; two peaches and two plums. He hadn't had those in a while.

Jade took the bag and gave Tiger a nod. After an exchange of money and goods Jade walked back to his bicycle. It would be an hour long bike ride back to Moros, but his pockets were full and he had a good dinner for him and Kerres.

In all respects it was mission accomplished, though it was never enough for the golden-eyed Morosian. Even though his jacket pockets were full of his spoils, his eyes automatically fell on every lit window he biked past. They all sung to him like angels from the heavens, suggesting what wonderful treasures could be nestled inside, just ripe for stealing.

What would Kerres say if I came home with a milk crate full of peaches for him? Jade's eyes followed a slightly ajar window, behind a concrete and barbed wire fence he knew he could climb. Nyx was just asking for some thievery, but no, he had to get home.

Patience wasn't one of Jade's strong points. When he saw an opportunity he went for it head first, but this time he kept turning the pedals on his bike and left the riches of Nyx for the next visit. It wasn't due to self-control, or even because of his success fencing his goods. It was because of the interesting man he had met the previous day.

Jade drew his hood over his head as he felt the first droplets of rain on his neck. The man he had met would be taking shelter under the Hallon Bridge tonight; the suspension bridge that connected Nyx and Eros over a river long since turned to murky ripples of ghoulish brown. The man, a pensive sort with a chip on his shoulder, had given him the most fascinating information.

It was the fact that the man was so close to Eros which had first captured Jade's interest, and his appearance was confirmation that he might actually be serious.

The man wasn't a slumrat like Jade; he was blond, slight, and beautiful with tawny eyes and white teeth. He looked as though he could have been a servant for the chimeras. If he had been another dirt-streaked waster in ratty clothing, Jade would have told him to fuck off.

The class difference between the elites, the middle class, and the slummers was distinct. Everything from their looks, to the way they spoke, to how they dressed was different. The elites draped their healthy bodies in new, fitted clothing suited to their status. They lived in refurbished homes without mould and water damage, and dined on fruit and vegetables. They were living the good life in the Fallocaust.

Jade's throat tightened. Though it was jealousy he was feeling, he would never dare admit that fully to himself. Instead he reminded himself over and over again that they were nothing but soft, pampered rich fucks who knew nothing of suffering; nothing of having to struggle just to stave off rickets and starvation. The only people who had it rougher were the greywasters, though at least they could scavenge anything they wanted out there. They just had to risk getting their faces gnawed off by the crazy people, or worse yet, King Silas's monsters. They were still poor as dirt though, with a life expectancy of around thirty-five. Or at least that's what the merchants Jade knew had said.

It was one of those merchants that had directed him to the man under the bridge...

Jade felt a quiver in his heart as he ran a hand over the breast pocket of his jacket; an electric percussion that filled him with a bright, shuddering anxiety. He pushed it down with a discipline he only liked to imagine he had and carried on towards Moros.

It was a long bike ride, but it would be warm for at least a few more months. He, Kerres, and his friends had survived the last winter, though barely. The next one would be worse – every year it was worse. No matter how much fruit he fenced for himself and Kerres, it never seemed to be enough. Like every other Morosian, they were slowly starving, slowly dying.

Pulling into the long alleyway to their apartment, he heard an all-too-familiar voice calling from a recess in one of the buildings.

"J, you want something to warm you up tonight?"

Jade gave the man a glance and got off of his bike; his dwelling was near enough anyway.

"What do you have today?" Jade checked around him to make sure a thien wasn't in bothering distance and ducked into the alcove, a fire exit for a building whose upper half was just a shell of metal beams.

"Opium, weed, meth, got crack too, Skyland quality, bro." Fiere dropped his voice.

Jade had no desire to stay up for the next three days, and crack was always too addictive. He bought a small lump of opium and a dime bag of weed for the weekend. With the drugs, fruit, and newly-earned money in his pocket he made his way up the rubber-coated stairs of their apartment building. No one could say he was returning empty-handed. He felt like a pirate in the pre-Fallocaust days, his body fully stocked with stolen loot.

Jade reached into his pockets and dug out his keys. He unlocked the apartment door and walked in.

The apartment was small, but for the two of them it was a perfect size. One bedroom, a small kitchen they only used to boil ramen water, and a den. For a Moros apartment it was in fair shape; the paint was half scraped off, the couch old and torn, and the cabinets warped from water damage and mould. The rent was low though, fifty bucks a month and it included electricity and running water: cold and hot.

As Jade hung up his jacket and took off his shoes, he immediately sensed the aura of his boyfriend. It always seemed green to him, like the hues the ocean used to get on a sunny day. It felt like a cool breeze inside his mind whenever he was near it. It's what had attracted Jade to Kerres when he had first been put into the care of Edgeview. A breath of cold ocean air in the throes of his sickness, he could almost taste the sea salt.

Kerres turned his head and gave Jade a smile. He had hair-sprayed his reddish-brown hair today, which meant he must've been at the bar earlier; the faint aroma of alcohol only confirmed it.

"You look successful." Kerres got up and gave him a welcome kiss, taking the bag of fruit and looking inside.

He gave an impressed whistle and picked up one of the peaches. He held it to his nose and gave an exaggerated sigh. "It amazes me that you find this sort of shit. I'll cut these up for us; why don't you have a hot shower. I was just about to smoke a joint."

Jade was more than happy to oblige. It had been a long trip home and the rain water had soaked him to the bone. He stripped himself naked and stepped into the bathroom.

It wasn't much, but it was theirs and they didn't have to share with anyone else. A toilet with a broken lid, the bottom rusted from both water and stale urine. A white sink with pliers stuck to both of the hot and cold water taps. The taps were missing the turning mechanisms and Jade wasn't going to start looking for replacements since they only rented. Then there was the bathtub, with a stained blue shower curtain. The tub had been white once but now it was more a muddled brown. Not even Tate, who worked with cleaning chemicals, could scrape the grime that had stained the tub; they had given up long ago.

Jade stepped in and turned up the hot water. With a relieved sigh, relieved to have made it through another day, he let the hot water take him to places he knew he would never visit. A tropical island like the one on 'Gilligan's Island' was today's fantasy, where the sun was bright, and the plants green, the sand was white and not ruddy and full of diseases. It might be farfetched, especially in this world, but life was dull without baseless fantasies.

Though even if it did exist it would be no place for a Morosian slumrat like him. It would be full of Skylanders and chimeras; they would turn their noses up at Jade and shoot him in the leg for even asking.

Jade was the king of his little thieving world, and he had the connections to fence anything he stole, but in the scheme of things he was just a low class slumrat and he knew it. It was forgetting your place in the many folds of Skyfall that got you killed. Jade might've been a thief, but he never got too big for his pants. He took pride in his side-job, even if everyone else looked down their nose at him.

Never forget who you are. They had told all of them that as soon as they left the orphanage. *You are the lowest class of Skyfall; in all respects you are no better than the greywasters. Silas was just kind enough to let you stay in the protection of Skyfall, instead of kicking your worthless asses to the wasteland.*

Although at least in the greywastes they were free.

Jade scratched the microchip behind his ear. It had his name, his birth date, and his class imbedded in it, as well as his criminal and medical history. In the greywastes, they only had Geigerchips. They weren't known at all to King Silas and Skyfall unless they were in blocks, and even then all they had was their blood on file.

Jade brushed back his damp black hair, and sat down on the musty couch. He started to roll off a piece of opium, listening to Kerres chopping the fruit in the kitchen. It was the weekend now, and they didn't have to work until Monday. He wanted to celebrate his success a little bit differently tonight.

There was also another thing to be excited about…

He waited until Kerres sat down with two bowls of sliced fruit sprinkled with white sugar before he decided to tell him.

Jade took a moment to eat a few slices of peach. His taste buds burned with the intense flavour, the sugar filling him with an electric rush.

He licked his fingers and gauged Kerres's mood. He seemed in a good spirits, perhaps this would go over smoothly.

"So I got some interesting news today…" Jade let that drag; he glanced up under his brow and watched Kerres.

Kerres's stiff crimson bangs fell over his eyes as he paused. He swallowed the fruit in his mouth and looked at Jade, his expression skeptical but curious, two emotions he had felt many times in their relationship.

"The twin chimeras, Ares and Siris, are away for two weeks."

Kerres stared at Jade for a moment. "I hope you didn't pay money for this intel."

If Kerres wasn't a factory worker full time and more into the darker underbelly of Moros, he might understand why this was the information of the year.

"Are you kidding?" Jade said. "Their mansion is huge and borders on Skyland and Eros. Do you know the valuables I could rob from them? And they won't know for weeks. It would be laundered, fenced, and long gone before then."

Kerres leaned forward with an exasperated sigh. He grabbed a cigarette with fingers stained yellow from smoke and lit it. The red cherry brightened as he took a drag.

Still hunched over, Jade shook his head, the smoke dangling from his fingers.

"Have you ever seen those two, Jade? They're tanks; they'll snap you in half, literally."

Jade had expected this resistance and had prepped himself for it on the way home.

"They'll be gone, and they won't even know the shit is missing until…"

"They probably have some security measures."

Jade's lips broke in a grin; he had been hoping Kerres would voice the obvious. He reached into his pocket and slammed a keycard down on the table.

Kerres's dark eyes widened; he looked at the keycard as though Jade had just slapped down a gold bar. Jade couldn't help but revel in his boyfriend's surprise; he didn't even bother hiding the gloating expression on his face.

"Whose keycard is that?"

Jade picked it up and slid it over each finger. "I picked it up from one of their ex-servants. They broke his leg and sent him to Nyx but he managed to smuggle his card out. He wants half of the money profit I get from selling. Laundered and clean. He knows I have the skills to pull it off."

Kerres didn't doubt that. Jade's name was common with the lawbreakers of Moros; his shady reputation was as thick as the filth that collected in the alleyways. He was well-known as someone who could get anything done for a price and make any item disappear into the underground.

Jade watched as Kerres dipped the cigarette into their overflowing ashtray and then leaned back with a shake of his head, the couch squeaking under the pressure.

"You realize if they catch you – you won't be coming back, right?"

It was as if Kerres had brought a black cloud into the room; the reality Jade had been running from since he got the keycard from the servant coming with it.

Yes, it was dangerous, stupid in some respects, but...

He needed a change. This winter had to be different.

Jade put the keycard down to light his needle of opium. He dangled the pen straw between his lips and inhaled the bitter smoke.

Almost immediately he felt the colours around him brighten, and the waving cluster of orgasmic warmth. Jade drew his knees up to his chest and felt his head tip. His eyelids became weighted down and he felt them closing. With a pull of his spectral mind he went inside himself, where the colours were sharper.

I need a change...

He had been born in the slums to a mentally ill mother and raised under her sporadic care until the age of nine. Jade knew his place in Skyfall and he had grudgingly accepted it. When the thiens bullied them, or when the elites spat on them from above, he took it with a stiff upper lip and walked on. There was no use in kicking up a fuss or being resistant. All it earned you was a beating from the thiens or a verbal tongue-lashing from the elites. There was no winning, no use in writhing in your social chains. Jade had been dealt a shitty poker hand in life, but he had made the most of it.

Though he might live in a sewer, at least he was the king of his own sewer. As long as he kept himself a few paces ahead of law enforcement, and watched his back around people outside his core group, he was fine. A better existence than the fake reality of the Erosians, Skylanders, and even worse, the cum-sucking chimeras who ruled all of them.

Jade's lips tugged into a frown; he shifted himself feeling the thready couch on his neck. The chimeras, fuck them. They didn't give a shit about Moros; they had condemned the slumrats to rot in their appointed district. Unable to move up in the world, damned to spin their wheels in the slums.

Born in Moros, die in Moros. The only chance they got to make a life for themselves was if they defected and tried their luck in the greywastes, and that was as good as a death sentence.

In Skyfall, you could always be demoted to a lesser district, but it was a rare thing for you to be promoted without a large amount of money. It was unheard of in Moros. The only way you could move up was with an altered ID chip and those were so out of reach for the typical paycheck of a Morosian, it was laughable.

So they stayed, and worked in the industrial factories or did hard labour at the harbour. Then they died. Not 'got old and died' though, because no one really got old here.

"I'll come back." Jade flashed a confident smile and popped a piece of peach into his mouth. When Kerres didn't return his warm smile, Jade sighed and switched on Skyfall TV, though Kerres's glaring eyes remained in the corner of his vision.

And he never said more than a few words afterwards, even when their mutual friends Fiere (who knew from being their dealer that there was opium smoking going on tonight), Tate, and Pete came over to bullshit for a while; Kerres was still tight-lipped – never too old to give Jade the silent treatment.

They spent the evening doing opiates and taking dabs of mushroom powder that made everything in Jade's vision shimmer and pulsate. The drugs helped the evenings go by; when work was done and everyone had managed to find enough to eat, there really wasn't anything else to do.

Jade half-listened to Tate's story about robbing an Eros house, his mind more often than not drifting to the card key he had hidden in his jacket. Kerres's warning was fresh in his brain.

But though he should've known better, Jade knew this was an opportunity he couldn't cower away from. Besides the obvious: new boots and some winter clothing for Sheryn, this could fetch him enough money to buy his way to a promotion at work, or get into the manager's good books. So it wasn't just items he could gain from this, he could move up in the world. Maybe even eventually save up for a black market ID chip that could get him into Nyx or maybe even Eros.

Anything but here...

"Hey, Jade?" Pete hit his foot; a man shorter than most, wiry and with wild eyes that were unsuited to his calm demeanour. "I saw your mom down by Garrett Park; she asked you if you had any spare blankets. Told me a story about a man stealing hers. I dunno, sounds like bullshit but she made me promise to pass it along."

Jade's mood dampened, threatening to sour on him. "I'll go see her tomorrow."

He felt the aura around Kerres give a pulse, or perhaps it was his own. With the hallucinogens clouding his empathic abilities, sometimes it was hard to tell. Either way, someone in the room didn't like Jade's mom being mentioned and it was either him or Kerres.

She wasn't a good mother, and when Jade was nine the chimera state had had enough and Jade was taken away from her. He was thrown in an orphanage and she had continued to be homeless.

That had been one of the first times in his life he'd stayed indoors in the same place for more than six months. From his earliest memories he remembered being pushed in a wagon from place to place by her. Because of that, Jade knew every corner of Moros, both good and bad. He knew what abandoned houses were good for shelter, and what heat vents from buildings could keep him alive on cold nights. Thankfully, when he started to learn how to control his empath abilities, he could tell which man would help him, and which one would hurt him. Most men his mother brought home only wanted to hurt him, but that was no surprise. His mother had been the one who wanted to hurt him the most.

Well, hospital stays did mean a warm place, a nice meal, and kind nurses. The nurses had been the ones to finally surrender him to the orphanage.

"I'll do it," Kerres said. He looked over at Jade and lifted a bottle of root beer to his lips. "We have that blanket the rats chewed; I wanted to toss it anyway."

Kerres was always finding a way, any way, to prevent Jade from seeing his mother and for good reason. Seeing her usually caused Jade to feel down and depressed for the next several days and, if he didn't watch himself, he got sick.

Sheryn had a lot of problems, and she always elicited a mixture of guilt and anger in Jade, knowing he was the cause of most of those problems. To get attention she used to hurt him physically, mentally, and emotionally. Most of the time it was in a subtle way, like poisoning his food or infecting the cuts he got as a child; other times it was more obvious.

Her problems hadn't gone away when Jade had left Edgeview Orphanage. She was still the same woman when he and Kerres had gotten their own place and jobs. Still crazy, still homeless, and still keen on being in her son's life.

"I'll go with you," Jade said with a nonchalant shrug, though he might regret it once the drugs wore off. Though if he did see her, then that would do him for the month. He tried to go down to Garrett Park at least once a month to see how she was doing; make sure she had enough tact to keep her from starving, and blankets for whatever season was upon them. He had given up trying to find her cheap shelters to stay in; she always ended up getting kicked out or beat up in the hospital. He had stopped feeling bad about that years ago.

Kerres started playing with Jade's hair; the mention of Jade's mother always brought out the sensitive side in him. Kerres had seen first-hand the toxic effect Sheryn had on her son, and had been trying to steer Jade away from meeting with her. Over the years though, he had grudgingly accepted Jade's guilt and settled for being there to monitor their interactions.

"Please… don't go to Skyland," Kerres whispered to him that night, after their friends had gone home and it was just the two of them in bed together.

Jade could see the flickers of Kerres's oceanic aura around him; even in darkness he couldn't escape the odd gift he had.

Jade reached out and traced it; it was like a tick, he always had to touch his friends' auras, trying to make his mental abnormality as tangible as he could. "I'll be fine."

Kerres sighed and Jade felt the muffled sound of him shifting over in bed. Then a moment later he felt a kiss on his neck, signalling that he wouldn't surrender his boyfriend to sleep that easily.

To distract himself from Kerres's worried eyes he climbed onto him, though his mind was still in his jacket, resting beside the keycard.

His break… his chance… a risk he had to take.

CHAPTER 2

THE GRASS WAS COVERED IN A THIN LAYER OF DEW; IT stuck to Jade's sneakers which were now squishing with every step. He needed new shoes before winter, but that was a luxury he knew he would have to do without, at least until he robbed the Dekker twins.

Then I could buy army boots, the good kind. The kind the Legion wear, suited for any climate and even travelling in the greywastes.

Jade's toes wiggled with anticipation; he looked down and noticed Kerres's old boots were just as bad. He imagined the look on his boyfriend's face when he handed him a brand new pair of leather boots. Those full lips would smile, his deep brown eyes would squint under that same smile and, heck, maybe he would even squeak.

That thought made Jade happier than thinking of getting the boots himself; he loved making Kerres happy. He deserved it.

Jade shielded his eyes as he scanned the park, looking for the garbage-strewn roost that would be his mother's dugout. He couldn't spot her though, just their fellow Morosians loitering around, and some maintenance men clipping the bushes and mowing the green grass. Apparently in the Fallocaust there was no grass, the world had killed all of it. But in Skyfall many parks had seeds and the fertilizer to grow them, even with the grey sun. There was nowhere else besides Skyfall where grass and green bushes were found, only in the parks and in the gardens of the residents rich enough to afford them.

"There she is..." Kerres said, his tone dark.

Jade felt Kerres's hand slip into his and he held it tight. There, up ahead, was Sheryn.

The old woman, with bushy black hair streaked with white, a wrinkled face, and small dark eyes, was sitting on a ratty grey blanket. A shopping cart was resting beside her, full of her worthless possessions, and tied to that cart was a small rat-like dog. Jade had forgotten his name but he was a dick who growled at everyone until he got a good kick in the ribs.

When she saw them, she slowly got to her feet. She wasn't that old, only in her middle forties, but being homeless and a drunk her whole life had taken its toll physically, not to mention the lack of nutrition and clean water. Now her bones looked like they ached and she always had sores on her creased face, probably from heroin or meth; Jade never stuck around long enough to ask.

"Jade... Jade..." Sheryn smiled, only four teeth left in her mouth. She turned around and started rummaging through her bag. The dog gave a growl but as soon as he got close enough, Jade gave him a swift kick in the ass and the animal slinked beside the shopping cart.

"I made you your favourite..."

Jade tensed and he felt Kerres squeeze his hand. Out of all the things for her to say, she had to say those five words. They held more weight than anything else she could've said.

Sheryn turned around; she held a can of beans with a spoon sticking out from the top. She nodded, still smiling, holding them out to Jade.

They would be spiked with something... they always were... no matter how much he wished she would stop trying to poison him; they always had something in them.

But she could no longer drag him to the hospital to get attention from the doctors and nurses, or to neighbours for sympathy. Jade had his own life now, and his time being hurt by his mother had passed.

"Put that away!" Kerres snapped.

Inside Jade's chest stirred. Kerres knew how to handle her, Jade never did. He would just take a bite to please her, even if he was puking his guts out afterwards. He never ate enough to kill him and it made her happy...

Jade wasn't weak or submissive, and yet he was a useless slop when it came to his mother.

The boy pushed down his inner hatred at his own remark; his feelings towards his mother varied like the tides. Sometimes he hated her, but most of the time he just felt guilty. Like she had been telling him his entire life – it was all his fault.

The only break he had ever gotten was when he was at the orphanage. They wouldn't let her near him then, but once he was out of Skyfall custody and became an adult of Moros, his protection from her had ceased.

"Do you need any food? Or water?" Jade asked.

Kerres reached over and took the fringed blanket from his boyfriend and handed it to the woman, though his facial expression told everyone around him that he wanted nothing more than to strangle her with it.

Sheryn shook her head, but even though one shake or two would be enough, she kept shaking it; even when her eyes looked back up at them her head shook back and forth, messing up her already tangled hair.

Jade turned and walked away, to let her be with whatever was happening in her head when her voice sounded behind him.

"You think you're so much better than me?"

Jade turned around.

The can connected with Jade's forehead, skinning his eyebrow before falling to the ground with a clang.

"You're a thankless little shit! Don't go thinking you're something you're not... too full of yourself to take food your mother made for you? Not good enough for the Prince of Moros!?"

This wasn't new... it had never been new... he had grown up hearing this. Jade's teeth ground together as he flicked a couple of beans off of his jacket, ignoring the wetness he could feel trickling down his brow.

"I made you your favourite!"

"Mom... do you – do you need any water?" Jade stumbled, even as Kerres was pulling on his hand to steer them away. The dog, in all of the commotion, had started barking and growling at the two of them; his short shoelace leash taut as he lunged and tried to pull the shopping cart with him. People began to stop and stare, making the back of Jade's neck go hot from embarrassment.

"I made that for you! For you! You're a horrible son, you think you're so great... you're not!" the woman roared. Kerres gave Jade's arm a final tug.

"I would be in movies if it wasn't for you... in movies!" she screamed, and as her shouts grew weaker she started to get more desperate. "You aren't even my son! You yellow-eyed jinn! Get out of here, shapeshifter!"

Jade groaned and pursed the inner corners his eyes with his fingers, in response Kerres pulled him and, this time, even though Jade stumbled, he didn't stop.

"Why do you keep doing this to yourself?" Kerres asked sharply.

They leaned against the walls that separated Moros and Nyx, sharing a cigarette.

Because it's my fault she's like this. Instead of spilling his emotions, he just shrugged.

Kerres stared for a moment longer but didn't push it. Such was their relationship. Kerres knew Jade enough to not dig out information; he got what he needed when Jade was stoned or high as a kite. Any other time, Jade was a fortress of cold resolve and buried emotions.

Though in Moros you had to be like that. At the first sign of weakness you got your throat torn out and devoured. Dog eat dog, that was the rule both spoken and unspoken. And with that the residents of Moros grew up to be their own little statues of hardened emotion. Emotions were for the weak and showing them on your face was for idiots.

Jade looked around to make sure no one was watching. Then he scanned the evergreens and tall bare rocks for anyone he might know. He was one of the top thieves and all the fencers knew him. He had to keep up appearances; there were always Morosians in the dark, cloaked and daggered, waiting to stab Jade in the back.

Just look at Sheryn… she was weak and the Morosians preyed on her constantly and on Jade when he was younger. She had sold him several times for drinking money, and though he had been able to get away most of the time, it was still a display of everything wrong with their slum district.

But you can get away…

Jade stole another drag of the cigarette before passing it back to Kerres. He leaned his back against the cold concrete and tried to enjoy the silence. It was always quiet by the walls, too far out of the hub of Moros for most people to care. No one visited here anyway; it was the gates where the activity was.

The gates from Moros to Nyx weren't guarded or even locked. Everyone was free to come and go as they pleased, but if they got into trouble in a different district the penalties were worse. They had a friend who had gotten arrested for pick-pocketing in Skyland; he was never seen again.

Kerres picked up a rock and tossed it onto the empty paved road in front of them. Half-broken buildings revealed burnt skeletal beams underneath, the structures blocking their view of the rest of Moros. Most of the buildings here were in the same state; brick and plaster had shed away like skin, only steel beams and rebar poked through to taste the air. No one with a job would live there but the crumbling buildings were a haven for gang hangouts, drug dens, and the homeless.

These were empty though. Too close to the borders for most people's liking; humans by nature liked to cluster as close to the center as they could, the outskirts seemed to void that safe feeling.

Another rock got tossed; it bounced several times before laying to rest up against the cracked curb. Besides their breathing that was the only sounds around them.

"I don't want you seeing her anymore…"

Jade let out a laugh, making Kerres's brow crease, not impressed at his reaction.

"We're equal partners, Kerres; you can't tell me what I can and can't do."

Kerres shifted, and Jade heard him sigh. "I think I should have a say in something you obviously are blind to. Why can't you just do this one thing for me? She's toxic slime, you said yourself that you can feel it."

Of course I can; she's my mother. Her aura was sickly green like pea soup but fragile and delicate like a dry leaf. Perhaps it's the feeling he got when he was around his mother that made Jade so sensitive to her moods.

He wished Kerres would understand that but all he saw in front of them was a crazy old woman who wanted to hurt his boyfriend. Jade saw past that. He saw her illness and what she had endured in her life, and the blame she put on him.

Yellow-eyed jinn… or yellow-eyed demon, both slurs she tossed at him regularly. She said he got his yellow eyes because he was Satan's spawn, but word around Moros when he was younger was that his father was a half-raver merchant whose Geigerchip had stopped working long ago.

Jade wouldn't know. He had never met anyone else with yellow eyes. He always just accepted his mother's excuse: he was the spawn of a demon, and deserved to be punished and hurt for even drawing breath meant for actual humans.

Kerres shifted around and rose, he leaned his back against the wall. Jade got up too. "Will you just… promise me you'll think about it? If you really feel that badly for her, I'll continue to drop stuff off for her or get one of the guys to."

Jade sighed. "Yeah, I'll think about it."

Kerres lifted himself off of the wall and nodded for Jade to follow him home; but Jade shook his head no.

"I need some time to clear my head, alone…" Though from some people this would draw protest, Kerres knew his boyfriend liked being by himself when his head was troubled.

"I'll be back in a couple hours, I promise," Jade said when he saw the unease on Kerres's face.

Kerres brushed several strands of crimson hair from his eyes and smiled at Jade. He leaned over and kissed him on the lips. "Alright."

Jade gave Kerres a smile just to appease him, and kissed him back. A moment later he was gone.

Though it wouldn't be a couple hours, and it might not even be that evening.

Jade looked around and dug his hands into his pockets, absentmindedly feeling the keycard.

CHAPTER 3

THE COVER OF NIGHT WAS JADE'S BOYFRIEND NOW; with Kerres safe back in the apartment he felt free and for the first time in a long time – alive.

Jade's bluish night vision illuminated the dark looming buildings around him, shrouding the tall, slender figure like a concrete blanket. The buildings would be his partner in crime, and the thiens that stalked the outskirts and corners of Eros and Skyland, his only enemies.

The confidence was rushing through him; tonight would be the best night to do it. It was only a day or so since the twin chimeras, Ares and Siris, had taken their leave, and the house would be open and ready for him to pick.

Jade's chest vibrated as though an amp was buried in his ribs; it shot volts of excitement that were only intensified with the crisp night air.

He leaned up against the cleaned concrete wall and shifted his eyes from side to side. When he saw the coast was clear he quietly jumped up and grabbed onto the wall with his fingers. With a grunt and an adrenaline rush that twisted up his spine, he hoisted himself up and flattened his body like a ferret.

Jade wiggled himself between the razor sharp barbed wire and the cold concrete; he swung his leg over and slid down to the district of Skyland.

Jade let out a breath when both feet touched the ground and froze. He hushed his own breathing and craned his neck to pick up any noises around him, but all was silent.

The borders from Skyland to Eros were different than the ones from Moros to Nyx. Whereas the other districts' walls opened to industrial buildings or at most the abandoned neighbourhoods, Skyland's borders brought you to a beautiful forest of thick-barked trees and wonderful-smelling rich dirt. It was a forest, but bigger than the few acres of brown trees they had in their parks. The forest was almost half a mile wide, with many paths and walkways for the Skylanders to walk their cicaros or their animal pets.

Jade was a black-haired boy of fifteen, wearing a black-zippered hoody, black cords, and hell, even black shoes. No one would be able to see him with his hood drawn up, as long as they didn't see his ghostly pale face or his gleaming yellow eyes.

At this juncture in his plan, Jade mentally patted his pockets to make sure the carefully and tightly folded russet sacks were there, and they were. If a thien caught him, as long as he wasn't frisked, they would have no proof he was there to break into a chimera house.

I've done this many times... this time won't be any different. If anything it'll be easier, I have the keycard...

Jade pawed his pants pocket, feeling the rectangle outline behind the corduroy. With one last puff of the cigarette, he snuffed it out under his foot. The Skylanders would smell the toxic scents of a Morosian cig and that would no doubt bring questions.

Just lay low and move on, and Jade did just that. He lowered his head and walked through the forest until he found a path. With a glance at his watch, he got his nautical location and started west towards the chimeras' gated home.

So many trees... oddly enough it made him feel exposed and uncomfortable. His place was in the alleyways and the ruined buildings. They enclosed him like a comfortable coffin, and when the coffin cracked open revealing his position to whoever was after him, the rubble-strewn burned buildings offered mazes upon mazes for the a slumrat to hide in.

Trees though... they were different; unless you could climb them they would reveal your position easily.

Why did these elites like their plants and flowers and all that shit? Same with their cultural need to learn musical instruments and paint pictures. They had this thirst to try and make things beautiful when there was nothing in this world worth making beautiful. The earth was dying around them, and just beyond Skyfall the people were so fucked up and radiation-crazed they ate each other raw. At least in Skyfall they canned them first.

So why did the elites need to pretend it wasn't happening? No amount of flowers would bring the earth back; King Silas had made sure of that.

The same king who ruled them still... the immortal chimera. Jade would be robbing two of his disciples soon. Maybe that was his own personal fuck you for killing the planet.

Or saving it, as the elites and the chimeras said. Though the slumrats knew better; they didn't buy into the lies. King Silas had killed the world so he could rebuild it the way he liked. Now everyone he had a hand in creating were hot, gay, and talented. He tried to snuff out what didn't fit into his perfect image, or at least send them to the greywastes.

Jade drew his hoody over his face when he saw the first flickers of light start to play hide and seek between the trees. White lights, not bluelamps or candles like in Moros and Nyx, actual light bulbs with electricity that never had brownouts like Moros did.

He took a breath of the air around him and felt it cleanse his mind; even the air here smelled better.

Jade broke out of the forest and started walking down a sidewalk, a smooth, level piece of pavement that hugged a clean white building that had shuttered windows above it. The street lamps were glaring, so he had to hug the corners tightly; at least the thiens were too far away to catch his eye, unless he made it glaringly obvious he was there.

I can get Kerres his boots... and some for me too. I can buy Mom a proper jacket; maybe get her to a doctor to see if she can go on meds...

So many things I can do... I could even get more fruit when I fence the items I steal. Enough to last us for the winter, maybe this year I won't get sick. My lungs have always been shit...

A fresh determination washed through Jade as he ducked through the parking lot of an old community center and sprinted across an empty street. In the distance he saw Skylanders, but he would be invisible to them. To a Skylander, a Morosian was dog shit, something you ignored, something that only became obvious when you stepped in it.

Sure enough, as he walked the last block to the gated house of Ares and Siris he passed two male Skylanders. As soon as they saw his ratty, smelly clothes, they wrinkled their noses at him like he had been moulded from garbage.

But they walked by without a word to Jade (why lower themselves to speaking to such filth?) mumbling and laughing to each other, gliding hand in hand like they were walking on air, their long silver robes flowing behind them, encapsulating their beautiful features as if showing the slumrat just how big a space lay between the two districts.

Jade felt the bitterness flood his mouth and he was tempted to spit, but all of this would be in vain if he got beaten to death by a thien... not when he was this close.

When he saw the red-tiled peaks of the chimera house his pulse started to race. The first wave of doubt rushed through his system, resting its barb in Jade's heart. With every beat and every silent footstep the barb dug itself in deeper, but he carried on.

I can't back down now... not now, not when I'm so close.

The lights were off, all but a porch light and a string of old Christmas lights that illuminated a rabbit hutch and a chicken coup; animals that weren't going to make noise.

With his throat a parched desert, he slowly walked around the tall brick wall until he found the place the disgruntled servant had mentioned to him. Here there was a back door that the cooks and the other slaves used, one that was far removed from the spectacular entrance to the mansion-like house. It had a long black driveway with bushes and flowers on either side, leading to a staircase framed by pillars which eventually led to two double doors.

This was their mansion; usually chimeras lived in skyscrapers but while Ares and Siris's home was being upgraded they had taken residence here. King Silas's bodyguards always had the best accommodation, not to mention pools and weight rooms to keep their brute physique in top condition. Those two were machines and had no trouble showing the commoners their strength. Jade had seen it many times during Stadium. They were practically animals.

With his chest pounding and a cold sweat glistening his brow, he approached the large iron gate. His eyes shot in all directions as he reached into his pocket. When Jade was sure the coast was clear he slid the keycard through the small box above the door handle, and held his breath.

Jade muffled a hiss when the light turned green, then opened the well-oiled gate and slipped in unnoticed.

It took everything in him not to jump up and down with a mixture of joy and excitement. Suddenly everything seemed possible; the world was his oyster. Life was about to get better, for him and Kerres. He could do his job as boyfriend and take care of Kerres, his silent, protective, and strong boyfriend, who already worked his fingers to the bone to bring home shit money, knowing full well if it wasn't for Jade's on-the-side thievery they would've starved long ago. His and Kerres's paychecks every month barely covered rent, not to mention their other expenses and their drug habits.

Jade was practically on his tip-toes as he ran across the garden. With a shuddering breath, he ducked in between a greenhouse and the brick of the main building and listened.

Still nothing! Jade couldn't believe it, this was really happening... he was going to get away with it. Jade walked along the house, shrouded in the deep shadows of the buildings until he found a door leading inside.

Despite his confidence his hands shook as he slipped the card key through the keypad and slipped inside. The click behind him as he closed the door echoed like an ear-splitting scream to Jade's ears, so used to silence. Jade paused and listened, but there was still only a deafening quiet.

Without pause, he walked down the carpeted halls, but his eyes tried to take everything in as he did. The blue tinges highlighted beautiful paintings, crown moulding of white plaster and lamps that hung down from golden chains. The walls were without mould and water spots, and, stranger still, the house didn't smell of anything – it only smelled clean. Clean to Jade was bleach and vinegar but this... it just smelled like nothing.

Jade shook his head free of such distracting thoughts and pulled out one of his russet-thread bags. With a still trembling hand he opened the first door he saw and peeked inside.

He quietly walked inside, leaving the door open behind him. It was another hallway but with doors lining the left hand side. This mansion was like a maze.

Jade looked into the first door but it opened on to a dining room, the second though made Jade inhale an excited breath.

A media room! A large one that held back nothing, all to boast the wealth of the residents inside. The TV was giant with two pole-like speakers on either side, and a poster of *The Godfather* behind it framed in silver. A few feet away, hugging both walls, were black book shelves and cabinets, all of them brimming with things ripe for the stealing.

With an excited thrum that filled him with cold adrenaline, Jade stepped in. He immediately went towards a shelf of VHS tapes and video game cartridges. He left the DVDs behind, those were rarer and only the elites could afford the players. VHS tapes he could fence quickly, and for a good profit.

And an Mp3 player! Jade threw it into the bag; that alone would fetch him over a hundred and fifty dollars! A moment later he shoved in a handful of CDs and a stack of Game Boy games, before turning and taking a moment to admire the giant rear projection TV. That would have been worth a thousand dollars easily, but, of course, he could never get it out of the room, let alone back to Moros. Instead Jade unplugged and stashed the N64 and quietly slipped out of the room.

Now he wanted to find a bedroom, some place where he could get a hold of some jewellery. Already he had enough loot to get them four pairs of new boots each and a jacket for Sheryn, but some gold and silver, perhaps some gems if he was extremely lucky, would buy their rent, food, and drugs for winter.

For you Kerres… you're my boyfriend and my responsibility…

If I got enough… I could quit my job for the winter, Kerres too… we might get away with not getting sick in the cold if we could stay indoors where it was warm.

Jade paused; he was halfway down the hall and about to check the next room when he heard a noise.

He sucked in a tense breath and looked around, his heart plummeting as he heard a shifting movement.

As an orange and white cat with a pressed-in face looked at him from on top of a plaster statue; he let out a sigh of relief. The chimeras' special pug-faced cats might be rare and valuable, but they didn't speak.

As he reached out and scratched its ears, he briefly played with the idea of stealing the cat, if only to breed him or her and sell the kittens, but he dismissed the idea as quickly as it came. They were all tracker chipped and the plushy feline would lead the thiens directly to Jade's apartment.

So he continued walking down the hallway; he was about to enter another room when the hallway light turned on.

Jade's breath caught in his throat, and his chest constricted so tight he was sure he was about to have a heart attack.

And to his horror his night vision failed, the sudden light reducing it to a blinding burst of white.

He put a hand over his eyes and turned to run, when suddenly he was grabbed by two thick arms and lifted up off of his feet. Jade dropped the sack of loot as his hand automatically snapped up to his bound chest.

Panic coursed through him like electricity, ripping through his body and exploding his heart as if he had swallowed a grenade. Immediately he screamed and kicked, thrashing his arms wildly but all that met his desperate attempts to escape was a low but taunting laugh, and the smell of meat on hot breath.

As his vision adjusted Jade let out a low moan, his yellow eyes fixed on the towering, muscular figure of Ares Dekker.

The chimera kneaded his fist into his hand and licked his lips.

"My... my... my... we caught ourselves a rabbit," he growled.

The man holding him, who Jade now knew without a doubt was Siris, laughed and licked Jade's neck with his tongue. "Mmm, taste him... he tastes fresh and new. How old are you, cat burglar?"

"Fourteen!" Jade gasped, his feet dangling and desperately trying to find the floor. It was a lie, but the only one he could think of to save him from the chimera brutes. Silas killed any man or woman who touched a teen under fifteen; one of the strictest and well-enforced rules in Skyfall.

Ares seemed unfazed though; he took a step forward and leaned down so he was eye level with Jade.

His deep, unnaturally violet eyes shone with hunger; his square face tightening to hold the grin on his lips, such a sardonic smile through an expression of pure, violent hunger. "I guess we'll have to kill you after we fuck you then. Drop him, brother."

Jade immediately fell to the floor. He scrambled to his feet and tried to find the door but as he stretched out an arm to crawl he felt a kick to his side.

"Fifteen... I'm – I'm fifteen and a half!" Jade gasped desperately, feeling so foolish and stupid for risking so much for a bag of loot. He tried to crawl towards the exit.

Another taunting laugh, the brutes wasted no time. Jade felt one of them kick him again, this time making him roll to his back. He held his chest and coughed, struggling to rise himself.

And he did rise, with Ares's large hand clutching his black hair he wrenched Jade to his feet. The chimera's vivid but frigid eyes sweeping up and down Jade's body as if analyzing a piece of meat.

From passive playing to violence, the chimera threw Jade hard across the room.

Jade crashed into a table in the corner of the room with so much force it splintered, leaving him gasping and bleeding on the ground. A moment later Siris picked him up by the hair, dangling him over the splintered pieces, then dropped him back onto the sharp shards of wood. He then pressed a boot against his groin before dealing him three quick punches to the face. Even in his terror and pain Jade could tell they weren't anywhere near full force. They wanted to torture him before they killed him.

Shit... shit... is this really it? Fuck, what is Kerres going to do? He was right. Will he even know what happened to me?

"Look at his blood... I bet he even tastes like a slum whore," Siris mused. He grinned and exchanged a wry glance with his identical twin brother.

The only visible feature separating the twins were their earrings. They both had three in each earlobe, but only one on their upper ears. One had a silver loop on the right, the other on the left; other than that the two brutes were identical.

But what did it matter... Jade writhed and tried to get up, feeling his bravery leave with the blood flowing freely from his nose and mouth. He looked up and saw both twins towering over him with their arms crossed.

Then to Jade's surprise, they took a step back.

"Go... run little rabbit... go run."

Jade's body froze as if automatically programmed to do the opposite of their commands. He looked up at them through a blood-streaked brow.

The boy cautiously got up, but as he started to walk Ares put a hand on his chest.

Jade froze, feeling his shoulders tremble. He had heard that chimeras lived to play games, especially the immortal ones, which he knew all the bodyguards were.

Sure enough, his suspicions were only grimly confirmed when Ares's menacing face split into a grin.

Ares gripped Jade's hoody with one hand and unzipped it with the other, and he pushed the fabric off, before leaning into his face.

To Jade's disgust, he licked the blood off of his face, slow sensual traces of a tongue that lapped every strip of crimson – a moment later, Siris joined him.

Like a cat being bathed by Dobermans, Jade stood frozen and rigid, his heart beating ice water into his veins as his brain told him to stand and bear it, his once long life now reduced to living second by second.

The chimeras licked the blood from his face and neck, before kissing each other behind Jade's head.

Once again... from stillness to violence.

Jade's legs were kicked out from under him and he felt himself drop to his knees, a hand grabbed his hair again but this time his neck was wrenched back.

He closed his eyes as he heard pants unzip, and turned his face away when he felt something warm and fleshy against his lips.

"If you dare defy my orders or if you decide your life isn't worth my cock, I will rip your chip out right from your ear and turn every friend or lover you have into greywaste rats."

If it had been any other threat Jade would've spat in their faces... but... no, not Kerres.

But they're going to kill me anyway, they're chimeras... if they kill me they'll find Kerres anyway. Fuck, FUCK! What was I thinking coming here?

With his fears outweighing his reasoning... Jade found his legs. He wrenched his head away from the chimera's grasp, and bolted out of the room.

The taunting howls behind him sent a frozen rush through his body; he poured on the speed feeling like a deer dashing away from a pack of lions.

With legs that trembled underneath him, he weaved through the halls, hearing the booming footsteps behind him, thudding down against the wood and carpet like iron balls. He held back a scream of desperation as he ran through the halls, hoping to see a door to outside but there was none. If anything he was getting deeper inside the mansion.

Jade ran into a large dining hall and through a set of wooden doors.

To his horror he slammed right into something hard; as he fell to the ground the shadow in front of him dealt him a kick to the head that shot his mind out of his body. Then there was another blow, and at that point he forgot where he was.

Jade felt his clothes ripped from him; the only protest he could manage was an opening and closing of his mouth and the occasional groan. Not even when the light flicked on and he saw the two brute chimeras, did he scream.

Ares laughed a cruel, cold laugh, and pinned Jade's arms under his knees, his naked groin pressed against the back of Jade's head. As Siris ripped his underwear off and roughly grabbed his dick, Jade's legs gave a half-hearted thrash before Ares grabbed them and pinned them back.

"No – no – no!" Jade found his voice and screamed. He thrashed his head back and forth and tried to worm himself free, but the brutes had him pinned.

Though it was no use, there had never been any use. Siris took his dick into his hand and held the base like he was wielding a sword.

The rumours had been true; chimeras were huge, with their circumcised penises only looking larger with the foreskin gone.

It was a weapon and the chimera was going to use it as one. Surely when both of them were done Jade would be dead; he wouldn't survive the size and he wouldn't survive their stamina.

"Please… come on… I'll – I'll suck you off, just come on!" Jade cried, his bravery long gone. Now his mouth only held desperate pleas and half-hearted bargaining that he knew were no use. Chimeras fed on pleading and knew nothing of pity; they were genetically engineered monsters and these two were the worst of all. The only thing Jade could do now was die with dignity, but the hot tears forming in his eyes told him he wouldn't even get that.

Siris punched him in the nose and Jade heard it crunch, and as a fresh flow of blood ran down, the chimera leaned into him to lick it. Then Siris stemmed the flow with his hand and reached back down to his groin.

Then came the pressure between his legs he had been fearing. Met with a scream of agony, the chimera pushed his large member against the opening, wetted with nothing but Jade's own blood and the brute's precum.

But Jade was too tight. The boy screamed so loud he felt his head go hot, threatening to make him pass out; his hole wouldn't give to the large mass, though the chimera didn't stop pushing.

Jade squirmed and tried to thrash but Ares held his legs back firmly.

"Fuck, I think this bitch is a virgin!" Siris said with a grin on his lips. Jade felt him pat his cheek and take more of his blood, then a moment later Ares spat onto Siris's hand.

The rough pain returned with vigour. Jade clenched his eyes tight and shrieked before his voice broke with a sob, only to start up again with ferocity as the chimera finally broke into him.

The pressure and searing, ripping sensation was enough to throw Jade into temporary madness. His mind overloaded, he thrashed his body with every ounce of energy he had, doing everything in his weakened state to get the excruciating feeling out from him.

Jade wasn't a virgin, but besides a few times in the beginning of his relationship and several times when he was extremely drunk, Jade had always been the top during sex. He had never enjoyed the feeling of being penetrated and Kerres had never voiced complaint. In truth it had been over a year since something more than a finger or a roaming tongue had sunken inside of him.

When Siris started to thrust into the tight opening Jade felt his body contract in on itself, bowing his back and tensing so hard he felt every muscle in his thin frame turn to stone like he had gazed upon Medusa.

However, his mind was all too free to experience the pain and raw, biting horror. As the chimera ruthlessly hammered himself into him, Jade howled.

"That's right, scream – scream all you want." Ares's voice was a cold whisper against his ears. He felt a hand wrench his chin up and he saw the black-haired chimera grin down at him. His brother was only inches away, groaning and gasping as he fucked him mercilessly.

Jade gazed up at him, half with it, half inside his head. The chimera looked amused at this stunned stupor; in response he leaned down and sucked the blood still running from the wounds on Jade's face.

Siris moaned and joined his brother. With his hips slamming deeper and deeper into Jade's soft but lanky body, he drank up every flow of blood that leaked from Jade's open wounds and bruised orifices.

When Siris came inside of him, Ares egged him on. Jade watched as they kissed deeply, before Siris grabbed Ares's hard member and generously licked the crown only an inch from Jade's head.

When Siris lowered the cock to Jade's lips the boy licked it too, hoping to grasp at any chance they might release him, but that chance was long gone. A moment later Siris pulled out a blood-streaked and cum-covered cock from Jade's ass, and rose.

As if the physical connection between them had him held in a spell, Jade felt the feeling come back to his limbs. The twins laughed and pointed at Jade as the boy struggled to his hands and knees and started to crawl away, no longer bothering to suppress the sobs and cries on his lips.

They saw nothing of a boy trying to escape; they saw it as a little bitch ready to be mounted. Ares positioned himself behind the boy so desperately trying to crawl away, and with little to no direction skewered himself into the bloody and swollen opening.

The scream was so loud Jade's vocal cords broke from the strain, and only sounded again when Jade inhaled a rattling breath.

And it only got worse; a moment later the taste of blood and cum as Siris pushed his cock between Jade's lips. When it hit clenched teeth he brutally rapped the side of Jade's head with a closed fist until he opened his mouth and took it in with nothing more than a mournful cry.

There was no dignity to be had, no pride or willfulness to hold onto anything. Jade tried his best to suck Siris off as Ares grabbed onto Jade's hips and slammed him into his cock.

The submission was not lost on the twins; they took their turns wrenching his hair back to see the slum whore sucking the chimera twin off obediently, even giving his own cock some tugs for the sole reason of humiliating him further.

Cum shot all over his face and into his mouth; Jade didn't even have the strength to move away. The hot, milky liquid covered his face to the taunting laughter of the twins, a moment later followed by Ares's tense moans and the sound of deep kissing above him.

When Ares withdrew, Siris moved his dick away from Jade's mouth. Jade immediately collapsed on the ground, his limbs feeling like jello; battered, bruised, and dripping semen down the crevice of his backside.

He curled up on himself, the semen still covering his face. As he heard Ares and Siris talking to each other in growling tones, he shuffled to the corner of the dining hall beside a door and tried to make his body as small as possible.

With a dry throat that tasted like fresh cum and copper, he watched as Siris started eagerly sucking Ares's dick, the two identical chimeras going at it with a stamina that Jade had never seen. Chimeras didn't seem to get tired at all; even moments after they came they seemed ready for the next orgasm.

So how long would they fuck me for?

Jade whimpered, thankful for at least a moment's rest. He held his hot and sticky body tight against himself and counted every way he despised his reasoning for doing such a stupid thing.

Now he would never see Kerres again, or the guys. Kerres would be left to pay rent on his own, which he couldn't afford. He would be evicted – where would he go? They both had no family and Kerres could only couch surf for so long...

He would become homeless; he would turn into Sheryn and start ranting and raving.

The thought made Jade's throat tighten and the self-hatred only flare further. As he watched the twin chimeras eagerly sucking each other off, seemingly done for now with raping the slum whore, he could see very clearly just how worthless he was. So worthless everyone around him would probably tell him he was lucky to get fucked by royalty.

Jade wiped a piece of cum that had been slowly running down his temple; he looked at it and rubbed it between his fingers.

Why won't they just kill me...?

The boy stayed huddled in a corner, his naked and soaked frame shivering as he observed the twins going at it. A sickening sight that in all other situations would've enthralled Jade, but now they were nothing but two demons ravaging their doppelgangers with the thirst of a narcissist finally able to fuck himself.

With the matter behind his eyes a grey heap of useless flesh, and his body only just starting to find itself, he watched in a stupor. Ares had mounted his brother now and, with his body angled away from him, Jade watched Ares fuck Siris with deep rolling thrusts.

Then his eyes swept the room, passing over the long wooden dining hall, the blue fabric chairs, and the grey walls, the pictures and… the half-ajar door he was leaning against.

There was no time to debate the foolishness of this; it was either this or wait for the twins to remember he was there. With shaking limbs, Jade crawled through the doorway and into the long stretch of hallway that lay daunting and dark in front of him.

Using the walls as support Jade rose on trembling legs and limped through the hallway; leaving the sliver of light behind him and the groaning brutes still impaling each other's identical bodies.

The relief was short-lived. Several moments after turning to a different wing his heart froze inside his battered chest. Angry boot stomps echoed off the high ceilings, filling Jade with such a primal fear he felt his legs go light; with the new rush coursing through him, he ran.

But each door was the same; none of them looked like they led outdoors. Jade's heart was in his throat as he turned corner after corner and ran with fear down each stretch of hallway. He knew he was deep inside the mansion, but there had to be a door outside somewhere.

Where… where! Tears stung Jade's eyes. Even when they were raping him he hadn't cried, but being pursued in a dark and empty mansion by these two animals taxed every last resolve he had. His mind was ice and he was drowning in his own fear to the point where he felt his sanity slip with the blood and cum running down his legs.

Boom… boom… boom. The iron balls slammed onto the ground; they were getting closer. Jade swallowed a scream and opened a door, though it was only another hallway leading to a small sitting room. He wrenched open that door as well and closed it behind him.

"Go run, little rabbit… go run!" One of their voices filled the dark corridors between them, it sounded like he was getting closer.

Jade tried to run, but his weak legs gave out from under him. In desperation he crawled several paces, leaving behind a streak of blood. Then with a grunt and the image of his boyfriend's face in his mind, he brought himself to his feet.

Then the slam of a door. Jade jumped so high, both of his feet left the ground.

That was close – it was too close, they knew where he was.

Naked and battered, the boy held himself tight, and concentrated on putting one foot in front of the other. Though without even realizing it, he was the stifling sobs on his lips.

Then a hope…

Jade's mind didn't register the light underneath the doorway as anything but sunlight, even though it was well past midnight and such things would be impossible. Still, in his state he couldn't care less. It was a break of light in an otherwise dark and sinister mansion, filled with brute chimeras and terror at every bend.

Another door slammed. Jade screamed this time and let out a desperate sob, before turning the door knob to the lit room on the other side. He slipped in and shut it, before collapsing onto the ground, a groan of despair breaking through his bloodied lips.

The room was warm, the light coming from both a flickering fireplace and a dim halogen in the corner. Jade's teeth clenched, his mind finally releasing him to his fate. This was no daylight, no escape. This mansion had no exit; it was only a maze for predators to play with their prey.

At least he would be warm. The boy crawled over to the flaring fireplace, his frozen and bare body shivering from both fear and cold.

He leaned against the warm but rough brick and stared at the door, waiting for the twins to break through and claim their escaped prey.

Then a small noise, like the flutter of bird's wings. Jade's eyes flickered over, his mind a tangle of wires too knotted together to jump from surprise.

It hadn't been a bird; it was the page of a book turning.

CHAPTER 4

His mouth went dry as his eyes fell on the figure in the dim lamplight, and if he wasn't so tired and in pain he would've cried harder.

It was another chimera; he knew that from his looks alone. But it wasn't only his looks that made Jade freeze; it was the chimera's aura.

An incandescent brilliance of silvers strung between crystal white opal waves, lining the beautiful pearl-like flares like stars in an ocean. It was a light aura, but held within it a fiery grace and unwavering dignity that Jade had never seen on anyone before.

And his beauty didn't stop there; this chimera was absolutely mesmerizing.

Long blond hair that shone like a deity's under the flickering flames, drawn behind his head and falling over an alabaster face in bangs that fell past his ears. His face was also perfect, sculpted by a talent that could only come from an immortal's touch. Thin, shaped eyebrows, a triangular face void of facial hair over a defined jaw, and pink thin lips that held no hint of a smile or even recognition.

The beauty was sitting in a stuffed black chair, his legs crossed, with a book resting on his knee. He was dressed in white and silver with a cape stopping only inches from the floor. He was reading his book silently, with a grace that seemed so out of place in this mansion; a small oasis in the inner circles of hell.

This confounded and confused Jade to no end. It seemed impossible. Who was he? Why was he here, so casually reading when such a raw and ugly thing had been happening only a few halls down?

And why hadn't he said anything to Jade? Called Ares and Siris to fetch their captive, with a stern warning to play with their food elsewhere? Or at least banished Jade from the warmth of the fire-lit room with an upturned nose and a sneer of disgust.

But he only sat there.

Jade stayed huddled by the fire, drawing his knees up to his body in a half-hearted way to protect himself. He knew he was bleeding blood and cum onto the carpet, but what else was he to do?

The chimera had to have heard him. Even if he was deaf he would've seen Jade run in, and hear the door close and the stifled sobs on his lips. But he was ignoring him – why? And would he ignore him when Ares and Siris barged in to take him?

As if acting on his inner fear, Jade heard a commotion outside the door. His heart gave a lurch of terror, and he held his hand to his mouth to muffle a sob of fear.

The two were talking in angry voices, too muted by the door for Jade to hear. A moment later he heard their taunt:

"Little rabbit? Little running rabbit?"

Jade groaned through a mouth still being held in his hand, and backed his weak body further into the corner of the wall of the fireplace.

In response the blond chimera raised his eyes from his book. The purple crystals turned to the door for a moment, before falling on Jade.

To the chimera, Jade was nothing more than a dog hiding from a whipping. His eyes went back to his book, as if he had never heard the twins outside the door, or Jade's desperate muffled cries. He was still once again.

Soon the voices faded and they were gone. Jade stayed still in his corner, his right half in the shadows but warmed against the fire, and his left exposed in the lamplight and shivering.

As the minutes went on, he found his reserves unable to maintain the adrenaline that had carried him so far through the mansion. Jade's body slumped and crumpled like a dying insect, and with the rough brick fireplace supporting his head, he stared at the blond chimera with both fear and appreciation, even if he had done nothing but continue to sit and read.

Jade didn't know which chimera this was. There were over twenty, he thought, some immortal and some not. There was no mistaking that this chimera must be an immortal; his aura shone like a man whose grace and elegance had been tempered with time. His face held no age though, and if Jade was to guess, his aging had stopped in his early or middle thirties. Not a single wrinkle or permanent crease fell over his perfectly sculpted countenance.

Why didn't he sell me out...? Jade wracked his brains trying to find a solution. His mind was a hive of questions and fears. The stunned stupor he had been in before had slowly trickled away with time, leaving his mind, and his body, open and raw; a flurry of emotions coursing through him that he had never expected to feel.

Jade found himself angry at the situation he was in. The confusion surrounding him, as well as the silence, was starting to drive him mad. Time was ticking by slowly, in a room without a clock. He didn't know what was going to happen next, and it was insanity inducing.

As the minutes turned into an hour, he felt his mind flare with frustration. The man was just sitting there reading! Not another glance or even a recognition of his plight. The chimera was completely indifferent to what had happened to Jade, or the fear that was ravaging him. The silence was becoming heavy and weighted, making his skin crawl as time continued to flow unbidden. It was so maddening, like someone audibly counting down to them shooting you in the head. He wanted to get it over with; the anticipation was eating him alive.

But instead of voicing his frustration through an animalistic shriek he did something that would surprise himself. Something that was so out of place Jade wondered if he had gone mad.

"Will you read to me?" his raspy broken voice sounded weak and drowned out even in the practically muted silence that surrounded them.

To Jade's shock, the chimera gave him a fleeting glance, before looking back down at the tattered book.

And he started to read.

"In the evening they tramped out across a field trying to find a place where their fire would not be seen, dragging the cart behind them over the ground. So little of promise in that country. Tomorrow they would find something to eat. Night overtook them on a muddy road. They crossed into

a field and plodded on toward a distant stand of trees skylighted stark and black against the last of the visible world."

Jade stared, and he felt the threads that had bound his chest so tightly start to loosen, strand by strand.

The chimera's voice was liquid silk, deep but smooth without the slightest hesitation or waver even on words Jade didn't understand. A richness fell from those words, one that held an elegance the chimera's aura and appearance had solidified in this perfect being long ago.

In that moment Jade felt like an unworthy flea in the presence of a demigod. A dirty creature huddled in his filth, not worthy to taste such a forbidden fruit that was this man's aura. A part of him knew that if he wasn't in such a sad state he would've left the room from the pure humility of being near such perfection.

Jade's body unwrapped with every word, and he hung on those beautiful tones; his eyes never leaving the tall and encompassing frame.

In this room, he forgot that he was in the presence of a chimera, a ruthless immortal monster that he had grown up hating. Those thoughts belonged to a boy of the slums, ignorant and dragged down from the weight of existence. Now such thoughts so loosely thrown seemed to be a sin to even mention.

"The small fire burning in the floor seemed a long way down. He shielded the glare of it with his hand and when he did he could see almost to the rear of the box. Human bodies. Sprawled in every attitude. Dried and shrunken in their rotted clothes."

Wow, they found dead humans... Jade said in his own head. Though his mind was a murk he still followed every word the chimera spoke to him. If he could bottle it he would, but he didn't know when he would allow himself to go over the memories.

In this room it felt like the fabric of time and reality had been broken, and there was no Kerres, Ares or Siris, no Moros, no Skyfall... no planet. It was just the boy and the chimera, and nothing else around him mattered or made sense.

Just his voice.

What happened next? Jade wanted to ask. He shifted, feeling the now dried blood sticking with the cum between his legs. In his trance he had forgotten his injuries and the violation inflicted on his body. Only the ripping of the skin between his legs as he moved reminded him of the ordeal he had run from.

Who was he? That question had trumped all others but still he held no answer. No thinking back to the chimeras he saw on the news could bring up the name to the face. Jade knew the chimera must be important, but his name was lost on him. Jade felt frustrated by this, but that emotion was constantly outweighed and silenced by the sound of the chimera's voice.

Warm against the fire, Jade watched the flames flicker against the chimera's long golden blond hair, and reflect against his violet eyes like moonlight on an ocean. Though Jade was still afraid, hurt, and confused, in this moment, as long as the chimera read to him – he was okay.

Ares and Siris must be long gone, Jade concluded to himself, and there was no better relief than that. Even with all the uncertainty this predicament had brought to his mind, at least with this chimera, for now, he was protected from them.

"He reached and took the lamp from the boy. He started to descend the stairs but then he turned and leaned and kissed the child on the forehead."

Jade blinked and raised his head as his voice stopped. He looked and felt his heart plummet to his feet as he saw the chimera reach out and gently pick up a bookmark, before slipping it between the half-finished book.

Even his movements were elegant and graceful as he rose and gently smoothed his robes.

He was tall, least a foot taller than Jade; a towering figure in a silver cape, with his hair like spun gold that fell halfway down his back.

Jade felt himself cowering down as the warm, trance-like mood of the room was broken down piece by piece.

Then the chimera's violet eyes found his and Jade cowered. He backed himself further into the corner of the wall and the fireplace, feeling a shudder of fear well up inside his chest.

Those eyes… they were so cold, devoid of any warmth at all, they burrowed into Jade with brumal indifference. What solace and security he had found in the chimera's voice and the atmosphere of the room drained away, exchanged with an influx of ice water.

Jade found himself shaking in fear.

He was wrong – *he isn't nice, he's a chimera, you idiot*. Jade sniffed but didn't break his gaze, he only stared back, frightened, his hands clasped around drawn-up knees.

Was it his turn to have his way with me? Jade's throat was parched and dry, and suddenly every injury and patch of bruised flesh on his body ached with incomprehensible pain, as though his mind was making up for the pain forgotten during their hours of reading.

"Can you walk?" the cold deep voice asked.

Jade looked down at his entirely naked body, only wearing his ratty duct taped shoes. He shifted his sore, aching limbs and struggled to stand.

Halfway up he faltered and fell to his knees with a groan of pain; the searing ripped flesh between his legs giving an angry jolt. He stayed down for several seconds before attempting to stand again; this time he was able to rise.

"Follow me."

The blond chimera swept past him, his robes giving off the sweet scent of mint and nutmeg. He walked through the door, not even looking behind him to make sure Jade was following.

With his hands trying desperately to cover his nakedness, Jade followed the chimera, not knowing how his legs were still able to carry him after the beating and rape he had endured. Though he managed to remain upright, they bent and bowed every several steps, threatening to spill him onto the floor.

With several unsteady strides Jade found himself behind the chimera, keeping as close to him as he could without touching him, fearing the twins' wrath behind every dark corner. Although this cold, dark figure, surrounded by crystal and silver, was daunting and terrifying, the twin chimeras held a much more immediate danger.

As the chimera opened the door leading them outside, Jade tried to grasp what had happened since coming into this mansion. So many terrifying thoughts jammed themselves into his mind, mixing in with the brief moments of calm and warmth brought on by the chimera's silken tones. It overwhelmed Jade's mind, and filled him with such conflicting thoughts he didn't know whether to scream, cry, run, or thank him.

So Jade followed him instead, naked and exposed. His hands were no longer hiding his groin area, but were clasped protectively over his chest.

Jade had no more shame. How could he when the twins' cum was still stuck to his face and dripping down his backside?

It was still dark out, but there was a glow against the buildings that told Jade the sun was beginning to rise. The chimera had read to him the entire night, and now daylight would soon expose the rewards for Jade's attempted grasp at a better life for him and Kerres.

You were stupid to think you could ever escape from the pit of Moros... just look at these people in Skyland. Even if you got rich beyond your wildest dreams you still have sewage in your blood, you would still be a Morosian. And even worse, tonight you became two chimeras' slut. Would Kerres even want you now?

There was a buzz of voices and snickers. Jade looked over to see several people stopping to stare at them.

If there was anything to be thankful for, it was that he didn't care who saw him now. At least for now he was alive. They could gawk and laugh all they wanted.

"I suggest you carry on, lest this is the last thing you see." The chimera's crisp voice cut the cold morning air around them.

The group of men immediately looked flustered; they quickly bowed before scattering off like croaches after the light switch got turned on.

In a move that shocked Jade even more, the chimera unclipped his long silver robe and handed it to him.

Jade sniffed; he wanted to say thank you but his aching jaw seemed sealed. Instead he took the robe and draped it over his naked body and continued to obediently follow the chimera, though where he was leading him Jade didn't know.

The chimera led them back into the forest; with the trees shrouding Jade's robe-draped body he felt a glimmer of relief. The chimera was leading him to the borders – could he be that lucky to find one of the only nice chimeras out there? He had covered him... perhaps...

His thoughts were halted by a drop falling from his forehead; Jade looked down and with horror realized his forehead had dripped blood right onto the silver robes.

Jade swore in his head and lifted a hand up to stem the blood, only to crack the dried blood scab that had sealed almost the entire left side of his face. More blood fell, and more curses took shape in his head.

He felt himself almost drawn to tears over wrecking something the chimera had been nice enough to let him borrow. As they approached the walls bordering Eros and Skyland, Jade took the robe off with a rattled sniff and a mumbled apology.

The chimera stopped and turned around; his cold gaze fell to Jade's forehead and then the robes.

"I'm... sorry..." Jade's voice was still a broken, hollow rasp. He tried to hand the robe back with a shaky, bloodied hand. "Thank you for letting me borrow it."

The blond man took the robe from him before switching it to his right hand. He held the fingers of his left hand up, and rubbed the blood between his fingers.

"It was not for your benefit –"

Jade swallowed hard, the tone of the chimera's words sending a cold chill up his spine. Hollow and void of any warmth or shred of empathy. They were frigid and steeled, making Jade freeze on the spot.

"– it was for mine."

In spite of the raw emotion in his brain, Jade looked at him, offended. All of the chimeras were gay, that was well-known, so what was wrong with his body? It was a laughable thought considering the situation he had just come from, but it temporarily overtook the other thoughts in his mind.

But then Jade looked down at his bloodied body, red welts and dried blood mixed in with the fresh streams of disturbed clots. He was an ugly sight right now.

Chimeras were used to supple, fit little cicaros, freshly cleaned and trimmed. Jade was a garish gangly twig compared to them. Perhaps he was so revolting he needed covering.

But the chimera continued to stare at Jade's now naked body, shrouded in nothing with the sun now peaking over the buildings. He was exposed and out in the open, with no darkness to cover the battered remains of what Ares and Siris had left him.

"Turn around for me; I wish to see all of you."

Jade's mouth dropped open.

"Are you fucking kidding me?" he blurted. As though a cold arctic river had infiltrated his blood he felt his body freeze to a brick of ice.

The chimera's smooth face seemed to get darker as he drank Jade in.

He took a step towards Jade and dropped the robe onto the ground.

Jade felt his heart race; he watched as the chimera slipped off a white glove Jade hadn't even realized he was wearing.

With his index and middle finger, he traced down Jade's brow. When he withdrew it, Jade saw it glisten with blood, though only visible for a brief moment before the chimera brought the tip to his mouth.

"You should have kept that robe on…"

Chimeras and blood… god dammit… chimeras and blood – he was right, he was right. What the fuck did I just do?

Jade wanted to turn and run, but his legs could only slowly walk him backwards. Only his voice gave away the fast hammers of his pulse. "I can run faster than you." Jade took another step, but as if the universe wanted to humiliate him more, his back hit the cold concrete wall.

From stillness to the strike. The chimera grabbed Jade's wrists and pinned them with one hand behind his head, holding him firmly against the wall. Nothing separated their bodies but a white button-down shirt and silver belted trousers.

A thin smile appeared on the chimera's face as his eyes drew themselves up and down Jade's body, but though Jade expected him to demand he spread his legs, Jade felt his fingers only brush the solid curve of his body.

"So you just wanted me for yourself then?" Jade spat. He tried to wrench his wrists free but the chimera had a strength to him that trumped anything that could be considered natural. He was essentially pinned, one hand grasping his wrists like a steel bear trap, the other free to trace across his shivering, blood-caked body.

Jade gasped as he felt a cold hand rest up against his erect nipple; he felt the chimera take it between his fingers and start to rub it in an almost mockingly sensual manner, filling Jade's head with confusion over the spring of feeling that came from teasing such a sensitive place.

The boy closed his eyes for a moment, before he opened them to the top of the chimera's blond head; he gritted his teeth as he felt a warm tongue suck the bud with slow, drawn-out licks. Another round of confusing pleasure coursed through him. The blond man enveloped the entire piece of flesh with his mouth, and with a warm, bordering on hot tongue, he softened it.

His aura encased both of them, and Jade felt the silver strings and opal waves mix with the purple and black hues of his own. For a moment, and to his confusion, they melted into one another and he felt the first twinge of sexual pleasure.

Then an odd sensation; the mouth that so generously sucked his nipple became cold, a frozen blizzard that immediately hardened the bud in his mouth. Jade gasped and let out his first audible groan.

The wolves chased me and with my luck I ended up in the lion's den. Jade opened his mouth and muffled the next moan with every inch of his restraint, but it was no use, the proof of his pleasure was right between his legs.

It didn't go unnoticed to the mysterious blond chimera. He looked down with a wry smirk, before his head rose and his lips found the open and bleeding gash on Jade's forehead.

Jade cringed and tried to move his forehead away, feeling himself suffocated to the point of panic as the chimera's body seemed to envelope and encompass his own. With the chimera's mouth and tongue taking in all the fresh blood he could find, his hand trailed to Jade's rigid member.

Jade's teeth gritted together, but as soon as he felt the chimera's touch go oddly warm he could no longer restrain another groan. In spite of his racing emotions and the helplessness he felt, Jade's hips pushed forward towards the odd tingling touch.

"Fuck... off," Jade gasped. He bowed his head, but the tongue still continued to suck the red cruor falling from his face.

The chimera didn't answer, instead his response was to grab Jade's dick with his hand and strip back the foreskin with a gentle but firm retraction. With Jade's chest shuddering the chimera drew it back over the head and started to tug and pull.

"Let... go of me!" Jade gritted his teeth, trying without success to free some part of his body, but his hands were locked in the iron fetters of the chimera's grip, and his head craned to accommodate the chimera's bloodthirst.

Another moan, this one bringing a biting shame as he felt his hips thrust towards the chimera's soft hands. The monster had him firmly in his palm, both mentally and physically, and in one fell swoop he had disarmed every part of Jade's being. He was putty in the chimera's hands and that realization alone filled his mouth with acid.

This was worse... fuck, this was worse. Ares and Siris just raped me... this guy, fuck, what is he doing? As an electricity built up inside his groin he felt his teeth clamp down on his lip, so hard he felt it split.

Stop it... stop it! The primal instincts of every male flared up inside of him, his hard member pulsing under the chimera's fluctuating touch. Even with his mind spitting poison and hatred for the chimera, his body swelled and rose, responding to his touch like a horny teen about to lose his virginity.

In response to his cruel pride-stripping thoughts, Jade let out a frustrated scream. He tried to wrench himself free again but his efforts were only met by the travelling of the blond man's mouth, this time sensually licking the blood trickling from Jade's lips.

Jade writhed and contorted himself, his dishevelled mess of a body covered in angry welts and the shame at its own eager responses. He tried to refuse, and tried to refuse to like it but the root of his pleasure paid no mind to his desperation. He felt a wet trickle on his penis and looked down to see it glistening with precum.

He clenched his teeth and felt an energy burn in him, the physical evidence of his arousal searing his pride. Jade hollered and gave his body a hard jerk before he bared his teeth and snapped at the man like he was a feral dog. "I'll rip your fucking face off if you dare put that... fu-fucking..." Jade gritted as another rush of pleasure humiliated him. "...fucking face near me!"

The chimera cared nothing for his turmoil; if actions and heartbeats could talk, the chimera's inner monologue would offer nothing but bemused taunting. The cruel and indifferent figure continued to massage and stroke Jade's rigid shaft with a smooth rhythm, breaking for nothing even when he found a new source of Jade's blood to devour.

"Cum for me..."

"Fuck off!" Jade snarled, wrenching his face away from the chimera's travelling tongue, but the man only drew it back in to continue toying with him.

Jade saw an opportunity and snapped at him. He was too slow though, the edges of his teeth only grazing the chimera's pale cheek.

The chimera looked at him, his ice cold eyes only amused at the outburst from a boy in such a perilous predicament. His hand stroking Jade's member so gently, sped up, making Jade gasp and shut his eyes tight, unable to see his body respond so willingly to the touch any longer.

"Cum for me."

Jade ground his teeth and bared them at the chimera like the animal he had felt reduced to. "You're all a bunch of fucking vampires. Bring your face closer and say that to me again."

A shiver ran through him, as the cold chimera let out the slightest of bemused laughs; he felt his hot mint smelling breath against his ear. With an increase in his massaging of Jade's penis, he purred in his ear.

"Cum for me, and if you really want to please me… moan my name while you do it."

Suddenly the pleasure intensified, the touch from the chimera's hand seemed to suddenly become static, tingly almost, a touch that no natural man bore. It was a chimera perk, it had to be, he had the ability to manipulate his touch. It–

"Ah… ahh!" Jade gasped, his clenched teeth breaking apart. He blinked away a shameful tear and thrust his groin further into the chimera's hand. Even though the man's face was right by his, the thought of biting him had dripped away like the precum below him. "I – I don't even know your fucking name you – you pervert."

That was the last audible sound from Jade's lips.

The heat in his groin drew tight and snapped under the chimera's soft but rapid strokes. With a sharp inhale and a cry unbidden on his lips, Jade submitted himself to the pleasurable, overwhelming orgasm that ripped his body in half, and flooded his head with a dizzying flash of heat.

In the throes of his climax Jade felt his legs go weak; he managed to rip his hands away and automatically he grabbed onto the first solid thing to steady himself; to his further humiliation that thing was the chimera.

He dug his now free hands into the blond man's shoulders as his legs collapsed under the rush of knee-shaking pleasure, holding on for dear life as the cum shot out of him and onto the chimera's bare hand.

Jade panted heavily, his face buried in the man's robes, his fingers clenching the fabric with a white knuckle grip. As the orgasm coursed through him, the man held him upright, only lowering him to the ground when the last electric charge finally fell from his body.

Jade let himself be brought to his knees, the utter humiliation sending a heat to his face. He looked down at the ground, his chest heaving and panting, and saw his soft penis drip one last pearl of cum, right onto the chimera's white boots.

Without a word the man turned around, only the crunching of boots on dirt and leaves could be heard. Jade watched him, ignoring the leftover quivering of his body.

The chimera leaned down and picked up his robe, before walking back towards the trail.

He had forgotten something though – Jade watched as he walked on; not noticing that the dog-eared book had slipped out of a pocket in his robes.

There was a temptation on his tongue to point it out, but for reasons he didn't yet understand Jade said nothing. He watched the chimera walk out of the forest, his elegance and grace not lost, even though Jade had seen the demon stir.

When he was gone the boy rose up, and took the book into his hands, and with every mocking thought in his head attempting to destroy him, he climbed up the wall, naked, beaten, and bloody.

When he finally stepped foot in Moros it was evening again. It had taken him all morning and afternoon to walk from Skyland to the garbage-strewn dark alleys of Moros. With no money on him, his clothing lost and discarded in the mansion, he was nothing but a piece of bruised corpse that the residents avoided like the plague.

The only clothing he had on now were a pair of damp ratty jeans too big for him, and a moth-eaten yellow t-shirt that had several brown stains on the back, clothing he had found while desperately digging around in the dumpsters of Eros once he had scaled the other side of the fence. They smelled like rotting vegetables, but covered his outward shame and he took a small comfort in that.

Jade stumbled on, his steps heavy and bowed under the numbing pain that had embedded itself in his body, but even with the agony painted on his once-handsome features he felt relief. At least he was home – at least he had survived.

If those words were his truth, why did saying them in his head fill him with bitter indifference? It should've been a relief he had survived three chimeras but instead Jade was angry, frustrated, and overflowing with shame and humiliation. His brush with death had given him no thirst for the life he still had, just contempt for the man who had saved him from his fate.

That blond chimera... Jade gritted his teeth, and pushed the chimera's derisive smile from his memories. He crossed an empty street and walked into an alley, heading home with a clenched jaw and a look in his eyes that dared anyone passing to ask him what had happened.

There was nothing to describe the relief Jade felt when his eyes fell onto his street. He could see his apartment window, the blinds drawn and shut meaning Kerres was out. That would give him enough time to clean up.

Jade allowed his tormented mind a brief respite in the form of a relieved sigh, before he walked faster towards the metal door that would lead him to the stairs.

"Jade?"

Jade froze and turned around slowly.

Tate was looking at him bewildered, then his face took on an expression of horror seemingly adopted by everyone who had taken a closer look at the injured boy. Beside him was a man Jade didn't recognize, but he was tall and muscular with a thick neck and a sour face.

"He looks like shit... what happened to him?" the strange man asked Tate.

Jade stared at both of them; he had avoided looking at his reflection at all costs, he didn't know how bad he looked but every time he touched his face it felt hot and swollen.

"He tried to break into a chimera mansion," Jade heard Tate whisper to the man. The man's eyes brightened, like Jade had suddenly become interesting to him.

"Which ones?" But Tate ignored him; he went over to Jade and put a hand on his shoulder.

"Are you okay, bro?" Tate asked. "Kerres has been hysterical... my god, buddy, those chimeras –"

"Shut up!" Jade snapped, sending the man jumping up in shock. Tate raised his eyebrows and put his hands up in a submissive gesture. Tate had always been a nice guy, softer than most Morosians, but in that moment Jade didn't care. He was in no mood for conversation and in no state to answer any of their questions.

"You're hobbling bad, did they –"

"SHUT UP!" An explosion of anger tore through Jade with such a surprising energy that even he was shocked at the outburst. But Jade had never been one to apologize easily; he turned around and continued to limp towards the door.

"I want to know what those chimera fucks did now. Who is that kid?" The man's voice started to fade.

"That's Jade, Milos. He's… *aw, shit.*"

Jade heard Tate suck in a breath and he knew why. If the dampness between his legs was as bad as it felt he knew the back of his jeans were stained with blood.

With every last ounce of energy in his body he made his way up the stairs. By now he had been walking all day, and on top of that he hadn't slept the previous night, or had anything to eat or drink. He felt like a zombie and if everyone's stares were correct he looked like one too.

Could I sleep – could I sleep… how can I sleep when that blond fuck is out there laughing at me? Jade swallowed, trying to wet his permanently dry throat, and turned the doorknob.

It was unlocked… he was wrong, Kerres was home.

Jade pushed the door open and stepped inside, his foot leaded and clumsy and his head bowed from the weight of his own racing thoughts. Like a beaten animal he slunk inside, hoping Kerres wouldn't see him before he got to the bathroom.

He heard the couch squeak and a gasp.

As Jade fell to the floor he took in a raspy, broken breath; he tried to raise himself but his whole body had suddenly gained a thousand pounds. Each arm felt like it held a weighted brick but it was nothing compared to the compression on his chest.

"Fucking hell, what did you do?" Kerres cried. He rolled Jade onto his back but that only compressed his chest more. The next thing he knew Kerres was holding him in the kneeling position as he tried to fill his spasming lungs with air.

The raw determination to make it home left him, leaving nothing in his reserves to even help himself stand. It was all gone, every ounce of energy, he couldn't even talk.

Jade put a hand to his throat, in a desperate attempt to try and ease some air into his lungs, but everything burned. His mind was quickly slipping into the dark fringes he had been running from since he had left the walls of Skyland and Eros.

"Jade?" Kerres stroked his hair, his voice faint but full of fear.

"I just – I just need some…" Jade keeled over and gagged, trying to shy away from Kerres's touch. He didn't want his boyfriend to see the blood, he had to hide himself and quickly.

"Bathroom… I just… need a shower," Jade rasped. He tried to shuffle towards the hallway but Kerres stopped him.

"No, stay love, you're okay – you're okay…" Kerres whispered. He was trying to take Jade's clothes off. Jade voiced protests, not wanting his boyfriend to see the evidence of the multiple rapes he had endured. He had to think of an excuse, something… something.

"I'll run you a shower; you can get warm, hun," Kerres said through a sniff; he rose to his feet. "Then I'll take you to a clinic."

Clinic? No… we have no money, I stole nothing for us. I just – I lost everything.

Jade let out a groan, before doubling over and throwing up. Then as Kerres ran to turn on the shower he flopped to his side and drew his knees up to his chest. Closing his eyes tight he tried to will the energy back to his body, to at least get him to the shower to wash the blood from his flushed skin.

The next thing Jade knew the hot water was hitting his face, and the silhouette of Kerres could be seen outside the curtain, keeping silent vigil. The clothing was already tossed into the garbage and the blood was running, unnoticed by Kerres, down the drain.

Jade lay with his back against the tile and closed his eyes, wanting nothing more than to scrub his body until it bled.

At least he had made it home… Jade had made it home.

CHAPTER 5

THREE WEEKS WENT BY AND IN THAT TIME JADE SWORE his teeth had been ground down at least a millimetre; his hands now holding crescent rings from his fingernails digging into the flesh. Jade was a mess and it was taking every effort and every bit of strength to hide it from Kerres.

Though Kerres had known Jade since he had been put into Edgeview Orphanage so Kerres knew something was off. He had copped it up to Jade getting his ass kicked by thiens or the bodyguards of chimeras, but that was as far as his speculations went. Jade refused to talk about any of it.

Even in the night after purposely loading Jade up with opium and playing with his hair how he liked it, the boy refused to tell him just what exactly had happened.

Tate whispered rape, as did Pete, even going so far as to throw in the names of the chimeras they suspected could've done it, but at the mere suggestion Kerres had verbally snapped them in half. Jade was a figure of stealth and cunning and there was no way he would let them do that to him. Anyway, the chimeras never let their victims go; it couldn't have been a chimera. They purposely murdered their victims to prevent bad publicity; the disciples of King Silas cleaned up the messes they made.

It must've been a thien, that's what Kerres had concluded. Jade had gotten busted by a thien and pranced around Skyland naked to be humiliated. That wouldn't be out of character for the brutish bullies that never missed an opportunity to humiliate a Morosian, especially one that had dared come to Skyland, the district of the elites and chimeras.

That had been it... and Kerres had accepted that.

But even as the bruises and the broken nose slowly healed, and the splinters in Jade's back had been carefully extracted, the boy remained stone-faced, tight-lipped, and closed off to the world, often opting for sleep rather than socializing with his friends.

But in his rest he saw the blond-haired man, his cold gaze toppling any progress Jade had made in forgetting his existence.

Once again Jade's teeth ground, his jaw ached with the stress and strain.

It wasn't only the humiliation that the blond-haired man had forced him to endure; it was the fact that that single incident was the glaring ink spot in his mind, from the moment he asked the blond-haired man to read to him, to when he had left him.

It wasn't Ares and Siris raping him; that had been so overshadowed by that man's towering visage that it was but a small blip in his memories. He wanted to tell himself he had blocked it out, but the fact was the experience with the blond man had outshined it like a match to the beacon of a lighthouse.

Filled with rage, Jade clenched his teeth tighter, wanting to scream, throw things, and beat up anyone who asked for an explanation why. He kept telling himself he should be more affected by the brutal raping the chimera twins gave him, and the bruises and abuse of his flesh, *but he wasn't*! It was all him... all the graceful elegance and derisive smile of the blond chimera.

And Jade hated himself for it... the memory stuck to him like tar and refused to unstick itself from his mind.

The voice, before it turned cold and cruel, when it was a silken stir as he read the lines of the book to him, echoed in Jade's mind. It had been steady and not rushed, taking in every moment as if deep down... he had liked reading to Jade.

But in the next moment the violet eyes were ice, filled with callousness and a heartless cruelty only a chimera could wield. It was such a contrast, it baffled Jade to think they had come from the same man.

Why has he saved him from Ares and Siris? To abuse him on his own? No, if that was the case he would've killed him after, not let him go.

The questions filled his overflowing brain, with no answers on his lips but the ones he had tried to fabricate to appease his sore and overtaxed brain.

He wished he could drug himself to forget everything that had happened, but the insect had burrowed into his brain and laid its eggs.

Jade's amber eyes looked over at the tattered book he had brought home, hiding unnoticed under old magazines. He reached over and picked it up, staring at the cover. Though it was faded and partially ripped, it looked well taken care of; a relic that had survived the apocalypse.

He opened the book and turned the page. He read the first few lines to himself before reaching over and turning a light on. He flipped through several pages to try and find the part that the blond chimera had first started to read.

Jade jumped as a metal bookmark slipped out of its place; he had forgotten the man had put it there. He shuffled to a sitting position and looked down to examine it.

It was a thin metal polished to shining with a purple tassel hanging from the top; the string was braided together over three shiny gems: a purple one, a black one, and a white one.

Jade ran his fingers over the soft string and scratched his fingernail against the odd gem stones. In the reflections of the light he saw writing.

Elish Dekker.

The silver letters blurred with Jade's trembling hand. Like he had just unwrapped a secret best not known, Jade quickly put the bookmark back into the paperback and set it down.

He got up out of bed and walked towards his door, unable to even be in the same room with it.

Anger flared through him. *Why did he let me go!?* He roughly opened the door, ignoring Kerres and his friends' surprised looks, and sat down beside Pete.

"Drug me," Jade said with a barb lingering in his tone. Without speaking or asking why, Kerres got up and started preparing him a pin of opium.

Jade stared at the coffee table, fully aware of the awkward silence around him. There was not a single fuck to give about it though; his thoughts were deep inside his mind, wrapping themselves around those silver letters.

Elish Dekker.

Elish Dekker.

The anger continued to boil in his veins. The sting of being beaten down and made submissive weighed on him and plucked at his slum-born pride. Being raped was one thing; if you survived your first year in the slums without being forced by a man you considered yourself a rare gem. It was what this blond fuck had done, and how he had done it, that sprayed its poison on Jade's brain.

A rape I deserved. I had broken into their house with an intent to steal their stuff ... that I can handle, that I could work through and bury in my brain. Like the incidents with Mom, or that time she sold me, or the chaos in the orphanage, those are simple in all respects... something I could eventually talk to Kerres about.

But fuck... this was so different... my mind felt violated, not my body.

He had made me cum... he had revelled in enforcing his control on my body and my mind. He didn't rape me, or make me suck him off. Every piece of clothing, save his gloves and the robe he had given me to wear, were still on him. Why did he take me to the forest to subdue me and make me cum? If he had asked for a blowjob for saving me from Ares and Siris... fuck, I would've gave him one.

Then the words the man had said to him came to his ears, seemingly on a silver chariot if only to taunt his brain with their power.

"It was not for your benefit."

"It was for mine."

"You should've kept your robe on."

Chimeras and blood... a thing that was well-known, even in the slums. Hell, it was obvious from watching the skyboxes during Stadium. The chimeras revelled in bloodshed and they loved licking it and tasting it too. They weren't genetically engineered vampires, that was stupid... but there was something about their makeup that made them seemingly become a little less controlled around it.

Had seeing me bloody and naked sparked something in that man? Perhaps it had been my fault for giving his cloak back to him after I had started bleeding on it...

The thought only made Jade more bitter. If there was one thing to make processing this mountain of information harder, it was the thought that perhaps he was to blame for all of this.

Fuck everything... fuck Elish, fuck Ares and Siris, fuck everybody.

Elish... he had said his name in his own mind. A name for the beautiful blond statue that had saved him and in the same breath made Jade liquid in his hands, with such a practiced ease it made his mind reel. In just a matter of moments he had taken the thief and he had made him submit to his touch with just a flare of those talented fingers.

There had never been more of a gap between the two men who had stood near the borders of Skyland and Eros. An arrogant slumrat naked and beaten and the elegant shining beacon that was Elish Dekker. A chimera with a crystal aura, trimmed with silver ribbons, that had, for a brief moment, joined itself with Jade's own tyrian purples and onyx blacks; an aura so beautiful it had banished the pain and fear in Jade's body when he had felt it.

Jade felt humiliated and angry. He hated being reminded of his place in the world, of the mud that flowed through his veins; that no matter what, he was a slumrat, and no matter how high he climbed in the Moros streets – he would be nothing compared to the blond chimera. Elish had made sure he knew that in record time. Even if he had stolen a thousand dollars-worth of loot he would still be the same Moros slumrat in the same garbage-strewn alleys.

Jade ground his teeth and slammed his hand roughly against the arm of the couch, only increasing the awkward tension in the room.

Kerres took Jade's hand and he felt the cold needle against it, though his mind didn't fully return to the present until he heard the flicking of a lighter and felt a glass tube pressed to his lips.

It wasn't until after he took his second hit that he felt the tension around his small group of friends die down to the point where they felt like they could talk again.

Jade felt Kerres draw his head onto his shoulder and rub it lovingly with his hand, before he gently started playing with his hair.

Another week went by with the festering pocket still rotting in his mind, though the time had numbed the more raw feelings inside of him, it had done nothing to quell the anger he felt whenever he thought of Elish.

He looked over at Pete who was sorting eggs with him; the short wiry man was nodding his head back and forth to the music in his ears. He didn't do drugs often and could afford small luxuries like a Walkman, though if he got busted with it he would get his ass handed to him by the boss.

Jade was an egg sorter for Dek'ko Farms; though what constituted farms nowadays was shoving weak-kneed white chickens into wire pens and forcing them to lay eggs.

The factory smelled horrendous but at least the egg-sorting room smelled a little less like chicken shit and a bit more like hay. He had been promoted from shit scooper a year ago, and though there wasn't a pay raise it had made Kerres not send him to the shower as soon as he got home.

He pressed the blue *Dek'ko-approved* stamp onto the fragile white egg shell, wishing he himself had a Walkman. Work was tedious and boring and it allowed his thoughts to go places he disliked.

So to distract his thoughts he craned his ears and listened along to Pete's music, though the asshole liked country for some fucked-up reason.

Another batch of eggs rolled through the conveyor belt, and Jade was ready with the stamp. Everything went through unless the light underneath shone some odd abnormality, a crack, or a bubble in the shell or some sort of weakness. Hell forbid the flaunting elites got a bad egg; that would be just unfathomable for people of such high status. Or for their slaves anyway; most if not all elites didn't even cook for themselves, either their sengils or cicaros did it.

Jade picked up an egg with a small hairline crack. For a moment he held the smooth white shell in his hand and ran his fingers along it.

White like Elish's opal aura... white but translucent like crystal... such a soft elegance but hidden beside that aura was a violet-eyed monster just waiting to strike.

Jade threw the egg and it smashed, strewing its contents all over the grey brick walls.

Pete took his ear phones off. "What the hell, dude? You're going to get us into trouble; you know they feed those to the orphanage."

Fuck off, Pete... Jade ignored him and continued stamping eggs.

Though apparently he was being watched.

"Jade in Block C, come to my office."

Pete looked at the speaker with a grim expression. Jade clenched his jaw and threw his goggles onto the ground. That egg was going to get taken out of his pay; there was no way to prove it was bad. Well, that was a buck off of his fucking paycheck; he needed every cent of that.

Without a word, Jade turned around and left the factory floor.

He walked across the metal grating. He looked below for a moment to observe the white chickens and the noise that surrounded them, bocking and crowing as they fluttered around their wire cages. Hundreds, maybe even a thousand of them packed into their cells, not even knowing what sunlight felt like.

Jade looked on, sliding both of his hands across the metal railings as he made his way towards the red EXIT sign. He could empathize with the chickens below him and not even from pity; a part of him could even feel the hazy confusion of the chickens' weak but sporadic aura. They really didn't know any better, they only knew the basic instincts of all animals: eat, sleep, mate, and die.

What was so different when it came to him? Jade's brow creased at the thought. That's all he did when you got down to the base of it. Eat, sleep, fuck, and wait for death. It must be great to be an immortal chimera; you didn't have the die part. Though if immortality left you like the crazed mess that their king was – no thank you.

His duct taped shoes made the stairs give off a metallic twang as he climbed towards Bill's office. He was already prepared to apologize and offer to pay for the egg just to avoid a confrontation; he would just not eat for a day, or see if one of the bars would give him some leftover plates that people didn't want. He was cozy with Corban at the Monkey Tree; he would always front him some half-eaten bosen burgers or, if he begged, some of the fries.

If he played his cards right Kerres wouldn't even have to know. His boyfriend never got angry when he fucked up work; he just had that glint of disappointment in his deep brown eyes that always hit a chord with Jade. He would've rather Kerres just yelled and screamed; it was better than giving him that disappointed look.

When he walked into Bill's office, the man was sitting with his arms crossed in front of him. He was a thin man, with small eyes and a narrow face covered by sparse facial hair, a man of Eros that had inherited this wonderful factory from his father.

"You're fired."

Jade paused, his hand still on the door knob. He stared at Bill for a moment before trying to sputter a response. "What? For the fucking egg?"

Bill cocked an eyebrow at him. Jade realized that he had no idea what he was talking about. "No, not the egg."

"Then why?" Jade's heart began to hammer rapidly inside his chest; he could feel the anxiety breed and spread through his body with the speed of a virus.

This couldn't happen, this really could not be happening to him, not now. He had too much in his head dealing with Elish and the mansion – how could he sort through this too?

"I don't owe you an explanation… get out of here. I'll give your paycheck to Pete on Wednesday."

"Are you fucking kidding me?" Jade exploded. "I didn't do anything! I need this fucking job; I'm going to fucking starve during winter because of this!"

"You took four days off last week…"

"I got hurt! You said it was okay if I brought in Pete to replace –"

"It doesn't matter."

Jade's face went hot. In his anger he picked up Bill's table lamp and tossed it against the wall. As it smashed against the paneling as he made a mock advancement towards Bill.

The pampered son of an elite shrunk back, before remembering his place in society. He stood to his feet and pointed to the door. "Get out of my sight, and you can forget about that last paycheck. It will replace the lamp you just broke."

"I'll fucking break you!" Jade roared, slamming his fist onto the desk.

Then he felt himself restrained; he kicked and struggled until a thien punched him in the stomach. The bodyguards were never far from their fucking charges.

"Just throw him out, I don't want to waste my time with the paperwork," Bill's spiteful voice called. Jade hurled a few more insults his way before he felt a rough palm smack to the back of his head.

Every factory worker turned to watch the show, some of them

whispering things to each other and all of them looking on with wide eyes. Pete was there too, his mouth open from shock and surprise. They made eye contact for a moment before the thien grabbed onto Jade's head and wrenched him towards the doors.

Not now... why now? The injustice skewered him like a spear, he felt himself unable to even comprehend what was going on with his life now.

If he had gotten away with that burglary he would have had enough money to feed Kerres and himself, buy them shoes, buy Sheryn a jacket...

You're such a pathetic piece of shit, Jade.

He clenched his fists and spat on the concrete parking lot of the factory before, without a second glance, he left, hitting and tipping over everything he could get his hands on as he made his way down the winding, empty roads of Moros.

The boy was seething with a burning energy inside him that only wanted him to hit and destroy. He refocused his hatred and stalked the alleys, hoping to pick a fight, find a crowbar to swing at things, or at the very least a drug dealer who he could score something to numb the feelings raging inside of him.

Ever since the night at the mansion he had felt like he was losing bits of himself, getting angry at things that had once only given him a drive to better himself, and taking out that anger on everyone from Kerres to his own body. Since the incident with the chimeras, his mind had been travelling off without him, leaving him a walking time bomb that exploded on everyone without provocation or warning.

Just several days ago he had gotten into an explosive fight with Kerres, a fight so bad he had felt like hitting him. It was over money, which made being fired even more damaging. Kerres had said he was spending too much money on drugs, and they didn't have enough food for the week because of it.

Yes, he had been doing too many... but he had needed them. They were the only brief solace from his thoughts about Elish; thoughts that were always just simmering underneath the surface. For his own sanity he needed to numb himself.

Although Kerres knew this was something to do with what had happened, he didn't know the details and so became less and less understanding as the weeks went on. Now he even had the gall to tell Jade he should be over it by now, that he'd had worse beatings.

Jade visibly shuddered; he twitched his face away as if feeling Elish's mouth lick the blood from his wounds.

Why did he let me go? The million dollar question, but there were millions of those questions he wished to have answered, though it would never happen. The chances of him ever seeing the chimera again were slim to nothing. He hadn't even known which one he was until he had found the metal bookmark. Elish was on the news every so often when Silas needed him to fill in for conferences, once he might've spoken after someone had shot Legion ruler Kessler in the head, but who he was had been lost to Jade. He had just never cared enough to find out who was who; whenever the TV show he had been watching got interrupted by breaking news he turned the TV off. The chimeras didn't affect his life.

Or they hadn't...

Jade shot to his feet when he felt a tightening between his legs. He started quickly walking away as if blaming the spot he was sitting on for the tingled twitch. Every time he replayed the moments when his back was against the wall he felt the stirring inside of him.

It might've been because he hadn't slept with Kerres, or even taken care of himself in that time. His mind couldn't have been further from wanting that, though his body still craved it as all men his age did. The farthest he got was stroking or satisfying Kerres orally to take care of his partner's own cravings. That was his duty and he loved his boyfriend; he didn't want him suffering because of his own inner turmoil.

Perhaps it was time to appease his own body; maybe the twitching would end that way.

Though Jade wasn't sure... there was something that nagged at him, pulled the membrane of his brain with small needle-like pinches.

A reality he didn't want to accept... that the way Elish had touched him had set his mind on fire with a pleasure he had never felt before.

The orgasm... oh god, the orgasm had been so intense. He had to grab onto the blond chimera's robes to keep himself from falling. The silken hand still pulling and stroking him in a soft but firm grasp, the pressure varying at all the right moments as it glided up and down his shaft. The man had known when to speed up, and when to stop. It was as if they were a violin and a bow, two pieces of the same instrument that, when played correctly, could make beautiful music.

Jade pushed the disturbing thought from his mind, filling the empty spot with the bitter anger he felt towards the man with the long blond hair. Wherever his doubts had infiltrated, anger would replace those feelings, and he hated that chimera with every ounce of his being.

With his hands stuffed in his pocket and one of his last cigarettes in his teeth, he walked through the dirty alleyways, though instead of making a beeline home he kept his eyes out for open windows.

An alley cat ran past him and glared at him with green eyes as he walked past. He wished for a moment he was an alley cat, before climbing over a chain-link fence to check out several houses that bordered the harbour wall that separated Nyx's port from Moros's.

Though his last attempt at thievery was too fresh in his mind, he knew all he had now was his fencing. He would need to step up the pick-pocketing and burglaries to make ends meet now, at least until he found another job.

Or another keycard.

Jade wanted to hit himself for musing on such a cruel joke. In many ways Jade was his own worst enemy. No man was more cruel than the one in his head.

As if to prove to himself he didn't need a worthless keycard, he hoisted himself up a rusted metal fire escape and silently kneeled in front of a curtained window.

With an expertise only a slum-raised delinquent could temper, he brushed the curtain back and poked his head in.

Quick and easy, don't look, just grab the most expensive thing you can see.

Jade slipped in, hearing two men laughing in the living room with a television show blaring loudly on the TV. Jade silently grabbed a toaster and a spice rack resting on the counter, and without a second glance jumped back onto the fire escape.

Without bracing himself he jumped down onto the concrete. Though everyone else he knew would hurt or possibly break his legs, Jade could steel himself for the fall with barely a bend in his knees.

Jade sprinted away from the house and took off his jacket to hide the loot. Instead of walking home he made his way across town to find Tiger.

Probably in his cave with his broads. He had told Jade he could come whenever as long as it was afternoon. Not too many sellers saw mornings.

When he walked into Tiger's hovel though, he was greeted with a shocked look, like he was a ghost rising from the dead.

The man gave him a comical rub of his eyes, and shook his head with a gruff laugh. "You're alive? Well smack my ass... you lived? I thought the twins had fucked and eaten your sorry corpse already."

Jade's face paled, and immediately he felt his chest contract. "What?" he whispered; he tried to take a step forward but his boots felt glued to the spot. "How did you know?"

Tiger motioned him to sit down, and after forcing every neuron in his brain to obey he sat down on the swivel chair in front of him. Absentmindedly Jade put his jacket on the office table that separated the two of them.

"That boy you met... my my, was I surprised when your name came up as the boy he sold the card to," Tiger said, still using his fake Russian accent. He lit a blue ember cigarette and handed it to Jade without even taking an inhale for himself. "He's not a jaded serventmaid; he was Ares and Siris's cicaro. You were set up, all along. This is what those twin-fucks do apparently. They give out these card keys to their cicaros to give to cute little rats like yourself. Once you break in, they spring you, fuck you, eat a few pieces once they've seasoned and tenderized your flesh, and then murder you. In that order. How in Silas's name did you get out alive?"

The shock temporarily rendered Jade speechless; he could do nothing but stare at Tiger as though he had been smacked across the face.

Tiger chuckled and motioned for Jade to take another inhale, amused at the reaction he was able to drag out of the seemingly stoic man.

Jade took an inhale before leaning down and rested his forehead into his hands. Tiger gave out yet another amused chuckle and Jade heard him knock against the wood. "I know we do not converse, but my many damns, Shadow. I wish I had heard of this thievery first. I could have warned you; I lost several supple little boys to them last year. I send girls now with stolen card keys just in case. They do not rape them first at least, quicker death."

A groan escaped Jade's lips, he felt light-headed and nauseas; he just wanted to get out of there. "How – how much for the stuff? I just lost my job so don't jack me around with negotiating just this once."

Tiger pushed himself backwards onto his chair and spun around to sort through his bags.

This new information made Jade's chest hurt, though what did it matter now? Ares and Siris were nothing compared to what Elish had done to him.

Wait a second... Elish had saved him... he actually had saved him. Not just from rape, but from being eaten alive and murdered.

That thought did leak through the barriers Jade had hastily erected in his mind. The sullen and stark realization that Elish probably knew that if Ares and Siris had found him, they would kill him. The blond chimera had stayed silent, and had even walked him to the borders, telling everyone who stared to essentially fuck off.

The chimera had read to him for hours... in a soothing, graceful voice.

Only to spring on Jade, touch him, and bring him to a knee-trembling orgasm.

It made no sense... and the more Jade uncovered and thought about it, the less sense it made.

Jade took the five dollars and the two pears without haggling; he knew the pears were from Tiger's own sympathies. Though it had been weeks there were still small wisps of bruise on Jade's face, and a healing pink scar above his brow.

Kerres and his friends might've been fooled, but Tiger knew from his experience with the twin chimeras that Jade had been raped.

Afterwards Jade roamed the streets, bought himself a small supply of drugs for the night and picked up some half-off fries from Corban and a piece of battered fish the bar owner had set aside for the beggars. He gave it to Jade with a sympathetic cluck of his tongue when Jade had told him about getting fired from the factory.

It wouldn't do enough to not get the disappointed look from Kerres, but it was something; he wasn't coming home empty-handed. At least he had food, and two bucks left over after visiting the pharmacy.

Finally when the streets were dark, and he had roamed himself to exhaustion, Jade slunk his sorry ass home; his tail between his legs, and the cold and stale food tucked into his jacket pocket.

When he opened the door though Kerres was beaming at him and there was a pleasant smell in the air too.

Kerres leapt up from the couch and gave Jade a long drawn-out kiss, only broken when his lips tightened into a smile.

"What's that smell?" Jade looked around the dark apartment; scanning the empty soda bottles, the filled ash trays, and the dingy carpet that hadn't seen a vacuum since Tate's broke.

"I bought us some noodles and stir-fry from Nyx, come on, eat!" Kerres's smile was a mile long.

"We... can't afford that," Jade whispered, never feeling more useless and pathetic than he did now. He took off his jacket, hiding the stale food he had scavenged, and took off his duct taped shoes. A sigh fell from his lips, wondering if it was too late for Kerres to return the food, or at least offer it to someone in the streets to recover some of their money.

Kerres laughed a lighthearted laugh that told Jade there was more to this story than just spoiling their stomachs tonight.

"I got promoted!"

Jade stared at him. He should have been filled with joy, but it seemed to be the latest nail in the 'you're useless and pathetic' coffin that had been Jade's life over the past several weeks.

"That's... congratulations, love." Jade forced a smile, but he was transparent in front of Kerres.

Kerres's mouth pulled to a frown; he put down the plastic container of food. "What's wrong?"

Suddenly not very hungry, Jade walked out of the kitchen and sat down on their mouldy, stale-smelling couch. He picked up the small baggy of opium and started twisting off a small piece.

Kerres was right behind him; he felt his aura there even though Jade couldn't see him. Still a fragrant seafoam green, that washed over the heat of his mind like a cold river.

"I –" There was no way around it, Kerres would know tomorrow morning when Jade didn't walk him to work. "I got fired today."

There was no disappointed gaze. Jade lay against the couch and looked up at his boyfriend, but all Kerres did was smile wider.

Kerres swung himself over the back of the couch and landed on it, bouncing up and down as the rusty springs gave a twang. He then straddled Jade, his arms on either side of the boy's shoulders.

Jade glared up at him, not in the mood to deal with his playfulness. But Kerres knew him and pressed on with his advances, ignoring the poisonous looks he was getting.

"It was a big promotion, Jade; you don't need a job anymore." Kerres's tone was kind, and Jade felt his chest loosen automatically. It was that sweet and caring tone that had drawn Jade to Kerres in the beginning, when he was a cold and lost child, getting over nightingale poisoning courtesy of his mother.

Kerres had taken him under his wing, and even when he graduated from Edgeview soon after, he had immediately taken up a job as janitor just to be able to be with Jade until he eventually graduated as well. Their friendship had developed into something more when Jade had hit the streets of Moros. Soon they were in love, and … inseparable.

Jade had lost his virginity to Kerres and vice versa; they had starved together, celebrated victories together and had just experienced life in Moros together.

But it was an equal relationship. Even though Kerres was three years older, Jade held his own if not more. Kerres was more laid back, the 'what happens happens' type, whereas Jade was the type of man to charge into the dark and take chances. He had seen the under belly of Skyfall whereas Kerres preferred to follow the law and do as he was told. Though with the chances he had taken Jade had been able to carve out a better life for them and he took a great amount of pride in that.

Jade sighed, but let Kerres kiss and suck on his neck, though nothing was stirring in him but anger for the situation he was in.

"I'm going to buy you new shoes…" Another kiss landed on his neck. Kerres's voice was a gravely vibration against the nape. "I'm going to get us both vitamin shots… lots of food…"

Jade sighed, glaring at the hallway leading to their bedroom and the bathroom to avoid looking at Kerres.

"Your only job will be to stay home and be sexy."

"Okay, okay… get off of me." Jade pushed Kerres off and got up; walking towards the door, his body flushing with an awkward tension that he could no longer stuff down. The only solution he could think of was to leave the apartment and get some cold air.

"Stop right there!"

Jade froze, pressing his lips together, his back turned to Kerres and the sexual advances he had been trying to force upon him.

There was a sigh behind him, and soft footsteps. He tensed as he felt Kerres put a hand on his shoulder, and almost jerked his shoulder away when he felt Kerres start to gently massage it.

"You've never hidden things from me before, J... when did this start to become a thing?"

Jade could feel the tension radiating off of his own body; if Kerres had his special aura talent he probably would've taken a step back.

Instead Kerres continued to touch him in a caring, soothing manner. Though to a normal person the advances would bring warmth to their hearts, it further drove the stake into Jade's chest. To Jade it felt like Kerres was talking to him like a useless child, someone lesser than him.

The anger churned, Jade felt his fists clench. Their partnership had always been equal, both bringing in money, both supporting one another; it extended to all aspects of their life and only varied in the bedroom from Jade's top preference.

Now he didn't feel equal, he felt like the shivering naked boy by the fireplace, and even sickeningly still – the one pinned up against the wall like a piece of meat.

Jade was an adult, a man, he had always found his own way... he had taken care of Kerres once he had graduated from Edgeview. He made his way through life doing what had to be done for his partner. He wasn't some trophy boy stuck in a smelly apartment all day waiting for his boyfriend to come home.

Emasculated and defeated, he tried to walk away.

He almost jumped in surprise when Kerres roughly grabbed his arm.

Jade turned around with a shocked expression, and to further his confusion he saw a glint of impatience and anger in Kerres's eyes.

"You're either going to tell me what's eating you, or you're going to get over it and start acting like the Jade I know."

Jade jerked his arm away and glared at his boyfriend; Kerres challenged his stare and didn't back down.

The situation exhilarated him; there was something about Kerres showing this dominant side of him that made Jade's pulse race. In response he leaned into his partner until he was nose to nose with him.

"You want ultimatums, Kerres?" Jade growled, his chest filling with an electric charge. He took a step towards him and to his unbidden joy, Kerres didn't back down. He stared back; his crimson bangs the only thing that broke up his staring dark eyes. "Let me go, or else I will break every single fucking tooth you have."

Kerres had no idea what had come over Jade, but there was a small notch in his boyfriend's unrelenting anger that he had a feeling he could grab onto. In response to his challenge, Kerres took a step back and gave jade's chest a threatening push.

Jade seethed; he roughly pushed Kerres back but as soon as he did, Kerres raised his hand and smacked Jade across the face with his palm.

Not a punch, or even anything that could do physical damage, but it hurt and it was enough to spin Jade in a rage.

Jade charged at Kerres, and Kerres met his charge with a stealthy slide of his socked feet. Though when he spun around to get another shot in, Kerres let Jade hit him.

Kerres was knocked backwards, stumbling over the arm of the couch and landing beside it with a hard thud.

Jade towered over him, his shoulders heaving with emotion, his yellow eyes wild and unhinged. This was the moment, the moment where Kerres would pull out his knowledge of Jade's personality and try and channel Jade's anger where it belonged.

Kerres rose and wiped the blood off of his chin before roughly taking Jade into his arms and kissing him passionately.

It worked.

Jade's chest froze, and as his lips opened up to meet his boyfriend's sudden advancement he felt the anger inside of him boil down to a surge of sexual lust. A moment later their clothes were off and Jade was digging through the drawer by the couch for lube.

As he plunged himself deep inside the gasping Kerres, he felt his self-hatred and the uncontrollable anger transformed into a vigorous need to fuck and fuck hard. With every thrust, and drop of sweat that trickled down his body it disappeared like therapy. No drugs could ever give him the release that an intense session with his boyfriend could give him. Even if Jade knew the relief would only be temporary.

When they were both dissolved heaps of tender flesh and cum, Kerres found himself in Jade's arms. They had eventually made it to the bedroom, where they had stayed for the last leg of their exploits.

Jade found himself half in reality and half in a daydream, feeling more content now than he had for the last month.

He smiled when he felt Kerres kiss his cheek.

"I know you so well."

Jade's brow furrowed, making Kerres let out a playful laugh. Kerres kissed him again before laying his head on Jade's chest, his free hand stroking small circles on his boyfriend's bare stomach.

"You know I love you, right, J?"

J and K... the stupid little nicknames they had given us in Edgeview; that's how close we were back then, and how close we are now.

Jade sighed, finally realizing with a surge of guilt what Kerres had been seeing in him for the past several weeks. His attitude changing as the clouds continued to gather over his head, not understanding what had happened to his boyfriend, and why he had been so full of anger and self-angst.

But his loving boyfriend wouldn't understand. He would get upset about what Ares and Siris had done, and if anything, he would tell him to be thankful that Elish had only done that in return for saving him. The always rational Kerres wouldn't understand just how much it had affected him, how he couldn't get what had happened out of his head.

Though the confession moved on Jade's lips to the point where he took in a breath to speak, he stopped himself. Instead he stroked back Kerres's crimson hair, brushing it out of his boyfriend's eyes.

"I know, and I love you, K."

With the tightness coming back to his chest, Jade kissed the back of Kerres's head and closed his eyes. Wishing more than anything he wouldn't see the blond chimera in his dreams.

CHAPTER 6

BACK WHEN THEY WERE BOTH IN EDGEVIEW, KERRES could only hold his hand when the aids weren't looking. So they did their hand-holding in secret, sometimes in the janitor's closet, sometimes in the empty room Jade had shared with another orphan.

Now they could hold hands and do more, whenever they liked, it was a little gesture that reminded Jade he was loved.

Even when it was more a steel grip to keep Jade from running off than a need for Kerres to keep his boyfriend close.

Two months after his unsuccessful mansion break in, Jade and Kerres were sitting on concrete blocks, side by side and hand in hand.

Jade groaned and pulled his fingertips away from Kerres's grip one by one. Kerres laughed and pulled him close before planting a kiss on the side of his face.

They were in a busy area, and as he guarded the children during field trips many years ago, Kerres guarded Jade to make sure no harm came to him. It didn't happen often, but with Kerres's improved spirits over his fancy new job it had brought out long buried emotions inside of him.

They were standing outside of the stadium, selling ecstasy and speed at double the price they had bought it from Fiere. It would be a small contribution to their funds but one that Jade had been making since he had been old enough to have the connections to do so.

Usually Kerres took one side of the stadium parking lot and Jade took the other, but with a smiling suggestion and a flash of his puppy dog eyes, Jade had teamed up with Kerres this time and had stuck to his side.

Everyone who would be buying from them they knew anyway, so Jade really wasn't at risk.

It was a rarity for them to have any trouble while selling outside during Stadium Night, but it did happen, usually sometime in the middle or near the end when the convicts came out. When people were already hammered and looking for a boy to fuck; or looking for a fight because they'd lost money in a bet. Kerres, and especially Jade, were prime targets for people who wanted to cause trouble.

Kerres slipped several women tabs of pink ecstasy and took their tokens, before slipping them to Jade. Though the people tried to make small talk it was really too noisy to hear anything.

The place was crowded, even though Stadium had started over an hour ago. Right now it was opening shows, usually the lions and the rats, or little performances to warm up the crowd.

Another couple of tokens got slipped to Jade, who placed them inside his jacket before slipping his hand back into Kerres's. They both watched the people of all statuses mull around, making small talk and exchanging bets on convicts. Supposedly there would be five of them going against the twins tonight.

Knowing there would be no point in letting it affect him, Jade pushed down the very common knowledge that Ares and Siris would be the ones to challenge the convicts.

Stadium Night. A weekly event which took place in a refurbished stadium that bordered the coast deep inside an abandoned part of the city. It was for the entertainment of the Skyfallers, and was one of the only events in Skyfall where every class was welcome to attend.

Everyone with at least five bucks for a ticket would be treated to a three-hour show of everything from lions doing tricks, to rats being fed to Skytech's newest abomination, and even the occasional young chimera performing stunts to show off their skills, all ending on a crescendo of watching this week's convicts getting brutally slaughtered one by one.

By none other than Ares, Siris, and their Master and Commander: Nero.

They had a chance though. The point of Stadium was to pit the convicts against the chimera brutes for their freedom. If they killed the chimera, they got a pardon and could walk free; but that had happened only several times in the last couple of years. Most often than not they were killed in whatever grisly way King Silas had thought up that week.

Though, of course, even if the convict did kill one of the three, they would come back. King Silas's bodyguards had the gift of immortality; Jade figured it was easier than training a new brute every couple months.

An eruption of cheers came from inside the stadium. Jade looked up to see the lights change from white to deep red, showing a kill was about to be made. Sure enough, the roaring of the crowd got louder before climaxing with a collective hushed gasp.

The large circular building, repaired with rusty metal and the medians and pavement of old streets, seemed to make their voices echo inside of it, spilling blood like beer in a large and brightly lit fenced arena surrounded by red bleachers.

Jade had sat in those uncomfortable plastic chairs many times and enjoyed, as his own guilty pleasure, the auras of everyone around him exploding and shining with the almost visible electric currents around them, broken up only by the giant neon signs and strewn-up Christmas lights that hung over the arena like snared telephone lines.

Kerres squeezed his hand and gave him a grin. "Let's go in. My treat."

The mere idea of being that close to Ares and Siris filled Jade's heart with anxiety, though he forced it down with a smile. It was something he didn't want to risk, even if Jade didn't think the twins would be able to see him from the lit up arena floor.

But if the twins did see and recognize Jade a chain-link fence wouldn't be enough to keep those maniacs from doing what Elish had prevented them from finishing.

Kerres pulled on his hand, looking like the twelve-year-old boy he had first met, and playfully tugging him towards the stadium.

Jade let himself be dragged, though he slowed down his steps. Deep down inside he did want to go, though the fear was still there. Stadium could hold a thousand people and they couldn't afford front row seats anyway.

With a sigh and a nod, Jade decided to push through the anxiety and continue to do what he had been doing for the past month: getting over it and moving on.

Kerres jumped ahead and bought their tickets. After getting their hand stamped with the chimera's lion-scorpion emblem and a number, they walked through the open doors and made their way across the lobby.

The lobby was nothing much; it was stripped of anything of value to keep the starving Morosians from ripping something off to sell. The entire circular area consisted of nothing but cracked painted walls and dusty floors, with white linoleum, warped and missing entirely in some places, showing bare concrete underneath.

Jade walked through the lobby, his nose filling with the smell of cold concrete and sweat, and past the large metal beams that kept the once retractable roof in the air. The beams had no use now, because there was no roof to keep up. Though that didn't matter. Even without a roof Stadium was always rain or shine. It was an amusing treat to see the convicts slipping around in the mud.

The crowd exploded again as the two of them quickly sprinted down the open hall; the concession workers called out their specials but the food was always too overpriced, even for Kerres's padded pockets.

Jade hid his smile when they showed their stamp and walked through the doors.

The energy hit him like he had just slipped through an invisible wall; he immediately felt his chest shudder and tingle from pure bliss.

Kerres led Jade to their seats, several benches up from the arena and so far away that not even a chimera could spot them.

They settled in and turned their attention to the show going on below them, Kerres immediately whooping and hollering like the other Skyfallers – it never took him long to get into it. The deafening noise and the screams of dying convicts brought out the bloodlust in even the most law-abiding resident.

Jade refused himself a reaction when his eyes fell upon Ares.

The chimera brute was dressed to the nines in a leather jacket, a red shirt underneath, and black jeans, all of this topped off with a pair of sunglasses and a black cape trimmed with dark grey. Outfits were popular and well-anticipated during Stadium. Tomorrow the same outfit would be for sale in the high-priced shops of Skyland, bought eagerly by pampered men with a thirst to make themselves feel dangerous.

As Ares pumped his fists up in the air, the crowd followed. Jade craned his head but it wasn't until Ares stepped back that he saw where his victim was.

The convict was writhing on the ground in a seeping pool of his own blood. He was struggling to get up but he kept falling over onto the liquid mess, mixing it up with the pounded dirt until it was a sticky mud that stuck to every part of his body.

It took Jade a moment to realize why he couldn't get up. His right arm had been tied off at the shoulder and subsequently ripped off, and his leg was twisted completely backwards. Every time he would try to stand, the leg would bend like it was made out of rubber, spilling the convict back onto the ground to the crowd's delight.

Ares turned around and, with an army boot that just two months ago had kicked down Jade, he rested it on top of the convict's head before he tipped the man over, shifting him up onto his back. With a mouth open in a scream inaudible over the crowd, he looked up at the blinding lights above him.

Jade could see the faint ripples of an aqua aura, and as Ares pressed his boot against the man's throat he wondered what he had done to end up here. Stealing, raping, murdering… every offence could wind you up as a convict in Stadium, though the chimeras saved the most grisly of deaths for those convicted of espionage, terrorism, or anything that went against King Silas.

Jade looked up at the skybox, a special covered area that only the chimeras and their people were allowed to watch from. It was held up by metal beams, and had windows on all sides for the royalty to view the slaughter going on below them. From where Jade was sitting all you could see were the front windows and the tips of chairs sometimes filled with a chimera, or one of their pets.

Jade watched a chimera he recognized happily smoking a cigar, talking to the great King Silas, both with laughing smiles on their faces.

Jade looked away, feeling relieved that Elish wasn't there. He didn't know what he would do if he saw him, fake a stomach ache or something maybe. Anything to convince Kerres to let him leave.

The lights went red and everyone around them, Kerres included, gasped. Jade turned his attention away from the skybox to see Ares holding the convicts head in his hands, a fountain of blood gushing from the stump of his roughly torn-off head, the body still twitching and shaking as it died.

The blood made the crowd go wild, but it was Ares's need for showmanship that made him the star that he was. Ares held up the head before removing one of the convict's eyes. He walked over and gave it to a pretty-looking boy with a horrendously over-embellished bow, the way a man would give a rose to a maiden. It was hilarious but at the same time it made Jade's skin crawl.

Those hands – those hands groped me and savagely beat me... and now look at them. Fucking chimeras.

With a jaw clenched to the point where the now familiar twinge of pain shot through him, he looked away. But with a restraint he had developed since the incident, Jade pushed it down and went on with the show. Jade had never been one to linger in the past, if he had done he would've been declared insane and euthanized. He had a talent to him now that could stuff bad experiences deep inside him and close them off for good, even if at times they would break through the curtain, it was nothing his mind couldn't handle.

If I can deal with the wreck of a childhood my mother gave me, and if I can survive in the slums... I can get over what happened in the mansion, and afterwards.

Jade took a hit of a joint being passed around and passed it to Kerres. He found his boyfriend's hand and squeezed it, landing him another kiss on the cheek.

With the audience around them continuing to cheer as each convict was killed in amusing ways, Jade settled in and enjoyed the show, watching as all three of the chimera brutes took turns challenging and murdering the convicts that got marched (or sometimes dragged) to the middle of the arena.

An hour later when the last convict, a woman, was disembowelled and dismembered, Stadium wound down. Now the raffle prizes would be handed out, and after that they would be free to make their way back to Moros.

Relaxed and enjoying himself for the first time in months, Jade took in the smell of fresh blood and tasted the energies and auras around him. The auras of most Morosians were sickly and dark, tainted with years of toiling just to survive the seasons, but once they came to Stadium and had a chance to let loose and have fun, they did. It was an inhale of cold crisp air to Jade; he was in heaven.

Everyone watched as an older man walked up with a microphone. He was holding a small piece of paper in his hands – the winning numbers of tonight's raffle.

He called out number after number, giving away things like vitamin shots, microwaves, DVDs and even vouchers for rat meat. Kerres rose in his seat just a bit every time the man called out a number, but would slink back with a disappointed sigh whenever they passed over the digits stamped on his wrist.

Kerres lifted up Jade's hand and read his number for a third time before dropping it with a groan. A couple years ago he had won some wool socks, and since then he had been bit by the raffle bug.

"And our last prize! Our crème de la crème!" said the announcer who everyone only knew by the name Old Joe.

Kerres leaned forward, his fists clenched in what could only be described as pure bliss. Jade smiled and rubbed his leg, looking forward to getting the crazy guy back home so he could expend that bliss elsewhere.

"The number is… stamp 0901298!"

Kerres jumped up off his seat shouting. He reached down and grabbed Jade's arm before yanking it high in the air. "Jade, that's you! That's your stamp! You won!"

If Kerres had looked at Jade, and not jumped up and down wrenching the boy's hand up for all to see, he would've probably taken Jade out of the building without an explanation needed. But Kerres was too caught up in the moment to care.

With feet that felt like they would never hit ground again, Jade let himself be led to the gate of the chain-link fence by Kerres's excited pulls, the crowd around them cheering, and the lights fixed on him. Though he didn't feel like a winner, he felt like a convict being led to get his head ripped off.

No one noticed. Kerres attributed it to nerves, and the crowd paid no attention. Jade was walked into the middle of the illuminated arena alone, all around him a continuous excited roar that tickled the lower registers of his ears.

The auras and energies gave his mind such a rush Jade had to tune his abilities away to try and tone down the uncomfortable and overwhelming feeling of everyone watching him. His empath abilities were controlled, and he enjoyed the weird gift he had been born with but when he had hundreds, possibly a thousand people staring at him, blaring their auras at him, not to mention the electricity of the environment, it mentally seemed to knock him off his feet.

Old Joe smiled as he checked his hand, before turning and nodding towards the long fenced entrance of the arena, lit by strings of lights of all colours and neon *Open* signs.

Two blue-tinged figures appeared in the doorway, and when their tall and burly shapes began to take form during their slow walk to the arena Jade felt his body go stiff with overwhelming fear.

The prey took a step back, his chest a vibration and his mouth dry and tight. He watched with yellow eyes wide as saucers as Ares and Siris walked side by side towards him, with knowing smirks on their faces.

The two brutes only smiled wider when they spotted Jade; with confident steps that only reminded Jade of the ground shaking stomps of their boots on the mansion floor, they approached the Morosian.

"Congratulations." A grin that held a bloodthirsty menace appeared on Siris's face.

Jade's legs shook, his toes twitched in his duct taped shoes, wanting nothing more than to run out of the building and never look back. Like the burglar in the mansion, the fear welling inside him ripped apart every shred of resolve he had gathered in himself.

No longer the tough thief from the slums, in the presence of his rapists he was nothing. They knew he was nothing, and he knew he was nothing. A small bug, a piece of shit on their shoe that would disappear with the flow of time. Jade knew his place in front of these immortal monsters.

His eyes couldn't leave their twin faces. He felt himself stripped bare in front of the cheering, talkative crowd, leaving himself with nothing left to defend himself with. Once again he was to be humiliated. He wouldn't even be surprised if they announced his crimes and killed him right there.

To his surprise though, Ares handed him a small cardboard box. It was his prize. All the other prizes had come in similar brown boxes, with a single blue bow resting on top.

"Open it," Ares's hushed but deep voice said, still clearly audible to him over the noisy atmosphere around them.

Jade took the box, almost unable to hold it, his hands shaking like leaves during a wind storm. He lifted off the top and, though his mind told him to run, he obeyed the twin chimeras and looked down.

It was the Mp3 player… one of the items he had tried to steal from the mansion, the same one.

"A present from Elish." The words chafed his brain as though a dagger was scraping away the membrane.

Jade's mouth fell open. He heard Old Joe say something behind him into the microphone and the crowd cheered him on. He could hear Kerres whoop and holler behind him.

His eyes automatically lifted to the skybox above him.

And there he was.

Elish Dekker stared down at him from high in the skybox, his flowing golden hair cascading down his shoulders covering a white duster jacket belted in the middle. His long, strong arms were crossed over his chest giving him a menacing look.

He was looking down at Jade, with a pale face that encapsulated a beautiful grace that seemed unreal; staring through eyes like smouldering embers visible even though he was many feet above.

It was only him on that pedestal, staring down at the insect in cold bemusement, with a knowing smile that told Jade he had just been the victim of a cruel prank.

What the fuck is this asshole trying to do? Jade gritted his teeth as every bit of self-control left him. Unable to hold back the anger and humiliation, he stormed off the stage before running down the entrance of the arena with the Mp3 player clenched in his hand.

He was going to find him; he was going to find him and throw the Mp3 player back into his fucking face! Jade ran past a few bewildered arena workers and found a flight of stairs.

Jade had no idea where the skybox was connected, but he didn't care. He had to try; he had to do something to steal back the pride that Elish had taken from him, even if it was just to confront him face to face.

With flames of anger burrowing into his brain, searing the grey matter and sending pulses urging him to do things he never would've normally done, he stormed up the stairs.

Jade pushed the metal door open with both hands and took a step inside. He was in a white painted room, with plastic chairs and patio tables lining the left wall, but that was as far as he got.

Two thiens were standing in a corner drinking coffee from plastic cups; as soon as they saw the expression on Jade's face, they put their cups down and grabbed him.

Immediately Jade jerked his arm away from the first thien, only to feel the other one punch him in the jaw.

Kerres gasped behind him. *Kerres has followed me?* Jade groaned and tried to wrap his arms around his stomach, before feeling himself get pulled to his feet by the two thien enforcers.

When he heard that amused chuckle his courage seemed to turn to ashes in front of him, a single sound that brought him emotionally to his knees.

Not a sound came to Jade's pursed lips as he looked up and saw the blond chimera towering over him; his cold face only broken by the slight smirk he seemed to save just to taunt Jade.

"You didn't like your gift?"

Jade refused to look into his eyes; he glared at the grey linoleum floor not saying a single thing. Even when the thiens shook his body, urging him to speak to their master, Jade's lips were tight.

"Gift?" Kerres's voice was small and confused.

Jade shut his eyes for a moment, until several echoing footsteps could be heard. He smelled the mint and nutmeg, and when he opened his eyes he could see white trousers and silver-buckled white leather boots.

"Leave the three of us; I do not fear the bites of Morosian dogs."

Jade was dropped to his knees, his shoulders shook. When the door clicked closed he heard Elish bend over to pick up the Mp3 player that had dropped during Jade's struggles, before handing it back to him.

"Why?" Jade managed to croak. He took the player from him, if only in the hope that Elish would step away from him, but he didn't. Elish's legs were only inches away from Jade's face; he was so close Jade could feel the cold sweepings of his aura mix in with his own. He hated the memories that his exposure to Elish brought to him.

"I had such a wonderful time with you, I wanted to pay you for your –"

"I am not a whore!" Jade snapped, looking up and glaring into his eyes. He managed to rise to his feet, where he clenched his fists trying to look as intimidating as possible.

The blond chimera didn't even bat an eye. He looked like he was about to twist the dagger further into Jade's pride when Kerres spoke.

"Jade... how do you know him? What's going on?"

This was candy to Elish. The blond chimera tore his eyes away from Jade and looked at Kerres, then slipped a gloved hand under Jade's cheek and pulled his chin up.

Though the horror wasn't the act, it was the feeling his chest gave when Elish touched him. In a second he was transported back to the wall, transported back to that feeling welling inside him. How his body unclenched and unwound under those soft hands that could manipulate his touch.

It was such a... wonderful feeling. For a brief moment Jade felt his head crane towards the silk white gloves before he snapped out of it.

"Jade and I had a wonderful time as I was walking him to the borders... I was merely paying him for his service. He gave such an exquisite performance," Elish's smooth and cold voice said.

He heard Kerres's breathing behind him become rapid, so angry but restrained to the point where Jade knew it would be painful from him. They were in the presence of an immortal chimera, of the highest rank. A single slip and the snake would strike.

"You – you raped him didn't you?"

The glove stroked Jade's face tenderly, and though inside he wanted to pull away, there was something that was gluing Jade to him.

"Rape?" Elish seemed amused by this. "I was not the one to disrobe. Jade seemed very eager to take off the article of clothing I had given him, after my brothers had their way with his body. He was the one whose semen slicked my hand, not the other way –"

"Shut up!" A roaring sounded inside Jade's brain, it snapped the strings of his restraint and he felt an almost heated madness sweep through him.

Jade jumped to his feet; he pushed Elish away but it was like pushing away a concrete barrier. He raised a clenched fist and punched him in the chest, but still the mountain didn't move.

"Such a fight in your veins, yet such putty in my hands when you're in the throes of climax." Elish held Jade's hands back with amusement, before he turned him around and gave Jade a playful push towards Kerres.

Jade whirled around but before he could attack Elish again he felt Kerres's hand on his shoulders.

"You're lying..." Kerres whispered.

There was a pause, and though Jade couldn't see him, he knew Elish was relishing every moment of this encounter. Jade turned around defeated, and heard the chimera's cold voice behind him.

"Did I say something that was false? Tell him; tell him what part of that was a lie."

Jade couldn't look at his boyfriend, but out of the corner of his eye he saw Kerres's confused and anguished eyes switching from Elish to Jade's own. When his eyes finally rested permanently on Jade, he took a step back towards the exit.

"I'm – I'm going home now," Kerres whispered, and without another word he turned from both of them and started walking towards the closed metal doors.

That was when Elish decided to twist the knife one last time.

"I hope you're taking good care of my book, stray. It is one of my favourites and I do not lend items freely."

There were echoing footsteps behind Jade, and the closing of a door.

The shuttle bus, only available during Stadium Night, took them home, and the atmosphere during the long ride back to Moros couldn't have been thicker.

Kerres was silent beside him, his hand that had once been unable to let go of Jade's, was folded with the other on his lap. He was looking out the window with a distant expression on his face and not even the hint of a word on his lips.

Jade was okay with that, he himself was lost in his own thoughts.

The Mp3 player was in his jacket, and though a part of him wanted to throw it away, he selfishly held onto it. Though his emotions ruled him, the Morosian slumrat that had been a part of him since his conception reminded him that not only could he sell it for at least a hundred and fifty dollars, he could use it himself if he wanted. He had never had anything like this before, and he had trouble letting go of his prize even though it had only come into his possession through a cruel chimera joke.

When the shuttle stopped in front of Bluetone Station everybody filed out. Jade took several steps back and let Kerres lead the way home, knowing that as soon as they walked into their apartment a fight would break out.

Like a steel gate slamming behind him, the door closed with a silent click. Jade locked it and leaned up against it, watching his boyfriend take off his shabby boots and jacket. Without another word he took out a container of yesterday's fries and fish and started heating it up in the new microwave he had just bought last week.

As the time ticked down, and the apartment was filled with nothing but the cycling hum of the microwave, Jade saw Kerres's head slump. When the timer beeped he didn't move.

"I forgive you."

Jade felt his teeth grate together. He glared at his boyfriend's slumped shoulders, swallowing the bile rising to his throat.

"For what?" he asked coldly.

"Cheating on me."

The words hit him like an oncoming train; a wave of anger replaced the sullen hollowness he had felt since leaving the stadium.

"Are you fucking kidding me?" Jade snapped. He saw Kerres flinch, though it was enough for Kerres to snap out of his state and push the lever on the microwave.

"I didn't cheat on you… Ares and Siris… caught me."

"You don't need to lie to me, chimeras are hot… I get it."

Jade's mouth went to mush; there was so many things wrong with what Kerres was saying he didn't even know where to start, yet he knew if he started trying to defend himself he wouldn't be able to control the anger scalding his head like boiling water, filling him with what seemed like thousands of fireworks exploding inside his brain.

"The twins raped me… Elish – Elish saved me from them."

"And he gave you his book as a souvenir?" There was a dry chuckle and the scraping of plastic against fingernails as he walked towards the living room. "Was this before or after you came in his hands?"

The words were like a slap across the face. Though after seeing Elish again, and the heated and humiliating confrontation back in Stadium, Jade responded in a way he didn't expect.

He quickly closed the gap between him and Kerres and violently shoved him against the couch.

Kerres yelped with surprise, falling over the back of the couch and landing in front of the coffee table, his food spilling all around them.

"If you ever say something like that again I swear to god…"

Kerres didn't look scared; he rarely ever did when Jade got physical with him. He scrambled to his feet and held his arms out. "Then tell me he's lying, Jade. I'm begging you… tell me he's lying!"

The recall of what Elish had done to him made his soul smoulder. "It's – it's not what you think, he – he had me pinned!"

"And he made you cum!?"

Jade's ears went hot, his legs twitched, wanting to run out of the apartment like he had fled the stadium. To get as far away from this conversation and these recollections as he could.

"I didn't want to!"

Kerres made an annoyed noise and threw the now empty plastic container against the wall. "I don't understand! Just tell me what happened from the beginning, fucking make me understand, Jade! Why did he give you a book? Why did he go through all this trouble to give you that Mp3 player? I don't understand, make me understand!"

"I can't…"

How can I explain to him that I sat beside that fireplace and hung on his every word as he read to me? That I fell into a trance of pure bliss as those golden tones fell to my bruised and hurting head. That moment between us – it was our moment. A brief oasis in the terror waiting outside that door. Something happened in that room. Even though his expression went cold when his eyes fell onto my body… it was my fault.

I should've kept my robe on.

NO! Jade let out a cry of anger, he pushed Kerres again, and again, until his boyfriend restrained him with his own hands.

Jade's legs become jelly; as his pushes became weaker he slipped and fell to his knees. Sobs became muffled on his lips as his chest heaved and shook from his own thoughts.

How could he explain it to Kerres when even he didn't know what was going on inside of him?

"What happened to you, J?"

"Shut up!" Jade screamed. He put his hands over his head and clenched his hair, grinding his teeth back and forth, feeling them squeak and whine under the increased pressure.

I don't know… I don't know what's going on. I don't understand what

Elish is doing, or how I can explain it to Kerres and make him understand. I was a mouse with the predator looming over me, confused as to why he kept toying and playing with me. I was a slumrat. He should've, in all respects, let Ares and Siris kill me.

I could accept him letting me go, I could move past that… but why this prank on me? Why did he feel the need to humiliate me further in front of everyone?

As if wanting to pick the rest of the scab off, Kerres said to him in a thin voice, "I fucking told you not to go to that mansion."

This flash of anger brought an uncontrollable rage to Jade he didn't expect. Before he could stop himself he raised a hand and slapped Kerres right across the face.

Jade rose to his feet, feeling like a different person had possessed his body. Like a zombie he walked into his bedroom to fetch his old earphones for the Mp3 player.

He grabbed them, and with a flicker of his eye, he saw the book with the metal bookmark resting inside. He put both of them into his jacket pocket before grabbing a thin blanket from the bed.

When he walked towards the door he heard Kerres sniffing back tears of shock.

"What did he do to you?" Kerres choked, his wavering voice pierced the silence growing between them.

Jade gave him a single anguished look, before his eyes could no longer bear the sight of his boyfriend on the floor crying; tears running down his pale face that was twisted in confusion and shock. Jade turned the knob and opened the door, without looking back he left Kerres crying softly on the floor.

CHAPTER 7

THE STREETS WERE FILLED WITH MOROSIANS ON THEIR way to bars, or one of the hollowed out buildings that were a popular hangout. They filed past Jade without a second glance, chatting happily with each other with bottles of stout in their hands and cigarettes on their lips, sporting torn and roughly patched clothing, dark from grime and sweat, and shoes taped with the same silver duct tape Jade's own had.

Jade walked through an alleyway, hearing echoing voices inside the brick building to his left. He glanced up for a moment and saw shadows leaning against the exposed rusted beams, and smouldering embers that lit up and faded with their inhales. Friends hanging out with friends, or perhaps gangs sitting around enjoying a drink before they started prowling.

In the darkness Jade could hear them erupting in howling laughs followed by the clicks of bottles as they drunk under the cover of the autumn stars, making toasts and half-drunken cheers to everything from good cigarettes to tight asses, not even knowing the man dressed in black underneath them was in a state of complete self-contempt and misery.

Another cigarette was brought to his lips; the jacket was thin but the blanket he had thrown over his back warmed him. With his hands tucked inside he wasn't uncomfortable or cold, though as the night ticked past midnight and into the darker hours it would only get colder. Winter was coming, though for now sleeping outside wouldn't be too unbearable.

Jade couldn't crash at a friend's house, where he knew Kerres would find him, or at a shelter where he was sure to get groped by some horny guy. No, tonight his roof would be the stars, but at least growing up in Moros had revealed to him every safe place to crash. There were vents all over Moros that would warm him, and safe little alcoves tucked under stairs or underneath buildings that would be safe enough, as long as he didn't mind the smell of piss and decay, and, of course, the occasional radrat or croach.

With his own cigarette lit he looked up at a burned-out street lamp, a useless totem of what this place might've been before the Fallocaust. Moros was too poor to have street lights, even the shops and the bars had to shut off all their lights at night, and anyone caught with a light on that wasn't a bluelamp after midnight was fined and disciplined.

In Eros and Skyland though they could have lights on all the time, their street lights were always on during the night, and illuminated the streets in their safe glow. So many bad things were allowed to happen under the cover of darkness, and usually by day the only remains of those horrors were a blood stain and, if they were lucky… a used condom.

When he got to the harbour of the Moros District, Jade walked across the sea walk and fiddled with his Mp3 player. He managed to turn it on, which gave him a small spark of pride. Electronics had never been his strong point; he had electrocuted himself once trying to fix the old TV they had and had stayed way clear of them ever since.

He put the earphones in and clicked around the small device until he found a list of songs, and though he didn't recognize any of them he was able to make one play. He put one of his ear buds in and enjoyed the novelty of being able to listen to music in his ear. It sounded much better than Pete's shitty Walkman, crystal clear with no background static. This was one of the last electronics they invented before the Fallocaust happened.

The song was slow, and it brought up inside him feelings of loneliness and guilt over exploding on Kerres. The next one he chose was a bit faster which helped take his mind off it.

He would make up with his boyfriend soon but he needed to cool off right now. Kerres had plucked his every last nerve with his accusations and assumptions and it would be bad for both their mental and physical health if Kerres pushed Jade any further.

Those two might have a rocky relationship, but they understood each other. Though Jade had gone too far in hitting Kerres it was nothing he hadn't done before in the throes of his temper. He had always had trouble controlling his rage and lashing out physically had been his only known outlet. Being a hothead wasn't an excuse though, and it pained him; he would apologize for at least that.

He slept under a stairwell that night and remained unmolested and warm enough for an adequate night's sleep, though his dreams were always a different story.

Jade woke up several times seeing Elish in his head, but once he smelled the piss and sour smell of rotting plywood around him he was reminded that Elish was far away and he certainly wouldn't be found here. The thought itself was almost laughable.

The next morning Jade got up and bought himself a couple pieces of tact for breakfast. He ate the first one and made his way towards Garrett Park to see how Sheryn was doing.

His mother was in her usual nest of garbage; before the dog gave away his presence he observed her nodding her head back and forth as she tried to sort through the cans she had collected. To Jade it looked like she was just piling them from one grocery bag to another, what methods of sorting she was doing was lost on him. It all looked like the frays of madness to him.

"Hey, Mom, I got you some sweet tact." Jade leaned down and gave her the square brown cracker.

Sheryn looked up at him, and smiled her jack-o'-lantern smile. "You're alone? You never come alone; did you break up with that boy?"

Jade's mouth twitched, but he pushed aside the tender feelings still just below the surface and gave her a nonchalant shrug. He sat down beside her and started chewing on the dense cracker.

"No, he's just at work today. I got fired. How goes the can collecting?"

Sheryn looked pleased at the question; she coughed into her arm and started showing the different tin cans off to Jade. Some with their faded labels but most of them bare tin

Dek'ko gave five cents a can; they melted them down and made new cans with them. Apparently in the greywastes there were millions of cans still full of edible food, though the greywasters didn't have the resources to melt them down so they were worthless there.

"This... see this one?" Sheryn pointed a yellowed finger, more a talon than anything, to a can with a faded Campbell's Soup label. "Merchant gave that to me, he had just come back from the block called Tintown. He might be your father, but his eyes were blue."

His mouth twitched again, but he tried to steer away from that conversation. "Want me to take those to the recyclers? Save you the walk? I know how your knee has been bothering you."

Jade didn't know what had come over him, whether it was him trying to make up for the guilt he felt over his fight with Kerres, or just having a night out to clear his head, but he didn't feel impatient with his mother like he usually did.

The old woman bobbed her head in a nod and handed Jade the grocery bag full of cans. "Go around lunch. I'll make us lunch. When you come back, we can eat together."

Or I can get poisoned. Jade reached into his pocket and gave his mother the last dollar he had, more than enough to cover the cost of the cans. "I'll just front you the money, in case something happens and I can't make it back right away, alright?"

Sheryn nodded and that was the end of the discussion. Jade leaned against the tree and gave the dog a pat then spent the next several hours listening to her ramble on about the state of Moros, and the good old days pulling Jade in the wagon. She loved to talk to anyone that would listen, especially her only son.

"You looked like a little alien when you were a baby, loved to bite too... look, look at this finger... you did that! Swallowed it too." Sheryn waved her stubbed pinky finger at him. Jade was never sure if he had actually bitten a part of her finger off when he was little, but she never missed a chance to remind him of it. "I watched you eat a rat once too, bit its head clean off."

Well, maybe you should've fed me more. "What about the time I climbed to the top of the CIBC building? Remember the thiens had to get me down?"

Sheryn thought for a second, before her already wrinkled face broke into a laugh. She nodded in her over-exuberant way and slapped her knee. "You got on the news too! I wonder if your father watched that news? I bet he would know it was you."

"Did he have eyes like me?" Jade asked. Though sometimes weird eye colours showed up in Skyfall, it was rare, he had never met anyone else with yellow eyes like him. Though he had seen orange once and a brilliant shade of green on a kid he had mugged.

Jade took another inhale from his smoke. He was still leaning up against the tree; he had almost wiped out his entire store of cigarettes chatting with his mother. It was a good way to keep him from saying something that might set her off. At least talking about when he was younger was safe, he was usually the one that got upset before her. She seemed to laugh at all the memories that made Jade wake up in a cold sweat.

Sheryn shook her head. "No, no, he had brown eyes… but mine are blue, and blue and brown make yellow."

Jade stared at her; he raised a single eyebrow but didn't say anything to dispute her logic. It was better to just leave it alone, she was crazy and he accepted that.

"If my eyes are yellow, why did you call me Jade? Jade's a green gemstone."

Sheryn shrugged. She licked her fingers as she started tearing open the butts of Jade's cigarettes, no doubt to collect the leftover tobacco to try and make an extra one. "I wanted to call you Phillip, but they had a giveaway of baby clothes. Something that President Chimery organized and he was giving away baby clothes and baby things. You got a green jumper with the name Jade on the front. Well, it would be stupid to call you something different, confusing too. You wore that until you split out of it and then I sewed it into a blanket. Nice clothes, soft fabric."

Phillip… Jade couldn't help the snort. *Phillip, thank god for a green jumper. I can't wait to tell Kerres what my name almost had been.*

Kerres… I'm going to have to face him sooner or later.

Jade hung out with his mom for another hour, before he rose to his feet. With the cans in hand he declined her offer of the cigarette she had managed to make out of his cigarette butts and continued towards Nyx where the recycling depot was.

On his way back to Moros with thirty cents rattling around in his pocket, he was greeted by Tate.

He met his friend with a wave, but as soon as he saw his face, Jade's own tensed.

Tate's eyes widened and he shook his head looking relieved. He ran towards Jade and as he got closer Jade realized he was out of breath.

"We've been fucking looking for you all morning, where the hell have you been?"

Jade looked behind him, though he didn't know what he was expecting to see. "I was visiting with my mom; I got in a fight with Kerres…"

Tate put up a hand to stop him. "Kerres got arrested in front of Olympus this morning; he's fucking in jail right now."

Jade's heart dropped. "He's in jail? What… where the fuck is Olympus?"

"Elish Dekker's skyscraper – in Skyland."

The empty alleyway echoed with the sounds of Jade's swearing; enough expletives left his mouth to make Tate shrink back and look around in shock.

Jade walked towards the bordering wall before he turned around and swore loudly again. He gave a nearby stack of metal garbage cans a ferocious kick, sending even more deafening noise throughout the empty alley. He balled his fists and with all his strength punched a nearby wall before also giving it a sound kick.

Tate just stared, not knowing what else to do. He watched as his friend unravelled in front of him, wondering why he had to be the one to find Jade. All three of Jade and Kerres's friends had been out looking for the guy all morning and afternoon. Admittedly they never thought of checking Garrett Park; usually the kid avoided his mother like the plague. That was the last place they had expected to find him.

"Jade, do you remember that guy who I was with when you came back from… that place? He wants to talk to you, do you remember the Crimstones?" Tate stepped back as Jade paced past him, his hands gripping his hair.

Jade looked at him with a glare; everyone had heard of the Crimstones. They were a terrorist organization, a useless one though.

Every year or so they rigged up a car bomb or tried to wreak some sort of vigilante justice towards the chimeras, but they had nothing to do with him.

"I don't give a fuck about that, Tate, I have to – ah, fuck!" Jade swore. Why was Kerres so fucking dumb?

Tate raised his hands. "Just… come with me so he can talk to you, maybe he can help."

Jade shook his head, he wasn't about to go with Tate and waste time on some stranger, and he definitely wasn't going to get involved with someone like that. Not when the chimeras had his boyfriend.

"I – I need to go see Kerres myself." Jade shook his head. At least he still had the Mp3 player; he might be able to buy Kerres's freedom with that, or at least post his bail so Jade could make him disappear somehow.

Leaving a bewildered and scared Tate behind, Jade ran towards the border of Moros and Nyx, and soon he was sprinting through the districts as quickly as he could.

With only a cracker of tact for breakfast and no dinner at all last night, Jade's energy drained from him quickly, but he let his worry for Kerres keep him going.

His body was refusing to go on just motivation and love alone, and Jade had to keep stopping to throw up in garbage cans and back alleys. Even with nothing to throw up his stomach lurched and knotted. The residents passing by tsked and clucked at him, more than likely thinking he was high on something, or else full of disease.

But his determination kept him walking, followed by sprinting whenever he felt his body could do it. The faster he could get to Skyland the sooner he could bring his boyfriend home. There was nothing more in the world he wanted than to apologize and make up with Kerres. Even though he didn't think he could ever explain to him what had happened between him and Elish, he could make up a story that would make sense to Kerres. He didn't have a problem lying over this; it was better than Kerres doing something this fucking stupid.

What the hell was Kerres thinking? The boulder that Jade kept trying to swallow down only grew and churned in his throat and stomach. The fight last night must've affected him more than Jade had thought. Kerres wasn't impulsive or stupid – that was all Jade.

Kerres was the rational one, the quiet and law abiding one… what the fuck was he doing outside of Elish's skyscraper?

Kerres must've walked all night to get to Skyland, or else he might've caught a charter there with the money he had earned from his job. Though he wasn't wealthy in any sense, he had been able to put a few dollars under the mattress for their boot fund.

Jade looked both ways; he was in Skyland now and there were cars to watch out for. Jade hobbled across the street and started asking directions to the precinct.

No one was helpful though, most didn't talk to him and there were even a few with the gall to make smart quips at him about 'going to turn himself in'. In the end a shopkeeper answered him when he went to buy several cigarettes with the thirty cents he had earned from the cans. He was close, only several blocks away.

Jade lit a cigarette and took a moment's rest to have a couple puffs. They were silver cigs, the opiate kind. They cost more but having a bit of relief for the numbing and aching pain in his body made it worth the money.

As Jade enjoyed his small comforts he looked around the clean district. The sun was setting again, sooner now with winter around the corner. Unlike in Moros, the flares of street lights cut through the darkness, and with the lit up shop windows, the streets almost looked like mini strips of daylight. With the homeless stuck back in Moros and the dying in hospitals, it looked like the streets of the cities he saw on the television. Even the smell was pleasant, no stale piss and alcohol stink at all. It was clean to a point where when he passed a restaurant he actually smelled the food inside.

There was a double-edged sword to him being here though, mostly the blaring fact that he wasn't welcome. He would have to get Kerres tonight; if he tried to sleep in Skyland he risked being arrested by the thiens. Even in Eros you weren't allowed to sleep outside; it would be a long walk back to Moros tonight or at the very least Nyx where they did allow outside sleeping.

Jade killed the cigarette and continued to limp on.

His relief was palpable when he saw the Skyland Precinct sign hanging above a large building with a domed roof. The lights were on inside and he could see two thiens standing guard, armed with assault rifles.

Jade weakly walked up the steps, trying to look unassuming, but it was obvious from his clothes and the gaunt hollowness to his face that he wasn't from around there.

Sure enough, as he got closer to the thiens, they shifted their assault rifles and took a quick step towards each other, essentially blocking off the entrance.

"My boyfriend got arrested, I need to talk to someone in charge," Jade said hastily. He looked behind the thiens and into the brightly lit precinct behind the two guards, as if hoping to catch a glimpse of Kerres. In the lobby, a few thiens sat behind bullet proof glass clicking on computers.

"Inquiries are from ten until four, it is seven now, move along," one of the thiens said. His voice was commanding and held little space for negotiations.

Jade's jaw clenched, a quiver went through his chest that was quickly changing into anxiety. He was growing desperate; he couldn't go back to Moros without some information.

Against his better judgment he pressed on. "Is he okay? You didn't beat him did you? Did you see him? His name is Kerres; he's from Moros."

"Please move along." The tone was more forceful this time; Jade knew he was already testing the thien's patience.

With defeat on his shoulders Jade gave the warmly lit precinct one last glance before he made a move to turn around.

Then someone caught his eye; a lady walking past with a dark-haired man following behind. She gave the slightest turn of her head, enough for Jade to realize who she was.

It was the female chimera, Elish's sister, the only female one that existed. He recognized her right away. She was the commissioner of the thiens. No doubt she would know what was going on. If she didn't, it would at least get back to Elish that Kerres had been arrested if he didn't know already, it was a long shot but he could help him.

That thought alone showed Jade just how desperate he was.

Jade took a chance; with lightning speed he pushed between the thiens and opened the door.

Though he knew eventually he would get caught, he wasn't expecting the thiens to be so quick. He didn't even get a foot through the door before both of them yanked him away, and threw him down the concrete steps.

Jade fell roughly onto his back, before rolling down each step and coming to a stop. He stayed crumpled in the corner of the concrete barrier that lined the steps.

He groaned, feeling an overwhelming pain wash through his body.

The thiens must've thought that was punishment enough, they laughed and threw a few taunts, but otherwise left the injured boy alone.

Jade tried to stand but his head went dizzy; as the world spun around him he felt blood droplets start to run from his face, falling to the dark sidewalk like little raindrops.

With all his strength Jade managed to get to his feet, and with a stumbling, awkward gait he began to walk away from the precinct, looking for an alleyway to crouch into until he could make his way back to a district he could sleep in.

I just need to lie down for a moment... just a moment. I'll have a cigarette and get up in no time.

Leaving a small trail of blood drops Jade found a back alley. A small alley, not the wide alleys in Moros where you could fit a car, but narrow, with dumpsters resting in front of metal doors, and only minimal garbage crushed into the sides underneath the rough grey brick walls.

Jade shuffled towards a metal air vent; he put his hand underneath it and sighed with relief when he felt warm air coming through. This vent might save him for now; his fingers were starting to get numb.

He wrapped his brown blanket over him and shifted up to the air vent the way a newborn animal huddles up to its mother. Even though half of his body felt hot, he was still shivering.

Jade lay in the darkness, the bright yellow street lights not even licking the corners of his boots as he huddled in the cloak of night. He could see the blood spots on the blanket and on the concrete, shiny and purple with a glisten that reminded him of black oil. All he could do was lean his head forward; he didn't have the energy to try and bandage the wounds. The only cloth he had was his shirt, and he needed that to help keep him warm tonight.

Well, at least crashing here was a step up from Moros, though – and the thought made Jade look around and scrunch himself up smaller – if a thien found him here they would throw him in a cell and confiscate his Mp3 player and everything he had on him.

Kerres better be thankful I went all this way for him after the shit he pulled. What was he thinking? The phrase was usually reserved for Jade; he was the one always fucking up. If he had a dime for every time someone had said that to him, he would be the richest man in the world.

The question held its weight and continued to pick at Jade's emotions. What had Kerres been thinking? What would possess him to actually go to Skyland to demand to speak to Elish? Jade had been raised with the chimeras as far away power figures who he occasionally saw on the news channel but who, for the most part, remained shrouded authorities.

They were powerful figures that even Jade knew not to fuck with. Kerres was smarter than him and a law-abiding citizen, he must have been extremely upset to do this. Insane almost.

Jade gasped as he felt the concrete hit his face; his mind snapped back from his inner daydream with the realization that he had fallen forward. Unable to keep the weight of his head in check, he had spilled himself right on the cold ground in front of him.

Gasping, Jade tried to sit back up but found his back gave a surge of pain with every attempt; he rubbed it with his hand, the cold fingers kneading the flesh offering a temporary reprieve, enough of a break from the pain for him to pull his shirt and jacket up, and lay down on the ground, bare skin exposed. His whole body felt boiling hot.

I pushed myself too hard, and now I'm paying for it. No food besides a cracker of tact in over a day, no water. Walking through four districts at almost a sprint and now getting tossed down the stairs? You idiot.

Jade squinted hard, seeing the yellowy lights dim and blur as his vision distorted in front of him.

He didn't even have enough money now for food, and it was out of the question to beg. Jade groaned as he tried to get up again, but his energy was gone. He lay sprawled out on the alley and watched the street lamps blur and twinkle, going in and out of focus, occasionally blocked by night owls strolling on towards destinations unknown.

Jade's heart pounded as one of the people walking by paused and looked into the alleyway. His panicked eyes raced back and forth as the figure approached with the soft click of his boots growing louder with every step.

A tall man, with a cape flowing behind him.

No way...

A low and cold chuckle came from the towering silhouette. Jade watched as the figure stuck his foot out and tapped him in the side. Jade tried to recoil, but the pain that erupted from his body made him suck air through his teeth instead.

"You're far from home… miss me that much? We just saw each other yesterday."

Commanding every muscle in his body, Jade tried to make himself stand up, unable to handle the humiliation of looking so weak and pathetic in front of the immortal chimera. It was futile though; with every attempt his arms or back gave a jolt of pain that only showcased his sickly state. The apex was when his arms buckled and gave right out in front of him and Jade collapsed onto the ground with a painful moan.

To his surprise he heard a scraping of boots against pavement. It was Elish kneeling down in front of him. Not just crouching, he was kneeling in the dirt, getting dirt all over his white pants, ones that probably cost more than Jade had earned in all his life.

As if to further shock Jade's system, Elish reached out and brushed Jade's hair away from his eyes. "You will die tonight. Is your boyfriend really going to like that?"

There was no longer the tense unease that Jade felt in his presence; he looked up at Elish only feeling fear and vulnerability. "Is he alive?"

Elish nodded, tucking Jade's black hair behind his ears in an almost caring manner. "After the show he put on he shouldn't be, but yes, Kerres is in a lot better shape than you."

The relief filled Jade with an encouraging energy. He once again struggled to rise but only managed to tuck a knee under himself. Elish withdrew his hand, and watched Jade struggle to stand, whether from amusement, cruelty, or curiosity to see if he could do it, Jade didn't know. His face was almost completely covered by the backlights of the street. Only his crystal aura was visible and even that was distorted in Jade's weakened state.

But he fell back down. "I'll do anything you want… if you'll just take him back to Moros."

His heart fell to the point where he felt like he was going to burst into tears when he heard Elish's chuckle, dry and mocking, bordering on cruel.

"What do you have to give me? You have nothing I want, nothing that I couldn't purchase unspoiled and in better health."

The tears burned his eyes as Elish stood. He sniffed them back as the chimera turned around to leave the dark alleyway.

Elish paused for a moment though, his head downturned as if seeing something. Jade watched as the chimera bent down and picked up the dog-eared book that had fallen from Jade's jacket pocket. With a sweep of his cape and Jade defeated behind him, he began to walk away.

Jade was unable to stem the whimper on his lips, with the weak cry came all his fears and sorrows. The stark reality of his predicament was glaring him right in the face, and stripping him of everything he had left.

"Read to me..." Jade choked. His chest shuddered under sobs his shattering pride so dearly tried to hold back. Though he no longer had pride, Elish had already taken that away from him. Now he was taking away the man that Jade loved.

To Jade's surprise the chimera stopped, the book dangling from his gloved hands. The street lights in front of him lined his silhouette in their yellow light, as if he was an angel who had just been kicked out of heaven.

Jade watched as he turned around, fixing his eyes on the black heap in the corner. The boy stared back, blinking the tears that now flowed freely, and shaking in his fear and grief. He was unable to even stand on his own two feet, let alone survive the night.

In a move that for many years Elish would question, he took a step forward, his soft boots clicking one by one until he was in front of the boy.

In the silence only broken by the cars passing in the dark streets, he picked Jade up and walked with him out of the alley.

The street lights made Jade's eyes squint; he closed them and felt his head drop. With a shift of Elish's arm he lifted Jade's limp head and let it fall against his white overcoat.

Then they were both in a vehicle. Jade had only been in a car several times in his life, so he tried to look up to see the streets go by but his neck felt like it was rubber.

Elish was quiet the whole time; the car was dark but the auras around them made everything glow to Jade. Since the light was in his head it could never illuminate objects, but it was still a comfortable glow that offered its own type of solace in the darkness.

"Just Moros is okay," Jade rasped, once again trying to look out to see if he could recognize anything. He realized all of the windows were tinted.

"We're not going to Moros."

Jade was too tired and weak to have much of a reaction; he nodded and rested his head back in the crook of his arms. If he had been dropped off at Moros chances are he wouldn't make the night there either. Not without a lot of water and some food, and since Kerres was in jail he had no one to nurse him back to health. Though Tate, Pete, and Fiere were his buds, he would feel too ashamed to have them see him in such a state.

Elish had already seen him at his weakest, and the chimera was so above Jade he already saw him as a piece of shit, whereas in Moros – he had a reputation to uphold.

Oh, what shit have I gotten myself into... I'm in his arms now; he's holding me and getting my pathetic malnourished body some help. I'm supposed to be getting Kerres back... fuck that idiot. What was he thinking?

The door was opened for Elish, and with Jade still cradled in his arms, he walked out of the car and towards the tall skyscraper.

The light was blinding when they went inside, so bright to eyes so used to the darkness that Jade had to shut them tight and shield himself with his hand. He didn't get a good look at the lobby, or the elevator; it wasn't until Elish started speaking with someone that Jade opened his eyes.

"Oh wow, look at those eyes, did you bring me a boy or a stray cat?" An older man with greying blond hair peered down at him through rectangle-shaped eyeglasses.

"Well, he bites like one so watch your fingers." Elish laid Jade down on a small hospital bed and dusted off his robes. "I gather he was thrown down the precinct stairs after he ran from Moros to Skyland. Is that right, stray?"

As Jade nodded, the man who looked like a doctor took out a pen flashlight and started shining it in his eyes; then he told Jade to open his mouth.

"It's not the tumble that's about to kill him, it's dehydration. I'll get some fluids in him and see if we can get him at least stable. Do you want him alive enough to return to Moros, or…?"

Jade tried to sit up, his arms shaking from the strain. "I'll be okay with just some water… I need to go get Kerres."

Then the striking cobra but instead of a physical strike like Jade had seen before, it was a cold smile and a smooth glove tracing the chin of Jades jawline.

"Your days of making your own decisions have passed." His purple eyes lifted to the doctor. "Jade will be staying with me from now on."

Jade stared at Elish for a moment, struck dumb by the comment that took him a moment to process. It wasn't until he felt the stabbing jolt of a needle going into his neck that the realization dawned on him.

"What? With you? Are you fucking k-kid-" Jade's eyes fluttered; with his depleting strength he managed to reach out and grab Elish's arm, before he felt the balls of his fingers loosen on the soft fabric.

He passed out to a warm hand on his neck and a cold whisper in his ear.

"Sleep well, Cicaro."

CHAPTER 8

J ADE KNEW THAT SOMETHING WAS WRONG WHEN HE woke up warm and comfortable. Unlike the last night's sleep he'd had this was an odd contrast. He wasn't cold, he didn't have snot stuck to his face, and he couldn't smell any old piss or stale alcohol.

His yellow eyes slowly opened, and as they did the blurred room started to come into focus. The walls were painted maroon, new paint without a single chip or curl, and were adorned with framed paintings: one of a cat with a pressed in face, and one with a stormy ocean and a pirate ship.

Jade shifted up in his bed, clenching his jaw tight as a jolt of pain reminded him of his injuries.

With his last memories a faint smoke in his brain, he swung his legs over the large comforter-covered bed and rested them onto the floor.

Carpet... Jade looked down and wiggled his toes against the soft grey threads and tried to get up.

To his confusion his neck tightened, and in that same moment he heard the sound of chains. Putting his hand up to his neck, he felt a thick piece of leather studded with cold metal. He looked down at his arm and saw leather cuffs with a shiny metal hitch on each piece, below was an IV which went directly into his arm.

"Hi."

The soft voice snapped Jade's mind out of his confused and half-asleep state; he looked over and saw a young man in the doorway of the bedroom he was in.

The man, possibly in his late teens or early twenties, was sitting with his arms behind his back. He had wavy blond hair and a soft face that held two large green eyes. To Jade's perplexity the boy was wearing a headband decorated with two cat ears, black ears with pink in the middle, like you would find on a Halloween costume before the Fallocaust. He was an odd sight indeed, but he didn't look threatening. If anything the young man looked scared of *him*.

"Hello..." Jade said slowly; his voice was still raspy and it took every effort to even speak properly.

Jade's calm response seemed to bring relief to the young man; though it wasn't overly visible on his face, the aura around him seemed to brighten. With a small smile the cat-eared boy quietly pattered up to Jade and gave him a small bow.

"Why am I chained?" Jade rasped, managing to raise an arm and, with it, a small linked chain.

The man looked at it for a second, before his green eyes quickly went to the doorway and then back to Jade. He cleared his throat and bowed again.

"My name is Luca, Master Elish's sengil. I am going to be your serventmaid. If there is anything you might need, please just let me know and if I can – I will make it available to you."

Jade ignored Luca's greeting and tugged on the chain attached to his neck. "Take this chain off me, that's what I want you to do."

"Oh, I can't do that. My apolo-"

"You said if there was anything I needed then to tell you. I need this chain off me."

The young man named Luca chewed on the side of his cheek, before looking nervously at the door. "I'm not allowed. Would you like something to eat or drink? Or I can bring you a Game Boy –"

Jade ground his teeth. He looked to the doorway, where the kid kept glancing, and decided to cut to the marrow of it. "Where's Elish? I think we're overdue for a talk."

Luca stared at him for a moment, before he nodded again and walked over to a solid black dresser. He picked up a brown paper bag. "Elish is at a meeting with Master Garrett and has instructed me to tell you he will be home shortly." The sengil took out a piece of gold tinfoil from a bag and handed it to Jade. "Here you go. I saved it from my dessert last night… it's real chocolate."

Jade took the tinfoil and smelled it; it smelled good enough. He looked up at the boy and raised an eyebrow. "Where am I? Are you Elish's slave?"

The young man's eyes shifted from side to side; he crumpled up the bag before putting his hands back behind his back. "I am Elish's sengil and your serventmaid. You are in his personal dwellings inside Olympus, which is in Sky-"

Luca gasped as Jade pinched his IV and pulled it out of his arm; at the same time the servant reached his arms out to take it from Jade, the crumpled paper dropping to the ground.

But Jade wrenched his arm back out of his reach. "Why does he have me chained? What has he told you about me?"

The servant was still trying to grab Jade's arm, the loose dripping IV in his other hand. "He already told you, didn't he? You're his pet, his new cicaro."

Silence filled the air; for a moment Jade could only stare at the kid with the cat ears, trying desperately to grab Jade's wrist.

Cicaro? A slave pet? He had seen these collared slaves being dragged around by their leashes, but only glimpses of them on the television. Most of his knowledge of cicaros came from gossip around the slums and stories shared deep in the night after too much stout.

They were human pets for the chimeras and high-ranking elites. A person, man or woman, with no dignity, no life outside of their master, they were worthless slaves who got used up and tossed aside once their masters got bored of them.

That wasn't going to happen. Not to Jade.

Though the words wouldn't come to his tight constricting throat, the desperate and helpless anger burned inside of him, leaving him no audible outlet.

So instead, the hot headed fifteen-year-old did the next best thing.

Luca yelped as Jade lunged at him, a desperate yell from Jade breaking the silence in the room. They both flew off of the bed with Jade's fists swinging.

But though the unrestrained Luca fell to the grey carpet, Jade's chain yanked him back; ripping the air out of his throat and hanging him like a noose off of the bed.

The servantmaid scrambled away from him, and, with his tail between his legs, ran out of the room.

Jade snarled and swore at the servant, as the collar restricted his air flow. A moment later he managed to find his footing on the carpet and sit himself back on the bed.

His chest was heaving. He looked towards the chain which was connected to the metal bed frame and started pulling on it, snarling and growling in a way that he had never had before.

I'm going to rip that fucking chimera's face off when I see him! Jade braced his bare feet against the wall behind his bed and tried desperately to break the chain. It was no use; even at full strength he would never be able to snap the links.

This wasn't right. He was a slumrat, what did that motherfucker want with him? Jade pulled on the chain until he started to chafe his hand, before he finally gave up and instead slid himself down to the small space between the bed and the side wall; his chain barely letting him sit on the floor without choking him.

Jade stayed in the corner until he heard the door quietly open. He was about to tell the slave to piss off when he felt the cold electricity of Elish's aura creep into the room like tendrils.

"You attacked my servant? That is no way to thank me for my hospitality and medical care." Jade refused to look at him and instead he stared at the wall.

"What did you expect? He told me I'm your pet now." Even the words made Jade's stomach give a nauseas churn. His pride and his knowledge of the elite chimeras and their way of always getting what they want were battling to the death inside him.

When he was in Moros, he knew what to expect and how to deal with it. This was a whole new kettle of fish; he didn't know what to do, or if there was anything he could do. He had been imprisoned by a force of control and power, by a chimera whose master was the guy who killed the world.

Elish took another step forward and sat on the bed. Jade heard the sound of tinfoil unwrapping which automatically made him turn his head towards the odd sound.

Elish broke off a piece of the chocolate bar and reached his hand down to offer it to Jade.

Jade took it, but to his anger Elish nodded approvingly.

"Good boy."

"I am not your pet!" Jade screamed. In his rage he jumped to his feet and tried to lunge at Elish, but the chimera was just far enough away that he couldn't reach him. Jade's head snapped backwards and he fell back against the wall. Coughing and hacking, his fingers clenched tight claws against the fabric of the bed.

His mind went wild as the cold chortle reached his ears.

"You were starving and unemployed in the slums, with death only a winter away and now look at you. Are you really going to convince me, and, more importantly, yourself… that this is something to be angry about?"

Jade opened his mouth, but he didn't have an answer to that. How could he explain to a chimera who had been born into royalty that even slum life freedom was better than being someone's lapdog. Jade put his hand up to his throat, trying to rub the breath back into his aching chest.

"I just came back here for Kerres. What about him?"

It was as if the chimera had been waiting for this. Elish broke off another piece of chocolate and handed it to Jade. "That is entirely up to you."

The dangerous edge to Elish's voice made Jade obediently take the chocolate; with a nod of approval from the chimera, Jade put it into his mouth, resisting the urge to enjoy the sweet melting taste he had only experienced once, many years ago. When he was done, and though it was one of the most difficult things he had ever had to do, he talked in an even and neutral tone to Elish.

"What do you mean by that?"

Elish handed him another piece of chocolate.

"It means that Kerres's life now rests nicely in your hands. We shall discuss it later. For now, I think an apology to my sengil is in order. You gave him a lot of trouble it seems."

Jade watched as the chimera reached over and unlatched the chain from Jade's collar. He rose and started walking out of the room. When he saw that Jade wasn't following him he stopped at the door frame.

"It is unusual to leash a pet inside his own dwelling, but I fully intend to if you don't start obeying me." His cold voice tore Jade's resistance like it was a dry piece of paper.

Jade got up on shaky feet and, although he had to balance himself on the bed and then the door frame, he followed Elish out into the main area of the skyscraper apartment.

Jade couldn't stop his eyes from widening as he took in his surroundings. The open-concept apartment was full of new and beautiful furniture, without a spot of wear or stain.

Two grey couches sat around a white marble coffee table, with a black shag rug on top of the already fluffy grey carpet. The walls were painted dark grey, trimmed with white crown moulding that also framed large wall-to-wall picture windows that showcased all of Skyland.

Jade walked across the room to the windows and looked out of them, not hiding the awe on his face. It was as if he was a bird, flying high above Skyfall; he must be on one of the top floors.

There was a balcony too, a partially covered area with patio chairs and a table, a perfect place to sit out and have a smoke.

Jade's attention was only broken when he heard Elish talking to Luca.

He looked over to see Luca holding a bucket of dirty water in his hands, his head downturned with a blank expression on his face. He was nodding his head as Elish spoke to him in a low tone.

"Will you be able to handle getting the dirt scrubbed off? Or am I going to have to hogtie those spindly limbs?" Elish looked over at Jade; his face held a cruel glint that told the boy he wouldn't mind doing the latter, and had fully prepared himself to.

Jade looked at Luca, who was still staring at the floor beside the bathroom, his posture soft and delicate. Not a spine on that boy; Elish must've ripped it out of him during his servitude.

In the slums, the sengil would've been raped and murdered within his first year out of Edgeview. The weak did not survive, and if they did survive most of them wished they hadn't. It wasn't uncommon to look up an old friend in the orphanage only to find out they had committed suicide. Jade himself had lost a couple of friends to that, and a couple more to rape and murder.

Jade held no sympathies for the timid little sengil; he hated weakness. Weak people were useless unless they had something you could take advantage of and besides a small and hot little body that, if Jade wasn't taken, he wouldn't mind taking for a test drive, he had nothing to offer Jade except an outlet for his own aggression.

Though right now it wasn't about Luca, it was about doing what Elish asked until he could hammer out an agreement to release Kerres. With a nod, Jade walked into the bathroom with Luca.

"Please disrobe," Luca said politely.

Jade snorted but shook his head. "No, I am not inept and I can bathe myself. Go… I don't know, go clean the sink or something."

The sengil gave him a pained look; he looked towards the open door as if trying to telepathically give Elish a cry for help.

Jade crossed his arms over his faded black t-shirt. He was wearing the same clothes he had come in with, his t-shirt and a pair of jeans with holes in both knees.

Luca, on the other hand, seemed to be dressed in some sort of servant uniform. He was in a plain button-down grey t-shirt and a black vest, with a grey belt belting up black slacks. Everything on him was crisp and new and he smelled like Elish did: of mint and nutmeg.

"Please?" Luca's small voice was bordering on pleading. "Please don't make me get Elish." It wasn't a threat at all; he was practically begging Jade to obey him.

A tight little servant is asking to bathe me, this was a pipe dream in the slums, or at least something you had to pay for.

The first victory for Luca and, in turn, for Elish. Jade stripped off his old and smelly clothes, to the servant's relief, and got into the tub.

What followed was Luca scrubbing off the thin layer of grime that he had on his body. It went better than Jade had expected and he didn't even get hard once, which only went to show just how much tension was below the surface of Jade's mind.

What was Kerres doing? Was he being taken care of? He wanted to ask Elish, get any information out of him that he could, but he knew that was useless. If Elish had mentioned discussing it later, then he would have to wait for that time. If the worst came to the worst, then the moment Elish left the apartment he would make a break for it and run back to Moros with Kerres. There had to be a gun in this house somewhere.

Cicaro… what bullshit. Just try, you can shove a street dog into an apartment but you can't keep him there. I will fucking wreck them all.

When Luca had satisfied himself he handed Jade a fluffy towel. By this time Jade felt the tense anxiety in his chest start to give with the hot steamy water and liquid soap.

He was looking forward to eating some food when he looked around and realized his slum clothes had been taken out of the large bathroom.

Jade's brow furrowed, and when he saw Luca holding carefully folded clothes, which looked like they were made of leather, he cocked an eyebrow.

Without a word, Jade held up the top item of clothing. It unfolded and he saw it was a small mesh shirt. He wouldn't be caught dead in such a skimpy shirt… he would've been raped the moment his duct taped shoes touched concrete.

The tight leather pants weren't any better, or the close-fitting black underwear.

"I am not wearing this." Jade dropped the clothes and looked around for his old clothes. They were gone though.

"Please?" Luca said in a meek tone.

"No!" Jade stormed past Luca and spotted Elish clicking away on a laptop, sitting in a grey arm chair. "I'm not dressing like a brothel worker. Where are my real clothes?"

Elish didn't bat an eye, or even look up from his laptop. "You're a cicaro now; you'll be dressing like one."

Jade couldn't fail to notice the sardonic smirk just edging his lips. He was enjoying every moment of this. The notion filled Jade with even more rage.

"Fuck you!" Jade snarled. He picked up the clothes that Luca had been holding and tossed them at Elish's head. "I am not your fucking pet, and I am not dressing like a whore! Go fuck yourself, let me out of here…"

Jade jumped when Elish moved, but instead of rising to his feet to pommel Jade, to his confusion, he brought a small black device out of his blazer pocket, with a small silver chain attached.

The last thing Jade saw was Elish pressing the button, and the last thing he heard were two small beeps.

A searing electrical shock shot from the collar around Jade's neck, ripping its white lightning up and down his body. With bent talons, the boy grabbed his neck, but the shock only spread to his hands; in a moment, he lost his balance and fell to the ground writhing with pain.

He gasped and gagged before throwing up a mouthful of bile onto the ground. With the room spinning around him, he heard Elish speak. "Take his towel; if he doesn't wish to wear his clothing he can wear nothing."

Jade felt a sting of cold as the damp towel he had been using to cover himself was removed. He groaned and shifted his body until his back was against the couch.

Reality was beginning to sink in, along with the danger he was in. He wasn't used to feeling so helpless.

With all his strength, Jade curled himself up as small as he possibly could and tried to make sense of what he was supposed to do.

All his brain had been telling him was to get Kerres out of jail, but where that would leave him he didn't know. His mind hadn't even gotten to the complicated quick of the matter; it just told him to get Kerres.

Or perhaps Kerres was going to have to get him.

Even with his fingers and feet twitching from the electric current, he realized one thing was clear: He had made a grave mistake running into that warm room in the mansion. Somewhere along the way he had caught Elish's eye, whether it was his blood or just his looks, he had drawn the cold gaze of his chimera monster and now he was planted firmly in his clutches.

They left Jade alone and he didn't move. Even though he was cold, the apartment was warm and the carpet soft. It was a step up from shivering next to a fireplace; he had to give himself that.

"Come sit on the couch," the cold voice sounded only a few feet away from him. Though he said it in a casual way, there was the same air to it that said very blatantly that it was not a request.

Jade had been curled up behind the couch for at least an hour; he didn't have his watch on him anymore so the time was lost on him. It had been enough time for his legs to start cramping, and his chest to ache from his limbs being crunched together. He decided to get up, even though he was still naked, and sit on the edge of the couch, as far away from Elish as he could possibly get. He stared at Elish with vile contempt.

"No, sit beside me."

Jade looked down at his scrawny naked body. He rose, but testing the boundaries, he grabbed a couch cushion to cover himself before sitting down beside the chimera.

He had expected Elish to keep talking but he didn't. Instead he continued to click away on his computer.

Jade didn't mind, he liked watching the computer do things. He hadn't seen one since he had been in the orphanage, and even then that was only occasionally for lessons.

Elish was filling out graphs that Jade didn't understand, and typing emails about marketing things or boring stuff that made no sense. The most interesting thing was the minimized tab of solitaire right beside a graph of bi-annual something or other.

There had to be some way of getting the upper hand here. Jade wracked his brain, trying to think of something he could do to make Elish free Kerres. If Elish had gone through all this trouble to make him a cicaro, it had to mean he liked him, right?

And the blood thing, that seemed to have been what had set him off. Bleeding and naked… maybe if he gave him what he had seemed to enjoy so much, he might at least give out a little slack when it came to Jade's predicament.

Jade looked down at his hands, his knuckles were bruised with small cuts, but not enough to draw blood, and being thrown down the stairs had only bruised him.

Another series of clicking and typing filled Jade's ears as he glanced around for Luca, but he was nowhere in sight. Taking that as the all clear, Jade decided to lower himself even more, if for no reason other than to save Kerres's life.

Wincing, and with his hand clenching the cushion, he bit through the left corner of his lip, before moving on and biting through the right. As the blood started to flow into his mouth and down his chin, he started wiping it with his fingers.

"Go to the bathroom and clean yourself up, I will not be pleased if you get blood on my couch."

Jade looked over at Elish, feeling his plan deflate in his head. He had been sure this would work. Without any other recourse, he decided to make his intentions a little more clear.

"I thought that was your job?" Jade licked the blood off of his fingers, before wiping his lips again.

Inside Jade's heart gave a jolt as Elish put the laptop on the coffee table. Taking that as a sign, and ignoring the screaming voice in his head, Jade shifted his body up so he was facing Elish and lightly but sensually started kissing his neck.

I'm in! Elish didn't shove him away, or snap him in half with his cold voice. Instead, he craned his neck back and allowed Jade to keep kissing him.

Leaving blood imprints on the nape, Jade moved his body until he was straddling Elish. He put his hand onto the side of the chimera's face before he started kissing the other side of his neck, his hands slowly travelling down to his pants.

Okay... you can do this. Kerres will forgive you. Jade licked and sucked on the chimera's soft neck, and when his hand reached the rim of Elish's pants, he started to slide it in.

Jade rubbed the flat area below Elish's bellybutton, feeling the first short strands of his pubic hair. Then to continue on his advances, he moved his head up to kiss Elish on the lips.

With a lightning fast movement, so sudden it made Jade cry out in shock, Elish grabbed his chin with hands that felt like steel traps. He squeezed so hard Jade sucked in a breath, waiting to feel the crack of breaking bone.

Jade looked at him, his eyes wide and shocked. Then Elish's other hand rip Jade's own out of his pants.

The chimera's eyes were ablaze, though his face gave off the false air of still being cold and emotionless. Jade could feel it radiating off his body though, to the point that he felt his own naked body quiver on top of the chimera.

"Do you really think I am that stupid? That I do not know what you're trying to do?" Elish's voice cut him like a sharp edge, every word burned Jade like its own personal skewer.

Jade's blood boiled inside of him, he felt his pride get further plucked as Elish's taunting eyes tore him apart piece by piece.

"For someone with the pride to not put on his cicaro clothing, you sure do act like a whore," Elish said with a smirk.

Unable to restrain himself any longer, Jade snapped. He punched Elish in the jaw, his other hand clenching around the chimera's neck, squeezing as hard as he could.

It was a foolish move, and he paid for it dearly.

As though he was batting away an annoying fly, Elish pushed Jade off of the couch.

Jade tried to scramble away, but the chimera grabbed his collar and dragged him through the living room.

A scream fell from Jade's mouth as he writhed and twisted like the mutt he was, contorting the collar on his neck in all directions, trying to wrench it from Elish's grasp, but instead he only succeeded in restricting his own airflow.

Jade couldn't believe it when Elish threw him onto a king size bed covered in a black and silver comforter. He looked around with his mouth open in shock before he felt a chain being clipped to his collar.

The fear drained out of him as Elish partially shut the door; he knew fear wouldn't help him now. Instead he sneered at Elish like an animal, bearing his teeth as he switched gears inside of his mind; the panic rising in his chest pushing him farther and farther to the deep end of insanity.

"Just try it!" he snapped. He scrambled to the foot of the bed and held a pillow out in front of him. "I'll rip your face off; you think I was bad by the border? Try me!"

Jade gritted his teeth as an amused smile appeared on Elish's lips. He wrenched the pillow from Jade's grasp before flicking it across the room.

"I will enjoy every struggle – every bite and every draw of blood… even if it is my own."

Every attempt I make to get the upper hand he dismisses with a wave of his fucking hand. What other cards do I have? I have nothing on him; he has my fucking balls in a vice. All I can do is stop him in the only way I know how.

Jade lowered his head and glared from under his brow. He narrowed his eyes and flicked his head at Elish. "Then bring it on."

A swell of doubt went through him as Elish's mouth split into a smile, almost enough for Jade to see teeth. He knew from just the few encounters that they'd had… that this wouldn't be good.

The light flicked off, and soon even the light from the door was blocked as Elish descended on him.

Jade was ready; as soon as Elish crawled on top of him his hard-nosed upbringing kicked in. Jade balled his fists and punched Elish in the side of the head.

Elish let out an amused laugh. Jade howled as he felt his knuckles crack against the chimera's rock-hard skull. A moment later he felt the boiling hot hand grab his own and wrench it behind his head.

There was a clip and the rattle of chains, then before Jade could react, another clip.

Jade screamed and jerked his cuffed wrists back and forth. He thrashed his legs which were also cuffed, but with a practiced ease, Elish chained his left leg.

Fully bound except for his right leg, Jade writhed and contorted his body like a serpent, spitting poison like one too, as he swore and cussed out Elish.

The man was now standing over him, his hand covering his face as if not wanting Jade to see just how much he was enjoying himself.

"Oh, that was so difficult. You surely are a creature to be reckoned with." Elish opened the door wider, coating Jade's chained and thrashing figure in the light from the hallway.

Jade let out a screaming bellow. He could feel the blood flowing through his veins like little knives, stabbing and poking every sensitive part of his brain. He bared his teeth before another scream broke the agonizing and furious look on his face.

Elish watched him with his arms now crossed over his chest, his cold purple eyes alight with amusement that only showed on his face with an upturn of his lips.

Jade felt himself become more of an animal every second. Losing himself in the torrential thoughts in his brain, he started to gnaw at the leather cuffs on his wrists. When his teeth barely left a mark he took to yanking the chains on his feet as hard as he could; the links were small, if he just… put more effort into it…

The chimera glided over to him. To Jade's anger, he sat down on the bed and went to tuck Jade's bangs behind his ear.

As Jade had promised, he snapped his chin up and caught Elish's finger in his jaws, with all the strength he could muster he clamped his jaws down like a mouse trap and he didn't let go.

Elish swung a leg onto the bed, his ring and pinky finger still in Jade's mouth. With Jade's mouth full of Elish's flesh and blood, the chimera leaned down and kissed the corners of his lips, nipping the dried blood that had formed where the boy had bitten himself.

Jade tried to release his bite on Elish's fingers, but the blond chimera didn't move them away. Instead he pushed the flesh between his thumb and pointer finger into Jade's mouth, stretching the skin of his lips back; and though he could still bite down, it didn't break the skin, there was too much pressure inside his mouth.

With a sardonic smirk that terrified Jade more than the initial advancement, the chimera took his white leather glove off with his teeth and started stroking Jade's stomach.

Jade's throat spasmed with shock. He started choking and gasping as he felt Elish go lower, his touch cool and tingly, feeling almost sexual even though Elish was only stroking around his navel.

With a suppressed scream still on his lips, Jade tried to spit threats at the chimera but the hand in his mouth stopped him, instead he jerked away from Elish's touch and tried to kick him.

Taking the opportunity, Elish grabbed Jade's free leg and bent it back, exposing the area between his legs. With a muffled scream and a jolt of his body, Jade felt Elish's fingers trace lower.

Jade's mind swam, all the rage inside of him pooled in his chest, leaking into his other extremities in the form of jerks and twists. His yellow eyes shot around wildly looking for some way to defend himself but the chains on the bed didn't go far. He was trapped and the only weapon he had was already controlled by Elish.

But then Elish withdrew his bloodied hand from Jade's mouth, though not for Jade's benefit, it was to fully bend his leg back so Elish other hand could explore Jade's skinny, lithe body.

Panting as his body tried to catch up on the oxygen he had spent struggling, Jade watched helplessly as Elish's bare hands traced along his groin, before cupping his balls in his hands. Elish weighed each between his fingers before he moved lower.

Jade's whole body heaved as a warm finger probed the tight opening between his legs. He shut his eyes and clenched his teeth, suppressing a grunt as the chimera slipped a finger inside of him.

"What a grip you have on my finger," Elish purred before pushing the digit up to his knuckle. He felt around the inside of Jade's rectum before he found the root of his prostate. With a victorious smile, he curled his finger, switching the temperature of his hand to a tingling cold.

The next cry from Jade's lips was different. Instead of an animalistic bellow this one was a higher pitch and bordering on pleasurable. Elish watched as the slumrat opened his eyes to see just what the chimera was doing to him, before dropping his head back onto the bed.

"T-that's not fair…" Jade gasped. Already the sign of his pleasure was showing on his once soft penis. He groaned again as the tip of Elish's finger caressed and pressed against his prostate every time it met the spot.

Elish slipped another finger in, feeling pleased with the tightness this gutter rat had. It was obvious from how the tight opening clenched his fingers, that he wasn't the one to receive in the relationship he had previously been in. He was an unspoiled specimen – save his younger brothers' temporary custody of him.

With both fingers teasing his prostate, Jade's member went stiff and rigid, and though he tried to lay on his stomach to save himself the humiliation, the chains wouldn't allow it.

Instead he had to lay exposed, Elish not even needing to hold back his one free leg. Elish thrust his fingers in and out of Jade's ass as the boy freely held his knees, moaning and crying out between clenched teeth every time Elish's cold tingling touch pushed deep enough inside for him to hit one of Jade's most sensitive spots.

And Elish wouldn't stop; with his violet eyes fixed on Jade's face, the chimera kept pressing his two fingers in and out of Jade's body, encapsulating Jade with such a cold but satisfied smile Elish knew, just as much as Jade knew, that he was winning him.

Fuck him… he can't control me like this! Jade gritted his teeth, hating every part of his body for responding to Elish's violations of his flesh. He wanted the chimera to stop but deep down, in the darker recesses of his mind, he wanted him to continue – to do more to him. *Kerres would understand… fuck, he would understand…*

Jade twisted around in the comforter, feeling a slick of precum stick to his stomach as his hard dick moved with him. With a tingle of pleasure as it fell back to his stomach, Jade found himself moving his hips, trying to stimulate it. Jade couldn't help it; the vibrating static inside of him was driving him crazy. He felt like an overdrawn bow string waiting for a snap that wouldn't come.

Jade lifted his free leg and shifted his lower half onto his side, trying to grind the upper part of his leg against his penis.

Elish put a stop to that; Jade looked down and saw him shake his head. "Not that easy, Cicaro."

Jade groaned, and opened his legs back up. He tried to grind his hips against Elish's hand.

This amused Elish, of course it did. Jade blinked away sweat he could feel forming on his brow. "Don't try and manipulate me, you know as well as I do no one can fucking *not* respond to that!" Jade spat, temporarily finding his teeth. In response, Elish's fingers became almost electric. They ripped such a pleasurable wave through Jade's body, he was sure he had orgasmed, but his member remained stiff and rigid.

"Fucking chimera touch is it? Y-you can't please a guy without using your mutant magic?" Jade gasped, twisting his flushed face in emotional agony. He held his leg back further and felt his fingernails dig viciously into the flesh, the only outlet he had to vent his frustration, both sexual frustration for wanting to cum so badly and the frustration of even being in this situation.

The finger thrusts sped up, making Jade's inflamed and needley flesh twitch towards Elish's hands. Jade dug his nails in deeper and once again tried to move his fingers towards his dick.

To Jade's surprise Elish reached up and unhitched the chains on his wrists.

And just like the chimera had wanted, Jade's hands went straight between his legs.

With both hands he started pumping himself, in tune to the quickening thrusts of Elish's fingers. It didn't take long before the tight tension in his groin broke under the pleasure, and with a cry and a scrape of his fingernails against the flesh of his inner thigh, he started spurting cum all over his groin and stomach.

Jade fell back with an exhausted groan, and put his hands over his face with a grimace.

He heard the cold laugh, before a mouth started cleaning up the cum around his member. Though it made him cringe with repulsion Jade let him. He didn't have the energy in him to push Elish away.

Instead he tensed up like a spring, even though the orgasm had made him feel limber. He bit back an insult, and with every muscle, he resisted arching his leg and kicking Elish in the face.

"Is this all you want me for? Did I give you such a thrill, now my life is forfeit?" Jade mumbled. His arms were still crossed over his face like he was waving the white flag of defeat.

"I could get much bigger thrills from much tamer cicaros."

"Then what is it? Why me?"

"I enjoy a challenge."

Jade hissed. He threw his hands off of his face and sat up.

At the same time Elish rose, and, as if to prove his pet's obedience, he traced a hand up Jade's still bent leg. He looked at him with a curious but dignity-stripping gaze. The look alone made Jade see red.

"You could've let me die in that alley, and you could've let Ares and Siris kill me... you didn't. Why?" Jade snarled, feeling the hatred swell inside him, mixed in with confusion. "Chimeras are supposed to be heartless bastards. I saw you in that room, you liked reading to –"

The blow was striking, quick, and it hit its target, the strength of the palmed slap smacking Jade's head against the iron rungs of the bed.

"Do not make me regret my decision, Cicaro." Elish's voice was a harsh and threatening whisper.

Cicaro. Jade could feel the humid, energy-stuffed room drain until it felt like a cold cell, closing in on him with every passing minute.

But Jade couldn't quench his anger; the slap had only injected more fury into his blood. Inside he had to show that he had some pride left in him, that he would never bend his will to this monster of a chimera. Even through his humiliation with the way his body had responded, as soon as it was over he would bare those teeth again.

I am not his cicaro, I am not a slave!

I am a fucking Morosian.

He spat at Elish.

The spit landed on the side of Elish's face, and as it dripped down to his jawline the burning purple embers glared up at the boy.

Jade's face went three shades paler.

He froze as Elish rose, and trembled as the chimera opened a side drawer.

When Elish brought out a long horse whip, Jade started to stammer apologies, before giving up completely and trying to jump from the bed.

But he had forgotten his leg was still chained.

As his foot was wrenched back, Jade fell onto the ground on his stomach, ignoring the angry twist in his leg muscles as he tried to pull himself away.

The first blow made him shriek louder than he ever had before, the second brought tears springing to his eyes, begging and pleading in rapid succession for the monster to stop. But with no sympathy, and no more patience, Elish rained blow after blow on his upper and lower back.

It wasn't until he had reached fifteen lashes that Jade passed out from the pain.

CHAPTER 9

EVERY TIME JADE WOKE UP HE THOUGHT THAT THE nightmare was over, but the top of his head hitting the bars of the metal cage reminded him that it was only the dawn of his captivity.

He refused a desperate whimper and instead buried his face into the single blanket Luca had been allowed to give him during the night. By morning it would be gone; he didn't deserve a cover for his lacerated body during the day.

His back was inflamed and tender to even the gentle touch of his servant. By the time the sengil was done cleaning his wounds, Jade's jaw was throbbing from biting down on the towel Luca had put between his teeth.

Every day Jade begged him for some pain killers, for more food than the starving rations Elish allowed him, or even something as small as an ice pack for his back, but Luca never answered him. Jade knew where his loyalties lay; a trained sengil only answered to one owner. That was their nature - they were trained from birth to obey; it wasn't Luca's fault but it didn't earn him any favours in Jade's book.

Jade wasn't sure what day it was when he heard the voices across from him in the living room, day four or five perhaps. His mind had temporarily failed him under the influx of physical and emotional pain, and the days had fallen to a single painful blur.

It must have been guests because he still had his blanket. Jade peered out from under it and saw a man with oiled back black hair talking to

Elish with a cigar in his mouth.

"Oh, Elish, it's been years since I saw you with a bruise on your face. Did he really get a strike in on you? Losing your touch?" the man mused. He took an inhale of the cigar before his large prominent green eyes looked over at Jade. He exhaled and laughed. "He's awake? Hello, aren't you a sad sight?"

Jade threw his blanket back over his head, causing the man to give out a rich laugh.

But Elish wasn't laughing. "This is my brother Garrett Dekker, President of Skytech. I suggest you sit up and greet him back."

Jade rubbed his eyes, his nose curling at the smell of the cigar. Careful not to break the scabs that had now formed on his back, he gingerly tried to raise himself. He laid his palms flat on the plastic bottom of the dog cage and tried to shift his knees under him but his arms gave out, spilling him face first into the corner of the pen.

"I can't." The sound was almost strangled. He swore and tried again, but the painful lacerations on his back kept interfering with his own brain signals. With one last failed effort he fell back down onto his stomach.

"Oh, for Pete's sake… stay down…" Jade heard footsteps and the shuffling of clothes. He looked up and saw the man staring back down at him; he was kneeling in front of the cage. His aura gave off a warm red and white; it wrapped around him like a silk ribbon.

Jade had seen him before: a handsome guy with a shtick that had him dressed like the people in movies that were old even before the world ended. He had a thin moustache and a fancy hat on his head, and eyes that looked deceptively kind.

To Jade's surprise Garrett reached into his pocket and pulled out a cigarette. He handed it to him before flicking a lighter as Jade put the smoke to his lips.

"You're a sad sight. Obey your master, little cicaro. You'll give up sooner than he will."

Jade took an inhale. His body shuddered as the spiked tobacco spoke softly to him; he blew out an exhale of silver smoke. It was an opiate cigarette; this would numb the pain at least.

"Thank you," Jade croaked. He put his fingers on the bars, his eyes shifting behind the man to Elish standing not too far away. The violet-eyed chimera was looking down on him with his arms crossed. He had made no move to confiscate the cigarette dangling from Jade's lips.

Garrett gave him a nod and a smile, before rising back to his feet.

"Does Silas know?"

King Silas? Jade's eyes widened at the name. If the rumours were correct King Silas made Elish's cruelty seem like a full body massage. The king of the greywastes and Skyfall was sociopathic, a full-blown maniac.

Though, of course, it went without saying, it had never occurred to Jade that being Elish's cicaro would undoubtedly mean he would one day be meeting the king that had ended the world. That he was, in turn, a part of this fucked up family of genetically engineered psychopaths. It wasn't just Elish's cruelty he had to deal with now.

This notion made Jade question just how long he would have in this world before one of them killed him. He had to escape, and soon.

"Not here." Elish nodded Garrett towards the patio, and the two left him.

Jade buried himself into his blanket and lay there, feeling sorry for himself and his predicament.

Elish had made no move to discuss Kerres with him after the scene in the bedroom so many days ago. In all respects the chimera had been ignoring him, opting instead to have Luca tend to his needs at his orders, giving the injured and starving Jade nothing more than the occasional passing glance or nudge of his foot to see if he was still alive.

Jade ignored the growling gnaw in his stomach; it had been eating him alive. Dinner was the worst; though Elish usually went out for his breakfast and lunch, dinner was usually spent at home. In his practiced dignity Elish ate at the dining room table with Luca running around to cater his every needs.

Jade was forced to sit in his dog cage and watch, and in a further act of dehumanization, he was tossed a scrap of food here or there. That was the only food he got and he had lowered himself to reaching his fingers through the bars to try and pick it up.

Luca scurried past him with a bunch of sticks, as he waved them around Jade noticed the tips were lit and a smoke was coming from them.

Jade's nose twitched, the sticks smelled like perfume. Luca continued to wave them around the living room like a lunatic, and after five minutes of the boy looking like a cat-eared ballerina Jade couldn't resist a comment.

"What are you doing?"

Luca didn't waver; he moused over to where Garrett had been talking to Elish and shook his hand. "I'm trying to get the smell out... from Master Garrett's cigar. He never puts it out and Master Elish never asks him to. It's a horrible stink and Master Elish hates smoke."

The smelly sticks were an improvement but now the room just smelled like a cigar dipped in perfume. Jade watched with minimal interest as the sengil fluttered around, before his loneliness got to him again.

"Why do you wear those cat ears?"

Surprisingly, the corners of the sengil's eyes pinched as he gave Jade a glowing smile. He absentmindedly put his hands up to his ears and pulled on them. "They make me work faster." His smile was a mile long before he ran off to wave a stick at the entrance of the apartment.

I bet that kids gotten his head knocked around too many times... Jade shook his head and scanned the apartment for something interesting to grab his attention.

There was nothing though. He carefully positioned his aching back against the wire rungs of the cage and tried to stretch his sore and stiff legs. He had been stuck in this cage since he had awoken after Elish's vicious beating. The only time he was allowed out was once a day to use the bathroom, all the other times Jade had to go he was forced to piss in a glass bottle. It was mortifying, and, as with all the torments Elish had rained down on him... dehumanizing.

What was Elish even waiting for? Jade was close to admitting that he had known all along what he was waiting for. It was Garrett's jovial words that were starting to pull the curtains away on that mystery.

You'll give up sooner than he will.

The immortal Elish Dekker was almost ninety years old, and his brother, who, through eavesdropping, Jade had learned was about one fourth of a second younger than him, knew him better than anyone probably did.

With a defeated sigh Jade ran his hand over his ribs, sticking out like large fingers trying to push their way out of a balloon, then with a glance he eyed Luca.

"Luca? Could you bring me my clothes?"

The sengil gave him his usual neutral look from under a bowed head; his busy fingers re-lighting the sticks.

"I'm sorry Jade, I cannot give you your old clothes."

Jade pulled the blanket off.

"No, my pet clothes."

Luca raised his head and cocked it to the side, almost as though he was a dog hearing an unfamiliar noise, before, without a word of reply he dashed into the bedroom.

While he was busy, Elish and Garrett exited the balcony. The president of Skytech chattering happily with Elish looking on. Still the cold immovable figure of unwavering pride and solidity, but with a relaxed expression that was only noticeable to someone who knew him.

Garrett left, and, with the door shutting quietly, Luca came back holding Jade's clothes.

Jade's mouth twitched. He had been hoping the chimera wouldn't be here to witness his victory, but he would eventually see him anyway.

There was the soft creak of the dog cage door and Luca offered him a hand out of his wire cell. Jade took it, and with a painful grunt he rose to his feet.

Jade stumbled, and Luca's arms steadied him. Then the sengil started to dress him.

When the servant was done Jade sighed with defeat, and held up his arms to check out the tight leather that hugged his skin. He turned around and glanced at a mirror hanging beside the hallway leading to their bedrooms.

Well, don't I look nice... Jade craned his neck, revealing the first of many angry red whip marks on his back.

The mesh was thin and it distorted the lacerations strewn across his back like crimson crosshatches, but they were still visible. He turned back to the mirror and flicked his hair out of his eyes.

"So…the cicaro has learned how to dress himself? Very nice."

Jade glanced behind him through the mirror and saw Elish's towering figure behind him. Jade noted the approving tones of his voice, which he tried not to snip back at.

Jade walked back to the dog cage.

"Have you really become so attached to that cage?"

Jade's yellow eyes gave him an icy glare. "It's not like I have a choice."

Always needing to pick at Jade's scabs, Elish turned his head towards the cage. "It hasn't been locked for three days. I'm afraid your confinement was all your own doing."

He's testing me... Jade's mouth pursed. A part of him was tempted to crawl back into the cage in nothing but pure defiance, or the Morosian need to try and get the upper hand. But he was out of the cage, hungry and thirsty, with his bones feeling like rusty hinges. So instead he let out a sigh and shook his head.

"Can I have some food or something?" These questions usually fell to Luca, but since Elish was talking to him he might as well cut out the middle man.

Elish glanced over to Luca. The young sengil was standing beside the hallway, looking ahead like he did whenever there wasn't anything for him to do. "Go fetch him some food from the kitchens, Luca. Something bland. I think we have learned what happens when you give real food to greywasters and Morosians."

Well, that was nice of him. Jade knew what he was talking about; the few times he and Kerres had binge eaten fruits and vegetables and real bread they had both been puking and running to the bathroom every fifteen minutes. Their bodies were used to being starved and only fed processed chemicals.

Perhaps that's what he had been doing the entire time I was locked up? No, that can't be it. Elish doesn't have any consideration like that; he would probably love to see me puking my guts out.

After Luca ran off, Elish took his place on the couch and flicked on the TV, before he picked up the small black laptop and started clicking around.

Jade was amused when he noticed the small clicks and drags; he had remembered the patterns of Elish doing actual work, a variation of keyboard clacking and clicks. Only mouse clicks meant he was playing solitaire.

"Can I sit beside you?" Jade rubbed his swollen and hot back. He hadn't sat down in something comfortable in days; he had been scrunched up like a spring.

"Yes."

Jade hid his smile as he approached the chimera with the laptop, as soon as he came close a grid of work cells came up and he started typing.

The boy sat beside Elish, and, without realizing it, he was closer to him than he had been the first time he had been allowed to sit beside him. Whether it was by accident or an unknown force inching him closer to the blond chimera he didn't know. Perhaps it was the calm aura Elish was giving off, relaxed after a visit from his favourite brother. Jade was reminded of the man he had seen in the firelit room in the mansion, and the glint of the same one who carried him out of the alley.

"That's okay; it's nothing to feel bad about."

Elish gave him a glance, his depthless eyes questioning. Though he might've been questioning if his pet had hit his head a little too hard.

"Solitaire. Sometimes I have trouble with it too. It's easy to get the cards wrong and you lose. You lost right?"

"I did not *lose*." To prove his point the mouse scrolled over to the minimized tab, and Elish brought up the row of cards. Jade held back a smile, too caught up in the moment to stop what his pride would've under normal circumstances, never allowed.

With his back aching from the blows of Elish's hand only several days before, he pointed his finger at a red king, and then to a blank spot.

To his further shock, Elish actually sniffed in amusement. "No, in the deck of cards I already found a red queen, which is blocking the ace of spades. I'm looking for the remaining black king. Don't move the card to the first spot you see, analyze and plan ahead."

Jade scanned the cards. "And if you get the ace of spades, you can move that two of spades to it and reveal another card."

"Very good."

Jade hated the jolt of pride he got. He was slipping back into Elish's hands, just like the night he had read to him. As much as Jade wished he could, there was no controlling the warm feelings of recollection in his chest.

"But what if the only black king is behind that two?"

"Then I play mahjong for a while."

Did he just make a kind of joke? Jade couldn't hold back a small laugh, and was shocked to see the corner of Elish's mouth rise in a smile, though his eyes were fixed on the computer screen.

There was something about this side of Elish that attracted him to the chimera like a magnet. He was helpless to not feel the two of them connect, even if Elish was his captor and abuser. It was a confusing series of thoughts and feelings painting his brain like a baby with finger paint, making a complete mess of the ebb and flow of a mind he had been tempering since he could remember. The chimera was pulling every thread in Jade's brain, both good and bad.

"I have a real deck of cards, not virtual ones. We had a Nintendo we shared at the Edgeview though. I never was able to afford one once I got out. Those games are hella hard." Jade's eyes flicked up as Luca came tapping lightly into the room holding a white ceramic bowl. He placed it on the dining room table.

Elish looked up from his laptop to the sengil. "Give it to him on the couch. You do know how to use a spoon? Did they teach you that?"

Jade took the bowl and looked at the contents, it was gritty and yellow. "I find it ironic you're poking fun at the orphanage *your* family runs." He sighed and leaned back into the couch. They had fancy sandwiches and potato fries yesterday and he gets mush? Jade picked up the spoon and let the corn mush flop back into the bowl with a distasteful *shlop*.

"Thanks, Luca, reminds me of home." Jade tasted a bit, at least it had sweetener in it. He knew it wasn't to teach him a lesson, more for his health, but their normal food taunted him. Supposedly he was a chimera's pet now, but the fish got fed better than he did.

Jade ate his food without further complaint, never eating more carefully. He had a feeling if he got any food on the fancy couches he would be cleaning up not only the food but his own blood.

When he was done Jade leaned forward to hand the bowl to Luca, though he flinched and bit the inside of his cheek as the hot and inflamed scabs on his back became tight against his tender skin.

"Luca, get him some of the pain killers we discussed."

Jade gasped as he felt a cold hand on his back. He tensed up like a spring as the frigid tips of Elish's fingers traced the wounds; like a slithering snake they found each laceration and gently glided over them.

But it felt good, it cooled his swollen skin. Jade felt himself relax as he leaned his elbows against his knee. It was a light touch, like Elish was pressing ice against a sun-baked pavement. It was the first physical relief he had gotten since Elish had punished him.

Elish did this and yet I am submissive to him soothing my wounds. This made Jade's brow furrow and his body tense up. The conflict wasn't hidden on his face, or his own confused emotions.

This chimera was like his touch: hot and cold.

Unfortunately, I was gas to the flames, we clashed with one another. For obvious reasons, he has imprisoned me, and he has imprisoned my boyfriend.

Elish said Kerres was being taken care of... now what was I doing? Biding my time? Or was I in denial of the fact that Elish wasn't going to let me go.

Or he won't let me go if I resisted him, so I was being docile for him.

Jade blinked hard, seeing Luca's soft slipper-like loafers come close to him. As much as he wanted to kick and scream, he was tired and sore, hungry and miserably in pain. Once he got his strength back he would fight for his freedom, right now... he just wanted some rest, a temporary truce.

Luca handed him a bottle of pills.

Jade stared at them; he unscrewed the cap and looked inside.

They were Dek'ko brand Dilaudid pills, the same ones that would set him back a hundred bucks for a bottle; he could fence every pill for a dollar each. This bottle had a two hundred count, perfect to crush and snort and even better to inject.

The boy glanced up at Luca, who handed him a glass of soda and bowed at him before walking back to his hallway corner. With the relaxing cold touch of Elish's hand Jade popped three of the pills and leaned his body forward, exposing all of his back to the chimera's soft bare hands.

Except for when he was touching Jade, Jade had never seen him with his gloves off. He assumed he wore them for the sake of not electrifying people by accident; Jade wasn't sure how it worked.

Around him the room seemed to grow blurry and dark, not physically but in his mind, everything tasted like silence. As the pills released their golden tendrils, and with Elish's cold hands soothing the swollen lacerations; he felt himself fall into a deep state of relaxation.

With the only audible noise being the keyboard being typed with one hand, Jade felt himself fall asleep.

When Jade woke up, his body was a fuzzy sweater wrapping him up; his head resting up against something soft and warm. He opened his eyes slowly, and immediately smelled mint and nutmeg.

There was still computer clicking. As his eyes focused he saw a document open and words appearing on the screen.

Jade blinked and realized Elish had his arm over him. He looked around and blew a breath of air through his nose. This felt entirely wrong, but he was too stoned to care.

"How long was I out for?" Jade mumbled. He shifted his body, half lying down on top of Elish, and rubbed his eyes.

"Several hours. Enough for ten games of solitaire and one too many episodes of Law & Order." It was odd. Though Elish's voice never wavered from his cold unyielding pride, Jade was starting to sense the small variations that showed he was in a good mood.

I wonder if he enjoyed my company, not just tormenting me... or maybe he just liked both. Jade wasn't sure, but he wanted to stay with this good mood. A week into Elish's cruel abuse of his body, and his time in the dog cage – Jade could use the break.

If I keep this up... he'll let Kerres go. The thought filled Jade with a small light, and a pull on his heart. He and Kerres had never been apart for so long. *Does he miss me as much as I miss him?*

"You didn't move?" Jade gave him a questioning look. It would be more in Elish's nature to get up without notice and let him fall on the floor.

"When you have a starved dog huddled and shivering on your lap, it would be cruel to disturb it."

No matter how nice he was acting, he was still Elish. But the chimera had to push it. "Or pick it up and take it home; even if it bites you like a rabid pit-bull."

Jade bristled when he felt Elish scratch him behind the ears. "But just put it in a cage for a week and he'll eat right out of your hand."

Jade whipped his head around and took a snap at Elish's hand; Elish pulled it back with an amused chuckle. Jade got up and picked up the bottle of pills that had fallen from his lap and wedged itself halfway into the couch cushions.

"Maybe the dog wouldn't bite so much if you stopped taunting it and poking it with sticks," Jade said bitterly. He started walking towards his bedroom; he was still drowsy and nothing hurt when he slept.

His body gave a twitch, expecting a cold commanding voice to pierce his ears but there was silence.

Because he was young and incredibly stupid, Jade whirled around, waiting for a response. But to his chagrin, Elish was still typing on his laptop, not a care gracing his elegant pale face.

"And when is Kerres getting released? You said you would talk to me about it; it's been almost a week. When?"

Elish still didn't look up, but Jade saw his eyes slightly narrow. Jade braced himself, ready to run.

"Like I said that is up to you."

Jade hissed air through his clenched teeth. "What do you mean by that?" Jade threw his hands up in the air, letting out an audible cry of pain as his scabs split.

Elish's cold purple eyes looked up from his laptop. "Who are you?" His voice became hardened and even more authoritative than usual.

"Jade!" Jade said, exasperated. "Don't tell me you never took the time to remember my damn name? You seem to fucking know everything else about me."

Elish gave him a dismissive wave, which made Jade's blood turn to magma. He seethed and, if he hadn't been holding two hundred dollars-worth of pills he would've chucked them at Elish. Though as that thought crossed his mind, he wondered how much of his attitude was because of those very same pills. They did have a tendency to make him moody. He and Kerres had had brutal fights on those same drugs.

"What the fuck do you mean by that?" Jade exploded. He took several steps towards Elish before kicking the coffee table in front of him.

"If you don't know who you are, Kerres stays in jail. There is nothing more to say on the matter." A thin smile appeared on Elish's lips and suddenly Jade felt foolish and uneasy. "Do you know what day it is today?"

"Friday... I think?"

"The day before Stadium, how convenient."

And there was the iron fist to grab my balls.

"You have to be fucking kidding me."

But Elish was not a man to kid, or joke.

Elish gently clicked his laptop closed and slowly rose to standing. As he did this, Jade backed away until his back hit the closed door of the maroon room he had first woken up in.

There was the sound of fingers scraping against paint as Jade felt for the handle, though in a flash Elish was upon him.

"What do you want for him?" Jade's lips quivered, he pursed them to hide his fear from Elish. He stood up tall and squared his shoulders, though the pain of his last defiance still on his back.

"Who are you?" Elish's figure blocked off the light of the living room, his entire frame encapsulated and overwhelmed Jade trying, with every stained shred of pride, not to cower before him. Though Jade couldn't stop the shake in his knees, or his hammering heart about to burst from his chest.

"Jade." He took in those burning purple embers for a second before he couldn't bear to look at Elish any longer. They seared the soft flesh of his brain, before soaking like brine into the bleeding raw folds.

"Jade? No, you're more than that now. Who are you?" Elish pressed himself closer to Jade, who continued to look away, though he still held himself with dignity. Jade stared at the door frame, forcing his body to stop its aberrant quivering.

Then it dawned on him. Elish wanted Jade to admit his ownership over him. And now Kerres's life was being swung in front of Jade like a puppet on a pendulum clock; his life ticking down to his moment on the arena floor. A fight he would never win.

Jade swallowed, but his throat was full of small needles, constricting and binding him like the cold strands of Elish's aura. Jade pressed his back against the wall and gritted his teeth.

It was enough to make his eyes burn. His pride stood in front of Elish with a sword in one hand and a gun in the other; but no blow could rain true when his captor was holding the human shield of Kerres in front of him.

But Jade was strong, stubborn, and had a defiant streak in him that no chimera could ever understand. One that could only be born out of the shit-strewn gutters of the district of Moros. The hard-nosed brat who in all sense had no idea the weight the vow he was about to make would have on his soul.

With a flick of his eyes, yellow met with violet, and those golden suns burned into Elish. With Jade's own purple and black brilliant aura around him, he pushed himself and his aura forward as if challenging Elish's own. They clashed together, and with Jade's teeth clenching and his own throat vibrating a growl he spoke.

"I am your pet, *Master Elish*." The stray's voice dripped contempt and hatred. "And I will spend my entire life making you fucking regret that."

Elish smiled at his unpolished diamond, and watched with great inner contentment as Jade burned him alive with those brilliant eyes, focused and shockingly vivid, like that of a fox or a hawk. Elish rested a hand on Jade's cheek and felt the burn underneath it, his cicaro's face flushed and sweating from his own turmoil.

"Get away from me! Or I will hurt you!" Jade snapped, though he didn't wrench his face away, he was too scared to do anything and Elish knew it. Elish knew Jade had to restrain that untamed energy, for the sake of his former boyfriend, though the difficulty of it showed with every breath from his lungs. The stray's heartbeat in his chest like two baritone drums, with Elish's own heartbeat they seemed to create their own orchestra. In tune and together, though, of course… Elish's was calm and steady.

The chimera drank it in, though the intoxicating aroma the stray gave off didn't satiate him, it only made him thirst for it more. There was something about Jade in this moment that made him irresistible, like Elish could almost taste the power and anger radiating off his body.

He leaned in but Jade moved his mouth away. This amused Elish. "Mm? Resisting? It fills me with joy when you put up a fight."

"Fuck off."

Elish laughed at the absurd audacity of him; Elish had him chained and bound in all ways and yet the mongrel still chewed and lunged at his bars, even with the red-haired one's life on the line. It didn't anger Elish; if anything it gave him a sick thrill. Jade could be such a sullen thing, but when you lit a fire inside of him he burned like a red dwarf.

"Do you not want to bite me again?" Elish purred. He put his mouth over the stray's neck and sucked on it, before breaking his seal to reveal a small red patch. He moved up to Jade's jawline and did the same. "I would enjoy a little nip; a break of my own flesh."

"You're going to regret this, you'll be begging me to go back to Moros," the slumrat spat. Low but heavy gasps spilled from his mouth in short successions. "Even if you fucking manipulate my body, you'll never have my mind, you'll never have me."

Elish kissed his neck again and slid his hand down Jade's leather pants. "I do love this fire inside you. You sound like you want to just murder me with an axe."

"Give me a fucking axe!" the boy snapped. Unable to take the onslaught of touch from the chimera any longer, he went to shove him away, but Elish grasped his hands.

"You'll be joining me on my visit to the jail on Tuesday. Your boyfriend will see you in your leash and outfit. That would please me to no end."

Jade let out a frustrated snarl and tried to yank Elish's hands away. The thought alone made him boil with rage. Kerres couldn't know what had happened to him. No – Jade couldn't fucking bear the thought.

The humiliation broke his spirit, and Jade felt the thumping of his heart travel from his chest to the inside of his head; filling his brain with a low ringing and the beginning jolts of anxiety. Once again the predicament that weighed on the corners of his mind brought itself forth with brutal force. It extorted every emotion buried deep inside of him.

As Elish sunk his teeth into his neck Jade screamed, and with every fiber in his body he stood his ground and screamed from the top of his lungs.

"LET ME GO!"

The blond chimera's mouth flexed and licked the wound on Jade's neck. He travelled his mouth up and teased the corners of it, only backing away when Jade tried to bite him.

The smile on Elish's lips made Jade grow cold. His head went hot and the pain behind his eyes threatened to fill them with desperate tears. It had been five days since his last abuse, but he was still sore, he couldn't even lie down on his back. The last thing he wanted was a repeat.

"Never. Not tomorrow, not next year, not when you're forty. You are mine until you breathe that last breath and even then – your spirit and your soul will belong to me."

Jade went limp, and with this act of submission Elish let his arms drop, before he started unzipping Jade's pants.

With a turn of his head, Jade stared blankly to his left. He felt his mind start to retreat inside of him, in a vain but desperate attempt to protect himself from what was about to happen.

But in Jade's vision he spotted something, and though others would see it as a mere decoration, Jade saw it differently.

Like all Morosians worth their salt, Jade was as underhanded as he was devious. With Elish preoccupied with his body, the boy took his chance.

Jade's hand wrapped around the candle stick that rested on a cabinet beside him, near the entrance to his bedroom. Before Elish even had time to react, Jade raised his arm and slammed Elish over the head with it, throwing the chimera off balance. He fell to the floor with his hand to his head and a rare curse on his lips.

Jade stared at him blankly, before his eyes travelled to the candle stick. He gaped at it, his mouth open as the disbelief and horror washed over him.

Then he ran.

Before he could even reach the door though, someone grabbed him and yanked him back.

Though not the ice-cold fetters of Elish – it was Luca.

With a shocked and angry look in the sengil's eyes, Luca wrenched Jade back with an angry scream, but the insurmountable fear was ravaging Jade. In a panic he swung the candle stick at Luca and hit him across the mouth, and again over the head; blood spilling and flying in all directions.

Jade suppressed the sob on his lips. As he raised the candle stick to hit the serventmaid a third time, the boy put his hand up to shield his face. The stick rained down onto Luca's arm, so hard Jade could feel it break.

Jade knew he should stop, he knew he should stay here and take the death sentence with his Morosian pride; but his youth and the terrible week he had endured soaked into his mind like poison. Through sheer, unbridled panic Jade dropped the candlestick and ran through the doors, leaving master and servant bleeding on the grey carpets of Olympus.

CHAPTER 10

THE INSULATION HUNG ON ALL SIDES OF HIM; SMALL pink clouds chock-full of dust and sawdust from the building above him.

There were radrats too and croaches. He had found a long stick to fend them off but he had already been bit twice by a croach. Disgusting creatures, the size of a house cat and they hissed like one too. They were covered in brown armour and had many legs. They ate everything and they bit everything that ticked them off too.

But he had to deal with them, anything was better than facing the outside world. Even the streets of Moros seemed unsafe. The alleyways were now narrow mazes that left every dark corner a mystery.

He had tried to go back to his old apartment, but it was locked. Kerres was still not there, and his keys had been left with his clothes back in Skyland. It had been too late in the evening to ask the manager of the building, and when he had finally decided to hide underneath one of the buildings he had dismissed the idea altogether. Elish would check there first. No doubt he knew where Jade lived. If he didn't, he could ask Kerres.

Though it was a fantasy to believe he would still release his boyfriend. After his impulsive actions the previous day, he knew Kerres could very well be dead now.

What the hell came over me? Jade huddled into his corner, the soft threads of the spider webs tickling his back and sticking in his messed up black hair. His leather pants were dirty, completely covered in grey ash which also coated his mesh shirt. The only things recognizable were his piercing yellow eyes, which glinted and shone at the people passing by like an alley cat peering from the darkness.

It was evening again, of his second day here. His stomach was a painful knot and his throat was parched. All of his saliva had been dried up with the dirt and now he couldn't even spit properly.

Swearing and hating himself was the only thing he could do, and he did despise himself.

Jade wanted nothing more than to take back the last three days. Though before it had been Kerres who had condemned them by his show outside of Olympus, now Jade had sealed both of their fates.

He was back in Moros and now he was a fugitive. He was hiding like a radrat, more a prisoner now than he had ever been.

When it was dark enough for him, and the steady stream of Morosians had stemmed down to a light trickle, he crawled out from underneath the building. Without even dusting himself off he started to walk towards Garrett Park, ignoring the stares of the gathering gangs and the young men out and on their way to hang out with their friends. They snickered at him, called out to him, but for the most part they left him alone.

Cold and numb, he robotically put one foot in front of the other and stumbled on. His mind a haze and his body was crying out for a drink of water, or a bite of tact.

Jade looked around with eyes red from dust. He tried to tell himself he should be enjoying being back in Moros, but it looked gloomier and more desolate than ever. The buildings were dark from it being past time for the lights to be turned off; they stood like looming statues over the park.

A man on a bike rode past. A stray dog sniffed the chain fence that stretched the length of the park. And far off a group of guys stood sitting on a flight of stone steps, occasionally erupting into laughs. So carefree… in their cesspool of a district and okay with it.

But no, Jade had to wish for a better life, and now that he had seen it in Skyland he wished he could go back to the unassuming slumrat he used to be, to be ignorant about what was going on in the other districts, and most importantly… ignorant as to who the chimeras were.

Jade rubbed his goose fleshed arms and leaned up against the crumbling brick walls near the hub of the district.

"Yo, can I bum a cig?" Jade rasped to a group of guys walking by.

They looked at him like he had just crawled out of a gutter, which in all respects he kind of had. Then with a laugh they carried on, each one telling Jade he was shit out of luck in whatever rude way came to their heads.

Another group filed on by. These ones he almost recognized, but he had never cared to get to know the gangs that infested Moros like cancer.

"Hey, bum a cig? Or food? Anything, bro." Jade scratched his arm, and looked pleadingly at the darkly dressed guys who passed by.

"S.O.L, man!" one of them men crowed. "But I'll give you two bucks for a hummer behind those trash cans!" They all erupted into laughter.

Jade swallowed down an insult that would only get him beat up. If he ended up staying in Moros, if Elish never came for him, he would track down each of these clowns and leave their heads nothing but splattered remains. He tried to memorize their faces as they strutted past, half a dozen embers burning off until they were swallowed up by the darkness.

That was Moros District. It was filled with beggars, mostly the elderly who didn't want to be euthanized by Skytech, and hadn't been sold for experiments or food by their family. The younger ones didn't get much pity. If you looked able to work, then everyone expected you to work.

And Jade couldn't even hold a grudge against that mentality. He had never helped out a young beggar even if they did look in a sore state. He would laugh with his group of friends and tell them to get jobs, just as callous and mean-spirited as the men who walked past him.

Eventually he gave up, every response was the same. To lower himself even more Jade started digging through some trash bins, but eventually he made his way to Garrett Park, where he hoped to get some food and water.

Jade walked over to Sheryn's nest of garbage. She was sleeping in the middle, covered by the blanket Kerres and Jade had brought her, and many jackets. The dog wasn't around, or if he was, he didn't feel like barking.

Jade crouched down and found a half-empty water bottle beside her. Not feeling picky he picked it up and drank it all in one gulp. The fluid cleared out the chalky mess that had once been his mouth.

He poked around further but the cans of food were always hidden in the trash. Only she knew where each and every can was.

Jade sat down and leaned up against the tree his mother always tied her shopping cart to. He reached over and pulled out a small blanket she used to cover the items in the cart, and wrapped it around himself.

He was full of self-loathing but also fear. Fear of so many things, from his own health still failing him, to Elish's wrath. It wasn't a case of *if* the chimera found him, it was when. Jade only hoped he would make the final blow quick but even that was a pipe dream. As with Elish's intense sessions when he made Jade moan and writhe from pleasure – he liked taking his time.

But what was there left to do? Either survive or die. Though right now Jade would've preferred dying, but the hard-nosed stubborn nature of the Morosian refused to let his body give in. Too much of a masochist to give in to the demon pressing down on his shoulders.

He closed his eyes and tried to think of better things. The only better thing he could see in his mind was Kerres, and they had both successfully ruined their chances of ever going back to their old lives.

Jade pulled the smelly blanket up closer and closed his eyes to the dark ruins of Moros around him. He missed his old life. Why did he have to wish for better? Was this his punishment for daring to dream of a change in the day-to-day monotonous routine? If so, the fates were both cruel and unjust, or maybe they had more of a sense of humour than Jade thought.

Morning came with the sound of a tin can being scraped with a spoon.

Jade opened his eyes and saw his mother eating a can of peas; another can was open beside her with a spoon sticking out of it. She was humming to herself, with a new dog beside her. It was quiet as a mouse and chewing on a piece of plastic.

"Hey, Mom," Jade mumbled. He tried to stretch but his back was still sore and his limbs were stiff like he was in rigor mortis.

"The word was you disappeared. Did you go on vacation to the islands? Did you have a nice time?" Sheryn gave him a smile, showing off the remaining teeth she had. She passed Jade a can of corn and nodded to him to take it.

It was probably poisoned. Jade knew this, but his stomach growled at the prospect of food, and his mouth salivated with the sweet smell. He took it and started shovelling it into his mouth without so much as even chewing. The food was ambrosia on his lips, even if it was just old Dek'ko corn in a dented can. The last time he'd had a proper meal was lost on him, only the corn mush several days ago and before that he wasn't sure.

"Yeah, vacation..." Jade managed to croak. His eyes scanned the green park for any sign of the tall, elegant demon who would drag him kicking and screaming back to hell, but all he saw were the usual dark-clothed Morosians, milling around and minding their own business, taking kids to play on the metal bars of the play park, or walking small dogs with baggies in their hands full of their shit.

Jade smirked at them. If you didn't bag your dog's waste it got DNA tested and then you got the privilege of seeing your dog chopped up for food. The cats were free to shit wherever they pleased, but at least they buried it after.

He heard a rattling and looked down to see that his hand was shaking; a small clinking was coming from the can as the spoon rapped up against it.

Sheryn looked at him and handed him a bottle of water. "You drink that, got extra from the dollar you gave me. You drink all of this and eat well."

There was nothing else he could do. Jade ate the entire can and drank the rest of the water, before leaning his sore back against the tree and closing his eyes to let his body work through the shock of food. It was already making his body tremble from the sudden influx of sugar and carbs.

Within an hour of eating the canned corn, Sheryn was shaking his leg.

Jade opened his eyes and blinked, automatically putting his hand on his stomach as it gave an unhappy lurch. He hoped he wouldn't throw up or he might be screwed.

"Why don't you go for a walk?" Sheryn shook her head back and forth, and a moment later she dumped out all of her cans and started trying to sort them. She looked up again and patted her hands against the cans with a humming noise. "Go have a walk, Jade."

Oh, she probably did poison me... oh well. Jade rose to his feet and started walking down to the east area of the park, putting one foot in front of the other as though he was a walking zombie.

Usually when Mom poisoned me, she would wait until I was violently ill and bring me to the hospital. She would give all my information to the nurses and would revel in the attention we both got. The comments on my eye colour, and how skinny I was for my age. She would tell them everything she did for me, and offer to show them the wagon she would put me in.

Eventually they had no choice but to take me away. Mom had sold me to a man, and I had scratched his left eye out and bit the side of his face when he tried to fuck me at nine years old. When I stumbled back home, Mom fed me canned soup with bleach in it, which seared my throat and burned my stomach. I needed surgery and they didn't want to give it to me. But after consulting the higher-ups I got the surgery, in return, I was put into Edgeview and I didn't see my mom for almost four years.

But I had Kerres… he looked after me. He was the first person in my life to hold me close. Our small frail little bodies huddled together for heat. I gravitated to him like a lost puppy and I clung to him like one too. He said we could be best friends and we were. Then once our bodies started to change and our interests too we became more than friends, and we were still inseparable.

We were each other's firsts for everything. Not even all sexual either. We got our first apartment and our first job; we bought our first television with our pooled money. We experienced life together.

And now I am a runaway cicaro, and already I have had so many experiences under my belt that Kerres couldn't understand. Our joined paths have been severed by that blond-haired chimera, and now we're apart.

More doubts and self-hatred filled Jade's head, and as he stumbled on to a small thatch of trees his heart ached for the ignorant life he had been leading just a few months ago. There was nothing for him outside the walls of Moros, nothing good anyway.

There was a clench in his stomach, followed by a lurch. Jade walked over to a row of red-berried bushes and was sick in them. Leaning against a light pole for balance Jade threw up a stream of yellow liquid, before, with a wipe of his mouth, he found another tree to huddle against.

Jade's face felt hot, and his eyes were watering from being sick. Jade curled up tight against himself and shivered between chattering teeth.

Yeah, she poisoned me.

The realization brought an unexpected reaction: a shrug of his shoulders and a vacant stare. He didn't care anymore, if anything perhaps it was the last straw in his torment and soon silence would follow. Elish wouldn't even care, perhaps just a single prick of sadness that his torture instrument was no longer. But he was a chimera; he could find a new one with ease. He had said it many times already.

The daydreaming made Jade's eyes burn, his automatic response to blink washed away by the unknown poison soaking from his stomach lining into his body. He squinted tight and opened his eyes to the green park around him, scanning every red berried bush and counting each thick barked tree. He was too near the small forest and away from the usual trails for any stranger to see him. It was just the Morosian and the trees now, waiting patiently but in a great amount of pain, for death.

You really did it this time... Even in his sickness he still hated himself. If there was one last word for him to say it would be sorry. To Kerres for breaking into the mansion, to Luca for bashing him over the head, and the clean-up crew who would have to remove his sad, worthless body.

Jade opened his mouth and took in a cold breath, the air icy against the drool running down his face. He tried to raise an arm to wipe it off but it was heavy and dead beside him. If his mother knew his state she would've put less toxins in the corn. She never intended to kill him, but his body was a wraith.

Or maybe she saw me, and decided I would be better off.

Then a strange shadow blocked the daylight that had been pressing red against Jade's closed eyelids.

Jade opened his eyes to see what had blocked his vision, only to see the twists and shimmers of crystal and silver.

"Can you not even escape properly?" His voice was low, coated in a thick layer of ice and contempt.

Jade opened his mouth to speak, but every word was laboured and raspy. "Is Luca okay?"

There was a pause. Jade tried to look up but his head was a dead weight, it flopped to the side and with it his chest contracted as he tried to take in a rattling gasp.

"You've indulged quite a bit on those pain killers I see," Elish said lowly. "How many did you hide in those pockets?"

Jade tried to shake his head, to tell him he wasn't stoned, or even overdosing, but all that came out was another baritone growl. He tried to back himself away from Elish but he couldn't move, instead he tensed up his body and glared at him.

"Still have fight left in you I see. Kerres, pick up some Suboxone from the pharmacy; he'll be back to his slumrat self within the hour," Elish said with a dismissive air that made Jade clench his teeth.

Even in his sickness Jade's mind was able to catch that small slip of his boyfriend's name, with sluggish movements he looked up.

There he was…

His crimson hair brushed back, his face sullen and scared. He was standing beside Elish in his Morosian clothes.

"Mr. Dekker…" Kerres let out a strangled noise and made a move to go to Jade, but it was as if an invisible wall was separating the two of them. Instead he stood there with agony on his face. "He's not overdosing; please – sir – let me talk to him."

"Kerres?" Jade groaned. His eyes closed momentarily. The boy took in a congested breath and felt his arms tense around his body, each muscle contracting and squeezing the blood through his veins.

Kerres must've gotten the all clear; he ran to Jade and put his hand on his face. He dropped his voice and whispered to him, "Did you see your mom?"

Jade looked past him, and even in his deteriorating state he felt the same fear when he saw Elish's violet eyes burning into him, taking him apart piece by piece. "Are you okay?"

Kerres's dark brown eyes softened and he nodded. "He let me go; he came and got me when he said you took off. I'm okay, just… I understand, J. Just do what you have to do, I'll be okay." He sniffed and put a hand on Jade's forehead. "How much of that shit did you eat?"

"I told you not to touch him," Elish's voice snipped, sounding impatient and annoyed. Jade glanced over to see the chimera with his long blond hair, dressed in his usual grey overcoat, looking every bit a graceful beacon of elegance, but his face was dark and his eyes were narrowed.

"His mother is fucked up; she's always trying to poison him," Kerres said. "He's poisoned, not overdosing on drugs. He has to go to a hospital, a real one."

"I see."

The moods and their auras changed around them. Jade felt his body go cold, like the air had been sucked out from around him, even though he was outside. It became a dark-shadowed cloud, falling down on him like acid rain; stinging his shaking body and making him wonder what would happen next.

With a small cry of surprise and protest, Jade felt himself held in Elish's arms. Too weak to do anything he sniffed and trembled in his wool jacket, never feeling more pathetic. The last thing he wanted was for Elish to pick him up when Kerres was watching. What would he think? Kerres… Kerres… I wanted to go home with him.

"Kerres?" Jade whimpered. He looked around for him but all he could sense was his seafoam aura. He missed him so much.

Just one more touch.

"Find her, and find out what she poisoned him with. Do not dawdle or your ex-boyfriend will grieve over your remains." There was a vicious tone to Elish's voice, the one that reminded everyone below him that Elish Dekker had never made a false threat in his life.

"Let me at least say goodbye."

"Now."

With a hoarse and stumbling protest, Kerres's aura disappeared.

"That was a privilege you did not deserve. I hope that makes you happy," Elish said.

Jade shifted himself in his arms, and in response Elish's arms tightened. The boy looked up at his master, and noticed a bandage on the side of his head.

"It does," Jade rasped. He tried to sniff back the snot and saliva running down his mouth but he was a sore sight and a pathetic one. "Why bother saving me if you're just going to kill me when we get home?"

Jade blinked, red creasing the corners and irritating his eyes to the point that tears were falling.

Surprisingly, Elish gave Jade a wry smirk. He stared ahead and nodded to someone Jade couldn't see, before crossing the park with his pet in his arms.

"So you admit my apartment is your home now? Not this garbage-strewn slum? Well, well, we are coming along aren't we?"

At least Kerres wasn't here to notice that slip. Jade grimaced and swore at himself, before the image of the chimera started to blur.

Suddenly, his body started to convulse. He twisted out of Elish's arms but the chimera's hold stayed firm. Instead he turned his head and started vomiting.

Red vomit. Elish adjusted his hold and put a hand on Jade's chest as he let him throw up the red blood onto the blades of green grass below him.

Jade shook and coughed, at the same time trying to inhale a breath.

"Every time you get yourself in these situations you wind up in my arms. Do you slumrats ever learn?" Elish's cruel muse hurt Jade more than the pain ravaging his body.

With another heave, Jade threw up again before collapsing limply. He was shifted back to his cradled position and in the distance he heard the low rumbling of an idling car.

The only thing Jade could manage back was a whimper, finding his only comfort in the shreds of Kerres's aura he had sensed again for the first time in a long while. Kerres was okay. He had said himself he was okay and he looked well. Even being in jail.

Jade wiped his mouth and leaned his head against Elish's sweet-smelling robes, trying to capture the moment Kerres touched his face. If everything else fell to pieces around him, even if he was a prisoner for the next twenty years at least Kerres was safe, and at least he knew Jade hadn't left him.

He closed his eyes and heard another taunting word, but it was only a mumble to his clogged ears and his distant mind. Jade didn't remember much after that.

Jade's body was agony when he awoke in Olympus's medical floor. With bloodshot yellow eyes he scanned the area around him quickly before opening his mouth to try and talk, though his words were a jumbled mess flowing from a mouth made of mush.

Well, he was back in Olympus; his grand escape hadn't gone as planned. Jade blinked as he saw Lyle the doctor, nothing but a blurry haze, wrapping up the arm of a servant he had seen in the kitchens.

All he had succeeded in doing was condemning both Kerres and himself. Elish wouldn't let this go, no, this was a slap in his face and such disobedience wouldn't go unpunished. Once again his mind filled with self-contempt and more hatred for his foolish impulse than ever. A slum dog who ran away from a new master to hide with his tail between his legs in the alleyways. Not free at all, just cowering under buildings and begging for food from a mentally ill mother.

There was nothing for it. The demon standing on his shoulders pressed its weight down, crippling his fantasies of ever going back to his old life.

This can't be it... this can't be what ends up happening to me. Being Elish's outlet for his own sexual needs and the chimera-bred cruelty that all of them seemed to have. He was better than that...

Or was he...

Jade clenched his jaw, every breath hurt his chest and throat. He wanted to cry out for pain killers but if breathing hurt so much he shuddered to think what talking would do. Instead he closed his eyes and gave himself to the misery. Perhaps he would be lucky and death would take him. Make it easier on everyone...

Death, death was quiet.

When Jade woke up next, he was relieved to feel a glow around his body, a cold and soothing feeling that swept up his bruised skin, tracing every line of his aura with soft fingers.

It was that encompassing light that made him open his eyes.

Elish? Elish was sitting beside him, his hand tracing Jade's bare chest. That was where the relief was coming from. Jade looked at him with a blink, and watched Elish's gloveless hands trace up and down his skin.

Jade was surprised just how bad his body looked. His skin was unhealthy grey, and the veins were no longer buried under the surface. They stuck out like red and blue scars snared through his stomach and chest like wires.

One moment he's almost caring, but in a flash he turns into a monster. I don't understand him...

If he would just act one way or another, I might be able to build up my defences. But how can I hate and despise him when I see these small moments of him caring for me? When I see the man sitting with the book on his lap, reading to the boy by the fireplace. Or the same one who stayed still for hours so I could sleep in the crook of his arm.

The confusion brought a burning behind his eyes; his lips pressed together, trying to dismiss the emotions flowing through him. He had Kerres, that was the thorn inside of him that kept him from fully obeying the chimera, fully submitting to him.

Then why do I feel so safe right now? Why does my body thirst for this touch and, most importantly, why the hell do I glow on the inside when he's near me. I don't understand. Even when I was in Moros his image was a constant in my mind. Not the cruel man who manipulated my body, and controlled me with a whip and a shock collar. The man in the mansion room, the fleeting glimpse of who Elish could be.

Jade felt his heart start to open, and as it did he hated himself even more.

"I'm sorry," Jade rasped.

Elish gave him a glance, but he didn't remove his hand, he only drew it up to Jade's chest and pressed the frosted palm against it. Jade gasped and as he inhaled, his lungs filled with a soothing cold air. It was like the fires of hell being quenched by a nuclear winter. The relief was palpable on Jade's face, he closed his eyes and a sigh spilled from his lips.

"It's too bad you were foolish enough to get yourself poisoned. If you would've stayed awake you might've been able to see that ex-boyfriend of yours for a little while longer."

Jade's heart gave a jolt as he remembered Kerres; suddenly his mind became clearer. "Why did you let me see him?" Jade tried to sit up.

Elish's hand pushed him back down to the bed, the frosted ice cooled down his body, relaxing Jade even more. He nodded once and met Jade's eyes with his own. "You swore yourself to me, Cicaro. He is of no threat to my hold on you. Though do not expect it to happen again."

A wave of relief fell over Jade, but at the same time an ache. It was a life he was no longer a part of, at least for right now. The only way he could press on was to hold a hope that one day Kerres would be able to be with him. Once he was stronger. Jade had proven easily he was in no state to escape now. Even if getting back to Moros was easy, surviving in

Moros in his condition was not. Even Kerres wouldn't be able to protect him once Elish came to collect his pet. Kerres seemed just as scared of the chimera now; he must've had more than a few threats from Elish.

"Is Luca okay?"

"Luca is fine despite a broken arm and a cracked jaw. He will be staying with my brother Garrett for the time being."

Lucky guy. Garrett seemed nice. If only it had been that fancy fuck sitting in that room with a book, it might've been an easier transition from gutter rat to chimera pet.

Jade raised a hand and touched the bandage on Elish's head. "How about you?"

There was a faint smirk on Elish's lips, which made his left eye crease over the violet iris. He seemed amused by the question. "It would be better if you didn't poke it."

Jade withdrew his fingers. "Oh, sorry." He shifted back into the bed and watched Elish continued cooling off his body. "You're being nice. I thought you were going to just kill Kerres, or kill me once we got home."

"Oh? Why?"

Jade stared at him. For a man of cold dignity and unsurpassed magnificence he sure did have his moments of humour. Though Elish would never admit it, his pride would never allow such a display of human emotions. The chimera and his grace were much too sophisticated for that. Instead Elish's jokes were veiled and hidden in his words, but Jade was starting to catch on.

"You know why." Jade coughed into his hand and tried to give him a smile. Knowing Kerres was safe and home filled him with an appreciation for Elish. "Isn't hurting a chimera punishable by death?"

Elish pretended to weigh this. As he did, he reached over and started unhooking Jade from all the machines.

"Though I would've preferred you didn't hurt my sengil. I was waiting for those taut little strings in your brain to snap. It took longer than I expected. For a Morosian, you're quite docile and tame. I'm disappointed that small clip on my forehead was all you had. I had a gun in that same cabinet; I thought you would've found it by now."

When Elish's long fingers had gently unhooked the last device, to Jade's surprise, Elish reached into his pocket. The cicaro flinched as he brought out the small plastic device that triggered the electric shock on his collar.

But he didn't press it, instead he opened it up. Jade looked closer and realized it could unfold. Elish snapped it into place, and Jade was baffled to see it had a screen on the inside.

He handed it to Jade.

Jade looked at it in awe. The screen had a map on it, with a little red dot pulsating on a small white box that read 'Olympus'.

"You're tracking me?" So that's how Elish was able to find him. "How? When did you do this?"

Elish didn't answer; instead he reached over and pressed one of the arrow buttons.

The screen changed. On it was a series of numbers, all next to small icons. Only a few of them Jade recognized, a heart shape being one of them.

"I know your heart rate; I know your blood pressure, your radiation levels, and this one I just installed for obvious reasons… I can even tell if you're ill. Wonderful little chip, isn't it?"

The room fell silent, save the silent humming of the machines around him. Jade stared at the device, before handing it back, feeling queasy and uncomfortable, like Elish was stripping him naked and bearing his shame for all to see, all over again. "So there really is no escaping now, is there?"

"There never was."

Jade glared at him, though not a word of protest left his lips. Instead he watched Elish with a subtle defiance, wishing there was something he could do, some way he could get himself back. Though there wasn't. The chimera was right. During one of the times Jade had been knocked out or too sick to protest, Elish must've gotten that doctor of his to implant Jade with a tracking chip.

Elish's gave him a cruel but amused smirk. He calmly picked up Jade and set him down on his feet.

Jade's legs wobbled, he started to fall forward but to his surprise Elish caught him. With arms that held a strength Jade was always surprised to feel, Elish helped him stand and slowly walked out of the clinic with him.

It would be a normal sight for any human being, but to Jade that motion alone almost knocked him back off of his feet.

Elish had never caught him before. Every time he struggled to raise himself, no matter how pathetic the sight, Elish had let him writhe in his own misery and weakness. The only time Elish had done something like that, was when he had picked Jade up to carry him back to what was now Jade's home.

The two of them walked to the elevator at Jade's pace, which was an inconsistent shuffle.

They quietly rode up to the top floor of Olympus, only Jade's raspy breathing breaking the silence between them. The boy felt like he should say more, show his appreciation in hopes the treatment would continue, but he didn't know what to say, besides another apology or a thank you.

He decided to just say it, not to suck up, but to edge himself a little more into Elish's good books. Elish had let him see Kerres after all, if only to get information out of him, but it was something.

"Thank you."

"For what?"

"You know what."

The elevator doors opened but as Jade took a step forward; Elish's arm broke his vision. He was blocking off Jade's path.

Jade's heart fell; he knew the hammer blow was near.

Sure enough, though Jade was too much of a coward to look at him, Elish's aura gave a shock of electricity. It made Jade's body freeze like a bowl of arctic water had spilled onto him.

"If you ever try a stunt like that again, or harm my personal sengil or any of my family, I will not hesitate to kill him. And rest assured, Cicaro, it will not be with a gun, or a cloak and dagger in the dark. I will torture him, put him in front of a cheering crowd and drink every reaction on your face as Ares and Siris rip his spine out of his body like they were uprooting a flower." Elish's voice sliced him like a thousand paper cuts; it made Jade's legs shake and buckle. He had to steady himself against the wooden walls of the elevator to keep himself from falling.

"Do I make myself clear, Cicaro?"

Jade's lips disappeared inside his mouth; he gave a quiet nod.

"Look at me."

The cicaro's eyes rose up to meet the intense shards of violet ice.

Elish towered over him, his shining golden hair falling down his grey overcoat, and the shorter bangs touching his ears. Such a picture of beauty, with a devil stirring underneath the surface. Jade took him in, and looked at him as requested.

"Who are you?"

The words cut Jade's heart in half, a defeating blow in a battle he had never stood a chance of winning. Jade thought of Kerres, and the relief he had felt knowing he was safe in Moros.

I am a martyr now, for him. I will be his, if it means my boyfriend is safe.

"I am your cicaro, Master." The words left Jade's lips, encapsulating the sickness his entire self felt infected with. "I belong to you."

Elish removed his arm, and, with a sweep of his cape, walked past and down the hall, leaving Jade to limp behind.

CHAPTER 11

JADE STARED AT THE CUP OF WATER, SMALL BUBBLES forming on the outer rim as it stopped its rolling boil. The tea bag steeping inside was floating around careless as a teabag could be, unaware that it was being watched like a hawk.

"198… 199… 200." Jade took out the tea bag and picked up the mug. He placed it on the saucer and walked out into the living room.

Jade rested the saucer in front of Elish, and took a step back with a smug look on his face.

Elish gave him a passing glance before he went back to his reading. Jade didn't move. He stood staring at the tea, waiting for Elish to take a drink.

Finally after several minutes had passed, Jade not moving an inch and Elish only occasionally turning a page on a folder he was reading, the chimera picked up the tea and took a drink, before putting it down without a word.

"Well?" Jade said exasperated. Since picking up Luca's old sengil duties during his respite at Garrett's skyscraper, Jade had been slowly learning every trick of his trade; with the occasional help of King Silas's own personal sengil.

The tea had been a constant battle for him. Sanguine, the king's servant, had only shown him how to do things once, and if he didn't remember the sengil forced him to make it again and again until he remembered how to do it right.

"Don't you have anything better to occupy yourself with? Do you mean to tell me I haven't been giving you enough work to do?" Elish raised his eyes from the mug of tea. He was still drinking it so that was a plus. Elish wasn't one to toss the tea at him or dump it on the floor, on the contrary, he just never touched the cup and let it grow cold. Or even worse, if Sanguine was still instructing Jade, Elish asked Sanguine to make him another cup.

That was more of an insult than anything. For a smart immortal with the grace and dignity of a god… Elish was very passive-aggressive.

"Come on!" Jade raised his hands and let them fall. "I fucking counted to two hundred. It should be perfect!"

Elish stared at him, before glancing down at his teacup; his shoulders rose and fell with a sigh. "I said two minutes for this type of tea, not two hundred seconds."

"Yeah, and I did… two minutes, that's two hundred. I counted every second."

Elish didn't break his gaze. Jade wilted under the intense glare, wondering if this would be the first time he got the cup thrown right into his face. Jade couldn't help but feel his shoulders slump.

"Jade, grab a pen, and write a note for me."

Great, what way is he going to humiliate me now? At least Sanguine wasn't here, that asshole had a smile that cut you more than any laughter ever could.

Because Jade had no choice, he pulled open the cabinet door with the stationary and pens, and sat down beside Elish. "Alright."

"This note will be to my nephew Knight, you know him as the head of Edgeview Orphanage." Elish took a sip of his tea and placed his file folders down quietly. "Dear Knight, the gutter rat orphans that you have released into Moros are unaware that a minute is sixty seconds, and that two minutes is a hundred and twenty seconds. Please be advised that you may wish to educate these flea-bitten wretches further, lest they be even more of an embarrassment to your center than they already are. Your uncle, Elish Dekker."

Jade opened his mouth to protest the note, but then closed it. He had been steeling himself the past month to not bite back when Elish jabbed at him, and so far he had been doing a fair job. Though he still had gotten himself physically disciplined several times, the punishments were getting farther apart. Right now it had been four days since he had been smacked across the room for a few angry snips when Elish was taunting him about Kerres, and the bruise was almost gone already. It would be the first time in several months he hadn't had an injury to take care of.

He heard Elish chuckle, before a soft gloved hand came and took the half-written note from him. "Dear does not have an I in it, and gutter is not spelled 'guder', but I digress..." He gave the note back to Jade and rose to his feet. "Keep writing, this will only drive my point in further."

Jade clenched his teeth and cut Elish's head off in his imagination. "In Moros we don't have time learn to spell. We're too busy, you know... not starving."

Elish continued to walk towards the balcony, his remote phone in hand. He always made his calls outside, away from Jade's ears. "And you couldn't even do that properly." The chimera turned around and swept his placid gaze up and down Jade's body. "Though you are making up for it. We might need to get you new clothes soon. Getting some meat on those bones is filling you out nicely."

Well, I guess I'm in for another wringing tonight. Jade watched Elish put his phone to his ear before closing the balcony door. Tea still in hand, which Jade made a proud note of. While his master was out talking, he busied himself in the kitchen, loading up their silverware and plates for the skyscraper sengils to take to the main kitchens.

Elish hadn't stopped his abuse of Jade's flesh, but the difference now was that Jade had stopped fighting it. Although he had trouble admitting it to himself, sometimes he almost liked it. The process of bringing Jade to climax was a long and slow one, usually ending with him begging for his master to stop. Which, of course, was usually what Elish was waiting for. In his chains and splayed out in the bed he was at Elish's mercy, his master's fingers tracing his body, touching and caressing every inch of him, and his tongue on his neck and chest, or wherever Elish had decided to draw blood that night.

But, and Jade still found this rather odd, even insulting, Elish never removed so much as his shirt. Only his gloves wound up on the floor.

Jade had never pushed this, if anything he was relieved by it; but there was a part of him that wondered if Elish just didn't want to lower himself by fucking a gutter rat. Perhaps he saved his own sexual needs for others. King Silas's personal pet Drake was available to all the chimeras; Sanguine had filled him in on that one.

And on other things too. King Silas's sengil knew things about the Dekker family that made Jade wake up at night in a cold sweat. Fears driving nightmares into his dreams, about threats that he hadn't even thought had been possible.

A threat from a person Jade hadn't even met, and hoped he would never have to.

"Drake is a passive one, a very polite chimera." Sanguine had explained a week ago; when he was showing Jade how to properly clean the blood stains on the carpet, the ones that he had caused when he'd attacked Elish and Luca. "We're not all bad, though I would say a large percentage of us are."

Sanguine was a chimera himself, though like Drake and the exiled scientist Perish, he was a lower-ranking one. Jade liked him, he was polite and patient, and on top of being a sengil was also King Silas's personal bodyguard. Jade was skeptical when Elish had told him this at first, but once Sanguine glided inside the doors he brought no doubt in with him. The sengil was tall, with black hair that fell to his jawline and blood-red eyes. His body was fit and slender and his movements as swift as a carracat's. Sanguine Dekker was a man of many talents, everything he could do he did well, and with an air of nonchalant grace that told Jade he took the entire world in his stride.

"Who is the meanest? Besides Silas?" Jade had asked, watching the baking soda bubble as it soaked into the carpet. He could almost make out Luca's body shape in the blood splatters.

Sanguine gave out a soft laugh and tipped his head towards the balcony. "That would be your own master; now that is a cold, cruel creature."

A shiver went down Jade's back. He also looked past Sanguine, to the tall chimera talking to a visiting Apollo on the balcony. The servant sengil was going to be leaving with Apollo, the president of Dek'ko, to give his own new sengil, Lance, some pointers.

"Really?" Jade swallowed a lump in his throat. Sanguine was seventy, another immortal one. "Not Ares, Siris, or Nero?"

Sanguine shook his head, and handed Jade the coarse scrub brush. "That's your mistake, young Jade. You think brutality is cruel? No, it's the cruelty of the mind. Tell me you don't know this?" Then Sanguine laughed and said something that stuck in Jade mind even now a week later. "You forget it don't you? I see his patience with you… you should know, little cicaro. You're special to him."

Little cicaro, all of the chimeras and the servants called him that. He was looking forward to meeting other real cicaros to see if they referred to them the same. "I am? I'm a gutter rat; I'm just a project to him. A game."

The servant watched Jade scrub the stain, always maintaining a countenance of patience and authority even though he was only a chimera sengil. "You've slept with him, no?"

Jade shook his head. "Not in the way you're thinking of."

"Keeps his clothes on?"

Jade felt his face go hot; his eyes went to the balcony.

Apollo was sipping on tea, his mouth moving and his arm flying through the air like he was complaining about something. Elish was standing beside the railing with his arms crossed, looking placid and indifferent as usual.

"Yes."

Sanguine chuckled, before his hand brushed over the disappearing stain; he looked at his palm as if to check that the blood was indeed fading. "Elish never had much of a sex drive. He doesn't even come to initiations anymore."

It was Jade's turn to laugh. He pulled his shirt down and showed Sanguine the purple hickeys on his chest, mostly clustered around his nipples. "Does that look like someone with no sex drive? Please, he's a goddamn monster when he wants to be."

Sanguine smirked. He rose and dropped a dry rag on top of the stain and stepped a boot onto it. "And you say you're not special to him."

This knocked Jade off his feet. He got up, shifting his eyes once again to Elish outside, as if expecting him to be able to sense the conversation between the two. "You're saying… he's only shown that sort of interest in me?"

Sanguine gave a playful shrug, before giving his odd smile that made his eyes squint like a pleased cat. "Perhaps… you should enjoy it while it lasts."

Jade blinked, before the corner of his mouth twitched. "Before he gets bored of me?"

Sanguine put two hands on Jade's shoulders before slipping them down and picking up his hands. Sanguine made them clap together with Jade looking at him with a raised eyebrow.

"No, no, no, little cicaro… because King Silas is going to kill you because of it!"

"Sanguine!" Elish's voice cut both of them like a hot knife. The sengil dropped Jade's hands before giving Elish a bow.

"That will be all, you're excused."

Jade's face tensed when he went over the conversation he'd had with that demon-eyed sengil. There was no denying all of the chimeras he had met had some sort of inner need to stir up shit and manipulate people. What gave Sanguine's musings more of a solid base though was the fact that he had been in service of King Silas for the past seventy years.

Though Elish wouldn't let anything happen to him.

At least Jade didn't think he would.

Admittedly though, Sanguine's admissions about King Silas took a back seat to the most interesting tidbit he had fed him. He was special to Elish?

Jade's arm went to his lower back. He rubbed the tight whip mark scars. He certainly didn't feel special.

That evening they sat together in their usual spot, the electric fireplace bringing a pleasant ambiance to the apartment. It was just the two of them tonight. No Sanguine, no Luca still, and the skyscraper sengils had already cleared their dishes.

Jade sat with his Game Boy, his head resting against Elish's shoulder. Elish was, as he always was, forever working on his laptop, though he freely switched between solitaire, mahjong, and work, without hiding the fact from Jade. Jade even tried to help him occasionally when he hadn't heard clicking in awhile.

"Just ask for a hint." Jade glanced up from his game of Pokémon and noticed Elish had been staring at the mahjong screen without clicking for a while.

"That's cheating. There is no game if you just ask for hints all the time."

"I never lose in my game."

Elish tipped the Game Boy up with his finger to see what game Jade was playing. "Such a waste of time. Is there not something you need to clean?"

"Nope, just training Luca's Pokémon." Jade showed him the screen and pointed to an icon. "He named his Mewtwo after you. That's one of the most important Pokémon. He's psychic."

"Sounds like he needs more tasks to keep him busy." Elish gave it the most dismissive of glances. "And I am not psychic."

Jade clicked around a bit more, trying to find one named Jade but there was none. "You're close to being psychic."

Elish snorted incredulously. "I am not psychic, none of us are."

Absentmindedly, Jade looked down at Elish's gloved hands. He was typing on the keyboard, writing an email message, from the looks of it to Artemis.

"How do you do that, anyway?"

There was no need to ask him specifically, it was clear Elish knew what he was talking about. Maybe it was the calm and pleasant atmosphere brought by the flickering electric fire and the fact that they were alone, but Jade reached down and picked up Elish's hand, before pulling his glove off with a pinched finger.

Jade held Elish's hand with his palm, and with the other one, he traced the ball of his finger along Elish's smooth and flawless hands.

"Ouch!" Jade yelped. Elish chuckled as Jade dropped his hand as it suddenly became burning hot. Out of reflex, Jade hit him in the side of the arm. "You jerk."

Elish smiled and cooled his hand down immediately. He took Jade's hand into his own and soothed the singed skin.

"I was born with it. It is one of my enhancements, all of us have different ones," Elish explained. Even though his voice still had that odd cold sterility to it, Jade could sense a small flicker of warmth.

"Is there anything else you can do?" Jade asked. He felt Elish's hand start to tingle and shock his fingertips. That was the sensation that made his body go crazy. He could never forget that one.

"Most of us are born with enhanced hearing, sight, just normal senses but extremely sensitive. I would say in the past twenty years we have been making the most interesting advancements in genetic engineering. Caligula for example, he was one of four. Unfortunately he was the only one to survive."

"What happened to the others?" Jade weaved his fingers into Elish's; he could feel his teeth vibrate under the steady stimulation. He wished he could do neat things like that; his strange aura reading was more of an inconvenience than anything.

"There was a fire in the labs. King Silas didn't like what was being grown in that lab and he incinerated it. Caligula was in another lab at the time, and two other unnamed ones. In the end, only Caligula survived to take breath."

"You guys are so scary… but so fascinating." Jade shook his head and scratched his ears as the vibrations started to tickle the fine hairs inside his eardrums. He put the Game Boy down, and rested his hand flat up against Elish's palm. "What other sensations can you do?"

This question brought a sinister smile to Elish's face, but it didn't scare Jade, the mood was too pleasant between them for him to worry about the cobra striking. So in return, Jade only narrowed his eyes and rolled Elish's fingers with his own. "What? What is it?"

Elish shifted the tables on Jade, instead of Jade playing with the chimera's fingers Elish pinched them with his own and wiggled them. "You'll regret it…" Elish let his voice trail off.

Jade yelped and pulled his hand away as a slight but painful jolt of electricity shot its way through his body, with an intensity like he'd touched a live wire. Elish let Jade pull his finger away with an amused laugh, before he poked his finger into Jade's chest, shocking him again, and then a third time.

Jade howled and laughed. He tried to push Elish away, but the chimera was having too much fun. The cicaro tried to make a break for it, but Elish pulled him back with his fingertips like little sharp needles.

With no indication that he was going to let his prey go, Elish pulled Jade onto his lap, before grabbing Jade's chin in his hand. His touch turned from sharp and painful, to a soft warm heat.

Jade looked back at him, trying to suppress the smile on his lips, and even more so the real joy he felt in his chest. A strange feeling he hadn't felt with this much honesty in months.

Elish stared back with his cold smirk, his eyes alight and burning, taking Jade in with such an intensity it made his body fill with excited static.

Then Elish kissed him.

Jade's world froze in that moment.

Everything around him became opal and silver as Elish gently slid his hands to Jade's neck, drawing his pet in further. Jade closed his eyes to try and get his bearings, but even through his closed eyelids he saw Elish's aura sinking into his own.

It filled Jade with light, and put a heat in his chest that no one had ever been able to stoke. It made Jade press back, and open his mouth to take Elish in more. Together they kissed deeply, Jade feeling more energy and passion in that moment than he ever had with Kerres.

Elish broke their lips. Jade opened his eyes in time to see Elish lean in and start to kiss the corners of his mouth, before, with a soft but insistent nip, he found his neck. Then, as Jade suspected, Elish started to lift up his shirt.

Jade slipped his leather pants off and straddled Elish, not hiding his arousal on his now naked body. He brushed his fingers through Elish's hair and ran his hand down Elish's white button-down.

"What has gotten into you tonight?" Elish's voice was a deep and gravely purr, but he didn't resist Jade's advances.

Jade didn't stop but his mind was asking him the exact same thing. There seemed to be a fever that would sink into his bones whenever Elish would show him this side of himself. A thirst that burned in Jade's chest, aching for more. It was never enough, not even the first kiss between the two of them was enough. The addiction that had started with a simple verse from a book was starting to make him crave Elish's affection like it had been his first hit of heroin. Jade had to have him.

Sanguine told me I was special to him… that Elish was a chimera with no sex drive. I remember that amused expression on Sanguine's face when he looked at those red marks on my body. I am special to Elish, he enjoys me.

This past month… since he had taken Jade back to Moros after his escape, even though Elish still berated him, insulted him, and hurt him,

Jade had been starting to learn how the chimera worked. He had started noticing changes in him.

Subtle changes, that no one but Jade would notice. Like perhaps Elish only hitting him with his hand instead of a palm-out smack down, or allowing Jade small privileges like being able to order his own food. Things that would be met with a cold chuckle if he'd even so much as suggested it when he'd first arrived.

It was a dance between the two of them. Jade had realized once he'd come back to Olympus that if he danced well, and obeyed Elish, but at the same time still kept his master on his toes, he would be rewarded and treated rather nicely.

So what had gotten into him tonight? The thirst to take it further, to see how far he could go with him. To submit himself to Elish in a way that he would've hated himself for several months ago. Because for some fucked up reason, with Elish's aura seeping into his own, Jade was starting to have feelings for the monster.

"You know what." Jade's fingers started unbuttoning each button one by one, with the precision that only a guy who had done it many times could accomplish. He drew Elish's shirt off his shoulders and started kissing his chest.

If there was one thing to say about chimeras, it was that they all had beautiful bodies. As Jade brushed his mouth over Elish's nipple, his hand stroked the firm abs of his stomach, each one perfectly outlined and defined by a faint shadow.

"What an obedient little gutter rat. They told me I was wasting my time with such an arro-" Jade kissed Elish hard on the lips, before taking the lower one into his mouth and biting down on it. He opened his eyes before scraping his teeth away.

Elish raised a blond eyebrow at him, before his cold eyes narrowed just slightly. In spite of himself, and with the feeling that he was petting a sleeping tiger, Jade gave Elish a smile.

"Oh... look at that. I found a way to shut you up." Jade grinned.

With a shriek and a holler, Elish stood up, taking Jade with him. A moment later, Jade was thrown onto Elish's bed, with the blond chimera soon on top of him.

Jade's mind raced, and although so many thoughts pulled him away from what was happening, his flesh, and the nefarious corners of his mind, wanted Elish badly. The burning in his chest only intensified as the chimera's body encompassed his own, and Jade felt the warm hands start to find every sensitive spot he had.

Lost in the moment, with cascading blond hair all around him, Jade didn't even notice Elish removing his own pants. He was deep inside the chimera's fluctuating touch, a touch that after teasing Jade's body, started rubbing Jade's penis in firm but soft strokes.

This must be the most bizarre case of Stockholm syndrome ever. Jade ran his hands down the curve of Elish's stomach and thighs for the first time, memorizing every firm spot and using it as fuel for the fire inside of him. He didn't know if this would become something regular, or if it was a fleeting moment of overindulgence on the chimera's part. Either way Jade was going to memorize and take into him every moment.

Time began to distort for Jade. With the auras mixing in with one another, he fell into the blissful and pleasurable feeling of Elish touching him, bringing him close to climax many times before removing his hand to place it elsewhere. His lips were never far away from Jade's body, kissing and sucking and making more inflamed red marks, even the occasional and now familiar nip of his skin to let the blood flow to the sheets below. Jade was tempted to make his own on Elish's flesh, but that was one fantasy he didn't want to push, though he was curious what the fuss was about.

Then the final act, one that Jade had been waiting for with such anticipation he was sure Elish was going to hold back, if only to frustrate Jade further.

But it finally happened, Elish withdrew the wetted finger that had been inside of Jade for the past hour and separated Jade's knees further with his hand.

Then with a teeth clenching cry Jade felt a push between his legs. Jade dropped his head onto the pillow and cried out as the unimaginable pressure and feeling of girth slid into him.

Of course chimeras were huge, would you expect different? Jade sunk his fingernails into Elish's back and let out a string of curse words. Elish bit the corners of Jade's lips, and though Jade couldn't see him, he knew his master was enjoying every cry.

Elish shifted his body and grabbed Jade's knees and hooked them over his own arms. Taking in and unwrapping every single emotion in his cicaro, Elish watched with fascination as he broke himself into Jade's body.

Well, he had wanted it... Jade's body had been begging for him. Elish had taken this new attitude in his cicaro with a sick fascination. Never would he have thought the first time he took the pet would be in a consensual way. This arrogant, untrained little gutter rat was surprising him more and more each day.

He loved bringing out different cries in him. When he sped up his thrusts unexpectedly the cicaro gritted his teeth and cried out. When Elish slowed to a sensual rhythm more suited for love-making Jade's tones dropped, and he heaved his hips like he was half-starved. It was nothing if not alluring. And though the steeled mind of Elish chastised himself for indulging in such a way, he found himself just as thirsty for this gutter rat's body.

Jade's chest started to heave, and his eyes closed tight. With a desperate pull of Elish's long locks the chimera looked down to see semen spilling forth from him. Bringing a coy smile to his lips, he drew the cicaro's legs back further and started hitting the sensitive area inside of him, tensing up those strings that wound tight throughout his body, and like was Elish's favourite game, bringing Jade's body to climax again and again.

Jade sunk his nails in deeper, biting through the pleasure and the pain as they became one continuous earthquake in his body. Elish's hips rose and fell in variating rhythms, and, as with his touch, he always seemed to know what would make Jade scream out.

Jade's body shuddered when he realized Elish was making his own noise.

Before he was just the observer, wringing every drop out of Jade with nothing more than his own biting words and taunts to stimulate himself. Now though, small suppressed moans were breaking through his lips.

The chimera's own actions were no longer just a tool being used against Jade. Elish was inside of him now, feeling his own physical pleasure. It was blowing Jade's mind to the point where the room had disappeared around him and all he saw was Elish.

The final wave came with a stifled groan and a build-up of exhales through clenched teeth. The careful rhythm was broken and Elish pushed inside of Jade for his own pleasure, no longer toying or manipulating Jade's body. It was all for him.

When Jade thought the apex was upon him he closed his eyes, and through his eyelids he saw their auras intertwined tightly together. Jade groaned with him, feeling his own body build and gather, readying itself for another orgasm.

Then Jade screamed from surprise. As Elish reached his peak he sunk his teeth deep into Jade's neck, like a steel trap they broke the skin, spilling blood into the chimera's mouth as his cum rushed into Jade.

Jade tried to clench his teeth to suppress the pain, but in the same instant he felt his body climax under the intense mixture of pain and pleasure. With Elish's teeth firmly clamped, Jade screamed again, heaving his flushed and sweaty body still trapped underneath Elish's own.

Elish unhinged his jaw from Jade's neck, but still remained on top of him for several more minutes, both of them trying to catch their breath as their bodies wound down.

Then Elish eased their bodies apart and Jade felt him lay down beside him. He stared up at the ceiling, ignoring the wetness seeping from his neck and his backside, and counted the chimera's breaths.

Jade watched Elish's silvery aura make patterns on the ceiling; like the reflection of the ocean they rippled and shimmered, touching and binding with the dark purple flares of Jade's own.

Jade twitched his fingers and tried to pull his own aura into Elish's.

They mixed in with one another, they always had. With Kerres they had repelled each other like oil, Kerres's seafoam green either getting drowned out by Jade's, or it retracted away. Elish's was strong and as overbearing as Elish himself. The purple and silver liked to mix together, like glue almost.

It must mean something... it meant Sanguine was right. Maybe our attraction to each other was something neither of us could help.

I wish I could show him, especially now... Jade's eyes tracked them on the ceiling, before a warm hand drew him in.

Jade put his arm around Elish's body, and felt Elish's hand on his own.

CHAPTER 12

"WHAT A JOY TO BE ABLE TO SEE YOU, *GELUS VIR*."

The voice was a low purring noise, one that seemed to come in all directions. But Elish always knew where to look for him. On top of every shelf, or perhaps the refrigerator, occasionally hanging from the roof like a bat. King Silas loved heights, and like a cat it was his personal pleasure to peer down at his subjects.

With an upturn of Elish's purple eyes, he found his king perched on top of a large bookshelf, looking down on him almost playfully with his head cradled in his hands. The king smiled when Elish noticed him, then, with a soundless series of movements, he jumped off the bookshelf and onto the floor. The king rose and flicked his wavy golden hair back, before sauntering over like the soundless ghost he was; the coat tails he had decided to wear today following behind him.

King Silas gave him a nod of approval as Elish bowed, then with a snap of his fingers he summoned Sanguine over. The red-eyed sengil, just as soundless, pattered over and put his hands behind his back awaiting his orders.

"Sanguine, bring Elish his usual... I have new bloodwine from the stores. Cigarette as well? Surely not one of Garrett's god awful cigars. I swear I will make it a law soon that he has to stop smoking them." King Silas paused, every movement on his body became still, then with a snake-like hiss he whispered, "Or is it the Morosian cigarettes you're smoking now?"

Silas watched Elish with his intense eyes, analyzing his every movement, knowing that if Elish even so much as blinked he would miss the subtle signs.

Ahh, yes, there it was. The king watched as Elish's lip gave the smallest of twitches. *Mm, amor. I pulled you from the steel womb myself. The only baby that refused a cry, just violet comets that took in the entire room. I cradled you in my arms and hollered my success, your brothers soon squalling all around us.*

Letting out a languid laugh, Silas dismissed Sanguine with a wave of his hand, before gliding up to his first born. He swept around Elish, raising his head to take all of Elish in. *Such a picture of beauty. I would never replicate such perfection again. Even Artemis and Apollo's beauty is nothing compared to this elegance.*

The king made a slow circle around him, looking up and down at his creation's long slender body, adorned with a white cape that flowed beautifully with his long hair.

"Have I said something to upset you…? Tell me, love. What did I do to make my beautiful creature so cross?" Silas took a piece of Elish's hair between his fingers and started twirling it around. His green eyes flashed with a morbid curiosity, before he purred in Elish's ear. "Don't tell me… you thought you could keep him a secret from me?"

Elish's eyes burned into the window of Alegria, King Silas's skyscraper. They tried to find Sanguine but the shark-toothed chimera was in the shadows where he belonged.

With a tempered patience that living under his king for almost ninety years had brought him, Elish didn't flinch or waver. Instead he was steadfast and determined, focusing on the windows and the dark skyscrapers in front of him.

"It was never my intention to keep the boy a secret. He is merely a pet and while my sengil is being borrowed by Garrett, my serventmaid as well." Elish's voice was cold enough to quench the fires of hell.

There was a click of shoes against marble. Silas glanced over and so did Elish.

Sanguine stood with a smile on his face, the closed mouth Cheshire grin that made his eyes squint. Everyone thought he just had an odd smile and in truth he did, but the smile was to hide his sharp teeth, which had small serrated edges like a sharks. That and his blood-red eyes made him one of the most mutated abominations that had come from their metal mothers. Perish and Silas had been thrilled with the results. Elish at the time only shook his head, wondering what abomination those two would create next.

Sanguine bowed and offered them their refreshments resting on a silver tray. It was the same spread that Elish had been enjoying with his master since he was a boy. Bloodwine, thick crust bread, and whatever seasonal cheese could be paired with it.

Elish didn't care for the sengil, and it was an obvious mistake to have Sanguine teach Jade to be a proper sengil. The demon-eyed servant was sneaky and slippery, with a smile that was all but a curtain covering his nature.

Silas took the glass, and motioned for Elish to do the same, though the cold chimera made no move to sit. He only took a sip, his eyes never leaving the king's face.

Both were gods of their craft, their faces were neutral voids. Two lions circling each other, their eyes locked, with neither backing down.

"And? Do you like him?" The king looked down at the crimson wine, a perfect matching for Sanguine's eyes, and swirled it around in his glass. "It seems to me, he is growing fond of you. He was quite the devoted sengil when Sanguine was helping him scrub up... those blood stains."

Silas's eyes rose to Elish's forehead, the bandage now gone but a small brown scab still remained. "Did your little slumrat bite you? I hear he got to Moros and you just... picked him up and brought him home like a runaway child? Cradled him in your arms?"

Elish picked up a small piece of cheese and absentmindedly bit it in two, when he had swallowed he said in a placid voice, "The boy's mother is mentally ill and had poisoned him. Surely Kerres didn't leave out that detail? Or does Sanguine have crows in Moros as well?"

King Silas laughed; he tipped his glass and clinked it against Elish's. "Sanguine has crows in all corners, in all locations, amor. You know this."

The king drained the glass, Elish still only sipping on his. Silas gave it back to the sengil with a wave of his hand. Sanguine bowed his head and disappeared to refill it.

"And what other trouble has he given you? Surely, you don't want to keep such an unrefined gutter rat? I could offer you much more suitable candidates if you're lonely."

"I am not *lonely*." Elish's voice had a frosted tone. "He has merely captured my interest. My brothers have done the same; there is no difference between the two."

"Then you will not mind... if I... dispose of him for you then? He sounds more trouble than he is worth. His body bears the marks of deep discipline."

The thought made Elish's jaw clench, a small falter in his countenance that made Silas notice something.

"Oh... Elish, you deviant..." Elish stared forward as he felt Silas brush his golden hair back. Suddenly the room filled with a tense air. King Silas retracted his hand, and in that moment Elish felt the King's heartbeat rise. "You do like this one. You fucked him didn't you?"

"Indeed." Elish couldn't suppress the growl behind those words.

There was a silence between the two of them, a silence that spanned decades. Only their heartbeats could be heard at various stages of beating. Elish's was steady and calm, as was Sanguine's, but Silas's sped up as his eyes scanned the love bites and rosy patches on Elish's skin. A blighted mark on such a smooth ambrosia; Elish was an unspoiled creature that did not lend himself easily to desire.

Elish knew what was coming, and all he could do was stand and take it. Perhaps try and talk him down from the oncoming explosion of jealousy that would be soon spewing forth from his possessive king's mouth. His favourite chimera bedding an unkempt gutter rat, choosing his body over the king of Skyfall, the greywastes, and the surrounding dead world.

Silas loved all of his chimeras, and with exception of Elish's only sister Ellis and the ones not yet of age, he had bedded all of them; and treated them like his personal boyfriends and husbands. King Silas had free rein over all of them, and summoned them to his skyscraper and bed chambers as he saw fit.

Elish had never showed an interest in anyone, and, of course, as would naturally happen with a mad king when his favourite chimera took an interest in a slumrat... he was jealous.

Even if he had about twenty hot chimeras at his beck and call and over a dozen pets, King Silas would always want what was out of reach, and if he couldn't get it... he got angry. Because King Silas always got what he wanted, even if he didn't want anything more than to fuck with you.

"Well?" Silas tone turned to an almost sweet, cajoling nature. "Is there something you want to ask me?"

Sanguine returned with two more wine glasses, always the crow on his master's shoulder, remembering everything and repeating it like a parrot. He smiled and held the silver tray in both hands as he waited for there to be a job for him. If Jade had held any of that odd nature Elish would've disposed of him immediately.

"Well?"

Elish's mouth twitched again, and with a sigh he forced the words from his lips. "May I keep him, Master?" Elish asked coolly, bringing the bloodwine to his lips. He couldn't taste the coppery tones, all he tasted was bitter acid, which ran down his throat and pooled in his stomach.

"And what do you want, love? Do you wish to soil our family with such a wild, disease infested gutter rat?"

I had wanted to be left alone, but perhaps this was my own doing by saving the boy, three times now. I suppose our masochistic nature, the one glaring trait of all of us, was showing through. Maybe it was only a matter of time.

I had thought I would be smarter than this.

Elish drained his cup and placed it on Sanguine's tray, before immediately picking up the other one.

With this boy brought a slew of complications. What was once a morbid curiosity has developed into something more, and very quickly as well. In a fell swoop, or a series of painful jabs rather, the boy has burrowed himself into me like a parasite.

But still, what do I want?

The answer was obvious; Silas's answer to the problem of his chimera disciples finding mates had always been the same. "It doesn't matter what I want, you will break him, torture him, and kill him in the end."

Elish looked over as he saw Silas's head come into view. The king had a small smile on his face, with his green eyes only meeting Elish's in the reflection of the window, broken up only by his strands of wavy gold hair.

"You may keep him... that is... if you win."

Suddenly the wine cup shattered in Elish's hand, shards of glass flying everywhere around them like crystal raindrops. The three men stood without a single surprised movement, as the shards fell to the floor, silent like falling snow.

Elish's hand dripped blood, staining the remaining glass shards. He felt the graceful touch of Silas lift his hand, though Elish pulled it away from him.

"I will not play your games." As though the words held a physical current, Silas retracted his hand.

And though Elish refused to look at his master, Silas's eyes burned into Elish's. Intense emerald slabs that could cut a man with the sharpness of a diamond. The world had fallen because of this look, because the humans had the audacity to scorn him.

He ended the world because it was not to his liking, and here I am challenging the same monster for a fifteen-year-old rat from the slums.

The room darkened around them, even Sanguine took a step back to hide from the standoff.

The chimera stared forward, a statue of elegance and grace; and beside Elish with his head downturned but his eyes tracking his every movement, his master, king, and creator watched him.

Elish had always waited for those eyes to turn black, to be finally unable to project a false sense of humanity. Black would be a more suitable colour for his king. Black like the toxic waste flowing through his veins, and the iron slab of his heart. Eyes with the inability to feel any amount of restraint or empathy.

Though, of course, Elish was hardly any different. He was created from Silas, and the same darkness coursed his own body as well, but he was not dead yet. No… far from it.

"Then you will kill him." Silas's cold voice hit him like he was a ship crashing into an iceberg, though still Elish did not falter. "Sanguine will come to claim his body tomorrow, it would please me to add his head to my collection."

So it was over as soon as it began. Well, perhaps it was for the best, the boy would've only brought me trouble in the end.

If only this could have waited for a few more years, I might've had a chance.

Elish never regretted his own actions; if something didn't go his way he never complained or got angry. He analyzed every fold and crevice of the situation and picked apart every last detail, so next time he could handle things differently.

How would I have handled that boy differently? I suppose if another one comes along in a hundred years I will have to see. Though from how this situation had played out I would probably just kill him. It is less complicated that way.

Mercy is not in my nature, but I will make it painless. An overdose of morphine perhaps, something kind and without a mess for Luca to clean. There will be no need for the stray to know. I would dislike having to see those eyes gaze up at me with betrayal.

It is not like he has much of a life anyway, no Morosian ever did. If anything he should be thankful for the several months living in luxury.

"I will take my leave then." Elish took a towel from Sanguine and wrapped his bloody hand, before turning to leave the apartment.

As he left, Silas's words haunted his steps. "We'll see if you can kill him, love. Something does tell me though; you will be playing my game. But no... you may leave."

Jade looked up from his Game Boy when he saw Elish walk through the apartment doors. He set the device down and rose to greet his master.

He took a few steps towards Elish, but there was no mistaking the look on Elish's face. Jade stopped and looked at him curiously, though he knew better than to say anything.

Elish hung up his coat, and it was at this point that Jade noticed the rim of rusted blood gracing the right cuff. His eyes travelled and saw the bloodied dish towel wrapped around his right hand.

"Can I look at it?"

"No." Elish glided past him without so much as a glance of recognition. This brought even more questions to fill Jade's head. He watched his master go with a raised eyebrow.

The cicaro followed behind him at a distance, and noticed he was carrying a bag in his hand. The chimera placed it on top of the white marble coffee table, besides Jade's Game Boy.

Still not speaking Elish sunk into the couch, his purple eyes fixed forward in an iced gaze.

This was new, but Jade had been living with Elish for four months now. If only because of his arrogant bravery, he sat beside him and took Elish's towel wrapped hand into his own.

When Elish didn't pull away, Jade unwrapped the white cloth and tsked at his cut up hand.

"That could use some stitches, I have that first aid kit Luca kept for me." There wasn't even a question of him going to get Lyle; Elish would shoot that down in a second. Even if everything else around Jade had been thrown into confusion, this fact was sure.

"I will make us some tea." The placid voice caught Jade off-guard, not to mention the fact that Elish rarely made his own tea, only in the mornings if Jade was still asleep and he wasn't feeling cruel enough to wake him.

Jade watched him for a moment longer than would be deemed comfortable, before with a nod he walked into the hallway closet and brought out the white first aid kit. He rested it beside the Game Boy and noticed the paper bag was gone. Elish had it; he could hear it crinkling in the kitchen.

Must be a new type of tea, Elish enjoyed all types, though his favourite always seemed to be either green, chai, or sometimes mint. It was where Jade was sure he got that mint smell to him, mint and nutmeg. It was an amusing realization that Elish smelled like tea.

Jade threaded sutures and laid out the disinfectant. He looked over at Elish and smiled as he brought them both a saucer with a steaming mug resting on top.

Jade took it from him and put it to his mouth. He took a sip and winced. It tasted like bark but there was no way he was going to complain. Maybe it was an acquired taste. He raised the cup to his lips again but Elish held up his bloodied and cut hand.

"Should you not take care of your master's needs before your own?"

Jade automatically flinched as Elish pinned him with his cold gaze. He gave a nod and started wiping Elish's hand down with the disinfectant. As he did, he noticed glass shards stuck into the deep pocked cuts. Had Elish punched a window or something? No, not unless he did it palm out. It took every fiber in Jade's being not to ask, but he wasn't stupid. Instead he brought out some tweezers and started picking out the bits that wouldn't wash off.

"Tell me about your day."

Though Jade had been doing well to make his face as neutral as possible, he couldn't hide the upturn of his eyes at this question. Elish had never asked him about his day before, usually when he came back from his errands it was dinner and tapping on that laptop, or watching his crime shows, then making Jade scream for a few hours, then bed. This was an odd thing.

Well… remember what Sanguine said. Maybe he's slowly coming around.

The confused look turned into a smile at that thought. Jade tweezed out a piece of glass and wiped it on the cloth. "I found another one of Luca's Pokémon games, so I reset it, which I am sure he will be mad at, but whatever. So anyway, I named the head-dude Elish and I had to come up with a name for his rival. Guess what I named him?"

Elish gazed down at him, the same indifferent but cold look that didn't scare Jade as much as it used to. "Jade, I am assuming? Do you even know how to spell our names?"

Elish flinched as Jade dug the tweezers in deeper, then the cicaro sucked in a sympathetic breath and shook his head. "Oh sorry, that one was really deep."

"Mmhm." Elish looked like he was going to let that one slide.

"No, I didn't name him Jade. I named him Silas. He got a shitty, like, crocodile -thing… it looks like a wimp, but I didn't like the other two. So I transferred a charmander over and –" Jade glanced up at Elish who was giving him the same look. "Do you want me to shut up?"

"Believe me, Cicaro; I don't need prompting when I want you to shut up."

Jade smiled, and doused the now clean wound in antiseptic, before he brought out the needle and thread. "Good, so anyway, I renamed it Jade, and transferred it over. So that's his main Pokémon, and it will be his only Pokémon. I'm not going to catch any other ones. Just Elish and Jade, kicking everyone's ass."

Elish smirked and watched as Jade held the hook in his hand, and started putting in the several stitches into his more deeper cuts. "And won't he lose with just one… animal?"

"Pokémon –" Jade corrected, "– and nah, I'm a master at this game. I'll be able to do it, as long as Luca doesn't reset my game."

"I will not allow him to reset it," Elish said absentmindedly, his eyes shifting from his wounded hand to Jade's tea cooling on the coffee table.

Jade looked up at him, and gave him an appreciative smile. "I also want to show you something later. I hope it works. I've been working on it for the past month, just a stupid trick but I think you'll get a kick out of it."

"Indeed…" Elish raised his tea to his lips and took a sip.

After that there was a calm silence between them. Jade carefully wrapped Elish's hand in soft gauze, before giving it a pat. "There, see? Morosians might suck at everything else but we're good home medics. The health care plan in the slums is pretty bad." Jade reached over to grab his tea; he brought it to his lips and took another drink. The tea seemed to get even worse when it was cooling.

"Come here." Elish leaned back on the couch and drew Jade into his arms. The boy gave another confused look, but being in the warmth of his master's embrace was a guilty pleasure he had stopped trying to fight months ago. Jade let himself be held, though Elish's hold on him was tighter than usual. "Is there anything on TV you want to watch?"

Wow, how many times does Sanguine need to prove he's right? Inside the ice that continued to thaw around Jade's heart broke away, and deep inside he felt a warmth start to build inside of him. Almost like an opiate rush, it was filling Jade with a blissful happiness he had never felt before.

"What about… just some music? And you can tell me how your day went." Jade gave him a smile, now holding faint traces of fatigue.

Elish nodded and leaned over to pick up the remote for the CD player; Jade took this opportunity to drink some more of the tea, trying to see if he could get his taste buds used to such an odd and unappealing flavour.

The music turned on behind them, a low guitar being strummed and a man's soothing voice; a moment later the lights dimmed and only the fireplace lit the living room around them, shining its warm glow on the old furniture casting shadows and reflecting against the skyscraper windows. Everything was a peaceful silence, a moment of bliss in a grey world.

Jade rested his shoulders on Elish's arms and sighed. Elish gazed back down at him. His cold aura was an arctic air, but it was vivid tonight, so bright Jade found himself looking up at the ceiling to watch the flickers dance across the white stucco. He tried to bring his own up to join Elish's, and with a pull he saw the black and purple strands start to form around him.

Elish shifted his body so he was lying on the couch, and gently stroked back Jade's hair. His touch held a soft warmth with small sparks of static. Jade melted into him and let the joy and warmth take him.

What an odd feeling... I feel so tired, I wasn't tired before. Jade raised a hand and put it over Elish's.

"I think this is going to make me fall asleep soon."

"I know," Elish replied, his voice an almost inaudible whisper. "You can sleep, I won't move."

Jade smiled and fought it. He reached for the remote and turned off the electric fireplace, shrouding the room in darkness. Only the small lights of the electronics around them could cast a glow for the naked eye, though in Jade's mind the entire living room was a spectrum of their colours.

Jade rose, even though Elish put a hand on his chest to keep him down. He moved his body so he was kneeling in front of Elish on the couch.

"I've been practicing all month..." Jade whispered. The atmosphere around them was so tranquil and serene he didn't want to ruin it with a loud voice. "Watch."

Jade reached a hand out to Elish's chest and picked up a strand of his aura. He pulled it like one would pull a rope from a well and coiled it in his hand. Then with another hand Jade caught his own drifting around him, and though fatigue was starting to claim him, Jade coiled it around as well.

"What are you doing?" Elish murmured curiously. He leaned forward; amazed at how the boy's eyes were focusing on something that wasn't there.

"I can see people's auras," Jade whispered. He gently moved his hand over the ball of black and silver, with opal and violet flecks, joining the two together. They moulded and seeped into each other and became one right in front of him. "Look... can you see it?"

Elish stared at him, before his eyes fell to Jade's hands, holding nothing in their bowled position but darkness and empty air. Elish shook his head, but a moment later his hand rose and cradled Jade's chin.

The chimera looked into the boy's eyes, and in a rare display of emotion his mouth dropped open.

Flickering in the cicaro's yellow eyes he could see silvers, blacks, and violets, like borealis they swept through the gold and the black pupils, unseen by the visible spectrum but a brilliant display in the reflection of the boy's eyes.

"You – you're an empath? An aura reader?" Elish whispered. "You never spoke of this before."

In that moment Jade's eyes fluttered; as he started to fall backwards Elish caught him, and yanked his body back to his kneeling position. Elish aggressively shook Jade's body, until a sliver of yellow rose between his eyelids.

Jade's mouth quivered, trying to make words. When he spoke his voice was weak. "Ours mix, Elish. Kerres and I... ours were like oil. I think it means we're supposed to be together. Ho-horrible, huh?"

No... no, this can't be true, this can't be right. I had told him to dispose of the remaining two newborns. He had told me it had been done. That was it, it had been settled.

This can't be...

Silas. You bastard.

"We'll see if you can kill him, love. Something does tell me though; you will be playing my game."

Elish swore and dropped the boy onto the couch. With speed not seen on the graceful chimera, he ran into the bathroom and opened up the medicine cabinet.

When he returned Jade was still, his heartbeat was weak and his breathing a dying rasp. A small trickle of blood ran down his nose; silent and unassuming, it dripped onto the couch.

Elish opened Jade's mouth, and crushed the green pills between his fingers before he forced them down Jade's throat. Elish pushed his body against the couch, making him sit, and when he was steady Elish tipped his head back and poured his own chai tea between Jade's lips. Though it would burn his throat Elish could only hope it would dissolve the pills faster.

"You fucking bastard," Elish whispered, trying to hold Jade steady by the neck; his other hand clasped over Jade's wrist, feeling his pulse.

"You will pay for bringing me into this, Silas. One day soon, mark my words, you will pay."

Elish closed his eyes and listened. He tuned his own hearing, something he rarely did, and listened to every sound the boy's body was making.

Jade, you'll be fine. You're strong; it's in your blood.
You are a chimera, my chimera… you'll be fine.

BOOK 2

Awakening

CHAPTER 13

MINT AND NUTMEG. A FAMILIAR SCENT THAT brought with it the alluring aura that was imprinted on my mind. I blinked my eyes and tried to bring the world into focus, though it took several hard squints to make the couch and the coffee table stop blurring on me.

It took me a full five minutes to realize that this was something odd. I shouldn't be in the living room with Elish; I should be in my room... or his room, where I usually ended up over the past months. Certainly not in here... with him underneath me.

I yawned and moved around, realizing that I was practically lying on top of him, and also –

I glanced down.

He had his hand on my chest.

"Awake are we?"

I jumped, not expecting to hear him. I don't know if I thought he was asleep, or if it was my usual startled reaction to his voice, but I jerked in surprise, which brought an amused sniff from the chimera.

"Barely." I winced and rubbed my throat before coughing. My throat was raw, not the usual 'I've been screaming all night' raw, but like it had been burned.

I slid off of his body and stretched, feeling every vertebrae in my back snap and crackle. I gave a loud yawn and fell back onto the couch. I laid my head against the cloth backing and looked at him.

Damn, he looked well... tired would be a good way of describing him.

Elish's long blond hair was unkempt, his eyes had bags underneath them and he looked incredibly exhausted.

My suspicions got to me and only solidified when I thought back to last night, if only to try and figure out what must've happened during the evening. I was puzzled when I realized I didn't remember anything. The last thing I remember was telling him about that stupid Pokémon game. Everything else was shrouded in haze.

It looked like he stayed up all night, but why? I rose to my feet but stumbled and fell back onto the couch. I shook my head and tried again, a bit more successfully this time. "Want some coffee? I think we both need some coffee."

"That would be pleasant." Elish rose and took a moment to straighten out his robes. "I'll be taking a shower and changing clothing. Order some breakfast, something heavy, I have a feeling it is going to be a long day."

Okay, enough shrouded mystery. I turned around and crossed my arms; of course he ignored me and walked right past, but I wasn't one to let this go. "What happened last night? If I was naked and bloody I might let it pass, but I'm not… what went on?"

"Remember your place, Cicaro."

I gritted my teeth and mentally stabbed him right in the back of his neck, but I clamped my mouth shut. If there was anything I had learned from being Elish's pet it was to know when to shut up and do my duties, and I knew that this was one of those times.

So I did my busy work. I called for coffee from the kitchen and decided on eggs and arian bacon, hash browns, and a couple of pancakes on the side. While that was being made I set the table, yawning the whole time. I was just wiped out; it was obvious that Elish hadn't slept either.

I coughed and winced under my burning throat, the mystery a hovering weight above my head. I tried to dismiss it but it was still there.

The food was delivered and I was in the middle of making our plates when Elish emerged from his bedroom. He had a bit more energy to him but he still looked tired.

We sat down together and started to eat. I slipped some cold water into my coffee to make it not burn my throat so much; I wanted caffeine not heat.

As I took a long drink I watched Elish reach into his trouser pocket and pull out a small white sealed bag. His other hand holding up today's Skyfall bulletin, a routine he did every day.

With my mouth half-full of food, I watched as he opened the baggy and poured a good amount in his coffee, before casually putting it to his lips.

That type of packaging looked familiar, it fucking looked like coke.

"What is that?"

"Medicine."

I narrowed my eyes at him, but he didn't have a single fuck to give. I inched my fingers over to the small resealable bag.

I yelped as he slammed his hand down on my fingers. I retracted them and gave him a hurt look before violently spearing a pancake. We ate in peace after that, and even my plans to sneak a look into the bag later were dashed when he put it back into his pocket.

When I was preparing him to leave the apartment he surprised me.

There was no hiding the confusion on my face when he clipped the leash to my collar. I looked at him questioningly as he handed me my leather jacket. We were in the throes of winter now.

"I'd wear your gloves too, it looks rather cold outside."

"Where are we going?" I knew I was rarely privy to this information but I had to try. I started slipping my gloves on and putting on my leather boots. I wished I had dressed in a heavier shirt or a sweater but I assumed we were going to be inside. Instead I had on my usual tight leather pants and a thin blue t-shirt with no sleeves.

"You will be coming along with me to Garrett's office and along on errands. Luca will be moving back in while we're gone," Elish replied, placing an old school brimmed hat on his head and heading out the door, my leash in hand.

I followed him and closed the door behind us, before we both walked into the elevator.

Well, this was new; at least I was going outside. I had been an inside pet before this, not going anywhere unless it was with Elish when we went out to grab food at a restaurant. Besides that he hadn't trusted me outside on my own and for good reason too. Those thien guards holding assault rifles in front of the entrance weren't just for protection, it was to prevent me from bashing my way back to Moros like a few months ago.

Though my escaping days were over, with the knowledge that Kerres was safe in Moros and my last escape still fresh in my head, I had resigned myself to my fate. One day if he got bored of me he might let me go, and if he did, I'd go back to Moros.

My lip twitched. I wasn't ready to admit that I enjoyed Elish's company when he was in one of his good moods. I felt that if I admitted it, it would mean I liked him as a whole and I didn't. The douchebag who hit me across the room and shocked me when I finally bit back to his scathing criticisms of me I didn't care for.

But the guy who let me lay on him the entire night last night – that guy… he had grown on me.

I rubbed my hands together, the tips of my fingers frozen even through the leather. It was cold outside but the car was warm; even so it took the entire trip to inner Skyland for me to thaw out. It was so cold I could see my breath like it was cigarette plumes; it was like everyone around us was smoking winter cigs.

With my leash in hand Elish walked into the Skytech building. I continued to shiver and wrap my arms around myself, wiping the snot running down my nose with my gloved hand. We went up the elevator to where I assumed Garrett was.

"Look at that little thing; he's shivering like a Chihuahua!" Oh, Garrett always seemed to be in my corner. I liked that guy; his aura was pleasant too, like a candy cane almost. "Elish, put more clothes on the poor wretch."

Garrett gave us both one of his beaming smiles. He was in his usual suit and tie with a hat on his head similar to Elish's. I gave him a smile and a bow.

"Oh, and he's doing his pet thing! Very good, brother. He looks healthier too," the president praised, clasping his hands together. Strangely though a moment later, his usual permanent smile faded.

I glanced at Elish and saw a cold and intimidating glare on his face, which was usually directed at me. It was freezing Garrett alive right in front of me; I felt a shiver go up my spine.

"Jade, sit in the lobby, you may play your game. Garrett… a word."

They may have been born only seconds apart, but it was as clear as day who the dominant brother was. Garrett swallowed hard and I saw his skin turn several shades paler; his eyes following Elish as he walked into his office.

Garrett sighed and adjusted his red tie, before walking into the office after him.

I enjoyed this a little too much. No one who didn't bear the brunt of almost all of Elish's punishment would understand the sadistic joy of finally seeing someone else get into trouble.

Over what though? I dismissed even the thought of asking Elish, it was so out of the question that the very prospect of it made me want to laugh out loud. Instead I reached into my soft leather bag of pet entertainment, and found an overstuffed chair in the lobby to sink into.

Surrounded by grey swirly marble and white pillars I turned down the sound and started training up Jade the charmander. I was going to have to work hard if I wanted him to beat all the other Pokémon on his own.

I lost myself in the video game, which was good because those two were taking a long time. I sunk myself into the chair and swung my legs over the arm. Last night's lost hours had completely wiped me out, and I wasn't allowed cocaine in my coffee like some certain person.

"You seem to be well, interesting indeed."

I jumped a mile high, I knew that voice. I put the Game Boy down and turned around to greet Sanguine.

"I am, thanks." I started saving my game since I would be smacked if I didn't show proper respect. As I did I glanced around and realized he was alone. "Are you here by yourself?"

Sanguine smiled, creasing the corners of his eyes. "Yes, little cicaro. I am here for you actually. Come with me."

A cold air descended around us; though I had enjoyed Sanguine's company and he seemed like a nice sengil chimera, there was an uneasy feeling surrounding him. I tuned myself to his aura and felt myself visibly recoil.

Deep red and black, with the black fluttering around almost like they were crow's feathers. It was… odd. It filled me with such an anxiety I felt myself automatically pull back like I had touched a hot stove.

I found myself a moment later. He was a sengil; he didn't have the power to remove me from my master. I gave him a nod towards the office Garrett and Elish were in and turned my Game Boy off. "You'll have to talk to Elish about that. He told me to stay here and wait for him."

Sanguine didn't move and the squinty, closed lip smile didn't falter from his face.

Then I heard a click. I blinked and looked down. Without even seeing his arm move he had clipped a new leash to my neck. "Oh, no, no…" I choked, but with the same unnatural chimera strength Sanguine pulled me to my feet.

An eerie chuckle that rolled from his lips.

"Let's go, little one. We shan't make this hard. Off to see the king. " Sanguine's voice dropped to a low hiss. He started to literally drag me towards the elevator door.

See the fucking king? Without Elish? Well, that wasn't going to happen.

"ELISH!" I started to shout. I pulled on my leash and coughed as my already sore throat got constricted on my collar. "ELISH!" I hollered.

I grabbed onto the chain and tried to yank it out of his hand. The sengil chimera was ignoring me though, and through my shouting I thought I even heard him whistling a tune as he dragged me along. I clamped my hands around the metal frame of the elevator and held on for dear life.

Then my saviour. Just as my fingers were getting ripped away from the frame the door flew open and Elish and Garrett both rushed out.

Elish took one look at us and I saw his eyes narrow, though in his statuesque elegance that was the only window into his emotions. "Drop him, Sanguine," he said in a booming, authoritative voice.

I heard the blood-eyed chimera growl, before my chain went slack. I booked it and in my fear I ran to Elish and took my place behind him. If it were anyone else my slum pride would have shown through, but this guy had quickly turned into a very intimidating and rather eerie creature, a chimera with so much engineering he didn't seem human. I wasn't going to fuck with that. Not without Elish nearby anyway.

Sanguine's narrow, sinister eyes looked at Elish before travelling to me behind him, holding the entire time an unimpressed but rather bored look. "Did you misunderstand Silas's orders, Elish? I was ordered to collect him."

Collect me? My mouth was glued shut but that didn't prevent the questions from swirling in my head. I glanced over at Garrett for help but that guy looked like he was about to explode. He wasn't good at hiding his feelings, unlike my master.

A moment later I felt Elish unclip the leash from my collar, followed by the sound of quickly coiling chains as he dropped it to the floor. "The boy is testament enough to my decision. Tell that to our king and leave us. We're finished here."

Elish snapped my leash back on and started leading me to the door, before Sanguine's deep and rather nonchalant voice called out to us. "I do suggest you come to Alegria and tell the king yourself. He does love your visits. Good day."

"Garrett... I will be in touch," Elish called behind him, then, without another word, he led us to the elevator and after a very tense descent, to his awaiting car.

What the hell had happened? My heart was still racing when I took my place beside Elish. My throat was raw too. I massaged it under my collar, feeling it already start to swell, it felt hot under my touch especially around my now scarring bite marks. You would think my neck would be used to this now but it still got angry whenever my collar got restrained.

I shot Elish a sideways glance but it was like looking at a piece of molten steel. He was in that Elish-state where he would rip your arm off if you so much as asked him to use the bathroom. So instead I just shifted myself as close to the car door as I could and watched the cityscape go by, hoping he wasn't going to direct this anger at me more than anything, I hadn't done anything wrong.

Oh shit, had I? Maybe I did and they smacked me over the head or wiped my memory, could they do that?

I glanced back at Elish and felt myself shrink down; Elish's hands were gently folded over his lap and he was staring forward. Though he looked relaxed, even his face was a deceptive calm... it was the eyes that got me, like laser beams.

"Hey, I didn't... fuck something up last night, did I?"

"I would have told you if it was something you did wrong." His voice brought winter into the warm car, but it was a relief nonetheless. At least this trouble wasn't my doing, but still... it didn't answer my question. Why was Sanguine trying to bring me to Silas?

"Jade, what is Sanguine's aura? What sense of him do you have?"

The words brought a rush of prickles to my skin, followed by a sharp shiver soaking every bone in my body. I looked over at Elish and stared at him; feeling like my head had just been ripped open and exposed.

"You know about that?" I stammered.

Elish nodded slowly. "You told me last night. Please meltdown about my knowledge of this on your own personal time. I need an answer from you now."

I thought for a second, of the deep red aura, like his eyes, and the black crow feathers that swirled around him. I let out a breath and described it to Elish in as much detail as I could.

"I thought as much," Elish muttered, tapping his two pointer fingers together, "and Garrett?"

Now that was a guy I liked. "He's like a candy cane, red and white. More white than yours which is crystally and pretty, silver too. I like him; he's not full of fire and brimstone like that creepy sengil."

"Watch your words, he is still a chimera." Elish's chastising had really improved from shocking me or smacking me on the head. I watched as Elish reached a hand into his wool long coat and pulled out a small leather-bound black book; it had a silver lock on it.

He handed it to me, before handing me a small silver key. I opened it but every page was blank, it was a journal.

"I want you to make a list of every person of importance we meet from now on. I want a separate section for chimeras, a separate section for sengils, cicaros, and a section for others. I am expecting honesty, you will not get in trouble for what you write," Elish instructed. He also handed me a very fancy silver pen.

There was a swell of pride that rushed through me when he said these instructions to me. My aura reading had always been a neat trick, but nothing other than that, just a trick and occasionally an annoyance because sometimes I honestly didn't want to know what kind of person I was reading. If Elish was giving me this job, it meant he saw something in my abilities, and he had a use for me other than being a chew toy.

"I won't let you down." I gave him a smile and turned to the first page. The paper was snow white with small blue lines perfectly spaced apart. I furrowed my brow though and handed the book back to him. "Can you write down their names though? I can't even begin to imagine how Sanguine is spelled."

Elish took the book back and clicked the pen. "I suppose it would save you the embarrassment."

He started writing, and as he did he continued speaking. "We will be attending Stadium this week. My brothers will be there with their pets. I would like you to give me a report on the chimeras I have listed starting at the top. Do as many as you can but do not rush; the ones you may miss I visit monthly anyway. Do you understand me?"

Stadium? I was going to get to be in the skybox! All the other times I had attended with Kerres I was in the back sections of the bleachers.

Kerres. My lower lip tightened and suddenly my breath started to catch, gripping my chest like a vice slowly getting turned. That touch on my cheek... I missed him, even if his face was fading and slowly being replaced by Elish's. I swallowed it and tried to break the vice with a deep breath. With sullen regret, I banished him from my mind once again.

What had started out as something exciting had quickly filled me with sadness.

I sighed and watched the car turn down a main road, taking the repaired road to a different skyscraper to meet a different person.

This area was well-occupied and the repaired skyscrapers stood tall, with tinted windows and painted brick; unlike the burned-out ones in Moros and behind the stadium, where sometimes a whole side of the building would break away, leaving the apartments exposed to the elements.

A few years ago we actually had one finally fall down; a few people were killed but it was mind-fucking to see it come down. Moros even made the news.

In Skyland such things never happened. The elites and the chimeras paid a shit load of taxes and with that money the elite district of Skyfall was always under a state of repair, road workers with neon vests and giant industrial work vehicles making holes and pushing concrete. It was a well-paid job, but the commute every day would make it impossible for a Morosian to hold a job like that. There were no proper shuttles for a reason, to make it hard for the slumrats to loiter around in their district.

And now I was one of those Skylanders in a tower. I was lower than a

Morosian because at least they had their freedom. Maybe I was even worse than a pet now, because I woke up every day not minding ordering breakfast, ironing his shirts, and cleaning the apartment.

I didn't even have to do that anymore, Luca was coming back. This made my brow crease further. I wouldn't have much to do all day but I guess I could start doing the writing in the leather-bound journal.

"What am I going to do all day when Luca's home? I usually just cleaned and straightened crap out, before he was lent to Garrett I was locked in a dog cage."

Elish was still writing in my book; he didn't look up as he replied. "You will be coming with me while I am out, from now on. Unless you're locked back in that dog cage, but it seems we are over the worst of your little tantrums."

I felt myself bristle. He was the one that drew out those reactions in me but, of course, he would never say it.

"So I can start my aura stuff?"

"That's right."

There was a pause as the car pulled into the front of a skyscraper, one I hadn't been in before. I took off my seatbelt and waited for Elish to move.

Elish handed me back my book, but held onto it as I tried to grab it. I looked up and saw he was giving me the freezing look.

"Rest assured, Cicaro, accompanying me is a privilege. If you dare embarrass me in front of my brothers or the associates I have my meetings with, your small slumrat mind will not be able to fathom what I will do to you."

His voice was calm but full of sharp edges, with every syllable said with such careful grace it sunk into me like iron in water. There was no negotiating with that voice, and no response that could survive his piercing gaze. All I could do was nod; words would be useless fodder, even if I was only to assure my obedience.

Elish nodded back, and with that he got out of the car.

We didn't return to Olympus until the evening. If I had been home by myself I would've caught a nap on the couch or something, but I was the eye candy for the people Elish was meeting instead. Though I was used to being eye groped by people it felt a little bit more imposing considering I was dressed in my skimpy pet attire. At least the inside of the buildings were nice and warm and it was only a sprint to the car once we went off to the next meeting.

I didn't see any more chimeras though, all of the people Elish met with were presidents of small companies or fancy elite people wanting to broker deals. The most interesting was a factory owner for a factory in the greywastes. It was neat seeing the contrast between the elites and the greywaste people. They were a hardened type of arian with thousand yard stares, a look that told you they had seen some shit. It sounded like a fucking horror show outside of the boundaries of Skyfall, though they weren't under anyone's thumb, so they had that going for them.

After apologizing to Luca (without being ordered to I might add), who seemed more shocked that I was apologizing than anything, I settled in for the evening. Elish was nice enough to let me wear some jeans rather than the constricting leather pants and all three of us settled into our routines.

The next several days were the same. I accompanied Elish to his meetings and his office a few storeys down. The routine for being a pet accompanying his master was quite simple: shut up and look pretty at your master's feet.

When there were no meetings in Elish's office, I got to lounge around on a chair in the corner and play my video games, or write in my new book. When there were meetings I kneeled or sat down beside the desk, and stayed quiet, looking on as eye candy and only speaking when spoken to. Some of the people brought me presents or sweets which was a neat perk to my job, though most of them ended up in Elish's possession. I think he just re-gifted them to the other pets we met because I was sure he gave my chocolate bar to Artemis's little pet Tyan. I wasn't overly thrilled with that.

Then finally came the evening I had been dreading. I woke up with a pit in my stomach every day leading up to Saturday, and on the day of Stadium it felt like the pit had burst, abscessing my entire gut with anxiety and fear.

Without realizing it my anxiety translated to my body, and though Luca had tried to cheer me up with cupcakes they just sat in my stomach like an angry lump. I looked forlornly at him as I put on my jacket to go. I could see it in his eyes that he didn't envy me for having to go into the snake pit.

This will be... fun, right? You always enjoyed Stadium before...

"Master?" I asked when we were driving to the stadium.

"Mm?" Elish was looking through my leather-bound book; he looked through it every day almost. Thankfully, he hadn't checked the back pages yet. I had been learning how to draw Pokémon and something told me he wouldn't approve.

"Are Ares and Siris going to be there?"

"Of course. They're the main components of Stadium Night. Nero is currently away right now visiting our brother Perish in the greywastes."

Remembering the beating I had endured, and the rape in the mansion, made the familiar unpleasant feeling rise up in me. I felt like I was going to throw up, so much so I wished I could unroll the car window just to get some air.

"You're scared of them I see?" Elish observed. "Whatever for?"

"You know why." My teeth clenched together and I rubbed my nose before shifting uncomfortably in my seat.

"Do not be afraid of them; those two are the least of your worries."

My neck automatically jerked to him as he said those words; there was a tone to them that threw me off balance. Then I realized what he was talking about.

The king... that's right, tonight I will be meeting the king.

We pulled up behind the building, into a small unassuming door shielded by a big concrete wall topped off with a barbwire fence. Anyone who walked around this area wouldn't have given it a second glance. I was also glad for this. I didn't know what I would do if I saw Kerres or any of my old slum friends. At least Kerres would be able to see I was still okay.

With a creak of rusty hinges we both slipped into the door. Two thiens took one look at us and backed out of our way. With a nod at them, Elish and I walked through a small hallway and up a flight of stairs.

Our footsteps echoed on the stairs, and as we descended each step the voices in the room we were walking to got louder, and with it my anxiety. I didn't know what to expect and that alone was eating me alive. If I knew just an inkling of what was going to happen tonight, I could prepare myself.

But no, that would be too easy and it could never be easy, could it?

With a push of the door we walked into a large room with white walls and the plastic grey checkered linoleum that was standard in most of these types of industrial buildings.

In the building were several chimeras. I knew this because they looked attractive and were wearing the best clothes; some even holding leashes attached to cute little pets like me. Behind them were tablecloth-draped tables holding food and drinks, and even some sengils I had met previously walking around with trays full of alcohol.

I would have killed for some Valium, but instead I was led around to greet everyone, most of them chimeras I had met already, either during meetings or when they came to Elish for counsel or visiting.

I greeted Apollo and his new pet Todd, and Apollo's identical twin brother Artemis with his cicaro Tyan (the one who got my chocolate bar); both of the chimeras had silver wavy hair and purple eyes like Elish's but lighter. I was sure they must've taken some of Elish's makeup to create them because they had the same indifferent cold stare, which only intensified when they saw me. I had always got the distinct impression from them they didn't like me, which I suppose I was used to.

Then I was dragged towards one of the most badass-looking guys I had ever seen. He was Kessler, leader of the Imperial Army in the greywastes. He was immortal like the others but unlike the others he had a real family. A husband and two chimera kids, one of which was with him now.

The general had short black hair and a dead-eyed stare that told me he had experienced some bone chilling things in his time. He shook my hand so hard I could feel it crack and told me I had the eyes for a sniper.

I stood a bit taller after meeting him, he might be a hard-ass but he seemed genuine at least. He didn't seem to look down his nose at me like the others.

Then I was introduced to his son. He was also an intimidating guy. He had eyes like mercury and a stance that said he was a soldier even when he wasn't on duty. His glaring grey eyes were partially covered in twisted black curls that fell past his ears. Caligula was his name and I had the feeling he lived up to the guy he was named after.

That was it for the chimeras for now. I waited until Elish was having a conversation with Apollo before I inched towards the food. I managed to grab a plate of crackers and meat without him even seeing me. I got a glass of wine too but I had to quickly shotgun it before he noticed.

"Elish, love, I'm happy you came."

Love? I turned around to lay eyes on the guy who apparently thought he was Elish's boyfriend and almost started choking.

And there he was.

The bringer of the apocalypse was standing just two feet from me; I hadn't even felt him approaching. Like the man I had seen on the TV he had wavy blond hair several inches past his forehead, and eyes a deep green. His face was thin and handsome, a small nose, thin lips and eyebrows that only showcased the sinister nature I knew he had. He was a couple of inches taller than me and carried himself with a stealthy grace. Not the graceful elegance Elish had but one that told you he could slit your throat in a crowded room without anyone noticing.

It was different seeing him in the flesh. I could feel the anxiety in my chest freeze, like a rodent fearing the impending strike of a snake. This guy was fucking insane, to the point where I didn't even want to peer into his aura. I didn't know what I would find but I had a feeling the experience would give me nightmares.

I swallowed and bowed, hating my feet for buckling. My body seemed more scared than my brain, like it knew something I didn't. I couldn't understand or make sense of the feeling. It was like a demon had walked into the room and everyone else was chatting and visiting, when the natural response would be to scream and run.

"Oh… he is beautiful. Oh, Elish, he is a magnificent creature." Silas's emerald eyes became bright. My body recoiled in horror when he held a hand out to touch my cheek.

"No… no, little cicaro, stay still." Silas's voice became a low purr. As his cold hand stroked my cheek I felt the chain of my leash become tight. Elish making sure I wouldn't run, I gathered.

But I let him, if I ran now I would be screwed, if I showed weakness Silas would pounce on me. He was a predator and his instincts would push him to pursue the prey that fled.

I couldn't run.

"Look at those eyes..." Silas whispered. His hands trailed up and his thumbs wiped the bottom of my eyelid as if expecting there to be tears. "Beautiful... tell me, Jade, what do you see when you look at me?"

What do I see?

"My king," I whispered though it wasn't only a king I saw. I saw a ghost, a predator, a demon... I saw someone who had killed billions of people and continued to kill more. I saw the man on TV, fuck, I saw... I saw his disciples. Elish's nose, Artemis and Apollo's eyes... Sanguine's grace and Ares, Siris, and Nero's brutality.

I even saw the man who ignored Moros. Who looked down his nose at the Morosians and seemed to go out of his way to make sure we only barely survived. I saw the tact trucks get delayed another day, I saw water filters constantly going up in price. I saw everything and yet I still didn't trust myself to look into his aura.

My response made a smile curl his lips. I was relieved that he had normal teeth. I knew it was unreasonable since he was born immortal and not created like the chimeras, but I was still half-expecting him to be as demonic as Sanguine. Still though, the smile alone was enough to send an electric shock up my spine. I just wanted to get this over with so I could go home.

"We will gather in the skybox now, it is almost ready... come, come with me." Silas removed his hand from my face, before, without another word spoken, he quietly left for a door leading deeper into the stadium. I noticed then that everyone was looking at us, a spectrum of different-coloured eyes watching with curiosity, all the chimeras with smiles on their faces, and the pets looking just as intimidated as I was.

I followed the group and we all filed into the raised hallway that stretched across the stadium, a hallway made up of sheets of metal and wood, with mismatched windows that were thick and bulletproof. I had seen this area from below; it was being held up by pillars and thick logs of wood, bolted to the platform and welded in. This skybox towered over the main entrance to the arena. We had front row seats.

Elish and I walked to the window and I looked down with a small thrill sparking inside of me. The people were already in their seats, both the dark blurs of Moros and Nyx, and the brightly clothed Erosian and Skylanders.

It looked like they had busted out the glow sticks tonight. Small green sticks were being waved around, blending into the brilliant neon signs and strings of little lights that illuminated the large arena.

This is where Elish stood when he looked down at me in the crowd. I looked to where we had been sitting, me and Kerres, but, of course, there were different people in our seats. I couldn't see Kerres either, I didn't recognize anyone down there.

I wondered if he was okay. I swallowed the question I could never ask, but I badly wanted to ask Elish if Kerres was still okay. I hadn't seen him in months, before we had never gone a day without seeing each other.

Perhaps he found a new boyfriend... he must've known that I was Elish's pet now. How could he not know? Or maybe he just thought I was dead.

I turned away from the window and took out my black book, not wanting Elish to see the conflicting expression on my face. I brought out my pen and looked at my master.

He was holding a half-full glass of wine and was staring down at the arena.

"Can I sit and work on my book?" I asked, opening up to my chimera page. So far it wasn't filled in besides Garrett and Sanguine.

Elish nodded. He gave me back my leash and motioned to a couch that was in a far corner of the large skybox. "You may grab as much food as you wish, but keep the wine down to a glass."

"Thanks, Master." I wasn't in the mood to watch people be torn limb from limb anyway. I filled up my plate with food ranging from the usual crackers, meat and cheese, to snake cakes, vegetables and fruit. With that and my glass of wine, I sat down to observe the chimera family.

Though Elish would scoff at the word, I almost felt like a spy. I turned to the chimera closest to me first who was the Imperial General. Though he was a hardened badass, I saw small flecks of humanity in him when he was around that steel-eyed boy of his. A great military leader but he loved his family. I thought Elish might be interested in that so I jotted it down. If Elish ever had to get something from him he could probably use his husband and kids as a bargaining tool.

Within the hour the games were going on below me. I glanced up every once in awhile but for the most part I sat with my nose buried in the black book. As I worked, other chimeras filed in and out and I was able to mark a few more of them off my list. Artemis and Apollo were on top so I tried to go into as much detail as I could.

There was a trick I was having to learn with these guys though. Without a doubt, these chimeras had imposing and brilliantly lit auras. In order to analyze each one of them for Elish, I was having to focus my reading on one of them at a time. Usually I projected it as kind of like a flashlight in the dark, being able to see everyone's aura at once. But now I had been making it more like a laser beam, pinpointing each one and focusing on it. Otherwise it all seemed to overwhelm my senses. I didn't even want to think of what the king's would do.

And like he knew I was thinking about him, the next thing I knew the king was sauntering over me, a silent ghost with nothing more than a shifting of his robes to give away his position.

Wearing a denim shirt and black trousers Silas stared down at me with a creepy smile, showcased by his sinister narrowing eyes.

I rose up and bowed to him, since obviously he wanted something from me. As I did my eyes shifted behind him to see Elish on the other side of the room, watching the both of us without making it obviously known.

"Sanguine... a chair." I hadn't even seen Sanguine arrive. I watched as the red-eyed chimera set a wooden chair down for his king; Silas sat in it and motioned for me to sit back down on the couch.

My heart was hammering at this point in time; I knew the king would be able to hear it. He had all the enhancements his disciples had and probably more. It only accelerated when he took my hand into his.

Then Silas started touching and feeling my hands and my arms, with no care for social boundaries or my body, which was tensed and coiled.

I held back a shiver as he traced a cool hand up to my neck.

"Beautiful," Silas whispered. His voice was... odd, for lack of a better term. It was smooth and graceful, like he knew every word he was planning on saying a month in advance. It was calculated, not a single syllable broke the raspy flow. It reminded me of when Elish read to me, the same continuity, but with no text as reference. "I have gifts for you, Jade. Will you accept a gift from your master?"

Elish was my master... but I nodded. My throat was too tight to speak.

Silas raised a hand to his side, and in his palm Sanguine placed a small leather carrying case with a silver buckle. He carefully opened it with swift but delicate movements. By now everyone was watching us, the games below forgotten in favour of watching this spectacle going on around them.

My eyes widened as I looked at the leather case. Inside, on a velvet backing, were six little blades about an inch long and four small silver-looking objects I couldn't discern. I had no idea what they were but they looked like weapons.

Silas's hands were on me again. They drew down my collar, revealing the pink bite mark from mine and Elish's first time together, and past my shoulder where the whip marks started. I knew Elish was probably seething right now.

"Such abuse... would you not like something to defend yourself? Give me your hands."

My eyes seemed trapped looking at his face; his emerald eyes looked at me with an inauspicious smile that creased his eyes like his sengil's. I felt cold steel and looked down to see him slipping one of those small silver knives on my fingers.

They were rings... with goddamn claws on the end. When he was done adorning me with these murder devices, Silas held up his hands and made claws. I replicated and he laughed and nodded.

"Perfect, perfect... Sanguine, his teeth."

"Master... he already has biting issues –" Elish's cold voice sounded behind Silas, but with a flick of Silas's hand my master was silent. In the same motion Silas clasped my chin into his hands and held it tight.

Then the demon chimera was there, squinty and smiling; he picked up what I now knew were silver teeth implants and grasped my jaw.

"Stay still, little cicaro." Sanguine's voice was singy and light, though what happened next was odd and rather painful.

I sucked in a breath, feeling tears come to my eyes as Sanguine held onto the back of my head with one hand and the other pushed the implants onto my existing teeth, with a force that I thought would break my jaw. The pressure and pain were unimaginable, but I didn't cry out.

Then it was gone. I clinked my teeth together and felt them, two silver implants on the bottom and two on top. They rested oddly in my mouth but like the fillings I got a few years ago I knew my brain would adjust.

"There." Silas patted the side of my cheek. "Some proper defence when your master takes you. Does this make you happy, Jade?"

Still trying to adjust my jaw I nodded, though it really didn't. I would be too scared to ever use them on Elish, the thought alone made my flinch.

Nevertheless, there was only one person who outranked my master, so I nodded. "Thank you, my king. I hope I won't ever get to use them."

His hands slid back to my chin, and suddenly he leaned into me and closed his eyes.

My own eyes widened as he kissed me. My body wanted to pull back but my brain had me frozen. I opened my mouth instead and felt his tongue trace the new metal implants in my mouth.

There was something else though; as he pressed his lips against mine I could feel a deep void surrounding me, a darkness without colour that sunk everything into it like a black hole. Curiously, I pursued this odd feeling until I realized I was starting to touch the fringes of his aura.

With a snap I pulled back, lucky for me it was at the same time he did. Then with a trace of a hand across my jawline, he whispered into my ear.

"I can't wait to taste every inch of you, *Catullus*," he purred, before his tongue licked my earlobe.

Then he pulled away and rose, leaving me stunned and humiliated. My eyes fell to Elish who was looking at the two of us with a cold burning anger. I was in for it, I knew it. He was going to fucking kill me tonight. It wasn't like he could get mad at the king. I was the only vessel for his anger.

I tried to look as submissive as I could, trying to get across to him that this wasn't something I wanted or even liked, but he turned away. I felt a dagger shoot through my heart at his clear dismissal of me.

"Oh, it's time already? Wonderful!" Silas exclaimed as he looked out the window, and though I thought my time in the spotlight was over, the king looked over at me and another smile came to those thin lips.

Though this one was different. My body went cold as his eyes burrowed into me, a bright and morbid fascination plastered on his face. He motioned me over and tuned to Elish and said something quietly to him.

I got up with my legs feeling like rubber and walked to the front of the window. Silas was beside me and to his left was Elish. They were all looking down onto the arena below us, so I did the same.

The pounded grey dirt was covered in streaks of blood, with bits of hair and pieces of flesh scattered around like the arena was a predator's den.

And surrounding the arena, past the chain-link fence were the hundreds of Skyfallers, a hive of energy and bloodlust. Most were waving glowing green glow sticks, some out of their seats, others with their fingers in the chain-links pulling the fence as thiens thwacked their protruding digits with nightsticks. It was an insane continuous roar down there; a normal Saturday evening at Stadium.

Then Ares came out with the next convict, pushing the person forward as she looked around with wild eyes.

My heart wrenched in that moment, and inside I felt a pain grip my heart that I had never felt before.

It was Mom.

CHAPTER 14

"WHAT ARE YOU DOING?" PANIC QUICKLY COURSED through my entire body, pooling in my brain and filling me with a liquid cold adrenaline. I pivoted on my foot and turned to run out of the room to the arena.

Something caught me and yanked me back. I whirled around.

It was Elish. With an unforgiving grip he pulled both my arms around my back and pushed me back towards the window.

"What the fuck are you doing?" I screamed, the adrenaline filling my body with rage. I kicked my feet behind me trying to nail him in the shins but my efforts were for nothing. I could hear King Silas laughing. I tried to twist my body around, screaming things that didn't register in my brain but that I knew were insults and cuss words. They were met with absolute silence though, not even a scathing warning from my master.

I tried to pull my head around to try out my new fangs but my neck wouldn't turn that far; there was no way I was going to stop struggling though.

Then in a move of pure cruelty Elish grabbed my chin and forced me to watch the arena below.

"Mom?" My voice broke, my breath caught in my throat, and the bridge of my nose started to tingle and burn.

She was cowering in the middle of the arena, blood running down the side of her head. Her eyes were scared and her movements sporadic and jerky like she didn't even know where she was. She was a scared animal being tormented by a cheering crowd. The intense roar and low rumbling that had once filled me with excitement made me sick to my stomach, and full of a primal rage I couldn't control.

No, it wasn't rage, who was I kidding… it was incomprehensible sadness. That was my mom.

She had pushed me around in a wagon, rain or shine. Even though she tried to hurt me for attention, she still loved me. She had done her best even if her best fell short of what was needed to raise a kid.

It didn't matter.

She was my mom

"MOM!" I screamed.

Ares was flexing his knuckles, circling Sheryn and making mock advances that she met with a scrunching cower. Making no move to defend herself she stayed in the same position, the same one she was often in when I would visit her in Garrett Park. I didn't even know if she knew what was going to happen. Mom never went to Stadium; she wouldn't know.

Why was Elish doing this to me? I'd been good, I had been obedient!

I tried to unhook myself from his steel-fettered hands, but his grip was firm and there wasn't even a fraction of give achieved from my pathetic attempts. I was forced to watch, my mind drowning out the murmurs and chuckles of the other chimeras as they watched my reactions.

Fucking monsters, all of them. Motherless beasts who loved nothing and cared for nothing.

Ares raised his hand and struck Sheryn in the face.

I screamed again and this time the tears came. She fell to her side, her layers of old ratted clothing making her appear bigger than she really was; she tried to get up but fell down onto her back, her eyes looking up at the ceiling, bulging from their sockets.

Ares put his hands in the air and the crowd cheered. In that moment I could recognize some of the Morosians in the front row seats, not my friends but members of gangs and brothers of people I knew. They knew who she was and they did nothing, they didn't even remain sitting in silent protest like I had seen before. Wild crazed animals, waving their glow sticks making neon patterns, pulling at the gate like rabid beasts.

Siris came out; I let out a high pitched moan and felt my legs go weak. I closed my eyes and with another flare of adrenaline I started to fight

Elish more.

"Why are you doing this to me? I've been good!" I tried to scream, wrenching my neck back to the point where I felt my muscles pull. I wanted him to look at me, explain why he was doing this to me. I had been good, I didn't deserve punishment. I had fucking done everything he asked of me!

"Watch," was all he said.

My face twisted; he grabbed my chin and made me face the arena.

They had her now. Ares had my mom's arms pulled behind her, in almost the same way Elish had mine. She wasn't going anywhere, she was frozen in shock, staring ahead, her head shaking back and forth. But there was no tick in her movements like before, she was pleading for her life.

Siris had a baseball bat in his hand, and with Old Joe narrating nothing but a muffled static on the loudspeaker… Siris hit her in the face.

The blow knocked her head back, and with a wave of the bat like he was a baseball player, he swung it again, this time ripping off the side of her face.

My arms went limp, my body went limp, and many years later I would go back to that moment and I'd know that this was where it all changed.

It was like the world sunk to my feet, and all that remained was me. Everyone else was gone, and with it my sadness, my despair. There was nothing left of me; when she died in front of the roaring crowd a part of me died too.

I would no longer be scared; I would no longer be their victim. I wasn't helpless anymore; I was no longer a passenger in someone else's vehicle.

There was only darkness that remained, because in truth I never had much else in me to begin with. Just self-loathing and sadness, and those were two feelings I felt drip to a black puddle on my floor.

What was left?

Darkness.

Cold.

Nothing.

A deadpan look that told my own reflection that I had just lost a part of me I would never get back.

"Release him, Elish."

I looked down at my hands, three rings on each hand, with razor-sharp steel claws. My tongue traced my mouth, over each pointed stud that was surrounded by inflamed gums.

There were footsteps behind me, and with them echoing in the back alleys of my mind I looked and saw Ares raising the bat and raining it down on my mother's already brutalized body.

I turned and walked towards the couch where I had been sitting, my feet feeling like light feathers, my mind full of helium. With the other chimeras nothing but scenery, I glided by.

I picked up Silas's chair, and though I could hear the quick talking and the shouts, I walked to the window looking down at the arena.

And with every ounce of my strength I slammed the chair into the window.

The window was bulletproof, but the shitty welding job wasn't. The chair crashed through the window, taking the glass with it; it fell to the ground with a loud booming crash. I walked towards the frame when I felt Elish's arms around me pulling me back.

"Don't do this." His voice was silent and cold, quiet enough that only I could hear him. I reared my head back and smashed the back of my skull into his nose; at the same time Silas told him to let me go and I found my feet.

Without another word I stepped onto the edge of the window frame and looked down.

The arena had become so silent you could hear a pin drop. Hundreds, maybe thousands of eyes stared up at the skybox as I crouched down and focused my eyes on Ares and Siris.

I jumped down and, as I fell, I heard the crowd gasp.

My legs hit the ground, barely flinching from the twenty foot drop, and with my fingers flexing I walked down the light strewn entrance into the arena.

In a split second the dead silence brought on an ear shaking eruption of cheers. I tuned them out of my hearing and focused on my enemies, two twin chimeras that I had been meaning to get back at for a long time.

Bigger than me, stronger than me, but slower. I watched them look at me, before turning to each other and laughing, Siris still holding the baseball bat, which he threw down to the squealing joy of the crowd.

The part of me that told me I had just signed my death warrant was gone. Only a dark static and a bloodthirst that had washed every cowering thought from my body remained. It was like a blanket or a thin sheet of metal; it covered the undesirable parts of my consciousness and showcased the inner anger I'd had beaten out of me at the hands of my master.

Siris walked up to me in a cocky manner that only made the crowd cheer more. With a smug grin he leaned down and spat to his side.

"I can't wait to fuck you in front of this crowd, you little –"

In the slums, we do not fight fair. If you fight fair, you die. That was all there was to it. With this in mind, a boy in the slums could grow up learning a myriad of things. A man's weak spots, and blind spots, and also what advantages you had with your own body. Agility, strength, coercion, even sex could buy you out of a dangerous situation.

I was a man with no honour, because I was a cicaro, the pet of a monster with long blond hair and eyes that could melt steel. There was no pride in me, no moral code. I was in that moment a shadow, a devil and in all respects… I was no longer human.

See… the reason why Siris couldn't say that last word… *whore*, I fully believed it was, was because I had already slashed these metal claws at his eyes. So instead, as his lips were forming those remaining syllables, his mouth had decided to scream.

For a split second before he closed them, I saw red split the purple irises. Then, perfectly spaced above and below those same eyes, two slash marks that opened his face like an overripe fruit. I saw the yellow bubbles of fat, and in it, the seeping red blood.

Siris swore and put his hands over his face. When his hands went up, my claws flew, and to make sure he stayed down, I opened up the side of his neck.

Then I was grabbed and thrown on the ground; the power of it knocked me senseless for a moment and I heard the crowd go insane.

I looked up and saw Ares, his face a twisted snarl, Siris moaning beside me. I scrambled to my feet and dodged a kick and then a raining punch that sunk his fist into the compacted dirt floor.

I jumped behind Ares, but he whirled around quickly. I bared my teeth at him, hearing the people around us screaming and hooting, glow sticks waving around our circling bodies like giant fireflies.

The atmosphere of the stadium got to me; every breath brought in their energy and filled me with cold determination. If I could, if I was like Ares, I would rape him after he died, but that wasn't me. I wanted him dead. Even if he was immortal, I didn't care. I had to do this; I had to have this one fleeting victory to keep my soul alive. I had nothing else.

I had nothing else.

"I don't care whose pet you are now, slumrat. I will kill you." Ares looked up at me from tensed eyebrows; off to the left Siris was leaning against the chain-link fence spitting curses at both of us. His eyes were a ruin and his was neck bleeding heavily.

"Bring it on," I whispered. "I would welcome death, we're friends. I see him regularly every night I am forced to sleep with that fucking blond monstrosity. So go ahead and try."

Ares looked to the crowd, before he cracked his knuckles one by one, trying to showboat like I had seen him do dozens of times from the safety of the bleachers. I was the underdog, and they all probably wanted to see me die. Either way we were putting on a good show.

Then Ares snapped his attention away from the crowd and charged at me. I shifted away from him, his speed so fast his shoulder clipped mine. I pivoted and turned before I jumped onto his back.

I raked my claws, slashing right through the thin t-shirt he was wearing, exposing red flesh underneath. Ares snarled and whirled around, before taking a swipe at me, but I jumped away just in time. I bounced backwards like a grasshopper and quickly pushed my rings back on my knuckles as far as I could. Then with another jump, I dodged him again.

Bad move. I had forgotten about the other one.

I felt Siris grab me, and with a painful pull that made my shoulders pop he pulled my arms back. The crowd gasped and half of them cheered, while the other half yelled for the underdog.

Siris dragged my thrashing and snapping body to the middle of the arena, where Ares was waiting.

I swallowed through my dry mouth as I saw he was holding the bloodied bat in his hand, waving it around and raising his other arm to egg on the crowd.

I clenched my teeth and dug my feet into the floor, bracing myself for my death.

The red lights signalling an incoming fatal blow shone down on us. The neon colours flashed. I took it all in and watched Ares's movements as he closed the last step of distance between us.

He raised the bat.

The glow sticks fell around us; they were tossing them into the arena with their cheering. Like flecks of neon rain they fell, bouncing onto the floor.

Ares swung the bat.

And I ducked my head.

The baseball bat hit something with a sickening crunch. For what seemed like an eternity my mind raced like a trout going upstream to figure out if it was my head or not. All I could sense was the overbearing noise from the crowd, and a booming sound that seemed to come from inside my head.

"Shit, brother!"

I blinked, my head was staring at my boots, blood was making small crimson spots on the ground. With a rush everything came back to me, a flood I was unable to deal with.

The grip became loose and I heard a thud behind me, followed by a second one that brought the bloody baseball bat rolling to the line of my vision.

I picked up the bat and blinked, before I turned around.

Siris's head was caved in on the side. Ares's back was to me, his left hand on the back of his head. He was gripping it in his own grief and confusion.

"Strike! Strike! Strike!"

No... I dropped the baseball bat, and the crowd started to boo and jeer.

Ares looked up at them, and started mock advancing on them, thinking they were booing at him rather than me. He was distracted though, and Siris was obviously dead.

The sounds rushed through me, over every fiber and nerve in my body. The surprise that I had killed one sinking into me, bringing both a fear and a sick thrill.

The darkness edged the grey matter in my mind and sunk in its poison. His back was turned to me, and though it took several seconds of staring off into nothing, I realized this was my only chance.

I picked up the bat and I crunched the hard wood against Ares's leg; when he fell to one knee I raised it like an axe and brought it down on the second one.

The brute snarled and struggled to get up, but his legs shattered further under his weight, and I saw them bend like rubber before the tips of white bone broke through his skin. The brute chimera fell to the ground as he swore loudly.

I held the bat in one hand, the tip swinging back and forth with a sprinkle of blood going with it like it was a dripping hose. I watched him with a blank expression on my face as he looked down at his legs and sighed with a shake of his head. Only an immortal could be so calm in death.

Then to my surprise, he looked up at me and chuckled.

My rage inflamed at his dismissive nature to my win. I wanted him to scream, and beg for his life, but no matter what, he would return. Like every high ranking chimera fuck he would come back. I hated the world in that moment for his indifference to the fear of death everyone had. He was spitting in the face of nature, and life. Something that so many people deserved and yet these heartless bastards got to live forever. It wasn't fair… it wasn't right.

I raised the bat and cracked it against his shoulder blade, and with the same momentum I swung it again at the second one.

Then I did the only thing I could think of, the only way I could make it my own personal victory. I wanted to kill him with my own body, not this bat. I felt like I had to. For every person these assholes had killed, raped, and beaten. For every Morosian who bought a keycard and entered into their own crypts.

I wrenched his head back, and sunk my teeth into his neck. Though unlike what the chimeras would do I didn't rip out a chunk of bleeding flesh; I clamped it around his neck like a lion to a zebra and closed off his windpipe.

The crowd went wild and the glow sticks continued to fall around me, covering the domes of my vision in sticks of glowing green. With the brilliant light reflecting in my yellow eyes they covered the ground like radioactive rain and illuminated the arena in an eerie glow.

Ares jerked up several times, his gurgling breath near my ear; my nose and eyes filled with the warmth of his convulsing flesh. It was so warm, so… tasty.

I pulled my teeth back just a bit, Ares quivering under my body. The red blood flowed into my mouth and in spite of myself I started to drink it, closing my eyes as the coppery warmth dripped down my throat, filling me with a sickening pleasure that I couldn't explain.

I liked it.

Finally when he was still, I unhinged my teeth and stood.

They cheered; they threw their glow sticks onto the already radioactively green arena, falling over me as I looked around in a daze. Old Joe's voice was talking in an excited pitch. I didn't know if he had been talking the whole time or was just starting now – I hadn't heard a thing.

Then I saw her, and like I would do whenever I lost my mom but found her again. I made a beeline towards her.

I leaned down and kissed her goodbye, and touched her cheek for the last time. Before I rose, and without another glance to the hundreds, possibly even a thousand people making noise, I walked out of the arena.

I didn't know where I was going. I walked out and filed past people who took one look at me and knew not to go near me. I made my way down a grey hallway with wall-to-wall windows on my right, darkness hiding the cityscape and the bright reflection of the lights.

My boots clicked against the linoleum, echoing the tall ceilings and bounding off the rusted metal beams. I got through the first door into the lobby before I heard the chimeras walking down the stairs that led to the skybox, a flurry of hurried voices

"Don't touch him!" I heard Elish snap, a violent boom to his voice that filled the room with tension. I didn't look though and I didn't move, with my head lowered I walked towards the row of metal framed doors; several of them already open, anticipating the end of the games

I thought I was calm, but as soon as I felt the leash clip to my collar I went absolutely berserk.

I whirled around and punched Elish in the face, claws and all. I saw the familiar yellow bubbles as his cheek ripped open, and a spray of blood that fell onto my face. I swung my second hand and caught his other cheek, before I lunged at him and sunk my teeth into his neck, the same clamp I'd had on Ares.

Then Kessler grabbed me, and then Caligula on his left. I snarled through my full mouth before, with an electric jolt, my jaw snapped open. I twisted and contorted around making sounds that reminded me of two tom cats fighting. My body heaved, and the anger in me reached boiling point. I whipped around and lifted my legs from the ground; Kessler's lock on me retaining my balance. I kicked out and caught Caligula in the chest, and he fell to the floor beside Elish.

I howled and spat as Kessler dragged me away, before I heard Elish's order to release me. They didn't though; instead I felt a frozen hand on my cheek and Silas's golden hair came into my view.

"There, there, little cicaro," Silas purred. I growled a low susurration in my throat, not even knowing how I was making such an animal-like noise. A moment later I felt the soul-ripping electric shock of Silas's altered touch. My screams were the last thing I heard.

I woke up with a pounding migraine. I lifted a hand and placed it on top of my head and with it I realized I was in chains again.

They rattled around me, and made my flushed skin twitch when their cold links brushed against it. There was nothing I could do about it though but open my eyes and see where he had me.

The darkened room of Elish Dekker, ash grey with black trim. The furniture was polished and the paintings with shaded colours, with very little clutter on top. Only a few pieces of silver jewellery, a kerchief and some half-burned candles.

This was always a dark room, the ambiance only broken up by the silver vase resting on top of his dresser that always held purple flowers.

I inhaled a deep breath, my chest stretching with protest like a balloon being inflated for the first time. The air felt good though; the room always smelled pleasant.

Though there was nothing pleasant about me, or my situation. My mood and the thoughts crawling into my mind like insects were as dark and sombre as the room I was in. There were no purple flowers in my mind to break up the gloom, all I felt was darkness.

My mom was dead; they killed her. No… Elish killed her. He knew she had poisoned me, he had been the one to rescue me from Moros when I had eaten too much of her tainted food. This was him getting back at me, but why?

I rubbed the sleep from my eyes, the links attached to my leather cuffs rattling as I pressed my finger knuckle into my eyes. As my body moved against silk sheets I realized just how much it hurt. Though not from being beaten; I had gotten out of the stadium with barely a scratch, my muscles just ached.

From Silas probably…

I shifted up and tested my chains before leaning up against the iron rung bed with a sigh. I scanned my brain for any signs of feelings or emotions but just as I suspected they were gone. I wasn't sad, or hurt, I just felt nothing.

"Welcome back."

My eyes shot to the corner of the room, and there he was. In the shadows sitting on a dark grey fabric chair, his legs crossed and his hands resting on his knee. There was no part of him I could see but a small sliver of light from the doorway that fell on his leg.

His voice brought with it a feeling of recollection, and not far behind, the arid winter. Elish was reality being thrust back onto me; he was the hurt and the sadness.

When had he become everything to me?

"I don't want to talk to you." Each syllable that I spoke felt like they weighed a hundred pounds. I felt betrayed. Why was I so immature and stupid enough to feel betrayed by him? What had I expected? It was me that was the idiot for thinking Elish wouldn't torment me just because of my obedience. That's what chimeras did, they hurt you, they thrived on it.

Sure enough, I heard the amused muffled chuckle, and as the last rolling tone left him, he rose.

I scrunched into myself, my chains rattling as I covered my body, but Elish only reached his hand out and flicked on the light.

My eyes widened when I saw Elish's. I had forgotten what I had done to him in the throes of my manic anger.

His face had been slashed almost beyond recognition. The cuts were deep, splitting his face open and taking out his left eye. His teeth were exposed as one of the lacerations had cut through his cheeks all the way to his jaw.

Not only that, the side of his neck was partially ripped open. Both imprints of my upper and lower teeth could be seen; the piece of flesh in between hanging loosely off his skin.

And in a solid statement to his desire for me to feast my eyes on the damage I had done, the wounds were not cleaned, or bandaged; the blood had flowed freely and had dried where it stayed. All down Elish's face and his neck, his chest and his now stained clothing. It was a horrific sight that made my chest quake.

My mouth moved to make an apology, but I clamped it shut as Sheryn's face came into my mind. Her scared eyes under her wild hair, moving away from the two immortal brutes as they advanced on her. Elish had killed my mom. He had barged himself into my life, and with a single finger he disrupted the fragile balance I had maintained since childhood.

Moros was my old life. Elish might've stolen me and ripped me away from my world, but he had no right to go to my slums and fuck up the people I left behind.

"You deserved it," I whispered instead, and with a flicker my eyes took him in, all of him. I would look at Elish until he left the room; I would not give him the pleasure of thinking I was avoiding seeing what I had done to him. "And Ares did too, and Siris, and any other chimera fuck that pisses me off from now on."

The indifferent and immovable Elish, even in his state of disfigurement, stared down at me with his deity-like grace. His mouth was only slightly downturned but enough for me to know I was in trouble, but I honestly didn't care. I knew there was no going back, I was dead anyway. I had killed the brute twins and disfigured my own master. I was a Morosian slumrat with no future and now no past; there was nothing left to happen to me but death.

"And why do you think I deserve this, Jade?"

My insides boiled. What sort of fucking question was that? Like I had dropped the feelings I had been juggling my resolve scattered all around me. I desperately tried to pick them up but the countdown ran out before then. Instead the anger won out and I snapped.

"You know why!" I shouted at him. "You killed my mom! You fucking killed my mom!" I jerked my wrists in a wasted attempt to dislodge my chains but, of course, it was useless. "You set me up to witness that. Why? I was obedient, I was good! I did fucking everything you asked!"

Elish looked down at me, but to me he was looking down his nose at me, like the insect I was.

"I can do what I like with you, Cicaro. You are mine to use how I wish, if I wish to use you for my own entertainment, it is within my right as your owner and as a chimera."

"Fuck you!" I snapped, bearing my teeth at him though as I did I realized my metal implants had been taken out, my claws too. "Fuck every single one of you! You don't understand, none of you do." My eyes started to burn. "You don't have mothers; you're all heartless unemotional monsters who have no idea what it's like to love. She was my *mom*, Elish. She was fucked up but that was my mom. She didn't deserve that, and to fuck me over further you set it up so I had to watch? What kind of monster are you?"

"That's far enough, Cicaro." His voice did all but broadcast that I was reaching the end of his patience but there was no fiber in my body that cared for my own fate now. I had to say what needed to be said before he killed me.

"No, fuck you, Elish. Fuck you, fuck your family. Do whatever you you –" I swallowed hard as he opened the drawer and brought out the whip, but unlike last time I didn't scream and curl myself into the fetal position, I pressed on, " – whatever you want to me. Kill me; I fucking beg you just kill me because I'd rather die than have to live one more day with you. You're a monster. I can't believe I was starting to like you; I was starting to enjoy living with you. Fuck you. Really, fuck –"

I clenched my teeth during the first hit, and again with the second. I let out a breath with my nose and didn't look away from him.

"You're a coward. You whip me while I'm fucking chained? Like you send old ladies to battle two immortal mutants? You chimeras are a fucking joke," I screamed. "Just a bunch of bullies, a bunch of cowards."

To my surprise he dropped the whip. I stared at him with my chest heaving up and down and hid the quiver of anxiety as he started to unchain me. My limbs became frozen with his body closer to me; I could smell the blood on him. His injuries were horrific, anyone normal would be screaming in pain, but he was as nonchalant as he could fucking be.

"I have nothing to prove to you, slumrat," Elish said in a hushed whisper. The chains rattled as he threw them behind the iron rung bed. I didn't move; I stared at him transfixed by his remaining good eye. "You will take whatever I give you, and you will thank me for it."

Then his two burning hot hands grabbed my shoulders, I gasped and felt my teeth snap together. The searing pain rushing through every cell in my body. I could feel my skin burn under his touch, and a moment later I could smell it.

"You are my cicaro, and you will be mine forever. You are here to please me, that is the only point of your life now."

My eyes started to water from the pain. I saw wisps of smoke. I looked down and saw small white plums rise like fog.

"Why are you doing this to me?"

His disfigured face looked down on me like he was a thousand feet tall, a deity in the clouds, the rips and lacerations weeping blood through the inner flesh of his face. He was a monster now, both physically and mentally, in all ways this man was a demon.

"Because you are stronger than this, all of this," Elish whispered. He gripped my shoulders harder making me gasp, I could hear sizzling. "And if I have to leave you a screaming mess on the floor for the next thirty years until I temper your mind, body, and spirit, I will."

The words sunk into the pain and made little sense to me. I could only continue to clench my teeth together until the pain of his burning hands became unbearable.

I screamed and tried to wrench my shoulders away but he only grasped them harder. Then to my relief his hands became cold. I gasped and slumped down, my chest rising up and down and my eyes leaking tears of pain.

"Just kill me," I gasped, and in that moment I wished for nothing else.

Elish shook his head and released my shoulders. I looked down and felt a whimper come to my lips, one that was as unbidden as the tears running down my face. His hands had a layer of my own skin on them.

My head went hot and my mind went faint, the adrenaline faded and the pain started to come.

Sanguine said I was special to him.

Why would this heartless asshole do this to me if I was special to him? Chimeras can't love anyone. Silas can't, Sanguine can't, none of them can.

I watched Elish rise, hating every part of him, every inch of his being. My pain only bringing forth the despair and the feelings of betrayal; thrusting it into my face and mocking the feelings I had for him buried deep inside of me.

I had obeyed him; I had done everything he asked. I let him fuck me without a fight. I laid with him, he held me. He liked it, I knew he did.

I was a slave; I knew that, I had grudgingly accepted that.

But we were all slaves weren't we?

"You think you're different than me, but you're not," I suddenly whispered, catching this fleeting thought that had implanted in my head.

Elish turned and looked at me, but this time I couldn't meet his gaze. I sniffed and shook my head at the absurdity of it. "I get it."

"Get what?"

I swallowed the lump, but it brought more tears of pain as my shoulders burned from even the slightest movements.

"I might be your bitch, but you're Silas's bitch. At least my master is worthy of respect, you have to bow to a psychotic, perverte-"

I heard the beep of the remote and a moment later an electric jolt from my collar. I threw up but inhaled it as my body convulsed. I started coughing violently and in the throes I was electrocuted again.

I fell back onto the bed, not unconscious but dazed, my mind reduced to mush.

The room went dark and the door closed, and I lay in my half-conscious hell.

CHAPTER 15

"Good afternoon, Jade, have you been putting on the cream I gave you?"

I squinted as the door opened to the dark room I had been thrown into, the light forever trying to burn my retinas. I greeted the doctor, though I didn't bother trying to adjust my eyes to the light, he never stayed.

Though Lyle had come in to clean my burns and whip marks every day, I still backed away into the corner of my chained area like a beaten dog. It had been so many days now it was almost a reflex brought on by loneliness, and being so used to spending countless hours in the pitch darkness.

It had been a week now since Elish left, and he hadn't come back. I had been here alone with only Lyle to give me food, water, and the burn cream. I didn't remember much of what he told me but he said Elish was dead.

Elish was dead.

In anyone else's mind that would have brought a myriad of reactions but to me it meant two things: Elish was going to come back a new person, with not a mark of my violence remaining on his body, and that for now, I was on my own.

An overdose of morphine took him to hell's gates, a painless and wonderful way to die. If only I had such a luxury to go out that way, but there was no morphine for me. I got no pain killers; I was left chained in a small room I had previously thought was a locked closet, alone without any food or water.

Then Lyle came, on what day I wasn't sure, but he came. He looked at me and swore; Luca peered in behind him and whimpered his sympathies. I must've looked like a sad sight. The handprint burn marks on my shoulders had become raw and open wounds though at least the burn cream was doing a good job.

"This is Skytech's special burn cream, about a hundred dollars a bottle so enjoy the luxury." Lyle's gloved hands rubbed a generous amount of the thick opaque goo on my wounds. It felt cool and soothing on the hot skin which had been improving every day.

Lyle brought a bottle of water to my lips; I drank generously but coughed halfway through.

"I'm leaving you an ice pack; put it on your head you're getting a fever." I felt a cold object placed beside me, and I watched with sore eyes as Lyle rose to standing.

"When is he waking up?" I asked, moving the gel pack from one hand to another. It was a different sensation, which was a welcome one from the hot sticky pain I had been feeling.

"Sorry kiddo, you know I have my orders, I can't tell you anything." Lyle handed me half a chocolate bar and left the room. "I saw Elish before I dosed him – you know you deserve this."

I glared at him, wishing he would leave so I could tune myself out of this reality. Though he made my burns feel better he had nothing more to give me. Like Luca and all the others he was working for Elish; they were not my friends.

Then I was alone again. I ate the chocolate quickly and enjoyed the different feelings it brought me. I had become a creature of seeking stimulus, any change from the routine I had been accustomed to in this room. Even biting myself had become a pastime. When every sense was taken away from you, you started to seek any break from the monotony.

Sleep was the best breakthrough, and I slept a lot, but like so many things it was a double-edged sword. When my mind dimmed and carried me off past the velvet curtain only nightmares seemed to hide in the corners. Even my dreams were nightmares because they usually involved Elish.

The hatred in me burned whenever his face came to me, and I hated him more than anything.

I sunk into my subconscious and closed my eyes, blocking my mind off to all distractions and stimulations, which had become easier in my closet. This place seemed soundproof, and I was sure sometime in Elish's eighty-eight years he had locked other cicaros in here, probably until they starved to death. It was small and dark with only a soundless ventilation shaft above me to deposit new air.

I had found myself slipping into a vivid unconsciousness in this room, and I think it was because of that lost reality that made me rather numb to what was going on.

What happens to your mind when all you are experiencing is blinding hatred and pain? It goes inside itself and finds little things to destroy. My imagination was just nightmares upon nightmares.

The only joy I felt was when I thought of Kerres and the last couple of years I'd had with him when we left Edgeview. Now that I was a captive, even Moros seemed like heaven. The colours around my slum district seemed brighter, the people happier, the stout less bitter, and the drugs more potent.

Moros and Kerres brought a small light in the dark smoke, but they were the only light.

And even that faded into the hatred.

Mostly my mind touched the areas that Elish and his chimera family had tainted, and the cancer they brought with them had only been spreading further. Now even my happy thoughts of Moros had been destroyed by Elish. I saw him sitting on my couch, lording over me at my old job, and even in Garrett Park where my mom had been.

He was always there and the more I stared the more he changed in front of me.

Such bright images, even the smells were right. I recalled these waking dreams and nightmares with such vivid recollection that I woke up confused as to where I was. Wasn't I just sleeping beside Kerres? Why wasn't he here?

It had been months since I last saw him in Garrett Park and he had probably moved on. Unless on the off-chance my actions at the Stadium had gotten me recognition. Perhaps the faces I recognized in the crowd would run to my boyfriend and tell him I had snapped under Elish's control.

That I had killed Ares and Siris. I had avenged my mother's murder. Did Kerres know that she had been missing? Did anyone really care besides me?

What did it matter? At least Kerres knew where I was, he was able to see me for that fleeting moment. Enough to tell Elish that my mother had poisoned me. No matter where Kerres was, at least he knew I hadn't abandoned him.

I focused my little parlour trick on my own aura, just to brighten up the room around me. Even if it never really lit up the walls, it was still better than nothing.

This is how I had entertained myself when I was younger. When my mom left me in my wagon to go get a drink or entertain men I would sit and play with the bright colours. I had learned how to manipulate them and touch them from practicing just out of boredom.

I saw the silvery glow of my hand reach out and pull a thread of black; I wrapped it around my fingers one small strand at a time.

The more colours I grabbed the more my brow furrowed. The black of my aura wasn't as black as it had been, it had a silver hue to it I hadn't seen before.

There was a pull and like a string was tugging the corner of my lip, it turned down. I knew what that meant but I wasn't ready to admit it to myself. Instead I balled up the aura into my hand and started fidgeting with it, wishing it had some buoyancy to it so at least I could make it into a bouncy ball but unfortunately when I coiled it into my hands it really had no weight at all.

With the purple and black strands weaving between my fingers I stared forward at the metal frame of the door; a haunting blue sheen to it through my vision. I had never been alone for so long and I was lonely. My only friends now were the images I could see in my head, and even they were getting too vivid for my own liking.

It was like I could see Kerres in front of me when I thought of him, though his face was distorted in my memory. He seemed younger when I conjured him up, probably because I had spent so much time looking at his face when I was younger. He seemed to be forever sixteen to me.

Elish came too, and to my own self-contempt he was the brightest beacon of them all; coming down on high with his beautiful, perfect and unspoiled aura around him, a picture of unmovable tranquility and elegance. At first glance, he seemed, to be peaceful and serene, but with one look, those burning purple embers turned to black flames.

Then in front of me, more real than the walls and the stained carpet, Elish changed. The silver and opal crystals of his aura turned to the darkest of voids that sucked everything to it like a black hole. His hair became shorter and his eyes turned a deep green. His laugh got more loud and taunting and his hands became a claw wrapped around my neck; squeezing not only my life out of me, but every piece of me he hadn't yet broken.

Then like I had been struck on the head I came back. I shook my mind awake and chewed on the side of my cheek. Trying to make sense of this brief lucid dream, it didn't take my tired and feverish mind to realize he had transformed into the Ghost King.

Because Elish was the king; he was Silas's creation, which is why Elish had no conscience, had no trouble being a monster. No problems murdering my mother while I watched, or keeping me from Moros. Elish was just as much of a demon as his master was, even more so because he wasn't as straightforward about his cruelties as Silas.

I hated that man, and with that thought I purged his face from my mind, not allowing myself to touch or sort through the feelings of betrayal and hurt I had felt. Acknowledging those only meant I had to accept that he had enough of my heart to make me feel those emotions.

I let out a short sigh and wondered where my head was at with my own thinking. These thoughts were getting more and more vivid in my head, the hatred growing and forming into their own manifestations. I wished I could back away from them but they seemed hell bent on injecting me with more and more anger.

Though it wasn't an anger that would cause me to have an outburst, it was a silent anger, a smouldering flame inside a wood pile that continuously got rained on with gasoline. It hadn't spread enough to explode, but soon it would.

I stayed this way for a long time; the only indication of the days passing was Lyle coming to check my burns. By the time the door cracked open and the sliver of light fell on me he had come more times than I could count on my hands.

I stared at the door but I didn't move, my mind not even realizing I had been unchained for days. There were more interesting things to see in my head, better colours and fantasies to occupy my time. Places to fly to, things to eat and all the more ways to kill every chimera that had wronged me – and some just for the hell of it.

Lyle didn't come after the door was left partially open, and no one came to feed me. Sometimes I heard voices that I recognized but I still didn't move. There was a new current in my brain that made other things more important, and right now sitting in the corner of the room playing with my own head trumped everything.

I noticed my eyes burning, though the pain didn't make me close them. I was staring at the wall reliving my killing of Ares and Siris. One move at a time, each adrenaline rush going through me with just as much fervour as the last.

"The door has been open for three days, what could be so interesting about this room?" His voice cut the ambiance I had so carefully cultivated in this cell.

I gave no indication that I was listening, and if his voice didn't have the same graceful silk that it had in my mind perhaps I would have realized he was standing on the threshold of my reality.

Though as the chimera seemed to be able to do, he infiltrated my reverie like a splash of cold water.

"Jade? Your master is speaking with you."

No, in my mind he was whipping me, before he fucked me just so he could smell the blood and sample it when he got into the depths of his passion. When he was unable to control himself in front of me, the brief moments when we were alone in bed. How could he be standing in front of me when he was obviously swallowing every scream that fell from my lips?

My brows knitted together when I felt a hand rest on my forehead, before travelling down and breaking my eye contact with the staring eyes on the wall. I tried to keep the wall's gaze but soon there was a new person looking at me.

Elish? When did he come out of my dreams? My furrowing brow

deepened as I saw his eyes, both of them intact and healed now. No longer the ruined face I had massacred with the claws that King Silas had given me. Every part of him was as new and fresh as the first time I had seen him. Even his aura flowed around me like the winds of winter, bringing a coldness to the room that banished the stifling putrid aroma that my own disgusting body had stagnated in.

"Jade?" Elish patted my cheek, before flicking his finger against the corner of my eye. I saw him give his head the slightest of shakes before he picked me up.

"In so many ways you are a sculpture of strength and resilience, but in many others you are fragile and weak," Elish murmured. I looked up at him and saw him illuminate in the lights as he took me from my dark room, like a demon unexpectedly finding himself in heaven. How odd though, because this man looked like how you would imagine an angel, and I myself was the creature hiding in the cave. Perhaps I was the demon and this had all been a mistake.

"You can murder two brute chimeras yet your mind falls to pieces if someone isn't there to monitor it for you. I suppose cutting off your other senses and leaving you alone with that brain is a rather cruel punishment for an empath. Your mind is like a moth's wings – beautiful yet fragile."

It was painful for my eyes to adjust, but I saw the grey couch and the white marble coffee table. Elish's laptop was in its usual place, turned on and showing a game of solitaire half done. It disappeared and my body turned to the windows of the apartment which held the view of Skyland and further back, the ocean. Though inside I knew this place, it was almost intimidating to me. I was used to my small room; the whole world was inside that closed off, stuffy sepulcher.

Elish set me down but as soon as he spoke to Luca, I rose and started to walk back to the room I had been shut up into, where the colours were better.

A hand stopped me. "Sit on the couch; Luca bring him his food."

Out of the corner of my eye I saw movement. The sengil with his black cat ears and small vest walked up to me with a small smile on his face. An unusual display of emotions for the sengil, it made me question his existence. Perhaps he was just another hallucination, though the food looked real enough.

Luca tried to give me the plate but I didn't take it, I wasn't hungry. The empty gnaw in my gut wasn't enough to make me put the effort into eating. I just wanted to be in the dark, it was the only help I got to shoulder the burden of my own reality. Why was Elish trying to force me to come back? It was horrible here. In the room I could be anything, here I was just a pet with a cruel master.

"Master... his expression is so vacant. He hasn't eaten for three days and he isn't even looking at the food. What's wrong with him?"

"He's been alone with himself for over ten days; he will be fine."

There was more movement beside me and I saw a piece of breaded fish waved in front of me.

"Take it," Luca whispered. I scrunched myself away from him and drew my knees up to my chest. I grabbed a pillow and put it over my knees before burying my face into it and locking my arms behind my head.

There, there was some darkness.

"You broke him!" My ears perked up as I heard the harsh and accusing tone in Luca's voice. "Dr. Lyle told you not to leave him in there for so long! He warned you –"

I heard a yelp followed by a thud. I raised my head and saw Luca on the floor, his eyes wide and brimming. Elish was standing over him; I could see his palm, red now from the strike on his sengil.

"Get out of my sight." Even my mind edged back to reality as his tone sliced through both of us. I watched as Luca scrambled to his feet, before he grabbed his shoes and jacket and with nothing more than a sympathetic glance for me, he left the apartment.

When the door slammed Elish turned to me, he picked up the food and put it on top of the cushion. "If your mind is so pathetic and weak that you can't snap yourself out of this, I wonder why I bother with you in the first place."

I stared down at the food and picked up a potato fry. "Then take me back to Moros," I rasped through tight vocal cords. "I think you're just as tired of this as I am."

"Tired of what?"

"You know what." I stared at the fish and chips, not wanting to look at the cold monster. If I kept looking at him I knew eventually the anger would come back and I would attack him again. And I was too weak to even get a single hit in. "I want to go home."

Elish still hadn't moved, I could see his white leather loafers, the ones he wore inside, sinking into the thick carpet. I watched them move as he turned around to stare at me.

"You are home."

My hand picked up the piece of fish Luca had dropped back onto the plate and put it between my lips, chewing slowly as the greasy mess dissolved in my mouth.

"I'm going to defect into the greywastes." My tone was flat, dead, and as hollow as my body felt. In all honesty this thought had never occurred to me until I voiced it, though I had a feeling that it had been something I had absentmindedly been considering. "You don't have power in the greywastes. I would be free, free of you."

A heavy silence fell between the two of us. I swallowed my food and picked up another fry and put it into my mouth.

"I would hope you would return to see your ex-boyfriend's execution, if you can actually find a shuttle before I have every legionary and thien from here to the greyrifts looking for you."

I shook my head, still not able to meet his gaze. Though I knew he was staring at me, his feet were turned towards me. "Go ahead and kill him. That would be the only two people I cared about out of the picture; you would have nothing more to take away. You would've taken everything from me."

I felt the hair on my neck prickle, and the heat that came with his intense gaze. I closed my eyes, wanting only to see the colours in my imagination and take myself from this situation. Fly away and be anywhere from here.

"When you're done sulking, put the dishes out for the sengils."

Like an underground volcano cracking through the earth's crusts, and as unexpected as the quake that brought it, I exploded.

With an angry cry, I jumped to my feet before picking up the plate and winging it at Elish's head.

He was waiting for it; he caught it in the air with an expert raise of his arm and quickly walked up to me.

I heaved, my fists clenched and the veins pulsing out of my head. I roughly pushed the him, ignoring the burning on the bridge of my nose. When Elish didn't move, I continued to punch his chest; the fire ripping through my arms and giving me a strength and stamina I didn't even know I had.

"Oh, there he is. Why hello, Jade. What kept you?" I could hear the smile lace his cold and taunting tones, it only infuriated me more. I snapped my arm back to hit him in the face, but in a display of his stealth his hand shot up and he wrapped it around my fist. Elish clenched it, before he quickly grabbed my other arm.

"What do you want?" I screamed at him, to my embarrassment the burning between my eyes producing tears. "You already killed my mom, you already made me obedient, and you already torment me all you want and I take it. What the fuck do you want from me?"

The burning only got worse as I looked up to those purple eyes, still cold and cruel and reflecting nothing but my own pain-filled eyes back to me. I was unable to contain it any longer.

He was silent, and in that silence his features didn't change.

"You don't even know!" I suddenly screamed. In a burst of anger, I wrenched my arms from his fetter-like grip and pushed him again. "What is it, Elish? You want my blood? Is that what you want so bad?" I turned and stalked to the kitchen; I grabbed a knife and stormed back into the living room where he still hadn't moved.

"Put that down before you hu-"

I raised the knife and slashed my arm with it; with my teeth clenched I switched hands and raised it to slash my other one.

I held my bloodied arms out to him, the nausea rising in my throat. I let the sheets of blood fall to the carpet and offered myself up to him.

"Is this what you want?" I asked, tensing my muscles to try and push the blood out of me. "You've taken away everything. You've killed or alienated me from everyone I loved, and you know what? That's not even the cruelest joke you've pulled on me." I picked up the Game Boy that had been sitting peacefully on the side table near the hall and threw it at his head, but he caught it without effort. He still wasn't showing any emotions, just placid calm; it infuriated me even more.

"I was liking... this... all of this." I couldn't believe the words were coming out of my mouth. "I looked forward to... to all of that... that stuff.

But I guess like all your black-hearted brothers, it meant nothing. I'm just a toy for you to play with, lock up when you're bored and beat in front of your family."

Elish blinked, took a single glance at my arms before his eyes fell back to me. "Are you done?"

I looked down at my arms, never feeling so much self-loathing and such hatred for that chimera. I broke down before his eyes and he brushed me off like I was a stray strand of hair on his shirt.

Why did I have to get brought out of that room? I wasn't used to him anymore. I'd had some quiet, some rest for my head and my beaten raw emotions. This was the last thing I had needed tonight, but like always he had to push me.

No, Elish always pushed me; I just didn't have the will today to ignore his jabs.

But things couldn't go back to how they were, not after he did what he did at Stadium. How could he expect me to forget about it and go back to how things had been? Until what? Until the next cruel idea that came into his head?

Until he decided that Kerres had to die? The last thing I held close to me, my last tie to Moros. How long until my boyfriend died like Sheryn did?

Rooms held no aura of their own, only humans did, but around me the room was filled with a black smoke, thick and with a dry soot that filled not my lungs but my mind. It clung to me and got its grit into every part of my brain. It was like the Grim Reaper was pulling a curtain over me.

And I think in that moment I realized I'd had enough.

"Yeah… I'm done."

I opened the cabinet drawer and, sure enough, there was a silver handgun. I picked it up, clicked back the safety and before I could convince myself not to I held it to my head and pulled the trigger.

The sound knocked every single sense out of me; my ears rang and throbbed in protest. But to my confusion, my body got pulled roughly.

No, no… I was dead. I blew my head off, why was I being yanked back?

As I fell my arm went tight and there I dangled for a moment. I realized Elish had the barrel of the pistol in his hand. I was blinking hard and looking at the floor for the blood.

I had watched movies, there was lots of blood. Lots of…

Everything went black. But I wasn't dead. A smell of mint and nutmeg filled my senses and there was the feeling of cotton on my face, followed by a tight constricting of my body like I had been trapped in the arms of a python.

"Why must you be so dramatic?" Elish hissed, though there was an odd tone to it; it was a single octave higher and his words came just slightly quicker. "Do you really value your life so little that you would kill yourself to get my attention?"

I tried to move my crawling skin away from him, but he wasn't letting go. I managed to move my face away from his chest so I could speak. "Why do you care? You don't give a fuck about me, or anyone."

"Is this what this tantrum was about? Do you need some reassurance?" Elish said, his voice brimming with taunting.

I growled, my whole body jerked to try and break his grip but it didn't. He still held me tight against him. "You killed my fucking mom! You made me watch! Stop treating it like that's no big deal."

Elish was silent for a moment, his steady breathing the only indication of the time that passed.

I had a sense he was thinking about something, not just silent because of indifference of cruelty.

"I have to follow orders, as you do, Cicaro."

I wasn't prepared for the impact those words had on me, it made me open my eyes and tense my brow in the confusion they brought.

"You didn't plan that?"

Elish let go of me, but I didn't move away from him.

"What part of your train of thought assumed I had? When I restrained you and asked you not to jump into that arena? When I ordered my brothers not to lay a finger on you afterwards? Or perhaps the glaring clue to my complete involvement over that spectacle, would be King Silas purposely arming you beforehand, just to see what would happen when you realized she was down there."

There had never been a doubt in my mind that Elish hadn't planned this. But now that the cold and resounding voice spoke with the same confidence, my previous assumptions died before the last syllable left his lips.

"He ordered me to force you to watch."

The realization made my stomach drop. But instead of saying something, my face dissolved. I felt so humiliated over such a brash display of emotions that I turned to hide my shame.

Instead he took me into his arms again, and though the tears kept being shed, mostly I just trembled like the pathetic little pet I was.

"I really thought you would be smart enough to figure that out afterwards. Have I ever punished you for no reason?"

"No," I said quietly. All other words left me. I had been positive it was him. Who else could it have been? But as I went over the horrible memories of that night, now with a different light shining on them; the more I looked, the more obvious it became.

Elish had obeyed Silas's orders, but at every turn he was trying to protect me from Silas. But why did Silas want to do that to me? That was a question not worth asking. If the rumours of the Ghost King were true, he didn't need a reason. King Silas liked playing games and fucking with people; I guess his own chimeras were not immune from that.

Would he hurt Kerres next? Another question I couldn't ask.

"So weak and so strong. You're a walking conundrum that never ceases to confound me." Elish let out a breath and shifted me away from his body. "I suppose praise is in order though, you took out both brute chimeras with nothing but those claws and teeth. I was impressed." Elish brushed a hand over the knife slashes on my arms and shook his head. "Come, you smell like gun powder and urine. Make yourself a bath. You can eat some hot food after, if you don't accidentally drown yourself."

I rose and cringed at the sight of his blood and tear-stained shirt. I knew the laundry sengils probably hated me.

"Is Silas going to do this to me again?" I asked as Elish started unbuttoning his shirt while walking towards his bedroom.

"Yes."

The nausea rose from my stomach to my throat; I loved and hated his brutally honest nature. "Why?"

I saw Elish's shirt come off, and with his blond hair swaying slightly, he threw it into his bedroom, before he tucked his hair behind his ears. "King Silas is almost two hundred and fifty years old; he has led a long and tragic life. All those he loved before the Fallocaust are long dead, and those after as well." Elish glanced at me and I noticed his eyes were narrowed. "Silas is a jealous ruler with his chimeras; he gets threatened easily."

Threatened easily? "I'm just a cicaro; I'm not a threat… am I?"

Am I? Sanguine… he said…

"I am almost eighty-eight years old. You are the first cicaro I have owned in forty years and the first from the slums. That should answer your question."

"Why me?"

Elish gave me one more passing glance before he opened the door to his bedroom.

"You know why."

I was in dangerous territory and I knew soon he would close himself down; I had already gotten a lot more explanations from him than I ever thought I would.

Still though, he hadn't answered the question that had been burrowed inside my head since the day he started reading to me. I didn't know why, and I didn't know if I ever would.

I lay in bed, my hands folded behind my head and my eyes staring up at the illuminated ceiling, watching the purples and blacks twist into one another. I hadn't been able to fall asleep; my mind was functioning like a turbine.

In another way, it felt like I was being pulled through a tube I was three sizes too big for. My mind felt exhausted going over how I felt about Elish. I had spent ten days in that closet hating him, and obsessing over the details of what had happened that night.

Now I had seen it differently, but it didn't leave me any less confused. If he had done it out of cruelty it would've made sense, because that's how I knew him.

The small things he did do though, when it came to Elish those things had been gigantic – and all of it had been happening right in front of King Silas's face.

How could someone so unemotional and indifferent go through such extreme changes of emotions? I didn't understand him, and being his pet and being around him almost constantly made that a dangerous thing to deal with.

The purple and blacks disappeared as my eyelids closed; immediately the colours I had been forced to leave behind came back. My mind started to relax.

Elish was the same bright figure in my mind, the lighthouse in the storm. Though as I would've expected he didn't have the same features of Silas, he was just Elish.

We were walking along the rocks, on the seawalk in Moros, though something was different now, he was holding my hand and smiling too.

I didn't know how he looked when he smiled, all I got were small upturns of his lips and that smirk I knew so well. I had never seen his teeth in his smile or even a lightness in his eyes. The graceful Adonis always wore a stone mask; I had only seen brief glimpses of him but never enough to form a proper visual.

His hair was flat against his wool overcoat. I looked up at the steely grey clouds and realized there was a cold rain falling on us. When it rained in Skyland we always had sengils waiting at the doors with umbrellas. Now he was walking with me smiling, and I think I was smiling too.

There was something else different too. I put my hand to my neck and I felt nothing but the warmth of my own skin. I had no collar and no leash, and as my legs shifted and walked I noticed I was dressed in normal clothes.

Suddenly I gasped and clenched my chest; I looked down and saw a hole in front of me, a dark black pit that seemed to suck everything into it. It was like I was feeling the aura of the devil himself; yes, that's what I had been feeling. That's the gnawing sense of foreboding I had been feeling since I had been thrown into that room.

Elish turned around and I saw his eyes narrow to slits, the smile long gone replaced by an ugly sneer that looked unnatural on his stolid face.

With my mouth still open in shock, I turned to see what had garnered such a horrible expression on his face.

King Silas.

Oh my god, King Silas.

Suddenly the scene changed and we were in a dark room surrounded by so much energy it made my teeth rattle from the vibrations, colours all around me of all shades, from bluey green, to bright orange to... to... that.

Then I heard screaming. I was screaming? My body spun and I turned around to try and find the source of the scream I was hearing. The tone shocked me to my core; I was in pain, horrible pain.

As if to confirm my emotions, I heard another scream; one that made me jump and gasp inside my own head. I was in incomprehensible pain. What was happening to me?

The dark voice that sucked all the other colours into it only grew larger, drinking every scream and agonizing emotion that fell from my lips. It grew on them, it loved them.

Another spin as I heard a laugh, before I screamed as I felt my hair being pulled back. I heard a snap, and cried out for mercy, but none came. The black void only fed off of it, and I knew with every expression of pain it would only feed more.

I woke up half out of my bed, my eyes bulging and my ears ringing, still trying to process the loud screams even though the room had fallen silent.

With my heart banging in my chest, my eyes scanned every last corner of the maroon bedroom, and finally, like a scared child, I even checked under the bed. I could still feel that cold void, sucking in every aura and emotion and eating it alive. Though my brain raced after my emotions, trying to calm it down with fleeting comforting thoughts, the feeling was relentless.

Silas was in my room; I knew he was.

The fear ravaged my body, my heart beat anxiety through my chest making my pulse quicken to the point where I thought I was going to have a panic attack. There was something out of place, something wrong and though I didn't know what was happening, I knew I had to get out of that room.

I got out of bed and closed the door behind me, my hands trembling so hard I had to use my palm to turn the handle.

The couch? No, it was too open; anything could hide or come through the windows or the door. He could come, King Silas was the Ghost, he was stealthy and silent. He had keys to every skyscraper, every chimera's den. King Silas was going to come for me, and eat me inside that colourless void.

My heart threatened to rip from my chest, the apprehension boiled with my own panicked anxiety. Even looking around the living room was making my breath short. Fuck, what was wrong with me? What had happened in there?

I walked towards Elish's room.

It felt like I was walking out of black tar, the void clung to me like a stink though it had no smell, no solidity, and no colour. Even though I ignored my aura ability and shut it to the back of my mind, I still could sense that foreboding; I could still hear my own screams.

What did I see and why?

I put my hand on the door knob and as the cold metal touched my skin a quiver shook my body, but the fear was overtaking the man I was. I sought the only comfort I had, even if it was the comforts of the python… the dragon.

I quietly walked into the darkness and closed the door behind me, before looking into the room.

He even slept elegantly. I had never risen first when I spent nights in his bedroom, I stayed where I had collapsed after our love making and in that position I stayed until morning. This was the first time I had seen Elish asleep on his own. He was lying on his back with a hand on his chest, the other one at his side.

I listened and I could hear his breathing but he wasn't snoring. Elish never snored.

With a lump in my throat, I walked over to the side of the bed; when I crawled in I heard his breathing change.

"What's wrong?" Elish mumbled, still sounding half asleep.

I stared at him; his eyes looked like moons to me, his face a snowy backdrop. He gave me a questioning glance. "You sound like you're on the verge of an anxiety attack. Whatever for?"

There was no way I could explain myself without sounding like a child scared from a nightmare; I had already humiliated myself by crying earlier. "Nothing… can I sleep with you from now on?"

Elish looked like he wasn't going to let me get away with the dismissing of his question, but to my surprise he let it go. "Yes, you can."

My chest calmed with his warm skin against my own; his aura seemed to push the dark void way from me. Oh, what was I doing... what was I doing? I was jelly in his hands. I knew with one peer into Silas's aura it would fuck with me. I just didn't know it would overcome me in this way and after so many days since I had seen him. Was he that strong?

I felt Elish's arm around me, and I lay my head in the crook of his arm, hating myself for this docile gesture and hating myself even more because I did feel safe in this embrace.

Another piece of my Morosian nature crumbled in front of my eyes; I could feel each brick get chipped away. I was becoming more and more Elish's pet, and I never thought I would feel okay with that fact.

The feeling in the pit of my stomach grew, the odd feeling I got when he was in a good mood multiplied. There was more confusion in me now than there had ever been. A tearing between two worlds and two natures. Jade of the slums and Jade the cicaro.

Right now I was Jade the coward, whose own head had made him afraid of the dark. Driven into the arms of his captor and master.

So much self-contempt, and so much disappointment. Two emotions that ruled me with an iron fist, like Elish ruled me.

With a sniff, I turned to my side, and put my arm over his chest; in response he drew me close.

Not a taunting remark left his lips, or a scalding word. He held me tight; in a way that made me suspect that he knew how much I needed it in that moment.

And with that, I fell into a dreamless sleep.

CHAPTER 16

I**T WAS NICE WHEN GARRETT VISITED ELISH IN HIS** office. Though I still had to get up off of my chair, bow, and do all the normal courtesies, he was one of the only chimeras to let me go back to doing what I was doing after that was done.

I was training up Jade the charizard now, he was kicking ass with Elish and kicking his rival Silas's ass too. The victory was all the more sweeter considering what he had done to me.

Elish had been avoiding him at all costs since Stadium months before. He had been putting off his calls and waiting until he suspected Silas would be high as a kite or drunk to make his calls or visits. I never came to these outings anymore and I was glad for that. I didn't want to see that aura; it had been giving me enough waking nightmares as it was.

Those hadn't gotten any better, if anything they had gotten worse, but only when I wasn't sleeping next to Elish. It was odd to get accustomed to at first, but now I was used to it and he was too. We had our sides of the bed, and if I had done something to piss him off sometime during the day I got the floor next to the bed.

He had also been feeding me pills to help me sleep deeper; I wasn't sure what they were but after waking him up several times with my tossing, turning and mumbling he'd had enough and consulted Lyle about it. So I was on my very first prescription, even if I wasn't even sure what I was taking.

Garrett was sucking on a candy cane, playing an intense game of chess with Elish, though you could only see the strain on the Skytech president's face. Elish was cool and calm, each move done with the precision of someone who had already planned out the entire execution in his head.

It was the end of February; I had been Elish's cicaro for nine months now. I had turned sixteen in January and had been surprised that Elish had remembered the date, along with the others. From Elish I had received a new Game Boy (which made Luca happy since I had pilfered his) and a Zelda game; Garrett had given me winter clothes because of my constant shivering and even Ares and Siris had sent me a gift basket full of drugs and alcohol. I didn't know what had happened to the last gift; Elish had taken it away rather quickly.

Now we were right into the major holiday of Skyfall. Though usually it was celebrated in December, because this was King Silas's world he had moved Christmas to the end of March and had renamed it Skyday. A day to celebrate surviving the winter and not getting eaten during the colder months. Though it was a bit of a copout because everyone busted out all the Christmas decorations anyway, cheap plastic had survived well in the Fallocaust and I guess before Silas killed the world people were really into cheap Christmas things.

With the candy cane moving around his mouth Garrett moved his piece, without so much of a blink of his eyes Elish picked up his bishop and took out Garrett's queen.

"Fucking hell, you demon-eyed shit!" Garrett said incredulously, slamming his hand on the desk. Elish gave him a plain look but I knew on the inside he revelled in one-upping his favourite brother.

"If you wish, you can move again."

Garrett's hands made claws against the office desk; he moved his mouth mimicking Elish before he bit down on the candy cane and pointed it at him. "I don't need your pity, brother. Just move, get it over with. Kill me."

Elish raised his hand and moved his knight; I didn't understand it but this infuriated Garrett even more. "I had my king open! Checkmate me!"

I snorted back a laugh with garnered me an evil glare from Garrett; he turned to me as if pleading for some emotional backup. "This is what he does, he can't just win. He has to humiliate you for a while first, give you a false hope that maybe, just maybe, you can win the game and then…"

Garrett made his hand into a gun and made like he was shooting the air. "– he kills you mercilessly."

As Garrett said this to me I couldn't hold back the laughter much longer. "Yeah, I certainly haven't figured that one –"

"That's quite enough, Cicaro." Elish watched Garrett's desperate move to try and save his king, but the next move from Elish checkmated him. With a slam against the wooden desk and a few more vicious crunches of his candy cane, Garrett rose.

"I will take my leave with my tail between my legs, as usual." Garrett raised a manicured eyebrow at Elish and started packing up his chess board. "Have you looked into my request at all?"

Elish nodded, and handed Garrett back his slaughtered king, as if to rub his victory in just a little bit more. "Unfortunately, there is no one that comes to mind that I could match you with, but I am looking. I can give you my word on that."

"No one in Moros District?"

This piqued my interest, though I pretended I wasn't paying attention.

I watched as Elish shook his head. "No, none of them possess any redeeming qualities; they would be more trouble than they are worth with very little payout."

Garrett sighed. I heard him place the chess pieces into their compartment in his suitcase. "Well, I have one boy in mind. I was wondering if you could do me a favour with him. Jade has that ability of his and well… could you?"

"Perhaps, who is it?"

Now since my name had been mentioned I couldn't help but look up from my game.

Garrett was clipping his briefcase; Elish was sitting in his office chair watching his brother's every move. Two opposites in almost every way I could think of, even down to the colours they wore, Elish in light shades most of the time, and Garrett usually in blacks and whites with some colour thrown in. Opposite but still close, a week didn't go by that Garrett and Elish didn't see each other. It was nice having Garrett over, he brought out the best in my master, even if Elish enjoyed acting like Garrett's visits were annoying.

"His name is Killian Massey, a factory worker's son. I met them by chance while looking over some safety issues. He's just cute as a button, very polite and shy. If Jade sees us as a match I would like to have some guards start to follow him around, make sure he stays alive and unspoiled until I can purchase him. Could you, brother?"

A moment passed between the two of them, and all I could do was watch as they spoke their inaudible chimera language, done with nothing but locked stares, something only two brothers who had spent the last eighty-eight years together could do.

Finally, Elish nodded and Garrett smiled from ear to ear and almost looked giddy. I still barely knew what was going on, but I gathered that Garrett wanted a boyfriend and my aura reading was about to be used for chimera matchmaking.

"But –" Elish's voice was sharp; he held up a hand and Garrett immediately dropped the happy expression, "– my terms are as such: If Jade finds you two would not be compatible you drop this interest in the boy; if that happens I will keep looking and Jade will do the same."

The president of Skytech nodded and picked up his briefcase. "Thank you, brother. It gets lonely in that skyscraper, and you've had so much success with Jade."

Elish gave me a bored glance. "I suppose he hasn't bitten me in a month; if that is what one would call success, so be it."

Garrett laughed and I rolled my eyes, wanting to say something sly back but I didn't trust the waters enough, since Garrett was in the room and Elish still had to maintain his overlord authority.

"You're so modest, Elish. Well, let me know how it goes when you return. I'm off to challenge Grant and Nero next. I do love our weekly games. Good day!"

As soon as the door closed, I lowered my game and glanced over at Elish who was looking through his address book. I was quiet but watching as he picked up his remote phone and dialled a number.

He spoke briefly with someone in a factory town I had heard of called Tamerlan, making an appointment with the Massey guy. Then he started thumbing through his file folders. Something he did regularly.

"You're doing well, I expected you to pepper me with questions." Elish gave me another glance before opening up a brown folder. He could sense the questions dancing on my tongue; in a rare act of consideration he decided to spare me the torture of keeping things from me. "My brother has grown quite fond of you and wants a pet of his own. Morosian preferably which I have almost talked him out of, considering the rest of your comrades are nothing but flea-bitten, disease-ravaged, drug addicts. He has, as you heard, taken a liking to a boy in Tamerlan."

I stood up a bit straighter and saved the game on my Game Boy, trying to look the part of being someone worthy of receiving this information.

"We will be going to Tamerlan factory next week to meet with Jeff Massey, and while we are there I want you to write down the aura of that boy, am I understood?"

I nodded. "I know Garrett's aura well, I can match that guy in a second."

Elish started placing folders in his own leather briefcase. "No, this isn't to match him with Garrett. The boy cannot become Garrett's pet under any circumstances; which is why I am firing Jeff Massey next week."

The room fell to a silence so thick it seemed to swallow up the hum of the laptop and the heating vents on the floor. I stared at him for a second; Elish's tone was nonchalant but concrete.

"Can I ask why?"

Elish rose with my leash in hand, my eyes never left him as he walked up to me. "I am exiling Jeff Massey into the greywastes, with his wife and their child. They will build a life elsewhere, away from my brothers' prying eyes." The leash got hooked to my collar and I rose, stuffing the Game Boy into my pockets.

"And so –"

Elish paused as his remote phone rang; he handed me my leash and picked up the small flip phone.

"Hello?"

I was taken aback as I heard the voice on the other end of the line start off as calm, but quickly, as the person spoke on, his voice got louder, and though it was muffled – more desperate and shrill.

"Calm down, Lycos. Tell me what happened?"

Oh, it was him… the friend in the greywastes, or that's the only information Elish ever gave me about him. He seemed to call at least once a month in the evenings and usually their conversations were taken outside. This was one of the first times he had called Elish during the afternoon.

I had already put my Game Boy away, and I didn't want to insult the both of us by trying to convince him I wasn't listening. So I sat in my chair and twisted Elish's silvery aura around on my fingers; there really wasn't anything better to do.

"Well, I don't know what you expected," Elish said with a hint of amusement in his voice; a moment later he took the phone away from his ear, just in time for Lycos to start shrieking at him. It took every ounce of restraint in me not to laugh at that gesture, or at the balls of this guy, no one I had ever met had spoken to him in such a way.

When he was done Elish put the phone back to his ear; surprisingly he was calm and unfazed by Lycos's outburst, which stoked my curiosity even more. "I have been wanting to take some time off. Why don't I come and visit and we can have a more personal meeting regarding this *teufel* of yours. I'd like you to take a look at my own anyway."

The tone dropped as Lycos responded to him. Elish shot me a glance. "Well, if he is as bad as you say, perhaps we can trade. I barely broke a sweat breaking this one; he eats out of my hand now."

I shot him a dirty look.

"Yes, it will take us a day to get there, a day back. Expect us this following Wednesday." Elish wrote down something on his folders and a moment later he hung up the phone.

"You – you were just joking, right?" I asked cautiously.

My master picked up my leash and we left his office. "You wanted to defect into the greywastes, did you not? Perhaps it would put a bit more force in your bite; you have been rather tame recently. Maybe I want to ruffle those feathers a bit."

I sighed with relief, he was just joking. If he was serious he would've told me to be quiet and to watch myself. With that worry laid to rest I decided to bring up the next worry I had.

"Are we really going to the greywastes?"

A chill went through me as Elish nodded; we started towards the elevator.

"Just the two of us?"

Elish nodded again. "Who else would accompany us?"

My mouth pursed to the side, I pressed the lobby button on the elevator and felt the familiar queasy feeling in my stomach as we started to rise to the top floor, where Elish's apartment was.

"Isn't it dangerous there? Like… ravers, creatures you only see in your nightmares, all the horrors I've been hearing about since I could remember?"

There was a ding as the elevator stopped; Elish started to walk out. "I am immortal, I have nothing to fear."

I stayed where I was and glared at the back of his head, with only a moment to spare before the slack of the leash snapped my collar, I closed the space between us. "And I'm not."

"Really?"

I furrowed my brow and sighed my defeat, knowing I wasn't going to get anywhere with this. We got back to the apartment where dinner was ordered by Luca. It wasn't until we were halfway through our meal that Elish decided to spare me the wondering for the rest of the night.

"I will be having Sergeant Sterling give you some drills at the Legion base in Skyland for two hours a day until we leave. He will teach you how to use an assault rifle and perhaps a few techniques on using a combat knife since you seem to hold any knife you get a hold of like a baton. And yes, Jade, you will be armed, and yes, I will skin you alive if you so much as point it at me while we're in the greywastes."

My eyes widened; in spite of myself I did a little dance in my chair. "A real assault rifle? Really? That's going to be amazing. Thanks, Master." The last part was purely to suck up a little bit; this trip to the greywastes was fast becoming something I was looking forward to.

Elish nodded, but the glance he gave me made me cower in my seat. "I am warning you now, Cicaro. While we are there I expect you to keep your mouth shut, and obey my every word. Nothing that is spoken or discussed during that time will be ever spoken about again unless I prompt you first, am I understood?"

I was already picturing what I would look like with an assault rifle. I nodded and chewed dreamily on the end of a bread stick. "If I see a radanimal can I shoot it? Just one?"

"Perhaps."

This was going to be a great vacation.

The next week was busy, but in a good way. Sterling was a tough guy who had been training the legionary in riflery for the last thirty years. His son apparently was glued to Kessler's son Tim's hip as well which had brought him many favours within the chimera family. I didn't mind him, but he put me through the wringer every day, to the point where I now had to wear leather gloves to practice because Elish didn't like my hands being so callused and chapped.

The two hours of training with Sterling were intense, and for the first couple days I could barely walk or lift anything besides Elish's tea. That on top of me and Elish's rather physical sex life left me feeling like my body had aged ninety years. Every joint was lubricated with acid and each muscle felt like it was full of spurs. Though my body was in better condition after my months eating well, fifteen years of being half-starved had done permanent damage to my physique.

Luca peeked over at me over the arm of the couch, his black cat ears as always resting on his blond head. "Would you like some more ice, Master Jade?"

I was laying on my stomach on the couch, watching TV and feeling sorry for my poor body. I nodded and glanced over at Elish sipping tea and watching the cityscape framed in the windows. "I'd like a massage; we're going away today so at least this combat training is over with."

There was a clink as Elish lowered his teacup onto the saucer. "That's too bad; it looked like you were getting some strength in those feminine arms of yours. I may require you to use the weight room a couple times a week."

I lifted my head and gave him a glare. "My arms aren't feminine." I lifted a sore arm and waved Luca over, and a moment later I felt his delicate hands start to knead themselves into my back.

"You prefer scrawny? Malnourished?" Elish mused.

Muttering under my breath I ignored him and let Luca do his work. The cat-eared sengil had the fingers of an angel, though even when we were packed up and ready to head to Tamerlan my body was still aching.

The two of us got into the awaiting car, my leash clipped onto my studded collar and in Elish's hand. Both of us dressed in our usual colours, my dark greys and blacks, and his white and silver, both ready to do our duties in the borders of the greywastes.

After weaving through the streets of Skyland, we crossed the vehicle border to Nyx and headed towards the bridge. I hadn't been on the floating bridge that connected Skyfall to the mainland since I was a kid; my mother used to take me to it in the wagon to beg for food and money since this bridge had the most traffic. The crossing had been made while Skyfall was being built, and it connected Skyfall Island to the factory towns on the mainland.

Of course, always happy to teach me something, Elish started talking about the history of the bridge, "– and if you look closely you can see the different materials used from the torn down towns along the harbour. We have workers repairing it at all times as you can see," Elish explained. "After the Fallocaust, and several years after the trenches that separated Skyfall from the mainland were made, a ferry took cargo, cars, and passengers. But that ferry was stripped for scrap metal years ago. Which is just as well, it was using too much fuel. We do have smaller ferries in use for the military though."

I nodded, and tried to think of a question I could ask back just so he knew I was paying attention, but I had never paid much attention to architecture. All the buildings in Skyfall were the same; just some of them had been more repaired than others.

"You guys should charge tolls." There, that would do.

I looked up as we passed an old bridge light; a man in a reflective vest was chained to a metal pole, he was doing repairs.

"True, before the Fallocaust that would've been a wise idea, but since everything is either run by the council, Dek'ko, or Skytech we would just be taxing our own earnings. Very intelligent idea though, it seems you have been paying attention during my council meetings."

I smiled at the compliment. I had been learning a lot listening in; Pokémon could only tune out so much and I was taken to all of his meetings. Running Skyfall was complicated and it involved a lot of economics I hadn't even thought of.

Tamerlan came into view about an hour later; it was one of the first towns off the main road. There were several large factories there, two harbour side and one inland, and the town that surrounded them was where the workers lived. It was quaint and gave off a feeling of being a close-knit community. All the houses were in fair condition with new tarmac roofs and scooters parked in open garages.

The town was surrounded by a large wall that kept out the greywastes, which, when coming in from the wasteland road to the inner gates, showed what a contrast the two worlds were – a small piece of Skyfall sitting on the very fringe of a land of death. In Skyfall you never saw the real greywastes, not the rock and the despair. It was easy to forget this desolate wasteland even existed.

And once we drove into the gated town you forgot all about it once again; the walls were twenty feet high and surrounded by thiens. Unless you climbed the walls you couldn't even see the wasteland. It was a bizarre notion that even though they were technically in the greywastes, the towns had carved out their own sustaining existences.

The car slowed down; I looked out the window and saw the houses go by slowly. Small and cute, well-maintained, with scooters in covered areas and even kids playing with barely a care in the world. I wondered if the block we were heading to the next day would have the same homey feel; somehow I doubted that, but I hoped they lived an adequate existence.

Then the car pulled into a driveway of a two-storey home. It was painted white with a blue trim, with new windows holding the warm light of the interior, and even showcasing colourful curtains which had been tied back. The front yard was well-groomed too; it was planted with green bushes lining the driveway and small tufts of green grass that grew in sporadic places, almost like someone had only had a single bag of seed and had just tossed it wherever they felt like. It seemed like a nice place to live; a lot better than where I had come from.

The door opened and we both got out. I quickly straightened up Elish's robes and adjusted the collar of his shirt.

"I will go in first; the boy will not be attending the meeting." To my surprise Elish pushed a bottle of rum into my hands. I looked down at it and raised an eyebrow. "Make conversation, get your reading of him and make sure it is correct no matter what it is."

I bowed my head and unscrewed the cap off of the rum and took a swig; without another word Elish turned, and with an elegant and authoritative walk, he made his way to the door.

Almost out of nowhere several thiens swooped in behind him, their assault rifles in tow and the usual no bullshit look on their faces. They stayed behind Elish as his bodyguards even though no one was expecting anything to happen.

When they were inside I saw that the door was ajar. I took a minute to myself to drink a couple more swigs of rum before I sauntered up the stairs, rum in one hand and my leash in the other which I spun around nonchalantly.

And that was the first time I saw Killian Massey. The young boy had his back turned to me, with an ear pressed up against the door behind which I assumed my master and his parents were conversing. I almost laughed out loud at how juvenile and silly he looked. Like a kid trying to figure out what his parents were getting him for Skyday.

I decided to break the ice; I took a swig of rum bottle and spoke. "You shouldn't snoop so much," I said casually watching with a smirk as he jolted from surprise. "It will just get you into trouble."

The kid quickly turned around and I saw his face for the first time.

What an angelic-looking little guy. He had large eyes of a deep blue colour and a small nose. His face was thin with a frail twiggy body to match; he had the gangliness of a kid halfway through a growth spurt but from the looks of his features he was one of those unfortunate men who were doomed to always look kiddish. I could see why he would catch Garrett's eye; this kid was the personification of a twink, the chimeras would eat him alive.

"Who... who are you?" The kid looked at me like he had been caught in headlights, the surprise only making his eyes more prominent.

"A mere cicaro," I said in a casual manner. I started tuning my aura abilities to him and suddenly a brilliant spectrum appeared around the kid; it made me smile. "My name is Jade."

My god. I took a step closer to him as the boy backed away from the door. His aura was attracting me like metal shavings to a magnet.

The blond boy was like a little sun; his aura was yellow and silvers, so light and feathery I felt like if I got closer it would lift me up into the air. This child had had a peaceful and sheltered life; not a single blemish or mark was on his soul; he was a perfect innocence, an angel taken from above that had somehow managed to stay pure on the fringes of the greywastes.

Poor creature, soon this perfect aura would undoubtedly be spoiled by the wasteland.

Then something strange overcame me.

My gaze drew itself up and down the kid's body and to my own shock... I didn't feel badly for the kid's bleak future. Instead I felt almost validated that he would soon experience the real world. For some odd reason I wanted this perfect creature to become spoiled. I couldn't stand such a beacon of purity around me, knowing I was a cesspool compared to him.

I was so overcome by these dark emotions my body twitched to run, but a bigger force seemed to be drawing me to him. Like a moth to a flame every cell inside of me pulled to get a closer look, though with malevolent intentions that I had never tasted before.

I found my eyes travelling his body and with a hard swallow, the feeling overtook me. "It's too bad about you leaving Skyfall; you would have done well as a pet." My chest quivered and other places too. Unbidden, my body jolted to take another step towards him.

Just... one... more step.

"I bet you would taste nice."

The kid cautiously inched himself away from my small advancements, his eyes more apprehensive than curious now. "I'm not going anywhere."

Yes you are... I eyed him, every inch of his body, every slender curve, every piece of marble skin exposed, it looked so soft. This kid, I wanted him for myself, I wanted to be the one to corrupt him, and take him for the first time. I wanted to see those eyes change expression as I tongued every inch I could find. To corrupt and draw out every moan and scream from his lips.

I wanted to spoil that aura with my own; I didn't want the greywastes to have him. No, I didn't want him to be defiled where I couldn't watch and devour every scream.

What the fuck...?

I blinked and pushed the horrible thoughts out of my head. The kid was staring at me, not knowing what the hell was going on below the surface.

I swallowed through my parched throat, noticing that my heartbeat was a rapid thrum. "Whatever you say." My voice was dry. I tried to solidify the nonchalant feeling I had been trying to give off previously and gave him a passing wink before tossing him the bottle. I then turned and got the hell out of there.

Once his aura broke from mine and disappeared with his innocent face I felt a flood of relief wash over me. All the nerves in my body were taxed and strained; I got into the car and leaned back into the seat, trying to figure out what the hell was happening to me. Never in my life had I felt such a corrupting, malevolent feeling when looking into someone's aura. Usually the feelings I drew from my abilities were from them and them alone. I had never had my own reaction to them, besides I suppose the awing feeling I had gotten when I'd looked into Elish's aura.

But that kid. I took one drink from that liquid sun and nefarious feelings stirred inside of me. Something uncharacteristic – a feeling a chimera would have, not a gutter rat like me.

I closed my eyes and let myself come down from the overbearing experience, then, with a sigh of self-derision, I took out my leather book and started writing. I honestly did consider not telling Elish about the strange transformation that had happened to me while peering into Killian Massey's aura, but I knew better. Perhaps this was the sole reason Elish was sending him into the greywastes. Though mercy was not known to my master, maybe this kid had struck a chord in him and Elish had been inclined to protect him from whatever horrible future being a chimera's pet would entail.

No, that wasn't my Elish at all… he had different plans, ones I would probably never know about.

After a half hour of writing, the door opened beside me and I smelled mint and nutmeg. When the door closed once again the car started. I didn't stop writing the entire time.

Finally when we were pulling out of Tamerlan, I sighed and closed my eyes, leaning my head back. I handed Elish the book which he took with gentle hands.

There was a row rumble of the car, and the feeling of rough pavement under the tires. We coasted along in silence, only the sounds of turning pages broke my inner thoughts. With every page turn my heart thumped harder in my chest. I remembered every word I had written down and I knew which parts he was reading whenever those pages shuffled.

With anticipation that soured my stomach I listened to Elish read. The chimera, a picture of calmness and tranquility, and me, a pathetic frame, a twitching, fidgeting mess that couldn't calm himself down. Not with the knowledge that my master was reading the horrible inner thoughts I had just had.

"You are becoming quite the writer." The confused tendrils of my aura only wound tighter together at the amused tones of my master. I brought reality back to the eyes and turned to him as he continued to speak. "You're vocabulary is improving. Depredate? You even spelled it right."

I sighed and wiped my hand down my face, staring up at the fabric ceiling of the car. "I've never had that happen to me before. Usually I feel what the person is feeling but with Killian, I felt both. He drew some sort of primal need to corrupt and spoil innocence I had never felt before."

Elish only nodded, a gloved finger lightly turning the page back so he could read through the beginning again. "He will be out of everyone's reach within the week."

I wanted him to say more, but he went back to his reading. Inside I itched to look in that brain, to pick apart every fold and peer into the thoughts lurking underneath the surface. What a taunting existence for myself. To have all this information around me but to never know what was going on. It was a tease; I felt a burning thirst inside myself for an explanation. Enough to draw the question out of me even though I knew better.

"He's different... how, Master? Are you sending him away so the chimeras won't be able to hurt him?"

My master was quiet, his blond hair reflecting the sunlight like it was spun gold, his purple eyes fixed on the pages of the black book, moving back and forth as he read to himself my own words. I wondered if he read it in my voice or his own.

"You risk a lot by asking me such a question, Cicaro. Is the answer really worth the possibility of discipline?"

My mouth twitched and I nodded. The gap between Elish's knowledge and my own was frustrating. I wished he would just forget this cicaro master bullshit for a second and just speak to me. "Only because I never had a reaction like that before." The bitterness on my tongue filled my mouth. "I felt like I was about to lose control and that doesn't happen when it comes to shit like that."

To my surprise he didn't turn into the quick striking cobra, even though my eyes kept blinking and my body winced in anticipation for a rapid strike. Instead Elish gave a nod with his eyes still fixed on the book.

"Well, Cicaro, I cannot tell you as of right now how young Massey is different, or why I am sending him into the greywastes, but I can tell you that one day you will know. Will that suffice those tumultuous thoughts in your head?"

It wouldn't and he knew it wouldn't, but his response to my question was appreciated so I didn't throw it back in his face. Instead I nodded and leaned my head back against the seat of the chair.

"You've been exposed to a lot and you have learned a lot, Jade. Now you must learn patience."

My brow furrowed and when he saw my expression he chuckled. Both of us knew that I had been forced to be patient many times, most of the times without reward. Patience was my middle name now.

But this was different; this wasn't waiting with bated breath for him to finally let me cum, or waiting obediently for his last council meeting so we could go home. This was an underlining mystery that stemmed far beyond my small world; something that I knew must be big.

I watched the greywastes spread out in front of us, the walls of Tamerlan now lost in the rocky and uneven terrain.

Patience was overrated.

"Can I ask one question, Master?" I spoke honestly. We were on the floating bridge now, Skyfall in all its brilliance on our horizon. I could even see Olympus in the distance. I knew the skyscraper well; it had a flat roof and tinted windows.

The weighted silence fell between us as it always did when I was testing the waters. My heart was a motor inside me as I waited to see what his reaction would be.

My master's only physical response was a slight twitch of his lips. "Go on."

I gathered up my balls and clenched the side of the seat as if preparing myself for impact. "Are you sending Killian into the greywastes to die? A quick death rather than… Silas?"

The lump in my throat didn't move as I swallowed, and when his violet eyes turned to me, the lump turned to a smouldering piece of lava.

"The boy will live."

I nodded, and in spite of myself and my already over-taxed emotions I found myself growing a bit jealous. Was Killian important to my master? Did he want to keep him from Garrett so once Silas killed me he could have Killian for himself? A nice piece of virgin flesh for my master to corrupt and control. Sanguine said –

"No."

My brow furrowed deeper, and I realized he was still looking at me.

"No, what?"

"You know what."

I glared at him, he stared back at me and I knew he wouldn't break his gaze first.

"Do not tell me you need more childish reassurance?" His voice was taunting, but my yellow eyes were just as fixed on his as his were on mine. I was desperately trying to draw out explanations though those eyes were immovable fortresses that revealed nothing of what was happening behind their walls.

"So what if I do? I don't know what's going on; what else am I supposed to think?"

Elish smirked, his eyes all but seeping amusement at my insecurities. "I would think you would be happy. It would take less attention from you, wouldn't it? You could see him break in front of you, would that not please you?"

A burst of anger and jealousy shot through me. I'd kill him first!

"No!" I snapped, before clamping down on my lip trying to physically stop the intangible thoughts rapidly being shot through my mind. "You're… you're…"

"I'm?"

I gritted my teeth together and debated opening up the car door and jumping out.

"You're mine!"

As if to drive in the humiliation that was bringing a heat to the back of my neck, Elish reached his hand out and brushed my bangs back, still looking at me with derisive mirth. "A pet trying to possess his master? How amusing." I ground my teeth harder but he went on. "But no, Cicaro, it was never the plan to covet that boy for myself. At this point he would wilt and die under me in a matter of hours. I prefer boys with a bit more… *bite* to them."

The relief washed over me like a tidal wave, but in the same moment I despised myself for feeling that way. In the deep corners of my mind it was all but obvious that I had grown an unhealthy dependency and attachment to my master. The thought of sharing his attention, both good and bad, drew jealousy from me. If he ever brought another pet into the household I would kill it as soon as Elish's back was turned.

So with the relief I felt I became playful. I turned my head as he brushed back my hair and tried to nip his hand, only to prove that I had more than enough bite to me.

Elish gently grabbed my chin and raised it as if examining my mouth, he tilted it to its side though what he was looking, at or looking for, was lost to me. "Though more well-behaved, you will never lose that bite. I have no need for other pets; my hands will always be full with you."

I beamed when he took his hands away from my jaw, and with my mind flooding with emotions I leaned over to him and kissed him on the lips, his strands of hair falling between my fingers.

CHAPTER 17

"UNCHAIN THE LITTLE MUTT, ELISH; LET HIM CHECK OUT the plane." Kessler must've sensed the excitement when the tarmac came into view. He was walking side by side with Elish as we approached the open airfield, a military base that was now used exclusively to house the Legion's aircrafts, military vehicles, and arms. I, of course, had never been near it. It was in the borderlands, still oceanfront but miles away from Skyfall and any civilization. The city was nothing but a charcoal drawing against the backdrop of grey skies and deep brown oceans.

The base was huge, with over a dozen single-storey buildings that looked like reinforced forts, all perfectly spaced apart and stained the same colours as the greywastes ground. There were paved roads going to each building and a long one surrounding the outskirts of the base. Large concrete walls enclosed it, topped with razor wire and surrounded by more legionary than I had ever seen.

Legion soldiers were different to thiens; thiens were just armoured cops that kept the peace in Skyfall. The legionaries took care of the greywastes, led by Imperial General Kessler Dekker and to a lesser extent his husband Tiberius and their two chimera spawns.

The greywaste soldiers were nasty-looking people with authority complexes, who carried around their assault rifles like they were their own cock extensions. I wouldn't want to fuck with them, that was for sure. At least they were on our side.

I heard my leash unclip and as the two chimeras talked about the planes refuelling and things I wasn't really interested in, I sprinted off to get a better look at the plane.

It was called a Falconer; it was a small military transport plane and the biggest machine I had ever seen. It boggled my mind to think that this plane would actually be flying around in the air; I had only seen things like that in movies.

I kicked the tires and ran my hands along the smooth grey metal, over each small bolt and rib, shaking my head in awe. I did a full circle around it, before I climbed up the back of a metal ramp that had been lowered, and whistled inside of it to see if it would echo.

In the inside of the cargo hold were two wooden benches on each side. Large plastic crates lining the rear of the plane. I tapped my foot against the metal ground to hear the noise it made, before I went to the cockpit to look at all the mechanics.

There were so many buttons, switches, and toggles. I sat in the captain's chair and found a pair of aviator sunglasses I was assuming did not belong to Elish. I put them on and sat back in the chair, pretending I was a pilot.

If only my Morosian buddies could've seen me now. I wished I had a Polaroid or something so I could take a picture of myself.

The voices of Elish and Kessler came closer and soon I heard the echoing steps of their boots.

"After the holidays send him down to the base. I'll be teaching Caligula and Tim to fly the Falconer; it's a good opportunity to get your boy started as well."

My ears perked up; I looked at the two of them with a grin.

"Really?" I raised the sunglasses and put them on my head.

"No," was Elish's curt reply. Kessler laughed, his grey eyes had a playful glint to them. It was always amusing when Elish interacted with the brothers that didn't have sticks permanently shoved up their asses.

Kessler sucked on a cigarette and blew the smoke out, his expression amused. "You need to start putting the boy through some drills, he's what… sixteen now? He should've been started on basic training when he was six. I saw what he did to Ares and Siris; you could have a machine on your hands if you put the effort into him."

I think that was a compliment…

"Pets do not go through basic training." Elish's tone was edging on the danger zone. I quietly slipped the sunglasses off and stepped further into the cockpit, mentally hearing the time bomb start to tick down.

"Even Drake went through basic training," Kessler pointed out, dashing his cigarette onto the floor. The leader of the Legion was a tall and burly man with arms the size of my head. He was immortal but it must've happened later in life; he looked to be in his late thirties.

The serene but icy gaze didn't falter in the least on Elish's face, his voice didn't change either. "If you have more to say on the subject we can have a meeting in my office once we return." Elish gave me a hard glance out of the corner of his eye.

Kessler nodded and flicked his cigarette out of the cargo ramp of the plane. "Just think about it, thoroughly. He's well-bred."

I crossed my arms but I saved my dirty looks for the metal door frame of the plane. I wanted to point out I wasn't bred, I wasn't a genetically engineered monster like they all were.

"I will." And with that dangerous tone I sat in the co-pilot's chair. Then after a few minutes of conversation as Elish walked Kessler out of the Falconer, Elish returned and turned on the plane.

With a glee that rose with the Falconer, I watched the base become smaller under my fixed gaze. The long and symmetrical buildings became children's toys and quickly were swept underneath the line of my vision. Then there was nothing but grey rock and black trees so small they looked like the bristles of a hairbrush. It took my breath away, and I couldn't help but look awestruck.

After a few minutes I saw the remains of my first city; I gasped in awe and pressed my face against the window. "Can we land? I want to walk around it. Please! Please!"

Elish glanced out the window. "That's Irontowers; you wouldn't want to step foot into that city."

I craned my neck as we flew over the tall structures, with roads carved through the buildings like rivers, showing a lighter grey than the decaying buildings that rose up from the wastes. I could see small patches of red, from rusted cars I guess, and black marks from fires that had died hundreds of years ago.

"Why?" I asked, watching a particular road that had bumper to bumper cars, going through the main four lane highway of the city.

"Since it is close to Skyfall we found that we were beginning to have a problem with fugitives or illegal defectors hiding in that town. So we thought it would be a suitable place to release some of our breeding pairs of altered radanimals. You would find there is a very unique ecosystem in that town, prey and predator animals alike," Elish said, his voice switching to its teaching tone. At one point in his long life he had been a dean and professor in the college and taught most of the chimeras. He left that about seventeen years ago for a position on the council and to aid King Silas in the running of Skyfall. Though he hadn't been a teacher in awhile, every time he took a moment to teach me something new, he seemed to glow a bit brighter.

"Would you take me to a real abandoned town one day? Without abominations?" The adrenaline of being high up in the air and seeing the world pass by below me was making me a bit soft.

Elish seemed to sense this. When I tore my gaze from the window he was smirking. "There are a few nice places in the greywastes I could show you."

"What's your favourite?" The city passed by, but the cars were still lined up, some even laying to rest a quarter mile from the road, probably in a desperate last ditch attempt to get out of the city. I wondered what they were trying to escape.

There was silence between us and I thought he wasn't going to answer, but eventually he spoke. "There is a place southwest, where the greywastes slope down to a large valley with a lake bowled in the middle. A friend and I found a string of houses on a sheer cliff with a view and tranquility unmatched. I always enjoyed that place; it has been almost nineteen years since I've been there."

"Can we go? If it's still there?"

"Sure."

This made me smile. I turned back to the window and watched the road snake down the rocky ground, stretching off into different directions and eventually going to long abandoned towns.

It wasn't until we had been flying for almost two hours that I saw the smoke of occupied towns and settlements.

Elish told me about every town and block we passed; the blocks he knew more about since they were under King Silas's control. The towns he said he knew mostly by merchant word of mouth or the occasional visit by a chimera, though they weren't as welcome there; some people didn't even know what the heck a chimera was.

Soon Elish was landing the plane; it made a pit in my stomach form, almost like when the elevators in the skyscrapers were descending. I watched from my seat as the ridges of the greywastes came into view, and soon the terrain was all around us.

Then to my surprise the roof of a barn could be seen, and finally the entire open building, grey and faded and almost empty save for some old tool benches.

We landed with a thunk and a moment later I felt the Falconer roll forward as Elish steered it into the barn.

The cockpit got dark. I let Elish get up first after he killed the engine and a moment later he was opening the sliding cargo hold door.

I jumped out after him and immediately scanned the barn. It looked old and in ruins, a lot like the old buildings in Moros but worse. This place looked like it was going to fall down at any second.

I picked at a grey wooden beam, the spongy wood coming off in my fingers. I ran my hand up the prickly wood before kicking the dirt with my boots. It was so fine and dusty, like ash. I bent down and rubbed a bit of it between my fingers, before I walked to the back of the plane and started checking out some old tool racks and work benches.

I was opening drawers and stashing a few screws I had found when Elish called for me.

My eyes widened when I saw him; in about ten minutes he had turned into a greywaster, so much so the shocked expression was clear on my face.

He had tucked his long golden hair into a cowboy hat and that alone made him look completely different. He was wearing a black trench coat, belted pants, and a threddy grey shirt with faded blood on the collar.

He swung an assault rifle over his back and glanced over at me, then pointed to a bundle of folded clothes. "Put those on and don't complain; they're supposed to smell like filth."

I had to smile at how weird he looked, with his hair gone and his usual white and silver colours back in Skyfall. He just, well... I actually found it a bit attractive.

Elish noticed my smile but he ignored it; instead he handed me a shirt and pants and started to get several things out of the crates.

I grimaced at the smell; he was right about that, they smelled like dirty bodies and gun powder. I put them on without complaint, and when I had finished fastening a faded brown belt he handed me a similar black long coat, a duster from the looks of it, and some sunglasses.

"Do not take these sunglasses off, purple and yellow are not natural colours and it will just bring unneeded attention," Elish explained before reaching over and unlatching my collar. "This is also getting put away for now."

I rubbed my neck; usually I only took off the collar when I was bathing, my neck felt weird without it now.

Elish took a step back and checked me out, before making me turn around. He nodded when I looked back at him. "No one will ask, but either way we'll have a back story. My name is going to be James and your name is Michael, you're my travelling partner, we are from Tintown. Now say that back to me."

Travelling partner? I guess father and son would be too creepy for him. "You're James, I am Michael from Tintown; we're partners."

"*Travelling* partners."

"Travelling partners."

Elish put on his sunglasses before handing me my assault rifle. This was what I had been waiting for; I'd had a great time at the base learning how to use it, though the Sergeant was a bit of a tool.

"One more thing." Elish took out a small leather case and gave it to me. "Put those in and keep the claws inside your coat, then look at me and listen."

I opened the case and swallowed the rock that dropped into my stomach. In my case were the teeth and the claw rings. Before my mind had a chance to tell me how I felt about seeing them again, considering what King Silas had done, I started pushing the fangs onto my canine.

I clinked them together and clamped down trying to force them the rest of the way in. I flexed my jaw before shutting my mouth, hearing the unique sound inside my brain of the metal resting on metal.

"Now listen as we walk and listen well." Elish took one last look around as he walked outside of the barn. I followed him as he headed towards a broken up strip of pavement.

"As much as I would rather drug you and have you forget everything that is about to happen, I don't have that luxury," Elish began. His tone made my head snap towards him, I gave him my full attention. "I must warn you, Cicaro, if for any reason I ever fear you will leak this information, I will have no choice but to kill you."

I blinked, but no words left my lips. Elish continued.

"I will only tell you what you need to know; the more you know the more you're at risk. So do not ask questions – you will receive no answers."

A chill went up my spine. Elish was trusting me with something big; the thrill this brought me was unmatched. From a slumrat to Elish Dekker's trusted cicaro; no matter how chaotic our pet and master relationship could be, this was something to stand up straighter about.

"Lycos is called Leo in this block. He has a son named Reaver whom we will be discussing. While we discuss him you'll be in the yard. Once we return to Skyfall you must never mention those names again to anyone; this is imperative, understand me?"

I nodded. I had already been given the 'don't mention anything about everything' speech during my first several weeks going to his office. I was well-versed in that.

"Now, about your aura ability… if you can and if he isn't skulking in the shadows, get me a reading of Reaver, also Leo, and his husband Greyson. No one else is important, just those three."

I nodded, before almost tripping on a jutting out piece of pavement. I wasn't used to such uneven roads. Nothing was straight in the greywastes; even the wooden beams I had seen back in the old barn were bowed and warped from age. It was all grey and jagged, not a single thing smooth or without a thin coat of grey ash.

I looked into a rusted car as we passed it, completely gutted and reduced to deteriorating twists of metal, most parts not even recognizable anymore. I kicked the frayed tire anyway with my boot, though it was completely flat, only a limp tongue underneath the metal rim.

Soon I was looking around in every direction, though unfortunately it looked like my assault rifle was going to be for decorative use only. I couldn't hear anything let alone see a radanimal I could shoot. This place was absolutely deserted. I didn't know why but I kind of expected the place to have more abominations in it, but it just seemed like miles and miles of nothing.

I let out a yelp as I almost tripped again. Elish looked at me, and though I couldn't see his face properly through his sunglasses, I knew he was giving me an unimpressed look.

My excitement about being in the greywastes was dampened a bit when I saw the block we were heading for in the distance. I suppose when I saw the towering walls and the chain-link fence in front of it, everything became real. I would be meeting greywasters soon. I had been hearing how wild and savage they were since I was a kid.

The corner of my eye caught Elish taking something out of his trench coat. I was surprised to see it was a bottle of rum. Elish only drank a glass of wine in the evening, two if his day had been long.

He took a drink, and I saw the corner of his mouth twitch under the taste; to my further shock he handed it to me.

"Drink."

I didn't need to be told twice; I put the bottle to my lips and started to drink right from it.

"Not the whole bottle, just enough to get it on your breath." There was a popping sound as Elish took the bottle right out of my mouth, but he didn't put it back into his coat, instead he just put the cap back on. "Greywasters are usually either drunk, high, or both."

"Sounds like Moros," I said wiping my mouth before he gave the bottle back to me.

I got the shock of my life a few minutes later when we approached the chain-link fence and concrete wall that surrounded Aras.

I sprung up into the air, my heart lurching in my chest as I heard the sound of wild dogs barking and snarling with such a deep, baritone growl it made my chest vibrate like the subwoofers we hooked up in the underground clubs.

"Those are deacons, they're guard dogs, ignore them. They sense apprehension and it will only make them worse," Elish said loudly over the insanely vicious snarling. I shrunk near the chimera as I saw gigantic, hairless dogs lunging and snapping at the thick bars. They were huge, especially their shoulder blades which jutted out of their scabby and patchy skin like mountains.

"Where's their fur?" I asked, feeling my shoulders rub against his arm.

"That's the radiation; they don't have Geigerchips so the radiation has made them hairless and mad from poisoning. Only cats, dogs, and the crossbreed deacdogs are allowed chips without special permission," Elish explained over the racket. In front of us I could see black figures appearing on the walls, all of them watching us like ravens. "They're good guard dogs but are not domesticated. As you can see Aras is surrounded by their pens; they act as not only guard dogs but alert systems as well."

I cringed as a large black deacon lunged at the bars, before letting out a yelp. I heard an electric snap before it fell backwards and had a small seizure. The fence was electrified; I made a point not to touch it.

We approached a gate, a small pathway that was enclosed on all sides by chain-link before it led to the gate that would bring us inside the block of Aras. Without acknowledging the black figures watching us the gates opened on rusty hinges. I held back until Elish started walking through, then I followed him.

There were two men waiting for us at the end of the inner pathway, a blond-haired man with a kind face, probably in his early thirties, and a tough-looking guy with a cowboy hat similar to Elish's. He had light grey eyes and a stern face, with a strong build that was only accentuated by the thin t-shirt he wore; it showed off every muscle he had.

All colours of grey in that guy, I only saw his aura for a moment before my eyes snapped back to attention as the blond-haired one spoke.

"Welcome back," he said with a smile; his eyes fell on Elish and then to me. I saw for a moment a strange look pass through him, before he recovered himself and motioned the both of us to follow him. "Did you have a nice trip?" He looked behind his shoulder. Elish started following them and as such so did I. I was already feeling nervous though, I was glad Elish was close by.

"The weather held up." Elish's voice was casual; I wasn't really paying attention though. It was my first time in a block and there was a lot to see. It was, well… the buildings were crap and everything was falling apart, but still it was amazing to look at.

It was like Moros, but the buildings were smaller, there were no skyscrapers here. This town looked like it had been cut out of a residential area, though in the distance I could see bigger buildings, possibly office buildings or apartments.

The windows were bare of actual glass, but had been boarded up by the scrap wood of their neighbours. A lot of the roofs had collapsed too; it looked as though some giant had put its foot down on the building and stepped on it. Everything was in ruins, or had shoddy repairs done from cannibalizing other houses.

Though that being said, the buildings had an odd comfort to them, the ones with smoke billowing out of the chimneys seemed cozy inside. On first glance it might look like a dump, but there was an air of safety here I could feel. No one around me seemed nervous or on edge; there was a sense of community I had never had in Moros.

I saw a couple of feral cats slink through the debris surrounding us to peer out with glowing eyes; we had cats in Moros too but these ones seemed more wild. They must've had more game to catch here; ours loved eating handouts, though we had a nice supply of radrats and regular rats for them to eat as well.

I followed the group as we made our way down the main street; all the vehicles had been pushed off to the side to make a space big enough for a vehicle to go through. It didn't take long before I saw other greywasters checking us out, a simple glance before carrying on to whatever duties they had planned. Everyone was skinny and dressed in old clothing, with the same smell of dirt and gunpowder.

No one was speaking, which I found odd. Besides the short back and forth when we arrived everyone had maintained a muted silence. It wasn't until we stopped in front of a house with windows and a bluelamp glow that the blond one spoke.

"Come on in, we have beer and some snack cakes."

Awesome, I was going to pack away a few of those. I hadn't eaten anything since breakfast.

The two men walked up the several steps onto a dusty porch with five wooden chairs circled around a sun-bleached coffee table, an ashtray set in the middle overflowing with cigarette butts. We all walked inside.

Their furniture looked worse than my Morosian crap, but I didn't judge. From the looks of the greywastes around us everything seemed rat-eaten or decayed from time; it was probably hard to get functioning furniture not to mention things that required padding like couches and chairs.

The blond one walked into the living room and we followed.

It was a simple living room furnished with a coffee table surrounded by couches, and desks up against wallpapered walls. Most of the surfaces were covered in papers and folders. To my left I could see a kitchen, and beside the kitchen a sliding glass door leading into an enclosed yard.

Everything was clean when you really looked at it, just old and with the faint smell of mould and must, a smell that seemed to stick on everything in this place.

I watched with surprise as Elish took his glasses and his trench coat off, though he kept his hat on. After taking a bottle of beer from the blond-haired one he gave me a glance.

"You can take your sunglasses off, Jade. No one will come here without announcing themselves first." He handed me the bottle after cracking it open for me. "This is Leo, you'll recognize his voice from the remote phone, and the other is Greyson, the Mayor of Aras."

I put my hands behind my back and bowed in my usual cicaro custom. When I raised my head I saw two very different expressions. Greyson was drinking from his beer bottle looking amused, but Leo, well… I think his eye was twitching.

"Lycos, Greyson… this is my pet, Jade."

Leo continued to twitch but Greyson chuckled; he peered down at me and shook his head. "Look at those eyes, he's a beautiful creature, isn't he, Leo? What a catch, Elish. Good job."

I felt the back of my neck go hot, but the more interesting thing was the shade Leo was changing. I realized two things in that moment: Greyson was purposely trying to make Leo react to him, and my master and Leo might have had a bit of a past. This notion made me bristle, which made me annoyed as hell at myself considering it was insulting for me to feel possessive of my captor.

Even if he *was* mine.

Greyson reached a dirt-stained finger out and pointed to my neck. "Look at that bite mark on his neck. Leo, show him yours."

Oh really? I narrowed my eyes and realized Leo was glaring at me right back; his face didn't back up his aura at all. His aura was a light green surrounded with a dark grey blending perfectly with his husband's, very light and ribbony, showing me he was a good person at heart. Perhaps he just had a jealous streak to him, one I wasn't about to dance around to make him comfortable. If anything I was going to prey on it like any other Morosian.

He started it.

"Shut up, Greyson. Elish, can I put your pet into the yard so we can get down to business?" Leo said with an icy chill to his voice. Greyson chuckled at this; his tough appearance seemed to only be a cover, in all respects he seemed like a jovial person.

"You will not put a hand on my pet, Lycos. Jade, please play your Game Boy outside for this duration. You can grab some of the cakes, but do knock if you need anything inside, alright?"

Alright? I had never heard Elish give me an order with an 'alright' at the end. I felt like I had absentmindedly walked into the twilight zone. I would've given anything in that moment to stay and listen to the conversation. One thing was for sure; all three of them were playing their own games, even my master.

Well, I could play my own game too, and I knew whose side I was on. "Yes, Master," I said with a loving smile. I laughed on the inside as Leo's hazel eyes pierced me. I rose and stuffed several cakes into my pockets before taking my beer outside.

I found a bench and sat down. I brought out my Game Boy and started to play and eat at the same time, shooting the occasional glance to the sliding glass door and the living room window, but I couldn't see anything, the glare of the sun was working against me.

I squinted my eyes at the grey sun beaming down on me. At least it wasn't cold, and this yard was enclosed like an aerie, surrounded by tall slabs of broken off pavement and what looked like the entire wall of an old house. It was a tranquil oasis with the faint smell of charcoal from a fire pit a few feet in front of me.

"Hey... *psst.*"

I looked up from my game and saw something out of the corner of my eye.

A guy in his early twenties or late teens was holding onto the corner of the house, only his top half and his leg poking out; he was smiling at me.

"What?" I said cautiously. The guy looked friendly enough, an oval face covered in black bangs and big blue eyes that shone with an impish glint.

The guy raised his hand and I saw he had an unlit cigarette in it. "You wanna smoke? Come have a smoke with me."

I narrowed my eyes and saved my Game Boy before turning it off. I looked towards the sliding glass door where my master was still conversing with Leo and Greyson. Nothing but my own reflection stared back at me and even he was telling me to stay put.

"No, I gotta stay in the yard."

The man, dressed in jeans and a grey t-shirt, walked to the side of the house and leaned against it. I heard the metallic noise of his refillable lighter before the turn of the flint wheel. He took an inhale and held out the cigarette to me. "I'm in the yard, come on. I don't see new boys here often. What's your name?"

I opened my mouth to say Jade, but I caught myself in time. "Michael." I rose and tucked my Game Boy back into my duster before walking over to him. I leaned up against the side of the house too and took an inhale of the cigarette.

I coughed and looked at it; it tasted odd, almost like the opiate cigs we had in Moros though it was hand-rolled. "What about you?"

The guy gave me a flashy smile, he seemed friendly enough. "My name is Reno Nevada."

Reno gave me a confused look as I laughed, then I realized greywasters probably didn't even know how to read, let alone know pre-Fallocaust geography. "That's the name of a city before the Fallocaust – Reno, in the old US state Nevada."

Reno blinked for a moment before I guess it clicked with him. He laughed and nodded. "Yeah, that's right; I think my pop mentioned that." Reno peeked behind the house, before he glanced up and reached out for my cigarette.

"Hey, you want to come to my friend's house and do some drugs? We got pills there; I bet you fucking Skyfallers have better though."

Skyfaller? My insides turned to ice, and the feeling only solidified when I realized I didn't have my sunglasses on. Well, shit.

"You got any on you? That stuff is rare here." Reno's casual conversation was lost on me as I began to dread what Elish was about to do to me. With a mumbled excuse, I handed him back the cigarette and went back towards my bench.

Suddenly, a black figure dropped in front of me. I immediately jumped back as this guy seemed to come out of nowhere.

The man had black hair, and black eyes that seemed to cut through my body like a hot knife through ice. Immediately my stomach jumped up into my throat. I took another step back.

He had a cigarette dangling between his lips, and a menacing smile on his face. The guy looked to be my age, with slightly arched eyebrows and a shaved face. In all respects though he was very attractive, he had a... chimera attractiveness to him.

Oh...

I was too shocked to do more than blink as the man slipped behind me. With a graceful stealth I had only seen on Sanguine, he put his hand around my mouth. A moment later he was walking me to a small space between the side of the house and a pile of debris

"Don't scream, we're not going to hurt you," the man I knew was Reaver said. His voice was low and smooth but it gave me chills. "I'm only holding your mouth because when we return you to your boyfriend, you can say we kidnapped you. Pretty nice of me, huh? Show me how much you appreciate it by shutting up."

Boyfriend? I wondered how much Leo and Greyson's son knew about me. Reaver took his hand away from my mouth as soon as we were out of sight. I contemplated screaming for Elish but I didn't want to bring unwanted attention to us, not with my stupid yellow eyes uncovered for everyone to see.

"What do you mean boyfriend?" I asked instead. Reaver still had his hand on my duster, pushing me forward as the two of them walked. I decided that I might as well try and shed some light on this weird little family Elish had just thrown me into.

Reno thought this was funny and gave off an amused chuckle; Reaver only pushed me forward. I was surprised to see we were heading towards the gates.

Reno answered, "We saw you cling to him when you heard the deacons, it's obvious. Though you're a little young, aren't you? Whatever, keep walking, Mikey."

"Where – where are we going?" I stammered, trying not to drag my feet. I didn't think I was in any danger; it was more disobeying Elish's orders.

"We want to introduce you to Aras properly!" I felt a playful bump of Reno's fist against my cheek, then a puff of cigarette smoke; he seemed to do most of the talking. "We're going to fish for deacons. Much better than playing that Game Boy, eh, Mikey my man?"

Reaver and Reno laughed over something I didn't quite understand. I tried to look behind me, wanting to perhaps communicate telepathically to my master but the house was out of sight now.

We reached cobblestoned streets, Reaver's hands still firmly on my duster. Around us were the same broken buildings we had just passed, caved in and looking forlorn to the world. We were heading to the same gate we had just come from.

When we approached the gate I was surprised that the deacons were quiet. As Reaver pushed me towards a lowered ramp leading up to the wall, I asked him why.

Reaver lit a cigarette and gave me no answer. His boots made no noise compared to Reno's clanging footsteps. He was a chimera alright; I bet all of his genes came from Sanguine. He was creepy as hell. At least his teeth were normal, but his eyes were so black you couldn't even see the pupils.

I reached the top of the gate and saw there was a several foot wide space in the concrete, a perfect walkway for the sentries I had seen coming in. Immediately I looked over the edge and saw two deacons lying beside plywood dens, surrounding by chewed up bones and big buckets of brown water.

The enclosure smelled horrible; no wonder almost all of these greywasters stank.

With the sun becoming hotter without the shade of the backyard, I took my duster off and hung it over the wall, before glancing over to see Reno dragging a white bucket towards us.

I shuddered as I saw it was full of limbs; brown, grime-incrusted arms and legs stuffed to capacity into the container; their flesh falling out of their stumps like old moss dangled from buildings.

Then I turned around and saw Reaver. He was pulling up a small crane and pulley with a thin metal wire coiled around it; the end of it had a blood-stained hook with several maggots wiggling around on it.

This entire place was smelly, dirty, and old. It made Moros seem like a paradise; at least Moros had electricity, hot water, and shops. Just the scene in front of me was a big enough testament to what the greywastes were like. These hicks only had severed body parts, deacons, and drugs to keep them entertained. It was like the wild west meets Deliverance out here; I bet they were probably all inbred too. I hadn't seen any towns nearby or settlements, maybe that was why Reno was always smiling. He was half-inbred retard; he followed this little psycho chimera around like a dog following his master.

Reno handed Reaver a severed arm, and with the expert hands of a murderer, Reaver stabbed the hook into the fleshy forearm before pushing the crane so the pulley was hanging into the deacon's pen.

"See, fishing!" Reno punched my arm and laughed; he looked over the edge and started calling the deacons.

"Hey fuckfaces, come get some treats! *Treat, treat, treat, treaties!*" the guy called in a singy voice. He jumped onto the edge of the wall and hung his legs down with a laugh. "The bitchy one is getting up; she's going to take the bait. Give it to Mikey."

Reaver took a step back but before he did he grabbed my shirt and pointed. "There, this pulley lever right here… up goes up, down goes down. You got that?"

I nodded; this was only the second time the dark chimera spoke. I didn't know why Elish hadn't warned me that Reaver was a chimera. I had spent so much time with chimeras over the past nine months, I could spot them in a second. What was he doing here and not in Skyfall under Silas?

And with that my thoughts went to the familiar way that Leo and Greyson communicated with my master; there was something under the surface that was going on, possibly behind King Silas's back. The notion both scared and fascinated me.

"Pull up!" Reno yelled suddenly. I jumped and looked down just in time to see the white deacon snatch the arm.

I pulled on the lever, and to the howls of laughter from Reno and Reaver I tried to pull the deacon up with the wire. The dog had its jaws locked, and though it was on its back toes, it still braced its front legs against the concrete wall and pulled, thrashing its large head back and forth.

I pressed my leg against the wall and forced the lever with all my strength; to their glee the dog started to rise up off the ground.

Reaver suddenly poked me in the side; I recoiled and lost my footing. In the same second the lever bounced up, taking me with it and throwing me up in the air. I landed right on my ass between the grooves in the walls.

They laughed and Reno pulled me to my feet. I let them do the work after that. I sat up on the wall with Reno, our feet dangling off and let Reaver have the next turn. He took the hook and released the safety clasp to start wedging the hook through the muscled area of the calf.

"Hey, cool leather cuffs, you into S&M or something?" Reno's foot tapped my bare ankles, exposed from my sitting position.

I flushed and wiggled my pants down a bit to cover them again. I didn't know what else to say, there was no real explanation I could give them besides the truth, so I decided to go with it. "Yeah, that's right."

Reno whistled, before lifting my pant leg up for Reaver to see. "Got silver links on them too; boy likes to be chained. Hot!"

My ears burned but thankfully they dropped it after that.

The deacons were gathering around us now, smelling either the meat or tasting the excitement of the first one as she ate her free meal. Though their fur was only patchy, their skin showed the colours their coats should be. Most of them were grey with white necks and stomachs but I saw one black one and two white ones slowly approach us with their heads lowered in caution.

Reaver dangled a severed leg in front of the now alert deacons. I could count seven of them now, making it easier to trick them into jumping.

The guy seemed like an expert; with the new cigarette hanging from his lips Reaver dangled the meat in front of the dogs, pulling it away just in time making the dogs crash into each other.

I pulled up my legs as a fight broke out underneath me; a white one and a grey one started growling and baring their teeth to each other, their snarls making their velvety muzzles wrinkle. Soon they were snapping and half a moment later they were rolling on the ground, white teeth flashing and grey dust being kicked up in the commotion.

"Watch this." Reaver pulled out an arm and flung it into the enclosure.

My mouth dropped open as the arm landed right in the middle of the two fighting deacons; in a flash every deacon in the pit was jumping onto the two fighting ones, creating a giant cluster fuck of fighting dogs, ripping and snapping at each other.

My eyes turned to the dark-haired man; a smile was on his thin lips and a flash in his obsidian eyes that set me on edge. I saw happiness on his face at the carnage he was causing below; it was painted on his countenance. He must have shared a lot of engineering with Sanguine and Silas; this guy seemed just evil.

My chest clenched, and, as I tried to stand, I could feel my heartbeat start to increase to a jack hammering speed. I rose and stood on the wall, readying myself to jump down.

Reaver noticed, he turned and gave me a piercing look. "What are you so scared about?"

"REAVER!"

I turned around, still standing on the wall and saw my doom below me. Leo was a picture of anger and so was Greyson. Then my eyes fell to Elish and as I saw the purple flames of a very pissed-off chimera. I found myself frozen in place.

"Get the fuck down here, right now!" Greyson yelled. "I told you to leave the boy alone!"

Reaver gave him a dismissive wave. "Oh, lay off, we're taking the kidlet out for a good time. I didn't hurt him." Reaver jumped down off of the wall. "He's like what, twelve? Let the kid play before he goes back to being that dude's sex slave."

My mouth dropped open, my heartbeat rose, and to show off what I had confirmed, the chimera enhanced hearing; Reaver looked at me and sniffed. "Look, he's fucking terrified. I think I'll keep him, yeah, I'm going to keep him. He's mine now."

I looked down at him and took a couple steps away, but Reaver grabbed onto my leg. I held out my arms to keep my balance but stayed where I was. One single move of this sociopath and he could throw me to the deacons below.

"Please take your hand off my travelling partner and return him." Elish's voice was an embodiment of smouldering anger; a dangerous tone I had rarely heard and had never heard directed at someone that wasn't me.

"Travelling partner? Nah, tell me to take my hands off your boyfriend and I might. Are you illegally banging him or what? How old are you, Mikey?"

My mouth opened and closed a few times; I tried to shake my leg free of him but his grip was like iron. "Sixteen," I managed to stammer, wondering if he was about to push me into the deacons' pen. I could hear the radanimals behind me shifting and sniffing around us.

"What? Really? Why are you so beaten down and timid then?"

I am not beaten down and timid…

"Reaver…" Leo's voice was a beacon of warning. "Bring him down; you've had your fun."

Reaver's shoulders rose up and down with a sigh, and I felt his hand loosen from my ankles. I was about to jump down when, to my horror, in a single sweeping motion, Reaver grabbed my ankle with both his hands and wrenched it out from under me.

I screamed and fell backwards, feeling a rush of adrenaline as I fell into the pen below me.

Then my whole body snapped tight and my ankle gave a painful yank, my other foot flying over my head. I was dangling?

My eyes went wide with fear as I saw the upside down deacons below me, my ankle dangling above me with the line attached to my ankle cuff. I screamed and hollered as I felt the line get pulled up, bringing the deacons' heads out of view.

That fucker! I gasped and tried to pull my body up as I heard the deacons gather below me. I couldn't see them but I could hear their excited panting and the sound of dry skin being scraped together. Their energy formed twisted barbs in my brain; a cluster of excitement and bloodthirst as they smelled the blood rushing to my head.

One jumped and, as it did, the pulley rose up some more. I screamed and thrashed my free leg but it was knocking against the side of the wall uselessly; all I could do was keep my limbs as close to my body as possible.

There was so much commotion above and below me, but what was happening above me had no bearing on my mind, considering I was being surrounded by giant radiated wolves. I concentrated at that point in keeping myself alive, though all I could do was try and raise myself as high above the deacons as I possibly could.

Then I felt myself get raised, the blood pooling in my head bringing with it dizziness and nausea.

I felt two hands on my ankle and a bunch more grab me and pull me over the barrier of the wall. With a gasp and a probably petrified look on my face, I fell onto the sentry space of the wall, surrounded by boots and angry voices.

"Jade? Are you alright?" Elish… thank god, Elish. I was pulled to my feet and a moment later I felt someone unclip my ankle.

Then a rush of anger found me; as soon as my mind knew I was safe it replaced the petrifying fear with more rage than my body could hold. My eyes quickly scanned the faces around me before it fell to the inner walls of Aras.

Reaver was walking away, as nonchalant as could be; he had just jumped down off of the wall.

Before anyone could grab me, I jumped onto the inner concrete wall and with a leap… I jumped on him.

I slammed down onto the asshole with my hard leather boots digging right into the small of his back; as soon as he hit the ground I used the only weapon I had on me - my steel teeth. Though I knew Elish would be pissed off, and I knew even more that Reaver was a chimera, there wasn't a single fuck for me to give. The only lucid thought I had in my mind was to not make it a fatal neck blow, opting instead for the soft muscle of his shoulder.

I clamped down on it and squeezed my teeth together.

"You little shit!" Reaver snarled. With strength only a chimera had, he shifted his knees forward and stood. I clung onto him like a brain-sucking leech and took another bite out of his shoulders.

"Get 'em, Mikey! Get 'em!" Reno hollered; he was laughing but no one else was, they were yelling again. Reaver was on his feet now, spinning around and trying to snatch me with his hands but I had a good grip.

Then I felt him run backwards; before I could figure out what he was doing I was slammed into the wall, the force knocking me off of his back and onto the hard ground.

I bared my teeth at Reaver like an animal as he spun around, his eyes like black flames burning me with every passing millisecond. I watched him reach down to his belt where his combat knife was and with the thought that I was probably about to get killed, I shot to my feet and started to growl.

I tried to take a step towards him but my ankle was buggered; instead I took a swing at him which he easily ducked. Then he took a swing at me himself, hitting me in the side of the face with the handle of his combat knife. I lost my balance at that moment and fell to the ground. Reaver circled around me.

Then the others reached us; another set of hands wrenched me away from Reaver and a moment later I was off the ground entirely. I heard a struggle and a lot of swearing, before witnessing something rather satisfying.

Greyson hit Reaver right across the mouth, making the chimera stumble back. "What the fuck is wrong with you?" Greyson roared. Greyson raised his hand and hit Reaver again before Leo held him back, though he wasn't putting much effort into it.

"Fuck off, he was chained, nothing would've happened to him!" Reaver snapped. Holding his cheek, but to my surprise the mad chimera didn't hit Greyson back. "It was a bit of fun, get the stick out of your –" Another blow, before Elish turned away from them and started heading back towards the gate.

"Hey…" I looked over as Reno jogged up to us, he put my bundled up duster on me and put several cigarettes down on top of it. I couldn't help but think of it as a peace offering. "Sorry about psycho-pants, he has the social skills of a raver; it means he likes you, really. Come visit us soon!"

Reno gave me a warm smile, but it faded when his eyes looked up to Elish's face. Without another word he sprinted off.

Red and black, those were his colours; oddly this brought a feeling of recollection to me. The aura that twisted around him in tight coils reminded me of another certain person back in Skyfall. Same warm energy and the same docile and friendly nature; they would work perfectly together.

Reno disappeared out of view and it was just the two of us, though I didn't trust myself to speak. If I did it would be the start of a lot of yelling and possibly me getting physically punished by my master. I wanted to put that off for as long as possible.

The deacons were quiet as we walked through; there was really no noise around us besides our breathing. I was still being carried, which I didn't mind. I was watching my ankle swell up around my boot and, as the shock and adrenaline wore off of me, it was starting to hurt too.

"Elish." Lycos sounded out of breath. I heard the sound of boots scraping against dirt as he approached us. "I'm sorry; I told you he was fast. Don't blame the boy, he –"

"I do not blame the boy, and I do not blame Reaver. I blame *you* and that mongrel husband of yours."

I cowered, even though I was off the hook – there was something about being close to Elish and hearing that tone that commanded my body to do nothing else but feel fear.

"I told you he's out of control, he has his good moments, he does listen but… when he feels that spark, he can't control himself. I think Reaver sensed Jade's apprehension and… wanted to exploit it. Fear awakens something in him." Lycos, or Leo as he was inside of Aras, was right beside us now. I could see his arms crossed tightly over his chest.

"Not in front of the boy," Elish's voice almost growled.

"I know…" I blurted, though I couldn't look at them. "I know he's a chimera, I'm not stupid. You should be putting that fucking maniac in a dog cage not letting him roam free, or give him back to Silas since obviously you two fucking clowns –"

Elish cut right through the anger bubbling up inside me. "Enough, Cicaro."

"We're doing our best; he's a teenager, Elish. He'll grow out of it; he'll start dating Reno soon and that should calm him down. You know their hormones, he's testing boundaries, he's –" Lycos sighed, wrapping his arms tighter around himself. "What do we do?"

The answer Elish gave confounded me. "I told you, Lycos… love him. Just love him, that's all you can do. Be patient, be forgiving, and let him work through it. Everything else would be trying to swim up a waterfall."

"Love him?" I snorted incredulously. "He's a feral monster; he's demonic like Sanguine and sociopathic like Silas. Take the fuck out back and shoot him before he starts another Fallocaust."

I was expecting to be told to shut up again, but oddly everything went silent around me. I looked up and saw Elish's eyes staring forward, his lips tight together, but Lycos was staring right at me, his eyes wide.

"Elish… about Jade –" Lycos dropped his voice. "If Silas finds out…"

"Goodbye, Lycos. We'll talk again in a month." The tone made me quake, and I found my already over-taxed body start to tense up and shake.

"We agreed that Reaver is too young to face his future, and I'm telling you Jade is too young. You've seen Silas and I have; if you love him as much as I think you do, spare him this. Wait until he's had time to live. You know what Silas will do to him."

My brain jammed on itself, I couldn't even process what Lycos was talking about. I watched Elish's throat move as he swallowed. "He is my cicaro, nothing else, Lycos. Leave us now."

"Elish… Silas will kill him if he finds out you –"

Suddenly my master whirled around. "NOW!" Elish snarled. Never ever in my time with him had I heard such an outburst of anger; the raised voice was new to me and it brought with it a fear I hadn't felt since my first few months with him. I couldn't even escape either; his grip on me was tight and restricting.

I stared at my feet, my body trembling. I think Lycos got the hint because I heard boot steps fade into the distance. Lycos was gone and Aras was behind us.

Like the greywastes that surrounded us, we were silent; there was nothing save a nuclear missile that would make me talk to Elish as he walked back to the plane. My body was still twitching and trembling under his firm hold, trying with minimal success to calm my nerves down; though in all respects I was fried.

Though I felt a bit stupid, I was content to have Elish carry me, not just because my ankle was swelling like a balloon but because in his arms

I felt safe; safe from that fucking psycho and his minion.

When we reached the plane, Elish opened the sliding door with one hand and put me down on the co-pilot's chair. While he was closing the hatch, I took a swig of the rum for my nerves and took out one of Reno's peace cigarette and lit it.

Turning a cheek to my smoking, Elish pulled the plane out of the barn hanger and soon I was feeling the familiar nausea in my chest as we rose into the air. It wasn't until the Falconer was on its way back to Skyfall that I decided to break the silence between us.

"So… I saw something that might be useful," I said quietly, blowing the smoke into my greywaster jacket. Elish hated smoke, but his distaste for it usually fell to only wood or fire smoke; cigarette smoke he was able to tolerate, didn't have a choice with Garrett around.

"Since this whole trip seemed to be useless, I would enjoy hearing something redeeming." Elish's tone was bitter; in spite of my slum pride telling me not to care I felt like trying to cheer him up.

"That guy, Reno Nevada… Reaver's friend, he's a perfect match for Garrett. Like, exactly perfect. Their auras would stick together like Velcro." I shrugged and took another inhale of the funny-tasting cigarette.

I watched his face for his reaction but there never was any. He stared ahead, as the greywastes disappeared below us, nothing but roads and bare rock and the occasional cluster of buildings.

"Interesting, I would have never figured," Elish murmured; he seemed to be deep in thought for a moment before he spoke again. "Unfortunately, Reaver needs a friend more than Garrett needs a companion. Perhaps a time will come where I will have need for him, but, as it stands, his place is in Aras."

"Reaver's a fucking prick; he'll kill Reno before you give him to Garrett. Why is a chim-" I cut myself off before Elish could tell me to shut up. Instead I quickly turned away from the questions I knew Elish wouldn't answer. "Are we heading home now finally? I'm tired and hungry."

Elish accepted my quick turn of conversation and nodded. "Yes, we'll be home fairly soon. Why don't you change and bring me my clothing as well. I want to get out of these rags."

"Of course." I rose up and put some pressure on my leg; I hissed as a jolt of pain ripped through me. Elish noticed and put up a hand to stop me.

"No, if it is that bad I prefer you to stay." My eyes widened as Elish himself rose, sliding his hat off of his head, his blond hair tumbling out and falling over his face. He brushed it out of his eyes and motioned for me to sit in the pilot's chair.

I gawked, but Elish wasn't paying attention, he was pointing out the controls to me.

"It isn't rocket science, and this has auto pilot. Just keep your hands on the stick and do not touch anything. Remember if this crashes you will die, I will not." Elish put a hand on the back of the chair and stepped back. I hopped over on one leg and sat down in front of all the fancy controls. There was no holding back the look of glee.

"You impressed me with how you handled Lycos and Greyson's passive-aggressive comments. It would be easy for you to slip into your old ways and try your teeth around men you might've believed would back you up. Not only did you remain obedient, you bit back in your own subtle way. That did not go unnoticed."

I beamed, like a fucking flood light, I beamed. Praise did not come easily to Elish, and I soaked it up like a sponge. There was no witty retort in that moment, I just smiled at him and said thanks. My heart was glowing inside my chest and flooding with emotion.

I put my hands on the funny-looking pilot wheel and looked ahead, feeling the pride I felt inside myself mix with the rush of being in control of the Falconer. I had never driven anything more than a motorbike before, and that was only several times when I was testing the waters with a gang in Moros. Usually I had my old work bicycle and everyone knew how to ride a bike.

Elish's praise helped quell the anxiety that my time in Aras had given me, but it didn't overshadow it. My abduction by the strange chimera had filled my head with questions, and it was frustrating knowing I would have no answers.

This was something Silas didn't know about, that part of it I could be sure of. Elish was hiding this boy in Aras, but why? Lycos, the mysterious guy on the phone, and his husband Greyson were in on it obviously, but what their ties were to my master was also a mystery.

I sighed and concentrated on flying the plane, though I knew the computer was the one really controlling it. More so than any other time, I wished I was privy to this sort of information, but I was just a useless pet and I only knew what my master wanted me to know. Unless I could figure it out myself the way I had figured out Reaver's genetic makeup.

In addition to those questions were the things that Lycos had said to Elish while he was leaving Aras. Things that had always been in the back of my head, but during the last few months had faded to the deep corners. Silas wanting to hurt me, or at least wanting me to suffer. It had been a long time since that incident in Stadium, a long time since my mother had been killed. I knew it was foolish to believe he was done with me, but I was banking on it being a long time before he did it again.

Was Lycos right? Was Silas going to eventually kill me? The greywaster had told Elish I was too young, which in all respects I found insulting. I was a Morosian, and we grew up quickly, I was sixteen and once winter came I would be seventeen. I wasn't some child that didn't know how to handle things. I had grown up in the slums and then I had grown up more under Elish's whip and dog cage. I wasn't some fucking pampered little Skylander.

My mouth downturned.

"For someone flying an airplane you seem rather miserable," Elish said behind me.

I glanced up and saw he was back in his usual clothes, his white button-down and a pair of black trousers, all cloaked by a white and silver cape. Now he was back to being normal Elish, not wastelander Elish who just seemed alien to me.

"It's nothing, just going over the events of our visit." I slowly rose and took the bundle of my clothing from Elish. "I'm not weak."

"I am aware of that." As I was putting on my leather pants, Elish zipped up my vest. It was nice to be back in my pet clothes – I had never thought I would think that. "If you were weak, I would've killed you long ago."

Elish patted my cheek and sat back down on the pilot's seat. I stood there, leaning against the back of my own seat, wondering if that was a compliment or not.

CHAPTER 18

I FLEXED MY BACK AS I LOOKED INTO THE MIRROR, MY shoulder blades sticking out of my skin. They used to push out the crosshatch scars on my back, but over the last couple of months the procedures Elish had arranged for me had made them fade back into my skin.

Along with my weekly rifle training Elish was sending me downstairs to his personal clinic to get my treatments from Lyle. Apparently it had taken thousands of dollars but he was able to get a scar removal machine refurbished. It didn't look like much, just a white machine on wheels that had a little wand attached. For an hour, four times a week, I got to lay on my stomach and play Game Boy while Lyle or one of his assistants ran it along my skin. Each scar took several sessions over the course of many weeks, since they had to heal before they could be lasered again. But the end results were worth it; my skin was almost back to normal and I didn't look like a woven basket anymore.

Except for the new ones that were added; our relationship wasn't perfect. I still pissed him off and I still got disciplined. Even now I had five scabbed strips along my backside that had to heal and scar first before they got removed.

"Very nice, Cicaro," Elish praised me. I could see him in the mirror; as usual he was in his chair reading a book, the fireplace aglow behind him. Off to my left I could also hear Luca in the kitchen preparing the dessert Elish had brought from work; some chocolates and ice cream that an associate with some sucking up to do had brought him.

I stretched out my arms and pushed out my chest; the handprints I had gotten burned into my flesh from Elish were still there, prominent and silver. They had only received two treatments and were in the process of healing; those ones I despised the most. Something about them being the shape of his handprints put me on edge. It was a time in my life I wanted to forget. Though I still got hit and whipped and beaten down, we hadn't clashed that badly since.

The bite mark on my neck though I had requested Lyle to leave; that was from our first time together... I kind of wanted to keep that one.

I turned around and stretched, popping the joints in my bones as my muscles tensed. I zipped my vest back up and started walking towards Elish on the couch.

Suddenly, the door to the apartment swung open. Elish and I turned towards the door and watched as Garrett stormed in, cigarette in hand.

"You, get dressed, put something nice on." I blinked as Garrett pointed his cigarette at me, before turning to the kitchen where Luca was looking bewildered holding two bowls of ice cream surrounded by chocolates. "You, bring me something with liquor in it."

I froze, my hand still on the tab of my vest zipper. I looked over to Elish for help but he only stared at Garrett, before rising with a sigh.

"What do you need my cicaro for, Garrett? What did you do now?"

Garrett glared at him, and in his usual animated manner he outstretched an arm towards Luca. The sengil handed him a tumbler which he shotgunned before grabbing the whole bottle from him.

"This is your fault, Elish!" Garrett took a drink from the bottle, and as soon as the seal broke his lips he was sucking on the cigarette. "I asked that boy from Rocksalt if he wanted to grab a drink with me... He *fucking shot me down*, in flames! I'm taking your little twink and I'm taking him out for dinner at Rocksalt and we're going to have a fucking wonderful time, then I'm executing that snippy little waiter. Don't argue this, brother, you refused me that Killian boy, you pony up a replacement for me tonight. Go, Jade, you're not going dressed like a cicaro; go put a suit on. You have one don't you? Forget it, I have one. Just go downstairs, my car is waiting."

To my amusement Elish smiled, a bemused smirk. He crossed his arms and observed with a cocked eyebrow as Garrett took another drink.

The president seemed absolutely livid; his usually slicked back hair was messy and the hat resting on top was crooked. His green eyes were burning and just a bit glassy from shotgunning so much booze so quickly.

"A mere waiter shot down the president of Skytech? My, my, I would be embarrassed too." Elish chuckled.

Garrett seethed; he turned his attentions on me and dashed his cigarette onto the carpet. "Why isn't he doing as I asked? I said go down to the car!"

I put my hand to my mouth to hide my own laugh, though truth be told it would be an interesting night to try and make the waiter jealous before his eventual death. I smiled at Elish and raised an eyebrow.

He shook his head in a subtle warning not to even voice my agreement; I tried not to look disappointed.

"Jade eats like a stray dog let loose in a chicken coup. I would not suggest letting him eat in public if you're wishing to make someone jealous. Now if you wanted to make yourself look pathetic, in need of sympathy…"

I opened my mouth at the uncalled for insult, but before I could defend myself I saw Garrett narrow his eyes. "You do know you're only insulting yourself, right?"

Elish held up a dismissive hand. "All I am saying is there are reasons I only take him on errands and business meetings. He's not trained for public."

So I suppose the brief moment where Garrett was the brunt of Elish's taunting jokes was over, it was back to ragging on me. I felt rather pissed off at this unnecessary jabbing, especially in front of Garrett whom I did like. I couldn't hold back any longer.

"I've gotten better!" I said back with an edge to my voice. I crossed my arms and turned to Garrett. "If my master allows it I would be happy to make him jealous for you, Master Garrett. If you want, I'll even wait in an alleyway after and hold him down as you bash his brains in with a baseball bat."

Garrett smiled at me hopefully, but behind us I heard a frosted, "No."

The Skytech president's chest rose and fell as he sighed; he leaned up against the wall and swirled the bottle. "He's not worth the trouble of taking him like you did your boy; I didn't like him that much. I mean, for fuck sakes, why is it so difficult to find someone nice? How did you manage to get that yellow-eyed bastard to like you so quickly?"

Quickly? I glowered at him. I saw out of the corner of my eye Elish walk over and take the liquor bottle from his brother's hand.

"Bring Luca, he's much better trained than the cicaro, and he's small and easy on the eyes. I am saying, in all honesty, that Jade will only make an ass out of you. You don't have the heavy hand he needs and he has few redeeming qualities."

Luca perked up, and I saw him bounce up and down on his tiptoes in excitement, his small black cat ears shifting on his head. My ears went hot as I felt a mixture of my own humiliation and embarrassment. The sengil was going and the feral mongrel had to stay behind? That hit me where it hurt, in the small shreds of dignity I had left. I would've liked going to dinner with Garrett and I would have been on my best behaviour; why did Elish have to humiliate me in front of Garrett and Luca this way?

I had to say something. Garrett had paid me many compliments and had shown he thought more highly of me than I previously thought. I wouldn't let Elish take that away from me even if it meant I got punished for it after.

"I would be good, and you know I would be good," I snipped with a tilt of my head. "I don't see why I can't go."

Elish shot me an icy gaze. "I don't see why I have to give some groomed gutter rat an explanation. Luca, go with Garrett and enjoy your night off, but please... leave your ears behind."

The glee radiating off of the sengil only filled me with more bitterness. I snatched my bowl of ice cream from Luca and without another word I went into my bedroom with a slam of the door.

Sure, it was juvenile, but I didn't care. Screw all of them.

I felt my brows draw together, and with a narrowing of my eyes I shovelled the ice cream into my mouth, surprised my anger didn't melt it right off the spoon.

Just when I thought we had been getting along, he still had to mortify me in front of his brother and the sengil. I hadn't done anything to deserve it this time, so why not just let me go? It wouldn't be any skin off of his nose. Garrett was his younger brother by like ten seconds; he obviously knew how to hold his own. The change in scenery would've been nice. I was cooped up in this house if I wasn't out being dragged to Elish's office and on errands, and even when I was out with him, I had my leash on.

With a gnawing bug eating my brain, I lay on my bed with my hands behind my head, staring up at the ceiling. I hadn't slept in my room in months; I always slept with Elish now. Even if he was pissed at me, I slept on the floor beside him. I still got nightmares when I slept without him, so I had stayed away from my bedroom.

"Come out." I scowled at his voice. Garrett and the sengil had left over an hour ago and all I had done in that time was stare at the ceiling and fill myself with self-loathing and just plain loathing for Elish.

I opened the door and walked out with my bowl; without saying a word I grabbed the three empty bowls of ice cream and put them in the sink for Luca to wash later. Then I flopped down on the couch in the most slacking manner I could and watched the muted TV.

There was silence between us for the entire duration of the show on the television, and several minutes into the next. It was so quiet that when I finally spoke out of sheer frustration it was like a remote phone going off in the middle of a quiet theatre.

"Did you need me for something?"

My ears perked at the rustling of robes, but it wasn't until I heard the beep that I turned to him in shock and opened my mouth to protest.

But it was too late; a moment later my open mouth filled with a scream as an electric shock emanated from my collar and ripped its way through every muscle in my body. I clenched the chair and snapped my jaw tight to stem the shriek but it only erupted through my teeth.

When it subsided I was panting, my head bowed and my body still twitching. I gasped and took several breaths before I tried to rise.

The next shock made me fall back into my chair. Unable to stand I instead tucked my legs under me and curled up in myself. My eyes were twitching and squinting in anticipation of the next painful shock.

"So why this little outburst? Don't tell me my brother stirs your loins that much?" Elish's taunting banter was nothing new to me, but to my own further embarrassment it made the space between my eyes burn. "He may be an enjoyable man, but he's clumsy in bed when he's drunk. Luca might be –"

The lid blew off of my temper. "I'm not mad because I wanted us to fuck, and unless you're stupid you know that as well as I do," I snapped, my body recoiling more and more into itself as each word tumbled carelessly from my lips. "I – I didn't…" I chewed on my lip, before another spur of anger went through me. I rose on shaky legs and turned to him. "I'm not saying shit to you, or else you'll just mock me and throw it back into my fucking face."

"I'd watch your mouth unless you want it on the other side of the room." His voice was a frosted whisper, so cold against my ears the fine hairs froze in place, but I was too pissed off to care. Instead I flipped him off and stalked to my bedroom.

In a moment his shadow got bigger, and as Elish descended on me my heart gave a nervous jolt. Before my brain could even debate a reaction he grabbed my arms and slammed them behind my head.

"You're an untrained piece of shit on my shoe, Cicaro, not worth accompanying my brother in public. You are a slumrat, a cesspool of filth and scum. Don't forget it."

I glared back at him, my arms firmly behind my head, and my body so far off of the ground my tiptoes only glided against the carpet.

I wanted to bite back, but suddenly the anger fizzled, the boiling water burned dry. I knew the routine, I would say something back that would get me beaten, then fucked mercilessly and eventually I would sleep on the floor.

For some reason tonight was different and I didn't know why. I didn't know why the conversation with Garrett had gotten to me, why his comments had seeped through my barriers.

Instead of insulting him back like he wanted, my face fell and I felt my lower lip quiver.

"I know." My voice emerged in a clumsy and hoarse whisper. "You make me forget, but yeah, I know. I'm shit."

Elish's face changed, in the subtle ways his cold countenance would allow. He looked at me with an expression of someone beholding a strange shiny object that had just shot down from outer space. I tried to look away, feeling my lips pull tight and my eyes start to water. I wanted so badly to hide this outward expression of emotion, but he still had my hands.

"Well, this is a new facial expression from you," he murmured curiously. He dropped my hands but before I could even lower them he was wiping the tears from underneath my eyes. He looked fascinated with my reaction, but I only felt my ears go hot. I wanted to get out of there and quickly; this was only making the humiliation worse. "My blade has pierced that armour before, but never have I made you cry like this."

I pushed him away but it was like pushing a boulder; to hammer in the notion that I wasn't going anywhere he put a hand against the wall, trapping me with his body and aura. We were forced to be face-to-face, though I was always looking up at him.

In that moment my chest burned with degradation. I tried to become strong and gathered up the last of my balls. "Just let me go." My voice cracked and broke as I said this, and with that the last of my pride spilled from me.

"Why now? I've said worse to you." Elish narrowed his eyes. "Tell me."

I gritted my teeth, and with that the hinge broke, letting the tears flow freely down my face.

"Fuck you, Elish!" I snapped, balling my fists so tight my nails dug into me. "You'll only laugh at me, taunt me, throw it back at me." I sniffed and finally was able to turn my face from him; I couldn't bear looking at those cold mocking eyes, but for some reason I couldn't bury it any longer.

"Before, it was different... I didn't care how you treated me, or how you degraded and mocked me. You were the asshole chimera and that... I knew that, but now..." Fuck, what was I doing? "The more time that passes the more every single thing you say about me I believe, because you know me now, not like before when I could convince myself you were only tossing insults around to get to me."

I wiped my eyes; the tears kept coming. I was turning into a pussy right in front of him. "When it's just us, you treat me like I might be important to you, then the next moment you treat me like I'm shit. How can I build a thick skin being your cicaro when with one compliment, one kind look... I... dissolve."

Elish was silent. I wished I could read his face but I was turned from him, the will for me to not look at him beating my own curiosity.

"You're my cicaro, nothing changed."

I sniffed. "No, it did change. I – I changed." I ducked under his arm and tried to escape to my bedroom, when he grabbed my wrist with a firm hold. I tried to wrench it away but it was tight.

I stopped, my tears hot against my burning skin. The salvation of the bedroom seemed a million miles away even though it was only down the hall.

"I'm sorry," I croaked.

Elish pulled my wrist and spun me around; he put his hand on my shoulder and gripped it.

"For what?"

"You–know–what."

Elish's eyes burned mine, his face still as beautiful as the day I first saw it in the flickers of the fireplace, almost a year ago now. That cold glow, like fire reflecting against ice, and his smooth voice, like every word was a jewel on his tongue. How that image had burned itself in my mind, a hot brand that had seared the folds of my brain. So many nights I tried to push him from my mind without avail, and now I knew… I was fully in his clutches now. There was no going back, there was no saving my heart, though perhaps there never had been.

"Say it." Each word cut a piece of me away, what was left of it anyway.

My aura shone around me. I looked at the silvers, now an equal contrast to the black. In every way I was becoming his. My aura was even changing, slowly but surely, in front of my eyes.

I shook my head with another sniff, my mind unable to embarrass me further, though my physical responses continued to shame me.

"Say it, Jade."

Say it, Jade. Was it when I realized he had been the one trying to spare me from the stadium death King Silas had arranged for me? Or during one of the times I laid with my head on his shoulder while he played solitaire? Maybe it was even in the greywastes, when he stopped me from walking on my twisted ankle.

I looked at him and saw the beautiful silvers and opals surround him, mixing in and flowing like a crystal river through my own aura. We were a perfect fit, we always had been. This had been a fight I was never meant to win; it was inevitable, and perhaps he knew too. Maybe that's why he saved me from Ares and Siris in the first place.

"I think I love you."

My heart fell about the same time as his mouth downturned, and when he dropped my hand I could feel my heart getting ripped out of my chest.

As Elish turned and wordlessly walked away from me, I felt an incomprehensible pain grip me. A sense of abandonment, of being discarded, and the all-too-familiar gnaw of humiliation.

It would be worse from now on, much worse.

The cold chimera stopped in his doorway and I saw a hand lean up against the frame.

"Are you coming?"

My mouth went dry, and it wasn't until I had to be reminded to breathe that I realized it had dropped open. I walked on jellied legs towards his bedroom, and when I entered it, he closed the door.

Then I was literally swept off my feet. Elish picked me up off of the ground and tossed me onto the bed, before, with expert hands, he undressed me, his lips kissing my neck lightly as he exposed my chest.

Coursing with fervour, I thought my body would explode. I squirmed out of my clothes with his help, and before my pants even hit the floor, I was unbuttoning his shirt and pulling it off him. My chest was aching from my own emotions quaking under the sudden display of passion.

His hands were cool and static, making my skin tense and shudder as he stroked down my stomach to my inner thighs. So soft and delicate, but holding underneath them a power that pulled out every emotion buried deep inside.

My own hands ran themselves down the curves of his sides to his hips, where I rubbed and grabbed them, wishing I could melt him into me, dissolve and bottle him so I could take this feeling with me always.

Oh, how far I had slipped under the chimera's spell, my body once recoiled from him, it once hated his touch, but now I swelled and bloomed.

And as if to highlight my own thoughts, I groaned when his hands brushed between my thighs, not even aware that his body was slipping off me and going lower.

A different kind of rigor raced through my body when I felt his tongue test the tip of my member. I put a hand over my face and groaned, not knowing if I was going to die from the shock or cum from the unreal realization of what he was doing.

Instead my body responded for me. I separated my knees and took in the feeling of his mouth now fully encapsulating my dick, drawing a deep suction that intensified with each movement. My mind was exploding all around me and all I could do was moan and take in every feeling.

The peak came sooner than I wanted, but even if it lasted the entire night it would come sooner than I wanted. The coils inside me were burning hot and dripping lust, and though I held back as long as I could, soon, with a fist full of his hair and my other hand digging the sheets, I came.

I expected him to stop, but in his usual fashion, he didn't even allow me a moment to catch my breath. Introducing a finger inside of me, he continued to suck and lick the head, stray bits of cum falling onto his tongue before disappearing into his mouth.

The flesh of my penis and the crown especially was swollen and sensitive, but the chimera's tongue broke right through my twitches and gasps and brought my half-erect shaft to fully hard. This time with more of a squirming squeal to my lips than a moan, the tongue teased and taunted the soft skin, before he put his mouth over it once more. Wanting more, always wanting more.

I did nothing to stifle my escalating groans. No chains of restraint held me back tonight, no biting of my lips and no thrashing of my body to escape the automatic response that his touch drew from me. Tonight something was happening, and I wondered if he was as caught up into it as I was.

The next climax curled my toes, and made me pull on his hair to try and stem the overwhelming pleasure that took me. This time, with my body panting and heaving, he released my dick from his mouth and withdrew the two fingers that had been digging into me.

I positioned myself for him to take me, no forceful jerking of my leg back, no shackling the cuffs on my wrists and legs; with my own strength, I moved my knees back and drew his face down to my lips.

With our lips locked, he grabbed the lube always resting on the night table, and with a bite of the side of my lip, he pressed himself against my opening. I groaned before gasping in pain as he bit through my lip, at the same time breaking into me and sinking himself up to the hilt. I chewed my lip harder to encourage the blood for him, and as he rocked his hips back and forth into me, I let him lick and draw the blood out.

I loved the burning and I loved the pain. I kissed him deeply and sucked on his tongue, my mouth filling with copper which was soon licked and taken in by Elish's own tongue. There was no place in the world I would rather be than here, being devoured by him, taken by him and claimed by him.

Who was I in that moment? I played his tongue with mine, and tasted my own cum in his mouth. Was I his cicaro? Or was I becoming more to him too? One thing I knew for sure, I was no longer a Morosian; I wasn't a slumrat, and if I was, I was in name and blood only. The person who tucked himself into the corner of the fireplace had disappeared into the shadows, burned alive for someone different to resurrect.

I had no answers, I had no right to ask questions. Elish would tell me who I was; he knew better than I ever had.

I noticed his breathing quicken, and in response I choreographed my hips to intensify his own pleasure. When I knew he was close, I pulled my lips away and welcomed his teeth into my neck. The chimera love bites that everyone seemed to notice, from Garrett, to Greyson back in Aras, the physical proof that you had breached their walls and had captured their hearts if only for a second.

"No... bite me." I opened my eyes, and saw his head was bowed, his chin resting loosely against my head. He breathed out a light moan and shut his eyes before saying it quicker this time. "Bite me."

I put my left arm around his neck and drew him in closer, then, without hesitation, I clamped down on his neck and sunk my teeth into him.

My body shuddered with emotion as I heard his unhinged gasps break through his steeled steadfast. I bit harder and felt his own blood start to wet my lips and mouth, filling my brain with fireworks as the cinnamon-like taste coated my tongue. It set my mind alight, it was as though I was tasting the liquid of the gods and I wanted more.

Drawing it in, I enjoyed the taste as much as I did his moans, indulging myself and drinking it in in all ways. I didn't release until I felt the last quake leave his body.

My head hit the pillow and I watched his skin, silvery blue, drip black spots onto my face, surrounded by his blond hair. My chest heaved with his but our bodies stayed joined, our auras a luminous candescence around us.

Then a hand on my cheek, drawing my face upwards. I looked up and into his eyes.

"Your aura… it is violet and silver." I stared up at him and it took me a moment to realize how mind blowing that admission from him was.

"You can see it?"

Elish stared at me intently. "I always could, but in your eyes' reflections only."

Leaving me with a feeling of emptiness, he withdrew himself from me and laid down on his back. But channelling Elish's own chimera nature, I crawled on top of him and straddled him. When he didn't push me off, only looking at me with a curious smirk, I picked up his still hard dick and pushed it inside of me. Then, with a sharp intake of breath, I leaned down and rested my forehead against his.

I started riding him, my body rising up and down on his, and seemingly singing with joy as he put his hands on my hips to help increase my thrusts. I bit my lip again and leaned down to kiss him.

When I broke away from his lips, I realized his eyes were still looking intently at mine, glossy amethyst with a glint in them that only drove me deeper into his grasp.

"It's turning to mine, isn't it?" Elish murmured.

I nodded, and when his hands braced themselves against my shoulders, I let him support me as I continued to ride him. "It's never happened before, so I don't know if it will fully… I just know it used to have black in it, and it's almost gone."

Elish nodded but didn't say another word; a moment later he lowered me onto him and started pushing himself into me, my body still straddling him but fully in his warm embrace.

With no more words exchanged, time around us, as it most often did when we were together, became meaningless. The only indication of a passage of time was every orgasm we shared together, never moving from our positions, only indulging in the occasional kiss and playful nip.

When my head was swimming and my body exhausted like it had

never been before, Elish withdrew himself from me a second time and leaned his head back with a final gasp. Unable to move I waited for him to roll me off of his body; I laid my head against his chest but he didn't move.

Still no words were exchanged, and not another kiss shared. I listened to his heartbeat through his chest, and felt a swell of happiness as he put a hand on my head and brushed my bangs from my eyes.

Then at rest, my body no longer having to fight fatigue, I fell asleep still naked and on top of him, his soft skin warm against my own, clammy and flushed with heat. It was the last sensation I felt.

I woke up sweaty and sticky and alone which wasn't an odd thing. Sometimes when the mood struck him Elish would jab me awake and tell me to make coffee if he had risen before Luca, but most of the time Luca woke up early and had everything ready.

With a stifled yawn I went into the shower, still damp from my master using it before me. I washed myself and put on my pet clothes – a skin tight mesh t-shirt with slashed sleeves and tight black jeans with laces going up the sides.

I walked into the living room and rolled my eyes at the sight. Garrett was passed out on the couch wearing Luca's cat ears with the sengil leaning against him. Both of them were naked with only Luca's blue quilt covering their shame. It looked like we weren't the only ones busy last night. They would both probably wake up hung-over as hell and hopefully embarrassed.

Well, whatever. I called in some breakfast though I left out Elish's breakfast since it looked like he had gone off to work. It was nice of him not to drag me out of bed to go with him but I wished he had; I kind of wanted to be near him today.

I sat down with a cup of coffee, sitting in Elish's grey chair with the couch in front of me, almost like those two were my own personal television.

I eyed a pack of cigarettes that Garrett had obviously thrown down while he was defiling our sengil and lit one. I crossed my legs and watched as the president of Skytech lay naked with Luca's black cat ears resting on his head.

I wished I had a camera.

The food came with a light rap on the door, not loud enough to wake up the two naked men on the couch.

I opened up my cardboard container. Inside were eggs fried with potato, meat, and onion with two pieces of toast on the side. I sat their containers down on the coffee table and took a fork to my breakfast, my other hand holding the cup of coffee.

I took a drag from the cigarette, the blue ember lighting up and fading as my lungs filled with the smoke. When I inhaled I saw the first stir of wakefulness from Garrett.

The president blinked and squinted at me. I watched the loose fabrics of his mind start to mesh back together and when they finally brought him back to his situation his green eyes widened.

I grinned and raised my coffee cup to him before taking another drag from the smoke. "Good morning, Master Garrett. Did we have a fun night?"

Garrett stared at me through half-asleep eyes before he put a hand to his head. "If you even knew how much you looked like Elish in this moment you would have a heart attack."

The corner of my mouth rose and I smirked at him, before saying in the coldest voice I could muster, "Indeed."

Elish's brother gave me a look, before a sigh came to his lips. "One day I will have one like you." He looked down at Luca who was now sitting up, his blond hair tussled and sticking up in all directions; his eyes were dull and puffy and he looked incredibly sick. A moment later he rose and sprinted off to the bathroom as naked as a jaybird. We both heard him throw up.

Garrett leaned over and nudged the green pill with his finger with a chuckle. "I told him to take that before he passed out, he must've forgotten. He'll be sick all day now."

I nudged his food towards him and finished the last few bites of mine. "So? Did you kill him?"

Garrett scratched his head and looked around, before leaning over and grabbing his blue button-down. He started putting it on and as he buttoned each button I saw the blood splatters on the breast of the shirt.

"Yep, it looks like I did. Well, I hope Saul took care of the clean-up. I don't remember a bloody thing," Garrett laughed with the same lighthearted air that always seemed to brighten up the room. I hoped eventually Reno would find himself in Skyfall; Garrett deserved a companion. Though as I was having these nice thoughts about him Garrett was in the process of picking off of his shirt what I think might've been a piece of scalp.

Luca came back with his sengil uniform on, looking green. He was holding a coffee cup in his shaking hands, looking like he was getting over cholera.

"Hey, Luca!" I said loudly, drinking in his obvious wince at the octave of my voice. "Do you even remember getting laid last night?"

Luca, calm, patient Luca gave me a pained look and popped several aspirin into his mouth. "Everything I remember, this headache I'd wish to forget, Master Jade."

I laughed and pushed his own food towards him before leaning back into the couch with the cigarette. Garrett rose, taking the blanket with him, mumbling something about me being the picture of Elish. He disappeared into the bathroom before emerging half an hour later dressed but still with a fatigued look on his face.

"I'm going to slink off and try and get home before someone I know spots me. I wish the two of you a good day." Garrett took the coffee cup with him and left with a quiet shut of the apartment door.

The rest of the day was spent with Luca looking pitiful on the couch, and me in such good spirits over what had happened the previous night that I decided to take on his duties and clean the apartment. I needed a way to burn my energy off anyway, and keep my mind from going to places that would only get me into trouble.

I wished saying that I loved him out loud would've brought me some sort of bitter regret, but his reaction afterwards had only shown me he had liked what he'd heard.

Maybe one day I wouldn't just be his cicaro…

I wiped the counter of the kitchen a bit harder; it was thoughts like this I was trying to dash from my mind. They would only get into trouble. I knew Elish, and I knew he would never go for something like that. He wouldn't relinquish an inch of his power, or his hold over me. Being a boyfriend or a lover or anything would be downgrading his control. With the exception of Silas, Elish had to rule everyone in his life with an iron fist, and that was just how it had to be.

I was okay with that, there really wasn't anything more I wanted. I knew him well; I had been glued to him for a year now. The thought of ever being a boyfriend or being anything but his slave was so far out of the realm of possibility, it was laughable.

When it came down to it, I was happy being his cicaro outside of his bedroom, and his lover inside of it.

My eyes kept watching the clock; we ordered lunch and then dinner.

I sat at the set table and waited for him to come home; there had been only a handful of times that we hadn't had dinner together, usually only when he was meeting with Silas and I had warning when those days were coming, usually because he was in a foul mood.

Luca noticed my apprehension and sat down at the table beside me, still sick but looking a little less pale and sickly. He waited with me in silence as the clock ticked past seven.

When it hit eight o'clock my impatience finally got the best of me. I grabbed my remote phone and dialled Elish's number to at least see if we could eat without him. I was hungry from cleaning all day and also hungry from overthinking every moment from last night.

My heart dropped when it started ringing. I glanced over at Luca and saw a look of worry on his face as well. It went to Elish's voicemail and I didn't leave a message; he knew my number and he would know why I was calling.

Where was he? I tried not to worry like a distraught woman but the fear was already starting to eat at my stomach. I looked at Luca for help but the worried look was all that I got from him.

"It is late enough... let us eat," Luca said quietly; his eyes shifted towards the door. "Master Elish will be eating on his own if he isn't here."

I nodded and reluctantly started opening up cardboard containers.

We ate in silence, both coming up with our own ways to deal with the building apprehension. I kept telling myself I was being stupid, he was an immortal chimera and nothing bad could've happened to him... but considering what went on last night, it stung me a bit more than it would have under normal circumstances.

The evening dragged on, and though Luca had eventually gotten up to tidy our plates and finish the cleaning I hadn't gotten around to, I stayed sitting at the dining room table. The food was sitting badly in my gut, drawing out nausea in me that had me almost running to the bathroom.

This... this was out of character. My mind kept contradicting my own emotions, telling me at one moment that I was stupid, considering Elish was the personification of strength and power, and telling me the next moment that he would never come back.

If it had been any other day... I wouldn't care, but now...

I wrung my hands over the cloth napkin and stared at a bouquet of purple flowers he had received three days ago.

Now I just sat there, uneasy, wishing he would walk through those doors.

Finally when midnight came around and I still hadn't moved, I called the only chimera I could think of.

"Hello?" Garrett sounded like he was at another bar; I could hear music and talking behind him.

"Elish never came home; he was gone when I woke up and he's still gone." The tone of my voice climbed with every word I spoke, like saying it out loud only made it more of a reality.

There was a pause. "Hm," Garrett said, "alright then... well, let me make some calls and if something's wrong I will call you back."

I sighed, feeling some relief that I had at least one chimera on my side. "Thanks, Master Garrett."

I made my way to the couch and sunk into it, my eyes still going to the apartment door every few moments.

My gut twisted and formed a pit inside my stomach, leaking bitter fluid that only fuelled the anxiety in me. There was something wrong and I knew it.

I fell asleep on the couch, my Game Boy humming its midi music as it lay forgotten on my chest.

My dreams were nightmares without Elish, but I didn't wake up. I slept through the horrors only because I couldn't escape them. They spread their poisonous seed throughout my brain, growing abscessing boils and harvesting their sores only to plant them once more.

I awoke to a light hand on my cheek.

My heart jumped as I felt his touch, but when I saw his face my happiness turned to dread.

His face was calm dignity, but his eyes were made from ice, void of any of the warmth I had managed to draw out of them. There was something different... something had changed.

"Come..." Elish whispered, before he rose and turned from me.

I got up, my heart a hammering drum in my chest, beating a fresh wave of anxiety through me. "Where are we going?"

"Come, Jade," was all he said.

I got into the back seat of the car first, and noticed Elish was holding a black duffle bag in one of his hands; he slammed it into the trunk and, to my shock, he got into the driver's seat. I had never seen him drive before; we always had someone do that for us. I made a move to open the door, to get into the passenger front seat, but before I could get my hand on the handle he was putting the car into drive.

"Where are we going?" I asked quietly.

Elish didn't answer, but I saw his gloved hands grip the steering wheel harder.

This only drove the anxiety already flooding my body; I swallowed hard and looked out the window for help. We were on the main road, but after a few moments we turned towards the concrete walls separating Skyland and Eros. We crossed the border and Elish took us towards the looming walls that divided Eros and Nyx.

There was only one place we could be going. My mouth went dry and I swallowed through a parched sandpaper throat, my hands trembling as I gripped the back of Elish's seat. I dug my fingers in, hearing the sound of ripping leather as my nails pierced the seat covering.

This couldn't be... it didn't make sense.

He... he was taking me back to Moros.

He got out of the car; it was parked beside an old barely used gate separating Moros from Nyx. I stayed where I was, in the backseat of the car, staring at the slashes I had made in the upholstery. I heard the trunk open and the sound of the duffle bag being tossed onto the ground.

"Get out of the car, Jade." His voice was cold, black ice on an abandoned road.

I stayed where I was, and a moment later the car door opened.

He asked me again, and I shook my head no.

When his hands grabbed underneath my arm, I jerked them away. In response, he snatched me with both hands and pulled me out of the car. I struggled to get on my feet and when I stood he let go and started walking back to the car.

Desperation coursed through me, mixed in with the confusion I felt and the bewilderment. What was going on?

Then despair replaced itself with anger; a burning started in my chest and spread rapidly through every muscle in my body, ending with a surge of frustrated hatred that brought embers to my tongue.

I spit the coals at him. "Scared are we?" I said, in a tone he had used with me many times.

Elish froze, his hand on the hood of his car. "Watch yourself, Cicaro."

I gritted my teeth before I grabbed my collar and unlatched it. "I am obviously not your fucking cicaro, you chimera scumbag." With the last word I pulled off the collar and tossed it at him; it hit the side of the car with a clang before falling onto the ground.

My neck felt cold… it was bare… it shouldn't be bare. I put my hands up to my neck, feeling my eyes well. Moros wasn't bringing me the warm feeling of home – that collar had brought it. Why was he leaving me in this place? My home was with him, didn't he know that?

Elish bent down and picked up the collar, he ran his hands over the soft leather, in a tender fashion I had seen last night, before his hand retracted like it had suddenly become hot. "I put your things in the bag, and some money to keep you from starving this winter. Be happy I did that."

The tears came as he spoke; I couldn't hold them back any more than I could hold back my own heart breaking in half. "Why are you doing this?"

There was a pause; he put the collar on the car's dash and turned to me.

His eyes were burning in a cold and cruel gaze that stabbed me like two icicles. His face held no emotion, no remorse. Not a single strand of hair was out of line, not a single crease on his face; he was the picture of frozen beauty.

In a resounding air of confidence and grace he tipped his chin up in a way that always made me think he wanted to literally look down his nose at me. He sneered at me like he was smelling something awful and spoke in the same tone.

"You fell in love with me, which means I won the game I set out for myself. Did you really think I would soil my image any more by keeping you around longer than necessary? You're as stupid as you are weak. Get out of my sight."

I thought I had been hit, but in reality I had only fallen to my knees. My face dropped and I stared at him with shock, trying to unweave his words to make them make sense, because they weren't registering in my brain.

"W-what?" My strangled voice broke.

Elish glared down at me, and I watched the corners of his mouth turn up. "It took less time than I thought; you really do have a weak mind, curling up to any man who strokes you even if he takes joy beating you like the dog you are. Just be happy I didn't kill you, gutter rat."

My lower lip quivered, but I was frozen on my knees. Only my eyes could move but even they were fixed on him. "Master?"

When he got into the car, I found my feet and my strength; out of desperation I ran to the car and put my hand out to stop the door from closing. Biting through the pain, I grabbed his shoulder and tried to pull him out.

"NO!" I screamed, tightening my grip and pulling on the fabric. "You're fucking lying! You're lying!"

He stared forward until he'd had enough. I watched him reach into the overcoat resting on the passenger side and pull out the whip.

I shrunk back and cowered down, my arms automatically shielding my head. I squinted and blinked, tears running down my cheeks and falling onto the grey ground below.

When he didn't hit me, I looked through my hands at him, and shook as I saw the violet embers burn with a hatred I didn't understand. There was nothing about him in that moment I understood, nothing made sense to me. Elish was an enigma of his own, a perfect deity that held in him many layers, but this betrayed all of him, every part of him I thought I knew.

But as I stared I noticed something. "The bite mark I left on you –" I croaked, my voice hoarse and raspy. "– it's gone, you died. Silas killed you didn't he?"

I screamed as the whip's sharp tongue licked my arm, and continued to scream as he laid blow after blow on me, so many of them I lost track of the world around me, only sharp stinging pain and the smell of my own blood filling my head.

When he stopped, I could hear him breathing. I lay on the cold ground trembling and shaking.

There was a scraping of boots as he turned to walk away, and with a blink back of tears I said quietly,

"Read to me?"

He paused for a moment, but it was brief. Soon the boot steps could be heard again and a second later, the slamming of a car door.

I watched the tail lights leave, and a kick of dust and exhaust. The motor faded, the lights of the car dimmed, and I was alone.

Back in Moros.

CHAPTER 19

They stared at me, the same dead eyes, the same sunken-in, gaunt faces from missing meals their entire lives. Sullen ghouls, walking zombies, my former people gawked and pointed at the former thief. Someone who was a lot like them… though I had known what living was. I'd had a life outside of this hollowed out corpse of a district.

It had been a year, but where else could I go? With my bloodied arm clenching my chest and the other carrying the duffle bag, I walked with my tail between my legs to my old apartment.

My mind was covered in a nauseas haze; every movement I made was robotic, only my muscle memory carrying me down my old haunts towards what had once been my home. A place where I dreamed of, and had missed for so long.

Now it was… I don't know; I didn't know what it was. All my thoughts were focused on what the hell had just happened.

I touched my neck, my bare neck, before dropping my arm to my side. Why did he just free me? Was he telling the truth?

My feelings welled up again as I remembered that Elish had never been one to lie. He held himself to a higher standard and saw liars as people who had something to prove. Elish had nothing to prove and never spared anyone's feelings.

The vultures continued to watch me, peering through alleyways and craning their necks as they walked past, whispering and snickering as I left a trail of my own shame behind me. I passed the café and the old bar.

Nothing had changed here... nothing, everything was the same, Moros never changed.

I looked behind me, as if thinking in this dream I could see Olympus over my shoulder, but all I saw were empty buildings with windows black and without life or warmth, rust and black mildew dripping from their gaping openings like tears.

Everything was so grey and dark, so dismal. I inhaled the stink of rotting garbage and the sour smell of decaying wood. I was once used to this smell, now it made my nose want to wrinkle. Why did it have to feel so alien to me? I felt ashamed at my own distaste for this place. I wanted to welcome it with open arms and a warm homecoming, but that had been thrown away the moment I walked through the walls. I now only saw myself as someone who had escaped from the slums for new and better things, only to come back a beaten coward, chewed up and spit out by the world I had found.

Chewed up and spit out by Elish Dekker.

Yeah, that was it.

My feet scraped the concrete, and caught in the chunks missing from the cracked and broken sidewalk. Bikes and motorcycles passed me and foot traffic, but unlike Skyland there were no cars. No one here could afford them.

My eyes burned and I blinked away the wetness, taking a glance at the first whip blow from Elish. It had left a thin red mark on the arm I had been shielding my face with.

A tear drop fell onto it, but I couldn't feel the sting.

I heard someone say *shit*, but he didn't talk to me. I thought I recognized the voice but my eyes only watched my boots. Boots that I could never wear again, because I knew I would be robbed if any Morosian saw them. I knew this because I would've robbed them myself.

I turned a corner, and that was when I heard his voice. I knew I would never forget his voice, even though it had been almost a year since that brief glimpse in the park.

"Jade?" he choked.

I looked up, my head a heavy weight. I stared at him, almost not believing he still existed. My mind had had to cut off any thought that he could still be a part of my life, to protect my own emotions.

But there he was, looking at me with a shocked and anguished expression.

Kerres looked older and I knew I did too. His bright crimson hair was longer, and he had more earrings in his ears; he was wearing blue jeans and a clean purple shirt underneath a member's only jacket.

Then he disappeared, because he was taking me into his arms.

He grabbed me and squeezed me tight. I heard a strangled sob come to his lips and a force from his embrace that gripped me so hard I thought my ribs would break.

"What did he do to you? Oh, baby… what did he do?" Kerres cried. He pulled back and reached a hand out to brush along one of the lacerations, before he pulled back and gently rubbed my hand.

"Did he free you? Did he free you, J?" Kerres's voice was strangled and breaking, he looked behind me and to all sides as if expecting to see Elish not far behind.

But he was gone…

Elish was gone.

"Yeah." My voice broke too as Kerres put his arms back around me. I knew he thought it was from relief, but my voice was failing me because I couldn't hold back the despair.

Elish had left me.

I could feel Kerres's breath on my shoulder, and the sniffing near my ear as he shed tears of relief. When he had gathered himself, he pulled back and put a hand on my cheek.

I stared at him, not knowing what to say, or do. He smiled through wet cheeks and gently took my duffle bag from me.

"You – you're so stunned, baby. Come with me… I'm so glad Fiere saw you before you came to my apartment. I moved. I got a better one for us, two bedrooms too. Come with me, J. I've been waiting for you, for a long time."

You have? He watched me for a moment, for any reaction but my lips only pursed in response to his warm voice. Had he really been waiting for me all this time? I felt a surge of guilt, because I had stopped waiting for him; I hadn't had a choice.

Elish said I was his forever… that he would temper me and make me strong even if it took the rest of my life.

Kerres led me by the hand, gently as if he was directing a lost child, his other arm holding my duffle bag; always a warmth to him that showed through his seafoam aura, light greens and blues.

Oil against my own.

What did it matter? Elish and my aura had been a perfect combination and look where it had got me? I didn't care. I snapped my mind out of my aura reading and pushed the ability back into my head. That would be the last time I used it, it had never brought me any good anyway. Fuck it, fuck him, and fuck everyone.

While we walked Kerres fell back so he was walking beside me, the direction we were heading told me which apartments he lived in now. The nicest ones in Moros, still shit, and less than shit considering where I had just come from, but the best ones Moros had to offer.

Coaltowers loomed over us, surrounded by a chain-link fence topped with razor wire and with an iron gate that had video cameras always watching. You paid for that protection, for the security that a crackhead wouldn't break into your apartment and steal you stuff, or people like me, or who I had been.

Kerres opened the gate and let me through first, before closing the rusted hinges with a small click. My mouth down turned. The sound of a gate closing behind me bringing back my first memories of meeting Elish.

Why, Master?

My hand went back to my neck, it was still gone... still bare.

"Jade?" Kerres whispered. He squeezed my hand which brought me partially back to reality. "Did he hit you on the head?" His voice was sweet and not at all patronizing. He wanted to know why I wasn't jumping up and down for joy, maybe?

We walked past a row of green bushes, being held back by a concrete barrier that reached my knees. To my right, past Kerres, was a small stretch of dirt that had a green mist of grass, too shabby and patched for it to make this place look anywhere near beautiful. It was the same bleak grey; the only colour was from where a chimera had touched it, from where a member of the Dekker family had decided to throw a couple of tokens to make something look a little less dismal, usually trying to win favours from the public when public opinion dropped.

This place was so cold... it made Aras seem warm and inviting,

Moros was just saturated under this imposing cloud of constricting gloom. I felt claustrophobic just being here. I wanted to go home.

"Jade?" Kerres whispered. We were inside the building now, walking up stairs. "Are you okay?"

I realized I never answered his question before, fixing my eyes on my boots to make sure I didn't fall.

I gave him a nod. "I just hurt."

He lived on the third floor now; he fumbled with the keys before he opened the door. I walked in and as the door closed behind me I stood there, not really knowing what was supposed to happen now.

Same furniture, but the couch was newer, the living room was larger than it had been in our old apartment and the kitchen had cabinets without mould on them. Everything was painted with old blue paint that changed shade according to which wall it was on, and on the carpet was a stained brown shag rug.

The place smelled like beer and cigarettes, which… which kind of reminded me of my old life.

"Where did he hurt you, hunny? Anywhere else?" Kerres sat me down on the couch and started trying to take my shirt off. I recoiled a bit and he drew his hands away.

"Do – do you want me to leave you alone?"

Who asks that? Elish took what he wanted when he wanted it, there was never a question of whether I wanted to be touched. If I resisted him he just grabbed me harder or hurt me until he beat the resistance out of me.

My eyes flickered to Kerres's. I stared at him, trying to force my brain to calm down and remember this man who had taken care of me since I was nine. I took a deep breath and shook my head, reminding myself again and again that this wasn't Elish; I wasn't a cicaro anymore.

"No, I'm… no, I'm sorry," I said taking my own shirt off. I wiped my face with my hands and inhaled another deep breath of stale cigarettes and booze. "He whipped me; I don't know how bad it is. I didn't look."

Kerres checked out my back and my chest. I saw fresh tears which he wiped away as soon as they formed. "You have so many on you, and handprints… he really hurt you. You…you've gone through a lot haven't you?"

You have no idea.

"I had been having them laser removed," I said through a dead voice. "It was a lot worse before I started getting treatments four times a week."

Kerres swore. For a moment he just stared, before he put his arms around me again and held me tight, more chokes breaking from his lips. I heard him sniff and whisper into my ear, "It doesn't matter, you're safe now."

My own chest tightened from his emotion radiating through me. I didn't know what to say, so I only murmured into his ear, "You waited for me?"

Kerres pulled back and looked at me in sober disbelief. "Of course I did... it was my fault, I got myself arrested. I know he used me as blackmail, he fucking told me. I... it was my fault; I'm so sorry, Jade. Please forgive me."

Forgive you? He was stuck in something that had happened a year ago; he was freeze-framed in that day and here I was... a different person, a year into the future where Jade the Morosian had died, and Jade the cicaro had sprung forth.

But Elish had killed that cicaro. My hand clutched my throat again and I blinked away the burning in my eyes.

Kerres rose and came back with the same first aid kit he had mended me with last year and started cleaning my wounds.

"I can't believe he just let you go, I was so scared he was going to kill you." Kerres's voice wobbled with emotion. I saw the wet cotton he was stroking against my lacerations come back rosy pink. "I had heard so many rumours, I – I heard what happened at Stadium, that you killed Ares and Siris. I wish I would've saw I –" he sniffed, "– I would've cheered the loudest.

"I can't believe he let your mom get killed; that's a low only a chimera could come up with."

I chewed on my lip, scabbed over from that night a few days ago, from the intense session of love making. It felt like it had happened years ago, how could such a switch happen in such a short amount of time? I didn't understand.

It had to have been Silas, right? But... Silas had threatened before and he still kept me. What had changed?

My face dissolved, and in response Kerres hugged me again. "It's okay; you're away from him now."

It was almost funny, in a weird ironic way. My ex… my boyfriend thought this was because of my captivity; what would he say if I told him it was because I loved Elish? And in response he broke my heart into a thousand pieces. Kerres would probably start hitting me. How could he fathom that I had grown so attached to my beautiful captor?

Kerres pulled away and gently wrapped some white gauze around the worst of the whip marks, the first one on my forearm. When he was done he rubbed it and gave me a smile.

"I know you're still in shock, I am too, but it's alright, you don't have to talk or do anything, just… get used to being back home. You're home now, that's all that matters, J."

Elish never called me J, or Luca, or Garrett… I was just Jade, or cicaro, or pet, or gutter rat…

"My poor baby, you're… it's like you're in shock."

I am.

"It's over now."

I know.

"He's gone."

I know.

There was a coldness that stuck to my bones, that no amount of warmth could fill in the slums of Moros. I watched as Kerres worked on my wounds, trying to give me false reassurances that rolled off of me like oil off of water. They meant nothing. His words were just background audio meant to fill dead air, in a desperate attempt to bring the old Jade back. But I had been trained to not react, not bite back, be tame, be sweet, be obedient.

"There… it looks like the ones on your back aren't that bad. I just cleaned them."

Not as bad? Was it hard for Elish to beat me one last time? Or did his arm just get tired?

I heard Kerres sigh, before he handed me a blanket that had been folded on the couch, I put it over me and curled up.

"I know you've been through hell over the past year, but I promise… I make okay money now; I can take care of you. It will be just like before but better, J. Take all the time you need. I know you'll get yourself back."

What if this is me? What if this is just the person I am from now on? Will you still love me?

I curled up tight and sniffed; my brain was tired and my mind was tired. I looked at the old television showing a TV show I used to watch with Luca when I wasn't out on errands.

Kerres stroked my side in a caring manner, and I heard him whisper under his breath. "I'm just happy you're home."

Home.

Was this all really a game for you, Elish? Were you really just like your king and creator?

The more his face bore down on me, taking over every thought and memory I had... the more I feared I had been taken for a fool the entire time.

I held the grey pillow to my chest; it smelled of Kerres but I was used to it now. Still for some reason I had to hold something when Kerres was at work; it felt odd sleeping without Elish beside me.

No... no... NO! I gritted my teeth and threw the pillow down on the bed, before, with a grinding of my molars, punching it hard several times.

Anger... today would be an angry day.

I screamed from my own despair and laid a punch right into the wooden frame of the bed, before recoiling back and hitting it again.

He fucking played me, fuck him! FUCK HIM! I hit the bed frame again before throwing my covers off in a rage.

My eyes burned and I closed them, refusing to watch the tears fall to the dirty carpet. Only in Moros was I finally allowed to hide my shame. Elish couldn't see me now.

It had been two weeks.

Every day since I had gotten back was different, but it was only a different-coloured hat on my head, in reality it was all the same just different feelings got drawn out of me.

Sometimes I woke up so depressed and sad I didn't get out of bed. Somedays I woke up feeling like I might be okay. Today I had woken up pissed off and angry, wishing nothing but to take that fucking blond shit in my hands and squeezing the life out of him.

FUCK HIM!

The tears leaked through my eyes, tears of anger, my mind weaving through my brain like a serpent, touching its poison and leaving behind it infected flesh. It was a part of the dark cloud that never left my head; I fed it with my own acidic thoughts.

I loved him… and he had played me like a violin, plucking each string to find out which sound he could make me make, which emotion he could draw out of me. When he was done, when he had drawn the last sound from his rosined bow, he had tossed me back to where I came from, like a puppy that had grown into a dog and was no longer cute.

In all respects I had been fooled; the star of a cruel joke.

But this is what chimeras do, you knew this. They play games for their own amusement, especially the bored immortals. Jade, you fucking retard, it's all your fault.

ALL YOUR FAULT!

"Fuck!" I screamed at the top of my lungs. I walked over to the black duffle bag and kicked it viciously. I hadn't even had the balls to open it, and the more days that ticked by the more I didn't want to. It would only tear open these rotting wounds, or pour more bacteria into them.

"Jade?" Kerres was standing in the doorway, knowing better than to interrupt me when I was raging. I had almost gotten physical with him when he had tried to restrain me the first time. Now he just let me bash things. "I got some Valium–"

What… drugs?

I wasn't allowed to take drugs unless…

Right, it didn't matter anymore, because that blond piece of shit couldn't tell me not to take drugs or smoke. I nodded and continued to stare at the floor. Kerres had only smoked around me; I hadn't seen him take any drugs but I didn't want to ask him if he'd quit. I had been forced to quit under my master's iron fist.

I held out my hand and K popped three pills into my palm. I swallowed them with a glass of brown-tinged water. It had been too long… way too long.

"I wish you would talk to me, J." Kerres's voice was high and pleading, I felt the bed shift as he sat down beside me. His smell mixed in with the scent of old musty blankets. "It would make you feel better."

I swirled the glass, my shoulders still trembling. I was used to his presence now, enough to not recoil when he came near me. Though I didn't like his touch unless I was half-asleep in bed, then I clung to him and I didn't let go until morning.

But not for the reason he thought.

"What do you want to know, Kerres?" I said with no life behind my own words. That was my voice now; Elish had even taken the strength of my own words. He had left nothing for me and my boyfriend to pick over but an empty shell of a body, its soul sucked out like marrow from a bone.

Kerres hand rested on my knee, rough from working them relentlessly since we had left Edgeview. "I want to know how I can bring you back… it's been two weeks, J. All you do is sleep and go through all those moods. I want to help."

"What else am I supposed to do?" I whispered. My life was meaningless now; all I had in my future was getting a shitty job and waiting to die.

In Skyland with Elish… I might not have known my future but I knew it was with him. I knew I could see the greywastes, learn more writing skills and instruments, learn how to use a rifle better and continue laser treatments. Learn who Jade was, not just struggle to survive each day.

It was better than rotting away in the slums, worthless and starving.

No… it was all a lie, it was all a cruel joke. Just to give me a taste of the outside world, so when I went back to this shitty slum I wouldn't be ignorant to how good living could be. How exciting and thrilling. Not just my life in general, but what it was like to experience real sex, real passionate, thirsting love. Real emotions, not just the dull grey I experienced here.

"Live?" Kerres rubbed my knee; his voice was so gentle, like he was coaxing a kitten from under a garbage bin. "Just… live, Jade. You're not living, you're just existing. I want my J back."

J died, Kerres. Now you just had Jade the pissed off Morosian, who wanted nothing more than to torture and kill Elish Dekker in the most painful way possible. To somehow pay him back for what he had done to me.

I loved him.

No… NO… NO! FUCK HIM!

Kerres leaned his head against my shoulder, though I was seething again, but as we sat still together the Valium started to kick in.

I sighed and felt my chest loosen; Kerres noticed and kissed my cheek. "Feeling a bit better?"

The tension drained from my shoulders, calling out my little friend called drug high. I felt myself able to nod and say in a quiet voice, "Yeah."

His hands massaged my shoulders, clumsy big hands I wasn't used to. The only hands that had touched me in Skyland were Luca's small and delicate little paws and Elish's gentle long fingers that brought on their tips multiple sensations.

With the drugs sinking in, each breath brought its own burst of relief; a dangerous feeling that my inner Morosian instincts told me to exploit.

"I forgot how good drugs were," I whispered. I felt my own head lean back exposing more of my neck to him. He lovingly rubbed my shoulders and my back with gentle variants of pressure.

"I'll buy you some if you think it would help; he made you quit I guess?"

I nodded. "I couldn't even smoke, except when Garrett came around. A drink or two in the evening with him, that was all." Our matching glasses of wine that sat on beaded coasters, purple and grey beads that matched the décor around us. We would drink and play solitaire or –

SHUT UP, JADE! I shut my eyes tight and beat the thought from my mind. It was fake, it had all been fake. He was playing the game the whole time, even our evenings of mocking banter and insulting nips back and forth had been pre-planned. It was all fucking fake.

It wasn't fake to me, my feelings had been real. The hardest blow of them all, what a laugh the chimeras were probably having right now. Elish beat and humiliated the Morosian boy and he still managed to make him love him.

My stomach soured. I shifted away from Kerres's touch and laid back down in bed.

"Drugs would be nice," I whispered, before my eyes shot to the duffle bag. He had told me he had given me some money to survive the winter… maybe it was time to open it.

I drifted off with the Valium coating its magic on my brain; I didn't wake up until late in the evening.

Groggy, and with a head full of lightning storms, I opened my eyes, hearing a group of people talking in the living room. I recognized their voices, they were my friends.

Inside the bedroom was dark, a little cave hidden around a bustling city of laughing voices and the normal conversation that comes along when men cluster together for booze and drugs. I debated staying asleep in the cave, but tonight I didn't feel like being alone. I was seeping self-derision and hatred for that chimera and perhaps some drugs and booze was what I needed.

I turned on the light in the bedroom and wiped my face down with a napkin soaked with water. With a comb through my hair I decided I looked acceptable. I had black circles underneath my sun-fearing eyes and I looked like shit – it probably would just help me blend in more.

Leaving the lurking shadows behind in Kerres's bedroom, I walked down the hallway and into the shabby living room.

A hush fell on the group of men when my silhouette darkened the hallway. The eyes of Fiere, Tate, Pete, two guys I didn't know and Kerres, fell on me.

"Jade..." Kerres sounded surprised. He got up with a smile and grabbed my hand so I could sit beside him. "I thought you were asleep. Sorry if we woke you."

"Aww, he's such a little suck!" Tate raised a beer at me and tried to chink it against my arm as I was led by Kerres. The others started greeting me in fast succession, offering me beer, cocaine, and cigarettes.

I withdrew myself to the furthest corner of the room, even though Kerres had been sitting on a chair next to Tate. Kerres didn't protest, he dragged the chair beside me and rubbed my arms.

"Want a drink, love?" he asked sweetly. I nodded and he jumped up and grabbed me one of the piss water Morosian beers. I took it and tried not to make a face at my first drink.

This was my life now... I sighed and hated myself even more. Fucking pampered little cicaro, is Moros not good enough for you now? You really are a piece of shit. No wonder Elish fooled you so easily; you were prancing around thinking you were better than everyone else and the chimera just knocked you down a few pegs. If anything, Moros is too good for you now, because at least the residents accept their fate and make the most of it.

You'll just be stuck here for the remainder of your shit life, knowing there is better out there but having it forever just out of your grasp. You tasted ambrosia and now you have to go back to tact. You had so many intense emotions drawn out of you, mind blowing orgasms, explosive feelings of pleasure and pain – now it's over.

But it made me feel alive; it reminded me I was living –

– *and now you had to go back to the clumsy touch of...*

My mouth downturned at the cruelty over what I was about to think next. Kerres didn't deserve that.

"Jade, come on, tell us how those chimeras live? My god, I would give my left nut to be able to suck chimera cock; they're huge right?" Fiere quipped.

My body retracted like it had been hit with an electric bosen prod; I looked into my bottle and mumbled. "Dunno, man."

The jackals around me laughed and a few of them said things to each other. I wasn't listening.

"Shut the fuck up, Fiere. He doesn't have to say shit, just let him hang out," Kerres snapped putting a protective arm around me, I could smell the liquor on his breath. "Why don't you tell us the time you got raped by that dude at the Laundromat first?" There was a pause. "No? Then don't ask him shit like that."

Fiere sniffed, but the atmosphere around us was still light. I could feel he was annoyed though. "Whatever, sorry, J. We've been pushing garbage in the slums, so sue us if we're curious. No one has ever been near a chimera, ever."

I gave him a nod and continued sipping my beer, a part of me missing the days where I would be the center of attention, the charismatic Morosian heading every conversation and laughing the loudest at the jokes and playful banter. I had been the prince of our little group, and well-known in the slums as the man who could fence anything and steal anything.

I felt like a kicked dog as I sat in a dark corner sipping my beer, forcing myself to at least appear normal, even though my thoughts were far from here, far from the slums.

The night dragged on and everyone continued to get more and more drunk and stoned. I nursed my beer slowly; I was only on my second when the conversation started to turn again.

It was one of the new kids, Loni, who started talking shit first. He seemed to be giving me the most sideways glances; the rest of them had started to ignore me the drunker they got, Kerres beside me answering most of my questions for me.

"I was there, I saw all of it." My ears perked up as I noticed he had dropped his tone; he was talking quietly to Tate who was taking long drinks from his freshly cracked beer. "They took a baseball bat to her fucking head, man. Jade broke the window like a maniac and jumped down. His teeth were plated metal and pointed; he had these metal claws on, dude."

I felt cold; I clenched the bottle in my hand and took another drink. Kerres was half-awake with his head resting against the wall, dazed and obviously drunk.

Tate whispered something to him and Loni went on. "He slashed and sliced those two brutes up. I swear to fuck he was out of control. His eyes glowed, you know like when you shine a flashlight on an alley cat? Like that, they reflected. I swear he's a fucking chimera and he just won't tell us."

That snapped my attention, my vision tilted and swirled around me as I jerked my head towards him. I could ignore a lot of things but accusing me of being one of those fucking assholes was going too far.

"His legs didn't even bend when he jumped." More shit spilled from his mouth. "I saw him drinking Ares's blood and I saw his master smile at the carnage from the skybox. *Smile*, dude.

"I'm telling you –"

My mind snapped and with a snarl on my lips, I threw the beer bottle.

Alerted by my scream of rage, Loni ducked just in time for the beer bottle to fly past him and shatter against the living room wall that separated it from the kitchen. It shattered into a thousand pieces, leaving a hole in the painted drywall.

Glassy eyes, lucid from shock, stared at me like diamonds sparkling in a cave. I stood, and felt my chest rising up and down with rage. The room fell to an awkward silence that bounced against my own aura with dismissive indifference. I only saw the fear in Loni's eyes. Brown eyes, and auburn hair, full of fear… he seeped fear.

"Sorry, man… sit back down, we're –"

I had no master; I had no one to hold me back. I was my own man again, but a different man, a new one. I had been trained under a chimera's cruel gaze and now I was stronger. I wouldn't take their shit, they were fucking below me. I was a chimera's cicaro; I was fucking better than them.

Yeah, get him, Jade, the cold voice in my mind hissed with sardonic glee.

I raised my hand and as it swung down on his ugly, pock marked face, I made a fist. It hit the side of his head with a sickening crack, landing the new kid onto the dirty carpet with a cry. I jumped on him and started pounding him in the face with my fist.

Like Ares and Siris had hit me… before they raped me, like Elish had hit me, when I was his cicaro. So many beatings I had endured, so much humiliation.

I wasn't them!

Around me the whole room erupted into action, some flying to pull Loni away, some holding me back.

In my drunken state, I was surprised to find myself fall back to the feral dog state that only Elish and his chimeras seemed to push me to. I started to growl and bare my teeth.

Kerres swore, his arms were around me. In front of me Loni was holding his mouth, babbling incoherently as blood ran through his fingers.

Blood… blood… chimeras and blood.

Want me to be a chimera? I'll be a chimera. I tried to thrash my body away from Kerres and Pete as they pulled Loni towards the door. I snarled at them and tried to break free, yelling things I didn't understand and letting the taunts fall from my lips like the blood from Loni's face.

"You ever compare me to them again I'll fucking show you how much chimera I am!" That I understood, and I screamed it with so much rage stars flashed through my vision.

I screamed like a wounded animal. Behind me Kerres was crying and pleading to Pete who had my other arm. They stayed with me, talking in hurried voices as I snarled at the now closed door.

Then the rage ended; like someone had pulled the plug on a sink full of grey water it disappeared into the darkness, and I felt all resistance drain away.

Though they both didn't trust me at first, after a time their grip lessened and finally they let me go.

"Jade?" Kerres whimpered. He sniffed and spoke to Pete, "I lost him, Pete. I don't know what they did to him; I don't know what to do."

"Are – are those... are all those scars?"

"Yeah, you have no idea, Pete. It was bad, real fucking bad and he was in it for a year."

"Shit... I'm... wow, Ker."

I watched Kerres's green-blue aura swirl around Pete's orange and black. I pushed them away and found my own.

My hands rose and I touched it, drawing it back with a pinch of my fingers. Already I saw the silvers fading but I coiled it around my fingers regardless, like a string being shaped for a cat's cradle.

"What's he doing?"

I walked away stretching my aura out, and walked down the hallway, moulding it and shaping the colours with my fingers. I went into Kerres's room and shut the door, before I laid down in his bed. I looked up at the ceiling and watched the swirling happen like my own drug-induced hallucination.

That – that had felt good.

I went back and replayed the moment in my mind. The feeling of my fist connecting against his face, the satisfying crunch as I hopefully broke some teeth or bone. The rush was delayed but now as I stared at the dark ceiling the energy coursed through me like I had been loaded with rocket fuel. Every replay of the television in my imagination brought with it a mini-orgasm in my brain. It was marvellous.

My heart beat quickly in my chest, and my body felt alight. Somehow, just a tiny bit, I felt relief coat my burned emotions like a gel pack. It made me take deep breath after deep breath, until my whole body was coated in the afterglow of pure physical violence.

Like when I had killed Ares and Siris. I remembered that rush, though it was overtaken by the despair of them killing my mother, and my hatred for Elish at the time. Now I refused to let any sad thoughts kill the moment. This feeling was all mine.

"Jade? Everyone is gone…" Kerres whispered. I heard a creak of the door open and a small sliver of light shed itself onto the room. The silhouette moved towards me, and as the light disappeared, I heard the soft click of the hinge.

"Are you okay?"

I nodded and patted the bed. Kerres laid beside me and put his arm around me. "You scared me, J."

"Next time he'll watch his mouth, and if he doesn't… I'll punish him more," I whispered, Kerres's aura joining mine and, though they didn't mix well, they still meshed into each other.

"Punish him?"

Watch your mouth, Cicaro.

"And if he defies me again… I'll bash him with a baseball bat, and pick his brain matter off my shirt."

Kerres froze and his aura froze too. The room fell to a cold silence, thick and heavy with unspoken words and emotions.

"Let's just go to sleep, J. You've had a bit too much to drink."

I'd only had one and a half beers, and he knew it.

But I spared him; it wasn't him I wanted to beat and kill. It was that smart mouth Loni and any other person who dared look at me with an expression I didn't like. It was any person who dared ask me questions about my whereabouts the last year, anyone who snickered or commented on what they had seen at Stadium. I had been trained by a chimera, I had been tempered by a chimera, and if I wanted to kill these flea-ridden parasites I WOULD!

I closed my eyes, the anger was still there, but something else was happening… the thoughts of hurting and bringing physical pain to these people were overshadowing my despair over what had happened with my master.

It wasn't a lot, but it had taken my mind off of it, it had expelled the pent-up anger and hate that I had been burying inside of me for the past year. Every snip, every attack on Elish I had to withhold and swallow seemed to release itself from my body.

A smile came to my face, and as I replayed the attack on Loni, I gave myself my steel implants and my razor-sharp claws. As I drifted off to sleep I brought us to Stadium, and with the dancing images of revenge and murder fresh in my mind, I transformed Loni into Elish.

And I killed him… over and over again.

CHAPTER 20

I DIDN'T GET OUT OF BED THIS COLD MORNING, EXCEPT once to get up and pee. Even when Kerres came back from work and peeked his head into the bedroom I didn't even look at him. My eyes just stared forward, memorizing the chipped paint of our bedroom. I think I knew each corner, nook, and cranny of the room now.

I hadn't been outside in a month, not since Kerres had closed the rusted gate on my past with Elish and introduced me back to what had once been my life.

I'd forgotten Elish's smell. I had forgotten the finer details of his opal and silver aura; sometimes in the middle of the night I woke up crying because I had heard his voice in my head. That was the only time I got to hear it now, and even then I wondered if it was the same silken tones, or just my brain trying desperately to remember.

My hand traced the curves of his torso, the smooth flat stomach, the night where I had touched him back, been the one to kiss him passionately, and the most hurtful memory of them all… when I had been on top of him, riding him and making him feel what he had been making me feel for the past year.

But no, Jade, it had all been a lie, and that brought with it a balanced level of both depression and anger. Both emotions had mixed into one emotion, an emotion I didn't have a name for.

I brought my breathing corpse out of bed and walked into the living room after reliving myself. Kerres greeted me with a smile, and offered me a pin of opium. I nodded and gave him a thanks. I had been making an effort to be more in reality for him. My boyfriend had been so nice to me, supportive and patient, and I had barely been giving anything back.

He hadn't even been trying to get sex out of me, which was surprising since we had shared an adequate sex life before. I think he knew what I could never voice out loud; that the number of times Elish had taken me numbered in the hundreds and letting someone touch me again would take a long time.

He assumed it was a byproduct of being raped, but in truth I still felt like I belonged to Elish.

But Elish wasn't coming back… nah, it had been a month now and my life with the chimera in Olympus had disappeared as quickly as it had come.

From inaction to the cobra strike.

I smoked the pin and curled up next to Kerres, wearing a sweatshirt two sizes too big and baggy sweat pants. He put his arm around me and kissed my forehead.

"Did you have a good day today, handsome boy?" Kerres asked gently after I had inhaled some of the bitter opiate smoke.

Feeling more relaxed I nodded and let him touch me. I was falling back into that routine. "I went out on the patio for a smoke, it's gotten cold outside."

Kerres chuckled and kissed my forehead again. "Yeah, it's the end of September, kitten. Winter is coming again; I could see my breath this morning."

When Elish had dumped me near the walls the sun was still warm and shining during the day. Fall had come quickly and brought with it harsh weather. We never had much of a spring or a fall here, it was just sunny, then rainy, and then slushy snow. Grey snow that brought with it a tinny sour smell that would coat all of Skyfall. It had been my job to clear the snow from the railings of Olympus and the fringes of where the grey snow would build.

Letting the opium wash some of my depression away I glanced at the rainy cold day outside, painting everything a darker shade of greys and blacks. We had a view of the walls of Moros, though where Elish had abandoned me was several miles to the north. It wasn't much of a view, just more grey.

"I'm going to start fencing again, contribute a bit," I whispered after we had been quiet for a while.

Kerres squeezed me harder. "No, don't worry about it. Since I cut down on the drugs I have money saved. I don't want you to risk shit like that again."

It was hard to tell if Kerres really didn't want me to risk it, or if he just didn't trust his half-feral boyfriend around the public anymore. He should know above anyone else that I was at no risk of being caught.

But I didn't need his fucking permission; he had given me my own key and I could come and go as I pleased. Kerres wasn't my master. I was my own man now and I could do what I wanted.

So I let his resistance to my idea wash over me, and I made plans in my head for places I could hit. Maybe that would snap me out of this depression; maybe it was time to put Elish and Skyland behind me.

Because Elish wasn't coming back, and he didn't care about me... so why did I keep caring about him?

Fuck him.

Why would I care? Why should I care?

Oddly my thoughts went to the duffle bag I still hadn't opened, and that brought an overflow of emotion. The chimera would always have his hold on me, and I was realizing a piece of that hold was showing in the fact that I couldn't open that bag.

I was a captive to the past, and I always would be if that bag was sitting in our room unopened; perhaps it was time to cut the abscess and drain it once and for all. It would hurt, but with Kerres and drugs I could kill the infection and maybe once and for all... I could move past Elish.

The next night after Kerres had gone to sleep early for his job in the morning, I took the duffle bag and carried it to the empty second bedroom – a room with a mattress on the ground and our old couch, used for storage or when one of his friends were too drunk to walk home.

My heart started to vibrate with anxiety when I closed the door. I flicked on the lights and sat down on the couch with the black bag in front of me.

So many haunting thoughts trapped into a single bag; the only thing I knew was inside of it was money, and from the feel of it, some clothes.

The room was filled with the sound of the zipper, and when it reached the other side of the nylon pack my stomach filled with a churning nausea.

No... get a hold of yourself. I felt fed up with myself and the feelings Elish's memory brought so, with a curse of inner hatred, I threw off the flap of the bag.

Money and clothes from the looks of it... I picked up a bundle of clean hundred dollar bills and swallowed down the shock of seeing so much money. If only to put off having to dig further into the bag I counted the cash, it was over two thousand dollars, over a year's worth of wages.

Thanks... I guess? I put the money back into the elastic band it had been folded up into and put it into the pocket of the bag. Did the cold, cruel chimera really care if I made it through the winter? Maybe Garrett had made him, or perhaps it was just the going rate for keeping a whore captive for a year.

I picked up the clothes that had been carefully folded and noticed it was the clothes that had been ripped off of me when I had been caught by Ares and Siris; my old Moros clothes but washed now. I held the clothing up to my nose and smelled them, they smelled like the apartment. Not quite like Elish but clean and like laundry soap. I put them beside me and reached back down.

My eyes stung when I saw small triangles of pink.

I picked up Luca's cat ears and pursed my lips; with a soft touch I brushed my fingers over the small pointed ears, and swallowed the emotions that came with the realization.

Luca... patient, kind Luca, Elish's sengil. He would miss me... sengils didn't know how to play games or be fake. He loved those ears; why would he give them to me?

I'll miss you too, Luca. I'm sorry I never got to say goodbye.

With a sniff I put the cat ears on and took out some other clothes that had been packed for me. My winter jacket and leather gloves that Garrett had gotten me for my birthday, and even...

No... what were these? I picked up what I had assumed were my old duct taped shoes but when I examined them I realized they were different. The duct tape was new, and the shoes were new.

The corner of my mouth raised in a sad smile. It must've been Luca, he had duct taped the new shoes I wore during the summer, to make them look cheap and undesirable for thieves. The sengil had gone to all of this effort to make sure I would have proper shoes this winter, suited for Moros.

With a glance down I saw that the lump in my throat wasn't going to get any smaller.

My Game Boy with Pokémon, the Mp3 player, and three bottles of pills. The medication Elish had been giving me for my nightmares, a bottle of aspirin for when I was hurt and some vitamins.

Thanks, Luca, you're a real friend. I sniffed and started putting everything away. I picked up the duct taped shoes and noticed something sticking out from the tape.

I brought the shoes into the light.

The thoughts that went through my mind when I saw a long blond hair stuck in the duct tape made no sense to me. It dashed away the kind sengil packing my bags and instead brought forth the image of my master carefully wrapping the tape around the shoes as I slept quietly on the couch.

The thought strummed a chord in my heart, but the sound was cut apart by the sharp shards and broken pieces. With a muffled scream of rage, I threw the shoes across the room and kicked the duffle bag.

It flew across the room and spilled; my hands flew up to my head and with every ounce of effort I tried to withhold my mind from flying into a confused rage.

It didn't make sense!

FUCK HIM!

"FUCK HIM!" I screamed into the dead of night. I picked up the shoes again and threw them, before throwing my clothes and chucking the pill bottles against the wall. Each expense of energy only encouraged the flow of more and more anger. Like an erupting volcano, I shot the toxic smoke up into the air, and screamed as if to try to force my inner poison onto the world.

"Jade?" Kerres cried, opening the door.

I whirled around, the expression on my face stopping my boyfriend in his tracks.

"GET OUT!" I snarled.

With his eyes wide with shock and his face pale, he closed the door and didn't say another word.

I bellowed my despair and confusion again before dropping to my knees, I grabbed the duffle bag and swung it across the room, its contents spilling completely.

A burning smouldered in my throat, and I couldn't catch my breath. I turned around and was about to leave to get some Valium when I noticed a box resting beside my knee.

I picked it up and motioned to throw it, when I realized that I recognized it.

It was a velvet box with a hinge, the same one–

No, he wouldn't have given those back to me.

I opened it and gaped at them, the blood draining from my face. My head snapped over my shoulder to make sure Kerres was gone, before I grabbed the first of the four implants and started roughly shoving them over my canines.

I didn't know why I was doing it, all I know was it made me feel better.

The next thing my mind registered I was looking in front of the full length mirror of the second bedroom, the last fifteen minutes a blur in my mind.

I was dressed in my old pet clothes; tight leather pants, a restricting vest over a mesh shirt, and black boots, just broken in and comfortable against my feet. I had Luca's cat ears on my head, and Silas's steel claw rings on my fingers.

I smiled wide and saw the steel teeth sharp and wedged into my canines, the gums red from me forcing them on tight.

My own eyes were a blaze of yellow, wide and staring like I had just peered into my own soul and had been shocked and what I had found. I was staring back at this maniac who looked like someone who had finally danced his last dance with sanity.

I looked beautiful; a mixture of the slumrat and the crazed cicaro who had murdered Ares and Siris, who had slashed his master's face and disfigured him. If I could have fucked myself right there and then I would, because I was the most dangerous-looking nutcase I had ever seen. Even my eyes were burning eclipses, golden suns around black circles and a marble white face, like some fucked up super villain in a world where the heroes had died off long ago.

My hands made a fist and I tilted that fist so the light reflected off of the razor-sharp moulded steel. I clinked the claws on my fists against each other, then walked out of the bedroom and into the living room.

The dangerous thoughts coursed through my brain like a sweet elixir, quieting down the despair and hatred. As I opened the sliding glass door that led to the balcony the living room overlooked, I could almost feel the medicine cure the burns on my heart.

Outside, over the dark streets of Moros, the cold fall air stung my roasting hot body, but the adrenaline-filled chill that night brought to the soul of a man, only carried with it more morbid and unthinkable thoughts.

I swung my legs over the balcony, and I jumped off the third floor.

My boots landed on the concrete with a loud snap, and as Loni himself had observed, my knees barely buckled under the weight. With no second thoughts and no doubts on my mind, I started walking down a small cracked path that led to the iron gate of Coaltowers. I crept into the alleyways with dark oaths on my mind and sunk into the shadows.

To hunt.

I saw Moros differently as I stuck to the shadows of the alleys. No longer the garbage-strewn cesspool that I had seen coming in, now, with the moonlight hidden between the thick fall clouds, it was my own personal playground. The steel beams that poked out of buildings, like bones erupting from a corpse, were my jungle gym. With a new fire inside of me I climbed them, and stalked the people mulling around unaware under my feet.

Like a panther that had just emerged from his den for the first time, I climbed and explored Moros like I never had before, slinking and following my potential prey. Sizing up victims and weighing their lives in my hands.

Though there were no moral decisions over who I would kill tonight and who I would let live. I wasn't some fucking vigilante of justice; I was the villain in this story and whoever I fucking felt like killing I would kill.

Because fuck Moros, fuck my life, and fuck Elish Dekker. I didn't care, if they caught me, whatever, put me in front of the crowd in Stadium and I will kill Ares and Siris again. At least Elish could watch me die and know in the black coal of his heart that he had done this to me.

I held onto a cold steel beam and watched the insects below me, a gentle breeze blowing back my hair. They were returning from a bar and two of them had companions in their arms, talking in loud and obnoxious laughter; there were five of them.

I followed them, not even needing to outstretch my arms to keep my balance. On solid feet, I lightly, but quickly, stepped along a metal beam and ducked between two crosshatched supports. Then I jumped down to the lower level and landed quietly onto the second-storey's broken and partially missing floor.

Using their voices to direct me, I stealthily walked through the room. My boots crunched against the drywall from the collapsed ceiling, a noise the insects below me wouldn't be able to hear.

The rooms I slinked through could barely be called rooms. What parts that had been exposed to the elements had been stripped down to their support beams, and the parts that were sheltered were mouldy, fragile to even the slightest weight, and collapsing under their age. It wasn't safe for a normal person, which meant that I would be undisturbed.

I kneeled down over a place where the floor had collapsed into the second floor underneath my feet. I grabbed onto a joist and swung myself down; with a pivot, I turned and found a blown-out window and looked out of it.

Unaware of the shadow stalking them, the five people carried on down the alleyway, talking shit and holding bottles of Morosian swill; taking long drinks and hollering their drunken talk for all to hear.

There was not an inch of me that felt nervous or hesitant; if anything, every step I took towards these people felt like salve on my wounds. I kept wanting to feel like I was becoming Jade again, but this wasn't Jade. I was hatching a new person out of the cocoon of this aura, one that had now become purple and black, and as polluted as all hell.

I wanted this, badly.

The despair and the depression in me was being replaced by this feeling of bloodthirst, and I felt no need to complicate things. By now, a month after Elish had abandoned me, I would take anything to anoint the ripped open, festering wounds on my heart, mind, and soul. If it took murder, and showing Skyfall just how much I was hurting – so be it.

And it was when one of the men, the one who didn't have a kid hanging off his arm, branched off with a drunken goodbye, that I felt the black shell around my heart start to burn.

Like a shadow against the lampless alleyways, I slinked along the walls, my leather boots making no noise against the trashed dark corridors.

Only my heart was a hammer in a black-echoed darkness, a piercing ring in a part of my heart that used to be alight with song, but had now grown silent.

The distance closed, and I could smell him now. A red plaid shirt, messed up black hair and a bottle of booze he brought to his lips as he stumbled home on unsteady feet.

My eyes scanned the makeup of this alleyway and in my mind I calculated my attack. I sprinted down an adjacent passage and took a sharp turn into a hollowed-out building that had been gutted and lit on fire long ago. I weaved through the charred wreckage, ducking under burned beams, and jumping through windows until I was ahead of the man.

Unaware of everything, the man kept walking. I jumped up onto a metal ventilation box and crouched down like a cat, even adjusting my feet like they did before pouncing. I could see his face now; an ugly face with the puffy features of someone who drank too much and slept too little. If he was missed, they would get over him quickly. Which in my mind at that moment was a pity; I wanted to kill people who would be missed and cried over. People whose absence would ruin lives and cause families to starve.

Suffer with me... suffer with me.

The anticipation became audible on my lips, a susurrated gasp which turned into a trembled vibration that tore up my chest. The closer he got, the more my body shook, knowing the line I was about to cross.

"You're as stupid as you are weak, get out of my sight."

I'll show you weak.

Before he even had time to react I lunged at the drunk, my mouth opening and my steel implanted canines ready to taste the coppery blood, anticipating the first bite.

When they sank into his throat, the animalistic growl that I had somehow been able to produce sounded, and as his hands grabbed my head, I closed my jaws over his throat and windpipe.

Like a lion attacking a gazelle I stayed with my jaws locked; even when he stumbled backwards and slammed down onto the ground my teeth remained clamped. Useless arms hit my head and clawed my neck in a desperate attempt to save his weak and pathetic life.

I let his life drain out of him and into my mouth; the thrashing became weaker and his desperate attempts to grab breath faded into the darkness. The sounds of me breathing through my nose becoming louder and louder as his death thrashes stopped, before finally he submitted to darkness.

I pulled his throat out when I was done, and spat it out onto the concrete, watching the trickle of black blood spill from the wound and onto the floor. I knew he was stone dead then; if he was alive his arteries would be spraying the cruor all over my body.

Leaning back onto the balls of my feet I watched the blood trickle out of him. I absentmindedly wiped my mouth free of the flesh stuck between my teeth.

My heart was pounding.

Wow, was it ever.

It hit me like a tidal wave of ice water. My body became extremely aware of my surroundings and what was happening inside of me. My hands were shaking from the adrenaline and my pulse was racing like a motorcar. I was light, light as a feather, to the point where I knew if I jumped high enough I would fly. What was this feeling? I was… I felt–

I felt… happy.

What Pandora's box had I opened?

I got up and looked around in all directions but it was only me; without looking twice I slunk back into the burned-out building I had emerged from.

And with black flames soldering the shards of my heart back together, I went out to find my next victim.

I pressed my body against the brick walls of Coaltowers, and tried to catch my breath, but I had been sprinting up and down the alleyways all night and now my chest was a crackling fire.

There was no stopping now though.

Still in the dead eves of night, I silently ran across the small courtyard of the apartment buildings and jumped onto the concrete barrier that held in the dirt for the plant beds. I glanced up and tested my fingers against the fire escape on the side of the building and with one last burning breath I started to climb.

I opened the window of the second bedroom and climbed inside. I closed it gently and collapsed beside it, my sweaty back under the window frame.

I smiled thinly and turned my head to the full length mirror.

With the smile still derisive on my face, I pressed my stained lips together and devoured my own image with the glowing hungry eyes that belonged to me. My black hair was damp and pressed against my forehead, contrasting my cold-bitten face, though the black and white wasn't my only contrast now.

My lips and around my face held red, of three victims I had murdered that night, and if I ran my tongue along my serrated teeth I would be able to pick out flesh. I had been out all night, and I chewed the tender skin like it was gum. Releasing wave and wave of pleasure from each piece of flesh and blood I tasted, and each scream I drank before my steel implanted teeth cut off their cries.

Yes… I took in the image of his former slave, this cicaro of Elish and I liked what I saw.

I couldn't be Jade the Morosian, I couldn't be Jade the cicaro.

I was a shadow, a super villain like in the comic books. I was a murderer with canine teeth, horrific metallic claws and motherfucking cat ears.

Wow… this was me. This would be me. I could do this; I could live like this and kill until the pain of Elish's abandonment was washed away in a flow of coppery, sweet blood.

I closed my eyes and to my surprise I felt them burn, my heart filled with reprieve to the point where a tear dripped down my cheek, the overwhelming feeling of relief that I had an outlet to shake my obsessed mind from that blond monster.

Murder quenched your pain like a bucket of ice water on hot coals. How – how chimera-like.

I undressed in the dark. After a quick shower to wash away the sweat and blood, I changed into boxer pants and a t-shirt and opened the bedroom door.

I watched Kerres asleep on his side of the bed, crimson hair tussled and partially covering his face. He had always been beautiful, though more handsome than beautiful; square face, rough prickly beard that he tried to shave off every couple days, perfect eyebrows above chocolate-brown eyes.

My throat began to tremble as I watched him sleep, and deep inside me something stirred, a feeling I hadn't felt for Kerres in a very long time.

Every inch of him I took in with my eyes, and when I couldn't withhold the burning between my legs I crawled onto the bed and started to kiss his neck and cheekbone.

Kerres woke up with a start. "Jade? What are you doing?"

I moved my lips to his face; with a few open kisses on his chin he realized just what I was doing, and let me take his mouth into mine.

My tongue found his and we kissed deeply. With movements automated and automatic I started taking off his t-shirt and he took off my own.

"What's gotten into you? Are you sure?" Kerres gasped; already I could feel the hardness between his legs.

After several minutes of making out, I took the elastic waistband of his boxers into my grip and pulled them down; his member, one I hadn't seen in a long time, sprung out hard as rock.

With a few more licks I took it into my mouth and started sucking on it with a firm suction, pushing his legs back to give my fingers easy access to the spots I wanted to reintroduce myself to.

My probing finger sunk inside of him, and with his shuddered gasp came a string of curse words that only egged me on. The heat and sexual desire was radiating off of him, making me suck harder, my free hand stroking his shaft up and down.

When he came into my mouth, I realized it had been a very long time since I had tasted his cum, or anyone's cum. I had never given Elish oral because he had never asked it of me. I would've died and gone to heaven if he would've let me suck him off during the last few months when I fell in love with him, but before I had gotten the chance he had dismissed me.

I sucked it out of the crown and took in every last drop, then, with his glistening chest heaving from the orgasm, I pushed his legs back and opened the nightstand drawer.

There wasn't anything there though. Kerres smiled coyly before grabbing my neck and kissing me deeply. "I haven't had anyone over, idiot; I don't have lube just use some hand lotion."

No one at all? I pushed away the feeling of guilt, and with my hormones raging it was easier than it should've been. After rubbing moisturizer into my dick and fingering some into Kerres, I grabbed myself and started easing myself inside of him.

Another thing I hadn't done in over a year, been the dominant top during sex. I closed my eyes and released a moan into the pillow Kerres's head had been resting on, feeling the tense constriction of Kerres grip my member. I sunk into the base and withdrew, my body drawing even more heat as I heard Kerres moan loudly. I thrusted back in.

I was in control... I was the one in control now. I was the dominant one, I was my own master. I was fucking the boyfriend I owned and claiming him as my property.

My teeth clenched and ground together as I found my rhythm; Kerres's sharp moans and cries lubricating my lusting desires to claim and own. Like I was murdering all over again, I was taking control.

I was in control.

My thrusts sped up, and in response Kerres cried out and started beating himself off, his mouth open and gasping in a permanent chorus of moans.

I did him hard, as it was my right to; without pause I drilled into him and felt the pleasure take my body. Pleasure that was my own and not given to me under that chimera's staticy touch. I was doing it on my own. Look at me now, you fucking piece of shit. You would've whipped me to a bloody pulp if I fucked someone under your control, but now you don't own me.

You gave me up; there is nothing you can do now. I can fuck who I want, kill who I want, and do all the drugs I want.

FUCK YOU!

My mouth opened and I felt the growls come to my lips, as I pushed harder and harder. As I did I felt Kerres body retract and shudder as he orgasmed, his moans reaching a higher pitch with my name mixed into their cries.

Stimulated by the noise he was making I reached my peak, with the throated growl that surprised me whenever I made it, I came inside of him.

"*Ah–Fuck!* Jade? Let go!" Kerres suddenly hollered. I felt a hand on my forehead push me away.

My mind snapped to reality and I realized in the throes I had bit his shoulder, and to my own shock and guilt I remembered I still had my steel implants in.

I let go and rolled off of him, stammering an apology through the electricity still coursing through my body.

Kerres turned the light on, his hand over his shoulder, a red and angry bite mark leaking small trickles of blood.

"What the fuck, Jade? What's in your mouth?" Kerres gasped. His eyes were wide as saucers but he wasn't angry, more scared.

My attention was elsewhere. Without answering him I leaned down and started licking the blood off of his wound.

Kerres tried to push me away but I grabbed his arm. "Stay still."

"Jade? *What–the–fuck.*"

"Stay still."

He cringed as I licked the blood from his wound. It was sweet tasting, and I swore it tasted different to the blood of the drunks I had just come back from killing. Because he was mine, he was my boyfriend and even his blood had been made for me.

Kerres's heart was hammering, but his hand stroked my neck as I drank from him.

When I could finally pull myself away I stared down at the wound, my quickened breath blowing on it, cooling down the angry red that was quickly swelling each small pocked mark.

"Jade?" Kerres whispered. "You're not okay…"

I shifted my body and laid down on the bed. I put a hand on his shoulder and pulled his blue-tinged silhouette beside me, before taking him into my arms.

"I'll be just fine."

"No." Kerres's voice was a bit firmer. I felt him try and pull away but I only held him harder, he was my prize, I owned him. "Something is wrong with you, and… and I tried to give you time to adjust but… Jade, I think Elish brainwashed you… or… or something."

My body automatically tensed at the mention of Elish's name, and, as always, his name brought the perfectly sculpted face, the cold cruel purple eyes and that thin sardonic smile he had when at his most dangerous.

Beautiful blond hair, long graceful fingers and a smooth voice I craved to hear. My perfect cold chimera, who with every touch had brought me to my knees in a wordless bliss.

"Don't say his name."

Kerres shifted his body so he was facing me; he ran his hand soothingly against my shoulders. "Love, I just want to understand what happened… so I can understand your actions." Kerres took a deep breath. "When I saw you at Garrett Park you looked so sick, so small and helpless as he carried you… but now that you've come back, you're – you're just, it's like you're unstable and full of anger."

"I am."

He continued to stroke my arms, as if trying to physically soothe the sting he knew his words would bring me. "Did he rape you?"

My heart dropped, my body went rigid but that only increased his soothing touch. I wanted to shake him off but every muscle had frozen into ice.

"Almost every night."

I liked it.

I watched his handsome face fall, but it disappeared as he buried it into my chest. I squeezed him tight and patted his back.

It was okay, Kerres, because every time it happened my body thirsted for his touch, and lusted for every painful thrust. I ached for each orgasm and loved nothing more than feeling his cum inside me, lots of cum from him orgasming until he was tapped dry. It was my pleasure to let him use my body to bring himself to his peak. I was honoured to take that beautiful blond fuck's semen. I only wish I could've tasted it before he threw me back to the gutter like an unwanted dog.

So it's okay Kerres, because I loved Elish, and though I love you… I am the one who owns you now.

And I'll take care of my little cicaro.

I patted Kerres's head and kissed his hair, and held him until we both fell asleep.

CHAPTER 21

*T**HE MORNING OF SEPTEMBER 13**TH* *THE BODY OF KENNETH of Moros was discovered behind a dumpster, near Finn's Bar on the 4**th* *street of East Moros District. The next day, after two missing persons reports were filed, thiens found the bodies of Gregory Hatt and Jeremy Fisher in an abandoned building on Goodal Avenue and on the corner of Rudolph and Salih Road."*

I watched him walk by from a small recess of an old closed down restaurant, his taped sneakers echoing against the tall buildings around him, solid brick on either side.

His footsteps hadn't quickened yet, he didn't sense me near, and I knew he wouldn't. After doing cocaine and drinking down beer after beer, he wouldn't hear me coming if I was stomping on metal shoes.

A smile creased my face and, like it was a throttle in my chest, the bloodlust controlled my movements.

"– two weeks later the partially dismembered body of Sven Sears washed up on the harbour with the same identifying cause of death as the previous murders – a single bite to the neck. Morosians are urged to avoid all alleyways and walking alone after night. Ellis Dekker, Commissioner of the Royal Skyfall Thien Force, had this to say:"

My silhouette stretched out under the moonlight, encompassing Loni's shadow. It moved up and down with my steps, the steel on my fingers making my hands look like long knives.

He turned around and his face blanched; I drank his fear and let my body absorb it, before he gave off a stammering scream and started to run.

"There is a serial killer loose in Moros, and my precinct is determined to bring this murderer to justice. We will exhaust all resources to find out who this person is, and make the District of Moros safe for everyone."

I leapt up onto a dumpster and, without pause, I used it as leverage and jumped onto his back, like I had done to Reaver months before. A pounce from a Morosian, more rabid monster than man, a man who no longer held a shred of guilt inside his broken heart.

I grabbed Loni's hair with my claws and wrenched his head back.

"Jade?" Loni gasped. He stared at me in disbelief, like his final moments in this world were nothing but his mind playing tricks on him.

I bit his neck and clamped down on it, before clenching my teeth until they touched. Then I ripped out his throat, and with his hair still in my hands – I watched the pulsing blood drip out of his body and onto the paved alleyway below.

Shit! The blood was dripping not gushing. It should've been painting the walls, I had gotten the angle wrong.

Loni screamed a little too loud, and with the echo of the damp bricks of the alleyway it all but announced what was going on in the darkened corners of East Moros.

The man grabbed his neck with another gurgling scream and started to run from me. I closed the distance quickly and pushed him down to the ground, watching his face smash against the pavement below us.

To make this damage control quick I put a hand over his mouth and started dragging him into one of the abandoned buildings.

His boots scraped against the ground as he thrashed and cried his muffled sobs into my hand. I dragged him through a blown-out room, and down the hallway littered with gyprock and crushed brick; feeling the spider webs and the strands of insulation brush up against my face.

I looked around and got my bearings. There was a giant hole through a brick wall, scorched black from a badly aimed Molotov cocktail, that would lead me to my lair. My abandoned basement with a hidden door, where I had started collecting my little prizes.

"We would also like to show the artists sketches of two Morosians who are currently missing, Hank Guillier and William Frank. They went missing after leaving the Monkey Tree Bar last Tuesday."

Loni moaned loudly, so I clasped his face harder with my palm; watching my steps behind me to pinpoint every single blood drop the idiot was shedding from his open wound.

I dug my free hand into the neck wound and as he screamed into my hand, I found his wind pipe and pinched it.

He passed out soon after and he was easier to drag after that. Luckily, the alleys that would lead him back to the apartment he shared with Tate were near my lair. I would be there soon.

With the silent moon judging my every action and the stars quiet spectators, I pushed the wooden door open with my shoulders and dragged Loni inside. Blood was still dripping down his chest but soaking into his thick jacket rather than the ground.

I was quite pleased with myself; the opportunity to bring a live one down here hadn't come to me yet. Though it was my own obvious blunder, it brought a myriad of pleasing images to my brain.

I dragged Loni down the stairs and dumped his passed out body onto the floor.

With a click in the cold damp darkness, the bluelamp illuminated my evil lair and the bodies in it.

I had strung them by their necks.

They looked nice.

There were four of them; the other two hadn't been announced on the news yet because they had been originally from Nyx. I almost laughed out loud when I realized they were purposely leaving them out. If the public knew I had moved on to killing Nyxians they would assume the Erosians were next and then the precious elite Skylanders. So they kept the killing to Moros District, because you couldn't expect anything else from the slums. The starving, drug-addicted, alcoholic Morosians were one crayon away from being batshit crazy anyway; it was only a natural occurrence that every few years one of them would snap and go crazy.

I smiled and looked at the men hanging from the rafters, their necks wrapped tightly with nylon rope; so tight against their neck it throttled their jaws like Chinese finger traps.

I enjoyed watching them hang; sometimes they even swayed back and forth without me touching them, like their own disgruntled spirits were trying to raise their bodies from the dead.

There was a bundle of coiled rope in the corner of the basement, next to a grey-bleached desk that held in it dismembering tools I had collected from open windows. Most of them were stained with rusted blood and held notches full of serrated flesh. They smelled; the entire basement was starting to stink of rot.

I picked up a length of rope and sawed off the amount I would need, lightly running my hand along the tight braids. I turned and sauntered up to Loni. I always enjoyed it when they died with their eyes and mouth wide open in inaudible terror. It pleased the very cockles of my heart.

Though he was only passed out, but for how long?

He almost looked like a piñata…

Loni woke up when I started wrapping the rope around his neck; he tried to scream but I had already cut out most of the air to his neck.

If I was Elish I would rape him, or jack him off like the choking game that some of my friends had played, but my sexual lust was always saved for Kerres. I had no urge to touch another man, not even to sexually assault them.

When I had wrapped his neck I swung the rope over the calcified-looking wooden beam and pulled.

Kerres's former friend (who was thrashing and clawing bloodied fingers against the binds) lifted up off the ground and hung with his new buddies, on a backdrop of grey brick and crumbling mortar. I admired my handiwork.

Then because I felt like hurting him more, for no other reason than I was extremely disturbed, I spun him around a few more times before I raised my hands in the air and sunk my claws into his shoulder blades. Then, like a cat was shredding drapes, I dragged them down Loni's back all the way to his ass. His choking screaming falling from his blue lips as his red flesh and yellow fat split from my steel talons like an open sack, running blood down my hands. With his wails music to my ears, I spun him around again and delivered my last slash. I cut three thin but deep lines across his stomach, and watched his steaming entrails spill to the floor like slop from a pot.

I didn't know why I did that… caught up in the moment perhaps.

When he was dead I gave him one more spin; his intestines wrapping around his thighs before I left him to hang with the others.

I just had to admire the collage of beaten and mutilated bodies that I had collected myself. The display of art in my basement made my heart shudder with joy. I wished I could show someone; I wished I could show Elish just what he had made of me.

Would you be proud, love? Or would your cold countenance hold deep inside it a look of horror?

I would know soon, when they caught me. That's what I wanted. So go ahead and try and catch me, Ellis. Put me in Stadium and let me kill the brother of your choice once again. I had killed two, I certainly could kill another one.

And if they kill me, so be it... the joy I felt taking lives only told me that I was too far gone now.

Before I left I pushed each one and made them swing, then with a glance behind my back at the bodies swaying in the decaying darkness, I turned off the bluelamp and made my way up the stairs.

Elish would have heard by now, if not from the television reports then from his only sister. He would know it was me, all of the chimeras would know it was me, but would they come and get me? That was the million dollar question. I challenged them to, I wanted them to. I would like nothing more than to feel the energetic atmosphere of Stadium again. I really didn't give a fuck if they killed me this time, then Elish would know what he had meant to me.

No word of him at all. I hadn't even seen him on the television, only Ellis and Artemis once to announce the opening of a new library in Eros.

I hadn't seen Elish's face in almost three months.

And something told me that if he saw me, he wouldn't recognize me as the boy he had left bleeding and sobbing on the walls of Moros.

Click... click... click... my boots echoed off the alleyway walls, a higher octave than Loni's had. He had sneakers, my boots had a two inch high heel that had been specially made for my feet. One of the fringe benefits of being Elish's whore.

I licked my fingers clean of blood and climbed my way up to the fire escape back to the apartment.

It had been an easy routine to master; the longer I stayed up roaming the alleyways for fresh prey, the less sleep I found I needed. I was down to needing only four or five hours every evening whereas Kerres was cranky unless he got eight. That gave me a window of three to four hours to do my prowling and to play with my hanging corpses, and more time if I drugged him which I sometimes did. I was only killing once every two to three weeks; it didn't happen often enough for him to suspect I was doing anything to him.

I changed out of my cat ears and villain clothes (or former pet outfit) and tucked them back under the mattress, where I hid them when I wasn't out murdering. Then I showered, walked naked into our bedroom and fucked Kerres into oblivion.

Two days later was Kerres's day off. I made us both some boiled eggs mashed with margarine and put his bowl on the coffee table.

Kerres came in, walking a bit crooked. I gave him a knowing smirk. He had been walking with a wobble all day yesterday, so to be cruel I was just as rough with him last night. He liked it though. "A bit sore today are we?"

My boyfriend gave me a playful smack upside the head and sat beside me, putting the bowl on his lap. "You never used to be this rough. I wish I knew what dreams you have to get you that fired up for me at five in the fucking morning."

I growled and craned my head to give his neck a lick. He squealed and rubbed where the saliva had cooled his skin, before he turned to me with a tsk. "I really wish you wouldn't keep those teeth in."

I shovelled food into my mouth and shrugged. "I'm not getting rid of them. I told you that five times already." My voice held some bite to it. I had gotten tired of him asking me to remove them a long time ago. It was my right to wear them. I was free and I belonged to no one.

"Yeah, I know." His hand reached over and he grabbed the remote and turned on the television to the news. Like a lot of Morosians I had been watching the coverage of the Morosian serial killer when they reported it. Though considering how many people I had murdered, there really wasn't that much coverage.

The thiens didn't like to advertise the fact that they still hadn't caught the murderer, and the chimeras didn't want to advertise the fact that it was their councillor's former cicaro doing the killing.

I took the remote from him and changed the channel to SpongeBob. I wasn't in the mood for hearing the bullshit that spilled from their mouths.

When there was a flurry of knocking on our apartment door, however, I had a feeling that it would be unavoidable.

Kerres got up and opened the door; immediately I felt the nervous and desperate aura of Tate, Loni's boyfriend.

"Ker... Loni's been missing, fuck, I thought he was sleeping at Pete's last night but I just went there after he didn't come home again. He's missing, man. I think that serial killer fuck got him!" Tate's voice was shrill and desperate. I glanced over my shoulder in a casual fashion, deciding if I should pretend I was upset since I really never cared for the asshole. The first time we met had gone badly and since then he had been a snippy, glowering fuck to me. Though instead of blatantly comparing me to the chimeras and telling everyone who would listen that I was a manic-depressive maniac, he left his insults to passive-aggressive picks.

"We'll go and look for him, let me grab my jacket," Kerres said hastily as he turned and ran into his bedroom.

The door shut and I looked back to the television. Patrick was doing something stupid. I loved that dude.

"Jade?" Tate was suddenly behind me. I could see his reflection in the sliding glass door. Same old Tate, full beard and long hair usually hidden underneath a blue beanie; nice guy, never caused me any trouble.

"Yeah?" I said, my one word response would be nothing new to him. I barely spoke to any of them anymore. When I came out to drink and do drugs with them I stuck to my dark corner, being the listener more than the person contributing to the conversation, and since I had punched out Loni no one pushed conversation on me. I still suspected they talked and gossiped about me, but they were smart enough to do it out of my ear shot.

"Do you know where Loni is?"

I kept my face placid and calm, knowing he was watching me in the reflection of the glass door as much as I was watching him. I stared forward and said in a cold voice, "No, why would I?"

I saw his hands clench the blanket we had over the couch. I could hear the fabric scraping against his fingernails.

He stared at me, and I could read the expression on his face. I knew in that moment that he suspected me, but he didn't have the balls to say it.

I glared back, challenging him with my eyes to say it out loud but he only pursed his lips and gave me a nod, before turning just as Kerres came back dressed in his jacket, wool hat, and gloves.

"Kerres?" I called from my spot. I watched Kerres walk to the side of the couch, straightening out his thin fabric gloves.

"Yeah, hun? I'll be a couple hours I won't be long."

"No, it's not that. Put a scarf over your mouth, I don't want you getting sick this winter."

Kerres gave me a warm smile before leaning down and kissing my cheek. "You take such good care of me."

You're my pet, it's my job.

I switched over the television after Kerres left and watched with inner joy as the news went on as usual. Now they were talking about the new library that had opened, and a robbery that had happened in Skyland which was getting all of the coverage. Before long I got bored of the news and went back to the television channel of Skyfall. Now Everybody Loves Raymond was playing, which as the title suggested, I also loved.

I put my legs up on the couch and became a limp noodle as I watched the television, chewing on a piece of sweet tact. Debra was being a bitch and Raymond was being a whiner, so it was a typical episode.

Suddenly, there was a slam on the apartment door. I shot up to my feet and looked at it, my eyes wide and my heartbeat going from normal to jackhammer in a matter of milliseconds.

Another slam, but I was frozen. I eyed the bedroom, wanting to grab my claws, a knife or something, but before I could react the door was kicked again. This wasn't Kerres returning, this wasn't one of my friends. The atmosphere in the room suddenly became cold and imposing; the hair on the back of my neck stood up.

The third kick brought the door slamming open.

"Thiens! Put your hands up!"

Oh shit.

I turned and made a break for the sliding glass door but then I remembered that Kerres locked it whenever he came back from his cigarettes. I swore and flicked the lock but it was too late; their hands grabbed me and slammed me onto the carpet.

"If you resist, it will be marked on your record, Jade of Moros District," a voice barked. I growled but let them wrench my arms back. I felt the clinking of handcuffs and several people hoisted me to my feet.

A man dressed in thien combat armour glared at me, a black beret on his head and a stone-cold expression on his face. He raised a scanner and waved it over my ear. When it beeped he brought it back and looked at the screen.

"It's him, this is Jade. Bring him to the precinct, don't hurt him unless he struggles," the man said addressing the three armed thiens that were holding me back. The man stepped back and let the thiens walk me out of the apartment.

"Shut the door when you leave," I called back to him. "In case you haven't been watching the news –" I couldn't hold back the smirk. "Moros has become a pretty dangerous place."

"Yeah, I bet you know a lot about that, don't you?" the man said crisply. I heard the apartment door close behind me and I was walked roughly down the stairs, almost falling several times.

They shoved me into an old army vehicle and, because these types of things were never seen in Moros, everyone was watching, the gawking, hollow eyes of the starved residents, wondering if they were witnessing the serial killer of the slums finally getting carried away.

Well, I guess I will see you at Stadium, guys. I bet I'll sell a lot of tickets.

I wish I could've said goodbye to Kerres first, I would be leaving my boyfriend once again, but he would be fine. I hadn't even been home for three months, and previously he had been alone for a year. If I died in front of him, he would know I was really gone and be able to move on with someone else. And if I survived – I'd fuck him all night long and celebrate my heroic status from once again wasting one of those cum-sucking chimera brutes.

Look at me now, Elish, look at me now.

I glared at the buildings going by. I could tell which district we were in just from the state of the structures we passed, and the number of pot holes the military vehicle drove over.

Though with all the dark feelings inside me, and the complete acceptance of my fate I still felt nauseas when we crossed the walls to Skyland. Not from the fact that I knew we were close to the precinct but because Skyland brought with it the feeling of recognition and the knowledge that Elish was close.

So I stopped looking out of the windows and looked ahead instead, at the brown hair of the main thien who had arrested me.

I looked at him through black bars that crisscrossed over the space separating the driver and passenger side of the vehicle and the pen they kept the convicts in. It was its own small prison in here; no handles on the doors and the seats were covered in hard plastic, assumingly so the prisoners' blood would be easy to wipe away.

Was Kerres back in the apartment yet? It was a forty minute drive in the best of traffic; though I think because we were a thien vehicle we had gotten there sooner. I wondered if he was sad right now.

My thoughts darkened as I played with the idea that perhaps Kerres would be happy I was out of his life again, especially when he and his friends found out I had killed Loni. I had probably disrupted his perfect little existence in the slums.

That opinion was hardly a consensus in my brain, more my own self-loathing trying to convince me that everyone was better off without me. That even though I now belonged to no one, in all respects, I also belonged nowhere. I was a roaming monster with no home, no master, and no future.

Well, whatever, it didn't matter now, I was caught. My fun time stalking and murdering people under the cover of darkness was over. Now I had Stadium to look forward to, and I could meet the final boss. Though it would be villain against villain which would be a nice little twist in the comic book I was creating in my brain. Wouldn't it be great if they let me wear my pet outfit and those cat ears, even more so if I got my claws and teeth again. I could see King Silas allowing it just for his own amusement.

They opened my passenger door in front of the precinct. I wondered briefly if the thiens holding their bushmasters were the same ones that had mercilessly shoved a sick and exhausted boy to his fate, or if they were different people.

I looked around the lobby as they walked me through the doors.

Grey tile floor, white walls and ceiling, with a secretary's desk that curved in a semi-circle against the wall, walled off with bulletproof glass from top to bottom with a small slit open in the middle to accept papers, and holes above it for people to talk back and forth. A small lady with glasses was behind that glass talking on a landline phone; only Skyland had landline phones and only chimeras and their minions had access to remote phones.

"Good, you have him, it doesn't look like he fought." Ellis Dekker was standing with her arms crossed over her chest. She had black hair that fell a few inches past her cheekbone and deep royal blue eyes. Like all chimeras she was beautiful, for a chick anyway, arched eyebrows, red lips, and a smooth complexion.

Though she was good-looking, she looked really fucking dangerous too. If anyone should have *Don't fuck with* written across their face it was this broad.

She walked up to me, wearing a black turtle neck and standard-issue black thien pants with the blue stripe up the side, and locked her blueish-purple eyes with mine.

"Yeah, that's him... let him go, I'll take him from here." Ellis grabbed my arm and started walking me towards a metal door with a glass window, framed between several red fabric chairs and a green potted plant.

"Yes, Commissioner, do you want guards outside your door?" I blinked with confusion as I was dragged away. All the times my friends had been arrested they were brought to the interrogation rooms in the basement. The soundproof ones without video cameras, where it was obvious what went on behind the Styrofoam-stuffed walls.

I was expecting to have the shit beat out of me, I wanted to at least get a few hits in before I confessed to all the murders. Take a thien or two out. I still had those implanted teeth in my mouth, though my claws were under the bed.

"No, it won't be needed, if anyone goes near my door – kill them." Ellis had the same poisonous edge to her voice as her brother. She seemed like a real piece of work, and a dangerous one at that. I guess she was the leader of the thiens in Skyfall for a reason.

The doors opened and closed and she marched me towards her office in a way that reminded me of how the nurse mothers at the orphanage marched me to the head mother's office whenever I got into trouble. I half-expected her to grab my ear.

Surprisingly, she let go of my arm as soon as she got into her office, and to my further shock she brought out a set of keys and started unlocking my cuffs.

"Sit." The sound of her voice brought out the inner ten-year-old in me, being scolded after doing something wrong. I automatically sat down, but I crossed my arms over my chest; I wasn't going to sit here and have a conversation with a fucking chimera. She might be a chick but she was one of them, and worse of all she was from the first generation... Elish's generation.

Ellis brought out a file folder and slapped it in front of me. She opened it and a single piece of paper was lying inside, with rows and rows of peoples' pictures.

I stared at each of them and laughed internally, yep, I recognized some of them.

"Point out which ones you killed," she said before slamming down a red marker. I heard the scrape of a chair as she pulled it up to the other side of her desk. The desk was just as obsessively neat and tidy as Elish's was, though this one had pictures of her kids; one of them was actually the man who ran the orphanage: Knight.

"All of them." I shrugged nonchalantly, and in the most arrogant manner I could muster, I flicked the file folder closed and crossed my legs. "Every single one and more."

Her face tensed and her eyes narrowed at me; the chimera woman realizing in that moment I wasn't going to play the sobbing murderer terrified of his own fate.

She reached across the table and opened the file folder back up. "You didn't even look at them, Jade. Circle the ones you killed and we can move on from there."

I glanced down at the pictures, and in truth there were a couple that I hadn't killed, but who cared? "Am I not doing you a favour, Commissioner Ellis? If I confess to all of them is that not less work for you?"

The dark-haired woman shook her head in a subtle fashion, then said something that made my heart freeze, "Sardonic and patronizing with a subtle wry smirk; you sound like your master."

I recoiled like she had just smacked me in the face. I swallowed hard, feeling my jaw tighten. "He's not my master anymore."

The smile that appeared on her red lips told of a spider who had just caught itself a fly. "Not so cocky now are we? Your heart is like a hummingbird."

Fucking chimera hearing…

She didn't stop there. "I know what you're trying to do, Jade. You're the most clumsy, foolish serial killer I have encountered in all my time on the thien force."

With everything going down around me I still had emotion left to feel stung by that remark. I thought I was a good super villain.

"It wasn't like I was purposely trying to cloak my actions," I recovered quickly enough to snip back, weaving the red marker through my fingers. "So just arrest me and get it over with."

Ellis snatched the pen away from me, like I was a child who was playing with his food, and slammed it down over the folder. "I know this is your pathetic little cry for attention, and I know you would like nothing more than for me to send your Morosian ass to Stadium so you can show off some more."

"Then do it," I said coldly, though it gave me chills to hear her say my plan out loud. I wondered what else she knew about me. I wondered if Elish had talked to her.

My heart started to hurt, but with another dry swallow I pushed it down and replaced it with the burning hatred I felt for that blond chimera.

Ellis uncapped the pen and handed it to me. I took it and stared at the crimson tip. "Jade, my precinct and I could care less about your teenage angst over my brother. Kill all the Morosians. I have better and more important things to do with our resources." I looked up over my brows at her, unsuccessfully hiding my shock.

She carried on, "I want two things from you: circle the ones you killed, and do not kill beyond Nyx. Besides that, kill until the pain goes away. The Moros District is filling up too quickly anyway; my family would not mind a cull."

"A – a cull?"

"No one will miss a few less vermin." Ellis seemed to be enjoying this. "My family would expect nothing less when a cat gets released into a town of rats. Luca's ears, that cute little outfit Elish made you wear, and, of course, the weapons my father gave to you. Are you trying to be some sort of evil villain?"

I felt humiliated once again. I stared at her, and watched the left corner of her lip rise. She knew she had me – fucking bitch.

"So you're not fucking arresting me?" The heat made the hair on the back of my neck tingle and burn; I started getting angry at the injustice of there literally being no justice. "I want to go to Stadium. I want to –"

Ellis held up a hand. "I know what you want to do, don't embarrass yourself saying it. Just circle who you killed and stop wasting my time with your petty teenage angst."

I flicked the cap of the pen and circled every single dipshit I had throttled. When I was done I pushed the papers towards her.

Ellis looked at them and nodded. "I thought as much."

"Can I go?" I said bitterly, the black cloud over my head only growing blacker and more dismal. I hated myself for even feeling sad at this point, not just because I was showing emotion in front of a chimera, but because I had just been given the license to kill and I was still pissed off at the world.

Surprisingly, Ellis let out a sigh. She rose and put away the folder in her desk. "Jade, a word of caution." She motioned me to rise which I did.

Her dark blue eyes stared at me, ripping away my own pupils to peer into my brain and pick it apart, though I suspected she already knew everything. If Elish hadn't told her, Garrett would have during his weekly games of chess with his siblings. I wondered if she had empathy in her, because it seemed to vary from chimera to chimera, but maybe, being a mother, she did. Then again, my own mother had never had any empathy.

"If I were you, I would end this killing spree; you're very close to grabbing the attention of my father, and you don't want that."

I was confused for a moment; but considering Silas would have no sexual use for a female chimera it made sense he would raise her as a daughter.

"I don't care, I'm out of that life now. I'm a slumrat again."

Ellis opened the door of her office and stood back for me to walk out first. "Even so, if you want to make things easier on you and Elish –"

At the mere mention of his name paired with mine, my anger flared again. "Fuck Elish!" I snapped. I started walking down the long empty hallway. Then with my heart threatening to thrash out of my chest, I whirled around to her. "Why would I want to make shit easy for him?

Fuck him! Fuck all of you!"

Suddenly in a flash, Ellis grabbed me by my collar. She locked her eyes with mine. I was temporarily stunned by this quick change in her mood.

"Keep your voice down, you obnoxious little pest." Her voice was a thin razor blade that cut through my emotions like they were paper. I bit down the next insult that was about to emerge from my lips and swallowed it down with the bitter acid that was filling my mouth.

She nodded at my silence and dropped me. When my boots hit the ground I shoved my shoulder away from her arm and started stalking back to the metal door.

"A car will bring you back to Moros, and remember what I said, Jade: only Moros."

I took a deep breath and collected myself, enough to know to keep my mouth shut. I pushed the metal doors open and quickly walked out of the precinct.

My plan had gone to shit, utter fucking shit, though I suppose being able to murder whoever I felt like was a nice perk. I wasn't the sort of idiot who would lose interest once the thrill of getting caught was gone. The elixir of excitement I got was from murdering and sinking my teeth into hot flesh, not getting away with it.

Though now I wouldn't be able to make my statement in Stadium, perhaps I could make my statement some other way.

Fucking Ellis... culling Moros? Too many of us? That bitch had systematically insulted me and called out every emotion I was feeling; shoving them in my face and blatantly calling them 'teenage angst'. Fucking ancient bitch hadn't been a teenager in seventy years, fuck her.

With an angry beehive swirling over my head I let the assholes drive me back to Moros, keeping silent even though a part of me wanted to flaunt my freedom to the fucks who had carted me out of my apartment.

Why the hell was that bitch even giving me a free ticket?

Because that was exactly what I didn't want.

Because she and all the other chimeras who knew that Elish had grown tired and abandoned me back in Moros knew I wanted to go to Stadium. They knew I had a fucking death wish.

I bet they were all having a good laugh at me, smoking their blue-embered cigarettes and drinking their fancy wine. All those immortal fucks who had nothing better to do than destroy mortal's lives for their own amusement.

With a sigh, I watched the other vehicles pass through the city. In that time, I had a pep talk with myself, trying to figure out what it is I wanted, what I was feeling, and what this conversation with Elish's sister really meant.

She had said I could keep killing them because Morosians were the scum of the earth and the Skylanders didn't care, further proving that we were gutter rats void of even the most basic rights.

Morosians were worthless and I was worthless. I was right back to being just another hollow face in the crowd. Because no one cared about Morosians, not even when someone was murdering them left and right.

I sighed and closed my eyes. Perhaps it was time to hang up my claws, because the statement I had been trying to make hadn't been made. This was teenage angst to those fucking chimeras, and nothing but something to laugh at.

I bet Elish was laughing at me… having a cold, bemused chuckle every time the bulletin came out highlighting all the recovered corpses and missing people in the gutter district that nobody cared about.

My eyes burned, but through my closed eyelids I made sure they didn't water.

I still missed him.

So much my heart hurt.

Kerres's voice broke into a thousand pieces when I walked through the apartment doors. He ran into my arms and babbled incoherently for several minutes before I could comfort him enough to pull his talons from my skin.

"I thought he stole you again! Then Pete said thiens took you! Oh, J, baby, fuck – fuck!! How could they think it was you? Those fucking morons. It was Tate, I think Tate tipped them off. I punched him in the fucking face when he brought your name up. Oh, my poor baby, did they hurt you? Elish wasn't there was he? I'm so relieved, my poor baby."

"Oh my god, Ker, stop rambling." His over-the-top desperation made my heart feel its first flicker of warmth. "I'm okay… they just wanted to question me that's all. They said they've been questioning a lot of people." A blatant lie, but it wasn't like he knew.

Kerres pulled back and I wiped his tears away, with a kind smile that I hoped would cheer him up.

But instead he frowned, and I saw his face tense. "Jade... I gotta ask..."

I walked past him and opened the paper bag I had picked up. I had gotten the thiens to drop me off at the pharmacy nearby.

"Please, don't be pissed –"

I waited for him to say it, because it couldn't be more obvious what he was about to ask.

"– are you the Shadow Killer?"

The Shadow Killer? I had a name now? I smiled at the thought. Yes, the Shadow, it had a ring to it. Tiger had called me Shadow a few times when I fenced things to him. I liked it.

I took out a bottle of rum from the bag and placed it on the coffee table. The drugs I had picked up were nestled nicely inside the bag for later consumption because I had decided that I deserved it. It was a quick hit of an all-in-one Eight Ball that was making me rather chipper right now; it had banished the overwhelming feelings for Elish that had developed on the way home.

"Don't be silly, Kerres." I poured him a shot in a cracked drinking glass because in Moros we didn't have a certain glass for each drink.

When I handed it to him, he looked at me guiltily but also wary of my improved mood. "It... it was just some of the things Tate told me. I don't have time to watch the news all day like he does and work is in Nyx so it's not talked about there. He... said all the victims had their necks bitten, like torn out."

I took a sip of my drink and leaned up against the couch. I watched it swirl in my glass. I dropped my voice and glanced up at him over my brow. "And?"

"Those implants you said Elish gave you–"

The vibe between us changed, and instead of feeling fear at his probing into my night time activities I only felt annoyance. "– will protect me if this person tries to come after me."

Kerres nodded to himself, and with a glance at his face I saw he was convincing himself that it wasn't me. "You're right, forgive me for even thinking it. Tate was just so upset over Loni missing, my emotions took over my reasoning." Kerres walked over and kissed me.

I resisted the urge to grab him, to hold his neck in my hand and force out every single lead he thought he had pinning me to these murders. Then tell him with a demonic laugh that I was above Morosian law and I could kill whoever the fuck I wanted. Just to see the expression on his face.

But he was Kerres not Elish, though sometimes I knew I took my deep rooted anger out on him. Instead I stepped away from him and took another drink, my trembling hands making small ripples appear in the liquor.

"– Jesus, Jade, slow down!"

I gasped and gave one last push as the strings of my sexual pleasure snapped. I bit the pillow beside Kerres and growled into it, thrusting the last of my cum into my boyfriend's ass.

I pulled out and rolled off of him with a groan, hearing the sharp gasps of Kerres finishing himself off; with a reach of my hand I batted his away and finished him off with my mouth.

Kerres came and dropped his head onto the pillow underneath him; after a few minutes of recovering from the climax I was annoyed to find his tone change towards me. "I tell you every time, J: *slow down*. What the hell is with you? You were never rough like this before."

"Shut up." I buried my face into his neck and kissed him. "I can do what I want to you, and you can like it."

I expected him to laugh, but instead he sighed and rolled over onto his side, his back facing me.

"What!" I said incredulously. I smacked his shoulder blade. "Stop being a bitch. What?"

Kerres rolled back around. I didn't expect him to look upset with me but he was. A moment later he brought his hands out of the covers and showed me the tips of his fingers; they were glistening with blood.

"That, that's what's wrong, every time you get on top of me you tear me and I've asked you so many times to slow down." Kerres sighed, wiping the blood onto the blankets. "It hurts, Jade."

The coppery smell reached my nostrils, and my throat felt parched with thirst. I found myself smiling and ripping the blankets off of him. "I got a way to make you feel better."

Kerres stared at me in shock as I bent his leg back. I lowered my head towards his blood rimmed opening and started to lick up the alluring blood that had collected.

But no sooner than I had tasted the first lick, than Kerres shifted away from me. "What the fuck, Jade? I'm bleeding down there, get away!"

My jaw clenched. I kneeled back on my legs and raised my arms and dropped them to my sides. "It's just some fucking blood. What? Are you suddenly some fucking prude?"

"No!" Kerres was sitting in bed now, looking just as annoyed as I did. "It's just fucked up, first you lick the blood when you bite me and now you want to lick it out of my ass? I gave you a pass when you first came here, but it's been months now. Did Elish make you–"

Kerres jumped and let out a shocked scream as my fist slammed against the headboard of the bed, only inches above his own head.

"Never mention his name to me, Kerres."

"Why the fuck not?"

I ground my molars; they whined under the stress. "Because I'll break your fucking teeth? I said shut up about it."

Suddenly Kerres shot up; he grabbed the pillow and threw it at me. "No, Jade, I'm fucking tired of walking on egg shells around you. I'm fucking twenty years old being bossed around by a sixteen-year-old ex-pet with no fucking job. You listen to me. Stop fucking me like Elish fucked you, and stop treating me like –"

"Watch yourself, Cicaro!" I suddenly snapped. I rose to my feet and gave him a violent push against the wall, but to my shock he pushed me back.

"I'm not your fucking pet, you maniac!" Kerres snapped back. "You're not Elish and I'm not you, and I'm not the Kerres you left behind. I won't let you treat me like this in the apartment I'm paying for; I won't let you talk to me like I'm your whipping boy. You can't come back after a year and think your re-emergence is enough to make me want to be your servant."

I glared at him, all my resentment towards him and Elish pouring from my eyes. My fists clenched so hard they were trembling from the strain. This was going to escalate, and I didn't know how to stop it.

I moved to leave when I heard my boyfriend speak, his voice a barely audible whisper, "Go out and kill another one of my friends, Jade, because every time you do you come back happier."

My veins turned to ice. I watched him in his blue-tinged glow as he stared at the floor, a dead look in his eyes, but he wasn't done.

"I bet your master would be pleased."

Darkness covered my eyes and with a jolt of such an incomprehensible anger I didn't realize I had, I lunged at Kerres until he was punching me in the head.

Punching me in my head because my jaws were snapping at his neck, my arms ripping and hitting him with fingers void of their clawed armour.

Kerres threw me off with a surprised gasp, but as soon as my back hit the floor I shot to my feet and hit him across the face.

Kerres was thrown backwards, hitting the night table and smashing the lamp against the wall. He looked stunned as I grabbed him by his crimson hair and wrenched him to his feet, before throwing him against the desk.

A deep growl reverberated from my throat as I walked silently towards him.

Kerres looked up at me in shock, the reflection of the moon outside the window bathing him in a silver glow, mixed with black from the blood dripping from his face.

"He killed my Jade." Kerres's thin laughter broke the heavy silence in the room. "He gave me a chimera back."

I didn't know what happened next, but I think he hit me with something. With an animal-like snarl from my lips, I was knocked off my feet, my cheek slamming into the frame of the window, temporarily shooting every sense out of my body and leaving me dazed.

In that same daze my mind took me to a place I hadn't been in a long time, when Elish would knock me senseless, when Ares and Siris would throw me off my feet. It drew from me a power that started in my chest and spread to every tight string in my body. I was their victim, but I would be a victim no more. I was the master. I was the king; he was my property.

The strings pulled me to my feet and turned my face to Kerres, who was staring at me in shock.

I jumped on him, half in reality and half replaying the fantasy of how I had always wanted to retaliate when those three hurt me. I found my jaws take Kerres's neck into my mouth and start to bite down.

Stop... stop! STOP!

My eyes opened and my ears did too. I heard a scared whine from Kerres that brought the situation I had found myself in flooding back to me with fierce fervour.

I pulled away and looked at him in shock.

My boyfriend was shaking, red puncture marks on his neck. One hand went up to shield the soft nape, his other one helping him rise.

"I'm – I'm sorry…" I whispered, finding my feet and standing up with him. I felt hot tears come to my eyes as I backed away from him. "I'm not me… anymore."

When Kerres saw my face, his own softened. He took a step towards me but I backed away from him quickly. His fingers brushed against my hand to try and pull me back, but I got myself as far away from him as I could. I ran into the second bedroom, mumbling nothing coherent but a small request to be left alone.

I closed the door and locked it, before I quickly fumbled with the paper bag I had filled with my small drug stash and started doing bumps right from the bag.

Calm me down... please, calm me down before I purposely overdose and kill myself right here.

I took in several lines of china white and curled up on the mattress. My body was shaking from the overwhelming self-hatred that I felt for myself.

A deep guttural feeling gripped me, a trickle of acid down a well without a bottom. I didn't fit in here anymore, and as much as I tried to go back to my old life, everything I did was wrong. Not only had I become a serial killer in three months but I had become even more abusive towards my boyfriend than I had been before, and he'd had enough of it.

Who was I now? The only identity I could scrape together was the Shadow Killer. I wasn't Jade from the slums and I wasn't Jade the cicaro, I was nobody yet inside of me I felt such powerful emotions I felt like I had enough in me to be several people.

Is this what happened when I stopped having a master to control me? I just turned into this loose cannon in dire need of someone to take my leash? I was a stray animal running around in the slums murdering without care. I was the one in control and this is where control got me.

I didn't deserve freedom. I wasn't even human anymore.

Automatically, not even knowing if I was going to go out tonight, I put on my pet clothes, buttoning up the tight pants, putting on the mesh long sleeve shirt and vest, and finally putting on the claw rings one by one.

I got up and was about to leave when I heard Kerres's muffled crying coming from the wall the two rooms shared. He was trying to be as quiet as he could but the sound was unmistakable.

Swallowing a boulder in my throat and using the china white as fuel, I got up and walked to the bedroom.

I opened the door and saw him with his head bowed and buried in his hands; his shoulders shaking from grief I knew all too well.

But when he saw me, I saw his pupils retract and I was reminded of my own stupidity. I was dressed to do what he had just accused me of doing.

"Get out!" Kerres suddenly screamed. I took a step back as he rose. "Get the fuck out of my bedroom! Get out of my sight, you murdering asshole! You fucking chimera-born scum. GET OUT!"

The door slammed in my face, and as the deafening sound faded, his hysterical sobbing came forth, with such agony I could hear him needing to gasp for breath between chokes.

The slam was more than just a door closing in my face, it was my old life finally closing on me. There was no going back, no recovering the scraps of the person I had been before Elish carried me into Olympus. I didn't know who I was, but one thing was for sure… I was no longer Jade.

With my heart a heavy, bleeding sore, I went into the second bedroom and grabbed Luca's cat ears. I put them on and walked out of the window and onto the fire escape. I would give Kerres some money to use the second bedroom and I would stay there until an apartment in Moros came available. I knew I was no longer welcome to share his bed, and in truth, I didn't trust myself around him anymore.

I wrapped my arms around my body; the cold fall was quickly turning into winter. I could see my breath when I ventured out in the middle of the night now. Soon I might need to add a cape or something to my outfit or else I would probably freeze to death.

I crossed the courtyard and opened the iron gate, leaving my troubles and my inner hatred behind in the apartment and focusing my attention on the license to kill that Ellis Dekker had been nice enough to give me. Who would it be tonight? For some reason the thrill of hunting and killing was lost.

I sprinted across an empty street and hopped up onto the sidewalk. I drew my eyes in each direction to try and spot any people I could stalk, but there were none. Still though, I stuck to the shrouded shadows of Moros. There were nooks and crannies, alleyways and more partially-destroyed buildings than you could count. Each I knew off the back of my hand, and every one of them I had explored at one time or another.

I took a deep breath and lit a cigarette, the burning ember giving away my location. But even if I came across a perfect prey, I didn't think I would care to kill him.

So I wandered around, and when I eventually did pass people I ducked out of sight. I watched them from above, usually crouched into a broken window frame, and wondered if they knew just how close they had come to me killing them.

Eventually my alleyway wanderings brought me to Garrett Park; subconsciously or not I didn't know. With a hesitant step I walked onto the grass, towards where my mother's nest used to be.

Unbidden a small smile crept to my lips as I saw the tree, but it faded into an ache in my heart when I realized all of her garbage had been cleared away.

I think a part of me still expected her to be there, offering me a can of poisoned food and yelling at whatever rat dog she had found to shut up, throwing things at me and calling me every name she could think of: demon spawn, shapeshifter, hell hound. She had a good imagination when it came to insulting me.

A plume of vapour fell from my lips as I sighed. I bent down and brushed my fingers along the bare spot where she always used to sit.

Like I had done in Stadium, I kissed my fingers and laid them on the spot and said another goodbye to her, hoping she was in a better place than she had been her entire life.

My mother had never led a good life; every moment had been a struggle and even the good moments were only brought forth from an oversaturation of drugs or alcohol. I had never made her proud, or happy… I had only brought her misery and eventually… her death.

I wondered what she would have done with me if she had known that I would grow up to be a serial killer. Would she have just smothered me? Maybe she would have just gone with it because it would've got her more attention.

Either way, I know she would've loved me, as much as she was capable of loving something with all her problems.

"Sorry, Mom," I said quietly before I rose and turned away from the spot, wondering if she was missed by anyone besides me. I hoped so, but somehow… I didn't think anyone had really noticed.

I closed my eyes for a brief moment, a moment of silence in a way I guess. She would never have a funeral, or a grave marker. My mom would disappear with the normal passage of time and just become someone's random memory. I would be the only one to remember her, and since I wasn't some immortal chimera, once I died she would be forgotten.

"The moonlight reflects so beautifully against your leather-draped body," a smooth voice suddenly sounded behind me. I whirled around and faced him with my eyes growing wide. "My my, little cicaro, have you ever been the most fascinating creature to watch in the dead of night."

He stood there, dressed in a tight open blazer, fitted on top of a black nylon shirt. He took a gliding step towards me, his crimson eyes drinking me in, matching perfectly the red bow tie around his pale neck.

He grinned, and in the moonlight shining like the sun above us, I saw two rows of sharp, shark-like teeth.

"Sanguine," I gasped

CHAPTER 22

I TOOK A CAUTIOUS STEP BACK FROM THE RED-EYED sengil, but at my obvious aversion to his presence he laughed at me and brushed his black hair from his eyes; with a casual flick he looked behind his shoulder.

"Cicaro, I am not here to hurt you. I saw you've been having trouble fitting in. I have come to feel badly for you. Come with me, little shadow. I think above everything right now, you need a friend who understands you."

I eyed him cautiously, but internally my heart almost seemed to pull towards any connection to Elish and my old life. It was a place I might not fit into anymore, but it was more familiar and comfortable to me than where I was now.

"Did Silas send you?" I asked quietly.

As the blood-eyed sengil shook his head, I scanned his face for any underlining deception but I didn't see any. "I am still a chimera, Jade. I am not bound with chains like Luca, Juni or the others. I can roam free, converse with who I wish and do what I like while my master is away or resting. And as of right now he is far away in the greywastes and will not return until the mood strikes him. I am here on my own accord."

Sanguine reached a hand out, and his eyes squinted as he gave me a closed lipped smile. "I think you need to be around someone who knows what you are going through. I only wish I'd had a friend when my own family turned their backs on me. Please, come with me, Jade."

When I was still with Elish, he would swoop in and usher me away from Sanguine with a firm shake of the sengil's neck to discipline him for talking to me, but Elish was gone and I was on my own now.

And with what had gone down tonight, fuck it... with everything that had happened over the last several months my body pulled towards a familiar face, and towards someone who knew the person I had been in Skyland. My own boyfriend in Moros didn't know who I was, but it seemed... that Sanguine did.

My heart filled with desperate longing for someone to understand what I was going through, because I didn't.

I reached out and took his hand. His smile widened to a grin, but it wasn't scary like it had been in Garrett's building over a year ago – it was warm in an odd way.

"There we go."

He didn't let go of my hand, and my heart betrayed me by feeling comforted. Sanguine... he seemed to genuinely want to help me transition back to my old life. "So... really no one knows you're here?"

The sengil shook his head. He hopped over the concrete poles that acted like fences, connected by two bowed chains stretched across, and held my hand up as I stepped over them, almost like an old-fashioned gentlemen helping a maiden. "No, no one, they would stop me. Once they let a pet go, they want to forget it even exists. They are chimeras born with ebony spoons in their mouths, they don't understand how difficult it is, how much... everyone turns their backs on you."

I saw Sanguine's lips downturn, an odd expression for a man I always saw either smiling or about to smile. He squeezed my hand and started taking me down a dark alleyway. I found a small splinter of humour in the fact that I had killed a man in this very alley just a month before.

"I kind of deserved it," I whispered. I glanced around as Sanguine led me down the alleyway, where, to my surprise, he took out a single silver key and approached an unassuming grey metal door half spray-painted.

With a chuckle and a shake of his head, Sanguine unlocked the door. "No, you don't. You are a powerful creature, Jade. Everyone in Moros should fall to their knees and worship you, just from being fucked by a chimera as powerful as Elish Dekker. No, no, *bona mea*, you deserve nothing but your own carnal desires. Now, come inside... you need to get wasted."

Despite the silent atmosphere that roaming around in the dead of night brought, I laughed at the incredulousness of his sudden statement. "What?"

Sanguine walked me inside and flicked on the lights. I blinked from the sudden flash of halogens before my eyes focused and took in a small apartment hidden in this unassuming alleyway.

It was a single room, with a small kitchenette tucked into an alcove, painted brown with purple trim, with a small double bed in a corner and a night stand. There was also a privacy curtain and to the right, a couch separating the kitchen from the living room.

I took a step in and couldn't help but feel in awe. My eyes swept the room to take in a coffee table brimming with drugs and an overflowing ashtray, with the television turned on and showing cartoons.

"We have little emergency shelters all over Skyfall; this one only I and the top chimeras know about, nice little nook isn't it? It's mine and as such, it shall be yours since everyone within a block could hear the fight you had with your boyfriend tonight." Sanguine shut the door behind me and I felt the click of the lock. "What's your poison, *mihi*? Opiates, meth, crack, weed? Let this be our little vacation."

I didn't move, my back leaning against the metal door. I watched the sengil stroll into the small apartment and crack open a bottle of root beer. With suspicion in my eyes, I tried to take in his face and his body language, appreciative of his kindness, but not forgetting that he was still a chimera.

"Why are you doing this?" I tried to hide the caution and skepticism on my face and in my tone but there was no getting away from it.

Sanguine took a drink, and sat down on the arm of the couch, a sad sigh coming to his lips. He looked up at me and gave me a small shrug. "Yes, you are wary of us, I do understand, and I would call you an idiot if you weren't. You want to know what is in it for me, since no chimera has ever done anything for you without wanting something in return. Am I wrong?"

The abrupt honesty took me aback, I felt for a moment stunned at his forwardness. "Well –" I had to be honest back, " – yes."

Sanguine nodded and motioned me to sit on the couch. "Jade, it isn't often my master leaves me to my own devices, and as a sengil I do not lead an easy existence serving him. Who else in my family do I have to sit and do drugs with for a while before I go back to being a slave? Someone I don't have to worry about degrading me or judging and patronizing my every move? This is my vacation from my troubles as much as yours. You are a creature in need of someone who understands you, and no one understands your situation more than I."

He looked at me with those wine-coloured eyes. "Is that a good enough reason?"

I stared at him for a moment, before a smirking smile appeared on my lips. "You had me at sit and do drugs." I flopped down on the couch and started rooting through his stash. "I don't want to be indebted to a demon-toothed chimera though." I gave him a wink, timing it perfectly because at my agreement to hanging out with him he had smiled. "So tell me how much all this shit costs and I'll front you some cash."

Sanguine tapped a plastic card against the table and flicked it towards me. "Fuck that, it's all Silas's money, even the cash blondy gave you. See that black card there?" He pointed to it. "No limit, only his chimeras get access to it. You could buy two restaurants and an apartment block before Domnik noticed the money missing."

I smelled one of the baggies and saw it was marked off with a CW for china white. I tapped it onto the coffee table and grabbed the fancy card. It read Sanguine S. Dekker.

"S? I never knew chimeras had middle names." I started cutting myself a couple lines, noticing Sanguine get up. There was a clinking of more bottles from the fridge. "I don't even have a last name, let alone a middle name."

A frosted bottle was set down beside me, just as I leaned down and took two lines, one in each nostril. I rubbed my nose and passed the small metal sniffer to Sanguine as he sat down.

Sanguine obliged and did his own share, before leaning a leather boot, much like mine, against the coffee table. "Stands for Sasha. I was born along with Artemis, Apollo, Jack, Valen and Ceph. All of us share the same middle name, each batch of babies has their own, back when being born in groups was more common."

I rubbed my nose again and sniffed, feeling the sour drip followed by the cold water flowing through my body. I shuddered and sighed. "Valen and Ceph?" Elish had never written down their names in my leather black book.

Sanguine turned up the volume on the television and put the bottle to his lips. "No, they died, not good enough to become immortal. Only the chosen immortals of second gen are alive; we're all seventy now."

I wonder if Sanguine missed his dead brothers, but I wasn't going to ask. "What's the first gens' middle name?"

"Sebastian, same as our king's."

Elish Sebastian Dekker, my mouth pursed to the side, but the drugs were grabbing hold of all the feelings associated with my former master, dismissing them with a cold kiss and a warm embrace.

I could get used to this hovel; it was a nice vacation, away from the judging eyes of Kerres and his nosey friends. I didn't consider them my friends anymore, that was for sure. The closest person I had to a friend right now was this demonic chimera who gave me chills back in Skyland. That said a lot about where my state of mind was right now, and my own confused emotions. I was clinging to whatever person would give me some sort of comfort and empathy. I really was pathetic.

I couldn't have cared less and I wasn't in the position mentally or emotionally to be picky. Sanguine had given me what I needed right now, and he was upfront and honest about what I was giving back to him.

So we shot the shit for the next couple hours and to my surprise he didn't probe about my fight with Kerres or the murders. If anything, I was the one talking to him about it and the one bringing it up. He laughed and listened to every detail with a judgeless shine in his blood-red eyes.

When the sun was coming up, he cracked open the door to the apartment and peeked out. "Are you going to be heading back to your apartment? If so you better hurry if that's what you're wearing."

I was drugged up on china white and from chain-smoking opiates. I lifted my head and blew the smoke into the already hazy fog that had collected from hours and hours of smoking. "Yeah, I'm getting tired anyway. I'll be sleeping like a baby from all these drugs. Want to hang out tomorrow?"

Sanguine squinted his eyes as he smiled. "Of course; use some of that money of yours and bring some food while you're at it. I do not go out during the day. I am an easy chimera to spot for obvious reasons, and I will get in trouble if a certain person catches me."

Drugged up and content I rose and stretched, before sauntering over and giving Sanguine a slap on the shoulder. "I'll bring you the greasiest shit you've ever eaten. I'll be by around midnight if not a bit after."

There was no mistaking the skip in my step as I made my way back to the apartment. My chest felt lighter and my problems a million miles away, and I didn't think it was just the dangerous amount of drugs I had taken either. Sanguine had put me in great spirits.

I stripped off and did my usual routine of showering and changing into comfortable clothes, but instead of fucking Kerres, who would be at work by now anyway, I rubbed one out myself and used that and the drugs to lull myself into the best sleep I'd ever had.

And such followed one of the most comfortable sleeps in my life, I curled up into my musty-smelling, thready blankets and buried myself in pillows. And with a blanket covering the window and the door closed I slept in my little nest having lucid pleasant dreams of murder, sex and drugs. Three things I have come to quite enjoy.

When I finally was awakened from my drug-induced hibernation, I was being talked to by the familiar voice that had been talking to me since I was nine. I ignored the voice and stayed as still as I could in hopes that he would leave me alone. I was having a pleasant dream that involved my ex-boss and a claw hammer.

I felt two fingers on my neck and a sigh; when I opened my eyes I saw two big brown eyes staring back down at me.

"You're out of luck, I'm still alive," I said bitterly before sitting up.

Kerres retracted his fingers and put his hands on his knees before hoisting himself up. "Don't say things like that…"

I rubbed my eyes and shook my head free of sand and rose, making a beeline for the bathroom.

"You've been asleep all day, where… where were you last night?"

I let out an annoyed breath. "Didn't we pretty much break up last night? You aren't privy to that information, so go back to your part of the apartment and I'll stay in mine. Math out how much this room will cost and I'll give you the money for it."

I heard Kerres swallow a choke. "Break up? You want to break up?"

"I assumed that was the next logical step since I'm a serial killer and apparently a piece of chimera scum who isn't the same boy that Elish stole." I partially closed the door and took a leak; somethings couldn't wait.

When I walked out Kerres was still in my bedroom, leaning up against the wall with his arms crossed over his chest.

"I'm sorry for saying those things, it's… it's just been harder than I thought adjusting to you being back." Kerres shrugged, but he didn't look mournful or sad, his brow was furrowed and his face tense. "I expected you to come back exactly the same, and considering what happened to you… that was a stupid thought."

"No shit…" I grabbed my paper bag full of drugs and made my way to the living room to dish out some more china white. Kerres followed behind me and hovered around the living room while I scraped the drugs into four neat little lines. I leaned down and took them all in and leaned back on the couch with a content sniff.

Deliberately, he waited until they kicked into my system before he said quietly, "These murders have to stop, love. I can take a lot of shit, but… you're killing people."

"Eight people," I said casually. My eyes flicked up to him and I weaved the sniffer between my fingers. "Six from here, two from Nyx. Is there anyone you want me to off for you, *love*?"

His narrow face blanched and I watched his Adam's apple go up and down as he swallowed hard. "Tate went right to Ellis about Loni; it's only a matter of time before they have enough evidence –" Kerres stopped talking when I let out a loud and obnoxious laugh.

"Being a former cicaro has its advantages, *mihi*. Ellis knows it's me and she could care less how many slumrats I kill. She just wanted to know who I killed and who was actually still missing. I'm above the law, I can kill whoever I want here." I grinned in the same flashy, tooth-filled way Sanguine did when he was content.

He looked at me like he didn't believe me, until I think he noticed the implanted teeth still capped over my regular canines. With that confirmation his expression got even sicker. "Is Tate already dead? Is that what you were doing last night?"

I sighed and closed my eyes as wave after wave of pleasure washed over me. "No, an old chimera friend paid me a visit. Someone who understands me, accepts me for who I am, and wants to help me adjust to life back in this shit hole."

"Elish?"

My eyes snapped open but I stared at the roof, I didn't look at him. "I said to not mention his name, and no."

"Are you going to kill Tate?"

I scowled at the ceiling, this was starting to kill my high. "Why do you care? Are you two bonding over the loss of your boyfriends now? Going to get together once we finally break up since I bludgeoned his boyfriend with a baseball bat and ripped out his throat?" I added those last two just to be an asshole; there was no other reason.

And it worked; the atmosphere tensed right in front of me, but I still didn't look away from the ceiling. I heard Kerres take a couple deep breaths and I knew he was trying to calm himself down.

"No, it's because when Elish took you, Tate, Pete, and Fiere were all I had, and they helped me get through the last year. I couldn't have survived without them... I – I missed you so much. It would be pretty fucked up if the three guys who helped me through such an awful time were murdered by the guy I was upset over."

"Tate ratted me out, that's a death sentence in the slums and you know it. He betrayed the group." Which was true; as soon as you became a snitch you were as good as dead, no questions. It was the rules and it always had been, that was slum life.

There was a pause. I looked over to see Kerres staring at the floor, and I knew what he was thinking. It made my insides boil. I rose and grabbed the paper bag.

"Oh, that's right... I'm not part of the group anymore am I?"

"You killed his boyfriend, Jade."

"And he can join him."

I started walking back to my bedroom when I heard Kerres sniff. I sighed, feeling my first sting of guilt that I had made him cry again.

"I'm sorry, Jade."

My eyebrows knitted together. I looked behind my shoulder and stared at him. "For what?"

Kerres was looking at me, rubbing his own arm with his hand as if trying to soothe himself. He shook his head and pursed his lips.

"Because... I think unbelievably bad things happened to you when you were with Elish... to make you like this. This is the first experience that we haven't gone through together."

That statement brought me pause.

Because he was right.

The small black-haired boy with cuts and bandages all over his face, and the tall red-haired boy had endured every hardship together. Starved together, got jobs together, had sex together and lived life in the slums together.

It all changed when I went into that mansion, after I had gotten raped and beaten by Ares and Siris and... and whatever you would call what Elish had done to me. I didn't tell him about that and I think that was the start of the rift that was separating two once inseparable people.

Either tell me what happened or get over it. Classic words from Kerres.

"Y-you're right." The words left my mouth, to my surprise and Kerres's, I turned around and looked at him. "And I can't tell you, because... because if you ever tell me to get over it and that enough time has passed, and I don't have the excuse in my head that you just don't know how bad it was... I – I might kill you." I said the last part with a derisive chuckle before walking back into my bedroom. It was almost humorous to me to think about having to tell him that I had loved Elish, that contrary to his beliefs, my master had never raped me. The first time he penetrated me I had wanted it, and every time after. How could I tell him that without him hating me?

The thought made me sick. I walked into my bedroom and got back into bed.

I shifted away and scowled when I felt Kerres lay beside me. He put his arms around me and held me tight. "Do you hate the chimeras?"

With exception to Sanguine? I wasn't even going to clarify that, since he didn't know who Sanguine was and I wasn't going to explain him to Kerres.

"With every fiber of my fucking body." That was the truth. I hated them all but I still held my same feelings for Elish. It was... complicated.

He squeezed me tight. "I was talking to Tate when we were looking for Loni, after he told me he suspected you. Have you ever heard of the

Crimstones?"

I had. Tate had mentioned them a long time ago when Kerres had gotten arrested, and Elish had too in passing. "They were responsible for those strings of car bombs in Skyland a couple years ago." I thought back to what Elish had mentioned. "And they shot Ellis in the head at one point in time."

I felt him nod. "Tate's coworker is a man named Dave Chel; he's a member… Tate told me you've been brainwashed by the chimeras which explains… your actions. They have former pets that they've been able to turn back to their old selves."

Seriously? My body shifted away from Kerres. I rolled over until I was facing him. "I'm not going with strangers to unbrainwash me; I'm not brainwashed, I'm just still fucking adjusting."

Kerres looked like he didn't believe me, but he still nodded before pulling the blankets up to his chest. "I know and I'm not saying to go with them. I just… Tate told them about you and their leader really wants to talk to you, if only for a few minutes. He might be able to help you, help us bring Jade back."

Jade's not brainwashed, you fucking moron. Jade was in love and he got his heart shit on.

"I'm fine with who I am and I'm not letting anyone near my head," I said flatly.

"Just meet with him, here in our apartment, in your comfort zone, please, J?"

I never imagined that Kerres still had sway to make me do things, but I had to give the guy effort for trying to fix this quickly failing relationship and the broken parts of my head. I gave him a sigh and a small yes, and as I did he hugged me hard and I could hear him sniff. "Thank you, love, thanks for caring that much about me. I promise, I'll get my Jade back, one way or another."

Jeez… what a guilt trip. I hugged him back and even though I wasn't tired I held him as he fell asleep in my arms. He had been working all day and I had been sleeping all day.

Even though he was on my mattress I let him be and went into the living room, hearing him snore lightly in the second bedroom.

Midnight couldn't come soon enough. I stayed indoors except for a quick run to the Monkey Tree for Sanguine's fish and chips. Then, with my boyfriend dead to the world, I partially lifted up the mattress and put on my pet clothes; I didn't want Sanguine to see me in cloth pants and a dirty t-shirt.

I was considerate though. I left Kerres a note saying I was visiting the friend I told him about and to not worry if I was gone for a while; even being considerate enough to tell him I needed time to think.

Then when I was all dressed in my villain clothes I slipped out and into the night, being the Shadow Killer in all my glory with a plastic bag full of fresh battered fish and fries hanging from my hand. I certainly was an odd serial killer, that was for sure.

Sanguine opened the door wearing sunglasses and his hair gelled up into shaggy spikes. When he saw me he bowed and smiled and motioned me in, taking the sunglasses off. "A part of me expected you not to return. Did you have an acceptable day?"

"Besides Kerres guilt tripping my ass it was good, slept a lot." I returned the customary cicaro bow and threw the food onto the blue counter top of the small kitchenette, before flopping down on the couch and dishing out the drugs. I hadn't taken a hit in about four hours and I was starting to dislike day-to-day life without powdered heroin.

"There –" I sighed, wanting to get it out in the open sooner rather than later. "– is some shit I gotta tell you about, do some lines with me. It isn't a big deal but the top dogs might want to know."

The demon-eyed chimera raised an eyebrow at me before he got out a metal spoon from the kitchen drawer and sat down beside me. To my surprise he started prepping a needle. "Really? Well, that spikes my curiosity."

My mouth pursed but in all respects… Kerres wasn't a part of this group so I wasn't betraying him. They were a group of people against the chimeras and no matter what Elish had done to me, my heart was still his, even if he had thrown it in the trash can. Anyway, I didn't want to risk any of the sengils or other cicaros getting hurt because I was ticked about what that blond fuck did. It was no skin off my ass to pass on info. "One of the guys I killed, a dude named Loni, his boyfriend was my friend at one point. He knows a guy at work who's a part of the Crimstones."

Sanguine's eyes immediately shot up from his syringe currently sucking up some water. It was obvious that I had caught his attention. I guess they were well-known amongst the elites. "The terrorists? Fascinating – continue."

I nodded. "First, you need to promise me, no harm comes to Kerres."

"Naturally."

That surprised me, but I guess sometimes I forgot that not all chimeras were dominant maniacs who couldn't stand any shred of control being taken away from them. Elish would've hit me and berated me until he hammered it into my head that I had no right to make requests like that to him.

"Kerres wants me to meet the leader of the Crimstones; he has it in his head I've been brainwashed and he says this dude takes former pets and can refine them I guess. There is no way I'm letting that happen but to make Ker happy I agreed to meet them. So if you want to scout it out and get some faces, you're quite welcome to."

Sanguine's red eyes became little rubies as he squinted at me, before a fire flared inside of them as he lit the lighter below him. He cooked off a dose of heroin with such a precision I had a suspicion he'd been shooting smack for the past sixty years.

"King Silas would be quite pleased that you are still loyal to the chimeras, even after Elish's dismissal."

Elish's dismissal. My gut ached and I think Sanguine saw my face fall; the next moment he picked up a band of rubber and started tying off my arm. I didn't argue.

"You did love him, didn't you?"

The space behind my eyes burned. I closed my eyes and held out my arm for him to prick and fill me with the only solution I had come up with for numbing the pain of being taken for a complete fool. "How can you love and hate someone at the same time? With so much passion behind each feeling?"

Sanguine let out a sigh. I opened one eye and saw he had a sad smile on his face. "I ask myself that every day, mihi."

That's right, the reminder almost made me laugh, Sanguine knew exactly what I was talking about, except his master never abandoned him, or if he did he took him back. This was why I had been magnetized to him in the first place; Sanguine was a sengil cicaro to the great and all-powerful King Silas. Not to mention a chimera on top of it. I bet this dude had even more issues than I did.

Which is why we were getting along just fine.

I felt my head tip forward, and with a laugh Sanguine pushed me onto the couch and I heard him prep his own dose. Time was lost on me for a while, until Sanguine's voice pierced my inner lucid dreams. "I will take you up on this show of family loyalty, friend. When Kerres has told you the day these men will arrive, take down the blanket in your window; that is the only sign I will need."

Oh my god, this heroin was good. I nodded and watched the cartoons on the television do their own stupid things. "As long as Kerres isn't hurt… for who we were in the past. I don't see much of a future for us anymore, it's ticking down until we're both fed up."

My words made my skin crawl, but the drugs in me were filling me with an honesty that I don't think my brain was ready to accept. "I'll never get Elish back; he played his game with me and discarded me, I know that, but I'm bad for Kerres. I'm making him miserable because I'm just miserable and I hate myself in general. Why drag him down with me, right?"

"It's unfortunate that Elish threw you away in such a manner, but you weren't the first and certainly won't be the last."

The comment cut right into the marrow of my bones. I found the breath in my chest become toxic. I blew it out and deflated on the couch. "You said I was special to him, man."

"I was wrong; if him dumping you didn't convince me of such, the fact that he seems to be quite content since ridding himself of you will hammer in the point."

My body crushed, I wiped my face quickly as my eyes started to burn inside their sockets and distracted myself by taking the tops off of some pixie sticks. I took a breath and dared my voice to crack or wobble under my own emotional devastation. But what did I expect? He had only used me for his own personal entertainment; it was me being stupid and still loving him that was my problem. Elish had made it clear that I was only a game to him. I was there for him to see how long it would take me to fall in love with him and that was it.

"I wouldn't expect anything different I guess. He did tell me it was nothing but a game to see how long it would make a gutter rat fall in love with him."

"Really? Elish is a cruel man, but did you really think he would like someone like you?"

The humiliation came back. I started tipping pixie sticks into my mouth, wishing the sour sugar was arsenic more than candy. I had to get away from his conversation.

I was so fucking stupid, and Sanguine was right… I was an idiot for thinking Elish's intentions were for me to be his permanent pet and in the bedroom, his lover; so unbelievably stupid it made me almost suicidal.

"Fuck him… just, fuck him and his fucking games," I said bitterly, scraping my claws against the couch, making a puff of foam split open beneath the tears. "I'll get him back for this shit one day. I fucking will."

I tried to take a deep breath but the toxic air inside of my lungs choked my trachea. I swallowed it down but found a hiss escaping between my lips. My own heart began to race as wave after wave of anger grew inside of me. I rose and grabbed Luca's ears which I had taken off when I'd arrived.

"I need to go for a walk, Sangy. I'll – I'll be back."

"He drives your thirst to kill, little cicaro?"

"Don't call me that."

"You murder to expel the energy he still fills you with. The rage, betrayal so intertwined with the cold, insatiable… *love*."

I put my hand on the door knob to open it, but suddenly a hand appeared. Sanguine shut the door and I felt his face near my neck.

"Bring me… let me watch you kill, mihi. Show me what he has done to you."

I gasped as he lightly blew a hot string of breath on my neck. I felt a shiver go up my spine and a burning feeling in my gut. It was a familiar, unworldly sensation that being around Elish had brought me, something that stirred feelings in me that I wanted to grab onto, like discovering your favourite drug after you had been forced to detox from it for three months.

My fists clenched, and my ringed claws knocked up against each other, making a chinking sound in the silence around us.

"Let's go."

Two blue embers pierced darkness in the cold dark alley, followed by white vapour, a mixture thickened by both cigarette smoke and breath caused from the late fall air. It rose up and joined the puffy white clouds, illuminated by the sliver of moon remaining. The night was frosty and cold, and we were dressed in skimpy revealing clothes but neither of us were cold. The adrenaline had warmed us, and the bag of cocaine Sanguine had kept in his pocket helped as well.

The red-eyed chimera had my hand in his again, our cigarettes moving up and down from our mouths to our sides in unison. I led him inside a semi-intact building and stepped up a flight of winding metal stairs to the third-storey.

I looked around the listless building and, with Sanguine's warm hand in mine, I crouched down and ducked into the second room, smelling a wave of must and the sour damp that all old buildings seemed to have.

This place was an old warehouse, and the only reason it was intact was because it was industrial and not made with plaster and wood like the other buildings.

To a normal person though it would be loud and full of echoes. The metal was rusted and the bars thin, laid in a clumsy way that made them easy to be nudged or hit even to the very careful. But Sanguine was the epitome of stealth and I had been trained in these slums, so we were nothing but black shadows cast against the steel iron beams; only visible to the layman by the silver moonlight leaking through the broken ceiling. This place looked spooky in a way; the beams used to be walled in to separate the warehouse rooms but now they stood in silence, crisscrossed like the steel webs of a giant spider until they disappeared into the hazy darkness.

The chimera quietly crawled up a beam to scout out a window. That Sanguine was fucking stealthy; the chimera didn't make a sound and he was quick. His feet barely seemed to touch the ground as he moved from one area to another, even on surfaces completely covered with crumbling paint, brick, and fallen beams.

After exiting the building, I brought him to one of my favourite alleyways. The chimera and the shadow walking along a strip of recessed brick ledge that wrapped around the industrial building, one of my guilty pleasures for stalking my prey.

Two shadows, as quiet as feral cats, stepped on light feet; even when we had to turn a corner, always a tricky edge for anyone, there wasn't a single step out of place.

I took this opportunity to talk to him; there wasn't anyone around us save a couple people loitering under a solar shop sign, but they were on the other side of the street at the end of this alleyway, far away from us.

"I'm killing Dave Chel's sister tonight; I want to send a message to those Crimstones," I said quietly to him. "I recognized that last name as soon as I heard it. She's also a waiter at Kiln's Bar, which we are above right now. Are you with me?"

Sanguine smiled and that was good enough. I walked along the brick ledge towards the back door to the pub where the workers usually left and stood over the exit sign, lighting another cigarette with Sanguine and waiting in our own silence.

I heard the sound of metal on metal and I looked over to see Sanguine sharpening two small dirks against each other.

I almost had to laugh. "You have piranha teeth and you're using knives?"

Sanguine's eyes narrowed in amusement; below us though I heard the door open and a voice speaking inside. "Killing with teeth is such an intimate, almost sexual experience, it would be strange doing that to a woman. I prefer to use weapons; we are genetically engineered to despise any sexual contact with women you know."

I had to laugh at that but I suppose it did make sense. "You're a strange chimera, but I can see your point. Man your battle stations, I think we're going to get people."

Sure enough, with the chimera and I standing side by side, two people, a man and a woman, emerged from the bar laughing and talking to the people inside. The woman was dressed in a short tank top and black pants with a purse slung over her shoulder. The man was a dishwasher, with a blue apron on over a white shirt and pants; both of them without a care in the world, shooting back a few comments as they talked unawares with the people inside.

I held out my arm to Sanguine and motioned him over; as the door opened I saw him smile and squeeze my hand. "I always enjoyed these nights with my family."

The chimera jumped down with his arms spread open on either side of him; as he landed I laughed at this odd creature I never thought in my life would become my friend.

I sprinted quietly on the ledge until I was several paces in front of the two.

My inner ego was stroked as both of their faces dropped and filled with terror, hands gripping their belongings and their feet pivoting and freezing on the spot.

The woman screamed, and the man put his hands out as if trying to talk me down with nothing but a pleading posture. I stalked up to them without a word and watched the shadow behind me grow as the shade that was Sanguine stalked his own prey.

Before they could make more noise, I persued the man. He turned and ran but in his own fear he was clumsy and uncoordinated. His arms flailed out and he had to grab onto the wall to keep himself from tripping over his own feet.

With a bend of my knees and a spring, I jumped, using the man's bent back as leverage to hop over him and land in front of him.

His face was red; he was bordering on overweight which made the job even easier. I flexed my fingers before raising my hand and slashing him in the face, my other one coming up automatically and opening his face from the bridge of his nose to his ear lobe.

Then the finishing blow. I sunk my metal teeth into him and held his arms down as he tried unsuccessfully to hit me.

I felt the life leave him, with a thrash and a gurgling that I could feel reverberating from the metal in my teeth.

But as my eyes looked forward, I saw the most oddest thing... especially considering what he had just told me before we had attacked the two.

Sanguine had the woman's face clasped between his two hands. He stared at her with narrow, sinister eyes and spoke to her, making sure she could see his teeth; though what he was saying was drowned out by the man dying and me having to breathe the frozen air through my nose.

The man gave a last gasp and with that I dropped him and watched with interest the spectacle happening before me.

Her eyes were wide and she was trying not to look at him, her purse forgotten and strewn over the cold ground, scattering her belongings across the pavement like spilled rice. Sanguine was as still as the shadows, but as I tuned into his aura it was as bright as the blue ember still glowing in his right hand.

Then, to my further confusion, the sengil reached one of his hands down and grabbed his knife; he flicked the metal pommel away with his thumb and took a drink from the bottom. The small dagger, it seemed, doubled for holding some sort of liquid.

When he had drunk his fill, Sanguine, a foot taller than the woman, leaned down and kissed her on the lips before retracting. As he pulled away there was crystal shine, a clear liquid that passed from his lips to hers.

I watched it drip down her upturned face, but before she could spit it out or scream, Sanguine raised his lit cigarette towards her lips.

I audibly gasped and took a step back; the moment the cigarette touched the top of her lip her entire mouth, and soon her face, erupted into flames.

Sanguine took a casual step back, his face splitting into the most horrendous grin I had ever seen. He watched with languid joy as the woman, screaming at the top of her lungs, ran into the streets; her entire head ablaze and her hands flailing, trying unsuccessfully to pat out the flames.

The smiling demon turned to me and put the smoke up to his lips. The fuel had covered the cigarette, setting the entire stick alight into a blue flame, which carried onto his lips, coating the red soft skin in an incandescent glow.

Sanguine sucked the ember. Even when the metal door opened and several workers ran out screaming, running towards the woman shouting their heads off in a blind panic, he did not flinch and he didn't waver from his casual saunter towards me.

Ignoring me and the demon chimera, the workers ran towards the female. Behind them the door to the kitchen went to shut on itself, but in a flash of black Sanguine stopped it with his foot, before casually lighting another cigarette. He turned to me and nodded his head for me to follow.

Inside the building? I didn't think I could stop now, even if I knew he was taking this too far.

We walked in to see everyone in a panic. When they saw us a few people stopped and looked at us in shock, and in truth I was shocked too, but I was just as much taken over by the bloodlust and it was easy not to be afraid of the workers in the kitchen. I had this demonic chimera with me and I think at that point I would have burned Moros down if he asked me.

Fucking chimera pheromones.

"Kill them, mihi," Sanguine said to me, momentarily brushing his warm fuel-slicked hand into my own before he turned towards the propane stoves.

I nodded and scanned the kitchen, my eyes picking up the three people looking at us with their mouths open. One woman and two men. The men were old, both of them balding kitchen workers I had never met, even though I had been to this bar many times for pub food.

I grabbed a butcher's knife, the florescent lights above me making the intimate act of eating their throats out seem out of place under such a glaring illumination of my inner transgressions. Instead I took a knife in each hand and cut them down one by one, saving the woman for last since she would be the weakest and indeed she was.

The two men got a few fair hits in, one of them slashing my arm which my adrenaline had no problem burying inside of me. The second one only got a punch in on my shoulder before I dug the blade into his stomach and opened him up from side to navel. More blood and more guts but I wasn't the one who was going to have to clean it up.

When I was done I looked around for Sanguine and almost had to laugh at he was doing. My chimera friend had all of the ovens open and the propane turned on; not only that but he was in the middle of spraying a can of stove polish on everything. I watched him spray the can dry before he smiled contently to himself. When he spotted me his eyes became as bright as blood drops on snow.

"Now don't go far from the exit, little thing, this will get hot fast." Sanguine took a drink from his dirk flask and brought up a barbeque lighter half a foot from his mouth. Then like I had seen circus people do in the movies, he craned his neck back and sprayed the fuel onto the lighter.

As the demon breathed his fire, the entire room exploded into an inferno, ripples of red and yellow flames seemingly coming out of thin air;

feeding on the leaking propane and the stove polish Sanguine had been spraying everywhere. In seconds the place was entirely up in flames, the shadow of Sanguine almost completely overtaken by the heat waves and fast gathering plumes of black smoke.

I shook my head in awe and made sure I had my hand on the metal door, knowing that sooner than I deemed comfortable this tinderbox would be our death trap and my coffin.

There was an ear-piercing scream over the roar of flames and I saw a human fireball run by me, collapsing with a wheezing cry beside the bodies of one of the chefs I had killed. A moment later the casual saunter of the chimera appeared, smoke seemingly separating to make way for him.

"Show off." I grinned at him.

Sanguine's mouth formed from a smile to a smirk, then, with a quick and artistic move of his body, he leaned into me and kissed me right on the lips.

Oh shit. My legs went weak and I had to grab onto the side of the metal prep table to steady myself; with the heat of the flames cooking his back Sanguine opened his mouth and I did the same.

For a brief moment we kissed deeply with a passion that only a chimera could wield.

Then he broke away and looked behind me, with a shake of his head and a sigh of dismay.

"Well, I suppose we must leave," Sanguine sighed, with such an air of nonchalant grace it was like he was complaining that it was raining rather than the entire bar burning around us.

It was my turn to hold his hand. I opened the door and we both stepped out into the frozen night air, my hot skin feeling like it had just been dunked into frozen water. I looked to my right and saw Sanguine's clothes were smoking and his skin seemed to be steaming as well.

There was a crowd gathering in front of the bar as black smoke poured out of the windows. I pulled on Sanguine's hand and the both of us ducked into an abandoned building.

But instead of taking him back to the apartment I only climbed higher. Sanguine gave me a confused look as I took him higher and higher up, each flight of stairs getting more decayed, bowing underneath our boots and snapping with the sudden increase in weight.

We reached the roof, a partially caved in hovel with strips of discoloured tar paper raising and curling over the rotting beams like frozen black waves. Then I led him to the edge overlooking the buildings below us. We sat down.

From our bird's-eye view we could see the pub burn perfectly, even the silhouette of the man I had killed, still splayed out in the position I had left him in.

Oily smoke was raising up from the building, not just from windows but from cracks in the badly patched roof and the mortar bare brick that held inside it the flickering flames that ate away at the inside of the restaurant.

I smiled and in return Sanguine squeezed my hand. I couldn't believe just how happy I was in that moment. It was in all respects like having Elish and Kerres combined. I had someone I could sit and watch people burn alive with; someone I could kill with.

Oh, what a lost boy I was.

And with that lingering thought in my head, I wasn't even surprised when he started to kiss my neck. Immediately I craned it, before straddling the brick divider we were sitting on to once again join my lips with his.

This time I slipped my tongue between his lips and felt every single sharp serrated tooth he had in his mouth, before finding his tongue and weaving it with my own.

He was a good kisser, but the sparks that flew between us were more suited for the burning coals below; it filled my body with an unnatural heat and I did enjoy it, but even in this new passion I still had no doubts where my heart grudgingly belonged. I knew it would take a while longer for me to regain what Elish had taken from me, if ever. Sanguine was a friend and he would stay a friend, but I wasn't going to deny I was yearning inside for an understanding touch.

I drew my hand up his arm, and opened my eyes to watch his clothing peel away, revealing red and hot skin underneath, I touched it with my second hand too and that one brought blood.

"Sanguine, you're burned." I moved my mouth to the side and tenderly brushed my hand against him.

The demon chimera didn't answer me, he stole away my voice with another deep kiss. I closed my eyes and let him take me in again, fuelled on the screams and terrified voices breaking the roaring inferno below us.

When we finally broke apart, Sanguine glanced casually down at the fire, embers shooting up into the night sky. The reflection of the flames in his eyes captivated me, like two living rubies, with souls transparent inside their prisons. I found myself more interested in watching them flash and flicker than the fire below me.

"Let's go back to the apartment," he whispered, before taking my hand and this time leading me back down the several storeys of the desolate building.

Hand in hand we sneaked out the back with our shadows hidden in the clusters of buildings. Every few blocks we stopped to steal a kiss from each other, before finally making it back to the apartment.

I knew what was coming next, and my body was already aching for it when the door closed behind me. With bloodlust rushing through my veins, and a love-starved thirst I hadn't had satiated in the least since Elish had abandoned me, I started immediately undressing the chimera sengil. I'd never wanted someone this badly since I had left Olympus, and not knowing why in all honesty. I don't think I wanted to play with the idea that I was replacing one Elish substitute for another. I just needed someone to fill up the crater Elish's abandonment of me had created inside my heart.

Because, and I knew this, I really did, I didn't want to start a new chimera relationship, especially with Silas's own personal sengil. I might be stupid but I wasn't that stupid. I just needed something stronger than Kerres, something more similar to Elish, someone who could take the rough sexual appetite my former boyfriend didn't have, someone I could fuck and release the anger and pain inside of me that seemed to fill the emptiness.

He took off my vest and I lifted my arms up for him to pull off my mesh shirt. We kissed as he started unzipping my pants.

"Sanguine, this doesn't mean–" To my surprise the sengil put a hand up to my lips and pushed me down onto the mattress.

"Must you complicate things, Cicaro? Can we fuck or do we need to talk about our feelings first?" Sanguine smirked, stripping his pants off, but to my inner kink, he kept the red bowtie on. "Stop being such a teenager."

I rolled my eyes before reaching up and grabbing the elastic of his boxer briefs. I pulled him down on top of me and ran a hand down his firm stomach, before slipping it underneath the elastic, feeling out the large chimera-quality member I had come to love. "Good, I'm glad we're in agreement."

I think Sanguine decided I talked too much. He pulled his boxers all the way off before dismissing my own from my body. He started grinding his hard member into mine before he straddled me, playfully resting the head between my thighs.

With a sick fascination, I watched the red-eyed sengil gather the blood from the forgotten knife wound on my arm. I sucked in a breath of pain as he squeezed and massaged it, collecting the blood as it leaked out with his free hand. And with that hand, he lubricated himself and me.

"You kinky fuck," I murmured, and with that he kissed me before the smile broke our lips. "I think I'm going to like you."

"Do you always talk this much when someone is trying to satisfy you?" His voice was a growl, and I realized that –

"– yes, yes I do actually," I chuckled wrapping both my arms around his neck and kissing his lips. I touched the razor-sharp teeth with my tongue and felt him do the same to mine.

Then I felt him position himself over the crown of my hard member, and with a teeth grinding growl, he lowered himself onto me; I watched his mouth open and his glistening teeth get bigger with a curl of his lips. My heart skipped as I heard the growl in his throat, the same reverberating tone that I never understood how I could make.

That was strange we could both do it…

I groaned with him and nipped the side of his mouth, watching his face tense and tighten as my dick disappeared inside of him, his burned arm only inches away from me. Sanguine was so close to me, his entire body seemed to join with mine… like the last time I was with Elish.

Sanguine moved his hips, and like Elish had done to me, I helped hold him up with my hands on his chest and my elbows and forearms resting on the bed. I was in control and drinking in every moment we were intertwined.

As we kissed, not breaking away this time, I felt our auras together, his black crow feathers and red strings weaving in-between my own aura, which I had seen grow blacker every day. The purples were disappearing into the darkness that had once almost entirely transformed into silver.

Now it was as dark as the shadows I had been named after, but it sank itself into Sanguine's like they were friends greeting each other after a long separation. There was no doubting the familiar feeling I got being inside of him, though I had no idea where. I had never felt like this with Kerres.

Sanguine growled through his pointed teeth and quickened the length and speed of his hips, in response I curled my fingers and started thrusting into him too, looking down to see myself sinking deep inside of him as his rigid member smacked against my stomach, wet and swollen, awaiting its own touch.

"Get behind me, fuck me." Sanguine suddenly detached himself from me, but he stayed in the same position. I rose immediately and got behind him, his firm and biteable ass in the air waiting for me to re-enter him. I eased myself into his body and grabbed his hips, before I started thrusting into him with the same speed we had finished off on.

I was fucking a chimera… a sengil, yes, but a chimera nonetheless. If Elish could see me now, oh what a fucking look he would give me, those cold eyes would rip a hole in me as soon as he saw me fucking the sengil like this. Elish detested Sanguine and with his former pet thrusting what Elish had considered his personal property into the sengil cicaro – Elish had every reason to hate him.

That only made me quicken my pace, if only to mentally send a *fuck you* to the master who had played me for a fool.

Sanguine groaned and bowed his back. I remembered the spot Elish prided himself on being able to hit inside of me, so I leaned myself forward and started aiming my thrusts downwards to try and hit the root of his prostate.

I had learned a lot with my former master and if one of those things was how to fuck a man properly, so be it. King Silas undoubtedly fucked Sanguine so I had a hell of a lot to live up to.

The burning in my chest blazed as the sengil let out a loud gasp. "Right there, harder – is that all you got? Fuck me, Jade. Hard."

My mind went crazy, as did my body. I sped up and grabbed Sanguine's shoulders, pushing his body towards me as I nailed him with every ounce of strength I had.

"I said harder, Cicaro, come on!" Oh fuck, was he trying to make my head explode? Kerres would be shrieking at me and hitting me if I fucked him this hard; even at what I thought was my usual speed that guy was whining that I was too rough with him.

I cried out from pleasure and dug my fingernails into Sanguine as I fucked him harder and harder, matching his own cries with my own. When I eventually felt his opening tense and quiver around my dick I reached down and gave him several strokes to help aid his climax, and in response he spilled cum right on my hand.

The growl in my throat turned into a clenched scream as I was thrown the same way, burying myself to the base into him as I collapsed onto his back, my hips still thrusting through the entire prolonged orgasm. It built and dragged on longer than it had with Kerres, its intensity bordering on the length of mine with Elish, but with a fiercer energy that only came with being the person in control and doing the fucking.

When the last shuddering gasp came through me, I separated us and rolled onto my back.

Sanguine got up without a word and I laid there panting. I watched him lean down to the coffee table and bringing over a baggy and the metal sniffer.

An inquisitive eyebrow rose as he dashed a lump of white powder below my navel, then leaned down and did a line off of my stomach, then another bump on the base of my cock, which he also snorted up through his nose. Fuck, I was just loving this guy's kinky nature.

The sengil looked up at me with a mischievous smile, a light dusting of white powder underneath each nostril.

"Take some of this." He made a fist and dumped the rest of the powder in the small space between his clenched thumb and finger. I leaned forward and took it all in one nostril then the other. I sniffed and rubbed my nose. Man, this stuff burned like hell-fire.

The sengil leaned into me and licked my lips with his tongue before kissing me, relighting the fire I had inside. He wasn't done yet and neither was I. I didn't think I would be done for quite a while. I wondered if I would put even his stamina to shame.

When he put his hands on my knees and urged them back, I knew he was just as versatile as I was. With a hunger in his eyes and the drugs, cocaine I realized, hitting us both, he took his own blood from the burns on his shoulders and back and lubed himself in the same way he had me.

Brushing my hands through our matching raven-black hair, I took in a short breath as he pushed himself inside of me, feeling almost tender towards him as his long, almost clawed fingers brushed against my cheekbone, turning me towards his lips. My heart skipped and raced as he moved himself inside me, kissing and playing with my mouth, using a gentle touch that I hadn't used with him at all.

Then he started to get rougher and I felt snapped back to my element, admittedly lost for a moment in a familiar feeling of me and Elish again. I was thankful for the roughness and speed, though I was more than happy to get fucked by the sengil; if it had been tender and gentle, the way Elish had done me the night I told him that I loved him – it wouldn't have sat well with me. I would've felt like I was betraying that moment, and all I had of Elish now were moments.

The rest of our night together I had no reason to worry about that moment being tainted; once he got his bearings Sanguine turned into his demon self and I turned into my own demon. Fuelled on coke and what I realized hours later was ecstasy, we fucked like insane devils, only briefly pausing to fuel up on more drugs and at my command, since I had done MDMA before, lots of water.

No one would believe me if I ever told them, but it wasn't until the next afternoon that we finally collapsed into a sweaty, bloody, cum-filled heap into each other and finally agreed that we were done. Because we were versatile to being tops and bottoms whenever one of us needed a break the other was more than happy to sink a cock or a mouth wherever it was needed. Sore asses got licked and teased (with blood, so fuck you Kerres), sensitive dicks got sucked and re-hardened (and even with his pointed teeth he was amazing at that), and every orifice we had we filled at one time or another with ourselves. The only breaks we had were an hour here or there for breathers to recharge our bodies, take in more drugs, and because of the water: piss. It was something else and something I would never forget.

Sweaty and damp, I panted into the pillow, a crumpled heap of rubber, too tired to move or even raise my head.

Sanguine though had the energy to put his arms over me and pull me close to him, his own breath quick and rapid. I had just fucked him for the last time. "I'm using the shower first when we wake up, mihi."

"What the fuck does *mihi* mean, Sangy?"

"It means my friend in Latin; an old language the king knows. It's a chimera thing. You may have noticed my brothers saying similar odd things. We have our own nicknames for each other."

Ah, I had heard Elish and Garrett do the same, which brought on another question. "What does cicaro mean?"

"A way of saying pet, though in an endearing way."

I smiled, of course it did. I shared one last kiss with him feeling my mind start to drift off to sleep. "Go right ahead and use the shower first. Just keep your hands off me. If anyone touches my swollen body for the next two days I'm going to break their faces."

I heard Sanguine laugh, before the light turned off, and without a word we fell asleep.

CHAPTER 23

I WAS RELIEVED WHEN I CAME HOME TO FIND KERRES AT work, he wouldn't be returning until about five, a little longer if he got a beer with Tate or one of the other guys down at the pub. Though with the Shadow Killer and his sidekick (yep, the news said sidekick; Sanguine gave me a very haughty look when the news reporter said that) moving onto arson and mass murder, I think everyone was staying indoors now.

We had killed eight people, and had celebrated making the news with another three hours of rolling around with each other, even though I had declared that no one was going to touch me for the next few days. I couldn't help it; knowing that Sanguine and I would never get caught for this made me feel like I was an immortal myself.

Now I was back home after being gone for two nights, but I didn't think I had anything to feel badly about; in my mind Kerres and I were pretty much done. He should've been happy that I had left him a note. In all respects he was a roommate to me now.

Though saying those words in my head did make me frown, but over the past three months since I realized I had changed and he had changed, it was getting easier to come to terms with that. I didn't have Elish anymore, and now I didn't have Kerres. At least I had Sanguine though only for as long as King Silas was busy... maybe he would still visit.

I sighed though as I got myself a glass of water and started prepping myself a dose of heroin, just to help me cope with the inevitable conversation I was going to have to have with Kerres. Whenever the drugs wore off, I found myself desperate to patch things up with my boyfriend but once the drugs calmed down my mind I realized the rift between us was too big and my drive to repair it was getting less and less. I think I was too broken and too far gone, and to be honest Kerres no longer had the patience to deal with my problems anymore.

And he deserved better. I'd had sex with Sanguine constantly for the last two nights and I didn't even feel guilty. Kerres had saved himself for a year waiting for me. Elish's cold heartless nature had rubbed off on me and I'd only hurt my boy more. It was for his own safety and his own good. I had never been a good person, but now... now I didn't even see myself as human.

I had been transformed into something horrible, and I didn't know how to get myself back and neither did Kerres, so all I could do was save him and face the rest of my life on my own.

I guess the note I had left him had been correct; I did need some time to think.

The strength of the heroin knocked all my doubts and insecurities out and I felt ready to confront him. Though when I heard the door open to the apartment, my heart still jumped into my chest.

Kerres saw me and I saw not the usual look of joy or relief on his face, just the tightening of his lower lip and a fullness to his eyes. "Hey... are you okay?"

I shrugged and since I wanted to busy my hands while I talked to him I started prepping another dose. "Yeah, I'm completely fine. What about you?"

The vibe between us was tense. I wondered if I should just get it over with so I could go back to my bedroom. I had just woken up beside Sanguine this morning so I wasn't tired, but I wouldn't mind just lying in bed and doing drugs in a dazed stupor. I had even packed all of my things into the duffle bag in case he kicked me out.

"Yeah, I didn't expect you gone for so long... but thanks for leaving me a note." Kerres sat down with a bottle of cola. I saw him eyeing up my awaiting needle. "Since when did you start injecting? That's dangerous, love."

My lips pursed and I flicked him over a bag of china white but he shook his head and lit a cigarette instead. "I heard you burned down

Kiln's."

"Yep." I tried to keep my voice level.

"Who were you with? There are two of you now?"

I sighed. So this was how it was going to start. "I told you, an old friend of mine has contacted me, someone who actually gets what I'm going through and what's happening to me. He's... I don't know, I think he's a bit of a pyromaniac."

Kerres nodded and stared at his cigarette; his body language made him look like he was bound tightly in invisible wrappings. "So you agree... something happened to you? That they did something to your head?"

I wanted to say no, but it would make it easier for him to understand. "Yeah, Elish fucked me up, I know, okay? Look we gotta talk about something."

But apparently what he wanted to talk about was more important. Kerres ignored me and pressed on. "How much longer are you going to do this, Jade? I know you said Ellis doesn't give a shit about Moros, but these are your people."

"They aren't my people anymore. I have no people, no friends, no family, no people." Saying that out loud only made it more real for me. I truly was alone. The realization made my stomach start to knot. "I'm alone, Kerres. I was always alone but now... my only friend in the world is Silas's slave, some demon-toothed, semi-human, sengil. I have no one else who gets me. Do you know how that feels, Ker?"

I didn't look up at him. I watched the tar liquid get sucked into the syringe through a piece of cotton filter. The cluster of emotions in me continued to bind tighter together, like I had swallowed a python.

"That's who you've been hanging out with, a chimera like Elish?" Kerres sounded surprised and hurt by that admission. "Has Elish contacted you?"

"NO!" I turned and snapped at him, making him visibly recoil. I couldn't help my eyes start to burn; why did he have to barge in here and start peppering me with questions? I was trying to gently break up with him, not give an interview. "He hasn't and he... he never will."

I tapped the needle with a sigh, before closing my eyes and squinting them tight trying to force the sting in my eyes to go away. I had started tying off of my arm when I noticed the look on Kerres's face.

It was a strange look. His complexion had paled and with the furrow of his brow he looked like he was seeing me differently. I turned away and pierced the needle into my flesh, a sting that brought only a feeling of pleasure. I was getting dependent on this stuff, to the point where if I didn't take a dose I started to feel nauseas and off.

"While you zone out from that... I'm going to get the batteries back Tate owes me..." Kerres quickly walked towards the door. "Um... thanks, you know... for not killing him."

"Yeah," I said sullenly, sinking into the musty couch and curling up as the cold warmth washed over me, taking small sips of my water as the door to the apartment closed.

When he returned I was still in my zombieland. He gave me a small basket of fries and brushed a hand over my hair. "I love you."

Kerres waited for me to say it back, but I couldn't. He noticed and I heard the whimper.

I might as well end this now. "Ker, I did a lot of thinking while I was away from home. I think you and I both know we aren't going to go back to how things were before Elish."

He was quiet, which was good and bad at the same time, I decided to press on, the heroin giving me the strength. I didn't think Kerres would be surprised though; he had yelled at me I was chimera scum, a murderer and a monster, and all those wonderful things he said to me. "I see what it's doing to you, and I well... love you too much to continue to keep fucking up your life. I know you're probably regretting me coming back... so I'm ending this relationship, and I'm going to get my own place."

The silence killed me, but I held myself steadfast.

"What? That's – that's not going to happen, Jade." I watched Kerres from the corner of my eye shake his head rapidly. "You're sick; it's your brainwashing that has made you this way, not you. You didn't change, they changed you and I'm not leaving you to just suffer like this. So no, you're not breaking us up. I told you I'll get you help, and I will."

Not that shit again. I put a hand up to stop him and wetted the rag I had used to tie off my arm before wiping my sweaty head. "Kerres, I'm sorry... but we're just not the same people anymore. Look at all the shit I've done since I got back. I'm broken goods and I'm violent, more than I was before. That's who I am now and I need to be alone for a while I figure out how I'm supposed to live like this."

But Kerres was insistent; he reached over and grabbed my hand and squeezed it. "But you don't have to live like this; you didn't change, Elish changed you. I know how to change you back and – and we can be happier again, love."

The pain of this prolonged conversation was turning into an agonizing ache. I swallowed it down but the emotion of it all was starting to penetrate through my drug-induced bravery. "I'll never be happy again," I found myself whispering, "but I won't drag you down with me."

His hold only increased and he started to cry. "I know it's hard, Jade. I know Elish really messed you up, I accept it. It took me a long time to but I accept he raped you, and tortured you and the Crimstones have dealt with that before. They've refined former pets, they've healed their scars. No matter how traumatized-"

I yanked my hand away and moved my leg away from him too. "I'm not fucking traumatized, Kerres." With automatic movements I rose. I had already broken up with him and said my piece. I headed to the bedroom.

"Where are you going?"

"Back to Sanguine's."

"NO!" Kerres screamed. I looked back towards the living room bewildered and watched with surprise as his face twisted into agony. He walked up to me, licking his lips from the stress. Automatically I took several steps back.

He grabbed me, and I could feel his breath quicken. "Don't go back to that chimera. Please, Jade, stay here. Don't go back to him; he'll bring Elish back. Elish will take you again, he'll hurt you again."

Those were the last words I heard. Though he kept talking I found his voice reduced to static, a low booming sound that rushed through my ears and in and out of the grey matter of my brain. It tuned out everything but the last sentence stuck in my head.

Elish…

I stared past Kerres, whose eyes were filling with tears, his mouth open as he yelled or pleaded, or something. I didn't know and I didn't care. My mind, like my heart, had gone back to the apartment, back to the blond chimera.

I remembered when I had fallen asleep with my head on his shoulder, smelling mint and nutmeg and a comforting warmth that being near his perfect aura always brought. It was such an indescribable feeling of security and safety, to be special to someone so powerful. I would be happy to curl up under his feet just to be close to that perfect Adonis.

My heart ... it hurt and ached to the point where it literally felt like it was breaking. I remembered that cold look in his eyes when he told me it had all been a game for him, that once again, like the Mp3 player at Stadium, I had been the victim of a cruel prank.

Kerres was shaking me, and it was only when my head snapped forward that the sounds of the world around me came rushing back.

"He left me."

Kerres paused; his brown eyes were red and shedding tears. I realized then that mine were too.

I looked at Kerres and pursed my lips, but my face crumpled. "He abandoned me, Ker, he left me. I thought I meant something to him, I told him I loved him, I loved him... Kerres. I loved –" My legs gave out from under me, and I felt my hands grab my hair as I let out an agonized cry. "He left me. HE PLAYED ME AND LEFT ME!"

My ex-boyfriend took a step back, his hands dropping to his side. "You – you love him? Elish... *Elish?*"

I pulled my hands down, my hair getting drawn down with it. I felt my chest rapidly quiver as my body started to collapse in on itself, unable to handle the sudden onslaught of the emotions brought on by my own shocking admissions. I had said it so many times in my head, but out loud? Out loud? *Shit shit shit...*

"I obeyed him, I was good, and he abandoned me here without a single fuck given." I sniffed and dropped my hands, trying to stand but my body swayed. I dropped back onto the floor and breathed in a sob. "He turned his back on me. I begged him not to make me come back here, I begged him."

Stop being so surprised; stop acting so fucking shocked, Jade. He's a chimera who never hid his nature from anyone; you were the one stupid enough to develop feelings for him. You dumb shit, you stupid, useless gutterwhore, he played you like an instrument. It's your fault, YOUR FAULT! And now you're dumb enough to tell Kerres how you feel. You're better off dead, you stupid fucking slut.

"It makes sense now..." I heard his dead voice whisper. "This murder spree wasn't because he fucked you and locked you up, it's because your lover abandoned you. This was all some cry for attention to try and get that blond fuck to notice you?" He was silent and I heard a drawer open. "Elish made you fall in love with him and then he dumped you."

I nodded, my arms wrapping around my chest. I leaned against the wall, my entire body a trembling mess.

"He brainwashed you," Kerres said after a while, in a firm voice of finality. He was convincing himself not me. "You're another chimera's game, just like Milos said. All of this... he said this is what they do. The Crimstones –"

Was he fucking kidding me? I pushed Kerres away, anger adding to the agony overflowing its toxic poison in me. "Stop fucking mentioning them! I'm not going to betray Elish, or any of the chimeras. They accepted me, Sanguine accepts me, and I'm not going against them. Shove it, Kerres, just let me go! LET ME GO!"

"NEVER!" Kerres screamed. He struggled to his feet and to my surprise he swung at me.

I wasn't expecting it; he hit me right across the face, throwing me off of my feet and landing me on the floor. I held my mouth and tried to get up but my limbs felt weighted down.

I heard his quickened breathing above me, and then he rolled me onto my back and hit me again in the head.

"I've talked personally to Milos. I talked to him a lot when I found out you burned down the pub. I told him everything... everything. I decided I would do what has to be done so I can break their hold on you," Kerres whispered. I blinked and tried to hold up my head but it was filling with dizzy nausea. "I'll never let you go, and if that means letting them take you, I'll do it for us. I love you, Jade. I promise I'll get you back."

I heard a series of rapid clicks, a sound I knew too well. I was being handcuffed. I swore and squinted. "I'm not brainwashed... Kerres." I spat up some blood and started coughing. "Just let me grab my shit and go."

My body roughly moved across the carpet as he dragged me to the second bedroom. "So you can leave and go back to that other chimera? He'll bring you back to the chimeras and I'll never let that happen. I love you, Jade, I love you. I loved you as a brother when you were nine and I love you as my fiancé now you're sixteen."

Fiancé? "We're not getting married, Kerres." I coughed again and felt him drop me beside the mattress.

I saw his feet move around, duct taped shoes; he shifted around and brushed my hair back gently. "We could be, once you come back from your time with Milos, when you're normal. We'll get married, and we'll be happy together."

Oh shit... I swallowed the next mouthful of blood and looked up at him. His face was tense but kind, his eyes full of emotion but red and puffy. I knew then that I had broken him, that under all the stress I had caused him I had drawn the last straw of his sanity.

"They'll be here soon, love, soon. I'll have you back soon. I love you, J. I'm sorry, I love you, I'm sorry."

With a kiss on my forehead he left the room with a quiet shut of the door. I heard it lock from the outside.

I was in trouble.

For a moment though my thoughts became crystal clear. Before I could fade back into the haze that drugs and my own throbbing head had brought me, I reached over and pulled the blanket covering my window and drew it over me. I put my head underneath the blankets to shield my eyes from the lamplight in the bedroom and tried to calm myself with a series of deep breaths.

Kerres had lost his mind, that I was sure of, but what the Crimstones honestly wanted with me I didn't know. The news coverage they got was always sparing; we usually heard about them through word of mouth. Silas didn't believe in giving terrorist organizations any media coverage, in the belief that the more exposure they got the more they would up their attacks to get exposure, and thus more followers.

I hated myself, and I hated myself even more for not caring about admitting it, but I was on the chimeras' side. There wasn't an inch of me that felt compelled to go to the Crimstones and tell them what I knew about the chimeras; I only saw them as my enemies.

That gave me a strange feeling in my gut. After Elish had treated me so badly, and dropped me with inhuman cruelty I still didn't want any harm to come to him, and I especially didn't want the chimeras and the sengils who had been kind to me to get hurt: Garrett, Luca, and Sanguine, the nice ones. King Silas might be a maniac and he might deserve to get his face blown up, but I didn't care enough to get involved. I wasn't going to be forced to join some terrorist organization; I was having a hard enough time adjusting to being in Moros and away from my former master.

I coughed, my chest burning like I was striking flint with every heave of my diaphragm. I wiped my mouth with my handcuffed wrists and stared off into the green fabric of the blanket, the bedroom light illuminating it to a fabricy candescence and filling my lungs with my own recycled carbon dioxide.

After what seemed like a long time, I heard a hard knock on the door and several male voices. As I expected, the bedroom door was unlocked and I could feel Kerres's aura edge along the corners of the room.

He spoke softly and kindly to me and pulled the blanket off my face. "I had to restrain him, Milos. I was scared he was going to leave and find the other guy. I was afraid he wouldn't come back; he was gone for two days after he torched the pub."

I let him pull me to my feet, my eyes upturned and glared at the dark shadow in the door.

A very intimidating-looking man was glaring at me, an AK47 on his back and a camo outfit fitted to his muscular frame. He was in his forties or fifties with a weather-beaten face and body and the look of a greywaster.

"Look at those fucking eyes; you're right Kerres, he is a chimera."

Of all the ways to start this off. I glared back and fixed my gaze on him. I recognized him, I had seen him with Tate once. "Fuck you, I'm not a fucking chimera, I had a mother."

The man didn't even listen to me, he grabbed my arm and when I jerked it back, he grabbed it again. "What's your name, chimera?"

He squeezed my arm tight. I looked at Kerres for help but he was small and submissive, inching away from us. He couldn't face me.

"Jade."

"Were you born with that name? Or do you just call yourself that?"

What sort of stupid fucking question was that? "My mother gave me that name when I was born. Her name was Sheryn and Kerres fucking knew her."

Milos looked over at Kerres and I saw my ex nod.

"They must've switched kids, they did the same thing with Ares and Siris."

My head went hot. I jerked my arm away again and grabbed my duffle bag. They let me push past them and I walked towards the living room. The only solid thought in my head right now was to get away from this guy, he looked nuts and dangerous and I had already had nuts and dangerous push me into a deacons' pen a few months ago.

I paused when I saw four more of them in the living room, all of them similarly dressed except with ski masks on their faces.

My mouth went dry. "Kerres... who did you just invite into our apartment?"

Kerres screamed. I turned around in time to feel an electric shock ripple through my body. I felt myself go stiff as a board before I fell hard onto the living room floor, every muscle in my body spasming and twitching, shooting fire throughout my veins.

"Don't hurt him, you said you wouldn't hurt him!" Kerres's hands went to my face. I felt wet drops as his tears fell on me. My teeth were clenched shut from the electricity; all I could do was stare at him.

"He's dangerous, an animal right now. You above everyone else know that. He has to be restrained before he hurts himself or us."

Kerres sniffed and gently rubbed my cheeks. I wanted to hit him in the face in that moment. How stupid could he be?

"He's not an animal, he's my baby... he's just lost, he's already down... don't Taser him again!"

My body, still stiff, was dragged to the living room. I watched my own fingers twitch back and forth as the furniture passed by me. When I was in the middle of the living room, with the coffee table pushed against the sliding glass door, they stopped.

Then they pulled me to the sitting position. I felt Milos lightly smack the side of my face.

"Look at those fucking eyes, how can you not see he's a chimera? You can read people, huh? Can you read me too? You mutant piece of shit."

"Don't talk to him like that!" Kerres screamed. A moment later I felt him being restrained, then Tate speaking to him quickly. My ex muffled a sob.

"Just tell them not to be so rough with him," Kerres responded in a broken voice.

"He's an animal, Kerres –"

Now what was that thing I did when Elish pissed me off? I raised my head and spat in Milos's face.

The reaction was basically the same, a bright light pierced my eyes as Milos punched me in the jaw. Kerres screamed and pleaded, his voice cracking.

"Jade, stop struggling! Please!" he cried. "They'll help you."

Milos looked over his shoulder, a rough and scaly hand on my neck. "We will help him, help him get reprogrammed just like it helped Shale and Vecht. You'll get him back, Kerres, but not before he gives me every last fucking detail about his time with those fucks." He turned back to me and smiled; his teeth were yellow and disgusting. "Every last detail whether he likes it or not."

And what was that other thing I did when Elish got in my face? With a flash, I lunged my head towards him and caught the corner of his mouth in my teeth. I bit down, catching as much flesh as I could.

Milos recoiled and snarled, then he hit me in the temple with a closed fist, before kicking me several times in the stomach. Kerres was still screaming but I refused to make a sound.

My head hit the floor and I coughed; my stomach was aching and my chest too, my breath failing to fill my lungs with enough oxygen. I gritted my teeth and let myself bleed onto the floor. They wouldn't get a sound out of me.

"Thanks, Kerres, this is helping me a lot," I managed to gasp before I had to attempt another struggling breath.

"Stop struggling! They won't hurt you if you stop struggling, J," Kerres sobbed. He sounded like he was being held back, but I couldn't see anything but the army boots of the masked terrorists around me.

"Put him in the bag."

The bag? For fucking serious? My body was yanked up again and I saw two of the people starting to unzip a giant duffle bag, one of the ones you used to carry military weapons.

This is how they were going to not make a scene? I looked around and swallowed the blood in my mouth; my eyes fell on Kerres.

He had his hand over his mouth, his face was terrified and pale, but still he wasn't fighting them. He was letting all of this happen... he was letting me get kidnapped by the Crimstones.

"Fuck you, Kerres," I said to him as one of them started wrenching me towards the bag. "Elish might've fucked my brain but at least he always protected me. This is on your head. Thanks, K. I love you too."

"Give him the injection, knock him out," Milos snapped. His hand pushed my head down into the bag, then he started kicking my feet into it as well.

Then a quiet chuckle, and even over the bustling noise around me, I recognized the source.

I looked up, and at the same time everyone else around me did too.

Like my saviour rising up from the bowels of hell, I saw Sanguine leaning casually against the entrance of the hallway; a cigarette in one hand and two of his dirks sheathed on his belt. When he saw us notice him, he gave a slight tip of his head in recognition and took a drag of his blue-embered cigarette.

"Good evening." Sanguine's eyes squinted but his smile was wide as the Cheshire cat's.

"Get him!" Milos suddenly screamed, breaking the surprised and tense atmosphere. "Sanguine, that's Sanguine Dekker. Get him!"

With their attention drawn, I jumped to my feet and pushed out every shred of pain and dizziness the attack had brought to me.

When his back was turned I put my cuffed hands over Milos's neck and pulled him off his feet.

I crossed my wrists, digging the chains in as much as I could and stumbled backwards until my back hit the wall. At the exact same time the four others brought out their AK47s and to my horror started opening fire on Sanguine.

The red-eyed chimera was fast though, but I saw the fabric explode off his shoulders and stomach as he, in his own rapid stealth, brought out both of his dirks and cut down the first one, before shifting over and opening a gaping hole into the neck of the second.

My head filled with distortion as the loud assault rifle fire cracked around me. I looked down and saw Milos's hands trying to desperately pull the handcuffs off his neck. They were dug into his flesh now, red flushed mounds swallowing the shiny metal; his entire face had gone purple.

Trying to ignore the gunfire exploding throughout the room, I clenched my teeth and pulled my wrists tighter, my body shaking as I extracted every ounce of strength to kill him.

I didn't even know what had happened when my arms suddenly snapped back. I looked down with a surprised blink as I realized I had broken the chains of the handcuffs. I stared at them for a moment before I wrapped my hands around his neck and squeezed.

Suddenly, I felt a faint cold sensation go through my hands and into the man's neck. I recoiled them in shock when Milos let out a gurgled yell, his body snapping away from mine like I had just given him an electric jolt.

He fell onto the ground twitching, before giving a shudder and staying still. I stared at him in absolute shock before I heard another crack of an assault rifle.

I looked up and saw the scene unfolding before me.

Sanguine was on his knees bleeding, one of the men was over him with his gun pointed at his head. Kerres was cowering under the kitchen table, his eyes wide and staring, looking like a petrified child trembling and hiding in the middle of a war zone.

I ran towards the remaining man with a scream and knocked him off of his feet. I grabbed a dirk Sanguine had dropped and stabbed him in the chest.

He groaned and shifted. The next thing I knew I felt a fiery wind graze my shoulder as he pulled on the trigger, a last desperate attempt to save himself before death's claws claimed his soul.

I was breathing heavily. I collapsed onto the man for a moment before I managed to wrench myself to my feet. I yanked the knife out of his chest, gave Kerres an uninterested glance and knelt beside Sanguine.

The chimera was in bad shape; he was breathing hard, each breath congested and laboured like it was going to be his last.

He tried to swallow but only coughed; foamy white blood dripped from his mouth.

I raised his shirt and gasped. My body went cold as I saw at least a dozen bullet wounds in his torso. I felt a clammy hand try and find my own; he took it and squeezed it.

"Jade, you... you must... my motorcycle is outside. I need to get... to get to the apartment. If I die here, Silas will know, he will kill your... your boyfriend and you. They know when I die, the Grim, my brother Jack – he collects us." Sanguine swallowed again, his blood-red eyes a perfect match for the seeping red on his face. "Now, Jade. I'm dying."

My mind flared with anger. I got up and in my rage I tipped over the kitchen table Kerres was under, my own eyes blazing. All the fear in my body was replaced with an uncontrollable anger.

"You're a fucking coward. I hope you're happy."

Kerres whimpered, and put his hands over his mouth with a shake of his head.

"We're over. I'm moving out of Moros. Never look me up, never contact me again, and if one of those Crimstones ever shows up on my doorstep I will turn you over to King Silas."

Kerres started to cry, tears rolling down his cheeks as he shook his head back and forth. "No," he whined. "They'll fix you, Jade... they'll fix you! I'll contact the others... we'll go to their base."

I stared at him, and inside I didn't feel a thing towards him. It scared me, but it was a relief in this moment; I couldn't let myself feel anything, I had to get out of there. Kerres was lost... he was one of them now.

"The last thing I'll do for us, is to make sure King Silas doesn't kill you, and to do that I have to leave. Take care of yourself, Kerres."

"NO!" Kerres screamed. He jumped to his feet and grasped my arm so hard I could feel the skin break. "They'll fix you, you'll be Jade again. I won't let you go, I won't let them fucking have you!"

I whirled around and raised my fist to hit him, but when I saw his face... I let it drop.

He was no longer my Kerres anymore; he was just another Crimstone.

A Crimstone and an ex-cicaro. We used to just be J and K.

Kerres took a step back, and his back hit the wall.

"There are others... many others. I promise you, Jade, this isn't the end... I'll have you back." His upper lip stiffened. "W-whether you like it or not."

"Bring it on, Kerres," I murmured, before turning around to help Sanguine to his feet. He leaned against me.

Kerres didn't respond to that and he didn't move. I headed towards the window leading to the fire escape, my duffle bag in hand. "Come on, Sangy. Do you have to be such a drama queen? Aren't you immortal?" I said to him in the most calming voice I could muster.

Sanguine managed a laugh. I helped him step onto the black metal before throwing the duffle bag over to the ground. I could hear sirens in the distance; someone must've alerted the thiens as soon as the gunfire was heard.

I tried to catch Sanguine as he jumped down the fire escape but he was so weak he collapsed into a black and red heap. With all my strength I dragged him to where a motorcycle was, hidden beneath some bushes, and tried to once again make him stand on his own.

With his last remaining ounce of strength Sanguine got onto the bike and put his arms around my waist. I turned it on and put the duffle bag onto my lap, and with the sirens coming closer and closer, I revved the engine and turned off into a side alley, towards Sanguine's apartment.

Whenever I felt his arms loosen around my chest I dug my fingernails into his hands to try and snap him back to consciousness. "Stay with me, Sangy. We're almost there. Don't die on the bike."

"Mmhm." I could feel his head leaning against the back of my neck; he was getting weaker.

Finally I pulled into the alleyway. Not knowing what to do with the bike, I got off and flicked out the stopper with the toe of my boot. I dug out the key from Sanguine's back pocket and dragged him inside, before wheeling the bike inside too.

The sound of the door locking behind me filled me with relief, the claws on my chest loosened just slightly. At least we were safe. The Crimstones hadn't got me and they hadn't got Sanguine.

Sanguine collapsed onto the bed, his mouth open and gasping each breath in, his bloody chest rising and falling. The chimera was ashy grey and already his face looked like that of a corpse.

I put my hands gently on his face. "What do I do, Sanguine? Do I stay here? Do I leave? Tell me."

His eyes were looking up at the ceiling, but he managed to talk in a small weak voice. "You take my black card, if they bitch, show them it. Get a place in Eros and hide, never come back to Moros."

The words stung me, but I had said goodbye to Moros over a year ago, it wasn't my home anymore. I nodded and felt him push the card into my hand.

"Will I ever see you again?"

He laughed, of course he laughed. I wiped the foamy blood from his lips and he smiled a demonic bloody toothed smile. "You're the stupidest genius I know, Jade." His face tensed and he put a hand over his eyes. "Stay with me – until I die. I'll hold off as long as I can but as soon as I'm gone, you must run little rabbit."

He smiled at my brow furrowing, before he waved me away. "Go, bandage your wounds while you have the supplies. Leave me to die in peace, mihi, turn the lamp off beside me and put on a cartoon."

The lives of immortals... *I want darkness and cartoons while I die.* I resisted the sarcastic quip hovering on my tongue and did what he asked, wishing he would answer the question I had asked him – if I would see him again. His answer could've meant both, I didn't know.

The lamp clicked off and with his ragged, wheezing breathing in the background, I sat on the couch and prepared myself a dose of heroin, my ears always craned and listening for his last breath to be taken.

It was such an odd thing to be doing. I was waiting for my only friend to die, fully accepting that he would come back because my mind was too shot to even process mortality right now.

Sanguine was safe and I was safe, that was all that mattered.

Kerres...

My face darkened. I had left him sobbing in a corner, cowering like a scared child. He had invited those men into our apartment, he had sold me out to them, believing with stupid naivety only a slumrat would have that they would actually help me and expect nothing in return.

I had tried to break it off, tried to end it as maturely and civilly as I could but he had to grasp onto this insane notion that Elish had somehow brainwashed me. It was too hard for Kerres to accept that I had changed more in the year with Elish than I had for the past fifteen years of my life.

I injected myself and turned the cartoons up for Sanguine. SpongeBob was on, he always loved that show.

The apartment was dimly lit, only a small lamp to my side and the red light of the heater, wafting warm air into the little shelter. I checked out my body and started patching up the thankfully small injuries. It looked like the worst was the gunshot graze but it wasn't as bad as it could've been.

I looked in the mirror and observed the swelling jaw and broken nose. I gingerly touched it and placed a book between my teeth before adjusting the bone back into place with a sickening grinding noise that echoed off of my brain. I shuddered and took the book out, ignoring the puncture marks I had made in the cover. It hadn't been the first time I'd had to set a broken nose and I doubted it would be the last.

After I had patched myself up, I laid on the couch and tried to force my mind to watch the cartoons, but my head was every other place but on the television. My future and what it involved kept overshadowing the flowing river of my thoughts, damming it up with its toxic questions that I was in no mental state to answer.

I snorted some china white and rubbed my nose before giving my head a shake, hoping a top off would help add more resistance to those thoughts, or at least make me so out of it that I didn't care.

I was surprised at how numb I was; I should have been freaking out and scrambling to make plans in Eros but instead I was just flat lined.

I had lost Elish and once he dumped me off in Moros, I had lost Kerres as well; the boy I had grown up with and loved, the one who waited for me for an entire year until the chimera had gotten bored of me.

Now what?

I didn't know, maybe I would defect into the greywastes and find a life there. Aras seemed like a nice place to be, or maybe I would live out my life in the factory town that the little blond kid had grown up in. His aura was like a marshmallow dipped in rainbows; I wouldn't mind that.

As if my cruel mind wanted to show me just how obvious it was that my aura could never be like that, I saw the blackness of my own temporarily waft through my vision. Black with barely any purple. Maybe that was why I didn't care anymore; my aura was as dead and hopeless as I felt.

My hand went to my neck and I stroked it, bare and slick with sweat. I still ached for that collar, and I ached for Elish's guidance right now.

My mind slipped into its lucid dream, fuelled by the extra hit of china white and the already strong venom of the heroin. Without realizing it, I fell asleep.

I woke up with a jolt and immediately my body became cold. Sanguine's raspy struggling breathing was gone.

Hating myself for falling asleep, I ran over to the sengil chimera, but I stopped when I saw him.

Sanguine's eyes were partially open, dim and lifeless, red embers choked with grey ash; his face once holding a squinting smile now hollow, even his lips had turned the black.

There was no time to gawk over the dead sengil; he would come back but if this 'Grim' found me here my life would probably be cut short. King Silas would kill Kerres for this, and as much as I was pissed at my ex-boyfriend I couldn't subject him to the king's torture, or his own Stadium death match. I knew it was over between the two of us, and the last thing I would do for him would be to save his life. We were toxic substances and I understood that, but I still wanted him to lead a happy life.

I grabbed my duffle bag and quickly left the apartment, hoping that I would see Sanguine again. If he knew I was going to Eros, perhaps he would find me. He had found me before, he could locate me again.

Another door closed behind me and automatically locked itself. My last oasis and my last haven, leaving behind my last friend. I was on my own now, really on my own, for the first time in my life.

Run little rabbit, go run.

...

The sirens were coming... what would they do when they got here? Arrest me? I hadn't done anything wrong, I – I had been trying to help him. I had to help him; he couldn't stop who he was becoming. It was beyond his power.

Oh, Jade... I'm so sorry. What I would've done to go back in time and grab that keycard from you. Burn it in the oven or chop it up into a thousand pieces. Everything changed when you went into that mansion.

Jade never came home.

"Get out from under there, the fucking thiens are coming, you idiot!"

Like a firecracker going off Kerres found himself shot back into reality, a reality he wanted to only run from. He wanted to burrow his head in the sand until it all went away, until this nightmare disappeared from what used to be a good life. This wasn't how it was supposed to turn out; they were supposed to be together forever. *How did this happen? How did I let it get to this?*

Kerres had his hands wrapped around his head, pressing against the base of his skull as if wanting to force what had just happened out of his memories. He didn't know how long he had been staring at that stained white wall, for all he knew the man could've been calling him for hours.

It couldn't be real, no this couldn't have just happened... I had to save Jade.

That fucking demon chimera took my Jade, just like Elish took him. He was mine, he was my boy, not theirs. I have to protect him, even if in the end I might be protecting him from himself.

"Kerres!?" Milos barked, grabbing onto the boy's shoulder and yanking him out from under the table.

The crimson-haired man looked up at Milos; his eyes widened as he saw the thick open wound on his neck, weeping blood freely onto the carpet underneath their feet. His entire body looked bruised and beaten but his stamina was the strongest Kerres had ever seen. He was still standing tall, acting like the giant gouge on his neck was nothing more than a paper cut.

"What about Tate?" Kerres rose before his head snapped to the left, he could hear hurried voices coming from the stairwell of the apartment. Before he could even process what was happening, Milos was pushing him towards the sliding glass door.

"Tate ran during the gunfire, he's getting backup, come on, we need to get to Garrett Park." Kerres noticed for the first time that Milos had a radio in his hand. Like everything around them it was slicked in blood; the entire apartment smelled like gun powder and blood. It was a war zone... so many dead bodies, all of them mangled messes of shredded skin, bone and so much blood. The demon chimera had done his job on the Crimstones.

And Jade is one of them.
No, he's my baby.

The next thing Kerres knew they were closing the iron gate and running towards the park. He didn't know why, he didn't know what the hell was happening. How was Milos even alive? The gouges in his neck… Kerres shuddered. Jade had a strength to him that Kerres had never seen before; he could have decapitated him.

Elish has given me a chimera… but where was that chimera now? Will he really leave me forever?

Kerres and Milos crossed an empty street, the sirens and the thiens far in the distance breaking the cold night with their shrill whine. Everything was near empty and desolate, only small dark shadows of forgotten people and the occasional roaming cat. The bleak towers of abandoned buildings seemed closer tonight, like taunting predators that only closed in on you when your back was turned. Moros didn't seem like his safe haven anymore; it was full of dangers and people who would do both of them harm.

As soon as Kerres's feet touched grass he could see more silhouettes, though these shadows were not hunched near heat vents to keep warm, or sifting through garbage. They were five men with their arms crossed, staring forward with stern and dead eyes. Crimstones, all of them.

How many of them were there? Tate made it seem like this was just a small group but I have seen over forty of them so far. Do they really hate the chimeras that much?

No one in Moros had ever taken the Crimstones seriously. King Silas never gave them media coverage, he didn't believe in it. So what bad things they had done were nothing but rumours carried through the districts. Car bombs here or there, and once they had shot Ellis in the head, but besides that they were just a small organization known for wanting to take down the chimeras.

But no one fucked with the royal family, or King Silas; so their threats were taken with a grain of salt.

Perhaps they were a lot more powerful than I thought; maybe the royal family just didn't want us to know that.

"Shale, do you have the body?" Milos jogged over to them, stuffing his blood-streaked radio into one of his cargo pants pockets.

Kerres looked on in shock as one of the men, a blond-haired young man, nodded. He looked down and nudged a black duffle bag with his foot, not unlike the one they had tried to stuff Jade into.

Kerres swallowed hard, though the events of the last hour had rattled him to the point where he didn't even feel sick or shocked by the body lying in the bag. He had no more emotions left to feel; they had all been killed brutally like the bodies they had left back in the apartment.

"We'll get his chip out of him, with a coat hanger and some luck we can put it behind this kid's ear without there being an incision. They won't do an autopsy on a Morosian," the boy replied. "Other than that… he has no tattoos, no identifying marks, just his hair."

Kerres blinked, then turned as Milos spoke. "And what are we doing about that hair colour?"

"We got the hair dye type from Tate too and a key to a hotel room. I want to take a look at the kid's hair in natural light so we can match the length," the boy said in a low tone, his blue eyes flicking to Kerres for a brief moment.

There was something off with that young man; he seemed… robotic, like every shred of his will had left him. His blue eyes seemed hard… and almost soulless.

Wait a second.

"Hair dye?" Kerres's mind finally caught up with what these men were saying. He looked around to make sure no one was listening in on them but not a soul was in the park this night. "For who?"

Then he saw the dangerous smirk on Milos's face, an ugly upturn of his lips that seemed to suit his rough appearance. Kerres didn't like it; he didn't like that expression and he didn't trust that man.

But… but I have to help Jade, they are the only people in this world who can help me. Who else do I have? Oh, Jade, I'm sorry. I don't want them to hurt you but when it is all said and done … won't the end justify the means? You'll be back; they'll make you normal again. You can be my J, and we can get married, live the life we were always supposed to. Without Elish, without the chimeras and anyone who would take you away from me.

Fuck, am I making the biggest mistake of my life right now?

Milos and the other Crimstones exchanged amused chuckles. They seemed to enjoy Kerres's confusion over what was going on.

Kerres took a step back as Milos walked up to him, and cringed as the Crimstone leader put a hand on his shoulder. It was a gesture full of false securities and sinister plots that Kerres knew he didn't want to hear. From what they were saying, Kerres was starting to realize just what this Crimstone leader had planned for him.

"Well, Kerres... I have use for you, and I can't get that use when you're roasting on the chimeras' spit... so..." The leader grinned and patted his shoulder; behind him the others continued to chuckle, like a group of hyenas who had just cornered an injured antelope. "I hope you said a big heartfelt goodbye to your friends, because you're about to commit suicide."

CHAPTER 24

It took me the rest of the night to make my way to Eros. Still dressed in my pet clothes with only a leather jacket for warmth, I stuck to the shadows of Moros until I got to a wall I felt comfortable crossing over. After that it was more difficult to cross the districts unseen. I didn't know Nyx and I knew Eros even less.

Of course, I was looking over my shoulder the entire time, expecting to see the camo-wearing Crimstones or even worse a chimera coming to take me to Silas to explain myself. I had a lot of enemies now and a lot of people I wanted to avoid.

Morning broke over Skyfall with my sore and tired body walking down one of the side streets, glancing in all directions for a hotel I could stash myself in before I went to find an apartment I could stay in. My head was bowed and my breath starting to get short, but besides a few confused looks people left me alone. It was because I was dressed as an elite, no longer wearing torn and patched pants and duct taped shoes. I was clad in extremely expensive bosen leather and hard-soled boots with two inch high heels.

I would need to buy new clothes; my serial killer days were over and Moros was over. My only decision now was if I was going to purchase a new ID chip and start a fresh life in Eros, or if I was going to extract my own ID chip and defect into the greywastes.

Jade the slumrat, to Jade the cicaro, to Jade the Shadow Killer... to who now? I was a wraith without a name, a shadow that slunk in the alleyways and hid in dark alcoves. Maybe I was never meant to be a real person, maybe my mother was right, I was a demon, a shapeshifting jinn.

I swallowed my sorrow and turned another corner. I looked up and saw a sign that read Redring Motel, a brown building with a green trim, with what looked like a dozen doors on the first floor and another dozen on the second-storey.

An older woman with dyed blond hair raised her eyes from a book she was reading, and smiled. "A room, dear?"

Dear? When I was a Morosian crossing borders they turned their noses up to me.

I nodded and reached into my duffle bag for some cash. I had Sanguine's black card but I didn't want to use that until my own money ran out. Not only did I feel like a bum using it, but I had no idea if these transactions were recorded. Sanguine was resurrecting in the shelter apartment in Moros, not checking into a hotel in Eros.

When I handed her the money the lady gave me a sad smile. I was shocked when she rested a hand on mine and said sympathetically, "Did you finally have enough, dear?"

I blinked but the moment my brows knitted together I realized I was a fancily-dressed young boy with a bruised and cut face holding a duffle bag.

I'd run with that.

I nodded. "Yeah… is it okay if this goes off the record?" I could use this to my advantage.

"Oh, of course." She seemed like someone who had at some point had to deal with domestic violence, so I had come to the right place. With a thanks she gave me my room key, and trying to avoid all the small talk I could, I turned and headed towards my hotel room. It would be mine for the next three weeks.

I immediately locked the door, drew the curtains and made sure the windows could lock too. The hotel room looked like every other hotel room I had ever seen except cleaner. Paneled walls and a double bed with a green and blue comforter, a clean bathroom, and a TV facing the bed. Besides a small dining table with two chairs that was about it. It was perfect to stay in forever, but I wanted to find an out of the way, small nook somewhere in Eros where I could hide out for a few… years.

Before my brain could catch up with the emotions I had left behind in

Moros, I prepared a dose for myself and injected the beautiful therapy into my veins. I didn't last long after that; I passed out cold still in my clothes and not even under the covers.

I woke up covered in drool with my whole body aching and feeling like shit. It was pretty obvious I was addicted to the heroin now, which was the last thing I cared about.

The tar made my head feel a little less like a beehive, and the more I did the more it seemed to organize my thoughts into a single file; but without the drugs I was a trembling shaky mess.

I injected myself and drank a few large glasses of water and for good measure I ate some complimentary mints, even though they had cloth fibers stuck to them. Then as the dose kicked in I turned on the television to the rerun channel and watched some sitcoms, still trying to run from my reality, a reality I didn't want to face.

Did Jack the Grim Reaper come and collect Sanguine yet? I hoped so; I had gotten that dude in enough trouble.

And Kerres... I wondered what explanation he would give as to why there were five dead people in his apartment with camo and machine guns.

I played with the idea that maybe they would praise him for killing five members of the Crimstones but who was to know. I just hoped he had a good explanation so he could go back to living his life. A life without me and not waiting for me.

Maybe I could bring him here... and we could start a new life.

No, shit... no, Jade don't think those things.

I closed my eyes and leaned my head back, feeling a surge of guilt I hadn't felt the previous day. My own anger at what Kerres had done had outshined the love I've always held for him. Maybe I was a bit too cruel to him; he was just trying to help. Kerres was naïve and trusting; he had always been such a sweet guy.

Had it been a mistake to leave him the way I did? My best friend and my boyfriend who had so desperately tried to get me back.

What had I done?

No. I tried to give myself a classic pep talk, to justify my decision to leave him. We weren't good for each other. I had changed too much; there was too much anger and hatred inside of me that I still felt. It was plastered all over my aura. I was a dark shadow, a nameless boy not even seventeen yet, with ties to the chimeras that would undoubtedly get Kerres killed. I had to leave him to protect him and to make him happy. My crimson-haired ex-boyfriend hadn't been happy with me, he couldn't handle me anymore.

But… we could… we could buy new IDs.

I hated myself… I really did.

A swell of self-loathing brought with it a string of vulgarities and insults for myself. There was no shortage of that in my mind, and though the heroin could dull the effects, it didn't dull my overwhelming internal hatred.

No wonder Elish hated me, no wonder he saw me as a snot-nosed little Morosian in need of a mental beat down. Who would want to be with me? I was worthless, a piece of gutter trash who couldn't handle his own emotions or his own life. No one wanted me, and no one ever had.

But Kerres…

I sat on the edge of the bed and buried my face into my hands with a groan. What had I done? I had turned my back on him like Elish had done me, when he needed me the most. I had literally turned away from him and gone with the chimera.

Was it really supposed to just be the two of us? But we had clashed so badly in Moros. I had lost control of myself and my inner turmoil with losing Elish. What would be so different if I went back? Now I would have the Crimstones after me, there was no escaping them. If they thought I was a chimera, and they knew Sanguine had helped me kill five of their members, where could I hide?

The greywastes…?

At first I had dismissed the idea, but I had been in Aras and it wasn't that bad. I could catch a merchant's caravan there with Kerres and maybe we could just start over. I would have lots of rats and ravers to kill and Kerres could scavenge.

We could leave it all behind… everyone. The only chimera we would have to worry about would be that psycho one and he didn't even know he was a chimera so he wasn't connected to the family.

My heart jumped with the prospect, but soon I was chewing nervously on the side of my cheek. I picked up the remote and turned to the news station. I would have to find him in the cover of night; I couldn't be seen in Moros right now and there was no way I could go back to the apartment.

I clicked the channel over, and felt a queasy churn in my chest as I immediately saw the front of our apartment building. An overwhelming urge came to shut the television off as the events of yesterday started to become a little too real, but I forced myself to put it down.

The scene switched to inside our apartment; I cringed as I saw the bloody outlines of dead bodies. It wasn't a video feed but photos, every corner of our apartment was photographed, even the second bedroom. Thankfully, all my things were gone.

"The living room shows where five members of the terrorist organization calling themselves the Crimstones were murdered last night by King Silas's personal bodyguard Sanguine Dekker, though reports are sketchy and updates few and far between." I smirked at that, but it was best that my name got left out. "The identities of the murdered have not been released and if the precinct continues their trend they will not be released and their families not notified."

"We also have an unconfirmed update stating that the tenant of the apartment, a possible recruit for the Crimstones, twenty-year-old Kerres of Moros was found dead early this morning in Garrett Park, from a possible drug overdose –"

My world went dark, like a stone lid closing in on my mind.

What?

The blood rushed through my ears like a steady roar, and as I tried to turn the television off, my mind went hot and a red haze covered my eyes. I stared dumbfounded and unbelieving as the reporter flashed to Garrett Park, where my mother had used to sit.

No…

I rose and tried to take a step, but my knees went weak and I sunk down to the floor. I let out a strangled sob and looked around the room. I was looking for my comfort, looking for the boy who had always been there to take me into his arms and hold me close to him.

But he wasn't there, he would never be there again. I had left him sobbing and pleading for me to go with him to the Crimstones. Instead I had gone with Sanguine and left him with the thiens on their way.

Kerres killed himself.

Kerres is dead.

What have I done?

In a trance I got up, my legs wobbling and feeling like strips of rubber. I stumbled towards the small dining table and laid out several lines of china white. My hands were shaking so badly as they clutched the metal sniffer that I kept messing up the perfect white lines.

When I was finished I leaned my head on the counter, feeling the heat of my own breath come back to me, the dull drone of the television only a couple feet away.

My eyes flicked to the screen, where they were now talking to a thien I had seen around Moros, a man with dyed blue hair and a pointed nose. I turned away but I was too afraid to close my eyes. Instead I stared at my leather boots, and let the drugs kill what emotions I had left.

And there were none.

There is not much to say about the next several days of my life, it was all a haze of drugs, throwing up, and drinking shots of vodka in hopes of being lucky enough to not wake up.

But I did wake up, and I only woke up to prepare my next dose before laying back down on the bed in my drug-induced stupor. I would never be sober again, I would die before I tasted cold reality. There wasn't a single cell left in my body to handle what facing the consequences of my actions would bring.

I had left my Kerres to die... my crimson-haired companion. What kind of monster was I?

A wetness soaked my lips and face, I was drooling again. I stumbled to the bathroom where I threw up the vodka I had been drinking. After taking a piss I staggered back and sat down on the chair, my head swirling a torrential rainstorm.

Monster.

Monster.

I reached into the duffle bag and pushed away the Game Boy and the velvet case holding my claws. I found the baggy of china white and tapped it onto the powder-dusted surface.

It was my last remaining powder. I was going to have to go to the pharmacy or find a dealer to score some heroin. Pharms sold everything but they were overpriced and cut, street drugs still had their draw.

My eyes closed and my head tipped forward. I caught myself and jerked my head up, the paneling ahead of me blurring and contorting under the influence of all the drugs.

I passed out again but when I finally came back into a shaky consciousness I grabbed my jacket, and, not even bothering to see how fucked up I looked in the mirror, I took some money and walked outside onto the balcony.

It was dark and I didn't even know what day it was. My boots clicked silently against the stairs as I drew my jacket over the old clothes I had eventually changed into.

I started walking down the street, looking out for a shady-looking character who would have what I needed.

Soon... soon I wouldn't wake up and this nightmare would be over. How would Elish react when he learned Kerres had killed himself followed by me? Probably smug. I could see that smirk come to his face, of sick satisfaction at the torrid chain of events he had caused.

Nothing but a game, and look at what happened when he was done playing with his pawn. Maybe that was what he was waiting for, to put the dog back in the slums after being a captive so he could patiently wait for him to self-destruct.

And I had... I explosively self-destructed and the force of the nuclear meltdown killed my boyfriend. The one person who would go to any lengths to keep me safe and to get me back.

The tension closed around my throat, wringing acid into my stomach, upset over its lack of food and the onslaught of liquor and opiates.

Soon my stomach would be full of maggots and rot, or chopped up and fed to the bosen or the abominations. The time bomb inside of me was ticking down; I knew there was no coming back from this and perhaps that's why I hadn't shed a single tear.

There was no more light in my mind, everything had gone dark. Places once filled with love, happiness, and comfort had become absolutely nothing. Like the universe before the big bang, it was just dark matter.

How could I feel emotions when I had ceased to exist? Just do drugs and enjoy your final days, drugs are a painless way to die; at least Kerres had died without pain.

Incredulously, I laughed at my own inner statement; he had died in agony, abandoned by his boyfriend after waiting so long for him, only to walk to Garrett Park, maybe hoping to find me, and when he didn't – he took the heroin I had bought and killed himself.

I'm so sorry… I couldn't handle it. I couldn't handle Elish's game and I couldn't handle life. I had made a fatal mistake. I had fallen for a chimera and had been punished for touching Midas's hand. Now I would wait, as the rest of my body turned to gold.

Turned to nothing.

Did Elish know he drove away with all of me?

Did I know I had walked away with all of Kerres?

I lit a cigarette and loitered around the alleyways, a light rain falling around me, soaking my head and my gloveless hands and creating small rivers which funnelled down to the drains below. The sewers below Skyfall knew no districts and stretched out in miles of brick mazes; maybe I could hide in there.

A sewer monster. I was a monster already.

I sucked the blue ember, one of Sanguine's own, and crossed the paved streets to a park.

Red embers lit up the black jackknife trees and faded like the glowing eyes of blinking creatures. I walked towards them and gave the four of them a nod. They were Erosians, dressed in denim and cotton jackets with their hair done nicely, casually chatting amongst themselves until they saw me approach.

One of them nodded at me. "What's up, bro?"

I gave them the customary nod back and cut down to why I was there in the first place. "Looking to score some smack, white or black, know anyone who is holding? Offering a finder's fee."

They all swept their eyes up and down my bruised body, sizing me up to see if I was cool. I guess I passed the test. The one who talked to me, a brown-haired guy with a normal aura of dark green and brown, gave a nod to a short black-haired dude.

"What sort of finder's fee are we chattin' about?" the short one asked.

"If I can get a regular dealer, twenty bucks. I'm looking for someone long-term who can help me out." I sucked back the ember and tried to shoot off as casual of a vibe as I could, though inside I just wanted to get a brick of black tar and slink back to my cave so I could be alone in my misery.

The short one snuffed out his cigarette. "I got a place for you, a safe injection den underneath a restaurant, got a guy there who can hook you up. I'll be back guys."

"You better bring us some fucking mickeys with that finder's fee of yours, Ronny," one of them quipped, holding a bottle of booze to his lips.

"Yeah, yeah." Ronny waved a hand and motioned me to follow him. "Let's go, this won't take long."

I followed the short one, not in the mood for casual conversation and he didn't seem like the type to talk either so we got along just fine. We crossed the park and jumped over an iron rung fence leading to a sidewalk lit by bluelamp street lights giving it an eerie glow under the drizzling rain above us. He walked on without a word, leading me down a dirt road surrounded by the chain-link fences of back yards before we cut across another park.

Finally, after ten minutes of walking deeper into the east side of Eros, he led me down a half-flight of concrete stairs. It was an unassuming location in a sketchy part of town; no doubt this was a drug den.

Ronny opened the door. I was surprised that it was open; we kept the ones in Moros locked but I guess people in Moros were a lot more desperate. These Erosians had the money to pay for their drugs and I bet if they got into too much trouble trying to get their fixes, they got demoted to Nyx or Moros.

Ronny told me to wait and he slipped in, though his hand was holding the door open. After a couple minutes talking back and forth he nodded me inside.

I pushed the door open and walked in.

Yep, this was a drug den...

The place was a dump, the same sullen hopeless vibe that the dens in Moros had, like I had walked into an open cemetery and the corpses were just waiting to get buried.

The inside was covered in spray-painted graffiti and smelled like piss and sweat, most of the walls had been stripped down to the studs, and the floor was stained and dirty.

There were people in here too, lumps of people with blankets pulled over them, tucked into corners or sitting on torn up couches; all with sunken, hollow expressions on their faces, mouths slacked open and white tongues dehydrated and swollen. They looked like the lowest of the low; I felt like I had walked back into Moros.

I guess drug addiction stretched to all districts; this place almost felt like the home I had left behind.

I stepped over a woman staring dead-eyed at one of several televisions, all with the sound turned up so they could hear it over the music. It was noisy, congested and just… miserable

My boots crunched on a dirty needle, shattering the plastic; they were everywhere. With a glance I found Ronny talking to a big guy with a plaid shirt and a thick beard.

The bearded guy looked me up and down like the others had and motioned me over.

"Looks like someone laid you out. Are you hiding out from another district?"

I shook my head; that would be an obvious ban from this place. Hiding out from another district would mean the possibility of thiens coming to look for you and though it wasn't illegal to have a safe injection den, it was illegal to use non-Dek'ko drugs. "My boyfriend kicked me out; he always supplied me. I just need connections and supply. I'd like to move up to larger purchases but I'll do small bags, whatever you want to do," I said with a shrug.

The bearded man nodded again, and I saw him looking at the blue ember of my cigarette; that was my ace in the hole that proved I wasn't from a lesser district. No one in Moros could afford these cigarettes; a single cig of Blueleaf could get you a pack of the Morosian shit brand: Herc.

"Okay, he's cool."

With that acceptance I drew out a twenty dollar bill and slipped it into Ronny's pocket; he nodded his head recognizing the exchange and bid us both farewell.

The man held out his hand and shook mine. He had a strong grip. "Just call me Ed. What do I call you?"

I guessed Shadow would be too obvious. My mind ran over every name I could think of, but only one stuck out. "Phillip."

"What's your poison, Phil?"

"Something to take the edge off, smack would be a preference." I took out a cigarette and gave it to him; he took it and I heard the chink of a Zippo as he lit it.

"This is my den, my rules happen in my den, you don't die in my den but you can hang out with purchase. My product is strong, not the usual stepped on shit your bubby bought you, if that is the story you're sticking too –" He let that hang with another puff, before taking the cig out and flicking the ash. "The first hit you do in front of me, I want to see your arms and I want to see you not throw up like it's your first roll. This is a safe injection site but the thiens get pissed off if we deal non Dek'ko products."

I wasn't used to the introductory rules, the drugs I bought in Moros I had been buying since I was thirteen and even before that the dealers knew my mother.

Well whatever, if I had to jump through hoops to get a steady supply then so be it. I sat down on a ripped up couch and took off my jacket, the track marks on my arms in full view, even more visible under my flushed skin.

Ed whistled and some chick in a stained tank top came over holding a needle. She prepped me with the smell of cigarettes and alcohol seeping from her pores and injected the tar into my skin.

The throbbing that had begun in my temples started to sink back into the bubbling toxins of my other emotions; my consciousness slipped and I felt my head tilt back with a satisfied sigh.

"Good enough for you, Ed?"

I heard the man chuckle. "Good enough, Phil." I felt a slap on my shoulder. "When you're ready to go, we'll do our buy."

I nodded, wanting to be left alone. When I heard the crunching of the dirty floor underneath his shoes I looked around and found a dark corner I could hide in. I grabbed a blanket from a pile stacked behind one of the televisions and curled up beside a bookcase, essentially wedging me between the corner of the wall and the shelf. It was a small and secluded place that made me feel like a rat hiding in a household.

I happily lost myself in the drugs; they were stronger than the shit I had bought in Moros, which was a pleasant surprise. Moros heroin had usually been stepped on several times and though it still knocked you out, once you had better you hated going back.

Maybe I wouldn't mind it here... the drugs were good and I didn't expect to be alive for much longer, so I might as well enjoy the potent drugs while I was breathing.

I came back to reality soaked in sweat, my feet cramped and aching. It was noisy around me, music still playing and the televisions still blaring so they could be heard over the heavy metal. My eyes focused and scanned where I was, seeing from my nook two couches, a television, and many surfaces to prepare drugs on. The bluelamps were on and so was a halogen on the water-stained ceiling, casting its light on the room below and creating large shadows that covered the naked studs and beams of the open walls.

People were chatting on the couch and two dark lumps like me could be seen; one leaning against what I think was a washing machine and one laying half in the hallway. There were more; I could hear their voices, but they were out of my line of sight.

I got up and took a piss in the most disgusting toilet I had ever seen and looked around to find Ed, my boots crunching everything from broken needles, to food wrappers, to bottles and cans.

I saw the woman exchanging money with a dude, but before they could go to the bedroom to do the obvious I stopped her. "Hey can you prep me another hit when you're done?"

She looked behind her shoulder. "First ones free, it's four bucks a hit, prepped and injected."

Twice as much as Moros drugs but it was more potent and if I didn't need to prep it, all the better.

I took out a twenty. "I'll buy four. I don't have change. I'll keep it on me and call you over when I need it, is that okay?"

The man looked at me impatiently, wanting to get his rocks on.

The woman gave me a nod. "Yeah, it's cool, I'll send Plinko over to sort you out. If any man but Ed talks to you you're being scammed. Only women distribute."

Good to know. I went back to my nook and curled up to enjoy what was left of my high.

I faded out and only came back when the woman was prepping my arm for me; I watched her with drowsy interest before the strength of the dose perked me up.

Surprisingly, she offered me a sandwich. I wasn't hungry though.

"No, you eat it. You can't die here, bright eyes. You've been here all day and all night."

"Okay…" I mumbled. I took a bite to appease the meth-addicted mother hen and took a deep breath as the cold heroin shot through my veins. When the withdrawal left my system I finished the sandwich in time for her to come back with a resealable bag full of heroin, and to my surprise some white rocks.

"You look like you need something stronger; Ed included some crack in the mix and a free pipe."

I smirked, the woman must really think I was an idiot, and Ed too. It wasn't a friendly gesture for a kid who looked like he had given up on life. It was because they knew I had money and they wanted to get me on the stuff you had to do more often.

I knew their game though, enough to take the free drugs and stuff the baggy into my inner jacket pocket.

It wasn't long until I started preparing my first hit of crack. I had to watch a woman sitting on the couch to be able to catch how to do it. I had watched Morosians smoke from pipes but it wasn't something I had paid attention to; they were a part of the scenery back in the slum district.

Would this kill me? I didn't know – I lit a lighter against the ball of the glass vial and took a hit.

Kerres would've killed me – Elish would've killed me, but they're both gone now.

My stomach churned and I quickly inhaled the smoke to try and get rid of the creeping thoughts. I coughed and wiped my sweaty head with my jacket sleeve, before my head hit the side of the bookshelf.

I heard the crack pipe tinkle as it fell onto the floor, and the rest of the outside world faded into melting colours.

Then it was gone… the pain was gone… they… they were gone.

I felt my eyes snap open, and then the sound of my knuckles rapping together. I smiled and sighed staring up at the ceiling, feeling happier than I ever had before.

It would be okay... my mind fully believed I would be okay and suddenly I felt excited for the future. The things I could do with Sanguine's black card; I could do anything now, anything, anything.

I heard someone laugh and I looked over and saw Ed pointing to me. I smiled at him and started telling him all the things I was going to do once I got out of there. The guy listened with the chick who had prepped my dose, an amused expression on his face.

"I'm going to buy a motorcycle, ever ride one of those? Fuck, I rode one just last week, or was it two weeks ago? No, I think it was one..." I rambled on, running my fingers up and down my skin. It felt nice to touch it. "I think after I get that and an apartment. I don't know you know I might fucking go on vacation. Why not? I have no one, Ed, no one."

Ed said something back, but talking was more interesting than listening to what he was saying.

Then after a while my mouth went dry. I swallowed some water and pulled the blanket over me; my body started to shiver.

It was fading, I needed more.

So I took more and it came back.

My entire body was vibrating, twitching, and moving. I couldn't sit still. I got up and travelled from one person to the next who was willing to hold a conversation with me, before I watched television for a while.

When I woke up again the crack had been done. I called over Plinko who got me a sandwich and prepped me a dose of heroin. This one knocked me off of my feet and shot my emotions back into the devil's throat of my mind, a bleak and dark place where I shoved my feelings in hopes that they would never come back. I sucked in the strong dose and let it over take me, and when they prepped me again and moved me to a bedroom, I didn't protest or care.

That night I was raped.

I didn't even know what was going on, he didn't even take my clothes off. I felt my pants get drawn down then penetration, and within ten minutes it was over. I barely lifted my head, and my arms were heavy weights; there wasn't an inch of strength or desire in my body to move. I just stood frozen and waited for it to be over.

At a time like this I really didn't care, even when it happened three more times I still didn't care. They were using protection, I couldn't feel anything inside me and I could smell the latex, but even if I caught a disease… I knew I was going to die here anyway.

The woman who had prepped me the first time, Helen, shot me up with more heroin, which was all I cared about. She then made me eat something and gave me a water bottle full of sugary water. She left and when the door closed I was left completely in the dark, only the glow of the VCR's clock could be seen. The time was always 12:00… it flashed at me.

I rolled over when the left side of my pillow was too wet from sweat and drool, and waited for the next man to come. The only time I saw light was when I was either getting heroin or a guy was coming in to have his time with me; the light brought either joy or pain.

Some were quick and rough, others slow, to the point where Ed would bang on the door and yell at them to hurry up. I wondered how much money I was getting them. I think they took the couple hundred dollars in my pockets, but I didn't check.

Every time I woke up was a disappointment and after a while I dreaded my eyes opening to the VCR clock flashing at me. Why wasn't I dead yet?

How long had it been?

Helen turned on the light one day; she had gauze and antiseptic on a tray. I got to look at my arms and saw I had abscesses all over them, but the first thing she started to treat was my face.

She didn't speak to me, but her hands were gentle. I wanted to say something to her but my mouth was mush. I was too out of it to care, and too depressed that I wasn't dead yet.

When would I be able to see Kerres again? I could see his face so perfectly in my head, though it made my heart wrench to even think about it. Even the thought made my brain pull towards the heroin, to fade his handsome face from the raw parts of my mind.

"Does he even know what's going on anymore?" Ed asked from the open door. I felt a cold stinging against my skin and focused my eyes to see her rubbing a pus-filled hole in my arm with a solution.

"No… he's the easiest trick we've had. He's just given up. I don't think he's going to last much longer. I really think we should dump him before he dies."

Do they think I'll die soon? Could I? Please?

"He's making me too much money; even once he's dead I know a few guys who'll fuck him just to say they did." The door slammed behind him and I watched the gauze come back pink and green.

After Helen had treated my wounds she dosed me. When she withdrew the needle I managed to raise an arm to catch her attention. I swallowed hard and tried to force voice to my lips.

"Another one," I rasped. I tried to squeeze her arms but my energy was gone.

She looked at me, her blond hair brushed back in a messy ponytail. "No, that will kill you."

I shook my head, and even with that slight movement of my skull my body felt nauseas and dizzy, my brain filled with a sickening heat. "I know."

She gave me a sympathetic pat on the shoulder and rose; she started gathering the tools and placing them onto the metal table.

"Please," I pleaded. As the heroin hit me I found myself unable to sit up properly. I swayed and landed on my side. I sniffed the snot that was starting to run down my nose and tried to say it a bit louder. "Please?"

She left, and I was back in darkness.

I looked up at the ceiling, the water stains showing up as ghostly waves of plasma with my blue night vision. My mind tried to bring up my aura but I immediately turned my ability off. It was nothing I wanted to see, blackness so thick I couldn't see the objects beyond it. It was covering me like a blanket, or a thick soup, enough to give any empath nightmares. There was no more purple, no more silver, those colours were long gone. All that remained was the darkness inside of me that rose from my chest like the smoke off Sanguine's clothes.

Another man came. I closed my eyes when the light infiltrated me. The light was just another way of telling me I was still alive. It put me right back into reality and right back into the continuous flow of time.

The fucking was the worst, but not for the reasons it should've been. It was because every thrust and every grunt was counted by me and timed. I knew how much time had passed and that didn't sit well with me. I didn't like reminders that my organic body was still working, was still functional. Why wasn't I dead yet?

Or why wasn't my body dead yet? My sullen and accepting attitude that I had been made into a prostitute had told me that I had died long ago.

I whimpered through a sting of pain as an old wound inside of my ass ripped open; the man dug his hand into the bed sheets beside my head and grunted. When he was done I felt wetness inside of me but it was blood not cum. I was sore down there, swollen and sore to the point where whenever Helen or Plinko made me sit up to treat the abscesses on my arms and the sores on my face, I cried out in pain. I didn't recognize my own voice.

After that I slept... I slept or accepted the muddled haze that was my reality. Never sober, never detoxing, I was always injected and always stoned out of my mind. My clothes were now gone and my money, everything else of value was far away in the hotel room which I hoped was still being paid for. I didn't know how long it had been, for all I knew I could've been here for over a month. I hoped the nice lady would keep my things once the time ran out on my room, or perhaps she would think I was dead.

I would be dead soon. This thought made me smile, and I welcomed my own Grim Reaper with open arms. I would die with a smile on my face and if there was any kindness in the universe my Kerres would greet me.

Yes... death.

My eyes didn't even squint when the door opened again, bringing in the blinding light. I had just received a dose not too long ago, so I knew it was another john to fuck me. I stayed still and awaited the penetration, awaited the pain and the reminder I was still alive and breathing. I despised the reminders.

Hands touched me, and though my mind was dull and listless it churned with confused sensations as I felt the hands pick me up. I flopped like a ragdoll before squinting as the light burned through my closed eyelids making me see red. What was this light? I had been the monster in the darkness. I felt nothing in the dark, but everything was getting brighter.

Brighter... white... strong arms.

I had died. Oh thank god, I was dead. Finally. Kerres, where was Kerres?

A hand held my head and I felt soft robes touch my cheeks. I tried to take a deep breath, the strength of the hold on me compressing my diaphragm; it was a tight constricting hold.

Mint… and nutmeg?

Boots crunched on the floor. I heard the music and televisions become loud and then quiet. I blinked and looked around, focusing my sore eyes only to see two silver buttons and an arm draped in such a candescent bright colour it hurt me to look at it.

Mint and nutmeg…

It couldn't be.

No… it couldn't be him.

BOOK 3

Resurrection

CHAPTER 25

THE CHILL OF WINTER BROUGHT MY EYES TO FOCUS. I watched with wave after wave of confusion as he carried me out of the door and up the steps. When my body jolted I felt a warmth around me and the feeling of fabric covering my skin; he had drawn his cloak over my body, as he cradled me in his arms.

"You know what to do with them." My heart started to hammer as I heard his cold low voice, edging the dangerous areas of his unwavering tones. My eyes snapped open at the sound and I sucked in a raspy, rattled breath. His arms tightened around me.

"Yes, Master Elish." Sanguine? His tone was suggestive and full of mischief, to the point where I could see his smirk in my mind.

I felt a hand on my head that drew itself away, before his boots clicked back down the stairs.

I inhaled another cold breath as Elish turned around and walked down the sidewalk. A moment later, he stepped into the familiar black car and I heard a slam.

He drew me close, and I felt a hand stroke my cheek in a soft and soothing manner. I stared at his sleeve, bewildered at the gesture, feeling my face and body tense like he had shocked me with a Taser. My brain jammed and froze, every neuron started to twitch and breathe back to life.

Then, like an overwhelming rush, every feeling I had felt being with Elish, that soft touch I had forgotten, came flooding back with a force that hit me like a speeding train. My body started to tremble and my breathing was laboured.

"Shh shh… calm down," his soft voice soothed. "You're safe."

My mind shattered under those words, and with a strangled choke, I broke down and started to sob.

Elish held me tight against him and continued his soothing sounds. I grabbed his coat with the last of my remaining strength and unleashed wave after wave of sorrowful sobs as Elish clutched me to him, harder than he had ever held me before.

When the car stopped, he drew the cloak fully over me, hiding me from view, or hiding the view from me, I wasn't sure. With sobs I tried to muffle through biting my lip, I felt him carry me inside of Olympus, giving people I couldn't see warning to stay back.

I heard the ding of the elevator. I sniffed and buried my face into his jacket which was now wet with my tears. I didn't want him to let me go. I didn't know why he had me, or what was going on, but all I knew was that I would die if he ever released me from his protective hold.

My eyes squinted when Elish withdrew the cloak that had been shielding me. I took in the apartment I had come to know so well with shock and surprise.

I heard Luca gasp, and a moment later, he was sniffing.

"Bring Lyle," Elish said to him and I heard the apartment door slam. Elish then lowered me onto the couch. I held onto him tighter and stiffened my body.

I felt Elish's chest rise with a sigh. "Come now, I won't be far."

"No," I managed a weak whisper; my voice was rough and raspy like sandpaper.

I felt Elish raise me again and he sat down with me onto the couch. "Okay." He started wiping the tears away from my eyes with a gloveless hand. I looked up and saw him looking down at me.

He looked beautiful, as beautiful as the night I first saw him and the day he abandoned me in Moros.

I turned away; even through the tightly woven emotions in my head it was still unbearable to look at him. My heart lurched and stung, and shied away from the soft coaxing of his touch.

Like an animal not falling for the same trick twice, I turned away and tried to force the anguish away from my face.

Elish had abandoned me… why was I here if I was just a won game to him? My face crumpled and my lower lip tightened, my eyes welled again.

"Look at me, Jade." His whispered words, drawn by chariot on a road of crystal, stung me like a thousand needles. Old emotions flooded me, but through the maze of the chaos I had endured they died, unable to penetrate the darkness I felt.

"Jade."

My brain urged me to look, but my heart wouldn't allow my masochistic nature to win this time. "Please?"

Please? He's never said please to me before. I blinked back the tears, feeling my lip quiver. I found my eyes draw towards him and I looked into those shards of purple ice.

Elish gazed down at me, his face was collected and firm but his eyes were fixed on my own, full of intensity and emotion; the placid stillness that his countenance could never hide. I gazed back and ran my vision through every feature I had once loved, wanting almost to touch the marble white face to confirm it was really there, that he was really there.

"I'm sorry."

You're... sorry? I stared at him as he mouthed those words to me, before stroking my cheek with his fingers. They were foreign to my ears and foreign to his mouth. I had never heard him apologize to anyone in his life, let alone the pet he had cast back to the slums with a cold shoulder and so many biting words – I'd had my heart torn to pieces.

What was happening? I was so confused, and when he saw the look on my face, a small smile spread to his lips.

"I did miss that confused expression that graced your face on so many occasions, but no, Jade, I will not say more. Just know you are safe and... no more mistakes will be made."

"What?" I rasped. I squinted my eyes and tried to raise my hand to wipe my face but he gently pushed my arm down.

"Not now, you do not have the strength."

Elish glanced up as the door opened. I was about to attempt to turn my head when I heard Lyle suck in a breath.

"Four and a half months and this is what you bring back?" Lyle whispered. I felt him approach before a light flashed in my eye. I didn't have the strength to even squint properly; I just stared at the beaming light.

"Pinpointed pupils, and look at those track marks." Lyle swore and I felt a finger pull my lips. "Burnt lips. I need a blood sample, I really have no idea how he's still alive."

Me neither.

Elish took my entire forearm into his grasp and squeezed it tight, his iron grip now acting as a personal tourniquet. Lyle found a vein and popped the cap with his teeth before sticking it close to one of my abscesses. I winced and let out a small cry; in response Elish petted my head.

"Nels… lab this." Lyle held up the vial and I saw behind him a young man I had seen in the hospital wing. He took the blood and disappear out the door. The old doctor turned back to me and shook his head. "Can he talk?"

"With coaxing he has spoken a word or two."

Lyle looked at me and waved a finger in front of my face, but I only fixed my eyes on him.

"You're lucky. He's fucked out of his mind and probably stunned, but I think physically he doesn't have any major injuries besides that gunshot graze. I'll go downstairs and bring you a detox kit."

Elish shook his head. "No, I will not subject him to hallucinations on top of what he has already been through. Bring me the powdered heroin; he will detox when I tell him he can handle it."

Lyle seemed skeptical but I think he knew better than to question Elish. I didn't even have the energy in me to be surprised that he was going to allow me to continue my drug addiction.

"I'll leave you some medicine and call in the tox results when I get them." Lyle raised himself from his kneeling position but Elish stopped him.

"I want those blood tests to test for everything, am I understood?"

Lyle nodded, and with that, he was gone. Once the door closed, Elish got up with me still in his arms and brought me into the bathroom.

I let out a whine when, with Luca's help, he started stripping off my clothes, but they continued and the next thing I knew I was being lowered into a bathtub.

"Make tea, some simple easy to eat food, and prepare the drugs Lyle is going to give you. I'll take care of him." I let myself sink into the tub, the water up to my mouth; the warmth soothed my skin though I was still shivering.

Then I felt a hand under the crook of my arm and he pulled me back up. "Are we trying to drown ourselves?"

I stared at the water, feeling struck dumb as the worst of the drugs started to slowly trickle from my mind. I didn't understand what was going on, or why. Was this all a dream and I would soon wake up in that dark bedroom awaiting the next man to pay for his fifteen minutes?

Or was this the afterlife?

I turned to him, and when I saw him gently start to wet my hair with the detachable shower hose I knew this couldn't be real life. Elish was doing things Elish had never done. I was in a place I had been forced to conclude I would never see again. Everything was strange. I shouldn't be here, something was off in my mind. Something had to be wrong, this… this was just not reality.

"Am I dead?"

"No, an immortal would not be with you in the afterlife." He put a single finger on my chin to direct my head back, then he turned the hose off and started massaging shampoo into my greasy, almost dreadlocked hair. I hadn't bathed since I had left Sanguine's, and from what the exchange between Elish and Lyle hinted at, that was almost a month ago.

"I can't be here… something's wrong," I whispered, blinking my eyes hard, confused at the strange sensation of him massaging my scalp. I had entered another dimension; was this what happened when the coils of my mind finally broke? If so, perhaps it wouldn't be so bad, a lot better than the reality I had left behind.

I knitted my brow together, then Elish tipped my head back and rinsed my hair. "Something is very wrong here."

Elish, obviously not content with only one shampoo considering my hair had become solidified grease, started over. "Nothing is wrong, Cicaro, your reality will come to you after you rest. I suggest you try not to think about it."

I shook my head and felt my head dip down. "I – I'm not your cicaro."

"Oh? And what are you then?"

I jerked my head up as I felt it fall, everything in my body was hot, but I was still trembling and shaking inside the warm, soapy water. I could see the porcelain tile glowing around me, bright and assaulting to my eyes.

I looked around at everything, so white, only the dark trim could break up the strange pure colour. I hadn't seen white in so long.

I didn't deserve white.

My aura was of darkness, it was born from it and so was I. I was nothing, a monster, a wraith in the shadows who killed and hurt, even those who loved me. I didn't deserve to be human let alone a cicaro. There was no redeeming quality in me, nothing that white could grasp onto; the core of my being was dead, I was dead.

I… had died with… *him*.

I looked down at my reflection, though the corpse that looked back at me didn't look like me. My eyes were dark, my face gaunt and a greying shade of tallow, sores were all over my face, stinging under the shampoo bubbles dripping down the creases of my troubled expression.

"As stupid as I am weak," I whispered to myself, almost surprised that the dead being staring at me mirrored my lip movements back. "A game that you won, a gutter rat, a… I am nothing. If I was anything before, even just a human, I am nothing now." I looked around confused, my brow furrowing. "Something is wrong here."

My head dipped back and he washed my hair again, before picking up a cloth and gently soaping my arms and torso. "I think you should try not to speak, though you are saying more words which I suppose is an improvement, even if they don't make sense."

After he had washed me, I was lifted out of the tub and draped with a towel that seemed to swim over my small frame. Elish carried me out into the living room and once again tried to put me down.

"No," I whined. Once again he relented and sat down on the couch with me. Now smelling a lot better, I scrunched myself into Elish's arms, then Luca put a plate of appetizer-type food on the coffee table and two cups of tea.

I perked up when I heard the crack of a plastic card against the coffee table. Elish gave an amused chuckle. "Of all things, of course your heart skips when the drugs come out. Are you feeling yourself detoxify yet?"

I nodded, though it was a lie. I had never stopped feeling like shit. I just wanted to do something that might make me feel a bit normal, so I could start to understand and process what had happened in the last several hours. The last lucid moment I'd had was entering that drug den, and the last sober memory I had…

I didn't remember.

Elish steadied me as I did a few lines in each nostril, before sniffing it up and taking my permanent place on his lap.

I relaxed and stared off into nothing as the drugs started to hit me, and I felt the gross feelings inside of me start to wash away.

My mind slowly crept back. I gave a satisfying sigh, enough of a sign for Elish to start trying to get me to take food from him.

"Luca, you are relieved for tonight. Take the car to Garrett's and tell him that I have him; I am sure that will calm him down."

I saw Luca bow out of the corner of my eye, before I saw him picking up… the cat ears? They had gotten my duffle bag, the bag that was full of my old clothing and the items they had packed for me. It had been the only thing I'd had to remind me of Elish.

I started to scowl again. I felt my lower lip quiver and the tears well up in my eyes. Elish put down his tea mug just in time for me to break down once again.

I gritted my teeth, my mind temporarily seeing the duffle bag in the second bedroom partially unpacked, the room I had stayed in when I had stopped sleeping beside Kerres. I could smell it, the musty blankets, the sour smell of a carpet soaked and air dried over and over.

Kerres sobbing under the coffee table, and protesting as they tried to shove me into that black bag. Losing control over the situation with every passing second, reducing him to a sobbing, pleading mess.

Kerres… oh, Kerres.

My heart lurched, feeling like two hands were slowly tearing it down the middle. I put a hand on Elish's shirt and clenched it hard, crying into his chest in a way that stripped every shred of dignity that I had never had with him to begin with.

I'm sorry, Kerres, I'm sorry because I feel so comforted in Elish's arms, confused, tired, and stunned, but comfortable. I don't know what's happening to me, I never did, which is why I could never tell you the truth. If only you had held on, I would've gotten us to the greywastes and we could've started a new life. But now I'm back here…

Am I?

Was I really here? I thought I was, but why? There was no part of me that understood what I was doing back in this apartment, high above Skyfall and far away from the dark alleyways of the slums. Elish had been a man of affirmative actions and resolutions he never went back on. He had never been one to lie or reverse a decision; I had taken everything he had said to me with truth and solidity.

So what had changed? Did these strange actions and gestures Elish had been doing since taking me from that drug den shed light on some change in him? No, Elish never changed, he was always the cold, stone-hearted chimera. There was no redeeming or backtracking. I was a played game to him; a useless naïve slumrat who was stupid enough to love a chimera. Every emotion I had expressed for him had been thrown back in my face.

Don't make the same mistake twice, slumrat.

I was a game to him, that's all. He'd played me.

What the fuck, Jade? Elish told you himself, he said those words to you. That I was a stupid gutter rat whose only purpose was for him to see how long it would take to fall in love with him. I was a game, reduced to a laughing stock. I was a feral slumrat on display to be seen as a testament to the feeble slumrat mind.

And I was falling for it all over again.

Suddenly anger flared inside of me and washed over every bit of sadness; it intertwined with the bounds of confusion and became a rabid beast in front of me, curling its lips over its sardonic snarl, taunting me with mock advances awaiting its time to finish me off for good.

No, I was stupid but I wasn't that stupid. I wouldn't fall for this again. I wouldn't be crucified a second time and stripped down to nothing for all of them to see and laugh at.

With a scream of anger, I pushed Elish away and rose to my feet. He looked at me with his calm unwavering face. I seethed as he casually picked up his teacup.

"What is this, round two?" I exploded, clutching my towel to me like a robe. "You can't even let me die? If I die it isn't any fucking fun, is it?

You only brought me here to make me well then you're dumping me back in that fucking slum! Fuck you!"

Fireworks shot off in my mind as Elish casually took a drink of his tea, before setting it down onto the coffee table with a small clink.

"I need you to save your mental breakdown for after you have rested, Jade. You're going to give yourself an aneurism."

"Don't patronize me!" The tears sprang from my eyes but I was so angry I didn't notice. I wanted to kick something but the coffee table only held the remaining food and his teacup. "Didn't you have your fun? Just let me die, Elish. You can't do this to me again, you can't... I can't be here. I can't... Elish, I can't." I looked around as if expecting someone to be hiding in a corner, waiting to help me fight this blond demon, but all my friends were dead.

I took a step back instead, my face hurting from my own expression of agony. "Please, just let me die, please. I can't do this again. I can't stay here waiting for you to win round two, waiting until you make me happy and make me love you just so you can fuck me all over again. My heart can't handle it, my emotions can't. I don't have Kerres to help me, I don't have anyone. I killed them all. I just can't do this again."

"Do what, Jade?"

"YOU KNOW WHAT!" I shrieked. I tried to take another step back but my legs buckled; I stumbled until my back hit a support beam that separated the living room from the sitting room by the skyscraper windows. "If this is just another fucking game you started because you knew I wanted to die in there, just let me die. Please, just let me die and move on to your next prey."

Elish shook his head and looked at me with a cold glint in his eye. "Why would I give you such an easy escape?"

My heart dropped, right to my stomach into a vat of toxic sludge, a substance I knew very well, but hadn't tasted in months. Elish had control over everything when he wanted it; he wouldn't even let me die.

I had no control, once again no control...

Kerres... I wasn't going to see him. I was going to be stuck here until Elish got bored of me once again, or until he split my heart open and drew out the emotions that he wanted. He was a succubus, his own demon masquerading as some sentient aural being. There was no way for me to free myself from this iron grip he had on me. I couldn't escape him.

Could I?

Fuelled by madness, confusion, and a mind not anywhere near thinking clearly, I looked to the balcony of the skyscraper. No, there was one way I could take my control back, perhaps one of the only ways.

I threw my towel at Elish and ran towards the balcony.

The cold air hit me with a sting as I got the sliding glass door open; my heart fluttering and jerking in prey-driven panic as I heard him swear, followed by the sound of breaking china. I sprinted across the patio and before a solid thought reached my mind... I leaped up onto the patio table resting against the iron railing and jumped.

Twenty-two storeys and I jumped.

For a brief moment I saw Skyland underneath me, the grey and black roofs and the small cars driving together like ants retrieving food for their nests. Everything was small like I was a giant looking down, ready to greet the tiny wisps of green trees and the grass; such a rich colour it looked like it had been painted on.

Then I was wrenched away, and with a fierce grip on my ankle, Elish pulled me down to the patio floor. I could hear his heart pounding as he paused for a second, before forcing me back into his arms.

Elish was out of breath, he was... scared? I could feel his fingernails digging into my scalp.

"You idiot!" Elish gasped, his chest heaving against my own, our hearts drum beats hitting the tight skin one after another, making their own music together. "You idiot, you fucking idiot."

Violently Elish pulled me away so I was facing him; he shook me until I looked at him.

His eyes were wide, his mouth a thin line in the middle of a jaw so clenched it twitched below his temples. "If you cannot wait until we have time to talk, so be it. You are too young to be involved in what my family will subject you to. I took you back to Moros in hopes you could go back to how you were, lead a normal life before I collected you in several years' time. I did it for *you*, you stupid mongrel; I only thought of what was best for *you*. I did it to save you the looming threat of that psychopathic, narcissistic, self-denigrating king I am forced to obey. Lycos was right, Reaver isn't ready and in no way were you ready. He saw it, I saw it, Garrett saw it, Silas saw it… we all fucking saw it, you immature little cockroach!" Elish's voice was twisted in such an angry snarl my body shook and my eyes went wide, but he wasn't done.

"The last straw was when I went pleading, *pleading*, Jade, for King Silas to grant you chimera privileges to save you from his fatal games. He saw that fucking bite mark on my neck and got livid with jealousy; he tortured me for the hell of it until I died with his body pressed against mine. Mulling over which way he was going to kill you. I had to get rid of you and strip you of your status as cicaro to keep his hands off of you. Are you really that stupid? Are you really that dull-witted that you think after all this time, after everything we, *WE,* have gone through I would drop you like that? Why would I not just kill you? Do you know nothing of chimeras? We kill cicaros, we don't give them a duffle bag full of thousands of dollars! You idiot!" Elish shook my shoulders, my head snapping back and then forward like a ragdoll. My head filled with haze and distortion as he literally tried to shake some sense into me.

Then he stopped, and it took me a moment to get my bearings. The world swirled around me with only his quickened breathing telling me he was still there, and I hadn't landed on the pavement.

Elish was always there except when I needed him, only there when he felt the whim to control and dominate me; even taking away my right to die under my own control.

Then my mind tuned and awakened to another shocking admission, one that seemed so out of character for my former master: he was angry.

I had rarely seen him actually angry but I could see it now. His aura of perfect features was shaken and his eyes were a blaze of violet fire. I half-expected him to throw me off the balcony himself to save him the trouble.

I shrunk down at his rage, my body shaking so hard my teeth were chattering.

"Get… just get back into the apartment." Elish rose and I did too, though my legs were still wobbling. The shot of adrenaline I had gotten had ran out of me like water through a strainer.

The sliding door closed behind me and I picked up the towel and wrapped it back around myself. I stayed with my back to the patio door and watched him sit back down on the couch and pick up his tea, his eyes glaring forward and his jaw still tight.

I was more confused than ever; had Elish really meant all of that? Which was the lie and which was the truth? One thing was for sure, I had been right when he was leaving me in Moros, the bite mark had disappeared and it had been from Silas. That much could be confirmed as true.

"Everything you said when you abandoned me in Moros was a lie?" I whispered.

"Yes," Elish said as he quietly drank his tea, "every word."

"You – you're not going to let me go again?"

"No."

"Promise?"

"I promise."

I felt stunned. My feet were glued to the soft carpet, my hands clutching the towel like it was my life preserver. I sniffed and tightened my lip to keep myself from crying again. I never cried. I was such an emotional wreck.

"Why couldn't you just tell me what had happened? That I had to go back for a while but you would come back for me?" I thought this was a valid question, though Elish confided in no one, with the small exception for Garrett.

Elish sipped his tea and I realized it was my teacup, his lay in shards on the coffee table, dripping brown liquid onto the carpet below. "Because your heart needed to be elsewhere, not with me. I had hoped the hatred for me would give you strength in Moros, to move past what had happened between us and use it to… grow up and come into your own."

Elish gave me a glance. "It didn't work out how I thought it would."

"You know what I was did in Moros?"

"Naturally, most of my brothers were following the Shadow Killer in the slums, they didn't want you to stop and were even hedging bets. I assumed you realized this when my sister questioned you."

Of course they were, I bet it was a grand game for them to watch me unravel in front of their eyes. "Did you send Sanguine?"

Elish shook his head, before he patted the spot on the couch beside him. I walked over but as I had done before I shifted myself until I was on his lap. I rested my head against his arm. "No, Sanguine approached you all on his own; not even King Silas gave him leave for that," Elish said, then he dropped his voice. "I think he sees a kinship between you two, two men with similar stories."

So Sanguine had really wanted to be my friend? With everything else that had happened I thought it might've been a set up.

But I suppose that meant the other thing would come to light.

"Did he tell you what we did?"

"In great detail."

"Even…?"

"In *great detail*."

I cringed and heard him take another drink of tea. Elish seemed amused at this response. "I would rather you dip your wick in a fellow chimera than that flea-bitten boyfriend you had."

The words scalded me like he had just dumped boiling water on my already raw burns.

"He killed himself because of this."

To my surprise he drew my chin up with his fingers and looked down at me. "No, he killed himself because he couldn't live with the guilt of essentially selling you out to a terrorist organization. Sanguine uncovered that Kerres was being groomed to hand you over as soon as you stepped foot in Moros. They have surgeries and mental techniques that would make you into a drone, and being the cicaro of King Silas's second-in-command you were indispensable to them. Kerres knew this, and in the end, he couldn't take his own guilt over letting them abduct you."

I shook my head. "No, he thought I was brainwashed and he was trying to get me help."

My expectation was for him to get mad at me for disagreeing with him but Elish extended the patience he had been showing to me all day.

"No, Jade, Kerres couldn't stand that he knew your feelings for me and decided a drone was better than the person you had become. Kerres changed more than you did. If you want to cry for him, go ahead, but cry for the right reason."

Surprisingly, he reached down to a small drawer in the coffee table and took out his laptop. I watched him click on it with the touch pad before he brought up a video.

"This is a former cicaro, of my brother Artemis, a boy named Shale. This video you are about to watch is a small clip to demonstrate what this organization can do. Within forty-eight hours, if Kerres had his way, this would've been you."

My body drew me away from the screen but my eyes were fixed on the video being played in front of me.

A photo of a man with blond hair, the cute small twink-type with a big smile. He had a collar attached to his neck like the one I had on and a short golden chain. I could see he was in a skyscraper, high in the sky like Elish's.

Ellis narrated, "Shale was kidnapped from a bar in Skyland two weeks after this photo was taken, two days later this video was released to the precinct."

My eyes widened when I saw the boy with the big smile, wearing the typical Crimstone camo, with a menacing assault rifle strapped to his back and his vest crossed with two belts of ammo. The boy's face was blank with two dead and vacant blue eyes stared forward, standing straight like a solider going through drills. He was standing in front of what I assumed was their flag; it had a green rock in the middle on a red background. The rest of the room was dark and even the floor was covered in thick canvas, hiding any identifying details of where their homebase was.

Then Milos appeared in the corner of the video; he started barking commands at Shale who obeyed without question, his eyes barely blinking and staring off into space.

I gasped when I saw the back of his head, it was shaved and there was a thick stitched surgical wound the shape of a horseshoe, unbandaged and inflamed.

The boy rose from doing pushups on the ground and resumed his soldier stance; a moment later I heard Milos say in a crystal clear voice, "Break your finger, Shale."

An audible crack could be heard as the boy grabbed onto his middle finger and snapped it backwards without a moment's hesitation, bending like rubber all the way until it was touching the back of his hand. He didn't flinch or show an ounce of pain on his face.

"This is the future every single fucking chimera has to look forward to. The human race will take back the world and exterminate every chimera scum –"

Elish turned the video off. "That would've been you, if Kerres got his way."

My emotions didn't rise up from the pit inside of me like I assumed they would; in truth I didn't feel anything but the last of my guilt disappear. "Kerres... knew this was what would happen to me?"

"Apparently this state is better than the person you had become in Moros – to him anyway."

"I was better off a mindless drone than a serial killer, a boyfriend beater, and a drug addict?" I said.

Elish chuckled. "And he said we do not belong as master and cicaro, what a fool."

I glared up at him and saw that he was looking down at me with a smirking smile; a moment later he brushed my hair back from my eyes and I sighed at the kind gesture. "I need drugs. I – I don't even feel anything hearing that, nothing at all."

Elish let me take another hit and I took my place on his lap.

"I didn't feel anything when I killed those people. I was emotionless until I heard Kerres had killed himself, then I gave in to drugs and whatever those drug den guys did to me to numb the guilt. Now I feel nothing all over again knowing Kerres would rather me be a zombie than who I had come back to Moros as." Elish drew his cloak back over me again. I was still wearing nothing but a towel. "Fuck him."

"We can discuss that later, now you need to rest, before your body fails you altogether."

I nodded and closed my eyes, feeling comfort in his arms, a place I never thought I would be again. Once again I was turning into someone else, or someone I had used to be, and once I'd seen the alternative... someone I was happy to be.

At least now though, I was under his control. And the feeling of having someone more powerful than me, who knew me, didn't fill my mouth with the bitter taste it used to. I felt comforted and okay, and for the first time in almost five months now – I felt safe.

I felt shifting and something being taken out of the drawer; a moment later my heart sang as I heard him read.

"The bunker was walled with concrete block. A poured concrete floor laid over with kitchen tile. There were a couple of iron cots with bare springs, one against either wall, the mattress pads rolled up at the foot of

them in army fashion. He turned and looked at the boy crouched above him blinking in the smoke rising up from the lamp and then he descended to the lower steps and sat and held the lamp out."

My eyes felt heavy, and I fell asleep; finding a small bliss in my complicated and painful existence.

CHAPTER 26

Elish opened one eye and swore oaths in his head as the shining turquoise gems of Joaquin Dekker glared down at him. How that sneaky nisse of a man got into his apartment without waking him was beyond him, though in the corners of Elish's mind he knew.

He had slept badly since he had deposited Jade in Moros, and it seemed with the boy safely in his grasp he had been enjoying the first proper sleep in months. His body must've commanded a deeper than usual slumber.

The black-haired Joaquin (pronounced phonetically as King Silas's orders had been) stood with his arms crossed, a look of derision on his face. He stared down at Elish with the distinct sneer of someone who was beholding the most foulest of things.

Elish didn't need to guess what that was. Jade was fast asleep and laying sprawled out on Elish's stomach.

"I see, four months and you bring him back? You failed to meet even the lowest of our wagers, brother." Joaquin, or Quin as his family called him, pursed his mouth. "And what is this? You're a mattress now? He sleeps so soundly on your body, a mere slumrat napping on the highest elite chimera, how quaint." Each word dripped from his lips like it was acid, and each one hit its mark.

Elish narrowed his eyes at him. "Speak one more snipped word at me, Joaquin, and Jack will be collecting your remains from the bottom of my balcony. Remember your place, subordinate."

Quin's pursed mouth twitched to the side, but the impact of Elish's words sunk into him like brine. "How am I supposed to react to this sight? Do you have any idea how bad this is going to look on you? You are Silas's prince, our brothers are talking behind your back enough already and I come to your apartment to see this? Tell me, Elish… you haven't overstepped boundaries with this boy have you?"

"What boundaries? You soak up the mockery and rumours of our brothers and yet you haven't heard he is a chimera?" Elish mused, but Quin's expression only hardened.

"So is Drako, and you do not see any of us show him the tenderness you have shown this alley cat."

Elish's face hinted umbrage at his choice of words, but Quin was a man of guileful strikes. He plucked at tight strings and pinched tender places to get reactions, then stored them in his computer-like mind to bring up as fodder later. Elish was no exception, but knowing his brother's backhanded ways of communicating he was able to brush off the pinch like Quin was a sugar ant.

"Jade is no chimera sex slave."

"So he is your partner then?"

"Of course not," Elish said back, a little too quickly to carry on the air of casual control he had been trying to exude, and for that he scolded himself internally. He had taken the bait, though if he was going to swallow it he might as well do it barbs and all. "He is a chimera pet, and what goes on in my personal life has nothing to do with you, or anyone else for that matter. Now is there something you need or are you going to continue to give me a reason to throw the boy off me in favour of painting the sidewalk twenty-two storeys below us?"

Quin flicked back his curly black hair, as if this display of elegance would wipe away the threat Elish had just made "Brother, you misjudge my questions. If you saw me dangling my pride close enough for the wolves to nip the edges would you not warn me? This whole pet nonsense and how you're treating him is spreading like cancer. Rumour says you shushed him like a child as you cradled and carried him out of that brothel, and swaddled him in your cloak to hide his shamefully used and abused body. Silas is going to be absolutely livid."

Sanguine's mouth is not just filled with pointed teeth, it also holds a lot of shit, Elish thought with disdain.

"He is an untrained feral beast, and all you're doing is rewarding his cries for attention. We told you his serial killing and brothel work was a way for him to manipulate you and you fold after so little time?" Quin continued to nip, and, as if to further drive in Jade's slumrat status he picked a piece of lint off of his blazer and flicked it onto the floor.

"The boy is no Ares, and no Siris, he needs different training," Elish answered coolly. "He is my property, my chimera, and I will train him as I see fit."

"Oh? And this training is cuddling him, rescuing him from a place *you* put him into? You've never had a sympathetic bone in your life! My god, Elish, what happened to you?"

"The mind of a feral chimera must be heated and cooled, a constant state of stress and emotional turmoil will only break –"

Quin let out a frustrated growl; he balled his fists and resisted the anger burning in his throat. "This is so out of character for you… if it was Garrett I would give it no passing glance, but *you*? No wonder Silas is so angry."

"If there is no more point to you being here but to spit nonsense, you may leave," Elish said bitterly. He lifted a hand that had been resting on Jade's head and dismissed Quin.

Joaquin glared down at him; somehow the fact that Elish still hadn't moved the boy's body off him filled Quin with such frustrating confusion it almost made him want to toss the boy off himself. Seeing this odd display in his cruel and emotionless brother, a man he respected without limits and knew as a cold, heartless being, made an unease churn in his gut. It flustered Quin to the point where he was left nauseas, *and Elish didn't even care!*

That part alone made his own mind reel and seethe.

With his only parting gift nothing but a final glare, Quin turned around haughtily and went to leave the room.

He glanced up at the doorway and saw Garrett taking the last several steps to Elish's apartment. When Garrett saw his brother, as usual, his green eyes brightened.

"Hello, Joey, dreary day isn't it? Come to welcome back the little petty have we?" Garrett grinned, but without a word Quin stalked past him and pressed the button on the elevator, so hard the sound echoed off of the ceilings.

Garrett cocked an inquisitive eyebrow but shrugged, before meandering into the apartment with a new smile on his face, Luca following closely behind carrying a tray.

The president of Skytech chuckled and sauntered over with a grin, beholding a sight quite pleasing to the eye; though obviously to the disdain of their brother Quin for reasons he quickly understood.

Elish was half laying and half sitting on the couch with the Morosian boy stretched out on his stomach over Elish's slender but tall frame, Jade's head turned towards Garrett and Luca with his mouth open, a damp patch visible through Elish's white collared shirt. Jade was fast asleep, with one arm hanging off of the couch and the other one tucked under the cloak with a towel half hanging off him.

"Well, he is right doublin' for a blanket this morning, eh? And how long have you been stuck in this precarious position?" Garrett grinned, fully aware that he could say and do whatever he wanted to his only older brother right now, without fear of consequence.

"He fell asleep at around nine, so I would say about eleven hours. He's in a dead sleep, not even Joaquin's ranting woke him." Elish glanced at Luca who was bringing in a tray of drinks and food; he motioned him over and grabbed a Styrofoam cup of coffee.

"Ranting? Well, that is like him, he always seems to have something up his ass. No matter, the boy has really been asleep for eleven hours?"

Elish nodded and took a long drink of coffee. "He's only woken up to sample the bag of heroin to keep himself from detoxing. Lyle called – the boy tested positive for heroin, crack, benzoids, and opiates. Thankfully he is clean of disease; I was concerned considering where I found him."

Garrett let out a breath; he took a white kerchief from his pocket and started gently dabbing the drool from Jade's mouth. "I just can't believe that cute little face murdered all those people; he really lost it when you left him. I haven't seen this much of a deadly rebellion since Sanguine and Valen."

"We've already discussed Jade's outlets at length," Elish said crisply.

And they had for the entire four and a half months, especially when the reports started coming in of murder upon murder happening in Moros.

Elish's brothers had been glued to the television and all information coming in. They devoured every news report like it was an alluring wine and feasted on every crime scene description Ellis's son Garren had given them with sardonic glee, the most delectable being when they had found Jade's kill den.

It was one giant joke to them; bets were wagered, rumours were spread, and at the heart of the matter was the most daring of questions they only shared in hushed whispers behind the blond chimera's back: what would Elish do? The cold, emotionless chimera was starting to act out of character; what was this fascinating development?

Then suddenly, when Jack had reported that Sanguine was dead and the boy gone, vanished without a trace to everyone else but Elish's own personal tracking device, the lighthearted shrugs shared with wry grins turned into low-toned whispers. The boy was missing, Elish was livid, unapproachable, and coming to council meetings more and more disgruntled and soured. Would he cave? Was he capable of caving? Elish had been a chimera who gave orders with a steel resolve that left no room for disobedience. To go back on his dismissal of Jade would be unheard of and would unleash a tidal wave of scornful gossip.

They watched like wolves waiting for any sign of weakness, testing fences and cackling like hyenas, watching with fascination these new emotions their oldest brother could only hide for so long.

Though not all of them laughed, some like Quin stayed in the shadows with an angry purse of their lips and sideways glances, hating the divergence from the norm they had been so used to seeing in their most solid and reliable brother.

Garrett Dekker on the other hand was neither laughing on the sidelines nor glowering; as Elish's closest brother and friend he only sought to help his brother in any way he could. He did not judge or condemn, but was a silent supporter at Elish's side, as he had always been.

The president of Skytech clicked and pursed his mouth to the side, before taking a look at Jade's arm hanging off the couch. He ran a finger up the abscesses and pock marks that spoiled the marble of the thin pale skin.

"Look at those marks on him." Garrett shook his head, feeling a surge of pity for the boy. "I told you, brother, I told you he was too in love with you for you to let him go. Cruelty, just pure cruelty, I am shocked he didn't die." This was another attribute of Garrett's; unlike the others he had the comfort around Elish to tell him how it was, without a condescending tone or a tail tucked between his legs.

Though this didn't guarantee it would be well-received.

Elish's face darkened; he wasn't in the mood to be scolded again, though Garrett's comments were a far cry from Quin's sharpened jabs. "You know why I did it. Do not chastise me now, what is done is done."

The president of Skytech reached into his suit jacket pocket and pulled out a large bag of powder; he placed it onto the coffee table. "This is from King Silas."

The room fell silent; even Luca paused in the middle of preparing the bag of food he had brought in.

Elish's eyes fixed on Garrett and his jaw tightened. "He's back?"

"Yesterday yes, today? Who knows, you know how our dear king is. Jack brought it to me this morning; our Grim of a brother did his job, he told our king Sanguine had died in the Moros shelter and that brought questions, but brother, it's not bad news. Silas is quite pleased with the story Sanguine told him, about Jade choosing him and telling that turncoat boyfriend to go sodomize himself. Keeping that dagger-mouthed brother of ours safe from the Crimstones. You do realize on top of Jade they would've taken our little Penguin too? In all respects Jade saved Sanguine, not his life perhaps, but he saved him from having his brain matter tinkered with. He saved us the pain of having to recover him as well."

Elish couldn't believe what Garrett was saying; it was a relief but at the same time it meant the boy was once again in the crosshairs of the green-eyed king. That was what Elish had been trying to avoid; he had taken the boy back to Moros in hopes of him flying under the radar for a few years; to give him a chance to grow into his own and hone his own abilities, like Lycos had insisted happen to Reaver.

"I'll be taking Jade out of Skyfall for the duration, to one of my shelters in the greywastes. He needs time to get his head back, and considering he's an empath I'm going to allow him the break, lest he snaps and starts pulling out his own eyelashes or something similar."

Elish started to gently get up, and with Garrett's help he managed to slide Jade off him without waking the young man. "There is only so much his mind can take, I forget he's only sixteen sometimes. Though we were running Skyfall by that age."

"But we were raised and trained to run Skyfall; Jade has no training in anything but using his fists and fangs to solve problems and shoving drugs up his nose."

Elish shot him a frosty look. "Then why in seven hells did you drop the baby off in Moros? Ares and Siris were raised in Moros and they're imbeciles."

Garrett frowned and pulled a blanket over Jade. "I was upset with you, over what had happened to Chimera X. Silas approached me with the idea when they had the fetus in stasis. At the time I thought it was harmless fun; a seed to plant to eventually pay you back for the hurt you caused the family with no serious repercussions. Now, of course, I regret it, but all in all… he's a good boy. Would you like him any other way?"

"No, it is more for his own sake than mine. His mind is as fragile as a moth's wings; he tried to jump off the balcony last night. From clinging and sobbing into my shirt to ranting and raving and back to clinging. Ares and Siris were brutes and Moros suited their personalities; if anything was cruel it was letting an empath chimera be raised in the slums with that mad woman."

Garrett suddenly chuckled and picked up the breakfast sandwich that was growing cold on the plates Luca had set out for them. "I can see why Silas hates him so much and why our brothers are so confused; you have never shown an ounce of compassion or empathy for your cicaros before. I bet Silas is regretting not terminating that baby."

"Where would the fun in that be?" Elish's voice was bitter. He disappeared into the bathroom; with the boy clinging to him for the last eleven hours he needed a break.

When he came back Garrett was still eating his sandwich, Luca hovering around them cleaning up the broken teacup from the previous night.

"I apologize for not telling you he was alive, Elish," Garrett sighed. The chimera had always been the most docile and sensitive brother out of all of them, or as Elish would put it… the most human. Garrett and Elish were closer to one another than any of their other brothers dead or alive.

Artemis and Apollo, the twins, were close to him as well, but since they shared so much of Elish's own coding their relationship was more based on a common personality type. Elish could never speak about personal things with them like he could Garrett. For some reason their completely opposite personalities complimented each other.

"I am happy to hear you think you're in my debt; I need a favour from you." Elish sat beside Jade and listened to his heart, to make sure he was still asleep and not just pretending so he could eavesdrop.

"Anything."

"I need you to give me a copy of Jade's chimera records. I need to know more about his mind. I want to know what his potential is before I move on with him. Could you make some calls and get them for me immediately? I wish to leave quickly before our king tries to summon me."

Garrett flinched at the request. He glanced down at Jade, then his gaze travelled back to Elish. "You know you're supposed to make a request to Silas first?"

"I am aware of that, but you know why I wish to not have him know."

Garrett chewed on the sandwich, deliberately taking it slow. When he finally swallowed his bite a sigh came to his lips. "Okay, Elish, I will. This is only to help the poor boy, right?"

"That is correct."

"Okay, brother."

A thin smile appeared on Elish's face, one that made Garrett look twice at him. He had seen that expression on his brother's face often since he was a small boy. It was the expression of a person with so many plans ticking in his head that to a normal man it would seem overwhelming. But Elish's mind was wired to perfection. His mind was like a garden covered in strings, where he planted each seed and connected them to a different string, before waiting patiently for them to grow. Sometimes the span between planting to sewing was twenty to thirty years. Elish was a lot like Silas in that sense; they were patient to an unbelievable level.

There was no mistaking that behind that smile was a plan that Garrett could only guess at, and also one he had no desire to know about. Garrett stayed out of his brothers' games and Elish's unspoken struggle with their master's command. The president had enough on his plate running

Skytech; he had no room in his life to become intertwined in one of Elish or Silas's webs.

Though as Elish smiled and Garrett looked on at him, Elish reached down to the drawer in the coffee table and pulled out a photograph.

"I was going to use this as an incentive, in case you tried to deny me those folders. Instead of saving it for some future thing I may have you do, I will let you have it. My appreciation for your counsel during the last several months." Elish handed Garrett the picture and refolded his hands over his lap.

"I cannot tell you where he lives and I cannot tell you his name. What I can tell you though, is that Jade has said your auras are so intertwined they fit together like pieces of Velcro. If he suits you physically then from what I have seen of him, he is who you were looking for."

Elish watched with a flicker of amusement as his brother's expression changed. When he took the photo Garrett gave Elish a confused and wary look, but as soon as he saw the picture of Reno posing with the severed head of a man, his face softened and soon a smile appeared.

Just as Elish had hoped, his brother fell in love before his eyes, though Elish could have probably shown him any photo of any teenage greywaster with the same results.

"Look at him, what a smile! What's he like? He looks so happy holding that head; he's a greywaster that much I can tell. How old is he?"

"He is a very cheery, charismatic boy, twenty, perhaps twenty-one. I could see no better fit for you, he can be all yours if you trust my decisions. Give me your word and when the time is right, I will hand deliver that boy to you."

"You have my word; when can I have him?" Garrett tucked the photo into his pocket, claiming it as his own automatically. Elish was pleased at this; if Garrett gave him the photo back he might grow concerned that his brother wasn't as excited as his heart was convincing him he was.

"Two years, possibly three."

Garrett's face fell. Elish raised a hand when he opened a mouth to protest. "You can trust my decision or you can try and convince King Silas to create a chimera for you; which at the very least will take sixteen years for him to become yours."

Garrett considered this, and brushed back his already slicked back hair. He rubbed his nose, something he always did when he was unhappy with what he had heard, but he nodded. "I suppose I've been alone for almost eight years now since my last one died. I can wait another couple years."

"Good, your patience is appreciated." Elish rose and motioned for Luca to take their plates. "Save some for Jade, since he woke up five minutes ago."

I opened one eye and saw them all staring at me; Elish looked amused and Garrett took one look at me and laughed his usual cheerful laugh. I pulled the blanket over my head; the light was a bit overwhelming right now – I was used to darkness.

Garrett pulled the covers off of my face and chuckled at me, looking as carefree and as bubbly as ever, it didn't match the throbbing headache in my head. "Look at him, didn't you just miss that cute face? I'm just in love with those little kitty eyes. Pleased that you're back. How do you feel, little cicaro?"

"Bad," I whispered, trying to shut my eyes to drown out the noise. "Can I go to the bedroom?"

"Yes, you may," Elish responded.

I gathered the blanket around me and rose, squinting my eyes and shielding them. I heard Garrett tsk.

"He was in complete darkness for almost a month," Elish explained. "Jade, that Ziploc bag is for you. Do not do any more than you do regularly."

I looked down and felt a small flicker of appreciation at the reusable bag of white powder. I picked it up, the sniffer too, and hobbled my way towards the bedroom.

I did my hits and grabbed Elish's comforter off the bed. I wrapped myself tight in it and to make everything darker, since Elish's bedroom had a window and light was shining through the curtains, I took everything into the closet and curled up with the thick blankets around me.

I sighed and felt myself enveloped in darkness and comfort; everything was quiet too except for the slight thrum of my heartbeat.

When I closed my eyes and tried to go back to sleep I could smell Elish's robes and clothes around me too, they smelled like him which was even nicer. I felt myself get lulled back into a peaceful sleep; the heroin my ship and the lack of stimulus around me my calm ocean.

Eventually I heard the door open and Elish's light chuckle. "I'll have to call maintenance, I'm afraid a gutter rat has made a nest in my closet."

I pulled my blankets over my eyes, and a moment later everything went dark as he turned off the bedroom light. I drew the blankets down and squinted my eyes.

Elish handed me something; I looked down and saw they were sunglasses. "We're leaving now, everything is all packed and ready. I'm taking you away from here for a while."

I looked up at him in horror, my mouth started to twitch and I felt my chest shudder with my quickened breathing. I think that was an automatic response now. I hated myself and how weak I had become, but I didn't fucking have anyone but him and this life. I had nowhere to go and no one to crawl back to. My horrible experience in Moros had shattered me.

Another chuckle – this one was bordering on cruel. "I hope you appreciate my restraint right now, you're giving me so many tempting opportunities to tease you. No, Jade, I am not dropping you off somewhere. I'm taking you to the greyrifts, to a house I have where you can spend a few weeks recovering."

"With you?"

"Yes."

My face brightened, I could use that, far away from here and safe, like we were during our time in the greywastes – besides the Reaver part. I rose to my feet and got changed into some warm pet clothes, the ones Garrett had given me for my birthday.

Elish looked at me up and down and shook his head. "They barely fit you. I suppose you weren't eating well even though I had given you money."

I shrugged, feeling a bit groggy but better with the sunglasses on. "I didn't eat much, and I only got a sandwich or two at that other place." My brow furrowed as Luca walked past me carrying bags; he was heading out the apartment door. "Sanguine… you sent him in there to kill them didn't you?"

Elish gave a nod of his head before picking up the last two bags; he seemed to know I was feeling pretty weak right now. "Yes, he burned them alive, it sounded like he enjoyed himself when I spoke to him last."

"I wish I could've helped." I followed behind him and shut the door. "Sanguine really likes his fire doesn't he?"

Elish nodded again. "Apparently he is quite fond of you as well. Would you consider him a friend of yours? Has his aura changed to you?"

That was right, Elish never cared for Sanguine from how he talked about him. I had told him Sanguine creeped me out and he did. Now though, as I delved deeper into my own dark thoughts, and had become a little less of a boy scout, I found myself more accepting of Sanguine. What seemed creepy and evil over a year ago was the equivalent to Sunday morning cartoons now.

As the elevator took us up, I explained all of this to Elish. He nodded to himself. "I thought that might happen."

The elevator stopped and because I was an idiot I realized that we had been travelling up not down, and a shorter distance. Sure enough, I shielded my eyes and looked away as the elevator door opened to daylight. It took me a moment to see that on the other end of a small concrete hallway a metal door was opening to the roof.

I stayed behind Elish to protect my eyes and as we walked down the hallway I could feel my feet vibrating underneath me. I realized I was hearing the Falconer idling on the roof.

Luca walked shoulder to shoulder with me, my old serial killer ears on his head.

"Thanks for letting me borrow those," I said as Elish walked ahead of us. "They helped remind that someone here still gave a shit."

The sengil gave me a small smile and looked at the ground shyly. "Thank you for returning them when you were done. I didn't have time to say goodbye, so Master Elish let me place them in the bag he was packing. I am very happy you're home."

So Elish did pack that bag... I swallowed down the feelings that the confirmation brought, as usual appearing as a hard lump in my throat. Everything in that bag seemed to increase in importance now. The claws and teeth to protect me, the money to keep me from starving and being homeless, the Game Boy because he knew I liked it... even the shoes. Elish really had taken me to Moros for my own protection.

I was constantly having small reminders that I was an idiot, but Elish was an idiot for doing it to me. No matter how he justified it in his head, I still felt messed up and I still felt fucked in the brain over what went on. If I hadn't gone back, Kerres would still be alive.

I lowered my head and wrapped my arms around my chest and jumped into the Falconer.

I stumbled as my legs buckled from the jump. Elish caught my shoulder and held me steady. "Sit in the co-pilot's chair and stay."

I did what I was asked and sat down where I wouldn't be in the way; a moment later Elish sat down in the pilot's chair. I heard the door close behind us and Luca give the clear for lift off.

I was happy Luca was coming with us, though I wondered if he would equally not mind going to Garrett's since it was obvious the retro chimera jumped his bones whenever he got wasted. Luca didn't seem to mind at all; he seemed like the gentle lover type.

I yawned and watched Skyfall pass us by and was amused when after an hour into the greywastes Luca brought us both tea.

"How did you manage that?" He put my sengil abilities to shame, even when we were high above the greywastes; in a world where everything was pretty much dead he still served his master.

I sipped my tea and watched a small settlement pass by, surrounded by concrete walls and shooting plumes of smoke up into the sky. If fate had unfolded differently Kerres and I might've been either on the outskirts waiting for a merchant's caravan, or already in the wasteland heading towards Aras or wherever they wanted to take us.

My lower lip tightened and my heart started to feel heavy. I missed him... I knew I had broken up with him, but I hadn't wanted it to end like this.

I'm sorry, Kerres, I tried. If you would've just held on... we could've escaped.

But no, that would've never been, even if he hadn't killed himself. Because chances were he would've just brought me right back to the Crimstones. We could go far away from here but I couldn't run from my nature and the person I was now.

The person I was now...

Kerres would've never left, he would've sold me out again. He wasn't Kerres anymore; he was a Crimstone.

But who was I?

My head was slowly starting to clear, and certain things were starting to come back to me, certain conversations and comments Milos had made, and also… what I had done to him.

I looked over at Elish, one hand was holding the coffee mug full of tea and the other one was adjusting a button on the Falconer. He was staring ahead at the rocky grey mountains, following a long straight strip of road, only broken up by the occasional jackknifed four wheeler, or chunk of road taken out by some violent way centuries before I was born.

I had been in denial for a long time, because it just couldn't be plausible. I had a mother.

Sanguine… he growled like I could…

Not to mention the way Milos jolted and shuddered at my touch, and how my hands felt cold and almost alive with a small vibration of electricity…

I absentmindedly touched my fingers against my hands and tried to concentrate, not even knowing if that would be how Elish would do it. I focused my thoughts on making the shock touch come back… but there was nothing.

It must've been something else; maybe Milos had set off his Taser accidently.

Yeah, that was it.

For the rest of the trip we were entertained by Luca and his Cilo guitar, a small portable guitar made out of metal and stained wood. It was compact and could fold into itself but the sound was perfect. It was expensive as hell so it was probably a gift from Elish since I didn't think that sengils got paid any money.

I had heard Luca play before and he was great at it. In Moros we didn't have the time or the money to learn instruments, but it was a must for the Skylanders since they loved their snobby elitist culture.

The entire time I tried to will my hands to do something but nothing was happening, by that time I had managed to convince myself it was Milos's own Taser.

Really, in all respects there was no way, I had a mother, and that should be the end to all my stupid overthinking.

When Elish started to lower the plane, I could see shadows on the greyscape became giant trees, ones I wouldn't have been able to get my arms around. They were larger and older than the ones in Skyfall, standing tall and for good reason, they had survived the Fallocaust and watched everything green around them die.

Then with the shadows around it, I saw the house Elish had mentioned. It was a large peaked building protected by a fenced barrier, with several smaller structures littered over the enclosed land.

We started to descend and I heard the motor kick into a different frequency. I looked down and saw the peaks of the house start to form through their casted shadows, tarred well and water tight. Slowly but surely it morphed from being just another greywaste structure to a picture of lonely beauty. An oasis in the deathlands, a piece of Skyfall so far away those who passed it wouldn't even know who owned it.

The house was red scrubbed brick with its white layers of mortar still intact, surrounded by large windows covered with dark curtains; there were balconies too and sliding glass doors all leading to a courtyard of grey ash and small shrubs. All of this was locked tight within a brick wall topped with barbed wire, a tall and looming barrier to separate the highest class from the lowest. Not unlike the walls that separated the districts in Skyfall.

The Falconer landed on what I think used to be a parking lot. When I stepped out and looked around I realized this house must've been a hotel once, or some place that required a spot to park cars.

It had a roundabout-type entrance with a dead and black-stained fountain in the centre, and further on, a covered area held up by refurbished steel beams. The doors were both metal and I could see that plates of metal had also been welded onto the sides of the lobby entrance. I bet not even a mortar shell could have penetrated this place; it was practically a fort.

"We'll be in the west wing of this house, to save on resources the other ones will be blocked off. Legionary patrol the outskirts of this base regularly to prevent greywasters from breaking in, so if you hear any gunshots you have nothing to fear," Elish explained, taking the bags with Luca behind him. He closed the Falconer door with one hand and I followed behind him towards the entrance. "They know we're here and no harm will come to you, but for obvious reasons there will be no venturing out of the grounds. Is that understood?"

I nodded. "Yes, Master."

Elish brought out a keycard and swiped the box by the door. It beeped and soon enough all three of us were inside.

What had once been a lobby had been transformed into a sitting room, with blue chairs and wood furniture, all resting on a wooden floor shined to a polish. The walls were half painted maroon and half paneled with many painted pictures and photographs, though what they were of I couldn't tell, everything was in shadow.

Elish kept walking and we followed him. He led us to a second door and then down a dark and musty hallway to a securely locked area. There was another beep and another pull and we were in the west wing where the three of us would be staying.

This area was painted in the same maroon and was also paneled, though the wooden floor was covered in overlapping rugs, the Persian patterned that felt squishy underneath my feet.

"Luca, the usual routine, turn the generators on and prepare some tea." Elish took the bags into a different room. I followed him and saw it was a large green bedroom with a black and teal trimmed comforter resting on top of a king size bed.

This one had carpet. I slipped out of my outside boots and dug around our bags for the loafer slippers that we all wore indoors.

I put mine on and rested Elish's white ones onto the bed, before removing his cloak from his back. I still remembered my cicaro training to take care of my master before myself. It wasn't taking me long at all to fall back into routines.

I folded Elish's cloak and took his jacket; he was taking out the important things he would need, tea and his laptop, the two things it would be unthinkable for Elish to not have.

My ears perked up as I heard a familiar rattle. I watched with Elish's white duster half folded in my arms as Elish quietly pulled out my old leash, before placing it on top of a white dresser. The chains made a coiling sound as they wrapped together on the bare surface.

I stared but he didn't notice me; he only kept unpacking his bag, silent and unaware of my reaction.

My hands went up to my neck and I rubbed it, feeling the familiar empty and bare feeling of not having my leather collar on my neck. Elish had claimed me again, so why hadn't he collared me?

He hadn't been calling me cicaro either... he had been calling me Jade.

Another familiar noise, this one the tinkling noise of the studs on my collar bumping against the steel loop where the collar clicked on. Sure enough, there was my collar, and in another moment all of my leather cuffs. I had taken them off the last time I had showered in Olympus and had never gotten the chance to put them back on.

Silence filled the air around us, a cicaro standing two feet behind him, staring intently at his old binds. Once the bane of my existence, fetters strangling me inside and out, now I wanted so badly for him to bind me again, to make me his. To give me the security my heart so badly needed, the confirmation he would never leave me again.

Did you miss me? The words crept to my mouth and stayed there, but my lips refused to give them voice.

When did you start to regret what you did?

That was another thing I didn't know if I could ever ask.

I jumped as the lights turned on around us, the generator shooting electricity into every lamp and every outlet. I quickly turned around and started unpacking my own bag, my heart hammering in my chest. I wasn't sure if it was from the surprise of the lights or my pain from seeing my old leather bounds.

Or perhaps it was the light being shed on my own guilty thoughts, forcing me to be fully aware that I was practically begging for Elish to fully commit himself to my enslavement. But I was done feeling bad about my own feelings. Kerres had betrayed me, and he had laid in the grave he had dug himself. I loved Elish... and no matter how fucked up that sounded I couldn't deny my own heart.

Before he could notice me I finished unpacking and took Elish's laptop to set it up in the living room, leaving him to change out of his travelling clothes. Luca was busy in another corner of the wing, where I assumed the kitchen was.

I started cranking up heating dials, still keeping my leather jacket on until it warmed up again; one odd side effect I found from my experiences was that I was always cold. I didn't know if I had lost a lot of weight or if it was just the drugs but I felt like one of those small useless dogs that just sit there and shiver.

When everything had been set up and Elish's laptop was turned on and ready for him to pretend he was doing work (when he was really playing solitaire), I curled up beside a heater and took up a couple keys of the heroin. Feeling warm and comfortable, I stayed in that corner and watched Luca set up Elish's tea and a plate of what looked like little snack cakes.

I eyed them, they might be about two hundred and thirty years old but they still tasted like heaven. The pre-Fallocaust humans really knew how to use their chemicals to preserve things.

Luca noticed me. "Would you like one, Master Jade? We have the chocolate cupcake ones with the stuff in the middle."

I nodded and reached out my hand, I picked up a chocolate one and a vanilla one and started undoing the wrappers. I ate both cakes in about four bites and curled back up against the heater.

Oddly once he set the tray down, Luca dashed into the other room for a moment before running back. He sat down right in front of me and I realized he was holding two of those Cilo guitars.

With small smile on his boyish face he handed me a guitar and brought out his. "Master Elish says it's time for your energies to be put elsewhere. I'm your new teacher."

I pulled out the guitar. I tried to pluck a string, the twang sounded like a thunder crack in the quiet room. "What energy?" I yawned and rubbed my eyes. I always felt tired and sleepy, but I was jealous of all these stupid Skylanders and their talents. I watched Luca take out a music book and lay it in front of me. Looking pleased with himself and content with the cat ears on his head, he started to teach me all of the basic notes and chords. I listened and tried to pay attention, Elish eventually coming into the room and sitting in front of his laptop.

CHAPTER 27

I SPENT A GOOD PORTION OF THE DAY PRACTICING THE guitar with Luca (who was an extremely patient teacher considering my hands would tremble if I didn't put enough heroin up my nose), and the rest of the day sleeping beside the heater.

In the evening Luca even lit a fire which I gravitated towards, and when he brought out old marshmallows that was the icing on the cake. I think Elish had deliberately told Luca to feed me sugars and fats because I had never eaten so much food in my life. I wasn't complaining though, mostly because I was too stoned to complain. The heroin seemed to make me crave sugar like you wouldn't believe.

When it was late I took my last bump of heroin and went into Elish's bedroom. I slipped my clothes off and put on some boxers and about a half hour later he joined me in bed.

He clicked the light out and was quiet. I rolled over onto my side and looked at him, mostly expecting him to start initiating something. It had been a long time and it would be in his nature, even though I was still torn up and sore from what had happened in the drug den in Eros.

But Elish was quiet. My brow furrowed as he closed his eyes.

He hadn't called me cicaro, he wasn't trying to have sex with me, and he hadn't put my collar back on. Maybe after everything I had been through, I was too damaged for him now.

Feeling a bit dejected I fell asleep, and during the middle of the night I inched over and curled up under the crook of his arm, where I belonged.

Three days later, after I had finished my guitar practice with Luca and he was off making dinner for us, I sat next to the fireplace bundled in my blankets, making sure to not burn the house down, especially as I had accidently singed the corners of one.

Elish was sorting files. He had brought a printer with him and seemed to be updating files on the people he wanted to keep track of.

He was still leaving me alone, and yes, at one point I would have wanted nothing else, but the stupid cicaro that had been beaten into me thirsted for some affection. He had been so kind to me when he had brought me from that brothel drug den, and he was still being kind… but he also wasn't touching me or making me do the things I was used to doing.

Or even inviting me to sit with him like he used to.

Was that a form of kindness too? Maybe he didn't know I had come to crave it.

I felt myself staring at him; he was paper clipping a photo onto a folder and setting it aside, before leafing through his file case and finding a piece of paper.

Maybe I was just trash to him now – more than I used to be anyway.

"Can I sit beside you?" I asked quietly, peeking up from my nest of blankets.

Elish glanced casually over to me. "Yes, but leave the blanket behind. I need a clean work area."

I abandoned the fleecy blanket and got up, stretching and popping my joints. They were so stiff and sore but at least my body was recovering from the physical aspects of my ordeal. The heroin acted as a pain killer so that helped a lot.

I leaned up against Elish and watched him sort his papers. I was amused to see that what he was paper clipping into these peoples' files were my write ups of their auras, now typed and spell-checked. That made me smile, at least I was useful in that respect.

My brow furrowed as I saw a file on top of a folder that just read 'Jade'. Clipped to the corner was also my work photo way back from when I was working for Dek'ko Farms. I tried to read everything on it but he tucked it into the 'Jade' folder and put it aside.

It was a really large folder… four or five times the size of the other folders. My eyes fixed on it and I felt my arm outstretch to read it.

"Retract your hand," his crisp voice said sharply. My hand shot back but I decided in my drug-induced bravery to be a jackass; I raised my foot and tried to pull it towards me with my toes.

I heard him chuckle, my heart swelled at making him laugh. "Hilarious, put your foot down, or else I might let you read that folder just for the sheer joy of watching your breakdown. Unfortunately, you're far from proper medical help and burying your body in the compacted dirt may blister my hands."

With a thunk, my foot dropped back to the floor and I stared at the folder like Elish had just told me not to touch the elixir of life. "What do you mean? What's in it?"

Elish clipped a photo I recognized as Luca's brother Lance and put it on top of my folder. "Do not let your curiosity get to you, Jade. Remember, if you snoop you will only discover things you'd rather not know about."

That didn't help my curiosity at all... I stared at the folder as the other ones piled on. I wasn't going to pry, not only because I knew better, but because I was beside him and he was engaging me which was what I had been craving.

"Can we update my photo sometime at least? I was like thirteen when that was taken," I said, smiling as I recognized a photo of Garrett with his huge grin. That guy looked like he had spent hours perfecting his smiles and poses in front of a mirror; he would've been a fun master to have.

"Sure, when we get home."

A little while later he was done. By that time I think I had seen every single chimera and sengil I knew and lots of business men I didn't remember. I didn't see several that I thought he would have on file though.

"Where's Reaver's file? And Lycos and Greyson and all them? Aren't they important? You wanted me to read their auras," I asked curiously, handing him a stack of file folders he had on the coffee table.

There was a click as Elish locked his briefcase before setting it beside him. "For the same reason I asked you to never mention their names."

I paused and remembered the conclusion I had come to last year when we had left Aras. "They're hiding out from King Silas, aren't they?"

Surprisingly, Elish nodded. I had half-expected him to tell me to be quiet or to give me a disciplinary smack on the head. "Yes, Jade, they're in hiding. King Silas thinks they're dead and it must remain that way at all costs."

Shit, I had guessed it but I still felt a rush as those words left his lips. I bit the corner of my mouth wondering how much information I could get out of him. My mind told me to press it, and in the coziness of the night I had to take that chance. "Why?"

My mind went to all different kinds of places as I saw a smile crease his face. He was silent to the point where I didn't think he would answer me, then he spoke.

"In time, Jade, in time."

I stared at him like an idiot, and tilted my head to the side. "You have something going on don't you?"

"I always have several things going on, that question is rather redundant." Elish's perfect pale face hinted at no emotions. He stared forward, his eyes melted steel. I knew my questions were over.

When it was quiet again I inched towards him and tucked myself under his arm; several minutes later though he moved it to start typing on his laptop so I had to settle for his shoulder that kept moving up and down.

"Perhaps it would be best for you to sit on the other side of the couch. It's hard to type." My heart sank a little bit as I was banished. I moved to the far end of the couch like a scorned pet and curled up.

The second banishment happened when he was out in the backyard going for a walk. I put on my winter clothes to go and walk with him but I was told to go back into the house because I was too weak to be out in the cold. I went back in with my head hung low.

This nice Elish was coming at a cost; he was kinder and considerate but for some reason he didn't want me near him as much. The old 'beat me bloody' Elish had been a dick sometimes but when we had our good times they were good. It was like trading two varying extremes for a continuous but monotonous stability.

I… I think I liked the old Elish better.

With the calm yet maddening Elish walking around outside, I went into the bedroom and stripped off my clothes. I put on a pair of leather underwear I had flatly refused to wear before and waited on top of the bed for him.

An hour later he came in, without a word or acknowledgement he stripped down into a white undershirt and cloth pants and slipped under the covers, not giving me a second glance.

He flicked off the light and closed his eyes without saying a word.

Without realizing the ticker of my patience with his new odd attitude had finally counted down, I gathered up every drop of bitterness in my stomach and exploded.

"So am I just too damaged for you now?" I snapped.

Elish sat up, but I stood my ground. I glared at him, tempting myself to start hitting him with something. I was about done with this attitude of his – it was driving me completely insane.

"What are you going on about, Jade?"

My insides seethed, my hands clenched the comforter in anger. "And why the fuck are you calling me Jade so much for? Where is cicaro? Where is slumrat? Where the fuck is that?"

Elish's violet eyes stared at me, weighing my reactions with that super intelligent brain of his, wondering what had caused it and what had finally made me snap.

Then he said something unexpected. "Why would I call you cicaro? I don't see a collar around your neck."

I glared at him, my jaw clenched and trembling, and my teeth squeaking under the pressure. I exploded again. "You haven't fucking put it back on me!" I yelled throwing my hands up in the air. "You've just been nice and it's fucking driving me up the wall. Stop it! Just treat me normally!"

"Oh? I'm treating you too well now am I? My, my, we *are* hard to please." Elish's gave me a bemused smirk. I let out a frustrated yell and got up. I snatched the collar off the table and threw it at him. He caught it, then he caught the wrist cuffs and the ankle cuffs.

I continued to rant, "I don't know what you're trying to do but stop it; if you want me to recover then let it go back to how it used to be."

Elish put up a hand dismissively and placed my collar on the night table. "You are so tame and submissive now, how could I treat you normally? All the fun is gone; you don't give me resistance at all anymore."

My body froze as I turned his words over in my mind. Was that really it? Was I too obedient and affectionate to get those usual reactions out of him? Was it my fault? When I was biting him and thrashing and resisting, he was at his peak, now my mind was messed up and my body malnourished and sore.

No, I still had fight left in me. I was still the hard-nosed Morosian brat and I'd prove it.

I took a step back and looked behind me. I faced him with my own smirk on my face.

Elish narrowed his eyes at me and that was the last I saw of him. I turned around and strolled into the living room. In a fluid motion, without even stopping, I grabbed his briefcase and started towards the door to the closed-off wings.

"Jade…" Elish was in the doorway; his voice was full of cold warning. I turned around and faced him, my hand on the door handle. I gave him a smile.

"I'm going to read that file on me," I said, my voice a song of mischief. I pursed my lips to give him a long distance kiss and slipped into the shadows.

"Jade!" I heard his footsteps click against the wooden floor. With a snicker I dashed down the long dark hallway and made a left.

The cold was stinging me; the rest of the mansion was dark and the same biting temperature as outside. I was hot though and my body was overflowing with adrenaline.

I closed the door of an oval-shaped sitting room and opened an adjacent door to poke my head inside, dead end though; I tried the next one and saw another hallway. On my bare tiptoes I silently ran to the other side and hid behind a piano to listen.

My ears filled with static as I craned them, listening for any sound that he was getting closer. When it was silent, I looked around the room and started picking out places I could hide if I needed to.

This was definitely some sort of music room; the piano was kitty-cornered against a wallpapered wall adorned with a picture of Artemis at the piano. To the left were violins and guitars and other instruments I didn't recognize.

I put the suitcase down and clicked it, not to look in it; I had no intentions of doing that, but to make the sound so that Elish would think that's what I was doing.

Sure enough, I heard the soft clicking of the footsteps. I smiled to myself and pattered towards the door leading out of this room before slipping through it. Without looking where I was going, I closed the door behind me and turned to start down the next hallway.

Well shit, it was a large storage room.

With a brief glance at the shadows of boxes and old instruments, I decided to take this to the next level and climb to the top of a large metal rung storage shelf. When I reached the dust-covered top shelf I crawled to the end of it and pressed my back against the wall that separated this room from the music room. I clutched the briefcase to my chest and waited.

I was smiling and I knew I was a maniac for enjoying this but if I pissed him off it would show him I wasn't some lapdog. I didn't think it was fair for him to judge me for being tame towards him; I was still recovering from what had happened in Moros. But whatever, if Elish wanted to see disobedience I'd give it to him with sprinkles on top.

I stayed absolutely still and waited, withholding the automatic jolt of anxiety as I heard him walking around the music room.

Plink... plink...plink... he pressed several keys on the piano, just to show me he was there. I stayed absolutely still until I heard the click of the door as he left the room. I think he was going back down the hallway.

I slid down and felt my feet hit the cold floor, breathing a relieved plume of white smoke as I opened the door handle and creeped out.

So quiet in here and freezing too! My heart was a pounding knot though. I felt like I was in a fucking video game, or a horror movie. No, it felt like I was back in the mansion with Ares and Siris stalking me, except this time I wasn't terrified, I was having the time of my life.

Like a shadow I tiptoed towards the door I had just heard him walk through, planning on following him while he thought he was following me. I put my hand on the knob and turned it quietly.

I shrieked as I felt arms grab me, strong arms with fingers digging into my flesh like frozen fire. I whirled around and planted a bite on his hand before ripping myself from his steel grasp, a laugh falling unbidden from my lips.

He let me go and I grabbed the briefcase and tried to make my escape but Elish caught my arm and yanked me back.

"What easy prey, stomping around the house like your feet were lead, no chase at all," Elish growled, though I saw the smirk on his face and a bright pull in his eyes. Then my eyes travelled to his pale, exposed arm, with a faint trickle of blood seeping down from the bite wound.

I tried to pull my arm away but he held onto it strongly. Instead, I leaned down and licked the blood off of the bare, warm limb. My chest shuddered from the taste; it tasted like ambrosia. Every time I sampled it it seemed to burn my tongue more and more with its pleasure. "And yet it's your blood on my lips this time."

I looked up at him and dragged my tongue slowly back along his skin.

Then Elish raised his free hand and roughly grabbed my chin, filling my chest with an electric energy that filtered through me like cocaine.

I smirked back at him and fixed my gaze on his.

"Bring your face closer, see what happens," I said, using the same taunt that I had when he had first pinned me against the walls of Skyland and Eros.

But this time he did. Elish leaned into me and I did the same, closing my eyes.

He brought his lips to mine, my heart skipping as he pressed them into me. I automatically opened my mouth to take him and we kissed deeply.

Though the pleasure suddenly turned to pain. I cried out and felt my knees go weak as he bit down on my lip, piercing my soft flesh and breaking through my skin. A moment later he pushed me away with a force that made me fall to the floor.

I licked up the blood that was falling freely from my lips and watched for his next move. I realized then he had a violin bow in his hand; a hard stick tight with strings made from human organs.

I knew what he was going to do; I got onto my knees never taking my eyes from his.

The first blow forced a grunt through my closed teeth. The next one I braced myself for but I still sucked in a painful breath. Every one rained down on me as if the bow was made of fire, breaking my skin and dripping ribbons of blood down my chest.

I closed my eyes and tilted my head back; the pain was overwhelming to the point where my head felt clouded and my mind started to go hazy, but still with every blow I felt myself back at home. I enjoyed it and I wanted it.

Though my body wasn't as eager to enjoy it, as the blows continued to break my body down I found my head bowing back, only jerking forward when the next smack of the switch shot my senses out of their distorted cloud.

My brain was going in all directions, feeling the sexual thrill from being whipped by him but also the searing pain brought from such transgressive strikes of love. I opened my eyes and saw his menacing smile, dripping with sadistic thoughts and his own love of seeing me hurt and bleeding.

"Do not make me do it until I get a scream out of you," Elish whispered, his voice bringing even more ice into the room. "This room is built for acoustics; a shriek of pain would be pleasing to the ears."

I looked down at my bloodied chest, hiding the surprise at the thin but swollen lashes. My yellow eyes flicked up and I found myself crawling over to him on my knees.

Ignoring his obvious taunts, I kneeled in front of him and leaned over to kiss his navel. Without permission or even the sure signal that this pain he was inflicting on me was taking a turn to a sexual nature, I slowly drew his cloth pants off his waist and brought my lips up to the base of his dick.

"What a brash little creature you are..." Elish whispered but he made no move to step away from me. Taking it as a good enough signal this might be wanted, I put him into my mouth, feeling him harden fully as my tongue massaged the crown.

I heard the scrape of a chair behind him and he sat down. I went back to the stiff member and ran my hand down its shaft, before grabbing it in a firm hold and taking every inch of it into my mouth.

I had never done this to him before. I didn't know how he liked it, so I did what I liked. I pulled back and started licking and sucking on the head, before drawing my mouth back down to the base with a firm suction.

He tasted good, and like the chimera's trademark, the thickness and length filled my mouth. Taking lavish joy in him not moving away from me, or whipping me further, I blew him. Keenly weighing his breathing and feeling nothing but a giddy joy as, fully hard, he put his hand on my head and started digging his fingernails into my scalp.

Then they shifted down to my lips, still dripping crimson droplets onto the ground; he collected some onto his fingers before bringing the bloodied digits to his mouth. I could feel his dick twitch in my mouth as he tasted me again.

Eventually I felt his own breathing quicken in just the slightest way, and his hand now resting on my jaw started to scrape his small nails against my skin. Soon his hips started to rock back and forth, and as I quickened my rhythmic strokes of his shaft and my mouth I heard a sharp intake of breath and felt the cum start to spout into my mouth.

I took all of it in and swallowed down the bitter but pleasing liquid, not letting a drop pass through my lips. I wouldn't waste it.

When the last shot coated my tongue I broke away, my own hands pushing down and palming my own rock hard member, almost poking through my leather underwear.

Then a cold hand rested on my neck and as the electricity shot through it, I screamed. My voice echoed and bounced off of the high ceilings, filling the room with my own pain-filled shrieks.

I fell down onto my back, my brows knitting and my eyes shooting in all directions, my brain temporarily being fried. I gasped and put a hand on my face trying to control the vibrating twitches going through my body.

I felt Elish behind me and my underwear slipping off of my body. Then heard it being tossed across the room with a small smacking noise. In a matter of seconds, he pressed my legs back and started to ease himself inside of me.

Oh, I had missed this. My mouth sucked in a breath of the musty cold air and I immediately drew my legs back. He roughly pushed himself into me and without pause, or even lube he started to thrust his hips. Ripping himself in and out, only the wet of my own saliva helping the friction between us.

It hurt. I missed it, and I fucking missed the pain as much as I missed breathing, but it hurt like it never had before. I cried out and dropped my head back onto the wooden floor and looked up at the ceiling; the encompassing aural figure of Elish looming over my skinny body, taking every part of me into him and melting us into one person.

To pacify my own pain, when he bowed his head to lick the blood running down my chest, I clawed and dug my finger into his back and shoulders as hard as I could until I could feel his flesh sticking under my fingernails and soon warm, wet blood. There was no wavering in his thrusts inside of me or faltering for a single minute, they were a continuous assault of pleasure and pain, so intense when the first orgasm came I had barely even touched myself.

And with the tensed snap of my burning pleasure I clamped my teeth against his shoulder, digging into his shoulder blade and piercing the flesh. In response he gasped and with the next quick succession of thrusts I felt him fill me. But he didn't stop and neither did I. Only half realizing I was growling I eagerly continued my own assault on his skin and let him pound me hard.

Like many times when he was on me, time ceased and drew from a series of slow ticks to a rush that coursed on like the speed of light. There was never any continuous and steady passage of time, it was just one intense burst of energy without form.

Finally though, the pain started to outweigh the pleasure, and the fatigue started to peak through the rushing emotions. My mind became more aware of time and each hard thrust of Elish's member inside my raw and filled backside. Even Elish's warm and encompassing body couldn't stem the feeling of anxiety slowly but surely building up in my chest. I was starting to feel trapped underneath him, being subject to torturous jabs that once brought me so much masochistic pleasure.

And he knew every tone and every scream, and I knew when my cries of pleasure turned to teeth clenching moans of pain that he was aware, but there was no stopping or slowing down.

Then, on a particularly rough jab as he came for what seemed like the dozenth time, I ground my teeth together and tried to push him off of me.

Like he was waiting for it, he grabbed my wrist with his hand and slammed it against the wood behind me, before with practiced stealth he drew back the other one. I swore and looked down to my stomach helplessly, seeing the red streaked member thrust in and out of me. Further on I saw my still hard penis laying in a puddle of my own cum, the tip swollen and still leaking onto my flushed stomach.

I struggled and in spite of my priggish confidence not too long ago, the post trauma memories of other incidents where I had been in a similar spot started to bare their teeth at me. My mind defaulted back to the normal instincts that being bound and fucked brought forth, and finally, to what I knew was Elish's joy, I let out my first desperate howl.

Sure enough, the thrusts sped up. I growled and tried to thrash my legs but they were cramped and frozen in place. I closed my eyes and screamed at him to stop but I knew better, and as expected my pleas went unheeded.

Then the tight feeling gathered again in my groin, and though my entire body was shaking with pain and anxiety I felt him push against my prostate, making my cries a mix of moans and howls of pain.

I came again with a frustrated cry, no longer shooting cum but a small clear dribble that mixed in with the puddle of seed resting in the concaves of my stomach. My mouth twisted and I called him every name I could think of as he continued to push himself mercilessly inside of me.

"Look at me."

"Fuck you!" I spat through my sore teeth. My jaw was on fire, the muscles worn and tired from clenching, screaming, and biting. I closed my eyes but felt his hand release me, only to clench my jaw in his grasp.

"Do it, now."

I gritted my molars and looked up at him.

His eyes were calm and cold in their sockets; I knew mine were a blaze of unhinged anxiety and pain. Like he had done many times before, the chimera stared down at me, and to my relief as he concentrated on my eyes his thrusts lessened.

"Draw up your aura," Elish commanded.

I stared at him, pursing my lips and twisting my face into an angry snarl. "Why?" But as I said that I did what he asked, seeing his blue-tinged frame suddenly surrounded with the beautiful spectrums of silver and crystal waves, wrapping around him in ribbons.

My own was black, still darkness with the purples and silvers dead in Moros. I drew all of my energy into flaring it around us, pushing my own darkness into his in my only act of defiance, even if it was pointless.

"Your aura is black now is it? Did they fuck the colour right out of you?" Elish mused, jabbing in a long thrust before continuing his relentless rhythm. His hands grabbed my shoulders and he pressed down the blades. I felt his hands go hot.

"No, your abandonment of me did. This is all you, asshole!" I snapped, closing my eyes and letting out a particularly loud scream. I dug my fingers into my sides before putting them on his shoulders, bracing against him and trying to shove him off me at the same time.

"Keep it up. I enjoy seeing the darkness in your eyes, a testament to what easy prey you were."

I growled and dug in my fingernails, before shrieking as his hands went hot, his fingers fitting against the old handprint scars like he was resting them on top of an old glove.

Then something happened.

As I opened my mouth and let out another scream, suddenly there was an audible electric crack that filled the room and my head with an ear-splitting sound. The next moment Elish was thrown off of me, as if he had just been electrocuted.

I tried to scramble to my feet but my body felt like I had been thrown into paralysis. After several seconds of tensing my limbs I managed to crawl towards him.

Not even wanting to figure out what the hell happened, I quickly went to him, the smell of singed flesh and hair filling the once cold and musty music room. Everything was covered in a thick, constantly moving blanket of electricity that brought out all the hidden smells of the room like the first of the spring rains.

When I crawled up to him, I realized Elish was out cold, and thankfully not dead. I leaned over him, thinking that it was so weird seeing him unconscious, and started patting his cheek to try and wake him up. Any malice I held towards him during our intense session had disappeared as soon as I realized he was hurt; that was just typical sex between us anyway.

When Elish opened his eyes I recoiled my hand, wondering if I was about to get murdered. A moment later, after he got his bearings, he sat up and to my surprise he gave me a flat, rather unimpressed look.

Elish didn't look surprised, shocked or even angry, more annoyed like I had just accidently spilled his tea or something. It didn't make sense and it filled my mind with questions.

"I would've preferred you just burn me, or give me frost bite. Do you really need to be that dramatic?" Elish rose to his feet and reached his hand down to help me stand as well.

I swallowed the boulder in my throat, realizing that this was the confirmation I needed that Milos's electric shock wasn't an accident, but did it mean what I thought it meant? I didn't know.

Though deep down, I had known for a while.

"How did I do that?" I looked down at my hands as if I expected to see the sparks fly off them, but they were normal, just streaked with blood and trembling – so yeah… normal.

Elish rested a hand on my back and directed me towards the exit of the music room. He slid his cloth pants back on and picked up the briefcase.

"You're an empath, you didn't think your abilities just extended to seeing fancy colours no one else could see, did you?" Elish said quietly; an echoed click behind me told me he had closed the door. I fell back so I was walking more beside him than in front.

"You seem to know a lot about my bar trick." I stopped and he took a few steps in front of me before he stopped as well. I leaned against the cold wall, facing a golden framed painting of a green landscape.

Suddenly, I felt dizzy and nauseas. A sick realization welled in the anxious pool in my stomach, one I didn't know if I wanted to draw attention to.

"Is my ability why you saved me in the first place?" I asked quietly.

"No."

My brow furrowed; he turned and started to walk again. I tried to catch up to his long strides, though my stomach was still a disturbed hive. "Did you know?"

I saw his hair, ghostly white in the darkness, shimmer as he slowly shook his head. "Though I have used it on many occasions to advance my own agenda, the answer is no. In the beginning I saw you as nothing but an annoying flea in need of being split in half with my fingernail."

I continued to follow him, clutching my stomach and hoping I didn't throw up on the wood floor. "How do you know what I can do? Are there other empaths?"

"None I know of, though Garrett seems to enjoy hiding things from me."

"Garrett?" My eyes widened; the president of Skytech? Elish finally pushed the last door open and a flood of heat washed over me. "What does he have to do with this?"

Elish turned around, his eyes looking into the heart of my own confusion. There was something else in there though. He looked almost… pained?

My heart dropped; I stared at him dumbfounded.

He read my expression and gave me no pity. "Really, Jade, are you that much in denial? Sanguine was correct, you are the most moronic genius I have ever met. How can one be so intelligent but in the same breath have something right in their face that —"

I knew what he was going for, but before I could confirm it in my own mind, my brain automatically went into defence mode. A thousand pieces of evidence to counteract this reality came shooting into my head. "I'm not one of you, I had a mother!" I snapped. My mouth twitched and I looked around the living room, feeling the cold sweat take away the reality-eating stupor I had been in earlier.

"I…" My mind suddenly flared. Instead of confirming it to myself I felt myself grow more and more angry. The more angry I got the less I had to think about what had been right in front of me the entire time. The glaring reality.

But my mind jumped into survival mode once again; in a desperate grab to steer my mind away from the glaring beacon it instead broke open another nagging reality, smashing it onto my emotions like a tossed rotten egg.

"That's why you brought me back from the drug den, that's why you saved me in the first place! Fuck Sanguine because he was wrong, I'm not special to you. I was your weapon like Reaver is to Lycos…" I licked my lips from stress and bared them at the floor. I couldn't look at him. I didn't know what I was more mad about, the fact that I was indeed one of them or the fact that that was the only reason he wanted me.

"That was it isn't it? Just training some stupid chimera so he can be given his assignment…" The thought devastated me. He hadn't done all of these things because I was special to him, because I had meant something to this cold and emotionless chimera. It was all a part of his plan to integrate me into his stupid fucked up family. Make me one of… *them*.

To my horror my shoulders started to tremble and right in front of him

I felt my eyes well.

Soon I was being drawn into his chest. I wrapped my arms around him and to my self-hatred I started to sniff through the tears rolling down my face, but I held strong and didn't give myself into sobbing like a child. I was past that, I had to be stronger than that, and I knew without hesitation now that I was made from stronger stuff.

"Why are you crying now?" Elish walked me to the couch and I shifted myself onto his lap, the only goddamn place I felt safe. "It really doesn't change anything."

I tensed up and shook my head. "There was something about you kidnapping a stupid slumrat that was endearing to me, it made it special. Now though… now you knew all along. You wanted me because I was a chimera due to be brought into this world, not because you liked me."

I pushed him away as he chuckled, but he held my arms back. "What a stupid thing to cry about. Here you find out your origins and you cry for that? You always had a knack for making me laugh."

When I continued to glare poison into him, he smiled slyly at me. "Now, how would that face look if I told you that I never knew you were a chimera until almost four months into you being my cicaro? Would you stop this hideous crying then?"

"How did you find out then?" I asked cautiously, then my mind travelled back to that time when he asked me to start writing down different peoples' auras. It had come out of the blue and he had never told me how he knew I could do it.

"King Silas made it rather obvious. He knows where all of the young chimeras are in the world. Garrett too which he conveniently hid from me."

"Garrett always knew?"

"Apparently yes."

Unable to handle much more information, I felt my temples throb. I leaned down and picked up the bag of heroin and when Elish didn't stop me I took a few bumps into my nose, more than usual, and sniffed it up. I rubbed my nostrils smelling the blood on my own hands and looked down at the briefcase.

"I have known for a while I think," I said quietly, waiting for the warmth of the china white to numb this storm of emotions under the surface of my skin. "I electrocuted Milos after I broke the handcuffs when I was trying to strangle him with them. I tried to convince myself he had just activated his Taser by mistake. Not to mention the glaring similarities I noticed between me and Sanguine."

"Denial is a rather powerful emotion." There was a hint of bitterness in his voice. "But now that this hurdle has been overcome, we can move on. I will be needing your skills in the future, and now that you know where they come from, you can start to develop them."

I nodded, not knowing what else to do, though the china white was soothing me to the point where I didn't feel like I had to reply. Instead I sighed and let the warmth envelope me.

"Did you not ever wonder why you can see so well?" Elish asked after it had been quiet for a few moments between us. "Or why you could jump and fall with such grace? Really, you are so thick-headed, mentally challenged even."

I smiled, feeling that I now had new ammo to use against him. "What shitty engineering; you dumb mutants couldn't even make me smart enough to figure this out sooner."

Elish returned my smile. "This may be on purpose. Reaver has ten times the abilities of you and he hasn't a clue. The same went for the other children we dropped off in Skyfall and the greywastes. Ares and Siris were from Moros too, did you know that?"

I shook my head, but his words brought a tug to my heart. I thought of my tangle-haired mother, with her circle of garbage around her as she sat in the park. Someone who couldn't raise me properly, but had to the best of her ability before the sovereign took me away.

"She wasn't even my mother?"

Elish shook his head. "No, her child, a daughter, was stillborn. There is a write-up I can show you, but for now I think you've been exposed to enough. We'll return to bed now."

"Can we talk about it more tomorrow? Would you show me more?" I slipped off him and picked up the plastic bag of powder.

"Well, that's part of the reason why we're here," Elish replied. "I don't plan on returning to Skyfall with a broken boy. I expect a lot from you in the next few weeks."

Oddly this filled me with a determination. I gave him a confident nod.

"I won't disappoint you."

My ears perked up as I heard the familiar rattle of the collar link; when I saw he was holding it my heart skipped inside my chest.

There were no words of happiness and pride when he put that collar around my neck and fastened it. A moment later he picked up each hand and screwed the small metal bolts on the cuffs so they were snug around my wrists. I sat down on the bed and watched as he fastened the ones on my ankles.

He leant down, grabbing my chin with his hands. I looked up at him and matched his smirk with my own.

Then my master pressed his lips against mine. I reciprocated though it was hard because I was smiling. I understood in that moment why he hadn't put my collar on as soon as I got back. I had to earn the collar; I was a chimera pet now, more would be expected from me.

Elish shook his head, looking pleased with himself for reasons I could only guess.

"Sleep well, Cicaro."

I woke up feeling like shit as usual. I crawled my sorry ass out of bed, ignoring the streaks of blood on the sheets from my beaten chest. The lashes hurt and I was bruised but for the most part the injuries were nothing compared to the beat downs I got with the whip. The violin bow just didn't have the right crack to it that the horse whip did.

After I was showered and had changed into my pet clothes, I flopped onto the couch with the bag of drugs, wanting nothing more than to feel the sickness drip away from me like rain on the roof of a house.

I did my lines and turned on the TV. We didn't get Skyfall TV here, of course, but we had DVDs and VHS movies. I popped in a recording of some shows and leaned back to watch them.

Luca brought some coffee and a plate of eggs and sausage on English toast to the dining room table. I got up and joined him just as Elish came in from outside.

I took a sip of my coffee and let the warm heroin hug me.

"You'll be taking Suboxone from now on. I think your mind is stable enough to be weaned off of the sludge you've been putting into your body."

I sighed and slumped in my chair. I didn't want to give it up yet. I decided to try and reason with him. "You know this stuff makes it easier for me to handle things and I think it's been helping me from stroking out. Can I just do it for a while longer?"

"No, the Suboxone will make you sure you don't feel withdrawal symptoms. Be happy that I am allowing you that."

I sighed at his reply and gave the sausage on my plate an annoyed prod; of course he noticed.

"Or would you rather go cold turkey? Or experience two days of hallucinations on a detox kit?"

No. I'd had to do cold turkey before and I heard the detox kits made you trip balls in a bad way. Neither of those experiences I felt like experiencing myself.

"No, you're right." I shot Luca a sideways glance and chewed on a piece of bacon; he was putting his cat ears on and adjusting them.

"You should wash those, they probably have more than a dozen people's blood on them by now."

The sengil didn't even waver at this admission; he gently picked up his knife and fork and started cutting his English toast. "Yes, Master Jade, I will hand wash them tonight with the other blood-stained items."

Typical laundry at Elish's.

I know I had asked it before, but the answer I had gotten had been so moronic I decided to go above his head. "Elish, why does he wear those cat ears?"

Elish dabbed the corner of his mouth with a napkin and said in the most casual manner, "They make him work faster."

I gave him a pathetic stare. He didn't look back at me, he only drank from his coffee cup and a moment later pressed something on his remote phone. I heard a beep and a whir followed by a reflection in the window of his laptop loading.

Luca was smiling though, a small smug little smirk. I brought up the same store of juice I used to flick on my aura ability and extended my finger.

Luca yelped as I poked him, before jumping up like a bee had stung him. His green eyes were wide with shock as he stared at me, trying to figure out what I had just done.

Of course I cackled at him and tried to poke him again but he jumped away from me and looked at Elish for help.

"Well, you figured out how to do it, very good, though you need to learn to focus it on just your hands, or else you will find yourself losing friends quickly." Elish looked up from his laptop, before going back to typing with one hand.

Luca took a step back, looking bewildered. "I thought you said he was an empath, Master. That he does not have the abilities that you do."

"He doesn't," Elish explained. "Jade is an empath, meaning he can sense people's auras and their beings. When it comes to a chimera if he is around them their abilities start to soak into him. Jade has been around me long enough and has picked up certain talents."

"Really?" I looked at him, fascinated. "Who else can do what? You got any ones who can fly or run super-fast or something?"

"We're not X-Men, Jade. We have only been able to master the normal chimera enhancements and the higher tier ones: thermal touch, intelligence, and your empath ability, nothing else as of yet."

I reached out another finger towards Luca, who was now sitting back down; he shifted away towards his master and tried to ignore me.

"What about the nimrods?" I tried to poke Luca again but he moved away just in time. "If I hang out with Ares and Siris will I get all strong?"

"You broke a pair of steel handcuffs, you're already strong. That was your engineering originally not some ability through osmosis," Elish explained patiently. "There is a certain set of default enhancements all chimeras get: night vision, hearing, strong bones, agility, and strength. All others are picked and chosen though some have failed. I believe your hearing never fully developed."

"But I'm the only empath one?"

"Yes."

"Why?"

Elish closed his laptop and finished the bite he was chewing; he never talked with food in his mouth. On top of the outpouring of grace and tranquility that seemed to radiate off this man, he was also as prim and proper as a real king. "I cannot answer that. I didn't know you existed; I left Skytech after the Skytech laboratories in Kreig burned down."

"Why?"

"Because the fire claimed the lives of Lycos and a small baby named Chimera X. It was a scandal and it caused a lot of problems within our family. I stepped down as dean of the college of Skytech and took a job as councillor. What Garrett did after that was not my concern; I avoided all aspects of Skytech and concentrated on running Skyfall."

I chewed on my toast; it took me a moment to connect who Chimera X was. "Oh, I understand. You saved them and that's why they're in Aras."

"Correct."

I kept eating, wishing I could ask just why he had done that to Lycos and Reaver, why he had saved them, but then I remember the tense meeting between Lycos and Elish.

The atmosphere had been heavy with unspoken emotion, a past buried deep but dug up and laid out on that dirty wooden floor for everyone to observe and analyze. I had seen it right away, and had sided with Elish instead of joining in on the passive-aggressive jabs.

There was history there, between those two. But with me standing beside Elish, and Greyson and their son standing beside Leo – it was obvious that it hadn't worked out.

I put my fork down and grimaced, a sudden realization making my stomach sour. "That crazy sociopath is my fucking brother?" Suddenly Reaver pushing me into the deacons' pen with the line on my cuff seemed like just a cruel prank an older brother would do to a younger sibling.

"Yes, you share very similar genetic coding, as with the others of your generation. Kessler's son Caligula, the three of you, as with every generation, are as close as brothers."

I made a face. I didn't like Caligula very much either. I had seen him more than a few times, especially during my rifle training. He was a sociopath like Reaver. "Am I similar to any of the other ones? Me and you, we aren't brothers are we?"

There was a clinking of dishes as Luca began to clear the table. Elish put his briefcase onto the table. A moment later he handed me something from what I assumed was my personal folder.

"In a sense, yes, we are all related but each chimera holds a certain percentage of a later generations coding and genetics. For instance, the twins Artemis and Apollo share mostly my coding. Here is yours."

I took the paper and scanned it. A lot of it didn't make sense but there was a line of text that I could make something of.

Chimera E.4

Sanguine: 55%
Apollo/Artemis: 22%
Garrett: 14%
Lycos: 9%

"Sanguine? No wonder we get along so well." I handed the paper back. "No King Silas? I thought all of you were like his genetic clones or something?"

Elish rose and smoothed out his robes, before taking his laptop and moving to the living room. "We all have more Silas DNA in us than any of the others. The first generation: myself, Nero, Ellis, and Garrett are almost completely Silas's, but with other engineering mixed in to change our features and abilities. So with the trickle-down effect, all the chimeras whose coding was sampled from generations before still have the king in their blood."

A moral person might see this as something bad, to have such an evil dictator's power running through their veins, but to me... a slumrat from Moros who had been raised thinking he was just a gutterwhore, a dime a dozen radrat... I felt an odd amount of pride at this.

The pride showed through a smile on my face. As much as I wanted this to be bad news to me, it wasn't. I was proud of myself. Though once we got to Skyfall and I would have to face the fact that this royal family were indeed a part of me was something else entirely. Right now, though, the mood was right, and the relationship between cicaro and master stable, so there wasn't anything nagging at me. Being a chimera was another reassurance that Elish wouldn't leave me and maybe it meant... that Silas might eventually leave me alone.

Wow, I was a chimera... I was different from everyone I had grown up with, not just because I could do my parlour trick.

I had a family, *the* family.

Kerres would never have been able to live with that... maybe it was best that he didn't have to see me go through any more changes. He had seen me transform into the Shadow Killer and now he would've had to see me transform into the chimera I was.

"Were you happy when you were told I was a chimera?" I asked when the breakfast plates had been cleared away and it was just me and him.

"Eventually, but at the time I was rather annoyed, solely because I had been played by a certain brother and a certain king."

"By saying I had been killed?" He nodded. "So… if I am a chimera, why does Silas want to kill me?"

"The explanation to that would be a long one, and not something I wish to divulge now. To put it simply… because Silas does what he wants, and gets what he wants. Remember this, Jade: he might have been a figure on the television, far away from Moros, but now he is more than a king to you, he is your master and the only person who will outrank me. You must obey him, as do I. No exceptions."

My mouth twitched. I watched his robes flow along the wooden floor as he glided towards where our coats were hung. There was a tone to his voice that suggested deeper truths to what he was telling me.

"What about if he ever asks about Lycos and Reaver?"

Elish paused for a brief moment and considered this. "If Silas ever questions you about them, it means he already knows everything anyway, but no, it is not information I wish for you to ever share willingly. But I wouldn't have brought you along for that trip if I ever expected you to be disloyal."

Pride shot through me like his words had just lit a stack of fireworks. "I'll only obey you," I said with a serious nod. I squared my shoulders and tried to look as much like a chimera as I could. "I'll always be loyal to you, no matter what. I really don't care for that asshole king. He can do what he wants to me, I won't say a word."

Elish gave me a sharp look and I deflated like a balloon. "Watch yourself, Cicaro. Watch your tongue and watch your ego. If you think being a chimera will allow you to speak as such to any of my brothers or, above all, our king, you will have a very rude awakening. Am I understood?"

I nodded. I didn't know my rank but I had a suspicion even Drake would be peering down his nose at me. "Yes, Master."

"I am warning you now and I will only warn you once: nothing has changed. You were given this knowledge for your own advancement. You are still a cicaro, and are expected to act as such."

"I know," I sighed and grabbed my coat. "Still a slumrat, still a pet. You just told a flea-bitten gutterwhore that he's royalty last night; you can't blame me too much can you?"

"Which is why you're not bleeding and twitching on the floor right now. Bring my tea. I'd like to go for a walk."

CHAPTER 28

I WEAVED MY FINGERS THROUGH HIS HAIR, ALL THE WAY down until I reached the small of his back, before trailing them up and resting them on his shoulders. I moved my hips up and down on him, taking him in as deep as I could with a clench of my teeth and eight fingernails digging into his shoulder blades.

We were in the bedroom, but he was sitting down on an armless grey fabric chair. I was riding him; even though it was the afternoon somehow we had ended up here. I couldn't complain; this had become my favourite thing to do with him.

He slid a hand behind the nape of my neck and drew me into him. We kissed deeply, my heart clenching and heating up with every taste I got of him. There wasn't a single part of Elish I didn't love, and the past three weeks in this house had only made me love him more.

Our lips broke apart as a knock came to the bedroom door.

Elish looked behind me at the closed door. I leaned in and started kissing his neck, ignoring whatever Luca needed. He knew better than to disturb us anyway; it wasn't a secret what we were doing. Usually Elish drew at least one scream out of me during our personal time.

There was another knock. "Master Elish?"

"Can it not wait, Luca?" Elish craned his neck for me. Running a hand down between my legs, he grabbed my member and started massaging it with his staticy palm.

There was silence, then a meek voice said, "Master Elish... a plane just landed outside."

I started to get up but Elish grabbed my shoulders and pushed me back down, smirking as I squealed at the awkward angle his dick went in at.

"That's fine, Luca, I am sure it's just Garrett with his chessboard, he seems to get annoyed when I miss more than two games. Tell him to wait, or if the mood strikes him he can join us in the bedroom."

I glared and pinched Elish's nipple really hard between my fingers; he smirked obviously trying to get a rise out of me, a staple when we were having sex.

There was another pause. I arched my back and stifled a moan as he started grinding his hips into me. Knowing he was trying to get me to cry out, I leaned down and took his nipple between my teeth in quiet retaliation, making him stifle his own noise.

"Master… it's… it's King Silas."

Never had the mood in our bedroom changed so rapidly. In a second I was off Elish, as he rose too. I handed him his pants and his cloak, making sure he was dressed and looking his best before I even found my underwear.

Elish quickly dressed without a word, slipping his white gloves onto his hands and white leather loafers onto his feet. When I had given him everything he needed I got into my leather and mesh, and for good measure, put a comb through my tussled up hair.

"Is there anything you want me to do?" The last thing I handed him was my leash but after he clipped it on he gave it to me to latch to my leather belt loop. It would be ready for him if he needed it.

"No, just remain silent, do what he asks and pretend you still have a spine with me, but not enough to make it obvious." Elish threw the bottle of lube into the dresser drawer and with a quick sweep of his cloak he left the bedroom.

I still have a spine. I glared at Elish as he left, trailing his steps as he walked towards the living room, Luca behind us in the kitchen quickly making tea and a plate of snack food. He looked nervous and I wondered if I did too.

I had to keep myself calm. I knew Silas could read heartbeats, most of them could. I had realized when Elish told me I could absorb other chimeras' abilities if I hung around them enough that my hearing was becoming advanced. It was still crap compared to theirs, I could only hear Elish's heart when it was quiet around me; I still didn't know how to tune it like my aura reading.

The door opened and any hope that I might be able to remain as stoic and in control as Elish went out the door like the sweep of cold air creeping in from the unoccupied areas of the house. My heart froze before thrashing wildly in my chest as I saw him.

Silas gave us both a smile and, in tandem, Elish and I bowed to him. Drake was with him, his own leather spiked collar around his neck and a silver chain held by the king.

"Look at my beautiful creations." Silas gazed approvingly at us; he walked up to Elish and clasped his hand before embracing him. Elish returned the gesture and kissed his king's hand. "My city has missed you, *gelus vir*, our family as well." Silas let go of his hand, and with another choke of my heart his green eyes turned to me. "And look at him, he looks much healthier now." I steeled myself as he brushed his hand over my cheek before tilting my head so I was looking right at him, the same thing he had done during Stadium.

But with Silas's touch came the familiar feeling of the colourless void, pressing down on my body with such a weight I felt my legs buckle under the knavish and steeping aura. I tried to shift my reading ability away from him but he seemed to force his darkness on me with or without my mind's consent.

And with the same overbearing feeling of him sinking into me, I felt his lips brush the corners of my own. I took a step back, seeing nothing but darkness, as though my eyes had become blind. I let him continue to kiss me, feeling myself being dragged down in his hypnotic, depthless aura.

I heard him laugh. "He's getting stronger. I could make him go mad right now if it pleased me. Just look at those eyes Elish, as golden black as the midnight sun. Do you see your aura when you look deep into those cat eyes?"

"I do."

I gritted my teeth, his eclipsing murk mixing in with my own black aura, only recently showing strings of silver and purple again. I tried to push his own away from me but it seemed to only sink into my skin like smoke.

Then Silas ripped himself from me. I stumbled back but before I could fall over I felt Elish grab a hold of my collar until I could find my feet.

Silas continued on speaking as though nothing had happened. I held my head and tried to shake the bugs free.

Fuck, I hated that guy. I hated everything that he brought here with him. This is what happened when you watch all your friends and lovers die around you; you became some sick weirdo who played with his creations for fun.

And I was one of them now.

"And? He knows now does he? Did he figure it out himself or did you finally spill the secrets on your lips?" Silas continued. I heard a tinkle of china as he picked up a mug of tea.

"Both, like some of the others he was in denial, but he is fine with it now," Elish replied, his voice tipped with both frost and authority. I knew him well enough to know he hated this unexpected meeting as much as I did. "I have kept him here to regain his strength after everything that happened. I wish to keep him here longer."

"Yes, I am sure you do." Silas reached over to me again and lifted my chin, before pulling one of my lips up. "You took his teeth out? Shame, did he become too powerful for you? Or perhaps the blowjobs were getting painful."

Wow, really? I bristled and bit the side of my cheek to keep myself from saying something that I knew would be my last words. What I did say was no better. "I lost the privilege from my biting. Master Elish told me I was full of disease and it would be inconvenient for him to catch my plague." My voice dripped ice and contempt, but it was for Silas not Elish.

The whole room went cold. I stared forward, unmoving and glued to the spot. A moment later I heard a low sardonic chuckle.

"Is that so? But you are no longer Morosian scum, you are Jade Dekker, my creation, my empath, my chimera," Silas purred, leaning down and kissing my cheek. His touch made my skin crawl. "Beautiful, Catullus. I can't wait to sample the fruit that Elish covets so much."

Jade Dekker? I swallowed at that name. I hadn't even thought about the smaller details of being a chimera. I not only had a last name now, I had *the* last name. The only one that mattered.

"Which brings me to why I am here..." Silas took a small red ball out of his bag and started throwing it up into the air. Behind him I saw Drake the cicaro tense up; he watched the ball move up and down as though he was a dog.

"Elish, it is time you returned home. I want to initiate my newest chimera properly; we're holding a party in his honour. There are certain things he needs to have done to be welcome into our lovely family. Many of your brothers will be attending. I expect you to bring my jade kitten with bells on when I summon you again." Silas threw the ball to me and I caught it, seeing a jerk of movement as Drake watched it rise into the air.

I held the ball and glanced at the king before my eyes travelled to Elish, to see if I could read him.

Elish was glaring at the both of us, his jaw clenched and his hands almost curled over his white robes; that was the only light that his body language shed on his emotions.

"Yes, Master," Elish replied. "If I could ask, I would prefer if we stay here until the party.

The king smiled, a closed mouth smile, kind of like Sanguine's. He started walking a small circle around Elish. "Oh? But it could be a month before I get everything together. Perhaps I could take him myself, spend a few weeks with his king. Sanguine... gave me such rave reviews." His voice was a low susurration draped in silk, and as slippery as silk too. "Did you watch the video I forwarded you? I was right, there was a thirst in him, covered in blood... with flesh between his teeth, thrusting himself into Sanguine."

"What?" I blurted, the hot blood running through my veins suddenly turning to ice. "There was a camera in that fucking apartment? Fucking serious?"

"Jade!" Elish said sharply; he gave me a withering look. "Go outside and throw the ball for Drake, now."

Thoroughly pissed off I angrily chucked the ball across the room; of course Drake bounded after it. I turned and started for the door leading to the hallway that would eventually bring me outside.

"No, stay, Jade," Silas's fluid voice whispered, deceptively smooth but barbed and dangerous. "I want to hear just why you decided to fuck my sengil? It has been a question on my mind for quite a while now."

Not trusting my eyes to stare at him since I knew he would see the contempt in them, I forced myself to speak. "I had no idea at that point who I was. In my head I was a Morosian slumrat and not Elish's cicaro. If a chimera wants me to fuck them, I'll fuck them and enjoy the privilege." Each word was spat from my lips like they were coated in bleach.

The hair on the back of my neck started to rise as the room fell to a hushed silence, even Drake was quiet. He had the ball in his mouth and was looking at me with wide scared eyes.

I could feel Silas behind me. The dark abyss was sinking into me and getting into my bones, pushing away my own aura and infiltrating it with that dark matter. It was like a vacuum, or a cancer, taking everything and leaving my brittle, drained body with nothing but the remnants of his presence.

And it was right behind me, crawling up my spine, weaving its tendrils around my bones and drawing me close. I wanted to run, my mind told me to run, but my feet were glued to the spot.

My heart pounded, my hands shook and when I could feel his breath on my neck a choking noise fell from my lips.

"If I fuck you… will you thank me for the privilege?" Silas whispered.

"Yes," I whispered back. "You are my creator, are you not? I wouldn't deny my king."

He put a hand on me and my back arched. I could see the black waves radiating off his hand, even though my back was turned to him. They had no sensation and yet I could see them, taste them, and feel their energy around me. Like phantoms in a haunted house, they were almost tangible.

I had prepared myself so I didn't even flinch when he kissed my neck, but I did tense up when he slid his hand into my pants.

My teeth gritted as I felt a finger slip between my cheeks, wiggling itself to my hole before slowly penetrating it. It hurt, but with my teeth clenched so hard my jaw spasmed and my back rigid, I managed not to move away from him.

He slipped his hand out and chuckled to himself, the same cold taunting laugh Elish had.

"So much cum, did I interrupt something? I thought I smelled my love's seed," Silas purred. His hand slid across the rim of my leather pants until he reached below my navel. I looked down and saw his slender fingers start to dance around the button of my leather pants. I was wondering how far I would let this go before I snapped.

No… no… Elish would kill me. Not only that, I would embarrass and disappoint him. I was a chimera and we all had to go through this.

I was glad I came to this conclusion. A moment later, like a cobra striking, he plunged his hands down my pants and grasped my soft dick.

I gasped as his touch became a vibrating static, even more intense than Elish's usually was. I bent my body over and groaned, as he clenched and massaged my quickly hardening shaft. Within twenty seconds I orgasmed.

No amount of control could keep the moan from my lips; I let it fall and tensed my body after wave after wave of tight pleasure shot through my veins like electricity. At the peak, I felt my legs buckle and give out from under me, but a tight hold kept me from falling. Like Elish had done one and a half years ago in Skyland, his master held me up with his own strength.

A low derisive laugh mocked every noise and movement my body made, filling me with humiliation and anger, before a slippery hiss fell to my ears.

"He cums so quickly… train him better, prepare him for our first night together."

I couldn't help it, I growled.

This made his small laugh grow. He slipped his hands out of my pants, and a moment later, his cum-filled fingers were brought to my lips.

"Lick it off, jade kitten, lick it clean."

I kept growling, staring forward, frozen to the spot and unable to move. I was too angry, uncontrollably angry. The humiliation was making my brain think of things I could never do, but I had to redeem my pride somehow. Once again it had been systematically stripped from me, a familiar feeling but one I would never get used to.

"Do not make me ask you twice."

I opened my mouth and tasted my own cum on his fingers. Obediently I licked the semen-slicked hand with my tongue, refusing to look at any of them. Most of them though, save Drake who was staring at me with his mouth open, were behind me. I didn't even want to see the look Elish was giving me, or his king.

"Yes, every little seed. Good cicaros clean up their own messes." Silas's voice was again the odd silk-draped purr. I could hear his heart beating wildly, enjoying every moment of this.

I could feel Silas's own sexual tension burning inside of him. I wondered if he was going to fuck me in front of Elish just to show that he could.

Though any ideas that that would happen were dismissed, when I was done he removed his fingers and handed me the red ball again.

"Now be a good boy, and take the fox outside. Luca… go with him. I'd like some time with my love alone."

I whirled around, my gaze going from Elish's controlled calm to Silas's brilliant piercing eyes. I wanted to scream and tell him Elish was mine and he couldn't have him, but my restraint stopped me. It didn't stop the space between my eyes from burning though.

Before I could shame myself further I took the ball, and stalked out of the apartment without another word.

I looked behind me and saw the blond-haired chimera eyeing the ball with his burnt orange eyes. They were still neurotically fixed on the red ball, as he obediently followed behind me.

"Master Jade, don't forget your jacket," Luca said. He jogged up to me and handed me my leather jacket with the fur trimmed hoody, the one Garrett had gotten me for my birthday. I took it with a mumbled thanks and all three of us went outside.

I noticed Drake out of the corner of my eye. He was staring at the ball, his tongue hanging out of his mouth like a dog, in between breaths of translucent cold air.

"Do you know how to talk?" I asked, watching his orange eyes travel up and down with the ball.

"Yeah, I can." His eyes rose again, and fell, then travelled from side to side as I waved the ball around. He was cute in a way, not just physically because, of course, every chimera was hot as fuck, but his mannerisms were like those of a golden retriever. He was docile and friendly and extremely ball crazy.

"Can you throw it, please?" Drake said politely; his muscles kept twitching every time I moved the ball in front of him.

Well, since he said please. I turned around and threw the ball as hard as I could into the courtyard. A blur of blond sped past me, and I watched the cicaro chimera dash off at top speed to catch the red ball.

The ball bounced several times before the cicaro lunged for it; he rolled around on the greywaste floor before rising, the ball stuck proudly between his smiling jaws.

It was really one of the oddest things I'd ever seen. The cicaro wasn't dressed in leather like me, but in black cargo pants and a zipped up cotton sweater, winter greywaste clothes he could freely roll around the dirt in. I on the other hand was not dressed for the weather. I still had my inside shoes on. I had stormed out before I'd had a chance to change them.

Drake stood up and shook his head and body like a dog, ash flying up into the air around him. He brought the ball back, and dropped it at my feet, before giving me a huge smile, which to my further amusement included his tongue lolling out again.

"Good boy!" Luca said beside me. I heard the sound of a wrapper and he broke off a piece of vanilla snack cake. Drake stuffed it into his mouth.

"He isn't a dog, Luca, he's a person," I said bitterly. I snatched the cake out of Luca's hand and handed the entire thing to Drake. "Do you want another one? We have lots, don't mind that dumbass."

"He likes being treated this way; he's used to it," Luca said defensively.

Drake took the cake without a word but his eyes were still looking at the ball.

"Do you want me to throw it again?" I asked.

Drake nodded, and swallowed the chemical cake. "Please?"

I had to smile back at this unbridled happiness. Maybe one day I could be as happy as this guy. He didn't seem to mind being Silas's pet, but then again he was another one of those mentally unstable chimeras, ones that might've been born with a screw or two loose. I had heard the exiled scientist Perish was even worse.

Drake nodded. "Yeah, yes... again. Can you throw it again?"

I raised my arm to throw it again but faked it this time; sure enough, like any dog, he started to run.

A moment later he stopped and looked back at me, scowling. I grinned and Luca held back a small chuckle. I threw it in a different direction and he dashed off to find it.

"See? He likes it, I'm not mean." It seemed Luca had been offended by my remark, whatever.

Drake came back panting and dropped the ball again; he bounced up and down on his boot-clad feet looking at me with excitement. "Again? Please?"

I picked up the drool covered ball and held it. "What are Silas and Elish doing in there?"

Drake stared at the ball. I raised it up to my eyes to try and make eye contact with him. His eyes were beautiful and large, but unfocused. I remembered I had seen him in Stadium though and he was focused then, so I copped it up to being the ball.

"Having sex probably," Drake replied in such a dismissive way it only added to the rot in my gut over leaving my master in there with that sociopathic pervert. I knew he was capable of defending himself, but it still sat badly with me. I saw Elish as mine now, even though I knew I was only a stupid worthless pet when it really boiled down to it. I didn't want anyone to touch him but me.

Especially considering Silas was his master, which opened up a few more doors with how they would be having sex. I had to make myself dismiss that thought before I went on a rampage. Silas might be quick but if I got the jump on him I could kill him quickly. I had gotten a few unsuspected blows on Elish before. Silas couldn't be that much better. And anyway, I was fifty-five percent Sanguine.

I threw the ball for Drake a few more times, before I sat down on the stairs in front of the house. I got another snake cake from Luca and started to eat it, looking at the jet plane. It was a bit smaller than the Falconer and was fifty or so feet from the entrance to the house.

Drake sat on the steps and put the ball beside him; he dug around his pocket and pulled out a hard tan cookie and offered it to me, before taking one himself to gnaw on.

I took a bite but it was rock hard, I guessed this was his human dog biscuit. My stomach was full of moths and butterflies churning in a bitter soup but I didn't want to refuse his offering to chew on things together. I sat beside him and bit down on the cookie

When Elish and Silas emerged from the front door I was tempted to remain sitting in quiet defiance, but I stood up, from automatic muscle memory than anything. I arrogantly kept chewing my biscuit though, noting that Elish's hair was damp; he had showered before coming out.

I stopped chewing though when I saw the red patch on the side of Elish's face, no doubt from being hit. My eyes automatically travelled down and, sure enough, a chimera love bite was covered by a bandage on his neck. I felt an uncontrollable amount of rage and jealousy at that.

"Oh look, our pets became friends. It's so cute when foxes and cats can get along." Silas smiled. Elish's stone-cold gaze didn't waver. It took everything I could do to hide my own.

"He has become obedient and makes friends easily now," Elish responded neutrally. He snapped his fingers and I obediently walked towards him, my body tense and full of rage.

Silas clipped Drake's silver leash onto his collar and ruffled his hair. "Did you have fun, Drakey? Did he throw the ball for you?" Silas turned around and gave both of us a smile. "Come home now, and I will summon you when it is time for his party. Goodbye, Elish, and do give that boy a haircut. He's getting rather shaggy and should look his best for his initiation. Come, Drako."

Before the plane door was even closed I started for the door, but as soon as I got two feet away I felt my chain go tight. Elish dragged me back to the steps until the plane was up in the air and disappearing out of sight.

When he made a motion to turn around I turned around quicker so I didn't have to look at him, with my mind still boiling over I stalked down the hallway and into the apartment. When we got in I clicked my leash off and stalked towards Luca's room.

"Jade," Elish called after me, he had that tone to his voice like he was calling a disobedient pet, where he carried the 'a' on my name longer than the other syllables. "Come here."

I froze and took a deep breath. "Can I *please* be alone right now?" I said through clenched teeth.

"No, sit beside me on the couch. I am behind on my work for today," Elish replied calmly.

I turned around and kicked off my dusty loafers and sat down on the couch. I picked up the remote and turned on a movie.

"If you think this immature little tantrum is going to get you anywhere you are in for a rude and painful surprise." The words hit my head like a hammer blow. I still stared forward. "You have nothing to be angry about, you did well with him, better than I expected. Though my pride in your advancement is being tainted by this pissy little attitude you're adopting."

My shoulders slumped. I stared at my socked feet.

"Are you going to tell me why you're acting this way, or are you going to just sulk around like some scorned damsel?"

I pushed down many urges inside of myself. "I'm not telling you anything, all you'll do is laugh at me, or beat on me for talking out of place," I replied, taking my tea from Luca and resting it on the coffee table beside his laptop.

He sipped his tea. "Then you must tell me now, I could use a laugh." His voice sounded just as bitter as mine.

My mind flared, thinking back to the both of them dismissing me to the courtyard, so Silas could do what he wanted to my master. It enraged me that he had that power over him. Elish was all-powerful, he was a deity in my mind, someone untouchable, there was no one better than him and here that slimeball was touching him and doing what he wanted to him. It was wrong and it filled me with so much rage I wanted to throw the fucking tea mug against the wall.

My voice dropped, as if my brain thought that if I talked quietly maybe the weight of my own words would lessen. I knew what I was going to say next was going to get me unconscious. "No one is allowed to touch you but me, especially not *him*."

Elish smirked, seemingly amused by my soured words. "Oh? Am I being possessed again? You do have such a jealous streak."

"You're mine," I said through clenched teeth, "and if he wasn't our king I would rip out his throat with my teeth. The way he talks to you makes my blood boil and the thought of him touching you enrages me. Funny enough for you?"

"Very… though I would keep this new found blood rage buried deep inside of you. If I have slightest notion that you might open that feral mouth of yours in front of him, I will break your jaw before you get the chance," Elish responded back coldly.

But I didn't care. "The only reason I will is because you told me to. I don't have any problem taking him on; I'm not scared of him. I'm fucking taller than he is anyway; I can take him. Where did he fucking grow up? Hollywood? He's a shithead."

Elish shook his head. "No, Silas did not grow up with the same luxuries as me and my brothers. He had a sad life, worse than yours, and from it he managed to do wonderful and terrible things all from the powers of his own mind. Do not judge him so carelessly, especially over things you do not understand. All in all, it is best you fear him."

"Fuck no, I'm not scared of him. Fuck him!" I snapped.

"I am sure he cares little for the opinion of the most pathetic chimera brought out of his steel mother, though if you prefer I will ask him." Elish gave me a dangerous look. "I have heard enough of your disrespect of our master, Jade. I let you get it out of your system and now I suggest you move on, lest I regret giving you that small amount of slack."

I pressed on though, unaware or perhaps uncaring that his voice was thick with warning. "He wants us to be as miserable as he is, he was a cowardly bitch before the Fallocaust and a cowa-"

I should've expected the backhand across my face, but I still didn't brace for it. My head snapped to the left and I almost rolled off the couch, the next one brought my head to the right knocking the vision temporarily out of me.

Elish's voice cut through the senses my brain was desperately trying to gather. "If you ever disrespect our master like this again, I will make it so you are unable to ever say a word out of line, slumrat."

I felt the blood rush through me, his striking me only made the anger inside me multiply. I made a deadly mistake in that moment as I glared at him, not dropping my gaze, only challenging it. "He is *your* master, not mine and I am not a slumrat. I am a chimera, one who can match *your* powers, Silas's powers, and any powers I feel like absorbing. One day you might bow to me!" I snapped.

Then I realized I was an idiot. He gave me one searing look, and I was out of there, wondering what the fuck I was on and why I was this stupid when I had been so obedient.

He grabbed onto my collar and yanked me back, in return I whirled around and went to touch his neck, my hands vibrating with tremors of electricity. He grabbed my hand and with a scream from my lips, he

491

electrocuted me.

I matched his own electric currents with mine, though the pain split every vein in my body open. I pushed on though, and challenged him with such fervour I felt like I was signing my death certificate.

Suddenly every single light bulb burst around us, and I felt the hair on my neck and sideburns prickle and rise. I fixed my eyes on his with my teeth clenched, forcing every bit of myself into matching every rise of electricity he pulled. Not out of defiance, but out of fear that the moment I withdrew he would electrocute me to death.

I screamed out of rage as he started to gain on me, our clasped hands radiating a white heat that I knew wasn't just my own aura reading. I forced another wave of energy through me but he was eating me alive; his eyes blazing so much raw energy they glowed in the darkness around us.

"You really think this is my strength, slumrat? I could make tea right now and still match this pitiful trickle of energy you've scavenged," Elish's low voice growled. I was surprised how calm he was. I was clenching my teeth and screaming, he was standing over me in confident and cold silence. "You've gotten too big for your shoes, stray. Apparently, instead of the usual self-loathing you seem to think you're now entitled to something."

I shrieked and felt my knees turn to rubber as he showed me just how much he was holding back. A spine-ripping electricity shot through me, blowing out every nerve and to my horror and humiliation, making piss start stream down my leg. I keeled over and threw up, a foot away from his feet.

But Elish had no sympathy. I saw his white loafers below the puddle of vomit. "If anything, learning your genetics makes you less entitled; you're a pathetic excuse for a chimera and a cicaro. I would take Silas to my bed over you any day, you disgusting filth."

I looked up at him, my lips trying to purse the retort my mind was already delivering.

"You're lying, and you know it, you like me, I am special to you. You hate him and I know you do, admit it!" I cried, hating how hurt those words had made me. He was lying, I knew he was.

My heart broke when he chuckled, then with a kick I fell backwards and onto the floor. I gasped and tried to catch my breath, my lungs fried and contracting from the pulses of electricity.

I looked up as he turned his back to me to walk to the study room.

I suddenly felt like I was in Moros again and he was turning his back on me, leaving me to go back to the slums, even after he had said I would be his forever.

He was dismissing me like a piece of trash. I couldn't... I couldn't go back there, I couldn't feel those emotions again. They had ripped my guts out. Elish hadn't been pissed at me like this in what seemed like forever. I was quickly realizing I didn't have the tools to handle it anymore.

"Elish!" I screamed, struggling to stand but I only fell back down on my knees. He kept walking, illuminated by several small candles Luca was lighting in the kitchen.

"ELISH!" I shrieked, my breath becoming short. I brought up our auras to see him better; I saw his colours swirling around him, wrapped ribbons of borealis mixed in with mine.

I closed my eyes and rose to my feet. I stalked over to him, still seeing the colours, and gathered up every ounce of my energy. "TALK TO ME!"

Suddenly Elish stopped dead in his tracks. My hand was outstretched in front of me, desperate and pleading. I felt a wave of relief wash through me and with that small act of recognition my body untensed and our auras disappeared.

Then he turned around slowly and looked down at me. I, the mess I was, looking up at him; emotions pouring out of me like the piss running down my leg.

My heart palpitated in my chest as he advanced on me. I shifted away from him and screamed from fear as he came closer.

When he grabbed my collar and started dragging me towards the bedroom I kicked and screamed with every fiber in my being.

I heard the rattling of the chains clip me into place. In response I thrashed with all my strength, the primal fear boiling over and pooling an unbridled terror inside of me.

I started to cry when his hands undressed me, and when I lunged to bite him I felt a blow on my face.

My head rolled back, and once again my mind was full of recollections, only fuelling the anxiety and panic I felt knowing what he was about to do. I managed one more scream and one more thrash of my legs as he pulled off my leather pants.

Then he descended and the cobra struck, though there was no toying with the taut coils of my body for his own pleasure; there was no coaxing my sensitive areas to perform for him again and again – this wasn't for this pleasure, it was for my punishment.

Elish thrusted himself roughly inside of me, and held my arms back with an iron grip. I screamed, begged, and fought but he took me anyway, drawing nothing out of me but my own agonizing voice, cracking and breaking under my despair and pain.

"Turn the light on," his emotionless but cruel voice said. I sobbed as my shame was illuminated as clear as day.

I looked over and saw Luca watching us, his hands behind his back and the cat ears resting on his head; he was watching obediently and I knew he had been commanded to. There was no way he would be in this room otherwise.

I cried out, hot tears dripping down the creases in my agonized face. I couldn't believe he was making the sengil watch me in this state. It was more than humiliating, it was an inhuman cruelty that only a chimera could think up.

"Go ahead, Luca. If his body pleases your eye, let him see it. He's just a bonafide chimera whore anyway; I'm sure he's used to it," Elish said. He pressed his hand down on my neck and I felt my breath choke as my Adam's apple pushed against my wind pipe. With his grip fully controlling my neck, he turned and made me watch Luca take his dick out of his pants and start to stroke himself off.

"Put it to his mouth. In this bedroom, at this time, you outrank him."

Elish pressed my head down onto the bed and I saw Luca holding a half-hard dick in his hands. His hands were trembling; the sengil's whole body was shaking in fear.

Elish tightened his grip on my jaw and I heard his hot breath against my ear. "You outrank no one, you are better than no one." I opened my mouth under his tight grasp and the sengil put his cock into it. With the blood roaring in my ears and the own pain from Elish penetrating me taking over, I sucked it... like the soulless shell I had become.

Luca let out a small moan; he put a knee on the bed to position himself before making me take his entire cock in my mouth. In response,

Elish released my jaw and grabbed my hair, pushing my face into Luca's groin.

Luca's moans mixed in with Elish's heavy breathing, his dick twinging and throbbing inside of my mouth. He was terrified, but there was no denying he liked it. I could feel how much he liked it with every twitch of his cock.

I muffled my own cries through Elish's intense thrusts, gasping and groaning with Luca's dick dripping precum on my tongue. I wanted to scream, thrash, and bite but there was no longer any will for me to do so; it had been eaten alive by the humiliation.

Finally the sengil came, and to further hammer in his cruelty, Elish grabbed onto the base of Luca's dick and withdrew it mid-cum, making the sengil's seed shoot all over my face. Thick spurts shot out with vigour, an intense orgasm from a man who didn't often get this sort of attention.

Luca withdrew and I could hear him panting.

"Sit on the chair; do what you like but do not cum again," the master ordered.

I stared forward, cum dripping off of my face, before I felt Elish's breath on my ear again.

"You're nothing, Jade, nothing, and you will always be nothing. Never forget your place, you were born a slumrat and that is how you will die, when I decide it is time for you to die. You are my pet, my property, your soul, your body and your breath belong to me, am I understood?"

His hand, now gripping my neck, became tighter, making my breathing a choked rasp as he started to pound me harder and harder. I needed to gasp, and I needed to cry but he was cutting off every bit of oxygen.

"Yes," I managed to croak, the cum dripping into my mouth as I spoke. "I'm yours."

I wheezed and coughed, opening my mouth to try and suck in any air I could swallow, but his hands were so tight my chest was on fire, my body was on fire. He was ripping himself in and out of me without restraint or mercy.

And Luca… the sengil had his pants entirely off now, his hand rapidly moving between his legs and his eyes fixed on me in shameful lust as Elish thrust into me. He wasn't done, I knew he wasn't. This opportunity might never come again for the timid sengil.

I closed my eyes and tried to move myself out of the awkward position Elish had me in, one knee partially up with my other leg practically pinned underneath him. But he tightened his grip, putting so much pressure on my legs I thought they would snap. He wouldn't even let me adjust myself to make his thrusts easier. It made me scream in frustration.

My head dropped as he smacked me again, the force knocking the sense out of me and laying me still. The fight died inside of me after that, and with a painful groan, I gave in.

Still, even though he had broken me, he didn't stop. I only cried silently to myself, trying to close my eyes so I didn't have to see Luca, but the sengil was there whenever a particularly painful jab brought my reality snapping back to me.

At one point I even lifted my hand to try and electrocute Elish, like I had done a few weeks ago, but in my weakened state it was nothing but a static shock. I whimpered and dropped my hand, and let him continue his violation of my body; feeling the cum inside of me more and more. Luca's cum was also still dripping down my face, the only signal that time was passing.

Then the last humiliating blow, hours into his first initial thrust inside of me. Elish took himself out of me and said to Luca, "Clean him when you're done with him. Do what you will, for as long as the mood takes you. He will not fight."

I closed my eyes as the door slammed, hoping beyond hope the sengil would leave me alone. But he crawled on top of me.

"Luca?" I whimpered. I had already blown him, why did he have to make it worse?

The sengil was breathing heavily. "I'm – I'm sorry, Master Jade."

A moment later there was a familiar pressure behind me.

CHAPTER 29

THE NIGHTMARES THAT NIGHT WERE HORRIBLE, BUT I had been battling my own mental demons for too long to do anything about them now. It wasn't like I was used to feeling the eerie horrors of Silas's aura creep into me, I was just too defeated and tired to care. What once would have me running to Elish for the protection of his crystal aura, now had me giving in to the colourless void without a single breath of resistance. I let it stick to my bones and I let it unwind the tight strands of my body to infect deeper and deeper.

What did it matter?

I stayed in the spare room until Luca came and got me in the morning.

He didn't make eye contact with me; he felt ashamed of what he had done and I was glad.

Luca packed our belongings, and with trembling hands, I served breakfast and tea. Elish acted his cold and unemotional self, giving me nothing but a passing glance when he told me what tea he wanted. He had returned to his normal routine as though nothing had happened, though I expected nothing more or less from him.

I sat and ate quietly, my face swollen and aching and covered in a black bruise that outlined the normal shadow in my jawline.

Though it was my body that ached the most. It was hard to walk, my legs were cramped and tight from the awkward angles Elish had fucked me. But what was new? I was a whore and that was what whores did.

When Elish was done, I rose and took his plate and helped Luca pack up the rest of my things, making sure there wasn't anything else I was forgetting. I didn't know the next time I would be back here, never probably. Why would he ever give me this sort of reprieve again? I didn't deserve it, and if he did give me another vacation from Skyfall, I would only piss all over the gift like I had done this time.

I was an idiot and I deserved all of this and more, but it didn't make me despise him less. I might've deserved it but the shit he said to me had stung. I thought I was more important to him than that. Important enough to not bring Luca in and make me blow him and have him fuck me, just to prove how pathetic I was. That was a new sort of low for him.

I just wasn't used to this treatment anymore; I didn't have the hard nose of a Morosian, or the iron will of a slumrat cicaro. I felt like an abused boyfriend and I hated myself for that.

Finally it was time to leave. Elish clipped on my leash and I took my share of the bags; Elish not carrying a single one, unlike when we had first arrived. Somehow it was funny to me that I felt like I was leaving even more miserable than when I had arrived. Though making me happy had never been the point; the point had been to make an obedient cicaro again and now I was. My mental health was the last thing on Elish's list.

When we were in the air, I did the only thing I could do to try and escape the dark cloud over my head. I drew up the hood on my jacket and closed my eyes, tuning out everything around me.

I felt a hand on my shoulder and a shake. I opened my eyes and saw the cityscape of Skyfall in front of me. I rose obediently and grabbed my bags before heading towards the door leading to inside the apartment.

As soon as I was in the apartment, I went to the only place I felt safe. Going back to old habits I dropped the bags, grabbed a blanket and stuffed myself into Elish's closet with the door closed tight.

I was relieved when Elish didn't come and force me out into the apartment; I wanted to be left alone in my silence and darkness. Undisturbed and where I had felt most safe, where I could see every wall around me and feel the soft confines of a small space. I didn't know the mechanics behind it, but being in a shut in space in complete darkness made me calmer.

Sometime later I woke up to yelling. Curious, I opened the door to the closet and tuned my hearing to the angry voice coming from the living room.

It was Joaquin, he sounded pissed off. I didn't hear anything more until the distinct biting voice of Quin said loudly, "Elish, he is *not worth it!*"

His tone brought a curl to my lips, but a moment later I remembered who I was, how pathetic and useless a chimera I was and I agreed with him in silent derision. I wasn't worth the trouble Elish had gone through to keep me. I wasn't worth anything. Kerres didn't like who I had become, and Elish didn't like me either. No one fucking did.

"You're making a fool of yourself, Elish! Ditch him before Silas brings you both to your knees!"

The back of my eyes burned and I wiped them before wrapping my arms around myself. As if hoping they could act like a barrier to my own loathsome thoughts.

It was a solid hour before I heard the apartment door close. I tried to go back to sleep but I wasn't sleepy anymore.

Eventually I got up and walked out into the apartment to face my reality, though in so many ways I just wanted to hide from it.

Elish gave me a glance, then he went back to his laptop. "Overheard my dear brother Joaquin, did we?"

I gave a half-hearted shrug. "He didn't say anything that wasn't true, did he?"

"I will decide if you are worth it, Cicaro," Elish said icily, but I caught a fleeting vein of warmth in his tone. "I suspect that Quin just needs a cicaro to keep his bed warm. He's a miserably little cuss but he has softness in him when no one is watching. Perhaps in time you can help me find him a pet to coo over. I am sure that would amuse you as much as it would me."

Help him? I was confused at what he was saying and the tone. I had expected him to be a lot colder towards me for a while longer, but I guess he never did what I expected.

"I'm not good at anything," I said quietly. I sighed and looked around before spotting my dog cage, still set up but now in a corner of the room.

I walked over to it and crawled inside.

My emotions crumpled as I heard him chuckle. "You're so dramatic."

"You hate me, Kerres hated me, your family hates me; though not as much as I hate myself," I said quietly, though I knew he would be able to hear me. "I can see why you threw me back to Moros. I can't stand myself either."

There was silence and then he spoke. "You are a jealous, possessive little worm who needs to be beaten down to remember his place, and I speak the truth when I say you must fear Silas. But I know that you do, your outburst was driven by emotion and jealousy, not a realistic bravery towards the king. Needless to say, you have been disciplined and you have submitted to my liking. So, you are forgiven for it. Now come sit beside me; you can watch me lose a game of solitaire, or perhaps indulge me with this idea I have regarding Joaquin."

I looked at him sitting on the couch with his laptop on his lap, always my graceful king and my master. He was looking at me with his piercing violet eyes, as if asking why I hadn't moved yet.

I stared at him dumbly, as if he had just spoken another language. In no alternate universe did I expect him to forgive me, or invite me to sit beside him. I… I wasn't worth that.

But I rose, because my heart still and would always ache for his affection. I stood and walked over to him, my shoulders slumped and my head hung in submission.

I sat down beside him and leaned against his arm; in response he put it around me. My heart did a flip-flop in my chest and automatically unclenched under his aura. So to further prove I was worthy of this attention, I indulged the idea he had spoken about.

"Joaquin's aura is light, but at the same time a bold, purply-blue that flickers like flames. He would be easy to match, but he wouldn't do well with someone like me."

"Oh?" Elish drew me closer to him and my heart swelled inside my chest; my body had been aching for a soft touch since that horrible punishment. I soaked up his affection like a thirsty sponge. "Do go on."

I remembered the aura of Joaquin Dekker. I had met him several times at Elish's council meetings and he had come to Olympus many times seeking Elish's counsel. "He wouldn't do well with some snarling Morosian; he'd need a soft timid-type he could spend time coaxing out from under the bed, someone love-starved in a submissive way. With someone like me he would just get offended by their dank presence and cast them aside. Quin hates filth, that's why he hates me and hates you owning me."

Elish patted my head. "Yes, I realized that some time ago, I believe you are correct. He would do well with a meek boy, a pure, tender creature that has been damaged but is not rotten. The complete opposite of you, very good, Cicaro. We will keep an eye out during our walks."

I smiled and, of course, he noticed it. "Such a proud smile you bear so freely."

"I like being included in your seed planting," I said. "Even if my greatest achievement is being your matchmaking service."

He scratched my head, but didn't say anything else.

Two months passed and things went normally, or what was normal in Elish's house. My wounds healed as they always did with the help of Lyle's Skytech medicine, and though he still avoided eye contact, Luca slowly forgave himself for not being able to control himself back in the greyrift mansion. I fully took advantage of his guilt though; he did everything I asked without so much of a mouth twitch and was even more patient when he taught me guitar.

Elish was very busy so vicariously I was busy too; he had a lot of work to catch up on since he had been gone for almost a month and it seemed like everyone wanted to have meetings with him, from roads needing to be repaired, to funding for the precinct, even family nagging him about plans for Skyday approaching in a few months, that was Garrett mostly. He had been visiting Elish at least twice a week for chess to make up for the time he lost.

Today found me leaning up against Elish as he tapped away on his laptop, two days until my birthday conveniently, though Elish had said nothing about it and neither did I.

I was raising up Jade the charizard, trying to get him to level one hundred, with Garrett the blastoise since I had needed a Pokémon to do HM moves.

In the months since our return to Skyfall I was feeling okay and at terms with my chimera status; if anything it had been a boon since I had returned. The word had gotten out and people were giving me even better presents now, and I was able to keep more of them than before. I think Elish wanted to put some more fat on my bones; he believed that my physical appearance was a direct reflection on him and me looking scrawny, bruised, and half-dead didn't make him look good.

It also was motivating me to better myself. Knowing I didn't have slum shit running through my veins had filled me with confidence, and in all honesty it also gave me a sense of belonging. I had a family now. Silas might've killed my mom, and Kerres might've killed himself but in return I had this group of twenty or so crazy bastards that I knew would look out for me from now on. I might be the lowest on the totem pole but at least I was on the totem pole, and Drake seemed happy being a subordinate.

I yawned and put my Game Boy down. I closed my eyes and made myself comfortable on Elish's shoulder, though it wasn't that comfortable a place to lay down; he had no problem moving his hand away if he needed something, even if it meant waking me up.

I was just about to fall asleep when his remote phone rang. He got up without a word and took the call outside. I took this chance to steal the warmth left behind from where he had been sitting and dozed off.

I woke up to the sliding glass door being slammed. I watched him walk in and to my surprise he slammed the phone down on the cabinet near the kitchen. He looked pissed.

"We'll be leaving soon for our get together with the family. I would suggest a shower and your best cicaro clothing," Elish said, his voice low and bitter. "We will be eating there too."

"Now?" I whispered. I could feel the colour draining from my face.

"Now, do it." Elish's voice was steel, and I knew better than to argue. I rose to my feet and went into the bedroom I shared with Elish. I did what he asked and as I showered I saw his clouded silhouette in front of the bathroom mirror. His moves were angry and he was tense; just watching him made the fear well up inside of me too. He left before I was done, slamming the door as he did.

I dried myself off and fixed myself up, wanting to dawdle but I sped up to avoid him getting pissed off at me. He looked like he was going to break someone in half... what was going to happen at this thing?

Elish was standing by the door talking on his remote phone. He had changed into a black vest over a white-collared shirt, no cloak or anything just his white duster in his hands. He had put new earrings in too, silver hoops with blue gems moulded into the small links. He looked nice; his hair shined against the fireplace across the room, and I could see flickers against his pale skin.

He nodded at me then took something out of his pocket. "Open your mouth."

I obeyed him, confused as to why he was giving me the metal teeth implants again and even more worried too. Not a protest left me though and I stood still as he pushed the steel teeth into my canines.

"Silas does not know about your knack of absorbing abilities, therefore I am telling you now, no matter what happens not a single jolt of electricity comes from your body, am I understood?" he said coldly. "I expect complete control, I expect stoicism, I expect you to act like a chimera and not a disobedient brat. Do not disappoint me, Cicaro."

I nodded, my shoulders slumped, realizing for the first time that this wasn't going to be some ordinary get together, and that he could possibly be taking me there to hurt me. The cold realization brought a sourness to my stomach, and I felt the first churn of anxiety.

"Is he going to kill me?" I asked quietly. "Is this some sort of blood sacrifice or something?"

"No."

"Is he doing this because it's my birthday soon?"

"It's your birthday today, did you not read the papers I let you see?" I slunk down. I hadn't noticed, but I guess it made sense. They couldn't have given me to my mother the day she had the dead baby.

So I was seventeen today…

I nodded and said nothing else. He let that go and didn't press it further.

The car took us to Alegria, driving through wet empty streets and the covered carts of determined merchants selling their products.

It was a dreary day and it reflected my mood; everything was overcast, grey, and dark, like the shadows over my head and the demons that were constantly on my back.

It was a long and quiet trip. I ran my tongue over my teeth trying to get used to them again, and also wondering why Elish had given them back to me. He had said that Silas wasn't going to kill me so perhaps that was it, it was my party after all, they couldn't beat the party guest to a pulp, what good would that do? Anyway, I hadn't done anything wrong, not to them anyway and Elish would never punish me in front of his family – most of them he didn't even like.

I stepped out into the rain and looked up at the steely sky; a moment later a blue fabric infiltrated my vision and I saw Elish was holding an umbrella over my head. Surprisingly, he let the rain fall on his hair and walked with me towards the doors of Alegria.

I stayed close to him and not just because he had my leash in his hand; it was because he was the only one who I knew would help me in there if something went wrong, if this was just another one of Silas's cruel games, like back in Stadium last year.

I didn't know the king well enough to gauge whether this was the same or not, but with King Silas I was learning to stay on my toes.

The thiens took one look at us and stepped aside, their guns always in hand and their dead eyes always a constant forward glare. They were ready and willing to lay their own lives down for an immortal king. Ellis's thiens and Kessler's army were forces not to be reckoned with.

Elish let us off on the fourth floor and we stepped out onto a large open hallway. As soon as the metal paneled doors separated I could hear the voices and feel the energy of chimeras.

I stayed behind Elish as he led me down the hallway, twice the width of Olympus and covered in pre-Fallocaust art work, from sculptures to statues to paintings, all restored to their former beauty.

This place gave off an elegance that was even more royal than Elish's skyscraper. The paint was trimmed with carved wood and the lower half of the hallway walls new wallpaper, floral patterns mostly blues but some greens. It smelled nice too, but I was now used to the smell of cleaning agents and air fresheners. The musty, sour smell of decay in Moros seemed farther away than the fading memories of my dead ex-boyfriend.

Like a lamb being led to slaughter, I walked behind Elish. His coat had been handed off to a sengil and I could only see the back of his vest; he looked so different now.

I found myself wanting to ask him for reassurance, just a small comment to keep me going, but we were too close to them and I knew he would never do it.

No, now was the time for me to act like the chimera I was and to greet them like family, not an inside pet put in front of a horde of junkyard dogs.

Then we turned and he entered the room. There were tables laid in a semicircle, with the middle cleared of everything but a red Persian rug. Each table had four chairs and on each of those chairs sat a chimera, some I had never seen before.

"There he is, finally, one minute late on my watch." I heard Garrett laugh over the low buzzing of voices throughout the room.

I spotted him as he pointed to his watch, a golf club in his hand, shooting balls off the roof again I guess. I had heard him mention before that there was a small section of turf on that roof for people to shoot golf balls off.

Garrett got up and in quick succession all the other chimeras and a few pets did the same; they all bowed to the both of us and we both bowed back.

When Elish put a hand up everyone quieted down, so quickly it was like there was an invisible remote in his hand only he could control.

"Everyone, this is my cicaro and our newest brother, Jade Dekker." Elish's voice pierced the quiet but electrified air.

Everyone started clapping for me. I had never had applause for anything in my life. I didn't know what I was supposed to do, so I stood there like an idiot and gave everyone a smile and a small hello.

Elish sat us down beside Garrett and motioned a sengil over, he said something to him and he went off to fill his order.

I saw Elish glance around the room, before addressing Garrett. "He hasn't shown up yet?"

Garrett had a wine glass in his hands; he shook his head and rolled a cigarette over to me. Half the people in there seemed to be smoking; I could see an air vent above us, a small wisp of cobweb blowing with the intake; sucking up as much of the cigarette and cigar smoke as it could.

"No, he will be soon, getting everything ready I suppose."

"Have you heard anything else?"

"Nope, you know I would tell you if I had."

Elish nodded. He reached into his vest pocket and put a blue lighter on the table beside him. I gave him a thank you and lit the cigarette. It was an opiate one to my relief; I had stopped taking the Suboxone last month and my nerves were screaming for something to keep my body together. All of these chimeras in such a small space were overloading my senses, each of them powerful and overbearing in their own way.

I looked around as Elish talked and saw quite a few of them I didn't recognize; though I wasn't surprised, there were still some names in my black book I hadn't filled in. One of them was probably Sidonius who was the chief medical chimera, and Nero, who was a part of the first generation.

Jack was also one I hadn't met, but I was guessing he was the creepy-looking guy talking to a nervous-looking red-haired sengil. He had hair the colour of silvery ash and black eyes, a thin face and… yep, I watched as he smiled, he had the creepy teeth too.

He must be a part of Sanguine's generation, another sharp-toothed nutcase.

Which reminded me… I glanced around but I didn't see Sanguine; he was probably with his king. I wondered if he missed me, we'd had some interesting times together. If there was one thing I missed about my time in Moros it was the two days of killing I had spent with Sanguine, and well… the sex had been awesome.

"Elish, it's been awhile, how is your new little project treating you?" I glanced over and saw a man with short blond hair looking at us with a smile. He was leaning backwards in his chair so he could see us properly; it hovered on two legs as he kept himself steady with a foot on the table.

I had met this one before and didn't mind him, his name was Teaguae, another chimera on the council though a mortal one. He was in his early thirties but showed his age very well. From his appearance I guessed he came from the same stock and possibly the same generation as Lycos.

"Just fine, Teag, he's made great strides and has come into his own quite nicely," Elish said casually. "Though I am looking forward to putting this stupid tradition behind us."

Teaguae laughed and tipped his wine glass back, before he slid his foot off of the table slamming his chair back onto four legs. I heard it scrape and a moment later he was handing an envelope to me.

"There you go, little man, this will take the sting out of it, seventeen is a good age. Make sure you get something from every one of these cheap bastards, and don't let your master take them away from you." Teaguae winked and left just before Elish hid the envelope in his pocket. I opened my mouth to protest but I remembered his words to keep myself stoic and maintain some sort of maturity, so I let it slide. I was curious to see what was inside though.

Teaguae was the first person to give me something but not the last. I received more and more gifts from each of the chimeras. Some of them were just envelopes and some came in boxes; each one that arrived was given to a sengil to take down to the car. I guess it wasn't tradition to open them now which was disappointing. This was turning into a nice welcome to the family birthday party. As long as I kept my aura reading offline and drank, my senses didn't bother me too much.

The room continued to buzz, like a family reunion of brothers who hadn't seen each other in years though since they all lived in one city I think going a week or two without seeing one another seemed like years; all of them seemed really close.

This was a side of the chimeras that I hadn't seen from the news; they had a real sense of brotherhood and though Elish looked like he would rather be pushing safety pins through his eyes, everyone else seemed to be enjoying themselves.

Even I was starting to enjoy myself; the snack food which kept being put out in front of us was good quality and the wine tasted great too. It was bloodwine, Elish's favourite, though as the iron taste filled my mouth I wondered just whose blood I was drinking.

After a while I was settled in and having a good time, chatting with the pet at the table beside me who I recognized as Tyan.

He was Artemis's pet and a cute thing at that, with short brown hair and deep hazel eyes. He was timid and friendly and didn't mind talking to me, though Artemis seemed just as uptight and disgruntled as Elish did.

Elish did say those twins had a lot of the same engineering; I wondered if he had inherited Elish's hatred for social gatherings and parties. They didn't like being forced to have fun; it seemed like Elish's life goal sometimes was to avoid anything that would make him let his stoic countenance slip. He always had to maintain his steeled air of confidence and grace, and letting loose at a family gathering would squash that in record time.

I sunk into my chair and sipped my full cup, munching on partially dried meats, soft cheese, dessert bars, and pastries. Elish, as usual, was only talking to Garrett, though he made polite small talk whenever a chimera came to give me a present and properly introduce themselves.

The atmosphere was buzzing and laid back, full of laughter and plumes of green cigarette smoke. The green was for cocaine and I wasn't surprised; alcohol and coke had always been my favourite party mix too.

I went to take another drink but a hand stopped me.

"That's enough for now," Elish said. He switched glasses and put his glass of tea in front of me instead.

I took a sip, though tea was the complete opposite of what the mood in this large room called for.

I took another sip and went to set the teacup down when everyone fell silent. I looked up towards the door and felt my heart jump into my throat.

"Our king has finally graced us with his presence! Come sit by me, you old bastard!" Garrett raised his glass; he was already half-cut.

King Silas laughed, a real laugh which I found odd since I had only heard his sinister bone-chilling laugh. He was handed a glass which he rose to Garrett. "I see we need to get you a bouncer again, love. Someone take his wine away before this party turns into an intervention again."

"Eat me!" Garrett raised his glass again. Everyone laughed and Silas shook his head, before slowly making his way down the semicircle tables, Sanguine and Drake following closely behind making small conversation too.

The both of them were dressed in their finest. Sanguine was wearing coat tails and his red bow tie. Drake was dressed in tight leather pants like mine with laces crisscrossed through silver ringlets going up the sides. His shirt was also similar to the clothing Elish made me wear: a leather vest open and revealing his washboard abs, and a spiked collar with a silver disk attached to a link.

Silas was dressed well too, in a grey open blazer with a tight white t-shirt underneath and black slacks. His hair was gelled, accentuating every blond wave falling over his white face and framing those two eerie green eyes.

They looked relaxed as everyone did, it seemed only the pets and sengils were nervous around him. They were used to Silas though; they had been raised under his feet or had been brought in like me, they were used to him and his games. I was the newest one getting broken in.

Would I get used to it too? I hoped I lived long enough to get the chance.

I felt the hair on the back of my neck prickle as Silas, Sanguine, and Drake finally made it to our table. I stared at my cup of tea as Elish greeted him politely.

"I'm about to start, do you have any requests, lovely?" I could barely hear Silas as he leaned down and whispered into Elish's ear. "Anything you want to ask me specifically?"

Nausea creeped into my stomach as Elish's face darkened. "Be careful."

Be careful? I swallowed a sack of butterflies as Silas laughed and whispered something into his ear too low for me to hear. Then with a pat on Elish's shoulder he moved on to talk to Garrett and the other five chimeras to my right.

Sanguine leaned down and licked my neck. I reached around and punched him in the arm playfully, he laughed and shook my shoulders. "I missed you, mihi. They're starting to leave their houses at night since we stopped; do promise me we will resurrect him one day, Shadow Killer?"

I smiled, thinking back to those fond memories. "I'd love that."

Sanguine ruffled my hair and walked past me and Drake came chewing on a biscuit. He grinned at me and offered me his half-chewed biscuit with his tongue lolling out. I shook my head with a smirk and reached up to grab the silver tag on his collar. I had noticed it when we were in the greywastes but I had never gotten a chance to read it.

Drake Dekker
Do not feed.

I couldn't help but chuckle. "Why can't we feed you?"

"I eat too much and then I throw up," Drake answered with a polite smile and with a slobbery lick on my cheek he moved on with Silas and Sanguine.

"That is why he gets those hard biscuits," Tyan leaned over and whispered to me. "Because they takes him a long time to eat. He's trashed his teeth multiple times so they just kill him and grow them back; sometimes they give him implants like yours but an entire set."

I cocked an eyebrow and shook my head. "Do you ever find it weird that they just kill themselves so easily? 'Aw, I have the flu… better overdose on fucking morphine and get rid of it.'"

Tyan gave a nervous giggle looking around the semicircle of wolves to see if one of them caught my comment but everyone was chattering away. He turned back when we both heard someone clear their throat in front of us.

I straightened up in my chair and looked forward, seeing the well-dressed King Silas smiling at all of his creations with a beaming glint. Just like when Elish had raised a hand, everyone fell silent immediately.

"It is always a pleasure when we come up with an excuse to meet with each other, get wasted, do lines off of hot boys, and indulge ourselves without the scathing judgmental glares of the insects below us." King Silas smiled, everyone around us clapped and raised glasses. "Though this time we have some business to take care of, many things actually."

Silas held out his hand and I saw Sanguine take out a brick of something out of his bag; my eyes widened as big as saucers as I realized it was a giant fucking brick of coke.

"Do not even think about it," Elish growled beside me under his breath. I sighed and watched him slam it onto the table in front of Quin and Apollo; two sengils appeared behind them and slashed the brick open with exacto knives. "Stay beside me and stay as silent and quiet as you can."

I looked over at Elish, but he wouldn't turn to me, he was staring forward, his hand clenched hard around my former wine glass. A small eclipse of black in an otherwise cheerful party, he certainly was hating every moment of this. Maybe he hated social gatherings and having a good time but I was a slumrat and this was my biggest dream.

"Jade." I felt my leash tighten, he pulled me towards him. "Remember what I told you, stay stoic, in control, calm and collected no matter what happens. You are a chimera, they're all watching you."

I tried to look at him but he roughly jerked my leash to keep me from acknowledging him speaking to me. "What's going to happen…?"

He didn't answer. I tried to shed the growing sense of foreboding and instead watched Joaquin Dekker take a line of coke off a sengil's exacto knife.

He was the chimera I was currently trying to match with someone, though it might be difficult. He always seemed to have a permanent stick up his ass and never missed an opportunity to be rude to me. Though now that I watched him it was probably from being fucked on coke all the time, he was devouring the powder like it was icing sugar.

As if to confirm this theory I watched Quin rub his nose and slam his hand on the table, shaking his head in the same common reaction that everyone had when they did a big hit of blow.

The brick got passed around, and I found it a bit funny that the sengils knew enough to not offer Elish any. It wasn't like he was clean and sober though. I had seen him put that baggy into his coffee cup on more than one occasion, so I knew he had done drugs, I guessed just not in front of people that could judge him.

I leaned back in my chair and tried to not have fun like Elish had commanded me to. Even when I saw Ares's pet Trig start to ride up and down on Ares with nothing but a cloak covering his shame I didn't make a comment. I didn't even point it out. I think at this point everything I saw had probably been going on at parties since there had been enough of them to throw parties.

Sure enough, no one batted an eye at this display, and after everyone was loaded on coke several other chimeras started putting pets and sengils on their laps or between their legs. Even Tyan had disappeared under the coffee table for a few minutes and emerged wiping his mouth with a sheepish grin on his face. I shuddered at the thought of what Elish would do to me if I even attempted to do the same.

Then Sanguine walked into the semicircle and raised his hand up into the air. I was amused to see that he was wearing a top hat to match his coat tails and bow tie, and funnily enough he held a wand. I realized as everyone quieted down that he was dressed as a magician.

"Gentlemen and gentlepets!" Sanguine declared. I laughed at the last part, typical Sanguine. "Your culture based on science disgusts me! I am here to show you that magic exists!" Sanguine waved his wand and out popped a fake plastic flower.

"Boo!" Grant hollered. He was another good-natured one; he was in charge of the factories and economics in the greywastes, he wasn't in Skyfall often.

Sanguine did an embellished wave as he took the plastic flower out of the wand and bowed as he gave it to Grant. "M'lady, will this flower shut your mouth? Or perhaps make that face of yours more pleasant."

Grant and everyone else laughed, I did too but Elish was still looking cold and annoyed; he didn't move an inch and as I noticed his body language I quieted down my own laughs.

After doing a few more card tricks to everyone's applause Sanguine stepped back again, and as he did two sengils wheeled out one of those old-fashioned boxes that they used to saw people in half.

Everyone started murmuring and it only intensified when King Silas glided in, holding something underneath a black silk covering. It was large but its shape was distorted in the darkness around us, even when the lamps above us focused on the semicircle I still didn't know what he was hiding.

I could feel a pulsing in my ears as I was filled with anxiety. It had disappeared from my body as the evening had gone on; I had been enjoying myself and naively hoping that this was all that was going to happen.

But no, that was too easy…

Something was up, something was about to happen.

"And for my next trick!" Sanguine took a step back and Silas walked to the spot where he had been standing. He slammed the heavy object onto the black box and pinched the silk cloth.

He whipped it back revealing–

A fucking chainsaw.

Everyone was quiet, staring at the machine. My own heart was inside my throat, beating a steady hammer that sounded like my own personal funeral march.

I looked around with my resolve and bravery depleting like an open valve. Everyone was starting at it. Some were nervous, others were smiling, and some, like Elish, wore no expression at all.

The familiar sinister smirk creased Silas's face. The one that made his emerald eyes shine with foreboding, and his aura seep and cover his creatures like a black cancer. Sanguine, of course, was behind him, matching his king's smile with his own Cheshire grin.

I wondered what plans those two had in their heads, and what things we were all going to see come from that box.

"Now, I would usually call for a volunteer… but it seems that a certain cicaro has become available to me." Silas smiled.

Oh, fuck no… my body suddenly filled with ice water. I felt frozen in fear like a deer in the headlights.

Sure enough, everyone stared at me. I looked around as the bile rose up in my throat. The panic only accentuated when I felt Elish tighten the slack on my leash.

King Silas looked over at me and the grin only widened. I knew why. I couldn't see him but I could see the white knuckle grip Elish had on the wine cup; it was lucky it was made out of metal because I think he would've broken it if it wasn't.

"No, not you, little cicaro, not yet… I am talking about a certain pet… Tyan is it? Tyan, you have come at an interesting time…"

A relief rushed through my body but it was short lived, wide-eyed Tyan was being pulled from his chair by sengils.

Artemis immediately rose as well.

"King Silas… Silas what are you doing?" Artemis's purple eyes were wide, he made a move to stop the sengils but his beaten-in loyalty halted him. He watched Tyan get dragged into the center of the room, fear and horror on the cicaro's face.

"Artemis, love, how old was Tyan when you first coveted his flesh?" Silas stepped back as Sanguine started shoving the terrified cicaro into the box. In a moment the mood in the room had switched – though it wasn't fear to match the expression on Tyan's face, it was energy and excitement.

The silver-haired chimera's face dropped, his pupils were small pinpricks. "Fif-fifteen, my king."

Behind the king, Sanguine closed the black wooden lid with a rusted creak. I could see Artemis's Adam's apple rise and fall as he swallowed hard.

"Such a liar, I thought better of you, Artemis," Silas tsked, the entire room was silent now. He took a step back and raised his hands to his creations that surrounded him. "It pains me that we have to besmirch Jade's party, so we will ask him… Jade? Have you ever fucked a fourteen-year-old?"

My face went pale as everyone's eyes turned to me. For some stupid reason I started doing the math in my head and said as loudly as I could,

"My boyfriend was sixteen when we first had sex, so no, I haven't."

Silas shook his head and walked over to the box, where Sanguine was now holding the chainsaw. He turned and tapped a finger against his chin. "Artemis, how does it make you feel that some feral, trash-eating slumrat has more restraint than you? That this Morosian boy knows and respects my rules. I do not have many rules, Artemis."

Artemis was just standing there, his body rigid and tight and his eyes fixed on the cicaro, the boy's head and feet sticking out of the box. The cicaro seemed to have driven himself into a catatonic state.

"I'm sorry, Silas," Artemis stammered.

"Fifteen, Artemis, they're children before they reach the age of fifteen. You fucked a child and you broke my rules."

A rip of horror ran through my heart at the sound of the chainsaw turning on. The sound filled the room, making the fillings in my teeth vibrate from the low but loud rumbling.

"Do not look away, not for one moment," Elish whispered beside me; his hand slipped to my knee and clenched it hard. "There is nothing you can do, so don't move."

"What?" I whispered, the thought that this might be a magic trick slowly trickling away. I looked back to the middle of the semicircle.

The demon-eyed chimera was holding a smoking chainsaw in his hand, his body cloaked in darkness and dim lamplight. He was smiling wide, showing all of his pointed teeth in a vicious display of his pleasure. Silas, beside him, was petting Tyan's cheek.

My eyes scanned the rainbow spectrum of eyes now cloaked in oily smoke; all of them were watching, some of them with sengils and cicaros riding their dicks, some with heads bobbing between their legs.

Even Garrett had someone servicing him; no matter how nice they were outside in the real world, every chimera here was watching the show with the same sick fascination, feeding on the energetic, heavy atmosphere and drinking in the fear of the boy with his head sticking out of the box.

Except my master, but I didn't look at him, I knew I shouldn't.

"And now, eager audience!" Sanguine yelled over the rumbling motor, "I shall saw this boy in half!"

I didn't want to see this, jeez, I had been talking to this kid the entire night. He was a cicaro like me, in the custody of a man like Elish. Was this really Silas enforcing his 'hands-off kids' rule or was he sending a blatant message to Elish?

The chainsaw changed tone as it hit the wooden box, speeding up and revving through the thin wood with ease. And then the tone changed again, drowning out the shrieks of pain and horror coming from Tyan. I couldn't look at his face, my eyes were fixed on the chainsaw and the black spots flying out of the cut it was making through the box.

In an instant the screaming stopped, but the chainsaw didn't; I heard it strain and whir as Sanguine sliced the boy in two, his face and clothes becoming drenched in the spraying blood. Everyone was getting sprayed with blood, even me and Elish, though neither of us made a move to wipe our faces, not even when a piece of flesh hit my neck.

My eyes fell to Silas, who had both of his hands on either side of the now dead boy's cheek. His blood-speckled face was alight with a lust I never wanted to see again, green eyes reflecting emeralds, contrasting the red as though he was made of bloodstone. There were no words for the expression on his face, or the energy radiating off him. I almost felt coy being able to see deeper into him than the others, like I was reading pages of his personal diary, full of nefarious and morbid fantasies.

I tore my gaze from him and glanced down to the floor, seeing streams of black underneath the box, falling to the floor and forming a puddle full of bits of sawdust and tissue.

Then the revving got momentarily sharper as Sanguine reached the end of the boy and the box, before he retracted the chainsaw and Silas pushed the boxes away; Tyan's insides hanging out like loose curtains before I saw some of his organs fall to the floor.

The entire room fell into a deafening silence as Sanguine killed the motor, all of us staring at the severed torso of Tyan the cicaro, and watching as a string of intestine started to coil onto the bloody floor with a sickening sound that took me all the way back to my kill room in Moros.

Sanguine looked at the chainsaw, and in a comical fashion he swore and face palmed. "Shit, well... science wins again!"

And they all erupted into laughter... of course.

I stared forward, not moving an inch as the chefs came to collect the body... chefs... chefs came to collect the body, I guess we were in the greywastes now.

I managed to reach a shaky hand towards the tea mug, but Elish slid over the wine goblet instead. I downed the rest of it in one gulp.

I glanced over at Artemis for just a moment. The silver-haired chimera also had a goblet in his hand, he was staring into it, a blank expression on his face. I wondered how many cicaros he had lost to Silas; it seemed to be a trend that they all ended up dying in similar circumstances.

But he did break the rules – didn't he?

I tore away my gaze wondering why I was trying to justify such fucked up thing, though I could talk… I had burned people alive with the same man who just chainsawed a boy in half. How was I different? I had never felt guilty and I still didn't, I guess it was something we were all predisposed to, perhaps I was no better.

I took another drink, the sengils still filling up my wine glass whenever they saw it more than half empty.

Elish still didn't say anything. My master had the same stone-cold expression on his face; like me I knew he wanted nothing more than to get out of here and go home.

Maybe this was it… maybe all the coked-up, drunken abominations had satiated their need for bloodlust.

They all looked happy and unphased by what they had seen, but that was no surprise; these men had been going to these parties and watching people die horrible deaths for years now. This was typical for these fucking monsters, and I was one of them. I wondered if I would cheer on a kid being murdered. I didn't want to be like that, my blood rage when I was in Moros stemmed from Elish abandoning me, not some sick thrill because my home life was boring. I was different to these people; I wasn't doing it for entertainment.

I saw a strong-looking brute I hadn't noticed before take a line of coke off Ares's arm, his pet, naked from the waist down kissing and licking his neck. He shook his head and smiled, before leaning in and meeting tongues with Ares. That must've been Nero.

I shuddered and looked away, remembering the game the twins would play, giving these same pets keycards to lure Morosians into their mansions to rape and murder.

They did all of this for fun, for entertainment, because in an immortal world we were all just parasites and pests raised to be their toys. I was just a toy to them; they didn't give a shit about me. I was nothing but a pretty piece of flesh. They had made that abundantly clear.

Or I was… now I was a chimera like them. They hadn't known when they had lured the slumrat into the mansion that I was their brother. I wondered how pissed off, if pissed at all, Silas would've been when he found out they had killed me.

I shuddered and drank more.

"Now!" My entire body jumped as Silas walked back into the room. He was wiping the blood off of his hands, though it was still sprinkled all over his face, the image broken up only by the rest of the dissipating chainsaw smoke. He strolled back in with his demonic chimera behind him chewing on what looked like… yeah, that was a finger.

"We can get to the fun part!"

The room quieted back down, but I felt the leash become tight again.

"Elish… bring Jade here."

CHAPTER 30

HE EXPECTS CONTROL, HE EXPECTS STOICISM. HE *expects me to act like a chimera…*
Elish won't let anything happen to me, right?

I rose with Elish, my confidence and my fortitude shattering around me, and my mind quickly trying to gather it up like scattering croaches. It seemed like I was in a dream as Elish led me past the chimeras and into the partially mopped up semicircle. I didn't know what was going to happen, or what they were going to do to me, I just knew Elish was there so it had to be okay. He wouldn't let anything happen to me.

As the eyes burned into me, I knew the fear that Tyan must've felt, though it was multiplied when I felt Silas unlatch the leash from my neck and hand it back to Elish. I noticed for the first time that he had a stethoscope around his neck, like he was pretending he was a doctor.

"Master, I would like to ask to do it," Elish said quietly. At the same moment I looked at him in alarm as Sanguine started unbuttoning my pants.

My mouth opened to ask what the hell was happening but I shut it, Elish's words echoing in my mind. Be stoic… be in control, act like a chimera, they're all watching you, Jade.

I let Sanguine slide off my pants and boxer briefs, leaving my bottom half naked for all of these wolves to see and drink in, and they did, but I ignored the comments. I was genetically engineered like they were; I would dare them to say something negative about what was between my legs.

I took in a deep breath, smelling the faint hints of mint and nutmeg behind me. If they were all going to fuck me as some sort of hazing ritual so be it. I had lived with Elish for one and a half years now; I was used to the abuse. They could bring it on; I'd be fine if Elish was there.

"Oh look at that, how horrible!" I blinked as Silas shook his head, staring down at my penis. I looked down too not knowing what was so bad about it, it looked the same as always.

My mouth went dry. I tried to swallow but I ended up almost gagging as Silas dropped to his knees, he took my penis into his hand and brought back the foreskin before pulling it over the head as far as it would go.

Then his emerald green eyes flicked up to mine and he tilted his head back with a smirk. "There will be no uncircumcised dicks in my family, not at your age anyway. Sanguine, bring your master his scalpel."

My legs felt weak, and to everyone's laughter I sunk to my knees, a cold sweat sweeping through my entire body. I stared at the floor and watched out of the corner of my eye as Silas took the scalpel into his hand, and put a lit cigarette between his teeth.

"You didn't think I'd want to fuck you before I made you pretty, right?" Silas said, his voice a low growl with blatant undertones of pleasure. He started massaging my dick but if he was wanting to make me hard he was going to be disappointed. "I'm going to make you a pretty bleeding pile of flesh before I fuck every drop of cum out of you."

His tone changed to a dangerous octave. I swallowed through my parched throat and felt Elish behind me, standing with me during this. I took in a deep breath, and let the energies of all the chimeras around me wash away my fear.

"I wouldn't expect my king to touch me before I was cut by you, King Silas." My words spilled forth, wavering under the anxiety trashing my insides, but still as strong as I could physically muster.

It was only for a moment, a brief moment that passed as soon as it came, but I saw it. I saw King Silas's brow furrow and his eyes narrow at the lack of fear I was showing him. He wanted screaming, thrashing, and pain; he wanted to feed on my agony and horror, this is what Elish had coached me for. Be stoic, be confident and do not feed into him, do not give it to him.

I looked ahead. I heard Silas say something to Sanguine but my ears were stuffed with cotton. Instead I drew up every aura around me, every swirl of colour on the visible spectrum and some that I swore were not. I took them in and let the overwhelming display of energy take my body away from there.

The first pinch of my foreskin made my jaw clench. I continued to steel myself as he pulled it forward as tight as it would go, before feeling a cold metal clamp pinch it.

My steeled screen was broken though when I felt the first cut. I gasped and like someone had pulled the plug on my aura reading I felt the colours drain away, dripping down to join the sticky blood of Tyan still on the floor.

I made the mistake of looking down; my chest quaked and tensed as I saw my foreskin sliced away with slight and deliberately slow movements. The sharp scalpel severed it, small droplets of blood falling like rubies over a gem-covered floor.

My head went hot and dizzy; the next thing I knew Sanguine was holding me upright.

I heard them laughing, the low rumblings of amused chimeras, revelling in the scene in front of them. They were all around me, watching, laughing, and absorbing my every reaction.

I had wanted to remain strong like Elish had commanded, but not moment after, Sanguine had to catch me as I threw up.

Now I was half laying down, the nausea not overshadowing the pain and pulling I was feeling, only amplifying it. As I gagged and got sick, I felt Silas continue to work, my mind only briefly rising from the drowning sickness to tune into the heavy atmosphere of cheering and laughing.

"He's taking it better than Ares did!"

"Hey, fuck off, he was fucking me while he did it! It was Siris that was the little bitch about it."

"Remember Ceph? I thought they were giving him a snatch with the tones of his shrieking."

"Elish?" I mumbled. I tried to rise my head and as I did I felt him help me back to a kneeling position. The room swirled around me, only the pricks of sutures keeping me from going completely inside my head.

Elish didn't speak. I tried to gather myself and bring up the strength reserves I knew I had in me somewhere, though it wasn't until I felt a wet suction on my dick that I actually looked down.

My stomach churned. Silas was sucking my dick; his mouth completely covered my shaft. When he withdrew I saw an inflamed row of stitches, and below that, the bloodied piece of flesh that used to be my foreskin.

I groaned as his mouth started to become tingly and static like Elish's touch. The feeling, to my absolute horror, was pleasurable and after a few more long, drawn-out licks and rubs of his tongue and fingers against my dick I started to get hard. Not a single neuron of my mind wanted to respond to the touch, but my body didn't care. I grew and rose in his mouth, feeling the stitches stretch to a painful tightness.

My teeth gritted; my knees spread apart to try and give it more room, around me the chimeras started banging their hands against the tables in a steady rhythm.

The light shining on me made the chimeras dark, only their shining eyes and moving hands could be seen, and the occasional flash of hair as the sengils and cicaros rode them; or in Nero's case, his cicaro was on the table getting fucked by him. The room was alive, in the controlled chaos of sharks who had just tasted the chum thrown into the ocean.

I screamed through my teeth as my cock got fully hard, the stitches stretching tight and threatening to rip the two pieces apart. My mind was hot and my senses overloaded and unable to process the intense energy these creatures were throwing at me. It could barely process the pleasure rising up from King Silas's talented mouth.

The hands slammed against the tables like drum beats, all in the same rhythm. As my pleasure and pain grew I could feel the steady beats get faster, weighing the pain-filled, agonizing look on my face to accommodate how quick they were slamming their hands down.

"Elish?" I bowed my head and let out my first actual scream as a rip of pain went up my cock, Silas's golden blond waves rising and falling as he sucked me off, taking every drop of blood with him. The pain was unimaginable, searing, and so intertwined with the pleasure I didn't know which was which.

Then the strings started to tighten, the pleasure in my gut rose and as the drum beats got faster... faster... faster.

Then finally, I came.

I came to them cheering, I came to the drum beats matching the thrashing of my own heart. I fell backwards with an agonizing scream, the tense overwhelming pain coursing through me like raw electricity blowing out every blood vessel in my body.

"Move aside, Elish." I saw Silas rise. I was on my knees panting, mine and Tyan's blood streaked against the wood below us, disturbed now by many boot prints.

"I'd rather –"

"Move *aside*, Elish."

My head was swimming. I sniffed and didn't even complain when someone pressed down on my back, making me brace myself with my own hands. I stayed there as I smelled something new; I saw sengils' feet and realized I was smelling charred human flesh.

They were serving Tyan now. Dinner and a show.

I gritted my teeth and gasped as I felt Silas penetrate me. I immediately dropped down to my elbows, feeling my knees slide apart on the slick floor before someone to my left braced my knee. I dug my fingernails into the far fringe of the rug that had been pushed aside and attempted to brace my body as the king started to fuck me hard. I couldn't see what he was driving inside of me, but it felt the same thickness as Elish. But he was rougher, violent, with a point to drive in as much pain inside of me as he could.

My teeth ground together, making spasms of pain run through my jaw, aching and sore from so much abuse. I tried to keep as quiet as I could as he relentlessly pounded me to the jeering and cheering crowd, hollering and carrying on like they were in the front row of Stadium, and as they did I heard the drum beats start up again. Every slam against the wooden tables brought a thrust from Silas's cock, going faster and faster as he panted his hot meat-smelling breath against my ear.

Then he got rougher, I cried out but then tried to remain silent. After a hard push of his cock he grabbed my hair and wrenched my head back farther than it should naturally go. I opened my mouth and gasped.

I realized he wanted me to scream, he was doing this to get the rise out of me that Elish coveted so much; a cry, a shriek, a reaction to show the chimeras and their slaves that he was in charge of Elish's pet. That's what he fed on, just like my master standing behind me. They loved to feed on the fear and unknowing; that was their favourite delicacy.

Then I heard his cold, silk voice sound behind me.

"Sanguine, escort Elish out of the room and take him home."

Fear claimed me, real, raw, unhinged fear. No, Elish can't leave me, I had been able to get through all of this so far because my master was beside me. What the fuck would these people do to me if Elish wasn't here? They would fucking devour me like the wolves they were, Silas at the forefront.

I was fucked, and at that internal admission the first whine of fear fell from my lips.

"I am not leaving."

The words fell on me like cold water, and seemed to have the same effect on everyone else, I felt the mood change around me quickly, like a bomb had just been dropped.

Silas stopped, but he remained inside of me. "It wasn't a request, it was an order. Go home, Elish, I'll drop off him off when we're done with him." His voice dropped to a whisper, and though it was a quiet sibilation it sounded like a thunder crack in the dead silent room.

"I am not leaving him with you, if I go, the boy goes." Elish's tones were dangerous; out of conditioning my own bones started to quake and shake.

Suddenly chaos. I heard a muffled struggle and at the same time the chimeras around us gasped and swore; a moment later I heard a crash and the sound of a table tipping over.

Silas withdrew from me. I scrambled away until my back hit the front of one of the tables.

My mouth dropped open when I saw Sanguine on his back, the table tipped over on top of him. Elish was standing in front of him, his violet eyes blazing with fire as he glared at Silas who was now on his feet.

My heart hammered, a tremor in my throat tightened like an elastic band as I watched them glare down at each other. The chimeras behind me were silent, the tension in the room thick as they watched King Silas and his first born chimera in the middle of the semicircle.

"Are you so desperate to keep that gutterwhore that you would defy me? My, my, Elish, I haven't seen this much anger in your eyes quite a number of years," Silas whispered. I couldn't see his face but his hands were belting his pants up.

Elish glared down at him, his visage an overbearing weight of control and power; it pressed against Silas's own, both overpowering beacons of white and black.

"I am taking the boy and I am leaving." Elish turned his back to Silas and started walking towards me. I whimpered and started to rise, feeling the relief wash over me.

"Pin him on his knees, get him down!" Silas's cold voice suddenly snarled.

In an instant Nero, Ares, and Siris jumped into the ring. I screamed as they grabbed Elish's arms and yanked him to the middle of the semicircle.

Elish didn't move and his expression didn't waver, not even when Nero kicked him in the back, bringing him down to his knees in front of Silas. He looked up at Silas with cold comprehension, his chin high and his shoulders square. He was the picture of pride and elegance, even when he was forced into this obedient position.

I sobbed and brought my knees to my chest. I wanted to jump up and save him, to fight every single chimera in here, but what use was I? I wasn't immortal and I had to stay a coward in the shadows with only that small comfort that they couldn't kill him.

Silas crossed his arms across his blood-stained shirt; behind me the chimeras were dead quiet, not even eating or whispering to each other. The room was full of nothing but reticent abominations watching their own family's Stadium. Juries on a stand without a say, observing the dictator discipline one of their own.

"You disappoint me, Elish. Have you forgotten your place?" Silas said in a low tone.

The hair on the back of my neck creeped up; he sounded like my master when I had fucked up. It swept my body in chills. I wanted nothing more than to take Elish and run. I didn't know what was going to happen; I got the distinct impression from how everyone around me was acting that this wasn't something that happened often, if ever.

"He is a chimera and he has rights, he's not a pet you can toy with, abuse or murder." Elish's resonance matched the dangerous tones of Silas's; two threatening forces meeting each other in a dark alley neither of them willing to step aside to let the other one move. "Nor will I let you do as you will with him without me present."

"Oh? You don't trust me, love?"

"With him? No, I would be a fool to trust Jade alone with you."

I held my hand over my mouth to stifle the gasp as I saw Silas raise his hand and violently backhand Elish across the face, then in the same motion he slapped him again, and again, each blow getting harder and harder. I counted ten times before he lowered his hand; by this time Elish's nose and mouth were dripping blood.

I couldn't believe that the room around me could go quieter but it did; a pin could drop and it would sound like a bomb going off. My gawking disbelief was joined with theirs. This didn't happen, this never happened and I knew it. No one fucked with Elish, and right now the only man who had a right to was practically spitting on him.

I couldn't see his face, but I saw King Silas's body go even more rigid; his feet were pivoted in a braced stance and his arms were tightly crossed over his chest.

Elish glared up at him, a stream of blood running down his face to join mine on the floor; his body still being held back by Ares and Siris, though he wasn't struggling or fighting. Nero was behind him too, a looming shadow waiting for the slightest resistance.

"This boy is a bad influence on you, Elish. Perhaps once I deliver his remains to you, and this spell he has on you breaks, you will see it."

That's it, I'm dead. I watched as Silas turned to Sanguine and he handed him the razor-sharp scalpel. My body started to tremble and I put my hands behind my neck, wondering if my clock had finally ticked down.

But Silas didn't go after me, instead he did something that was even more horrible than that. With the small knife in his hand, and Elish still firmly held back by Ares and Siris, he walked up to Elish, took a handful of his long, straight blond hair and started cutting it off of his head.

"Silas!" Garrett rose but the glare Silas gave him made him sit back into his seat. The president was sweating bullets, his hand shaking as he wiped the dripping wetness from his forehead.

The long chunks of hair fell to the floor in clumps, not a single chimera breathing or moving after Garrett had been put in his place. Everyone was tense and motionless, the fun carefree atmosphere dead and gone as soon as the first tone of resistance from Elish's mouth had fallen on their ears.

When his hair was cut down to only five inches off his head Silas stepped back and kicked some of the clumps of hair away. Once beautiful long shining locks, now reduced to dead strands on the dirty floor, covered in blood and the dirt off King Silas's boots. It was such a demeaning act I couldn't believe it was actually happening to the deity I had come to love.

When my eyes fell on Elish I couldn't recognize that the person I was looking at was him.

Elish looked completely different now; it was like Silas had cut away his very being. He looked almost… human, though that was the wrong word, he still wasn't human, the smouldering purple eyes showed a demonic anger that I had never seen in him before. I think instead of the angel losing his wings, the angel had just been thrown into the pits of hell. I didn't want to know what would rise out of those ashes, but something would. There was no disrespecting my master like this; no one did that to him, not even his king.

"Every time you look in the mirror, I want you to remember the consequences of disobeying me. Get out of my sight, the boy is under my care now. I will send you Drake for a few months; if you are that desperate to love an animal, you may love mine."

Elish wasn't looking at him anymore, his eyes were fixed forward but he was staring off into space, not seeing a single thing in this reality. I didn't know what was going to happen next; I didn't know if this public shaming was going to shake him.

"I will grab my coat and I will be going."

His cold, dead tones cut through the mood in the room, and like a trigger getting released as he rose to his feet, Ares and Siris stepped back to let him go. The brutes disappeared into the shadows and only the glowing aura of King Silas remained.

Looking very much a king, he picked up a long fist full of Elish's hair and dropped it down to the ground with a satisfied smirk on his face. The king had won, he had broken the unbreakable chimera in front of his brothers and me.

I couldn't look at Elish as he walked the semicircle to get to where our seats were. I wondered if he was going to tell me goodbye, or if he would leave me as a bloody, crumpled mess underneath his feet.

Elish grabbed his coat and put it on. I watched him slowly belt it, looking so different with his hair shortened, but still always my powerful chimera. The king could disgrace him in front of the chimeras but I knew it was nothing to him; Elish was stronger than that, he had to be, whether Silas realized it or not.

I wiped my red eyes and watched, trembling in my dark corner. The eyes were all on Elish, walking with his dignity and grace behind the seated chimeras and back to the opening of the semicircle. Silas had his back turned to him in an obvious display of rejection, his boots scraping against the floor as he kicked Elish's hair into a pile.

Then I saw something shine against the lamplight. I didn't even have time to react when I saw Elish pull Garrett's golf driver from his overcoat – and take a violent swing right to the back of King Silas's head.

The king fell to the ground like a stack of bricks, the circle of chimeras gasped and swore, and there was a scraping of chairs. In the same instant Elish raised the club again and viciously, with all the strength the chimera had, slammed it down onto Silas's skull; the room reverberated with a crack as Silas's head opened up like a dropped watermelon.

Elish raised it again and separated the top of Silas's skull from the rest of his head, the king's brain spilling onto the floor, the only movement a twitch of his fingers.

I gaped, frozen in place. I stared unbelieving as King Silas lay dead.

"Get your fucking hands off me!" Elish snapped. "He's dead, so I am in charge now. Ares, Siris, Sanguine, and Jack, all of you take the pets and sengils and go home, NOW!"

My eyes tore away from the grisly scene only several feet from me and I saw Elish. He was bathed in the lights of the room with vehemence clear on his face; his short hair only accentuating the eerily calm but burning expressions on his visage.

Elish's eyes scanned the room making sure the ones he had ordered to leave had left, and I watched him raise the bloody golf club and point it at all of them.

"I am king until he recovers as is my duty every time he dies." Elish's cold voice dropped, I looked and saw half of the chimeras standing, ready to attack him, but at his admission they stayed as still as statues. "And during this time, I will say to all of you: The time is coming where you all will have a choice to make, whether you want to deal with that insufferable lunatic for the rest of your lives or choose something better. I suggest you take the next several years to decide where your loyalties lie, and if you want to live the rest of your lives in fear of which game he is going to play next; which loved one he is going to murder on his whim." Elish raised the club and swept the room with it. "As your oldest brother, I ask you this: do not speak a word of this to him, or the others, let it sit in the back of your mind and permeate like the hatred and resentment I know each of you hold in your hearts. Choose your sides, because I have had enough, and unless you really are engineered to be slaves with no self-respect… I know my brothers have too."

Elish threw the club down, stepped over Silas's dead and almost decapitated body, and walked towards me.

Then he bent down and put a hand to my cheek.

"Are you okay?" Elish whispered to me.

I heard the chimeras around us talking, obviously confused by this tender display.

All I could do was nod and say a very weak *yes*. Elish nodded, and I raised my arms for him to pick me up. He held me against his chest, protectively and tightly, and without another word, he left the room.

The driver gave us both a shocked look but he knew enough to not say anything.

We rode home in silence, though my heart was hammering so hard in my chest I thought it was going to rip out and fly to the dash of the car. My body was still in survival mode, and being half-naked with a cut up dick didn't help.

But I was with Elish, so I knew I was safe.

He had done this for me, all for me.

He had killed the king.

He had told his brothers to make their choices, that he did indeed have something he was planning. Perhaps Silas wouldn't have the chance to kill me; maybe one day Elish would make me safe.

I looked up at him, watching the lights of Skyland illuminate his bloody face, sometimes pale from the LED street lights, other times warm yellow from the apartment buildings or stores. Every light showed me the same cold steel gaze, fixed on nothing and seeing nothing but the transgressive images I knew were in his head.

Elish looked so different, but he was no less beautiful and definitely no less powerful. The shorter hair, about the same length as mine, made his jawline look higher and his face more full of expression, even if to the layman he was still a marble slate. It also made his ears poke out more; I could see every earring in his ears.

Without realizing what I was doing, I reached up and wiped the blood running down his nose, and then his mouth. He didn't move or even flinch from surprise, he just stared forward, glaring into space and whatever was going on inside his head.

I didn't say anything during the ride, or in the quiet trip in the elevator back to our apartment; it was actually Luca who broke through the silent cloud that had encompassed both of us.

"Master?" Luca's voice was strangled. Elish swept past him and addressed him quietly.

"Luca, go to Garrett's skyscraper and when he returns do not leave his side. I would ask you not to come back here until I summon you. Take your things."

I heard the sengil sniff, before he disappeared. Elish walked me to the couch and gently set me down. "We will be leaving very shortly, grab your bag, the same one we took to the house, do you understand?"

I nodded.

"Shower, bandage yourself, dress in warm clothes, not cicaro attire, greywaste attire. Can you do this? Can you stand?"

Without a word I rose to my feet; though between my legs was aching and sore it didn't interfere with my mobility. I nodded again and he turned and walked towards his study.

Before Elish left I reached out and grabbed his arm, he paused and turned around giving me a questionable look.

"I love you," I whispered.

My master's face softened for a moment, before he gave me a nod and turned back around. I watched him go with a tug in my heart, before obediently I went towards the bathroom.

I quickly showered, scrubbing my body as hard as I could to get rid of the grime I felt after having King Silas inside of me. After I doused my penis in disinfectant and wrapped it up in gauze, I pocketed all three rolls of gauze in the bathroom and the bottle of antiseptic. I was changed into my old (but at least clean) greywaste clothes and put the gauze and antiseptic into my duffle bag.

When I came out Elish had his hat on; it made me sad to see he didn't have to tie back his hair and put it up in the hat anymore, now the uneven strands stuck out underneath the black rim.

He had several bags with him. I wanted to ask him where we were going, if we were going back to the house in the greywastes, but that was just one of the many questions on my mind. There were so many that my autopilot refused to even acknowledge them. I just did what I was told and waited for my next order.

Elish handed me a bottle of Dilaudid pills. "For the pain, grab a bag and follow me. I packed that Game Boy of yours and the rechargeable, if there is anything else you need grab it now, we'll be gone for quite a while."

I grabbed the bag and followed behind him, it seemed like we had just gotten home and here we were taking off again, though this time I didn't know if we were going to be returning. He had killed the king, in front of many witnesses. Maybe this was it? Maybe to keep me safe we were going to have to leave Skyfall forever.

I didn't know how that made me feel, scared definitely, but there was some sort of appeal to not having to watch my back and worry about King Silas coming to get me, or the remaining Crimstones. It would just be me and Elish; there was something morbidly romantic about that. What a fucking weird ass thing to think.

When the elevator opened in front of us and the two of us walked out I got the shock of my life.

Standing in front of the Falconer was Garrett.

"Don't try and stop me, Garrett," Elish said coldly, walking towards the plane and towards the black-haired chimera who was standing with his arms crossed.

"I'm not stopping you, you idiot, where do you plan on hiding the plane? Behind a crucified raver corpse? Just tell me where you're going, and I'll call you when it's safe for the boy to return." Garrett took a drag on the cigarette he was holding and hopped into the plane.

I heard Elish sigh and mumble something underneath his breath; he helped me onto the plane and closed the door behind us. Garrett sat down in the pilot's seat and a moment later the plane turn on.

Elish sat down on the co-pilot's chair and I went to disappear into the back, but with a grab of my arm and a pull I ended up sitting sideways on his lap instead; he steadied me with his arms and I wiggled myself into him.

Garrett looked over at us and smiled. "I knew it."

"You don't know anything, drive the plane," Elish said flatly.

The president smirked but did as he was ordered. I rested my head on Elish's shoulder and watched the control panel of the plane light up our faces with its different buttons. We had never flown at night before; Garrett was looking more at the screens in front of him than out the window.

"Elish… what you did back there…" Garrett said after a while, when the cityscape was far behind us and only darkness could be seen outside the windows. "What do you have planned?"

"I will say nothing on the subject."

Garrett let out a drawn-out, exasperated sigh at that response. "Brother, you know it will take at least a month for his skull to regenerate; you don't have to flee now."

I felt Elish stiffen underneath me. "I am not *fleeing,* Garrett. I have business I need to take care of and I would prefer to do it while that insufferable parasite is dead. I will be back, I will not hide from him and my pet will not hide from him. As long as he respects Jade's right to live, and my right to own my property without having to constantly dodge his games, we will get along."

"You know he… he won't do that… right?" Garrett said slowly. "He's insanely jealous of your relationship with Jade."

"There is no *relationship.*"

Garrett gave another exasperated sigh. "I say that in a broad sense. You're only prolonging the inevitable and focusing Jade into his sights even more. I'm sorry, Elish, and I don't want to say this in front of him but he *will* kill him for sure now."

Now it was my turn to stiffen; my heartbeat started to rise.

"Silas will not touch him, and I will not dodge his games for long. I meant what I said, Garrett, make a choice and choose your side wisely. Our lives are going to change in a couple of years, so decide if you want to be on the winning team or the losing one."

What was Elish planning? What scheme did he have going on that would result in King Silas being overthrown? The idea fascinated and scared me. I had gotten hints that Elish hated him, many hints, but as soon as I opened my mouth to help him bring a voice to this inner resentment he had regarding the Ghost King he snapped me in half. This was the first time I had ever heard him say out loud that he actually did have a plan.

Could I one day not have to worry about King Silas? Would… would Elish be king instead?

I felt a shiver go up my spine, one that seemed rooted in my soul. I knew after this things would change, in every aspect I could think of. Especially for my immortal chimera, who was finally trying to put a stop to the king's reign of terror.

I curled up on Elish's lap, feeling proud of him and feeling my heart grow even larger. He might not be the type of guy to express his emotions in words or even on his face, but through his actions I knew I was special to him. He had killed the king because he refused to leave me alone with him, and because Silas had dared try to humiliate him in front of his brothers. I was in awe of his strength, and the fact that even after this night, Elish had lost none of his grace and dignity.

"Elish… sometimes Silas's games can be trying –" Garrett started to say but Elish abruptly cut him off.

"You've sent ten pets, boyfriends, and fiancés to their gruesome, violent deaths and after each one I held you as you cried like a child, and counselled you as you moped around for several years after. Is your memory that bad that you forget this? Every man who gets too close for his comfort he murders, most of all the first generation. So am I supposed to hand that greywaster boy over to you so he can be tortured and murdered like the others? Do you have no spine? Or are you that cold-hearted and selfish that as long as you have someone for a year or two before they get skewered on a stake that is good enough?" As his cold voice sliced Garrett like a sharpened icicle I watched the dark-haired chimera slink down further and further in his chair.

"That's our life, brother, we were brought into existence for this. This is the reason why we exist, to be better than the common man, to obey our king no matter his demands and in return we rule the world. We have sacrifices we must make."

"Then I see no reason to subject the greywaster boy to this treatment. I grow tired of sending innocent unassuming boys to their deaths. You have been alone for the last eight years, you can be alone for another eight hundred."

There was silence; the tension could fill a stadium.

"Well, that was a mean thing to say."

I almost laughed at not only the choice of words but the hurt in Garrett's voice; he really was a docile, friendly guy.

"Make your choice, you promised me two years and you have the remainder of that time to decide. I ask no commitments and I expect none. Just observe that tyrant's actions with a new pair of eyes. I am offering everyone a chance to escape this."

"He's... he's immortal, Elish." Garrett stated the obvious, but it was a lingering problem in my mind too. Elish couldn't just kill King Silas; it wasn't that easy and it certainly wouldn't be easy with a pack of twenty plus chimeras still loyal to him, and a fucking city on top of that. King Silas had ended the world, he had killed civilization, so just what did Elish have planned that could top that? Manic lunatic or not, King Silas was fucking powerful, *he had ended the world.*

"I am aware of that, and it does not change anything. You are my brother, Garrett, my only confidant and my ally. I know you will make the right choice."

Garrett sighed, and I saw him nod, but his eyes were troubled and full of fear. He absentmindedly lit a cigarette and took a long drawn-out drag.

The broad and heavy silence fell in the cockpit again, the hum of the plane engine and Elish's heartbeat the only sounds I heard. Though I was wide awake and feeling the residual fear, I still jumped when Garrett spoke.

"Artemis and Apollo... you'll have them in this, Nero too, of course; he would never go against you. I hope with Nero, Ares and Siris will fall in with him. Teag will do whatever I tell him to do, and, of course, I know you will have Perish; he might appear loyal but befriend him and treat him with respect, he'll follow you to the end, Sid too." I watched him take another inhale. "Your biggest problems are going to be Ellis, Sanguine, Joaquin, Drake, Jack, and Kessler... Elish you need Kessler before you plan anything, the Legion cannot fall, and with Kessler you'll have Caligula, Grant, and the other legion chimeras."

Elish nodded. "I've been having Jade analyze their auras, I'm aware of the ones I will have trouble with. Garrett, this didn't start here, I have been planning this for the past nineteen years."

I heard Garrett swear under his breath. He wiped his head of the sweat that had started dripping down again. He looked like he was going to pass out from this influx of realizations. I hoped Elish would take over flying the Falconer if he started to look like he was going to pass out.

"Of course you have... of course," he mumbled.

Then to my surprise he gave me an unimpressed look. "Fancying yourself a prince then? Prince Jade, how fitting."

I heard an annoyed noise come from Elish. "He is not going to be a *prince*." His tone was arctic frost.

Garrett shook his head and started pressing several buttons on the glowing screen in front of him. "Right, he would be a king. King Jade, a real rags to riches sort of thing. King Elish and King Jade, royal leaders of Skyfall. I refuse to have a title lower than a seventeen-year-old boy."

"He – is – not – going – to – be – a – *king*." Elish's voice wavered on dangerous, but I had a feeling that Garrett couldn't care less.

"Then make me a king," Garrett quipped.

"I have more important things to concern myself with, Garrett. Get a robe and call yourself Jesus for all I care." Elish tone was still dark, bringing forth something the two brothers still clashed on. Garrett was the sort of person to try and lighten the mood with humour, whereas Elish preferred to seethe in silence. Humour was not his strong suit and I'd had to learn that during my time with him. His jokes were usually veiled in such a way that you didn't realize he had made one until hours or even days after.

Garrett let out a long sigh; he shook his head slowly. "I really should've just smothered that boy." The president gave me a look and I realized he was talking about me. I slunk down a bit.

"Another bad decision on King Silas's part," Elish remarked, displaying his version of a joke. I gave him a look and though he didn't look back I saw a slight raise in the corner of his mouth.

"We're getting close; are you spending the night in Anvil?" I looked out the window and far in the distance I saw white floodlights twinkling in the horizon. It was still pitch black and it would be for quite a while. We were still in winter, and I guessed that it was only midnight.

"Yes, probably. Park ten or so miles to the east, enough where no one will be able to hear the plane."

"In between Anvil and Aras? Alrighty."

My heart jumped, but with a squeeze from Elish's arms I knew better than to say anything, but I understood… we weren't going to Anvil.

There was a jolt of the plane, and the lights in the distance started to rise in the air before they disappeared from view. The Falconer slowly lowered to the ground, hitting the greywaste surface with a thud.

"Don't bother killing the engine, we have to make this quick." Elish rose with me and set me down on the floor. I grabbed two of our bags and stepped out into the cold greywastes.

A blast of winter air hit me with the fresh smell of damp dirt. I opened my bag and took out my gloves as Elish exchanged a few more words with Garrett.

"Alright, two months… in this spot, two months, early morning, don't make me wait… this place gives me the creeps." Garrett sighed, he was standing in the open door with his hands grabbing onto the top metal rim. "Take care, I'll do as much damage control as I can but he is going to be pissed off when he wakes up."

Elish didn't seem to care about that. "Do not let him near my sengil, if he makes so much of a veiled threat against him I want the phone call that you're on your way here to drop him off, understood?"

"I like Luca, you know I'll do what's in his best interest." Garrett nodded, he looked tired and with a lot on his mind; I knew the plane ride home would probably be the longest one in his life. He had a lot to think about, but like Elish I knew Garrett would make the right decision.

After the plane took off we were left in the deafening silence of the greywastes. I looked at Elish since I had no idea what direction we were going in, but to my surprise he was getting out a small syringe from his bag.

I took a step back as he came towards me; he didn't have any patience for it though. "I'm numbing your groin area; you'll thank me in about ten minutes. Unbutton your pants." In normal circumstances I would've protested more but we'd both had a long night. I did what he asked and only swore when he stuck the needle right into the base of my dick. He threw the needle and cap away and grabbed all of our bags.

"Get on my back."

I blinked at him. He stared back at me quickly losing what patience he didn't have. "Would you rather me carry you like a damsel? I have bags to carry; you're too slow and there are creatures that will make a fine meal out of you. Do it and stop looking at me like that."

Without a word I got on his back and hooked my arms around his shoulders. Elish grabbed the bags and handed me the third one, and we started walking towards the flickering lights in the distance.

"Elish?" I said after he had been walking with me for an hour; he was a fast walker, even when we got to a ridge that he had to skid down. I had thought he was going to fall several times but he had incredible balance.

"Yes?"

"Thank you."

"For what?"

"You know what."

Elish walked along a trickling three foot wide river that cut a small canyon down the middle of the grey rock; he reached an area he was happy with and jumped to the other side. I held on tight and managed to stay on, thankful that he had numbed my groin. That area had constant pressure on it from Elish walking with me and I would've been in agony.

"You know you would make a great king."

"You should really be listening for radanimals," Elish responded. He stepped onto pavement and I looked ahead to see a road now stretched in front of us; burned-out cars turned in all angles littering the curving strips of pavement. It bumped and dipped in the uneven terrain, remaining broken but steady until the glowing lights of Aras.

The cold air of the greywastes seemed to awaken the adrenaline inside of me. I felt a small thrill being out here at night. A part of me wished I had permission to get off of his back and explore the grey rocks around us. I felt the need to climb and take in this new terrain.

I jumped and gripped Elish harder as the sounds of the wild deacons ripped through both of us, making my chest vibrate and quake with such intensity it felt like my heart was skipping beats. Elish ignored them though and walked into the floodlights, the sounds of guns clicking and hurried voices filling the chaotic air around us.

CHAPTER 31

"You're out late, mate, is your boy there injured?" a male voice, belonging to a silhouette on the floodlights, sounded. Around him more sentries started crawling out of the woodwork like scavers smelling fresh meat. These people always set me on edge; if I was seen as a feral in Skyfall I was a refined prince in the greywastes. "I need to speak to Leo right now," Elish answered in a tone that left no room for further questions.

Unfortunately, greywasters played by different rules. The man stared down at him with an uninterested look and shook his head slowly, his gun still cocked and ready in his hand. I hated having guns pointed at me. I shuddered, remembering the Crimstones back in Moros. The anxiety and fear still woke me up in a cold sweat sometimes.

"Leo's asleep; it's past three in the morning. Come back when the sun rises."

That wasn't going to happen, obviously. Elish's tone didn't waver in the slightest. "Tell Leo that James and Michael are at the gate, and that Michael is hurt. He will put you on rat shit duty if he discovers tomorrow that you kept us out in the cold; mark my words, Matthew Donovan."

The silhouette paused and the one on the other side laughed, a female. "He's got you there, *Matthew Donovan*." I heard the click of a switch and the crackle of a radio. She called a name I didn't understand and I heard another static click.

All four of us waited. The deacons were still barking and growling at us but the guys on the walls were yelling at them, making them start to quiet down.

"Leo here."

"Yeah, Leo, we have a guy here with a kid who's hurt. James and Michael. They said you would know."

There was a pause and in my mind I could mentally see Leo start to have a mini-stroke inside that house of his.

"Let them in, now. Do not tell anyone they're here, go." The radio clicked off. I saw the silhouette of the girl glance down at us and then to Matt, then a moment later came the rusted creak of metal scraping against metal.

Without another word Elish walked through the gates with me, and into the familiar though much darker block of Aras. All of the lights inside the small town were turned off, kind of like Moros except this place had a distinct smell of rot and decaying wood. Moros had more of a stale urine, alcohol stench to it.

We got about half a block towards Leo and Greyson's when I saw two black shadows running towards us; there was no question who they were.

"Eli? Fucking hell, you... what are you doing here?" Leo slowed down; he looked the same, short blond hair, hazel eyes, and a handsome face that hid his age well. His husband behind him hadn't changed much either, dark brown hair and grey eyes with creases that pinched the sides and a face that told you he didn't take anyone's shit. Both of them already looked confused and worried, but when they realized Elish's hair had been cut their faces fell in shock.

"The boy is hurt, I need to get him out of the cold," Elish said, handing Leo and Greyson both his bags. Greyson reached up and I handed him the one I had been carrying with a small thank you. I tried to slip off Elish's back but he tensed his grip on my thigh so I stayed where I was. He really hadn't let go of me except in the apartment. I didn't think he trusted me more than a foot away from him anymore.

"Seriously injured? Do you want me to wake Doc?" Leo asked hurriedly, his face was pale and I heard a rattling sound. I looked towards it and realized it was the duffle bag clips rattling against each other. Leo's hands were trembling.

"No, it's bandaged." Elish started walking towards the house.

"Did... did *he* do this?" Leo dropped his voice, but it wasn't good enough for Elish.

"Not outside, fool. It's bad enough you went screaming my name down the streets." He gave Lycos a warning look and the former chimera, my other brother, clamped his mouth shut. We all walked towards their house in silence.

The screen door opened and the wooden door behind it. Greyson sprinted behind the house and as Elish set me down on the couch the lights around us turned on. By now the local anaesthetic was wearing off and my circumcision was starting to hurt. I got up and hobbled towards the duffle bag as Leo put a kettle of tea on and started closing all the curtains of the house; when Leo got in they locked the door behind him and the sliding glass door too.

"He doesn't know you're here, does he?" Leo asked Elish as he handed me a blanket and went back to the kitchen. I wrapped it around myself, taking my gloves off to reveal pale and sweaty fingers. I tensed them and hobbled back to the couch.

"He's dead. I killed him at the party tonight." Elish's voice had an even tone, contrasting the emotions in the living room and kitchen around us. "No one knows we're here. Your son is safe and so are you."

There was the familiar sound of breaking dishes. I shot up, wincing under the pain as I saw Leo gaping at him, a broken mug shattered on the floor. "In front of our brothers?"

"A good twelve of them at least, and about five sengils and six pets," Elish replied dully.

"Why?" Leo looked like he was about to have a stroke. In response Greyson put his hands on his husband's shoulders and walked him out of the kitchen. He sat Leo down on a blue chair beside the couch I was sitting on, then went into the kitchen to take the steaming kettle off the stove.

"Why do you think, Leo? The party was Jade's *Welcome to the family* party and his birthday party; you know as well as I do what goes on when they get frenzied, especially that poltergeist," Elish said quietly. He gave Greyson a nod as the greywaster offered him a cup of tea; he took the other one and set it down in front of me, then sat down.

I shifted closer to him and as I did, he handed me the bottle of Dilaudid pills.

"The tea will make them work faster," he said quietly.

I nodded and tightened the blanket around myself, as Greyson sat down too I swallowed two of the pills and washed them down with some old earl grey tea.

"Did he rape him? He's wobbling bad, shit, he didn't cut him did he?" Leo's eyes were still wide with panic. I scrunched myself smaller, wishing I could disappear into myself so I didn't have to listen to his conversation.

"In front of everyone, after our brother Sanguine sawed Artemis's fifteen-year-old pet in half with a chainsaw." Elish sipped his tea.

Greyson winced as he burned his mouth with what smelled like coffee. He sputtered and put it down roughly. "In half with a fucking chainsaw? In *half* with a fucking *chainsaw*?"

"That's right."

"The more I hear about you crazy fucking psychos the more I understand my kid," Greyson said bitterly. He wiped his mouth and shook his head. "What made you finally snap? I mean we've been waiting for it and I wish I had been there, but what?"

I could tell Elish didn't want to answer this question but I was curious as to what he was going to say. "He wanted me to leave Jade and go home and I decided I'd rather that not happen. It was apparent he was going to kill Jade the moment I voiced resistance. From my appearance you can guess what happened next, and after that was done I decided to take advantage of Garrett's new driver."

Like any socially retarded greywaster Greyson let out a laugh, though as soon as Lycos gave him the look of death he quieted down and coughed. It was such an out of place display of emotion it made my stomach sour towards him, but it seemed like it was just his personality. I suppose you had to be rather crazy to marry a fugitive chimera and raise his demon baby.

"And... and you left?"

Elish took another sip. I wanted to curl myself up on his lap, but at least I was close to him.

"I told them, Garrett, Grant, Quin, Teaguae, Artemis, Apollo, Kessler, and Nero, I told them that they were going to have to make a choice, not now, not soon but in the next few years. I told them that I knew deep down they were as sick of this as I, and that in time there would be an opportunity to change things and no Lycos, they will not tell him. As soon as that idiot took his last breath I was king, and they will say no such words to him, you know that as well as I do."

Lycos and Greyson both stared in disbelief. I stayed silent sipping my tea, watching the both of them go through a variety of emotions.

"I want to observe Reaver tomorrow. I'd rather he be ready for his mission sooner rather than later," Elish said quietly. "I want to gauge how long we have to wait."

This sparked my interest. "Reaver has a mission?" I asked quietly, looking up at him.

Elish nodded. "I'll explain everything to you in the morning. It's too late right now and the day has been longer than expected."

"What does he know?" Leo asked, turning his gaze to me. He didn't look at me with masked disdain as much as he used to, but I still saw hostility in his eyes. No one was really used to Elish treating me well, least of all someone who hadn't seen him in a year. Elish had changed how he acted towards me a lot in the time since he was in Aras.

"He knows he's a chimera and he knows we're hiding you and Reaver, but he doesn't know why. That is also why he's here; he's ready to know everything, keeping secrets from him is not only annoying but it's unnecessary now. It's time the ball started to get rolling, time is ticking down and I want to start seeing improvements in your son. If he is the same wild child who hung my cicaro over the deacons' den I am going to start stepping in and taking control."

The mention of Reaver brought a small smile to Lycos's lips; he looked at Greyson and then to Elish. "Well, he has gotten a bit better... distracted at least. Just a couple weeks ago he started following around that Massey kid. He hasn't gotten the balls to talk to him, but he never lets him out of his sight."

Massey kid? *That* Massey kid? I tensed at the mention of his name, and in the same moment Elish's hand resting beside me went hot. I almost cried out but I hid it. He didn't need to tell me twice; that burn was meant to tell me to keep my mouth shut.

"Oh? The one who came from that factory town? His parents died recently did they not?"

Ouch, tough break for the kid. He was such an innocent thing; to have luck like that in a place like this and with Reaver stalking him. He would probably be dead soon.

"Yeah, it's been rough on him, he's gotten a bit depressed and is a bit of a shut in. But Reaver's started noticing him; wherever you go he's right there. I don't even think the kid realizes it yet. Reaver's become a shadow. I even have trouble spotting him now. So I'd watch Jade, if you think he snatched him quickly last year –"

"Jade will not be going anywhere without me. I only plan on staying here for two or three days before we buy a quad and make our way to Halfton Valley. I'll stay there with him for the remainder until Garrett picks us up." Elish drained the rest of his cup and rose. "We'll be –"

"Halfton Valley?" Leo cut in, his face suddenly looked very dejected and offended. I watched him as he stared up at Elish with a hurt expression. There was obviously something interesting in that location, his next words confirmed it. "You're taking him there?"

Elish ignored him and I rose as my master started grabbing our duffle bags. "Is the east house still unoccupied?"

Greyson decided to speak from now on; he sounded a bit annoyed but to my surprise it was directed at Leo not us. "Yeah it is. I'll get one of the workers to wheel you over a generator. We keep them at the Slaught House. We don't have heaters in there; why don't you spend the night in Reaver's old room? He has a double bed, the east house is dirty, without heat or water. I'll have the workers set it up by midmorning."

"That will do, sooner rather than later. I would prefer Killian Massey not know I am here, he may recognize me." Elish started towards the set of stairs. I picked up my bag and my bottle of pills and followed behind him.

"Elish… I…" Leo stopped himself but Elish turned around and looked at him. Leo started to stutter, looking awkward and out of place. "I'm… it's nice to see you again."

Elish looked at him for a brief second before nodding and continuing to walk up the stairs. "We will talk more in the morning."

Elish closed the door behind us and locked it, before going to the window, locking it too and closing the curtains. Then he started to dig out clothes for us to sleep in.

Reaver's room was bare and it was obvious he had moved out some time ago. There was only a double bed in a corner with clean blankets and sheets, framed by bare walls with nothing more than several thumbtacks showing that someone had once lived here.

I got dressed and washed some of the grey ash off my face, using nothing but the sleeve of my shirt and some bottled water. I got into bed and after Elish flicked off the lights he followed me.

"Killian is bait isn't he?" I whispered as I crawled over to him. I got in my usual place, laying on my side with my head in the crook of his arm and my hand on his chest. "You sent him to Aras because you wanted him to attract Reaver; that's why Garrett couldn't have him."

"I have no idea what you're talking about," Elish said flatly.

"It's to calm Reaver down, give him something to focus on, and it's working. I bet that makes you happy, doesn't it?"

"You weave such interesting tapestries in that mind of yours."

"And what's the deal with Halfton Valley? Lycos looked positively pissed when you mentioned it," I asked. I ran my hand up and down his chest, something I had started doing out of habit to practice my fluctuating touch. My mind was more focused at night and I was able to do it better.

"As you know Lycos was a scientist, and I was the dean of the College of Skytech. We knew each other before he went to Aras," Elish explained patiently. I was surprised he hadn't told me to be quiet and go to sleep yet. I wondered if he felt a bit of tension lift off him over being able to finally smash King Silas's skull in. Though in a way I was a bit ticked that I had gotten beaten and fucked mercilessly in the greywaste mansion over not being able to control my feelings for the king.

"Did he like you?"

"Go to sleep, Jade."

Ah, there it was.

"Did he though? I should know, in case I need to start being jealous again; though I have a feeling his husband is already watching his every move." I made my touch as hot as I could make it, though it didn't even make him flinch.

"Sleep."

I pushed myself up by my elbow and kissed him on the cheek. I felt it tense.

"Why are you being so calm and affectionate? Six months ago you would have been terrified, giving the world that blank dead-eyed stare as you sat in a corner and shook like a wet dog." Elish took my hand and brought it up to his neck. I wondered if it felt weird for him to not have his hair to warm it. I made my touch as warm as I could.

"The same reason why you're not throwing me off the bed, because I disobeyed the order of 'sleep'," I said, almost playfully.

Elish was still for a moment and I thought he was done talking to me, when all of a sudden he grabbed me and started pulling me over him towards the end of the bed. "If you insist, go sleep on the floor."

I let out a holler and then a laugh. I squirmed away from him as he pulled on my arms towards the edge of the bed. I yanked them away and he stopped.

I could see a small smile on his face, nothing more than a slight raise of his lips, but I knew Elish's body language like the back of my hand now; what most people would miss I understood and he was telling me he was just fine.

I was relieved that he was okay, it wasn't like I expected him not to be. Elish was always okay, but I was worried he would well... turn into the other Elish.

I tested my luck. Before I moved back into my position beside him I leaned down and kissed him on the lips, he kissed me back. "Don't get any ideas, Cicaro, getting you to laugh was merely for my own sadistic pleasure. Lycos is probably seething in the other room right now."

That bastard! "You're using me for your own passive-aggressive needs? You're an ass." I leaned down and kissed him again. "You know what would also make him really fume?" I deliberately drew out the next kiss, but a moment later I sucked in a breath as a prick of pain shot from my groin. I rolled off of him.

He gave out a cold chuckle, knowing exactly what had just happened.

"No, but I know what will make you scream. You've had your fun, Cicaro, go to sleep." Elish closed his eyes and I did too, resting a warm hand against his neck. How odd it was that I felt so safe and content here, though knowing Silas was dead and hundreds of miles away gave me an idea as to why. Out here it was just me and him, not even Luca around. I liked that; I liked having him all to myself, far away from bad memories and experiences. Elish was a different person out here, and I was looking forward to spending this time with him.

As I drifted off, I remembered something. "Don't you have one more thing to say to me?" I said sleepily. I opened one eye and gave him a tired smile.

He was quiet for a minute, before I felt a hand brush back my hair. "Yes, of course. Happy birthday, Jade. We will have a real celebration when we get home."

I smiled and fell asleep soon after that.

Over the course of the night I woke up several times in horrible pain, but every time I did Elish was awake and he had pills for me ready and hot tea. Most of the time I woke up he was looking at the ceiling, lost in thought but a few times he was looking through folders. There was something comforting being able to wake up and have him already awake, especially since he seemed to know when I was waking up even before I did.

Eventually, I woke up to the sun shining and the room was empty; I could hear voices below me which I guessed were coming from the living room. I made a move to get out of bed but sucked in a painful shudder. Cursing Silas under my breath, I rose to my feet and found the bathroom.

There was no hot water but I had suspected as much. I had a cold shower in dingy water and examined my sore member; it was red and a bit inflamed but so far it wasn't infected. I changed the gauze and doused it in antiseptic and Polysporin and after making myself look acceptable I hobbled down the stairs and into the living room.

An interesting sight was waiting downstairs for me.

Leo was brandishing a pair of scissors behind Elish, who was sitting shirtless on a chair looking like he would rather be sitting in a sewer drinking cyanide. Leo was hovering around him snipping his hair, trying to make it even and not the mangled hack job Silas had left him with.

Elish looked at me as I appeared in the living room. "There is food for you in the microwave."

Leo glanced up from his clipping job. "I should cut his hair too, or do you like it curling like that? Reaver's would start to go curly on the back as soon as it got more than four inches. I think it's Garrett's DNA strain that does it. Reaver does have his nose."

I absentmindedly pulled on a lock of my hair; it had started to curl on the edges but Kerres had always liked it when it did that. I didn't care either way.

"You might as well while you're at it," I heard Elish respond behind me as I took a bowl of corn mush from the microwave. I walked crookedly to the living room and wheeled the grey chair so it was facing Elish and Leo.

Elish's hair was even now, coming to his jawline at about the same length as his bangs used to be when he still had his long hair. He looked nice; I was starting to like it more at this length though I was still getting used to it.

"How much Sanguine does he have in him? He carries himself the same way he does, don't tell me you haven't noticed?" Leo gave me a curious glance. I didn't know how Sanguine I could look though, considering I was hunched over, shovelling corn mush into my mouth.

"Fifty-five percent. Twenty-two percent Artemis and Apollo, fourteen percent Garrett, and nine percent you."

Leo was still looking at me. "I was gone before he got pulled out; did his teeth turn out normal or did you have to cap them?"

"Normal, but his jaw strength is impeccable. He wears implants now, not my idea but I think I'll keep them in his mouth permanently. He seems to get himself into trouble, and with his penchant for biting he might as well use his talents," Elish said placidly. I bared my teeth at Leo just so he could see the steel implants. Leo shook his head.

"I was glad when Reaver's teeth came in; though like all the little ones he bit more than a deacon did. I couldn't believe Silas slipped that demon's strain into all four embryos. I had no clue how I was going to explain pointed teeth to him or those around him without making it obvious he was different."

"Jack and Sanguine's baby teeth were flat; it wasn't until their adult teeth came in they become serrated," Elish responded. He got up and put his black t-shirt back on.

"That's good, it would be a pain if we had to cap them. Do you remember how many times we killed him when he was little? I counted seven times before he started losing his teeth."

I stopped, a spoonful of mush halfway to my mouth. "What? He's immortal? I thought you had to get some special thing done by Silas for chimeras to become immortal?"

Elish gave himself a passing glance in the mirror, and absently rubbed the back of his neck. "I wanted to wait until after tea, but I suppose this is as good a time as ever." I watched with confusion as Elish picked up his briefcase and brought it over to the table.

"Reaver isn't just a chimera, Jade, Reaver is about ninety-nine point nine percent Silas. The only part of him that is not Silas is a few strands of DNA here or there to change his appearance and give him those advanced chimera abilities. He is an almost exact copy of him, therefore instead of him needing to go through the necessary surgery to become immortal, Reaver was born immortal like King Silas."

As my brain tried to process this information Elish handed me a paper. I always thought it was funny how he handed me these papers like I would be able to understand perfectly once I looked at them, but most of the words and graphs on the papers were Greek to me. I didn't understand any of it.

"So he's special? Like really special? I don't get why that's such a big deal." I looked down and, sure enough, most of this I didn't understand. The top part read Chimera X and below were dates of things, math, and growth charts. "I guess that explains why he's such a psychopath; now that I think about it a lot of how he acted was a ringer for Silas."

Leo tensed at this; he was still holding the scissors and decided in that moment to motion me over to sit in the haircut chair. I wondered if that was a good idea. I got up and obeyed though.

"Yes, Jade, from what I have heard he is indeed a lot like King Silas, but in many ways that is good. He needs to be strong, mentally, physically, and emotionally. He needs to be everything that Silas is, without being what Silas is, if you understand what I mean," Elish answered. I swivelled the chair so I could still look at him.

"So why are you hiding Reaver? Why don't you want Silas to have him?" I asked, feeling the first snip of my black hair being cut away.

Leo started talking behind me. "Silas decided about twenty-five years ago that he wanted to have a partner, someone who he could rule the world with forever. Someone genetically engineered to be like him, be attracted to him, basically he was made to be his partner. Before, when I was still in training, Perish, Garrett, and Elish started working on genetically cloning a chimera that would be immortal from birth. As you know the chimeras have to have Silas's secret surgery to become immortal. Though it didn't work; all the babies would die which obviously meant we were doing it wrong." Another piece of hair fell down onto my shirt. I took this chance to take my shirt off, or else I would be itching for a week.

Leo carried on. "I was put on the project and as the years went on the interest waned and soon it was basically just me in the lab working on the babies. Eventually Elish started helping me; when we only had a few embryos left Elish took some to experiment on and low and behold he got one to stick. He delivered him to me, but as he grew... well, we discovered something fascinating. Or at least Elish did. Elish... you do the honours."

My eyes widened as Elish smiled, so wide I almost saw teeth, close but not quite. I hadn't seen him smile like that in almost a year. I stared at him as he sat in silence, looking ahead with his violet eyes deep and full of thoughts I knew must be dark.

"We discovered... that being born a natural immortal, gave Reaver a very unique gift... Reaver can kill immortals. Reaver can kill King Silas."

At this moment Elish's eyes drew up to meet mine, like he wanted to see every single reaction on my face. I wasn't sure what expression I was giving off but I knew I had gone three shades paler. I couldn't believe the words that had just left his mouth.

Reaver could kill King Silas? That black-eyed devil could kill King Silas?

"And... and he would actually stay dead?" I sputtered. When Elish nodded I shook my head in disbelief. "What the fuck? Really? How do you know this?"

Elish continued to smile; he looked quite pleased with himself and I could understand why. Now everything around me made sense. He had been biding his time as this boy grew up in secret, waiting for the seed he had planted to grow up and grow strong. Now the calls from Lycos made sense; their discussions and fights about Reaver made sense; Lycos's fear about how he was growing up made sense.

Elish was growing an assassin in the greywastes.

"It's complicated, and a secret I keep to myself, but being the oldest out of all of us I discovered some things about Silas that made me realize what a direct clone of his would be capable of with the right tinkering," Elish responded casually. "As soon as I realized that Lycos and myself had created a successful copy, and on top of that, one that could eventually terminate that mad hatter, I brought word to King Silas that the last embryo had died and on my consult it was impossible for us to create a viable Chimera X."

I nodded in awe, and as another snip of hair fell from my head, Leo said bitterly in the background, "And that's when the shit hit the fan."

"Indeed," was Elish's response. "King Silas had a tantrum and before I could warn Lycos, Silas decided that Lycos's punishment for failing was death, though I suspect he also didn't want a chimera around that knew so much about his coding and genetics, for not even Silas's blood is on file. He decided to incinerate the lab, not knowing that the baby was still incubating and Lycos was still looking after him. We managed to get both the child and Lycos out and conveniently Lycos had decided to start mounting a greywaster who apparently was foolish enough to hide a chimera and a newborn."

I could feel the heat of Leo's eyes behind my head. "You should be thanking your lucky stars he's a good person; Greyson's been an excellent father to Reaver."

Then in a sweep of movie quality coincidences the door slammed open and Greyson came stomping in. He threw his hat off, his face red with anger. "That little shithead, that fucking little shithead. I made the grievous mistake of suggesting he invited Killian over to his house for a movie night and he threw a grenade at me! It was a dud but I didn't fucking know that. The moment I even bring light that he just might, just MIGHT be crushing on Killian he –" Greyson stalked into the living room and shut his mouth as soon as he saw me and Elish. "Oh, you two, right, good morning."

"Reaver threw a fucking grenade at you?" I said bitterly. I shook my head feeling a sour taste come into my mouth. As the shock of Elish and Lycos's revelation wore off, I remembered just what kind of person Reaver was. "I was right last year, Reaver is insane. You raised someone worse than Silas, not better."

I didn't cower though I felt like it when all three of them glared at me. I didn't know where I had gotten the confidence from, but remembering the psychopath who had only laughed when he was waving my writhing and screaming body over half a dozen snarling deacons made me bitter towards him. And hearing how he treated his fathers had only hammered in the fact that Reaver was no assassin saviour. "I think at this point you three can safely admit you are now hiding Silas from Reaver and not the other way around."

"You don't know what you're talking about." Leo roughly snipped my hair. Elish rose at his tone and took the scissors away from him. Regrettably because I was still a young idiot this gave more bite to my words.

"Don't tell me you don't realize that kid is a dead ringer for the dude who sawed a fifteen-year-old boy in half because the kid's master petilized him when he was fourteen? The same guy who put my mother, an old lady with bad knees, in front of two brute chimeras who beat her to death with a baseball bat. The same –"

"That's enough, Cicaro," Elish said in his warning voice. I clammed up but it was Greyson who was giving me the dirty looks.

"He's gotten a lot better since he started following Killian, calmer, he's more introverted and quieter now. I think he really has grown out of his teen stage. Busying him with his sentry training, scavenging with Reno, and following Killian, it's stopped him from getting bored. Really, Elish, I think you'll be happy with his progress. He'll meet your deadline, I know he will."

I grunted at this. I still wasn't convinced.

"Is he still a drug addict?" Elish asked.

"Well... we gave up on that a few months ago." I guess Elish made a face at this because Leo's tone rose to a more pleading pitch. "Elish, I told you, when we stop him he pushes away from us; my god, it isn't like he's going to overdose and die. He, well... he has it in his blood. You know how much drugs Silas does and the entire family." There was another pause. "And I won't even bring attention to –"

"Then don't." Elish's cold voice cut him off.

It took me a moment to realize he was talking about the track marks on my arms; they were red scars now.

"I wasn't with him, it was when I was back in Moros, I've been off of drugs for several months now," I protested covering up my arms. I heard

Elish put the scissors down and I ran my hand along my head. They had only taken two or three inches off and made the back shorter. I walked towards the mirror, not even realizing I had said something wrong.

"You dropped him back in Moros? You never mentioned that when we spoke. Why?"

I cursed myself into oblivion in my head, leave it to me to open my big ass mouth.

"Jade, why don't you go on the porch and play your Game Boy."

I was waiting for that. I sighed and grabbed my jacket. "If Reaver comes near me I'm going to rip his throat out, just warning you."

"You'll be fine, just don't leave the porch," Elish answered. I gave another sigh and hobbled out to the porch and sat down on a rocking chair.

I turned on Pokémon and tried to concentrate on playing but every minute or so my eyes seemed to flick up and scan every empty building around me. If there was one thing I had learned while I was in Aras, it was that Reaver was quick. He also had a tendency to use bait to get what he wanted so I made sure to keep an eye out for Reno as well. Reno might be harmless but where he was, the slippery serpent that was Reaver wouldn't be too far behind. Those two were a dangerous combination in a way. Reaver gave off the aura of being emotionless and dangerous, Reno on the other hand was light and carefree. Combined, they could probably dupe anyone out of anything, including their own lives.

I continued to play and continued to watch the streets and the buildings, but besides a few people walking by nothing happened. Perhaps Reaver was too busy now to harass me, which in all respects was a good thing, even though it wasn't too good for the small innocent boy he was stalking.

A half an hour later the rusty door opened and then the screen. I looked up and saw my master exchanging the last few words of a conversation with Lycos. He was holding a needle in his hand and in the other, his jacket.

I blinked when he handed me both of them. "We're going for a walk; stick that in yourself."

I was starting to ache a bit again down there, so I did what he asked without protest. Deep down I wished for an endless stock of this local anaesthetic. I could use it the next time he smacked me around for doing or saying something stupid. "I'm not in shit for mentioning your ditching of me am I?"

"I didn't ditch you."

I smirked at him and decided to be a dick. "Fine, callously abandoned me."

I glanced up at Elish with a playful smile; he shook his head and started walking down the steps. "I don't know when you decided you were allowed to make such smart-ass quips."

I jumped over the railing and onto the greywaste ground, feeling much better after the local anaesthetic kicked in. "When you stopped smacking me across the room when I did it?" I jogged up to him and put my hand over my mouth to cough. "I wouldn't do it while other people were listening. I can stop if you wish though. Sometimes it makes you smile and I like seeing that."

"I'll tell you when it's time to stop." Elish narrowed his eyes as we passed a boarded up building; he scanned it from one end to another. I looked too. The decaying buildings seemed like they could harbour anything inside of them. I wanted to explore them but I knew better than to ask. I was still on the lookout for Reaver, though I wasn't nearly as worried about him kidnapping me now that Elish was beside me.

We walked on and I saw we were heading towards the square. I was about to ask him something when he held up his hand before bringing a finger to his lips; then slowly he pointed towards the square and pulled me towards a shed with an overhang.

I looked to see where he was pointing, and I saw someone I never thought I'd see again.

Killian Massey was sitting by the fountain on the square, quietly reading a big thick textbook. Even though it was January he was sitting in a ratty jacket with a hoody pulled over his head and sneakers.

His head was bowed but I could see that he had grown taller since I had met him back in Tamerlan; his hair was longer too. His bright blond strands fell over his face as he leaned against the upper ring of the circular fountain, his knees crossed and the textbook resting on his lap. The boy looked peaceful and, oddly enough, very clean. Cleaner than the usual greywasters I had encountered; he seemed to be taking good care of himself.

"I can't believe he's survived this far," I said. I was surprised though when Elish shook his head.

"No, not him, look on top of the shed."

My eyes travelled to a large shed with a tin roof standing beside the fountain; it was stacked with wooden crates. As I looked I realized there was someone sitting on one of those boxes. I hadn't seen him before, he was a shadow in himself.

I narrowed my eyes to bring him into focus. I saw that he was just out of Killian's eyesight. He had angled himself perfectly so the boy couldn't see him, though if you were looking from another angle you could spot him with a keen eye.

Reaver had gotten taller too, and if possible more menacing-looking, but, unaware that he was being watched his usual dangerous visage was softer and more toned down. Still looking as threatening as he ever had, there was something different about him. Even though he wasn't talking, walking or even moving, he just seemed to radiate silence, stealth, and stoicism.

Then Killian closed his book gently and put it back into a canvas knapsack that he had. Without a word or even an acknowledgement that Reaver was there, he got up and started walking down the cobblestoned streets of the square, far enough away that he wouldn't notice us.

We both watched him silently walk by us, a lanky blond kid who unfortunately looked very under-nourished even for his small size, and sullen too; though since his parents had died only a couple of weeks ago, I gave him a bit of a break. Kid was an orphan now and probably going through a hard time.

I felt a poke on my arm. I turned my attention just in time to see Reaver get off of the crates and, without a single noise, jump off the shed. Then with the same graceful stealth, he hugged the shadows of the buildings in the square to follow Killian wherever he was going.

The part that struck me most about this behaviour that Leo and Greyson had told us about, was that Reaver wasn't doing anything to hide what he was doing, besides leaning more towards the edges of buildings, but that was nothing outside of his usual skulking nature. Besides that though he didn't hide when Killian stopped to do something, or even stopped walking. He was just… following him.

"Jade, give this to him."

I blinked as I felt something pushed into my hand. I looked down to see I was holding a small bottle, containing some pills rattling inside. I glanced up at Elish like he was crazy, but there was no room for discussion, there never was. Elish pushed me out of the covered shed we were standing against and urged me on.

"W-why?"

"Just do it, engage him, apologize for last year, I don't care, just engage him in conversation. Do it," Elish hissed, giving me another push. I gave him an unimpressed look and started walking across the empty square towards the dark figure.

I got five steps towards him before Reaver looked over and noticed me. Immediately he narrowed those black demon eyes at me and nodded his head in manly recognition.

"They said some yellow-eyed bastard came into Aras, and I only know one yellow-eyed bastard. Did you finally kill that pretty-faced merchant?" Reaver's voice had gotten deeper too, though not tone-wise; his voice had been mature when I had met him last year. I think it had gotten more controlled and dark, a man who didn't like to say unnecessary words. I could definitely sense a change in him, though still dark and sinister, it was more a controlled blackness in his heart, not the wild, needlessly violent teenager who got thrills from dangling boys from deacon dens.

"No, he's around here somewhere..." I said casually. I pulled out a cigarette and handed it to him, he took it without a word and lit it. Thankfully they were Leo's, Elish would've murdered me if a blue ember popped up on that cigarette. "I thought I would give you a present." I tossed him the pills. "Leo and Greyson had to passive-aggressively mention you liked pain killers so I decided to be a bitch and pull these out of our bag."

Reaver smirked. I shuddered, seeing Silas in that cold upturn of his lips, he just seeped Silas's energy.

Then I made the mistake of peering into his aura, just to see if I would see and feel what I suspected.

As Reaver unscrewed the bottle I felt my knees start to go weak, a black smoke started to surround him, though as Silas's aura had been, black was the only colour I could use to describe it. In reality it had no colour, just a black hole, a depthless fourth dimension with no colour, texture, feel or sense but darkness, bloodthirst, masochism, and sadism. A pulsing barbed vein of just evil and dark thoughts that he didn't understand but at the same time embraced like family.

But there was more there... there was more there than Silas's void, but it was nothing good, because it was just filled with darkness. This was no human, no chimera; Sanguine was more human than he was.

This was bad, very bad. Silas might be dead inside but Reaver was very much alive and that scared me more. The more I looked into this black-flamed soul the more I was convinced that Elish and Leo had made a huge mistake. If Reaver killed King Silas he would be even worse than Silas was. At least Silas gave off rather controlled chaos; he tormented his creations more than he tormented his people, but Reaver... this man lived off inflicting pain; he was a sadist at the worst level.

This... this wasn't good.

Then suddenly Reaver turned from me, his black eyes scanning the building lined streets and I realized he was looking for Killian.

It was when his black eyes saw him, that I felt his aura briefly change. It wasn't much but it was there, a slight silver light in a cold, dark ocean of darkness. It was dim against the black depthless waves, but even the smallest match was a beacon when everything else was dark. It was incredible, I had never seen an aura physically change in front of me like that. It was like his heart was a shapeshifter, only briefly able to feel warmth before it morphed back into the nefarious void.

Then Reaver spoke and I recoiled my tendrils from him as quickly as I had infiltrated him. "Dek'ko Dilaudids? I haven't had the fresh potent ones before, thank you, Michael was it?" Reaver put the bottle into one of his many cargo pants pockets, before giving Killian another glance.

He wanted to keep following him, and I think I had gotten the sense of him that Elish wanted.

I nodded. "That's right, well tell Reno I said hello. If you haven't gotten him killed yet." I gave him a wink and turned around to make my way back to Elish.

"Not for lack of tryin', good luck, Mikey."

I made my way back to Elish, who was in the shadows of the shed we had been standing by. He looked at me inquisitively before we started walking through an alleyway.

"Okay." I took a deep breath and looked around for anyone listening, though I knew Elish would be able to sense them sooner than I. "You really… need to pay attention right now."

"I'm always paying attention, Cicaro."

I stopped and shook my head. "No, I mean you really have to listen…" I took in another breath, and breathed out a plume of cold smoke. "Your key to you three not ending up with someone worse than Silas, is Killian. That aura is the blackest, most desolate plain I have ever seen. Silas is dead inside, Reaver isn't… Reaver is –"

"Reaver is who Silas was when he ended the world, not the crazy, dead, miserable shell of a person he is now?" Elish responded. I looked up at him surprised; he had said exactly what I was feeling but didn't know the words for.

I nodded. "I saw a break in him though, for a split second when he saw Killian, a fleeting moment but it was there. That kid is your only hope. I don't know how you knew to send him to Aras but it was probably the decision that will make this plan of yours actually possible."

My eyes trailed up to Elish but he was easy to read, he was smiling silently to himself; I wished I could peel back that brain of his to see what was going through his mind.

"I couldn't have asked for better news, good work, Cicaro."

Our boots clipped against the pavement as we walked back towards Leo and Greyson's. I shoved my hands in my pockets. "I'm serious though, Master. He's… he's fucking evil. Are you sure Killian will do him good or are you setting up a lamb for slaughter? Because literally he's being stalked by a predator right now."

My master seemed to smirk at the last part of my comment, I was amusing him again. "Do not underestimate that young boy, he is very resilient. Killian would do well to have a bodyguard to protect him from the greywastes, especially since he is rather suicidal right now. Reaver watching over him will prevent the boy from doing anything foolish and it will keep Reaver occupied. It is a rather win-win situation if you think about it."

I considered this and tried to see it from Elish's perspective, but I remembered how soft and innocent Killian had been in Tamerlan, and being around someone like Reaver just seemed absurd. Those two didn't seem like they would get along at all, but perhaps that's why they would. Elish and I were complete opposites as well, though that wasn't saying much, he was still cruel and prickly and I was still a slumrat, we had just found an algorithm to live by. Not without a lot of scars, bite marks, and sore backsides though.

"So you're expecting them to start dating or something?"

"Eventually, it may take a while but with the interest Reaver is already showing, it's obvious he's in love. He will realize this in his own time and then he can claim his prize."

"When are we going to take him to Skyfall to kill Silas?"

"In time, things have to happen naturally, we must be patient."

"It's hard to be patient, I want him dead, I want you to be king," I said stubbornly.

At the mention of the word king, Elish smiled and put his hand on my shoulder. "Now don't go mentioning such things around Leo and Greyson. They have it in their minds Reaver will rule Skyfall after all of this."

I snorted at the thought. Elish smiled, sharing the mutual humour we found at this notion.

"Yes, I know, but you see Greyson absolutely despises me, and for me to be in power in his head would be exchanging one doppelganger for another; he has to feel like he is in control of the next ruler of the world. We will let his dream fall to cinders on his own time; we have more important things to prepare before we fuss over minor details."

I chuckled, not realizing my laugh had its own cold strands to it. I *was* turning into him. "I love how you say *we* now."

He paused and narrowed his eyes. He gave me a look but I didn't meet his gaze, I just carried on casually with a smile.

Then my eyes turned to the sky. I saw a snowflake lightly fall to the ground, another one close behind it.

In an instant my cocksure smile turned into that of a child seeing candy. It had been a long time since I had gotten to run around in the snow. I was usually high above Skyfall during the winter and there was no way I could play in it while I was doing errands with Elish.

"It's snowing! Oh my god, does it snow more here?" I exclaimed. I held out my hand to try and catch the snowflake. When it landed on my glove I vibrated with glee and held it out for him to see.

Elish shook his head like I was an idiot. "It snows a lot here, we're miles and miles inland, in what used to be the Okanagan Valley, or perhaps that's more west of here. I'm not sure. Most of the landmarks that would tell us were destroyed when the bombs dropped."

I blinked away the snowflakes as they kept falling. I was half-hoping it would start sticking. I put my hands out and started trying to catch even more snowflakes.

"You're acting like you've never seen it in your life. We get more than enough snow in Skyfall." Elish shook his head like I was a complete moron. "Stop acting like an idiot."

"Our snow was all grey and full of garbage and sludge, then it rains and disappears. Since we're out of the city, it will be more crispy and solid. Hey, can I go sledding?"

"You're seventeen, no."

"Can I make a snowman?"

"What do you think?"

I gave a loud sigh. Elish rolled his eyes but said nothing else.

After a couple of hours hanging out at Leo and Greyson's, we moved on to a small one-bedroom house in the east area of Aras, far away in a mostly abandoned part of the block, where the odds of Killian stumbling upon us were slim to nothing. I helped clean it with a couple of workers, sweeping and getting the heaters and lights working properly.

Elish took this opportunity to find a quad for us to purchase or borrow. By that time everyone had left and it was just me sealing up the windows with old plastic some asian dude named Chang lent us.

I finished the last window and stepped outside, not holding back the glee at all at there being so much snow; then, since Elish wasn't around, I started playing.

My boots made tracks along the porch. I paced back and forth until, with a shift of my eyes to make sure my master wasn't in sight, I started making a snowman.

The snow was freezing against my hands of course, but with a flick of my parlour trick and some concentration my hands became like little toasters and not only did that warm up my skin, it made the snow slick and shiny in my hands.

I rolled up the first bottom of the snowman, then worked on the second. Once I made the body of Mr. Snowman I dug into the greywaste ground and made two rocks for eyes, and a bent stick for a smiley face. I didn't have any carrots for a nose, like they used in the books I had read as a kid, but I did find a funnel from a gas cap so I used that. To top it off I put Elish's hat on its head.

"I thought I told you no snowmen," a voice as cold as the snow said behind me.

I jumped and turned around, my mind racing for an excuse. "I… I… uh, I… well… sorry."

"Bro, that's a badass snowdude," another voice I recognized said. I hadn't even noticed him in the darkness. "If you don't like him, I'll take him over to Reaver's, drink some beers with him." A small ember flared and Reno came into the warm light.

Reno, taller like we all seemed to be getting but with the same charismatic smile, gave me a nod as he took the cigarette out of his mouth. He dug it into the snowman's face to make it look like he was smoking.

"There, now he's a greywaster man." Reno looked proud of himself, but Elish was giving me a very unimpressed look; it looked like he had more things on his mind though.

"I will be right back, I am getting Reno his money for renting the use of his quad. Reno, come inside. Jade, you too."

I abandoned my snowman and came inside the warm, dimly lit house, Reno trailing behind me making a beeline for the heater to warm his hands. He glanced around and whistled.

"This place looks good, you sure you want to leave? You're welcome here. Reaver won't hurt the little dude, he's got other little dudes on his mind now."

Elish ignored him. He handed Reno an envelope of money and said in the most casual of voices, "There is the extra twenty in it, no questions, no answers, now smile."

Reno laughed. I looked at my master with a raised eyebrow, but realize he was holding in his hand a digital camera.

"Alrighty, no questions, even if I have a lot of 'em." Reno scratched his head and comically straightened his hair out and wiped his face, before giving the camera a big, wide smile. There was a flash and Elish nodded. "Good enough, deliver the quad to Leo and Greyson's shed. It will be returned within two months."

"Sure, you know for another ten bucks I'll take my clothes off." Reno grinned. "And fuck it, I'll give *you* ten bucks for a picture of *that* guy with *his* clothes off." He gestured to me.

For a moment I was sure Elish was going to consider this, but instead he motioned for the door. "You have my leave to go."

Looking visibly and comically disappointed, Reno left with his money.

"I'm not looking forward to having to deal with that boy during my weekly chess visits with Garrett," Elish said bitterly.

I took the digital camera from him but he snatched it back and turned it off. "I'm assuming that's further bait to get Garrett to do what you want?"

"You're learning my ways well, Cicaro. Yes, though I have no concerns over Garrett's loyalty it is always smart to dangle a carrot here or there."

"You should've taken him up on his offer of taking his clothes off." I took the kettle I'd had steaming away on the hot plate off and poured him some tea; he settled down in a rat-chewed couch that smelled musty. I took my place beside him and turned on his laptop. We didn't have a television but I had some music on in the background. It kind of looked cozy and homey this way; I liked it.

"The last thing I wish to see is a dirty greywaster without clothing."

That's true; they were rather dirty and probably very un-groomed. In a way I looked forward to seeing what Reno would look like cleaned and in pet clothing. I bet he would look hot as fuck.

It would be nice to have a friend in Skyfall. The closet friend I had was Luca and I couldn't talk to him about Elish. With Reno we could bitch about our masters, though I didn't think Reno would have much to bitch about since Garrett was such a nice guy.

"Do you want to see me without clothing?" I said with a coy smile.

He gave me one cold look and started bringing up his Excel sheets on the laptop. "Though I wouldn't mind a warm body curled up next to me, my mind is too preoccupied with other things and you need to worry about infection. Change your bandages and turn up the heat on your way back. I am donating too much money to Aras's coffers to not get some of it back in fuel consumption."

Feeling more than just a little dejected I got up and did what he asked, before pulling up a chair and watching the snow fall outside with my tea. A part of me was wishing we didn't have to go back to Skyfall. It was quiet here.

CHAPTER 32

SLEEP THAT NIGHT WAS JUST AS TROUBLED, BUT LIKE last night every time I woke up with a whine Elish was slipping pills into my mouth and holding his tea to my lips.

We spent the next three days pretty much snowed in, only seeing Leo and Greyson for dinner or tea in the later evenings. As Elish had requested we maintained a low profile here and the snow helped aid that.

Day four of us being snowed in had me shovelling the snow off the porch and Elish looking on with his tea mug in his hands. I was dressed in normal cargo pants and a long-sleeved shirt but my body was toasty warm, as was Elish's. He had eventually clued me in to the fact that we could warm ourselves with our own abilities. It was a novel idea that never occurred to me before, but it made sense; our clothing acted like insulators for the heat we gave off.

When we went back inside I started warming my hands on the heater. I noticed Elish was rooting around in our medical bag. I gave him a look as he took out some scissors.

"We're taking your stitches out, it's been almost five days now, let's see how everything looks."

It had been hurting less but itching more, I had to make a point not to itch myself when we were in the bar getting food, or in front of Leo and Greyson. I had been looking forward to getting the twine taken out of my junk.

I took off my cargo pants and sat down on the couch bare ass naked from the waist down. Elish kneeled down in front of me with tweezers clenched in his teeth, and though it made me cringe to have scissors so near my groin now, I let him unravel and snip away the gauze.

It was looking better at least, still a bit red around the stitches but now it was mostly mended together. I swallowed some pills and took a deep breath as he started snipping and tweezering my stitches out.

"It's healing quickly, a part of me worried it would get infected and we would have to cut it all off, then what good would you be to me?" Elish pulled out a small black string and put it in the pile.

"I still have my ass, I'm sure you wouldn't miss it too much." I smirked before wincing as he pulled out another piece of wire, it was an odd sensation but not without its charm.

And the charm seemed to be multiplying. I swallowed and adjusted myself on the couch, his touch plus the small pricks of pain drawing out some tight feelings in my gut. I curled my toes to try and get rid of it, but as he carried on I started to get hard.

Elish found this amusing; he chuckled and pulled out another string. "You have no restraint do you, Cicaro?" With a teasing stroke of his hand he rubbed his palm against the crown of my dick, before pulling out another string. He took a wash cloth, and with a smooth motion he washed my stiffening member up and down before cleaning the head. I clenched my teeth and groaned.

"It's been almost a week, you can't blame me," I gasped as he dug the tweezers in and pulled out the last stitch from the bottom part of my penis. I looked down and saw him test out my now foreskin-less dick in his hand; he grabbed the shaft with his fingers and tried to retract it but it only slid down to the base. It was gone, everything was gone.

I wasn't sure how I felt about that, but I had always enjoyed Elish's dick, so I guess I was used to it now. I wondered if he had ever been with a guy with the skin still on besides me.

"Looks like it fused together nicely, not a butcher job that's for sure. I was certain he would do something wrong just to spite me…" Elish responded, lowering his head.

Inside my body did a spasm of anticipation as he ran his tongue along the red spots where my stitches had gone in, and when he drew his mouth over my head and gave it a suck I swore and leaned back in the chair.

To my humiliation with no less than five long drawn-out licks to my sensitive head, I came with my hand clenched on his shoulder. He withdrew his mouth and let the cum spill freely as he stroked my shaft, encouraging the flow.

"You *do* cum quickly," Elish chuckled.

I put my hand over my head as he continued to stroke me, letting the cum ooze onto the couch and the floor, I wiped my hands down my face. "Don't stop, fuck, the first one doesn't count when it's been this long."

Surprisingly, he put his mouth back over the head and started cleaning the head of my cum, before drawing a wetted finger down to my backside. I shifted down even lower so he could find the right spot, not stifling my moan as he positioned his finger and started slowly pushing it inside.

"Is it –" I gasped and lifted up my knees, his suctioned mouth going up and down on my dick; it still hurt around the stitches but it was blowing my mind how good it felt. "– is it passing the test?"

There was a pop; I cringed as the air hit it, even though it was warm air it still made me tense up. "It will do, though do you have to squirm so much?"

"It's sensitive!" I dropped my head back and groaned. The pleasure was tightening every part of my body, bringing trembling moans that rolled off of my tongue and into the small house we were hiding out in. There was no one to hear me, not even Luca. I didn't hold back as he intensified his efforts and slipped a second finger in.

"I missed the novelty of hearing you scream without having to come to your rescue," Elish said before tracing his tongue down my shaft. "Just like the old times before you became as old and broken in as my shoes."

"Let's take Reaver home then, spice up this boring life we have, so I can watch with morbid glee as he rips you to bloodied shreds." I grinned, but a moment later I winced as I felt teeth scrape against my head. "The teeth just mean I got you. I'll take every –" I jumped a mile high as he gently closed his teeth over my dick. I smacked him on the head as he laughed dryly, before continuing to nicely suck on me.

I jolted as I heard the door slam. Elish didn't jump but he looked towards the door before rising with a glance out the window. I heard him mumble something under his breath.

"Put your pants back on," he said without an ounce of emotion in his voice. In a split second the mood in the room had changed, the lust and warmth radiating between us had disappeared with the cold chill of the door being half-ajar. I felt myself snapped out of my blissful daydream, and though I was confused, I felt like I'd been cheated.

I got up as Elish walked out of the partially open door and glanced out the window.

All the cruelty I had in my body was drawn out and put forth in the form of a single dry laugh. Lycos, or Leo as he was in Aras was stalking down our driveway with his shoulders slumped and his hands clenched in anger. I watched with glee as Elish stood on the porch with his arms crossed.

"Are you going to tell Greyson what's got you so pissed off, or are you just going to lie about it again?"

In classic chimera fashion, which was neat to see considering he seemed to be the least chimera guy I had ever seen, Lycos Dekker whirled around, his face beet red. "Don't patronize me, Elish; go back to sucking off that pathetic little lapdog you're so fond of."

"I will. My concern for your tantrum was merely a guest's courtesy. Enjoy your morning." Elish turned and started walking away; behind him Leo was fuming.

"What does he have that I didn't?" Leo suddenly screamed, loud enough for me to worry that someone else might hear. Though that wasn't my concern, I was glued to the window. Leo might slip some valuable information if he got angry enough and I had to hear it. Elish, though his treatment of me had improved, had never said anything that might suggest I was more than just a chimera pet to him.

Elish didn't move an inch. I wished I could see the look on his face, though I knew it was as cold as the snow around us.

"Chimera jealousy? I would've thought you would grow out of such a pointless emotion after I married you and your greywaster, then gave you a son to raise. Are you not happy, *Leo*?" Elish's voice became cruel.

I laughed in my head, but it showed with a smirk on my face. I admit it; I was loving every moment of this. I knew something had gone on between the two of them.

"I am fucking happy, don't twist my words, *James*! I love Greyson and I love Reaver. What I don't fucking understand is why you have that fucking kid hanging off of your arm? Why you're doing things with him you never did with anyone else? You told me you weren't even capable of loving something. It's so out of your character it makes me sick. What the fuck happened to you?"

The unspoken reality of what our pet and master relationship had been developing into hit both of us in the face, even though he was on the porch and I was half-hidden, looking out the window. It brought a chill to my heart, like it had been ripped out of my chest and exposed to the cold air. It seemed like a secret that needed to be kept in the dark, kept safe and hidden around strangers, never talked about and certainly not laid bare in the glaring sunlight for the world to see.

"I didn't change, I think you are confused. There was nothing between you and I, there never was. Stop making a fool out of yourself, Lycos," Elish said coldly. "I have had enough of this pointless display of emotion. Stop demeaning yourself. What happened was twenty years ago."

"Yeah and as soon as you got your fucking clone I suddenly didn't mean anything to you," Leo snapped, pointing an accusing finger. "So what does Jade have that you want? His aura ability? Does he know you're just using him to figure out how to sway our brothers? What about him? What happens when you've gotten everything you needed out of Jade? Are you going to drop him back off in Moros again? Or are you finally going to kill him this time?"

Now it was personal.

My insides boiled with anger. Unable to control myself I opened the kitchen door and slammed it shut.

Both of them turned to look at me. I didn't stop at the porch though. I stalked towards Leo. "He didn't know I was an empath until months after I became his cicaro. They had hid it from him. So sorry, *Leo*, he saved my life, twice, without me being able to give him a single fucking thing. Burns you up doesn't it?" My voice was a vicious taunt, but all the cruel enjoyment I had gotten from this fight had turned into anger.

"Get out of my face, you're nothing but a fucking slave and a tool to him!" Leo yelled back. He was taller than me and bigger too but I didn't let him intimidate me. "If you think he won't eventually get tired of you, and toss you aside once he's bored, you'll be added to a list of dozens of men before you. He only wants you because you can help him right now, and if it's not that, he only wants you because he enjoys breaking wild animals. Once you submit, you're gone, do you not see that?"

"He already tried that line on me and he came back for me!" I gave Leo a rough push; he was easier to push than Elish that was for sure but he still stood braced in front of me. "He always comes back for me."

Leo narrowed his eyes, he shook his head with a look that told me he thought I was an idiot.

"Yeah, I know how it works, he always comes back… until the day he doesn't."

Those words burned my heart and my head. I found myself almost choking on them. They weren't said out of anger, malice or jealousy; he said them with a force that told me he meant every single syllable.

Until the day he doesn't.

My face darkened, and anger crawled under my skin like a nest of ants. I glared at the chimera and forced my presence into his before lowering my voice to an evil murmuring taunt. "I enjoy tasting every drop of your jealousy, because you know what I do to him," I growled. "But go ahead, greywaster, tell yourself whatever you must to let you sleep at ni-"

I felt a crack against my chin. I didn't even know what happened as I flew backwards, but my mind worked quickly. As I hit the ground I sprung back up and pushed him roughly, before we fell down onto the ground tearing each other to pieces.

I choked as I felt my collar yanked back before I was airborne again. I landed head first in the pile of snow I had shovelled.

"If you touch my pet again –"

"Fuck your pet!" Leo snapped, then lowered his voice. "He isn't a pet, he's a fucking clone of you. Fuck both of you, fuck you whoever you've become. Do you know how much pain I've gone through raising that child?"

"You were the one who suggested raising Reaver with Greyson; you seemed very keen on having the ideal family, Leo," Elish replied calmly. I dug the snow away from my face, spitting out bits of wood and rock.

"Yeah, you spent two years putting those ideas in my brain; you spent two years slowly crafting me to do your bidding!" Leo hissed. I wiped away the last of the snow to see Leo pacing. "Well, you know what? You made a mistake, because I love him like he's my own son, and quite frankly I'm no longer willing to give him to you even when he's ready.

He's *my* son, *my* property, and you can keep your cold cruel hands off him and find another plan." With his hands shaking he pointed down the street. "Get out of my town and take your boyfriend with you."

I jumped to my feet and took a step towards Leo, knowing I was about to attack him, when to my complete shock it was Elish who grabbed him.

With his hand wrapped around Leo's throat Elish raised him off of the snowy ground and dangled Leo in front of his face; Leo's feet thrashed as he clawed Elish's clenched hand.

"If you ever threaten to take my property from me, Lycos, or continue to fill my pet with such nonsense, I will slaughter your husband, I will slaughter you, and I will take my property as the light leaves your eyes, am I understood?"

I stared dumbly as Leo nodded.

My mind didn't know what to make of what happened next.

There was a high pitched crack, and in the same instance a red mist exploded from Elish's neck, and as it did his body jerked back just slightly, dropping Leo onto the ground. As the greywaster chimera dropped to his knees a spout of blood shot from Elish's neck, leaving a trail of red on the snow-white ground.

I screamed and ran towards Elish, who was on his knees holding his neck, blood spraying between his fingers like he had clamped it over a high pressure hose. It was everywhere.

"Reaver, NO! Don't shoot the kid! DON'T SHOOT THE KID!" Leo's screams were desperate. I saw a flash of his jacket as he shielded me and Elish, his arms outstretched protecting me from the direction of the gunshot.

"Master? Elish?" I put my hand over the one clasping his neck and the other to his cheek.

Elish's eyes were focused ahead, his mouth open and speckled with coughed blood. I could feel his heart start to congest as his blood pressure disappeared with the blood spraying between his fingers, running like rivers down his neck and coat.

"Master?"

"Greyson, James's house, now! Fucking right now!" Leo snarled on the radio. Then he raised his voice. "Get the fuck out of here, Reaver. I don't even want to see you."

"He was holding you by the neck. You're welcome!" I heard Reaver say sharply.

I felt my throat start to vibrate, a growl rising to my lips. Then Elish gave a gurgling cough, and my attention went back to him.

"No, leave Reaver. Stay. Don't move from me, promise." Elish managed to raise an arm to touch my shoulder before he slumped into me, dead.

"Get that fuck out of here!" I snapped at Leo, but he didn't listen to me, instead he grabbed Elish's arm and started pulling him towards the house, the blood coming from his neck slowing down to a steady drip. I tried to get to my feet but I fell onto my knees; they were shaking so much I couldn't stand.

"Reav-, Jesus fuck, Reaver!" I heard Greyson scream a minute later. I didn't look but I heard the sound of a fist connecting with something.

"He was hurting Leo! He was dangling him from his fucking neck!" Reaver spat. "I did the kid a favour. I heard Leo say he was a slave."

"Go to your basement, wait for us there, that is an order, sentry!" Greyson roared.

I looked down at the red snow in front of me. It was steaming from the dissipating heat of Elish's blood. I picked up a handful of the crimson slush, feeling my body tremble as it melted off my hands, staining the pale shaking digits like rust after a rainy day.

Greyson grabbed me and helped me to my feet. Around me there was blood everywhere, thin sprays that shot five feet and droplets from the spouts that had been running through his fingers. They seemed to outline where he had collapsed kneeling onto the ground.

"There there, son, you know he'll come back, gunshots heal quickly. He'll be back by tomorrow morning, remember?" He walked me into the house where Elish was lying in the living room, a towel over his neck wound.

My legs gravitated towards him. With Leo talking in a strangled tone to Greyson I curled up beside Elish and tried to hold back the burning behind my eyes. I sniffed, missing the long hair that I used to feel on my cheeks and buried myself into his white duster instead.

"Oh, look at that, that's so sweet, poor kid." Greyson knelt down beside me. "Son, why don't you come with us and get some food? He'll be fine by morning, I told you." He put a hand on my shoulder.

Immediately I heard the growl come back in my throat.

"Greyson... take your hand off of him," Leo's warning voice sounded.

"Is he... is he *growling*?"

"Greyson... he's a chimera, he's Elish Dekker's chimera and our son just killed his master."

The mayor of Aras scoffed, he rubbed my shoulder and pulled on it. "He's a good kid. Come on, Jade. He'll be fine here."

I heard footsteps and I saw Leo's boots behind me, then his hand lowered to take his husband's own hand away from my shoulder.

An anger rushed through me, filling my brain with a sudden flash of rage. I whirled my head around and clamped it down on Lycos's arm. I locked my jaw and as he stepped back and tried to yank his arm away with a scream, I rose with him, growling like an animal.

Greyson laughed, which infuriated me. I unlocked my jaw and jumped towards Greyson but he was waiting for me.

He grabbed my collar and pulled me off balance, then, before I could reach him, Greyson pinned my arms behind me and crushed my back to his stomach. I thrashed and snarled, whipping my head back to bite him as he soothed me like I was some sort of animal.

"Boy, I raised a chimera ten times worse than you since birth, you can't break my hold on you. I've been practicing this move for seventeen years." Greyson's voice was stern and commanding. "I know you're pissed and I apologize for my son, if you can calm down, I'll let you go but keep those fangs away from my husband's arm."

I clenched my teeth and tried a few more times to thrash away from him, but eventually I gave up, though the anger was rampaging inside of my heart. The audacity of that black-eyed fuck outraged me.

"Elish told me not to leave his side. I won't leave him here, immortal or not," I spat when Greyson finally released me. In the corner of my eye Leo was holding his arm, droplets of blood falling to the floor.

"I don't want him outside. Reaver's too unpredictable with him, he's shown that," Leo said, he was out of breath. "I'll put Owen in front of his door and Houston so we have someone that isn't under Reaver's control. I don't want to risk Reaver messing with him, and if he gets bored tonight he will. If Jade dies while Elish is out he'll take Reaver just to spite us and you know it."

Greyson scratched the back of his neck, before clenching his fists, making a frustrated noise and declaring loudly, "I fucking hate chimeras!"

"I know the feeling." I didn't hide the derision in my voice. "I hope you whip that boy of yours from here to Anvil; he doesn't have nearly as many marks on him as he deserves."

"He's getting better!" Leo shot back. I bet out of all the words that come out of these guys' mouth, these were the most frequent.

Leo seemed to ignore the expression on my face at his comment. "His body is about to become boiling hot, if you want him to heal quicker help us move him outside into the snow. At about midnight it will cool down again and you can move him back inside. He'll be awake by morning; blood regenerates quickly, and it looks like Reaver hit only one artery."

Leo took the towel away and looked at Elish's wound. "Don't stitch it, it would only delay it ten or so minutes, but in the future, if any limbs get detached or his head, sew it back on, nothing fancy even if it's shoe lace. They regenerate from the brain down and if the skin is touching it will fuse back to it as long as it hasn't started to putrefy."

I wanted to say something smart-ass back but these were things I did want to learn for the future. "Okay... thanks," I said. "Anything else I should know?"

"Chimera blood is universal, you can transfer it to everyone; you should know that too." Leo placed the towel back on the wound and picked up Elish's leg, Greyson grabbed his other leg and I watched without stopping them as they dragged Elish outside. It was not dignified and I hated seeing it but if the cold would make him come back faster I'd allow it.

I followed them outside and heated up my body.

Greyson came back and in greywaster hospitality he offered me a cigarette. I took it and lit it but as I blew out the smoke Greyson let out another of his trademark inappropriate laughs.

"Leo, look!" Greyson touched my arm and gave out a guffaw. "He has that mutant touch going on. Feel, he's a hot water bottle. Why can't you be like that? You and Reaver are like freezers."

Leo dropped Elish and started covering him with snow. "Empaths can soak in the other brothers' enhancements, be lucky he didn't go after Reaver; one touch and he would shock him like an electric eel and we would have two dead chimeras on our hands."

As if it was my cue I poked Greyson, there was a snap and his teeth clenched together, his body going rigid. He took a step back holding his chest before he laughed again.

"You're such a boring chimera, Leo. How is being sciencey a talent? Oh well, Jade, we're going to set up guards around your house. Owen and Houston are friendly and they'll make sure not even Reaver messes with you, alright?" Greyson shook his head to try and shake the fuzzy static I knew was swimming in his head.

I nodded and looked over to the mound of snow that was Elish. I felt cold with him not being around. I had really gotten attached to him; I derived all of my safety from being beside him.

"Thanks, Greyson," I mumbled.

Greyson sighed. "So polite too. Maybe we should give Reaver to Elish. He's done wonders with the feral Morosian; he's ready to go up a level."

"Greyson!" Leo snapped. "He threatened to take Reaver if…"

Leo paused before he slowly closed his mouth, remembering just what he had threatened Elish with. This filled me with a fresh flood of disdain. I decided to give those two something to fight about, if I had to be miserable tonight they should be too. "Leo told Elish to forget training Reaver to kill Silas and he was keeping him sheltered in Aras forever. That's what pissed Elish off, all because Elish chewed him out after Leo hit me."

The cheerful grey eyes of Greyson suddenly hardened, and behind him I saw Leo's face drop. The mayor of Aras slowly turned around and gave Leo a glaring look.

"Alright, we're going home. Jade… we'll see you soon, come and get us when he wakes up." Without another word, with Leo's body language clearly showing his guilt and submission, they both left. I hoped Greyson gave him a few backhands for his actions, it would please me greatly.

When they had buggered off I grabbed my tea and pulled the chair out onto the porch, a mound of Elish buried in his snowy coffin a few feet away from me, safely underneath the canopy of the porch but outside in the cold where apparently he would heal faster.

Wrapped in a blanket I played my Game Boy and listened to music with my Mp3 player; between that and sipping tea I spent the day beside my dead chimera, waiting like an obedient dog for his master to come back from the dead. I couldn't believe I was used to this happening now, like it was second nature. Just waiting for Elish to come back from the dead, again. At least I wasn't locked in a room anymore.

Two men dressed in black bulletproof vests, with assault rifles and big boots started hanging around eventually; they didn't talk to me and I didn't talk to them but they patrolled and did their job so that was good enough.

I noticed in the late afternoon that Elish's body was melting the snow, so I piled more on top of him. When evening came and I noticed his body had started to cool I dragged him into the house and into our bedroom. Though I didn't have the strength to put him onto the bed, I was able to get the mattress onto the floor and roll him onto it. I curled up beside him after I had towelled him dry and laid the towel back over the wound on his neck.

There wasn't anything else I did that evening, except load myself up with drugs and get myself into a healthy stupor.

When I was ready for bed I walked out and turned off the generator and hooked up the inverters so we could still have a heater on, ignoring the water that had started to fall from the sky; it was raining now and from the looks of the grey night sky it wasn't going to stop.

I slept beside Elish that night, and at about two in the morning I felt the first weak beats of his heart. I slept easier after that.

I was woken up with a horrible start, with my head still in a dream I felt myself yanked to the sitting position and someone shaking me so hard my teeth rattled.

"Jade? Jade!"

I opened my eyes, feeling the world spin and my teeth click together as he shook me. "What? Stop shaking me," I protested sleepily.

Then to my further confusion he took me into his arms and held me so tight I thought my bones would crack. I hugged him back even though I didn't know what was happening.

The hug was short lived though, he pushed me away and with that his voice got frigid and biting. "Why are you so cold? Why did you not at least wash the blood off of your face!" he snapped before he got up and started for the bedroom door.

Still half-asleep and dazed, the first reaction out of my mouth was a whimper. He whirled around and opened his mouth, but stopped when he noticed the expression on my face.

"What is that look for?"

I slowly got up to my feet, shoulders slumped. "I don't see why you had to shake me like an unwanted baby and yell at me, that's all. You have no clue what I had to deal with after you got shot."

He looked at me coldly for a moment, his mouth a thin line. "You were cold, with dried blood stuck to you, there was a brief moment where I thought you were dead. You're obviously not. Get ready, we're leaving Aras."

I followed him outside, the rest of the house was so cold it made my nose go numb, but with a quick glance out the window I saw it was pouring with rain, the snow dissolving and washing away, forming small rivers that ran down our driveway.

"But it's raining…"

Elish started packing up all of our things. I rubbed my hands together and put on my jacket and my hat, before trying to warm my body. "We can use the quad in rain, you'll be fine. We need to leave this place quickly."

Elish handed me my duffle bag. I just stood there watching him walk around packing stuff, I couldn't move. I didn't even want to think about having to go out in the rain. It was pouring out, melting the snow quickly to the point where I could see the greywastes' ground again.

He put a blanket around me, took my shoulder and pushed me out the door, then with a slam he was behind me and I started to make my way towards Leo and Greyson's, where Reno had taken the quad we were borrowing.

I put the blanket over my head and walked beside him down the empty dreary streets. The sound of the heavy rain filled every corner of my mind, taking away any heat I had in my body. Soon my mood was dampened too, and a lump formed in my throat, but I followed obediently and waited by the shed as he rolled the quad out to the front of Leo and

Greyson's driveway.

I guessed he wasn't going to even say goodbye to them, but I didn't know what he would say to them anyway. It was obvious he was angry, and if what he had said was correct we had to leave Aras quickly, but for what reason I didn't know. Maybe he was worried he would twist Reaver's head off.

I got onto the leather seat; behind me Elish secured our bags with a bungee cord and threw a small tarp over it, then I heard a rusty sound as he checked the fuel supply before belting a gas tank to the back as well; his eyes hard were amethyst and his movements quick but angry.

I slunk down not wanting to talk, noticing with another lump in my throat that the jacket he was wearing was coated in dried brown blood. At least his neck was healed and new-looking again, soaked and blanched in the rain, only the hat protecting him from the elements.

"Move up," Elish commanded. I shifted my body up and he got behind me. He turned on the quad before putting his hat onto my head and pulling my hood up over it.

With a throttled rumble he pulled out of the driveway, just as Leo came running out.

Elish didn't stop or give him so much as a glance; he drove down the broken pavement into the dreary walls of the west gate. Like they had been warned, the gates opened up as we approached and without a word to anyone we drove off into the soaking wet greywastes ahead of us.

Elish turned the quad east, the sharp ridges and bare grey hills saturated and covered in a thin mist of rainy fog, nothing but wraiths with only a semi-solid outline. An uninviting place at the best of times, but in the rain it was absolutely miserable. I wanted to protest to Elish about this decision to leave Aras so quickly but I knew my words were pointless. My master had made his decision and I had to trust it, though I could already feel my body start to tremble, even with the warmth I was able to muster from underneath my skin.

We drove through a break of trees, and the quad slowed as it tilted down to reach a long road. It looked spooky to say the least; the road stretched off and disappeared into the mist, cars rusted where they had died, only shadows against the fog. It was eerie, and knowing we were in the middle of nowhere plus the cold in my bones made me shiver in my seat. Once the terrain got flat Elish wrapped an arm around me to hold me next to his hot chest, though most of the time he had to have both hands on the handles to steer the old quad.

Why was I out here? I sighed miserably as we drove through what used to be a neighbourhood, houses partially collapsed with roofs that sunk into rotting beams, shingles blown across the wasteland covered in dust or sticking out like the scales of some half-buried beast. There was nothing out here, everything was dead, and what wasn't dead had a quickly approaching expiration date.

Elish got off for a moment and checked out one of the houses. I waited, shivering, hoping we could stop but a moment later he got on and without a word we drove past.

He pressed his stomach into my back, but even the warmth of his body wasn't enough to kill the cold feelings in my chest; my own ability to warm myself had disappeared within the first two hours. I was just a shivering cold mass now, pressed against Elish as though he was a hot water bottle, though I knew he would run out of his own store as well. Bringing out this trick we both had cost strength and he needed it to drive over this hellish terrain.

The next several hours were misery, even with Elish shielding my back and his hat and my hood covering my head; I was a shivering shaking mess. I kept having to steady myself to keep my body from falling off the quad when the terrain got too uneven, which was hard with my arms wrapped around my body.

What was worse was that Elish kept stopping to look into houses but none of them seemed to fit his standards; whenever my hopes were raised, when he would pull in beside a house with a semi-intact roof, they were dashed moments later. It got to the point where the only reason I wasn't getting angry at him was because I was too cold and tired; speaking took energy I didn't have.

Night fell on us but he didn't stop, and because of his night vision he turned the single headlight off as well. We were nothing but a growl in the abyss moving along the landscape like a shadow beast.

I could understand why in my sombre, frozen state. A light that would be a boon for a man with normal vision was blinding with our sight; it caused more night blindness than illumination.

In the dark we rode on, for hours and hours; hours that melted together into one continuous frozen misery. Elish was cold now, his heat gone from his body but stubbornly he pushed on. His aura was nothing but contempt and annoyance, as if he had something to prove to this wasteland he had brought us to.

Though the greywastes knew no fear, not even the fear of my master. I think he had trouble accepting that the greywastes would take everyone's pride, even his.

The next stop didn't even bring me hope, just a bitter taste in my mouth to mix in with the rain water. But to my surprise he turned off the quad and wheeled it into an open garage that was attached to the small rancher. I heard him take off the bungee cord and the duffle bags, then with a screeching noise, he lowered the garage door and pushed an old tool box against the door that led inside the house.

"Get off, we're spending the night here." Elish's voice had lost none of his strength; he sounded as if he was giving me an order back home.

He never showed weakness, not even when he was dying yesterday did he give an inch to the world around him, even though the greywastes seemed to swallow even his crystal aura into its hundreds of miles of sepulchered misery.

I got off the quad but my legs were asleep and sore so I had to steady myself against the machine for support. In front of me Elish was getting things out of the bags and I heard the click of a bluelamp.

I looked around the garage and as I did I realized why Elish had driven us away from most of the other buildings. The interior was covered in spray-painted letters and images, and bloody nails which held leathery bits of flesh pinched into the crumbling drywall. There were work tables with axes resting beside them and chains hanging on steel latches, brown and covered in rust, staining the floor in their perfect outlines.

"I don't want to stay here," I whispered, my heart dropping into my chest. I felt the air around me suddenly became thick, every breath bringing anxiety and apprehension into me.

Elish took my blanket off me and hung it off of one of the benches. "We don't have a choice, you need to rest. We will leave in a few hours."

"But this is some sort of torture garage," I said quietly. I sat down beside the bluelamp as if expecting it to keep me warm but the LED light offered nothing but its cold glow. Elish started taking off his clothes and, without addressing my concerns at all, he told me to do the same.

The warm clothes from the covered duffle bags were a small comfort, though the blanket had helped trap in the body heat I was giving off. I had wished we would start a fire or something though, but as I looked around the blue-trimmed silhouettes of the tool boxes and plastic containers with lids ajar, I realized there was nothing we could burn. Greywasters or ravers had come in here, probably many times, and I knew this rotting frame of a house had been stripped bare and picked clean of everything but its beams.

I looked up from my lamp and saw Elish checking something in his overcoat, but he put it back in without a word. He looked angry and I was tired so the thought of asking him what he was checking on didn't even cross my mind. He hung up our clothes though I didn't see the point and put a duffle bag underneath my head.

Then he laid down in front of me and turned the bluelamp off; he held my shivering body tight against him and tucked the blanket underneath my back. I felt his stomach start to heat up, though he was tired and I could tell just from his aura alone.

"Rest now, I'll keep watch, no one will come here in this rain." Elish's voice was calm, but he tightened his hold on me. "You're safe."

I didn't realize how exhausted I was until I closed my eyes, safely in his embrace with his body and energy surrounding me. I wouldn't say I felt comfortable though, it was hard to feel comfortable in that place. Even in the darkness I could still smell the sour smell of rotting plywood and the damp smell of slowly decaying wood; it reminded me that I was far away from home.

I woke up to Elish's hand on my forehead. I looked around and immediately doubled over coughing, and as I hacked up onto the concrete I noticed I was extremely cold and shivery.

"Let's go." Elish's voice sounded behind me; he pulled me off of my feet before putting the blanket over my shivering body.

"How much further?" I asked, clutching the blanket to my chest. Elish bent down and lifted up the garage door with an assaultingly loud scraping noise, one that made my teeth get put on edge.

I sat down on the quad and ignored my aching bones. The greywastes were still dark, with no hint of sunlight shining on the horizon and no sign that the stars would soon give way to day. It was still the middle of the night, but that didn't shake my master's stolid determination. He was still focused on beating the greywastes, to prove that not even weather could stop him from getting what he wanted.

"I'm not sure, today I think." Elish wrapped the blanket up tight enough against my skin that he was able to get two layers on most of my body. "I wasn't expecting to have to drive the entire way."

He got on behind me and started the quad; it roared to life underneath me and the garage filled with the smell of sour exhaust. As he slowly eased the quad out I tried to talk over it. "What do you mean?"

Elish rolled down the carved out driveway, avoiding a large gouged out pot hole and a tipped over SUV. When he got onto flat road he answered. "I died, when we die Jack collects our bodies so those who killed us can't reign possession over us. We left Aras not because of Reaver, but because Jack knows Lycos well; I couldn't risk Jack seeing him alive. He's very much under Silas's thumb. We had to get as far away from Aras as quickly as we could."

Of course, I hadn't even thought of that, but then that drew forth more questions. "So why isn't he here?" I coughed into my blanketed arm.

"It's a signal in our brains that stops sending a relay to a device Jack has, usually he can track it. I took mine out years ago, but every time I am killed under Silas's hand, I worry that he will put it back in. Thankfully it seems he has not, though now I have to make it to Halfton Valley on my own steam, which I am not thankful for," Elish responded and at that moment he took a hard left. The cars in front of us were jammed together bumper to bumper as the people who had once lived in this neighbourhood tried to flee the city. The city itself was completely destroyed, and was nothing but beams and skeletons in the foggy distance, looking like tall metal trees reaching up to the sky.

A few hours into our journey my eyes got heavy and I felt sour pills come to my mouth. "Swallow them, they'll warm you up."

I realized we had stopped, though the roaring of the quad was still in my head, making my ears pulse and ring.

Then water was put to my lips and I swallowed it down, then a snack cake. "Eat."

"What about you?" The cellophane was already off. I put the sweet spongy cake to my mouth and started to quickly eat it. I was starving, tired, and thirsty.

"I'll eat when we get to the house. Are you cold?" Elish checked something in his overcoat then he looked at me with an emotionless expression and watched me eat, as if not trusting that I was able to do it myself.

I nodded and took the last bite of the cake and washed it down with some irradiated water. I could feel my Geigerchip vibrate as it passed through my throat. Not even the worst water in Moros made that thing go off; this must be straight unfiltered rain water.

Elish started on the quad again, permanently keeping one hand on my chest. I think I needed it, I really had been feeling sick and woozy all day, and a cold chill was settling into my muscles and bones.

"I think I caught a cold." I coughed into the blanket again.

"I know, it's from the dry air, we're inland and far from the ocean. I didn't expect you to be outside for so long, which is why we're getting to Halfton as soon as possible," Elish replied calmly. I felt the quad steer to the left as we passed a tipped over tractor trailer, its bones covered in prickly rust that dripped brown onto the pavement. Beside it a river had formed, cutting through the greywaste dirt and breaking concrete, forcing the small cracks apart to eventually form large fissures.

"How much longer?" I asked with another cough; this one scraped my throat.

"Not long, you can sleep if you want, we will not need to go off this road for another several miles, then it's off road until we arrive," Elish responded.

I nodded and he was silent after that. With the rain coming down and me in my dismal misery I wished he would keep talking to me. His voice was one of the few comforts I had in this miserable situation. I missed my warm bed, Luca doing everything I wanted, and the warm, dry apartment building.

The cold rattled my bones, the dampness seemed worse against my rain-washed skin. Sometimes I would feel warm but when I did Elish moved and the cold came back to me. I opened my eyes and watched the skeletons of cars pass by, with the black dead trees waving their spiny fingers at me as they swayed in the wind.

I think it was then that I realized Elish had probably never spent time in the greywastes, not the real greywastes where there weren't warm houses, underground labs or friend's houses that could shield us from this extreme weather. If he had and he knew how bad it was out here, he would've never left Aras. He wouldn't have exposed me to something like this; we were basically in the middle of a storm, and what broken-down houses we had come across were miles and miles behind us, only rocky valleys, mountains, and a single road kept us company now.

This thought sat like undigested food in my stomach, and as I felt him tense behind me with his aura as dark and cloudy as the rain drawn up mist, it was only further confirmation of my grim realization.

I tried to sleep, but whenever I would start to drift off the quad would take a turn, or a pot hole would jar both of us, sometimes even my head would rattle me awake with false memories of Elish's shock remote beeping. I managed a half awake half asleep state fuelled by the Dilaudids Elish had given me to swallow. They gave me a false sense of warmth, though a weight in my chest was making me cough even more.

Then the quad moved off road. I looked up after coughing a long bark into my blanket and saw sharp ridges rising their peaks over what looked like a grey canyon, one that seemed to swallow up mountains. I lifted my hand to point but it dropped.

"It used to be a lake," Elish explained, noticing I was looking at the sharp incline that led to the valley below. "But the water disappeared when a bomb fell, now though there is some water half a mile or so down. This is our valley, Halfton Valley. You'll be warm soon, let that keep you awake."

The remote beeped again and I jolted in my seat as if anticipating the shock, but it must've been in my head still. It was soon drowned out by rain and the shifting of greywaste mud.

My body leaned back as he drove up an incline, his hand resting firmly on my chest, an unsuccessful attempt to hide the fact he was listening to my breathing.

We went downhill next, the house must be near, but all I saw was the grey mud and rocks pass by, my eyes were fixed on the ground. I didn't even look up when he stopped the quad, or move when I heard a pressurized sound as he opened the door to a house I didn't see.

Elish got back onto the quad and slowly drove us at an incline, then everything went black. Cold, wet darkness, but in the distance I smelled bleach and indoors, if there was such a smell.

The quad turned off and a moment later I heard beeping; these were keypad beeps not the ones that shocked my collar. I looked around with tired eyes and though my night vision still worked I could only make out the slight shadow of a white ceiling, lined with removable tiles and a rusted unused sprinkler system.

Then bright light. I squinted my eyes and heard a small relieved breath from Elish; he grabbed me a moment later and walked me into a large underground apartment.

Blue walls, beige carpet, he walked with me down a hall and turned into a bedroom, he sat me on the bed with gentle hands. I could hear the heat clicking on around me, then the sound of wet clothing being pulled from soaked skin.

"The water will take time to heat up, in the meantime strip down and get under the blankets." Elish turned and left, leaving me half out of my jacket.

I fumbled with buttons with numb wrinkly fingers, managing to get my jacket and shirt off and leaving it in a wet mess beside the bed. I started shivering even harder, unable to keep myself from vibrating like I was seizing. I was confused at the sound I was making while shivering, but soon I realized it was the sound of my metal implants clicking together. It sounded like a sword fight inside my mouth.

When I had stripped down naked, I crawled under the fleecy red patterned covers and pulled them over my head, trying to breathe in as much warm air as I could, my lungs feeling like they were covered in a thin coat of ice.

Then I felt Elish get into bed beside me; he drew me into his arms and tried to make his body warm, though he was tired and I know he hadn't slept. The blankets would do it though.

I heard the beep again, but this time I knew it couldn't be in my head. "What's that?" I asked quietly.

"Just the remote, don't concern yourself with it. Just stay awake and get warm, the water will be hot enough soon for us both to shower. Then you can lay on the couch with some tea." Elish's stern voice was tight in his throat. I felt him rub his hand up and down my back. "You're trembling badly, it's like hugging an iceberg."

"Your fault," I whispered through my chattering teeth. I tried to make it sound playful but I failed miserably.

"I am aware whose fault it is," Elish said bitterly back, the self-derision in his voice surprised me. He heated up his hands and rested them against my chest. "Does this make breathing easier?"

I took in a deep breath, and though it still felt like I had a foot on my diaphragm the heat did help. I could feel the mucus in my chest break up a bit easier.

I nodded.

Eventually he rose and I heard him flick on a light in the other room and then water running. A few minutes later he took me into the shower with him.

As he looked down at me he chuckled before turning up the heat on the silver tap. "You're a pale, skinny little ghost of a boy. I've never seen such a pathetic sight."

Before I could answer back I started coughing, even though my chest felt heavy with liquid it didn't come up when I coughed. I stared at him miserably, hoping that if I was such a pathetic sight to him he would stop teasing me about it.

"I'll never forgive those idiots for putting you in Moros. Your immune system is horrendous, I've never seen a cold turn into pneumonia so quickly."

Pneumonia? I looked up at him, my eyes widened. Almost every winter I caught pneumonia, Kerres occasionally did too. I had almost died from it more than a few times. "How do you know?"

"Your heart rate, your breathing, your fever… I know your body and what your body doesn't tell me that remote does. Now try and wash yourself, turn the water as hot as you can stand it." Elish turned me around so I was facing the spray of steaming water. With his help I was able to wash myself, and when we were both done he walked ahead of me into the living room and turned on an electric fire embedded in the wall.

I sat by the fireplace and shivered like a wet dog, Elish was turning on lights and then I saw him place the kettle on the stove. I was so relieved to finally be indoors and out of the elements. This oasis in the greywastes seemed surreal, something that only a chimera with all the money in the world could build. I assumed this was like the safe houses littered in Skyfall; it would make sense for them to have small underground houses like this in a way, since apparently even the oldest chimera there was an idiot when it came to underestimating the greywastes.

I couldn't believe at one point I had wanted to defect here, I really would have been dead.

Elish brought me some antibiotics which I swallowed, before he gave me a book with some crushed yellow powder on it.

"There, you may take them nasally like you prefer. When you're done join me on the couch with your tea. You may put on a movie if you wish or I can bring in your Game Boy." Even when he was being kind he had to use his cold and commanding tone. I wondered if it was because he wasn't used to being kind like this. I appreciated it either way, I knew it was his way of apologizing for subjecting me to two days in the soaking rain and wind.

When I had taken in a good amount in each nostril I found my place in his arms. I sighed with relief and cupped my tea mug with my warming hands.

Slowly I felt the warmth come back to my iced bones, but still the chill in my chest remained, sending small trembling vibrations that I couldn't stop. My mind seemed to be jittering, like when you shake a jar full of bugs to see them fight, everything was quiet chaos though nothing loud enough for me to hear.

I coughed and he took my tea as I hacked into my arm. I apologized with a croak and he handed me back my tea. I felt a brush back of my hair, and a moment later the TV flicked on followed by a burned DVD of The Simpsons.

This was where I belonged, though what the toll would be on my body getting here I didn't know. I understood why he had to get out of Aras so quickly, but why he had to push us so hard to get to Halfton in almost two days I didn't know. There had been a lot of places we could've gotten warm in, though perhaps he had seen worse in those houses than the butcher's garage.

I sniffed back the sour drugs still stuck in my nostrils, and stared in a half-dreamy state at the television, only my coughing snapping the warmth coming back into my bones.

As he watched the television I glanced around the apartment we were in. There were windows that had blinds closed on them, and to the right a small kitchen with fancy stainless steel appliances and a clean linoleum floor. All the walls were blue or beige and the furniture as well, except for an area rug which was off-white and purple. This place was clean, and as the heat soaked into the rooms it seemed comfortable and homey. With the electric fireplace and Elish holding me, I felt safe, though this was a chimera's den so I didn't know how safe we really were. I guessed as long as King Silas remained dead. Hopefully for the next three weeks, I wouldn't have to worry about him coming after us.

"Well, we made it at least, are you warm now?" Elish asked. He rested a hand on my forehead.

I nodded. "I still feel like shit though, is this weather normal? I thought you told me once it didn't rain often and that's why so many buildings were intact?"

My master shook his head, his face darkening. "It does not rain often, unfortunately this is near the rainy season. We should be thankful the rain washed the snow away, there would be no way to come here in a foot and a half of snow, we would've had to walk to the nearest shelter and hope for the best, and knowing your frail, weak body, Cicaro, you would be dead by now."

I wiped my nose. "You wouldn't let me die."

"No, no I wouldn't."

Feeling like a puddle of muck, I shifted against him for reassurance. "Why?"

Elish looked down at me and raised one of his blond eyebrows. "You know why."

I decided to press past the endearing exchange of words that had become our thing since the beginning.

"Why?" I pressed lightly.

Elish took my delicate prying and in spite of his usual indifference to my need for reassurance he indulged me. "Because then I would have to finally get Luca the kitten he has been asking for every Skyday, and I would prefer to not have to."

I smiled and he smiled back for just a moment before he caught himself and motioned towards the television. "Now watch the television, and stop asking such nonsensical questions."

"Nope, you got me sick, I get to ask questions," I mumbled, though I did start watching the television again. I yawned and coughed at the same time, I *owed* and rubbed my chest, ignoring his amused snort behind me. "Can we stay here forever and say fuck you to everyone?"

"Tempting. I do get our network in this place so I can do some of my council work, but no, eventually we will have to return," Elish answered patiently. "But not for a while, until you're better and until Silas has had time to calm himself."

"Is he going to hurt us when we get back?" My voice dropped, I felt a shiver go up my spine, one not caused by the chill still embedded deep in my bones.

"I do not have an answer for that. Someone who doesn't know Silas would tell you he will without hesitation, but Silas is sneaky and devious; he never goes for the obvious kill, remember this. To hurt us on our return would be too easy for him… he is in the throes of his game with us and he will never hesitate to throw a curve ball. No, I suspect my punishment for killing him may go ungiven for years possibly. By that time Reaver will be ready and you will –" Elish cut himself off. As I looked up at him I saw him draw up those steel barriers.

Instead he said quietly, "No matter."

"Me what?" I found my own voice dropping down an octave, holding my breath as if breathing would break the silent honesty between the two of us. This small and fleeting state he rarely found himself in was a delicate one, and even the slightest movement might jar him into putting those barriers back up. I wanted to hear what he was going to say next; I had to know what part of this had to do with me.

I felt his chest rise and fall; he took a slow drink of his tea. I felt the fringes of his aura tickle the outskirts of my mind, even though my aura abilities were far from the realms of my strength. It was a testament to his strength, his control, and his willpower.

"I am going to make you immortal."

The words hit me, and for a few stunned moments I didn't know what to say back. What do you say to someone telling you he wants you to live forever?

I said the only thing I could manage through a mouth full of questions. "W-why?" I said in a stuttering percussion that brought out a crack in my voice, as if I needed to prove just how young I was.

Elish, with only his calm and controlled aura around him, replied in a simple tone, "Keeping you alive is distracting, it would be more convenient to not have to worry about Silas or any of the others trying to kill you."

A tightness took my throat as the weight of his words sunk into me, but not the words themselves, it was the unspoken string of realizations that always came attached to Elish's veiled truths. The puzzle that was given to you to crack: what Elish says and what Elish means.

Though he was a straightforward man who was supposed to only say how he felt, no matter how blunt and cruel. When it came to us nothing could be said out in the open; it had to always be cloaked behind half-truths for him to keep his label of being the emotionless ice-cold chimera. Elish would never be a man to tell me he had grown attached to me, or that I was something more than a cicaro pet; he would never divulge his feelings to me or anyone. I had accepted that, but accepted or not I still picked apart his words to try and find the hidden meanings.

"Is it just so I won't die before you're bored of me?" I whispered. Suddenly my mind had filled with new fears, of having to live through the day he finally has had enough of me, or had finally found someone new to entertain him.

Lycos had told me that Elish had done it with all the cicaros before me, that eventually he got what he wants out of them and tossed them aside. Those words had weighted on my soul, why should I be different from all of them? I hadn't been alive when he'd had other pets, I didn't know what had happened. Though we had been master and pet for one and a half years now he was still almost ninety years old; he'd had a long time to use and toss aside boys like me.

Like Lycos… from what he had said.

"Why must you always jump to the worst possible conclusion? I tell you I wish for you to live forever and you must make it into some foreboding of abandonment?" Elish said dully, taking my teacup away as I started to hack and cough again.

"I just –" I protested, wiping my mouth, but before I could get the other words out he hushed me.

"No more, I indulged you enough, Cicaro, rest now. Your questions can wait, you have an immortal lifetime to ask them."

I sighed and nodded, knowing that I had reached the threshold of his patience with me. Instead I sipped my tea and let him pet my hair back, wondering what was going on below his surface.

CHAPTER 33

I FELT ELISH GRAB ME FROM UNDERNEATH MY ARMS and rise me, then some cold water brought to my lips. I asked him where I was, and he told me I was safe.

My mind was pulling me in every direction possible and with that my eyes scanned the room. Was I in Moros? No, the place looked too nice, no apartment in Moros was this clean. Was I in Skyfall? I could be, but then why weren't we home?

His hand was cold on my forehead, then he wiped my face with a rough cloth. I could focus my eyes better after that, but I was boiling hot.

"Can I go sit in the snow?"

"Of course not, why would you ask such a thing?"

"I'm hot."

"I know, the antibiotics will help with that."

I nodded and coughed, he held a towel to my mouth and chuckled coldly when I was finally able to gasp for breath. "And you ask me why I wish to make you immortal?"

My head tilted forward and the world swirled around me, a feeling like I was floating on balls of cotton, which seemed to take me far away from the congested mess the pneumonia was bringing me to. I tried to talk, I did everything I could to form the words out of my mouth but all that came out was a mumbled string of nothing.

"Jade?"

I blinked slowly as Elish said my name, feeling a bit more with it than

I did yesterday. I looked up and saw he was wearing a blue checkered shirt; his hand moved in front of my vision and I felt my chin get tilted up. He looked at me, his shorter hair touching his cheekbone. "You must put some force behind those coughs, your lungs are congested and it's time you started clearing them."

I stared at his shirt and tried to cough. I heard him sniff. "Well, that was rather pathetic; for someone who can scream so loudly your lungs are just dreadful."

"Is pneumonia contagious?" My voice was like sandpaper scraping against needles.

"It can be."

I coughed a bit harder, and I heard him chuckle. "Hilarious, now remain sitting up. If you don't start coughing up that congestion I'm going to start slamming my hand on your back or electrocuting your chest, I haven't decided which."

I managed a nod though my head felt like a ball bearing. I tried to think of something else witty to say, but a sudden wave of hot dizziness dashed any retorts on my lips. Instead I inched towards him with a whimper.

"You're all sticky and sweaty, must you come near me?" Elish protested, but with a sigh he sat down beside me and I leaned against him.

"Once you're immortal, I can kill you with morphine and within four hours you will be recovered. None of this annoying sickness to deal with. This is a sengil's job not mine, when did I become your serventmaid?" He sounded impatient but I knew he was just protecting his chimera pride; at least no one was around to see him wiping sweat off of my brow.

"W-watch… watch yourself, s-sengil." My teeth started to chatter, he let out an unimpressed breath through his nose and put a cold hand against my chest.

"You still have your humour, your fever is one hundred and two point five though, and there is nothing funny about that. I'll be preparing an IV for you soon. Pneumonia is all the more deadly to a slumrat with the immune system of a premature infant."

I started coughing again, and this time I felt him hit my back. I doubled over with my chest feeling like it was caving in on itself, drawing up more and more of my strength to bring up the thick coating of mucus I could feel every time I breathed.

Chunks of green pus appeared in my hand, rimmed with red. I wiped it on the towel with a mumbled apology. It was embarrassing to hack up this gross shit around my master; I felt humiliated to have him see me in such a state. I was supposed to be eye candy, dressed in tight leather that brought out the slender lines of my body, cocksure, confident, and a force to be reckoned with. I was supposed to give off that aura, and keep up that appearance and now it was all being hacked away like the phlegm in my lungs.

"Good, keep coughing it up," Elish said approvingly.

I wiped my mouth and said through a raspy voice, "I don't want you seeing me like this."

He thumped my back when I started coughing again. I hacked up more green gunk into the towel this time and folded it over itself before he could see it

"Oh? Are you worried I will no longer see you as some demi-godly Adonis sex symbol? You destroyed that image of yourself when you had to piss in a bottle in the dog cage, then further on when you were nothing but a sweaty, vomit-covered mess when your mother poisoned you, oh, and let's not forget when I found your one hundred and fifteen pound unwashed body in a brothel covered in filth and abscesses. Oh and, of course –"

"Okay, okay." I wiped my mouth with the same towel. "I get it, fine. I still don't like you seeing me like this though. Until you make me into a god, I'm just a worthless slumrat succumbing to mortal afflictions."

"What a silly thing to say, even when you're immortal you'll still be my worthless slumrat." The words spun from his mouth in an oddly doting way. Elish hit my back again, until I could feel a welt forming. I coughed again.

I had to smile at the inner workings of my chimera. It was like watching a tiger try to bathe a duckling; you had to almost *aww* when the tiger eventually licked all of its down and skin off. The point was the ferocious beast was trying to be attentive, so you had to look past the bloodied feathers hanging out of its mouth.

I leaned against Elish and wiped the sweat on my forehead, taking in a congested, difficult breath. My lungs felt like a crackling fire every time I breathed.

"How do you make someone immortal?" I mumbled after he had turned off the light above us, only a table lamp bathed the blue bedroom in a dim glow.

"It is not a fun process. Silas prepares a piece of brain tissue beforehand, from his own brain and while the chimera is under he cuts a hole in his skull and slices their brain and puts the piece in deeply. The piece of brain attaches itself to the chimera's brain and fuses with it, giving the chimera's brain the regenerative abilities that Silas was born with," Elish explained.

Cut my brain open? I shuddered, but my body was still shivering so it went unnoticed. "And you had this done?"

Elish nodded. "The first chimera to have it done was Nero, since it was still experimental. When he survived and regenerated he was soon followed by Garrett, Ellis, and finally myself. Afterwards only the chosen chimeras got the gift of immortality."

"Does it have to be King Silas's brain since he was born with it? Or can it be any immortal chimera?" I asked, taking a moment to cough up more of the mucus in my lungs. The towel was starting to get damp and sticky. No wonder my lungs felt like I was trying to pull apart pieces of fly paper with every breath.

"Only born immortals can do it."

That raised more questions in me. "Can't you just make me immortal now then? We can cut out a piece of Silas's brain while he's recovering."

Elish shook his head. "No, I would despise having you stuck as a teenager forever."

I hadn't thought of that. "So I would be a teenager body and mind forever if I survived?"

"That's right, your frontal lobes won't mature until you're about twenty. Five years sooner than a normal man; you have your chimera engineering to thank for that."

"So... when will Reaver stop aging? Since he's a born immortal like Silas?"

"About twenty-four I believe. I was never sure, but from what I have managed to dig up regarding Silas's pre-Fallocaust life, he stopped aging at twenty-four. With us chimeras, once we're implanted with the brain matter we stop aging altogether mentally and physically."

"How old were you when you had yours done? The first generation?"

"Thirty-three."

"When do you want to do it to me?" I asked as Elish reached over and turned out the light. I heard him shift down and move me so my back was to him; I guessed it was so he could beat the mucus out of me during the night.

"Ideally I would want to wait until you're twenty-four, but I have a feeling I will need to do it sooner. It depends on King Silas and on Reaver's development. I will know when it is the right time, but I will put it off as long as possible… for my own sanity." I heard him yawn and a chin rest on the top of my head. "Now sleep, I will be awake, your coughing will most likely prevent me from sleeping long."

"At least I'll be young and hot forever then."

"More mature too, hopefully. Perhaps I won't have to exchange you for a newer model in time."

"If you ever leave me when I'm immortal, I'm going to devote the rest of eternity to finding new and painful ways to kill you." I grabbed his arm and pulled it so it was under the crook of my own. "And I'll rip to pieces any new cicaro you find, and your sengils too."

"Mmhm, go to sleep."

"I am fifty-five percent Sanguine and he's psychotic. I'd put him to shame, just warnin' you." My words were starting to slur.

"And yet you're one hundred percent idiot. I am counting the days until those frontal lobes grow. I do despise teenagers."

Clean water flowed into the tea kettle, copper bottomed with a stainless steel handle. I put it on the red-hot stove element and started looking for the cabinet that held the tea mugs.

"Do you have your favourite mug?" My voice wasn't my own, but that was a small glitch in my mind that I paid no heed to. So many other things were wrong compared to just the tone of my voice, it was easily lost in my head. "Or one you would like me to use?"

"My purple mug with the cat? No, I left that back in Alegria, it doesn't matter which one, just remember… one hundred and twenty seconds on that particular tea," King Silas whispered behind me. "Make sure the temperature is right, Elish, don't make me make you pour it down the drain."

"Yes, Master."

I looked down at my hands, they were bandaged, old bandages discoloured with bits of fabric stuck to them, and new ones from being scalded again and again. Some of the burns were half healed, others searing my skin as they ached for the relief of cold water. The burns spread up my arms and became different shapes the more they spread down my body. Cigarette burns, lighter marks, body parts held to smouldering coals, or stove elements, with the smells of my own burning flesh choking my lungs with its thick smoke.

I looked down at the empty mug, before turning around and sweeping the room with my gaze.

My feet drew me past my master, who was sitting on an olive-coloured wing chair, his legs crossed and his hands folded neatly on his lap. Then I went to the mirror.

My eyes had bruises under them, purple ones to match my irises. Though my violet gems still overshadowed the blackened blemishes on my face, they seemed to distract the vision from the abuse that appeared so obvious, that and my long blond hair that touched my shoulders.

I was young; I couldn't have been older than fifteen.

The kettle gave a whistle and I ran over to take it off of the element. King Silas would grow angry if it whistled for longer than necessary. I poured the tea with shaking hands and put a tea bag into each. I mentally counted every second.

"Why are you making… tea?" I looked behind me, a confused look on my face. It sounded like he was right behind me but he was still sitting on the couch with his hands tented.

I shook the voice from my head and grabbed the mug of tea. I brought it to Silas and handed it to him, before sitting down on the chair directly in front of him.

He had come especially to see me, but why?

"Did you get the… the research I sent? Perish and I have been making great progress with the teeth on the two chimeras you ordered. All we are waiting on now are your names for the two Chimera D's." I took a sip of my tea, watching his every move, despising my conditioned body for twitching every time he raised the tea to his lips. I anticipated the burning liquid on my flesh, soaking into my bandaged hands to trap the heat into my burns.

Silas took a small sip. "Sanguine will be the one with the red eyes, Jack will be the one with the black. Write down their names properly, *Elias*."

My mouth downturned. He always had to bring that up even though it wasn't my fault. The name they implanted me was supposed to be Elias, not Elish, though at least Master Silas liked the name I kept calling myself. Elish Sebastian Dekker. We shared a middle and a last name, but that was where our similarities ended.

"I'll… I'll write it down."

"Write what down?"

My eyes shot up to him, but it was as if he didn't say anything, he looked at his tea mug and I watched his lips slowly move. As he told me the spelling I wrote it down: S-a-n-g-u-i-n-e.

"Yes, that is the spelling…" Silas sipped his tea and lowered his coffee mug. I twitched in my chair but he seemed… calmer.

"Elish, love, did you enjoy yourself at my birthday party for you?"

A trickle of ice water slipped down my spine.

Nero told me I was next, but I had hoped… he would… I hadn't even seen Garrett since he took him to that floor in Alegria. Did he know the shameful things I did to myself while I watched Silas take him? The thought made my face flush with embarrassment.

A tremble of electricity ran up my hand, for a fleeting moment I thought it was mine but a moment later the flare intensified and I felt a scream come to my lips.

The tea mug fell to the floor, spilling the half-heated liquid onto the carpet. The boy screamed in the sepia-lit darkness, piercing the silence the deep of night brought. He gasped, took a step back but he was grabbed again.

Elish shook him, back and forth as his head whipped back like a ragdoll, it took every dug up piece of self-control to stop when he started crying out. He wanted to shake him until the memory he stole shot out of his head, never to be seen again. He had tried to forget those times with every ounce of his engineering

It's not his fault, it's yours, now put him down.

Elish stopped, his heart a rapid drum. He wondered if the boy's hearing could now pick it up, but no... he was almost unconscious. His golden eyes were almost rolled back into his head, and only a flare of heat from Elish's palms made them roll back to the world; small bursts of light on a body comprised of only blacks and whites.

"Jade?" Elish whispered. He brushed Jade's black bangs from his eyes, behind his ears flushed from his fever. "Who am I? What's my name?"

"Elish, but it was supposed to be Elias."

So it was true, a part of Elish wanted nothing more than to convince himself the boy was merely sleepwalking. But no, what scorn he felt from the boy's probing abilities would need to be discarded. In truth this was a very remarkable development, one Elish would undoubtedly use to his advantage at a later date. The anger he felt was drawn from pure embarrassment of the boy seeing him like that, so young and so... damaged. It was a useless emotion, without benefit than to further make his soul threadbare.

It would be tossed aside, it had no use. He had stopped feeling useless emotions years ago, they were nothing but toxic fog to distract him from things that were important. What was important right now was–

"Master? You forgot your tea, did I make it wrong again?"

Elish allowed himself a small sigh, he picked up the boy who was babbling incoherently and brought him back to the bedroom. Oh, why did it have to only happen when Jade was delirious with fever? To get the boy to do this when he was well and within his own mind would be near impossible.

But I suppose if it was this easy I would've drawn it out of him through pain and intense sessions of sex like when he had shocked me several months ago.

It would be a challenge, since he was a chimera and so close to the boy it would mean he would have to play Jade's guinea pig. Perhaps Luca could offer his services but Jade would be using it mostly on chimeras, and their engineered minds worked differently. It would be like teaching Jade how to drive an automatic when he would only be driving stick shift.

Elish needed Jade's abilities trained properly…

Oh, the things I could get him to look into… I could get him to finally unravel Perish's brain. I had thought it would be impossible.

A flare of excitement illuminated the opal hues of Elish's soul. This would be perfect, yes, this could be the key to putting all the pieces together, finally awakening the secret he had spent so many years trying to uncover.

But not him, no… he would have to find someone else for the boy to practice on. To have this young man probe Elish's own thoughts would be disastrous. Jade was a cicaro and had no right poking his roving nose in places he had no purpose being. The boy was still young and still had the rebellious, sneaky nature of a Morosian and he wouldn't hesitate to use the information against his master when he was in the throes of a tantrum. It couldn't be him.

No, this slip will be my first and last, I will allow my mind no more breaches like this. I will find another way, another chimera or similar. It will take time but that is one thing we have right now, we have time; the boy is advancing too quickly for comfort anyway. His head and body need to be heated and cooled, something I have been doing since the beginning, and the tempering process is a slow one. Though the results will last for the rest of his soon-to-be immortal life.

Elish leaned down and removed the sweaty hair stuck to Jade's face, he brushed it back and with his cooling touch the boy opened his eyes. Small burning suns, the pupil so black they were depthless and – yes…

Elish smiled silently to himself, yes, there were those silver flecks. It made Elish happy to see they were returning; he had wondered how long it would take. The blackness in Jade's eyes reminded Elish too much of the young boy's greywaster brother; he preferred the shining gold coins that gazed up at him with a thousand emotions at once.

"Elish?"

"I am right here, are you too hot?" Elish asked as the boy sat up in bed, looking around in a daze. His face was as pale as the moon but for the shadow of facial hair that grew quicker with every year. He was turning into a man in front of Elish's eyes but he still loved being held tight to his master's chest, though with all the horrible things that seemed to happen to him it was probably the only place the boy felt safe.

And though Elish complained in his own head whenever he had to carry Jade, he didn't mind nearly as much as he convinced himself he did. It was something he had gotten used to, and now it seemed odd not to have the boy beside him at all times.

"Your hands are burned," Jade mumbled. He raised a clammy hand and tried to pick up Elish's. He looked at them and traced a finger like he could actually see the bandages. "I would've never let him burn you."

Elish retracted his hand and his eyes narrowed; if only there was some way to wipe those images from Jade's mind, but even if there was he couldn't. It was for the greater good that Jade kept those thoughts; he might remember how he accessed them tomorrow if Elish was lucky.

But there had never been any luck in this, no, the only luck he ever got was figuring out how to make the first child immortal. After that his luck had seemed to run out, the burns still scarring Lycos's body was a testament to that, he had come dangerously close to having to find another surrogate family to take in the black-eyed child, and wild genes like that would be best handled under the care of someone who knew what they were dealing with. It was a miracle Jade had survived to adolescence.

"Yes, he liked to burn me and blow cigarette smoke in my face. He didn't burn the others so I have no answer as to why," Elish responded quietly. The boy nodded, still a mess of stray bangs and clammy skin.

Jade patted his hand in his delirious state. "We'll burn him alive."

"That would be enjoyable."

The boy got up again in the middle of the night to cough, long and hoarse coughs that made Elish wonder if he was going to break a rib, but he was hacking up the phlegm and really that was all that was important. When Jade was finished he curled his sticky self up to Elish's arm and fell back asleep. A noisy sleep, full of tossing and turning, whimpering and whining, but Elish never needed much sleep anyway, so he entertained himself with future plans and eventually, the television.

The next morning Elish woke and put an IV in the boy. After showering and making himself tea and breakfast he did his work while listening for signs that Jade was waking, but besides the hoarse coughing there was nothing.

Then afternoon came and Jade appeared, the IV bag was empty and had been detached which was good. He was holding all the dirty sheets and blankets and was, in a pathetic attempt, trying to drag them to the laundry room.

Elish didn't say anything; it was a rather amusing sight, the boy was dressed in nothing but purple boxer shorts, unless you counted green mucus as a garment. He was slumped over, sweaty and pale as the moon, trying to keep hold of the blue plaid sheets.

Jade sniffed and walked past him as if Elish wasn't even there, and five minutes later he came out of the laundry room with a fresh pair of sheets.

"That really isn't necessary." Elish sipped his tea, more amused than anything at the boy's lame attempts to keep the apartment clean.

The boy gave Elish a glazed over look, he looked down at the sheets, mumbled something, then walked back to the bedroom. Elish shrugged to himself and continued working on this year's budget for the districts of Skyfall. The weeder harvest had done well this year and with that would come more money; every district was clamouring for a piece of the pie and it was Elish and his brother Joaquin's job to distribute the extra funds.

Time ticked by and the bedroom became silent. After a while Elish got up and walked to the bedroom they had both been sharing.

It was cute in a way, Jade's had only gotten three corners of the bottom sheet on before he had given up and gone back to sleep. It was strange to feel pity for the young chimera, usually when Jade was injured it was well-deserved, but this time no matter how much Elish tried to convince himself it wasn't, it was his fault. He had put his stubborn need to leave Aras ahead of the boy's health, even though the weather was horrible and neither of them had proper rain gear. And further on when the weather worsened he had pushed the quad and himself to get to Halfton Valley as soon as possible. Opting to surge forward because he hated the thought of having to camp out in one of those disgusting houses, it had given him the impression of giving into the greywastes. He should've been smarter than that, but he underestimated the greywastes, the terrain, and the weather, and unfortunately it was the boy who suffered. Through no fault of Jade's own he was ill.

Which was why, though it was strange and something Elish was still learning how to do, he felt compelled to help him, even though this really was Luca and Lyle's job. Elish had never taken care of anything in his life bigger than a house cat, and he only fed them because they whined otherwise.

Elish picked up the ragdoll of a teenager and put him into the bathtub, the boy didn't even flinch even though the water was on the cold side to try and bring down his fever.

As Elish did, and had been doing for the past one and a half years, while he bathed the teenager in the cold water he mulled over in his mind just why he was doing this. Why he was right here, kneeling over the ceramic tub, taking care of this empath and keeping him safe. It had been a trial with Jade; never in Elish's life had he had to face so many realities and so many incidences where he had to admit quietly to himself that he should've handled things better.

What had started out as annoyance towards Ares and Siris and their decision to go on with their games (even though they knew Elish was caretaking the mansion that night), turned into something different very quickly. He remembered fondly those scared eyes peering at him from beside the fireplace and the surprise inside of him when Jade had quietly asked him to read aloud. In that moment Elish had felt a flicker of enchantment inside of him; the Morosian boy, a wild slumrat with a bad attitude, raised without discipline or even proper love, had bared a small piece of his heart to him, a chimera. Even though he was cut from the same cloth as the twins who stalked the hallways for his flesh.

Jade had put himself out there anyway, the bloodied, raped boy who had just gone through an evening of trauma, had exposed a part of himself to Elish... a man who was not just a chimera, but the highest ranking one in existence.

No matter how many times Elish replayed that evening and early morning in his head, he could never crack the puzzle; the mystery behind his actions and the boy's had never ceased to confound him. He had lost sleep trying to unravel the mystery, but he always came up with nothing and that conclusion had infuriated and frustrated him, to the point where he knew the only way he could figure out what had happened was to covet the boy himself, no matter how much his brothers snickered behind his back at this out of character reaction.

The first step was to get his file from Knight Dekker, Ellis's son and the man in charge of Edgeview, then he set up plants familiar with Moros to spy on Jade. His interest in the boy had grown when it was revealed that he was a thief and a fence in Moros, and that he'd had a boyfriend for as long as he had been out of Edgeview. A Morosian native with a mentally-deranged mother, a ripe fruit, spoiled but still on the vine. Elish had to have him so he started to pull the strings and plant the seeds needed to make it so.

It had been easy; the first thing he had to do was to start the rift with the boyfriend, and the most straightforward thing to do was to fire Jade from his job and promote Kerres. The imbalance there would be obvious and the slumrat pride would make Jade resentful of Kerres being the sole bread winner. When that was slower to take on than Elish wished, he planted the Mp3 player as the Stadium prize.

Now that was a plan he was proud of, and the other chimeras were more than willing to go along with it. They loved to play their games on the insects below them and revelled almost as much as Elish did at the expression on the boy's face when he realized just what was in the box.

After that things happened quickly, because Kerres had played right into his hands trying to get into Olympus... there was nothing more stupid and Elish had taken advantage of it. Ideally, he would've liked to sever their relationship for a few more months but when an opportunity like that presented itself –

No, that was the ideal memory... in truth Elish did almost leave the boy to die in that alley. Only now that he'd had Jade for so long did he disliked thinking of how close he had come to never having Jade as a cicaro, but it was the truth. Because he was starting to dislike the confusing feelings inside of him when he saw Jade.

Elish prided himself on the fact that he knew his own mind, body, and emotions inside and out, and this Morosian had thrown a wrench into all of that, making him do things he wouldn't normally do, and feel things he had dismissed as mortal emotions.

It was frustrating, but at the same time intriguing and for that he kept drawing himself back to the boy out of pure curiosity of how his own self had reacted. A morbid curiosity, or boredom, who was to know which emotion had been stronger.

Elish had enjoyed it, but at the same time he found himself hating it.

He disliked admitting to himself that Jade drew up a lust inside of him he had never felt before, a lust that he had pushed onto Jade hours after they had met. That slip caused Elish frustration, he had never been sexual in the least; it was a baseless emotion and feeling that clouded one's judgment. It offered nothing but a momentary release followed by fatigue. A nagging annoyance that Elish took care of only out of necessity, because he had to bitterly admit even if his mind didn't want it, his body would bother him until it got its release. He summoned Drake twice a week to take care of him orally, or if he decided he needed more he would take Garrett during his chess visits. Unbeknown to Jade chess usually meant something different between those two, though since the cicaro came about it had become just that and only that.

Which was probably why Garrett was whining for his own cicaro.

It wasn't just the sexual thirst that Jade had brought out of the immovable chimera, it had been other emotions buried deeply inside. Rage, worry, fear, and frustration, and oddest of all: protectiveness. King Silas had seen it before, he had and Joaquin and Garrett had too, something deeper was developing inside the chimera, and though he didn't know what to make of it, the thing Elish knew for sure was that he would burn down Skyfall before he let King Silas hurt Jade again.

Elish's brow furrowed, though it was an interesting turn of events in his life it did come with its own share of problems. He knew his brothers were snickering behind his back over his cicaro chimera, but as long as they kept their gallantry to themselves they could do as such. It happened to all of them; Artemis and Tyan were the latest in years and years of public humiliations to keep the chimeras on their toes and most importantly: loyal. Silas let them live their lives in comfort, but never allowed them to be too comfortable.

It was just the way things were, and with Reaver ripening nicely in the greywastes, and the addition of his future partner Killian, he would be ready to be plucked in a few years' time and Elish could finally be rid of their Mad King.

That thought alone made all of this worth it, and that thought alone made Elish patient with his own confusing emotions and reactions involving Jade. He would have all the time in the world to unravel that mystery.

"Elish?" Jade croaked when Elish was rinsing his hair under the detachable hose.

"Mm?"

"I'm soaking in hot water."

"Fascinating."

"– I'm a tea bag."

The boy looked at Elish, a grin appeared on Jade's face before he started laughing.

Elish could do all but stare at the boy, the thought once again crossing his mind that he had indeed gone mad himself for taking this Morosian as his cicaro, chimera or not. Sometimes Elish was sure Jade had some sort of brain damage caused by malnutrition or just the trials of being raised in the slums, but then again, he was only seventeen and teenagers were idiots.

Elish dumped some cold water on his head. "You would make the most disgusting tea."

Jade let out a delirious giggle, before sliding down in the tub, taking a mouthful of water and spouting it in an arch like a water fountain.

"You know, I could hold your head underneath this bath water and all my troubles would be over." Elish smirked.

Jade smiled, looking pathetic as usual, red rimming the bottoms of his eyes mixing with the black bags from being woken up all night to clear his lungs. When he is immortal Elish would just kill him and be done with such an inconvenient sickness, it would be easier then.

The thought soured Elish's mood, the others were right, he had taken the boy when he was too young. If he could've waited a few more years he could make him immortal now, then overthrowing Silas would be all the more easier. But what was done was done, and in truth, chimera or not, if Jade remained in the slums he would've died, or Silas would've harvested him himself like the other chimeras they dropped off to their surrogate parents to raise. At least having the chimera at the age of fifteen made him grow attached to his master; it would've been a much tougher fight to tame him if he had gotten him at eighteen or nineteen.

The boy still had a love-starved quality to him, that ached for approval, acceptance, and protection, things he never had growing up. Once you reached full maturity your brain hardened and if you hadn't received those things, your mind closed off their receptors. The boy hadn't been there yet, and he had soaked up Elish like a sponge.

Jade started coughing and as he always did Elish slammed his hand down on his back, watching the flecks of green, white and yellow fall into the soapy water.

"Thank you, Master," Jade croaked.

"Oh, hello, Jade, feeling a fleeting moment of sanity are we?"

Jade wiped his mouth and took in a deep breath, Elish could hear his lungs crackling. "Yeah, when I'm better I have to tell you about this dream I had."

Interesting, he isn't trying to hide it from me, I was so sure he would...

"Yes, I heard some mention of it. Do not think anything of it now, like you suggested once you're well we will talk about it."

Jade nodded and Elish helped him stand up and draped him in a towel. A small smile appeared on the boy's lips, and his eyes looked almost wistful. "In my dream you looked so small and innocent. What happened?"

Small and innocent? Even at that age they never described him as such, but Jade had only seen him in the presence of his master, and all of them acted on their best behaviour especially back then. Days long ago when King Silas had made it clear they were the hope for the future; the first of many chimeras who would rule the world, or what shattered remains Silas had left of the world.

King Silas taught them, doted on them, raised them but they never called him father, only his single daughter, an unwanted twin of Nero who Silas decided to let live from mere curiosity, had been given that privilege.

The reason behind that was made clear when the three male chimeras had turned fifteen.

Elish banished the thought from his mind and helped Jade into the living room. "When you get to be my age you'll see what happens, life happens. Now sit on the couch, some mint tea will help clear your lungs."

Jade nodded and Elish was happy to see that, though he was slow, he was able to walk. Elish saw him wipe his brow, his face the picture of fatigue and sickness. Only the slumrat could remind the immortal chimera just how fragile the human body could be. Though a slender solid creature, who usually radiated strength and endurance, when in the throes of pneumonia he was but a small waif lost in evanescent but damning mortal afflictions.

After Jade was warm and dry, and the electric fireplace had been turned up as high as it could go, Jade sat with both hands clasped around his tea mug, Elish keeping him close and engaging him in a two player game of checkers.

Jade coughed into a tea towel and put his hand over Elish's which was cupping the mouse. He slid his checker over. "King me."

Elish tsked at him. "You dare to become king before your master?"

The black-haired cicaro smiled and watched as the small pixilated black checker got a king's crown on top of it. "I'll take you with me. I am a stern but gentle king, you can be my mistress."

Elish rubbed his head affectionately and watched Jade as he raised a shaky hand and drained his mint tea. Elish tried to take it from him but he shook his head. "I need to pee anyway, can I get you more tea too?"

"Sure, do not scald yourself." Elish handed Jade his tea mug before ruthlessly taking down Jade's newly crowned king with a double hop of his white checker. As Jade left he saw Elish smirk smugly to himself.

Elish tuned his hearing to monitor the boy's every movement; after Jade was done in the washroom his soft footsteps took him to the kitchen. As Elish heard the scraping of the kettle against the stove element he mapped out the checkers game in his head and tried to challenge himself to predict Jade's next several moves. He would win this game, of course, the only time he ever lost was on purpose if Jade was acting too smug.

Jade knew he could never win a game against Elish but when he thought he was close he got excited and started squeaking like a mouse, then once Jade did win he was immediately deflated and whined knowing he had been strung along. It was fun to take the wind out of his sails.

Elish tapped his finger against the top of the mouse, debating if he should win sooner or drag out the game, when he noticed the kitchen had gone silent. He looked behind him and found Jade standing a foot from the back of the couch, a blank expression on his face.

"Jade?" Elish put the laptop down.

The boy didn't flinch, he continued to stare blankly at the wall in front of him, still holding both cups of tea in his hands. It was like someone had pressed pause on him, he wasn't moving an inch.

Elish rose, wondering if this was another aura thing; he took a step towards Jade when suddenly the boy's frozen body fell to the ground like a tipped over mannequin, the cups of tea shattering and spilling around him.

In a matter of moments, from calmness to chaos, Jade started violently seizing. His eyes rolled to the back of his head and his teeth clenched. Elish tried to hold Jade's arms down but they balled and curled so tightly against his chest Elish could see the taut veins popping through his flesh.

This wasn't good… this was a grand mal seizure. With a calm grace in intense situations only the Elish had, he got onto his remote phone and pressed the number at the top of his contact lists, at the same time trying to make sure Jade's airways stayed open.

"Oh, hello E-"

Elish abruptly cut Garrett off. "The boy is sick, he's having a grand mal seizure and he has pneumonia. I need you here now, bring Lyle."

There was a pause, and though it was only for a few seconds Elish found himself holding his tongue to prevent himself from delivering a scathing comment to hurry up.

"Okay, I'm at your place right now actually. Where are you?"

"Halfton Valley."

"We'll be right there."

There was a beep as Elish disconnected the call, he put his hand on the boy's chest as Jade continued to seize, his other hand steadying Jade's chin. Elish could feel the boy's muscles contracting and tensing all over his body, his eyes frozen and glazed, lost to anything that was happening around him.

Elish counted in his head, it lasted two and a half minutes. When the last spasm ripped from Jade's thigh to his chest he lay still; his chest a crackling heave as it struggled to suck in as much oxygen as it could.

Then Jade's eyes closed and he fell unconscious. Elish picked him up, monitoring and weighing each breath and sat with him on the couch.

Finally, after some coaxing words Jade's eyes opened, jutting around until they found Elish's. Jade stared at him in muddled confusion.

"What? You're here? Where's Kerres?" Jade looked from side to side delirious and unfocused. "What're… where… shit, where's little you?"

"Little me?"

Jade was silent for a few moments, his mouth opened and closed trying to find his tongue and words. When he did speak his voice was weaker and more strained than before. "When you were small, Nero used to put you in headlocks; you stuck close to Silas, you were real attached to him, what happened?" The boy's words started to slur. "He protected you from Nero, and Garrett's pranks. Golden boy, you were his golden boy."

Elish's face darkened but he reminded himself the boy had just had a seizure and wasn't in his own mind. "You should stop that mind from wandering into mine, it will only get you into trouble."

Jade's face suddenly fell, his bottom lip pursed into his own. "Is Kerres still dead?"

"Yes."

His face twisted in remorse, but like the thought was only a fleeting breeze his expression changed to wonder. "Why are we killing Silas if you loved him so much?" Jade raised a hand and touched Elish's lips tenderly.

"People change," Elish whispered. He reached over and turned on the television in hopes of distracting the delirious boy from asking so many inappropriate questions. He had his patience with Jade, a patience that he held for no other man or chimera, but even his patience would wane thin after too much prodding into his childhood long ago.

"Yeah, you changed."

"Apparently."

"I love you."

Elish sighed and shook his head. "Look, I put your favourite episode on, the Stonecutters one. Why don't you watch it?"

"The light hurts my eyes." Jade squinted and his yellow eyes disappeared under blackened eyelids. "And noise, noise hurts. Can we just sit in silence?"

There was nothing Elish enjoyed more. He turned off the television and the light on the side table to his left and held Jade to him without another word.

Elish zipped up the boy's jacket and sighed an exasperated sigh, for he was once again acting like the boy's sengil. He laced Jade's boots and buttoned up the leather straps of his gloves.

The elevator leading to the surface gave off a beep; it was five minutes ago that Elish had heard the Falconer land.

Jade held up his hands and stared at them. "One day do I wear gloves so I'll do not go electrocuting people?"

Well, he was almost speaking English.

"If you wish."

Jade flopped a hand on Elish's head. "Zaaaapp." Elish shook his head, wondering why he hadn't drown the boy in the tub, before he rose to greet Garrett and Lyle.

Garrett smiled when he saw him, followed by Lyle still dressed in his hospital coat with a stethoscope around his neck, further on Luca came hauling a big bag full of medical supplies.

"Alright, where's the sicky? Grand mal seizure you say?" Lyle was never a man to mince words or bullshit. He spotted Jade who had slumped over onto the couch and put his stethoscope over his ears, then kneeled down and slid the instrument up Jade's shirt.

They were all silent while Lyle listened, and a moment later the doctor cringed. "His lungs sound like someone sucking the last bits of soda from a straw. This is the most unhealthy chimera I have ever dealt with. Garrett, what the hell was your company thinking putting this boy in the Moros slums? Young chimera bodies need nutrients to grow not tact and irradiated water."

Only Lyle, who had been Elish's sengil before completing medical studies at the college, could get away with such a barbed comment. Lyle was seen as a part of Elish's small family now, and felt more comfortable around him than he did with most of his brothers. Elish's sharp chastising of him speaking out of place had stopped years ago, though sometimes Elish did dock his pay just to take his own jab at him.

"Yes, Garrett thought it would be funny to do so, it is his doing," Elish said placidly. "I already voiced my opinion on his choice of passive-aggressive humour."

Garrett gave him a sharp sideways look. "I was only following orders, and that's beside the point. Elish, I'm concerned about that seizure... has he been doing anything... *funny* recently?"

The scathing look Elish gave Garrett was all he needed to see, the dark-haired chimera nodded, his Adam's apple bobbing up and down as he swallowed hard. "He's... well, that's... that's great he's advancing so quickly…" Elish continued to glare at him, watching his brother's face start to pale.

"So…? What has –"

Garrett yelped as Elish grabbed his brother by the shoulder, then with a firm hold he walked Garrett into the bedroom he and Jade had been using. He shut the door.

"Spit it out." Elish's voice held a tone that left no room for Garrett to dodge or sway the demand.

Garrett looked up at Elish and swallowed hard, before his eyes shifted around as if hoping Luca or Lyle would defy their own personalities and come to his rescue. Though it was no use, the thought was so outlandish it was laughable.

"I think this is something you need to ask King –" Garrett yelped and jumped as Elish slammed his hand against the side of the wall, right beside Garrett's head.

Garrett looked at him in shock. "What… what has he been doing?"

"He's been invading my memories, he knew things that no one but the first gen and Silas would know, visions through my eyes of our childhood."

Garrett's pupils dilated, annoying Elish even more; he was interested with the advancements of Silas and Perish's creations, not the boy's failing health. "That's… that's amazing."

"And beside the point; what does this mean?" Elish hissed, quickly losing his patience.

Garrett pursed his lips until his pencil moustache was almost scraping against his bottom teeth. "You're not going to like this… he's advancing too quickly for his own brain. Elish, if he continues to get flashes and go into what I am assuming is a catatonic state… he's going to keep having seizures and eventually he's going to have a stroke or cause a bleed. It's a problem we've had with empaths before… Elish, we never told anyone but that's what killed Valen."

Elish's cold visage didn't waver, only his purple eyes got hard. "Valen was an empath?" Valen had died over forty-five years ago at twenty-four, Elish had never asked why. He had been involved with his work and his own problems back then; he had been teaching at the College of Skytech too.

Elish had had no idea his long dead brother was an empath like Jade.

Garrett nodded slowly, his body bracing for whatever reaction Elish was going to give him. "We didn't think the engineering took, he hid it from us. Valen was Sanguine's partner if you remember, from what Sanguine told me his ears started to bleed and he just... he just died."

Elish felt a wash of dread go through him, but soon it turned to cold anger. "Silas knew the last empath died young, didn't he?" he said in a dangerous whisper.

"Sorry, brother... but—"

Garrett jumped a mile high as Elish's fist went through the drywall in a rare display of his emotions. He tried to slink underneath Elish's entrapping hands but in a flash Elish grabbed Garrett's tie and yanked him forward so they were face-to-face. Elish's eyes were a blaze of unhinged anger and at that moment his younger brother feared for his life.

"Elish... Elish... listen to me, before you tear me limb from limb, I've been... we can do surgery on him. Sanguine funded research after Valen died, from his own cash sup- my god, stop looking at me like that! We can help him!"

Elish's dangerous expression didn't waver, he tensed his hold on Garrett's tie and started to twist it in his hand, constricting the air flow.

"What surgery?" Elish's frosted tones sank into his brother's bones, a chill rushed through Garrett.

"It's... it's a blocker, a series of small tubes we insert in his occipital lobes, it will block his empath abilities, all but his aura reading," Garrett stammered, his hands gripping Elish's hold on his tie.

Elish twisted his hold tighter, his mind trying to process the repercussions of this surgery. Cutting open the boy's brain, something that was already fragile was risky and full of complications. Anything happening to Jade's brain right now was risky, but what choice did Elish have?

But Elish had wanted the boy to develop this ability, hone it and polish it; it was something Elish could undoubtedly use in the future, on Perish and possibly Reaver when the time came to unravel those men's brains fold by fold.

"How long does he have if I don't opt for this surgery?"

Elish felt his carefully laid out plan start to deteriorate in front of him.

The boy's abilities were invaluable to the seeds he had been planting, without it he couldn't come close to amassing the support he needed. He had to unlock those carefully implanted–

"Two years."

That's all? Elish's face tensed.

So this is how it has to be…

Time was never on my side.

How can I, an immortal, still hold an enemy in the ticking of a clock?

Elish tried to do the math in his head. Even if he didn't do the surgery Jade's timer had started ticking down, he would be dead by nineteen, right as Reaver was coming into his own and right when his cicaro would be old enough to become immortal. There was no choice, Elish had to give him the surgery, but in doing so it would delay Jade's development, and coaxing the mind of an empath was a long process that took patience.

Meaning he wouldn't be ready for the task Elish had planted for him, a seed to be harvested in the future. One that involved probing into the thoughts of the chosen targets and unleashing the information buried so deep. Could Jade learn all of this that quickly? And find out the nagging question Elish had been plagued with since he had learned the name of King Silas's most hidden and coveted secret?

The boyfriend, the other born immortal…

Not Reaver

The one the first generation was forbidden to speak of.

– the one who had died long ago, long before the first chimera was even a dream of their king's.

He had no choice.

And Elish knew it.

Elish dropped Garrett, who stumbled and grabbed onto the headboard of the bed, clutching his throat as he wheezed for breath; his face was flushed red and his eyes bulging.

"I want scientists and doctors researching this surgery, I want it practiced on prisoners and perfected before you touch a scalpel to my property. No one touches Jade until I have a hundred percent success rate on implantation and removal; am I understood?"

Garrett's hand went back and forth as he loosened his tie; he glared at his brother as his face returned to a normal colour. "You don't need to threaten me, you shit. I like the boy too. Quin's right, your *boyfriend* is turning you into a deranged lunatic." The man's voice was caustic and biting; though Elish was always the most dominant chimera Garrett still showed his teeth whenever Elish's bullying singed his pride. "I hope love doesn't make me into such a mad man."

"I do not *love* Jade," Elish spat, "and he is *not* my boyfriend."

"You harbour no hidden feelings for him? Tell that to my neck! Or Silas's bashed in skull!" Garrett pointed at the red mark already starting to swell. "You're going to make him immortal aren't you? That's why you want testing on its removal."

"Once his frontal lobes develop and his brain is strong enough to fuse with the immortal brain matter, yes, I am."

Garrett guffawed incredulously. "Silas will never allow it; he will never give you a piece of his brain."

"I have already proven I can access that lunatic's brain. What I do is my business and to whom I want beside me as I continue my immortal existence is my say and my say only now," Elish answered coolly.

"Sounds like King Elish *does* want King Jade," Garrett snorted, but with an icy glare from Elish he ducked, even if Elish only gave him a frosted gaze. It seemed as quickly as his bravery came, it left.

Garrett's shoulders slumped and he sighed, his docile submission, an attribute unnatural for a normal chimera, overshadowing his wounded pride.

"I'm sorry, I hate it when we fight. It's just… it's strange for me to see you so… *this*. You've been my icy, emotionally dead older brother for almost ninety years, you've never so much as tipped over a bar stool and now you punch walls? Don't you think it would be healthier if you just admitted to us that you do… maybe… perhaps…

…a… teeny… tiny… bit…

… *love* him?"

"No."

Garrett sighed and watched Elish open the door and walk past him; Elish's head held high and his growing hair, now touching the nape of his neck, swishing behind him. Not even love could bring him from that pedestal, though to try and convince Garrett's carved from ice brother of that was a different story. Elish hated feeling endearing emotions and only saw it as a glitch in his chimera makeup. He prided himself on strength, stoicism and a cold visage of a man whittled from the strongest of stones. To waver from that was a flaw, not an attribute, and to admit love was to admit he wasn't the perfect specimen Elish prided himself on being.

Love was weakness, a vulnerability that the enemy could use against him, and to Elish Dekker, there was nothing more to say on the subject.

Without another exchange of words, the two of them walked back into the living room.

CHAPTER 34

I OPENED MY EYES, BUT AS SOON AS I DID I CLOSED THEM again. The light was assaulting, it seared my eyeballs like it was acid.

But a moment later the light turned off, and a gloved hand brushed my hair back in a soothing way. I tried to speak but my mumbled attempts were only met with a cold chuckle before he put his hands over my eyes and said silently, "Just give your eyes a moment to adjust; you've been asleep for a while."

I breathed in the smell of his leather glove; it felt cold and slick against my skin. While he shielded my eyes from the light I tried to take in a couple deep breaths and was relieved to feel that my lungs were clear.

"What happened?" I mumbled, as the dreamlike events before my long sleep started to slowly trickle back. "Are we in the greywastes?"

Elish took his hand away from my eyes. I squinted and saw him slowly come into my vision. My master held a small smile for me, his aura bright in contrast to the dark room we were in. I looked around and one of my questions was answered; we were in his bedroom back in Olympus.

"You had a seizure and with your sickness we returned home. Lyle put you in a medically induced coma to give your brain time to recover, that was two weeks ago now," Elish explained, he glanced behind him and I heard the soft footsteps of Luca.

As the sengil took my hand and helped me sit up in bed, I furrowed my brow. "Two weeks? No wonder I feel so groggy, is my pneumonia gone?"

There was the scraping of a cup against a saucer which made my teeth grate over the sound, then I saw Luca offering me a mug of tea. I took a drink of it; it was lemon, one of my favourites.

Elish gave me a nod. "Yes, your sickness has been taken care of. You are fully healed and as healthy as one can expect. Though you are in desperate need of a shower. Luca will help you and after you can attempt to eat some food. Get up now, you've been idle for far too long." Elish stood up and took my tea mug from me, before with a silent sweep of his robes he left the bedroom.

I sighed, my head felt like it had grown a layer of fuzzy mould on it, but I suppose lying in bed wasn't going to change that and more importantly… it wasn't like I had a choice. With Luca's help I got up and started towards the bathroom.

When I was clean and freshly shaved I hobbled my way out into the living room and spotted Elish looking outside the skyscraper with his mug of tea. He was gazing out at the blue sky; it looked like a beautiful day, only a few cottony clouds in the distance and even the sun was shining and reflecting off of the skyscrapers in the cityscape. I realized if I had been out for two weeks that we were into March now; I had survived another winter.

On still shaky feet I joined him beside the wall-to-wall windows, and noticed with a small smile that his hair was now long enough to touch his shoulders. Reading his mood as calm I reached out and touched the golden strands and smiled.

"Your hair grows back quickly," I said quietly, taking small bites of a butter tart Luca had given me to eat.

Elish didn't break his gaze, but only raised his tea to his lips. "It is a pill you take every day, to stimulate growth. It should be back to its normal length within four months."

I remembered seeing that advertised in the pharmacy; it was amazing what Skytech could come up with, and yet in the slums we still ate hard tasteless tact to give us the necessary vitamins and minerals. Well, priorities…

"Jade, what do you remember of our time in Halfton Valley?"

I slunk down. His tone had suddenly shifted to cold, the same frosted sharp tones the chimera used to use on me in the beginning.

I wracked my brains, and it didn't take long for me to dig up the treasure trove of memories my mind had already attempted to bury. I knew as soon as young Elish popped into my head why his mood had taken this turn.

"I... I will never mention it again, I'll do whatever I can to make it not happen..." I stammered, feeling an adrenaline rush of anxiety permeate my system. The same feeling you got when you uncovered a secret you weren't expecting, or one you didn't want to know in the first place. "Please, Master, I did *not* do that on purpose."

Elish didn't move, but his body radiated an emotion I couldn't taste, even on my aura reading. "You say you will do what you can to make sure it doesn't happen – but you don't know how, do you?"

Immediately my mouth went dry as he cornered me, a cat and a mouse. I shook my head in defeat, there was no use pretending. "No... it's never happened before and with no one else but you. I'll do whatever..."

My mouth locked shut like a steel trap as he raised a hand in a voiceless warning to be quiet. "You will be receiving surgery in the next several months, an implant that will stop this telepathy until I decide you are ready to develop it. In the meantime you are to report to me any mental wanderings, no matter what, no matter with who, am I understood?"

"An... implant?" My hand immediately went up and touched my head. "Like in my brain?"

"That's right."

"I... I don't want something in my brain."

"You don't have a choice," Elish said coolly. I saw his purple eyes narrow in the reflection of the window, and I knew I indeed had no say in the matter in his eyes, but in mine I did, this was my brain.

"It's my body, I can opt out for surgeries. I don't want something implanted in my brain. What if it makes me into a vegetable or something? Why can't you help me develop it now? This is shit!" I said bitterly. I glared out the window and angrily took a big bite out of my butter tart.

There was a heavy silence between us, before Elish answered in a low octave, one that did all but scream I was edging the danger zones. "It is not your body, it is *my* body, *my* mind, and *my* property. You have no say and you never did, do not take my decision to inform you of your upcoming medical procedure as some sort of request for permission, slumrat."

I glared at him, before saying simply but acerbically, "You're a dick."

Elish paused. I froze as his eyes finally left the cityscape in the window to fix on my own.

I blinked with confusion as he chuckled, before raising an inquisitive eyebrow at me. "That's it? Really? I'm disappointed, you used to be so ferocious. Did Silas neuter you as well when he took your foreskin?"

I glared at him but as those memories also came back to me I felt my legs press together. "I've been asleep for two weeks, cut me a break, I'm groggy."

Elish's mouth rose in a half-smile. "Yes, it has been an insufferable two weeks. Brother after brother coming to either annoy me or ask counsel. I do look forward to having the company of my gutter rat again. Come and put on your jacket, the day is warming and a walk with fresh air will do your body good."

I frowned, but there was a part of me that was pleased with how that exchange had gone, a year ago we would've probably come to blows but it seemed me and my chimera had found ourselves a steady rhythm. I finished my butter tart and got my jacket, though as I walked my legs kept buckling, especially my left leg. They weren't used to walking and my brain wasn't used to making them walk.

I yawned and held onto my tea mug as Elish clipped my leash onto my collar; to Luca's credit as soon as he saw me yawning and still looking sleepy he switched out my lemon tea for coffee which I appreciated. There was nothing like living with a sengil whose sole purpose in life was to figure out what you needed before you even knew you needed it.

When I was draped in my usual tight leather including my silver buckled jacket, Elish led me outside into the crisp but sunny day. I took a moment to breathe in the fresh springy smells and stretch my ropey muscles. I could hear my joints popping and snapping as they finally got a chance to stretch.

Elish, wearing his grey overcoat belted in the middle, and white trousers, led my silver chain with a quiet grace, gliding along the concrete without a second glance to the people parting to let us pass. Everyone stared and some people even inclined their heads to bow at us, or Elish anyway, they never really looked at me. It was my master they wanted to take in, I was just the gutter rat holding the tea mug, a black blemish that distorted their view of Skyfall's second most powerful resident.

I sipped my coffee and observed the green shoots of flowers start to rise up from the ground, pushing through the black dirt to reach the sun. It had always made me happy when I could see the green start to come back to Garrett Park; it meant soon times would be a bit easier for me and Kerres. That the food would become cheaper, the heat costs would go down and we could hang out with our friends outside in the burned-out buildings again. I wouldn't say it solved all our problems but it did cut a few of them off the list.

Spring in my seventeenth year, who would've known I would be spending it in Skyland with my master, being led by a silver leash. Who would've known I would be content with it?

I sighed, feeling a fleeting moment of guilt. I had been thinking of Kerres less and less, though with so much going on the last several months maybe that wasn't my fault. I still missed him, dearly, but I think I had come to terms with the fact that he had changed. At least now... he wouldn't have a chance to kidnap me, or hurt my family.

Oh, how far I had fallen.

I warmed my hands with my tea mug, before I remembered my abilities and warmed my hands myself. I smirked at the novelty of the gift Elish had given me, through something that could only really be called osmosis. I wondered briefly what else I could heat up.

But as if sensing my fluxating touch Elish glanced behind him. "No, Jade, you are no longer allowed to use those abilities. Nothing but your aura reading."

I stopped and threw my free hand up in the air. "Why?" I said letting it drop and smack against my leather pants.

Elish didn't answer. I went to protest more when my leash tightened. I choked and stumbled forward, my coffee upsetting over my cup and raining drops onto the concrete. I licked up the drops and let out a long unimpressed breath. The chimera paid no mind and continued to walk me along the sidewalk, strolling past large skyscrapers and flat-roofed buildings. Everything here was layered in concrete, only broken up by the raised beds of black dirt holding the small green shoots and twiggy bushes that had survived the cold brunt of winter.

I ran my finger along the rim of the mug to pick up the spare drops, feeling my hands go sticky from the sweetener sugar Luca had put in it. I probably looked like an idiot but I hated the feeling of my hands being dirty, so I proceeded to lick the coffee mug as Elish walked me beside an old and cracked parking lot, lined with a wall of half-concrete and half-chain-link fence.

Suddenly my foot caught on something, from sheer stupidity of not looking where I was going I flew forward, my mind only giving me time enough to put my hands in front of me to break my fall.

All at once the leash tightened, but that did nothing but yank my neck back. As I spilled to the ground the cup shattered between the pavement and my hand and forced the shards into my palm; to top it off my forehead cracked against the ground as well, filling my brain with a red flash of light.

I swore and tried to get up, Elish helped me with a sigh and a shake of his head. "Look at that, you're bleeding and you have shards all in your palm. No, don't try and get them out, we'll keep our path and return home. The walk we're on is just a loop anyway."

My eyes fell to my bleeding palm, I could see shards of porcelain shining against the sunlight above us. My chest rose and fell in a sigh and I wiped the small beads of gravel off of my forehead. "Sorry about the mug." I tried to kick the shards into the corner where the sidewalk met the half-chain-link wall but Elish continued to walk.

"We have thousands, tea mugs do not suffer from age." Elish handed me a white kerchief and pressed it against my palm, before he started walking with me again, slower this time. "It will require no stitches, just disinfectant, let's continue on now."

I nodded, feeling that my pride had been more injured than my hand and forehead. I followed more closely beside Elish now, pressing the white kerchief against my hand until I saw the fabric start to turn red.

"Excuse me?" I glanced up from poking at my wrapped hand, my eyes flickering towards the sound of a mousy and soft-spoken voice. We had just turned a corner in the road and were heading down the far side of the concrete and chain-linked fence on our way back home.

My eyes fell on a young man with copper hair parted on the side and brushed into a wave, with a thin and unassuming face highlighted by two sapphire-like eyes. He stared at us as a small mouse would staring up at two predators.

Elish and I stopped and looked at him for a moment. The boy was sitting on a folding white chair that looked like it came from Moros rather than Skyland, with a black briefcase in front of him and a small sign that read. 'Medicoal Servises.'

"Yes?" Elish answered for both of us, his voice making the boy visibly twitch.

I watched as the boy swallowed before rising to his feet, in a way that reminded me of a business man about to sell us a pitch. Sure enough, he straightened his shoulders and said in a rehearsed tone, "I offer medical services for Skyfallers, at discount prices. I have experience in stitching, bandaging, disinfecting, and minor dental work. My rates are rock bottom and match no other. I noticed that young man has suffered an ailment. I would be more–"

"I can take care of my pet just fine, thank you," Elish said coolly. He turned to carry on with our walk when I noticed something flickering out of the corner of my eye.

If Elish hadn't mentioned it months before I would've never caught it, but absentmindedly I had always been keeping an eye out. With a turn of my abilities I brought up the colours twisting around the young man and narrowed my eyes.

Like a flicker of aurora borealis I saw deep red and purple rise off of the boy's body, darkening only as he looked at the ground with his shoulders slumped, obviously feeling badly for being shunned by my master. I saw immediately that this boy was someone we could have use for; he was meek, scared, and undoubtedly not from here at all. To his credit as well he was cute, in a scared bunny sort of way. I think if I even so much as twitched towards him he would scurry away like a rodent.

"Wait…" I said quietly.

Elish froze and shot me a dangerous look, it was unheard of for me to challenge his authority especially in front of someone else, or worse, in public. "Why are you in Skyland?"

The young man raised his slumped head, but the question only brought more jolts of anxiety through his head. He looked around nervously. I noticed he had some bruises that tinted his jawline, all the way up to his double-pierced ears. "Well, I had tried Moros but they chased me out –" That wasn't surprising. "– and Skyland is so much… safer and they tip better."

Elish glared at him and I was surprised the kid hadn't exploded into flames from his smouldering gaze. He tightened my leash in a way that told me I was going to get throttled with it as soon as we got back home. "You need a license to act as vendor here, do you have that?"

"N-no…"

In Elish's usual razor-sharp manner he continued to verbally tear the boy to pieces. "Did you think that no one in the elite district of Skyfall had ever thought of opening up street shops such as this? Did you ever wonder why we have no panhandling here? It is illegal. Skyland strives to keep gutter trash and scum off of the sidewalks." Elish's voice became a low and dangerous threat, the kid looked like he was about to start crying and from his aura he looked like the type.

Though I would revel in kids my age getting a verbal tongue lashing from my master, I knew he would be interested in this kid. I decided to pull the ace out of my sleeve, wishing my telekinesis powers could implant the realization in Elish's head that this boy was someone we could use. He was a perfect match for the royal douchebag Joaquin Dekker, a chimera Elish had wanted to sway to his side the same way we were planning on swaying Garrett.

I glanced at Elish and absentmindedly pulled on my leash so he would hopefully clue in. "Yeah, I would hate to see what would happen to such a small, meek little boy like you in a place like this." I stared at Elish and said very carefully, "Especially if we had to tell a certain troublesome councilman."

I watched in my own fascination as Elish's dangerous glare turned to a sparkle of curiosity. His eyes fell back on the boy, cowering like a cornered rabbit, a wisp of bangs covering his soft forehead. He was a few inches shorter than I was, but his age was a mystery to me.

"I'm – I'm sorry, I'll leave," the boy stammered, the tips of his ears reddening. It looked like he wanted us to just leave so he could hide in a hole for a while; he looked incredibly uncomfortable in our presence – for good reason.

"No, that will not be necessary." Elish's tone changed to a more bored, casual octave. "I own this building, you can use this and this area alone until you can afford a vendor's license. Where are you from, boy? A factory town I am to assume?"

As soon as Elish said that I knew he must be right. If he was raised in the greywastes he would be more hardened, and if he was from one of the districts he would've known the rules and would've known it wasn't a good idea to engage a chimera without them engaging you first. He really didn't seem to know who we were, and if you had a television set and the news station you knew who Elish was.

"Well, I was originally from Blackbay Factory but I decided to try my chances here..." the boy said. "If I could have a small reprieve, a month or so, I can pay the vendor's fee, I promise."

Elish was unmoved. I watched his purple eyes sweep the boy up and down, analyzing the boy for himself in a new light. I remembered when that was me.

"What's your full name?"

"My... my name? Jemini, or Jem."

"I said your *full* name."

"I'm... I'm sorry, sir, I don't have a last name."

I saw my master's eyes flicker in annoyance. I knew why, the piles and piles of folders Elish had in his filing cabinet explained it easily enough. He wanted to dig up this boy's file and pick him apart.

Though his name must've been enough, Elish adjusted his hold on my leash. "If anyone gives you trouble about setting up your business here tell them Elish Dekker has given you his leave and if they have further questions they can bring them to me. My request is that you do not move from this spot and do not panhandle or beg for money, am I understood?"

The boy named Jem nodded, though as soon as the last name Dekker got tossed out there he suddenly turned a bit green. I had been waiting for that realization, it only hammered in the point that he didn't recognize my master. "Thank you, why don't I bandage his hand for no charge? It won't take long."

My left eye twitched. I knew I had no reason to be insecure (right?) but when little twinky boys showed kindness towards my master, as opposed to the usual stricken fear, it made my hackles rise. I had been happy that Killian was far in the greywastes probably getting fondled by Reaver by now, and now I had to deal with a new piece of submissive eye candy smooching up to my master.

"Yes, make it quick." Elish took a step back and gave my shoulder a small push. As I stumbled forward Jem gave me the old white chair to sit in and immediately started cleaning my hand.

"What's your favourite colour?" Jem said in his standard mousey tone; he started gently wiping my hand down with stinging antiseptic.

"Um, I don't know… I like the colour purple, and red, I like red too." I shrugged, not prepared for such an odd question.

Jem nodded and picked out a few pieces of porcelain still in my hand; he didn't say anything more, he just wrapped up my hand in a white gauze cloth. I could feel Elish behind me watching his every move, picking apart every movement and every word that came from Jem's mouth. I wished I could perch on Elish's brain and figure out what he was thinking. Perhaps he was doing his own quick readings of this boy to see if he indeed would be a suitable piece of bait for Joaquin.

The colour question made sense as Jem opened up his briefcase; I was amused to see that all the band aids he had were different colours, every colour of the rainbow and some of them with old cartoons on them.

"Interesting choice of medical supplies," I chuckled.

Jem took out several purple band aids and a red one and started putting them on my cut fingers; he gave me a shy smile. "Well, the Legion sells them to the residents at Blackbay at a discount; you see they have a base near us. Of course these types of band aids would be unsuited for legionaries, so I bought them. You don't mind do you? I thought it could be my thing you know? People might ask where my customers got them and I might get more business that way."

"Nah, I don't mind." I shook my head and after he was done I admired my coloured band aids. "We don't get enough colours in this world." I glanced up as he put a red band aid on my forehead before giving me another shy smile; this soft-spoken kid was a little enigma in himself.

"Want a sticker? I like stickers." Jem picked up a sheet of panda stickers and I picked one with a baby panda holding a stick leaf. I wondered if Elish was glaring laser beams into my back or if he was getting a kick out of this kid as well.

I held out my hand and Jem put the sticker on it. I looked at it and chuckled. "You're gay aren't you?"

Jem looked a bit surprised at my forwardness, and at the same time Elish gave me a good yank on my leash, but after a moment of getting over the shock of my very forward question he nodded. "Yeah, I am… I guess it's the stickers, right?" Jem got up off of his knees and took a step back. "You're all done, that didn't take long right? Tell your friends if you're happy with my services."

I got up and showed Elish Jem's handiwork, but that was the last thing he was interested in.

"Will do." I smiled.

Elish gave Jem a look that would shrivel the balls of any man; sure enough, the kid withered under his gaze and turned his blue eyes to the chain-link beside us.

"Remember what I said," Elish said coldly. "Have an enjoyable day." Without another glance or a word exchanged except for a small goodbye from Jem we started back down the street that would lead us to Olympus.

We walked back in silence to the skyscraper and it wasn't until we reached the elevator that Elish finally spoke. "Are you sure?"

I gave him a sober nod. "Completely, trust me on this one, he's perfect for Quin. You saw how he acts, he's a timid little fairy but I'd suggest you move quickly on this. He obviously just arrived from Blackbay, it won't take long at all for someone else to prey on him or scoop him up. He's lucky he got out of Moros with just a few marks on him; they would've torn a kid like that to bits, fuck it, I would've torn that kid to bits."

The elevator dinged and we both walked out and into the hallway.

"Yes, I can see that. I think a cardinal just flew into Skyland, it would be foolish for us not to take advantage of such a rare creature," Elish said as I pushed the door open, then held it as he walked through.

"How are you going to get Quin to notice him though?" I asked, noticing Luca was giving me a sideways glance. I was sporting a red band aid on my head now, and my hand was wrapped and stickered.

"I'll take a day to string a few ideas through my head. Joaquin has a meeting with me soon regarding marketing numbers. I'll request he comes to the apartment for that discussion. Perhaps something will come to me during that time." I removed Elish's coat and Luca scampered forward with Elish's white loafers.

The rest of the day we spent in the skyscraper, though Elish was still taking meetings and calls all day. Considering how much time he had been missing recently everyone was pawing for their time with him. Elish was in charge of all of Skyfall right now and his remote phone was always buzzing with calls. He was a man in high demand so I made it as easy as I could for him and behaved myself.

Throughout the day chimeras and several important city workers met with Elish in his Olympus office and I fell back into my usual role of silent eye candy. Everyone acknowledged me, asked about my health and made it clear they were glad I hadn't died.

I also got some nice presents too: chocolate bars from Grant who was showing off his newest cicaro, some little weenie kid named Kal, and five lollipops from Knight Dekker, the half-chimera son of Ellis, a man who had also been in charge of Edgeview. All in all it was a good day to be back and a quiet one, but once it came time to retire to the apartment I was more than happy to get out of my high-heeled leather boots. My feet were killing me and my boots were for sex appeal only, not walking.

I flopped down on the couch as Luca pulled my boots off and started massaging my feet. I stretched out and put a bottle of root beer to my lips as the sengil worked me over. Elish took a spot beside me with the phone to his ear; I only perked up when I heard a familiar name.

"Yes, from Blackbay Factory on the west coast, no last name goes by Jemini though the spelling I am unsure of." He became silent before glancing around. I leaned over and handed him a pen he had absentmindedly put on the coffee table; he took it with a nod of his head and started writing something down on his folder.

"Yes, I want a rush on it, bring them tonight and leave them in the lobby, my secretary will drop them off with my sengil, yes, tonight, no exceptions." Elish's voice was stern; he started writing something else down on the folder. I could hear the muffled voice of someone on the other end of the line. "Good, that is all." Elish ended the call and rested it on the coffee table. He looked tired too so I offered him some of my root beer.

Elish took a swig and handed me back the bottle. "Luca, order some pasta tonight, garlic bread, cheese, red sauce not white, and something for dessert and a tray of sweets for when Quin comes to visit tomorrow."

Luca nodded and rose. I leaned my head on Elish's shoulder and even though he had marketing information and grid sheets on his laptop, I drew up the mahjong tab. "You need to relax, that phone hasn't stopped ringing all day."

Elish didn't protest, instead he started clicking on tiles. "I am technically the King of Skyfall for several more days, once Silas wakes up my workload will minimize."

My body froze like someone had pressed pause on me. I grimly nodded but my sudden reaction didn't go unnoticed.

"Do not concern yourself with that, Cicaro, it is nothing I will not take care of."

There was still no hiding the hammering in my chest though. How could I have forgotten about the king? It had been over a month since Elish had rescued me from my coming out party, and the king would be waking up soon. What would that mean for me? Silas would be pissed right off, everyone knew that. Would he take it out on Elish?

I studied his face but that was as useful as studying a slab of marble, there was never a hint of apprehension or concern over meeting with our master and I knew there never would be. I still didn't like it; the last time he had a meeting with Silas I got kicked back to Moros.

"Your heartbeat is still speeding up, do you not trust your master?" Elish asked without turning away from the laptop. "I suppose it is time for me to give you your birthday present."

I couldn't hide the curiosity in my eyes as I watched Elish reach into his breast pocket; it only deepened when he pulled out a key attached to a small key ring with a green stone on it.

He handed it to me and I saw him smirk from amusement. I dangled the keychain and gave him a grin. "Did you get me a car?"

Elish chuckled. "Never... never ever would I trust you with several tons of rapidly moving steel. No Jade. I bought you an apartment in Eros, a nice one bedroom with an acceptable view of the ocean." Before my heart could rip out of my chest or give me a heart attack he continue, "It's in a secure building, much like the house Sanguine brought you to. It's a safe area for you to use if ever the need arises that I am… dispatched." He said the last part with a bitter tone. "Your orders would be to take Luca and stay there until I come and get you, no matter how long. No one knows where it is, not even Garrett."

"Sweet!" I grinned and put the keys in my pocket. "You bought it? I own an apartment? Since I'm a chimera, when do I start getting bucket loads of cash?"

"Oh, that reminds me…" Elish beckoned Luca to grab his jacket and when he did Elish took his snake skin wallet out of his pocket and handed me a black card. "There, your own black card, custom made for you. There is your 'bucket loads of cash' but just so you know I can read every transaction you make on the network, so do not go buying anything foolish."

"Really? Damn!" I took the card and started to admire it, but something caught my eye.

Jade S. Dekker.

"S? Is my middle name Sebastian too? Or Sasha like Sanguine's?" I asked. I had never even thought about what my middle name was supposed to be. I couldn't believe I had forgotten to ask.

"No, since you were a rogue child who was really supposed to be put to death, you were never assigned a middle name," Elish said in a casual manner, but as I looked at him I saw a mischievous glint shine in his eye. "I took the liberty to give you a middle name. It's now on your permanent record."

I stared at him for a second before my mouth dropped open. "You fucking gave me the middle name slumrat didn't you?"

My shock only furthered when Elish's lips disappeared into his mouth in a purse, before, for the first time ever… he actually laughed, a real laugh where I could see teeth. Just seeing him happy like this brought my own smile to my face, but to defend my honour I also gave him a playful push.

"I do regret not doing that, I really do… but no, Jade. I gave you a more suitable middle name. Shadow. Fitting isn't it, Shadow Killer?" Elish grabbed my collar and to my inner joy he drew me in for a kiss. "You have a unique middle name, one Silas did not choose for you, your master did."

We kissed deeply and as we did he parted my lips with his own. I felt his graceful fingers trace the nape of my neck, before slowly travelling down my back and slipping down the rim of my pants.

A rush went through me and I felt the fire start to ignite. I shifted over to straddle him but instead he pushed me down onto the couch and started rubbing my stomach and side, his warm fingers touching and stroking my eager flesh.

Then he got off me and grabbed my collar; he started pulling me towards the bedroom.

"But dinner… it will be here soon!" I looked around. Luca had made himself scarce, something the wallflower seemed to do whenever Elish and I started to get intimate.

"Perhaps I wish to feast on something else tonight?" The door swung open and with a yelp I was thrown onto the bed. I bounced twice before I looked up at him with a half-smile. I got onto my knees and took my shirt off, eyeing him as he started to remove his clothing.

When all I was wearing was my collar and cufflinks, I wrapped my arm around his neck and fell onto the bed with him on top of me. I pulled him onto me and we started kissing, his hands continuing to travel up and down my body.

Elish's touch drew out the flaming tendrils buried inside of my flesh and with each graceful stroke he only spread them to every corner, like he was painting my body. His movements were slow and deliberate, tracing his fingers as if mapping the veins underneath my skin.

My body flushed with want, as he started to kiss and play with my left nipple. I took in a rattling breath and clenched my teeth tight.

I heard him let out a cold dry laugh. "What eagerness, you're about to explode with just a lick here or there? I would save your stamina, Cicaro, I've been waiting for this dry spell to end since Silas cut off your foreskin. Since then you've either been injured, ill or unconscious; you've been a horrible pet."

He was right, besides the interrupted blowjob thanks to Leo back in Aras we really hadn't been intimate in a while, no wonder I felt like I was about to burst. I hadn't gone this long without one of our all-nighters since he had dropped me off in Moros.

I groaned as he pinched my nipple, before he started to lick around my navel, as he teased the soft skin I heard the chains rattle as he hooked my cuff links up to the chains in his bedroom. A cold thrill rushed through me and I found myself smiling from pure anticipation. "You got me injured, you got me ill, and you got me unconscious, you've been a horrible master."

A gasp spilled from me as he pinched my nipple harder. I heard him give me a disapproving tsk. "Such disobedience... my slumrat is past due for a vicious beating, he's gotten too big, too confident..." My lips curled as I felt the first lick on the base of my dick, weaving through my short public hair, just trimmed this morning by Luca. Conjuring a feeling of unimaginable hunger and lust for him to touch me, I lifted my hips almost pleading but he only played with the base.

I growled and pushed my hips up more, but he completely ignored my dick and instead continued to lick and nip around my groin; he was teasing me like crazy.

Suddenly though the pleasure turned into pain. I shrieked at the top of my lungs and pulled myself away as he sunk his teeth into my groin. Automatically my arms dove for the area but with a taut snap and the sound of tight metal I remembered he had me bound.

I gritted my teeth and jerked away from him. I looked down and saw his lips were already covered in blood. "What do you expect slumrat? A gentle kiss of my whip? Now, now... you're a chimera, and it's time I treated you like one." His lips went down to the bite wound he had made beside my dick, which was already trickling blood down onto the sheets. I weighed my options in that moment and decided to meet his challenge.

"Bring your face a bit closer, dear master, see what happens," I whispered. I licked my lips in the most vile manner I could and bared my teeth, still and probably permanently now, holding the steel implants. "Or am I too feral for you? Should I fetch Jem? Do you need easier prey now?"

With his mouth full of my own blood, he crawled over to me, and to my surprise he put his face up to mine and tried to stare me down. "Afraid of a slumrat? Don't make me la-"

In a flash teeth met flesh; with a trained bite I sunk my fangs into the soft area above his collarbone, near the side of his neck and tore two inch wide gaps. My heart shuddered as his blood started to trickle down my lips.

Elish put a hand to my forehead and pushed my head down on the bed, I saw his purple eyes glare down at me in a blaze, before his free hand cupped my chin.

I stared back up at him and swallowed the drops of blood I had gotten from him.

And I tasted him.

My mind went wild.

Like a forest fire had suddenly swept through tinder I felt a thirst suddenly scorch my throat. It was insatiable and all consuming, burning my chest and veins with a longing I couldn't control.

It was the most ambrosial taste I had ever had grace my tongue in my life, more powerful and intense than all the other times I had tasted him.

I had to have more.

Elish saw the change in my demeanor and body, and like a cold rush of water over coals he let out a taunting laugh. "Yes, my chimera, thirsty are we? How do I taste to you? Good?"

The blood drops from his neck were falling onto my own neck. I desperately wanted to taste them, I wanted to put my mouth over the wound and devour every shred of life he had in him. Even the smell was driving me wild, but he dangled himself over me like a piece of meat on a fishing line. Always just out of my reach.

I gasped, and felt a bead of sweat drip down my temple. "Stop fucking with me!" My own voice was twisted into submission; though obviously enjoying my suffering Elish only smirked at me. He ran a hand down to my groin to gather the blood that was trickling out, then with a smooth flick he coated his fingers in his own blood before bringing them to my lips.

I sucked on them eagerly and as I devoured the cruor I put a hand on his rigid member and started to stroke it. In response Elish pushed his fingers deeper into my mouth, but when they started to gag me I clamped down on them and bit through his flesh.

With my new penchant for his blood pacified with his fingers, he separated my legs and I drew them back. Soon I felt the familiar pressure that quickly increased as Elish penetrated me.

I screamed through his fingers, and as I did, with a quick and stealthy shift he pushed the skin between his thumb and middle finger into my mouth essentially pinning my mouth back. In the moment though I didn't care, I hadn't had anything inside me for a while and it was a tight fit.

Every time I opened my mouth to scream his hand pushed my lips and jaw back further, preventing me from biting him anymore, but not from voicing my pain. That only added to Elish's sadism, with a dry chuckle he pushed his hand back towards my upper jaw thus wrenching my head backwards, his finger digging my upper teeth back. It hurt almost as much as his cock driving in and out of me did.

As soon as I felt his hand pull away from my mouth I snapped my head forward to bite him, but with expert stealth he missed my bites and instead wrapped his large hand around my neck. I snarled at him, the growl rumbling inside of my throat, but with a series of rapid and deep thrusts they turned into high pitch moans. I gritted my teeth, hating his power over my body, but as I chanced further sadism and raised my shackled wrist to hit him, he only grabbed my wrist and twisted it over my head.

I was stuck now; one of his hands was on my neck, the other one holding my hands back, and as the mouse writhes under the coils of the snake I struggled to get away.

Elish's eyes dug into mine. With perverse joy he leaned down as if wanting to sample the anger for himself, and licked the corners of my lips with his tongue; his hand squeezing my neck like an iron shackle as if daring me to move away from him.

When he shifted his mouth away from me, I moved my own and found the wound on his neck. With a shudder deep inside my chest I felt the ambrosia taste of his blood flow into my mouth and down my throat. Elish didn't move, or correct me, he let me lick and nip the wound, opening it wider and drinking everything that spilled forth, the influx of pleasure driving me to the point where my mind was swimming from not being able to breathe properly. With Elish driving himself into me hard, and my mouth occupied with the bite wound, my breathing had become strained and ragged.

I couldn't remember how many times I'd orgasmed but eventually, with my body flushed and covered in cum, lube, and blood I found myself riding him, moving my hips up and down as I pushed my body to the very cusps of its limit.

My head was bowed and the only thing that was keeping me steady were his hands on my shoulders. I was tapped dry, sore, and ready to collapse from exhaustion.

When Elish and I shared our last climax, I collapsed beside him with a groan; he had wrung every drop out of me to the point where I ejaculated nothing but a small pathetic dribble of cum. We had been up all night at this point, I just hoped he didn't have any early meetings.

I laid my head against the cold pillow and a few minutes later he started cooling me off with his hands. I shifted closer to him and directed his touch to my chest; my lungs still burned like they were coated in sandpaper.

"What's with the blood thing? Is that something we're bred to like?" I asked, feeling my body uncoil and relax. I was so exhausted but it was a good feeling, like I had just released a mountain of tension that had been bearing down on my shoulders.

"That is actually a very complicated question. I will not confuse you with the origins of it, but a penchant for blood goes all the way back to King Silas's youth," Elish explained. He smirked as I let out a shudder from his ice-cold hands grazing my nipple; it had been bitten raw and was very sensitive. "He realized before the Fallocaust that immortal blood had a certain allure, and since when you follow the family tree we all end up to King Silas, we were all born with the same thirst for it."

"Just chimera blood?" I remembered my devouring of Kerres's blood, but I hadn't gotten the same intoxicating thrill as I had with Elish's. It was like Elish's blood was laced with heroin; I could taste him in it.

"Well, put it this way, chimera blood is like drinking a fine wine, wine is wine, but you'll not enjoy it as you would a finely-crafted brand." Elish leaned into me and licked a trickle of blood that had started to fall from my lips, sometime during the night, as he often did, he had bit them. "The more you feel for that chimera, the more you thirst for them. Which makes your frenzy all the more interesting."

I gave him a suspicious look before I felt a smirk come to my face. "Why? You know how I feel about you, I've said it."

"Talk is cheap and so are words, easy to say but harder to put into actions." Elish brushed back my bangs and looked into my eyes. "So much silver now, I will miss the black."

I lifted up my hand and focused my ability, the flares of my aura immediately coated my hand and I smiled to myself. "That's just what happens, or I'm assuming so. We'll have to see what happens to Garrett and Reno, and Joaquin and Jem; see if Elish and Jade's matchmaking service is as big of a success as we're hoping."

"There is no harm in trying. If the worst comes to the worst, I can train him to become a sengil or perhaps I can get a second pet, *ouch*." I pinched his nipple as those words left his mouth; in return he gave my hand a jolt of electricity. I snapped it back quickly. "Time will tell."

I yawned, and with that signal Elish put a hand on my back and drew me close to him, in the position I usually slept in. I rested a hand over his side and closed my eyes. "We'll think of something; too bad he's not begging for a cicaro like Garrett. Poor Jem, hopefully he'll be able to unwedge that stick in Quin's ass."

Elish chuckled. "Joaquin isn't that bad a chimera. His world doesn't involve anything small or delicate, just sneaky business men and our family. Which I suppose is why that boy would throw him for a loop. Enough of this now though, I'll think of something. Sleep."

I nodded and felt my mind start to wander, the fatigue and soreness of our night's events making my bones sigh from relief. Both satisfied and exhausted, I gave in.

CHAPTER 35

I COULDN'T HIDE THE EXCITEMENT WHEN THE ELEVATOR dinged, opening two metal doors to reveal my new second apartment. It was on the fifth-storey, high above the other buildings and as Elish had told me, it faced the ocean and Griffin Park below.

I squeezed his arm and started pulling him into the living room, *oohing* and *ahhing* over the two dark brown couches and the recliner, with my own browny-grey marble coffee table on black wood. In the corner was a large rear projection television framed by two large pictures, one picture was of a man holding a mask but his face was in shadow and the other was a pride of lions; all of it on a back drop of beige painted walls with white crown moulding.

"This place must've cost like five thousand dollars!" I exclaimed. I went over to an oak chest of drawers and pulled them out; inside were new blankets and, of course, a black teapot and tea set.

I gave Elish a dirty look as he let out an amused snort behind me. "Really? That's your understanding of how much apartments like these cost in Eros? With furnishing?"

"Well, how much did it cost then, smart guy?" I slid open the sliding glass window and was immediately greeted by the sea air, though the ocean was an endless dingy grey and as dead as the world itself it still smelled nice and refreshing, much better than Moros.

"It's rude to ask the price of a birthday gift, but be assured it's more than you would've ever made in your life time three times over." Elish walked behind me, enjoying my excitement over the apartment. "The pantry is stocked with non-perishable food, enough to last two people several months, though it will never come to that."

I checked out the bedroom but turned around when I heard Elish clear his throat. I glanced behind me and saw him open up the end of the hall closet.

My eyes went wide as I took in a gun rack holding three assault rifles and above it three hand guns, with ammo crates and nylon sacks stacked underneath.

"Oh my god, let me see…" I closed the distance between us but Elish held out a hand to stop me.

"I am trusting you with a lot of fire power, and you do not want to know what will happen if you betray that trust, Jade. The key for this crate will be kept hidden on your keychain. I will have a copy as well and so will Luca. This is for emergencies only. If anyone ever tries to get into this apartment by force that is not me, shoot them. If they're enemies they will die, if they're one of my brothers they will come back… the important ones will anyway." Elish closed the door and locked it with a small silver key, before handing me back my keychain.

"Even King Silas?" I asked, stuffing my keychain into my pants pocket.

"Especially King Silas," Elish said in a low tone. "There is no need for me to pretend I have loyalty to him with you; you know better than to act disobediently in front of him by now and you know at this point I still have little choice."

I knew how it worked, and I understood it. I might not have been mature enough last year to understand the complicated position Elish was in, but knowing everything he was planning and the time he was forced to bide as we waited for Reaver, I knew what he was talking about.

Elish had been sure to discipline me for talking negatively about King Silas not because he loved his master or respected him, but because of how dangerous it was to let someone like me think I had Elish's coat tails to hide behind if I ever ran my mouth. If I ever showed disrespect and hinted that Elish had been letting me get away with such actions it might alert Silas to Elish's disobedience. For our own safety I had to be scared of him, and punished if I showed even the slightest hint of disrespect.

I got that now, and Elish knew I was old enough to understand it, so he had lessened his chastising of me when we openly talked about the king. I was just pleased that I had broken through a bit of his light screen, and he was comfortable enough to talk freely to me about the king. There was no one in the world except maybe Lycos that he could do that with.

Elish handed me a leather vest; I took it and was surprised at the weight. "Is this… bulletproof?" It looked like the light one I sometimes wore; it even had the leather straps and silver buckles.

He nodded. "That's right. I also have a gun holster in there somewhere. There is nothing else you should need in this apartment. It will be a suitable shelter if anything goes wrong."

The way he said those last words send a chill up my spine. "Are… you expecting anything to go wrong?"

There was a snap as the gun cabinet closed. "Silas will be waking up soon. I don't know what mood we will find him in when he does. I have spent almost ninety years with him and I still haven't mapped his personality; he's a mental shapeshifter."

I heard him let out a breath. He turned around and gave me a cold look that made me freeze on the spot. I stood there like a statue as his overbearing elegance shadowed the small wraith that was me. I always felt like an insect in front of his presence.

"Listen to me, Jade, and remember this." His voice was cold, a slow trickling river in an ice field. "Never for one moment think you have King Silas figured out; he is a thousand people and more in one body. The moment you think you know his next move he may purposely do the opposite, and the next time when you plan on him to do the opposite he will do exactly as one would predict a man to act. Remember this, and do not fool yourself into thinking he is but a spoiled, pampered king, that would be a grave mistake. King Silas is a deity in himself, never take my malice towards him as him not being a well-matched foe."

I leaned against the wall, all I could manage from under the weight of his words was a small nod, and the realization that I had been fooling myself. "You're right, I was making that mistake. It's easy to see him as just an immature maniac with too much power. I keep having to remind myself he's over two hundred and fifty years old and that he started the Fallocaust. It would be easier to overthrow him if he was just a brat."

"Yes, it would, but he isn't. He's a dangerous and hyper intelligent creature, he is always ten steps ahead of you, but to my credit I have so far managed to be twelve steps ahead of him," Elish responded. "He can do to me what he will, I'll come back and I am too valuable to him to ship me off to Donnely like Perish. All that matters to me is that I have a safe place to hide you, and keep you alive until you can survive the procedure to become immortal." His eyes narrowed just slightly. "Which is my chief concern right now, everything else is a pot simmering on an element which will come ready in due time."

His concern was for me? That made a glow smoulder in my heart. "Do you want to stay in Aras for a while? Would that be more helpful? Or go back to the greyrifts?"

Elish shook his head. He started turning off lights; obviously we were going back home. I grabbed my jacket, watching my new apartment dim around me.

"You're health is too fragile for the greywastes; you need that surgery and time to recover. I also refuse to be out of town when he wakes. He will see it as me hiding and even the thought of that makes my blood boil." Elish snipped my chain onto my leash and we started walking down the hallway of the apartment.

The city swept past me and I watched it go by with a half interest, people walking down the streets, only briefly noticing the fancy, spotless car with the tinted windows. Not a speck of garbage to be seen, or a panhandler, all of that had been shunned back to Moros where it belonged. Moros was a place that I could finally say with confidence I would never be sent to again.

At this thought I looked at Elish, for my own silent reassurance but he was staring forward with his usual air of a man in deep contemplation, the computer that was his brain sorting through the gardens he had planted, mentally checking each seed to see how they were faring. Then once we got home he would physically check them on his laptop or his many folders, making sure with god-like precision that all of his plans were springing forth. I admired him for that brain, even though I felt like a knuckle-dragging Neanderthal next to him.

I let him be without bothering him and went back to gazing out the window; we would be home soon.

"Hey, Elish…" I raised my head which sometime during the walls of

Eros and Skyland had ended up leaning against the back of the seat. "Jem's gone, his chair looks like it has been thrown into the back of the parking lot."

Elish turned his head, but the car had already driven past the spot. "Stop here, Harvard."

Harvard, our driver, slowed the car down immediately. "Would you like me to wait, Master Elish?"

"No, we'll walk the rest of the way." Elish opened the door and got out, I did the same and immediately started walking towards the fenced in parking lot Jem had set his small kiosk up in, but I didn't get far before my leash became tight and he dragged me back. I gave a hack into my arm and let him lead.

I trailed behind his silver cape, and peeked into the far end of the parking lot, where the half-concrete, half-chain-link fence kitty cornered a blind spot, hidden even better by the shadow of the buildings around it.

I was surprised to see a pathetic little shelter made in the far corner, constructed out of scraps of press board and cardboard with a tarp tied on the roof to break up the spring winds. It was a derelict little hovel, only four feet tall with a door so small a large dog couldn't even fit through.

I saw a dirty plastic dinner plate beside the door and a couple of loose band aids still in the package, muddy and ground into the gravel with several cigarette butts.

"Shit, he's been living here too? I thought he had a hotel or something," I mumbled. "Where do you–"

Elish held up a hand; immediately I clamped my mouth shut.

It was faint, but my hearing had been getting better, a small heartbeat coming from inside the shelter that made Moros seem like a paradise.

"Why aren't you minding your shop?"

A small pathetic voice whimpered from inside the shelter. "Go away, I'm closed."

I raised an eyebrow. "He sounds hurt."

Elish handed me my leash and took another step towards him. "Come out and greet me properly, you may be from a factory town but you should know chimera respect by now," Elish said in a stern voice.

There was a rustling of paper and garbage and I saw a dingy green blanket move around; eventually after much shifting I saw Jem's bowed head poke out of the hole.

When Jem raised his head I cringed and sucked in a breath; someone had done a work up on his face. His lip was sliced and his ear had been partially cut; he also had deep black bruises on his cheekbones and a wound bandaged by a dirty white gauze on his forehead.

Jem stood and with his shoulders slumped he looked up at Elish, a pathetic and defeated slouch on his face. "Sorry… good evening, Mr. Dekker…"

I couldn't see Elish's face but from the submissive cower Jem gave him I knew he must be burning him alive with his eyes. "Who did this to you? I told you to tell anyone who bothered you to consult me if they had a problem with your location." My master's voice was like a hot knife, every word sharper and more direct than the one before.

Jem lowered his gaze and twisted the bottom of his ratty shirt in his hands. "They did this to me *because* I said to take it up with you. They came here… asking about some kid and giving me trouble. When they started taking my stuff I mentioned your name to try and scare them, and… I got this for it."

Asking about some kid…

"What was the kid's name?"

"Jade."

My heart dropped into my chest. I started walking towards him but Elish yanked me back. "Who was looking for me? What did they look like?"

Jem took a step back as Elish grabbed my leash and roughly dragged me back.

And as he did, I watched his lips move, and like he was saying it in slow motion four words left his cut lips.

"Some red-haired guy."

No.

No Jade.

There are… hundreds of red-haired…

"Was his name Kerres?" I opened my mouth to say it at a normal octave but as I tried to control the heat cooking my brain like it was inside an oven, I ended up half-shouting them.

"I… he didn't–"

I gagged as Elish yanked me back, away from Jem. I heard him say coldly into my ear, "Go back to the skyscraper, now."

I pulled back towards Jem, ignoring Elish's orders. "Did he have brown eyes? My height... a few –"

"NOW, CICARO!" Elish snapped. He threw me towards the opening of the parking lot. I stumbled and looked back to him; my whole body started to shake.

Elish glared at me, an imposing sculpture of ice and fire, with a danger surrounding him that was thicker than his aura. I cowered and looked at him pleading but his expression didn't change. Not an ounce of negotiation to be had, or an inch to at least let me listen in; his orders were clear and his face told me I wouldn't live to disobey another command.

With a muffled sob I turned away from him, and walked back to the apartment, a burning behind my eyes making a single tear drop slide down my face.

There was no way.

No way at all.

He wouldn't do that to me.

I came home and immediately got Luca to make me a drink. I sat down with it on the couch and stared at the windows of the apartment, my heart a steel locked box that refused to show me its contents.

There were a lot of red-haired people, Jade. Crimstones as well, don't get your hopes up.

Hopes? The inside of me laughed. As soon as the word *hope* came to my mind I felt the blood vessels in my heart retract, with a taste of bitter masochism I realized hope would never be the word I'd use to describe this.

If Kerres had done this to me, if Kerres had faked his death to get back at me... I would fucking kill him, with my goddamn bare hands.

He had told me before I left... he would do everything he could to get me back. Suddenly Kerres doing that wasn't out of the realm of possibility.

My eyes started to burn again, and I immediately slung back the drink and asked Luca to top me off again, my voice cracking and brimming with emotion.

"Are you okay, Master Jade? Did you and Elish get into an argument?" the sengil asked kindly as he handed me my lemon soda and vodka and started rubbing my shoulders.

I shook my head. "No, nothing like that…" I sniffed and pursed the inner corners of my eyes with my finger, before leaning back into the couch to let Luca work his magic fingers.

My own self-hatred slid down my throat like poison, with such a burning taste it made the vodka seem like milk. There was no hiding my feelings, and after everything Kerres had done for me, I hated the fact that I didn't want it to be true.

If it was true, every remaining good memory I had of him would be tainted for the rest of my soon-to-be immortal life. I wanted to remember him as the boy who held my hand at Edgeview, who took care of me and loved me through my young life and teen life, who made a mistake trying to get me help, and took his own life because of the guilt.

If he was alive, it would draw the entire event into a new and ugly light. It would mean he deliberately faked his own death to not only hurt me, but to run from Elish's wrath; it would mean he had always had every intention of trying to deliver me to the Crimstones again.

It would mean that in all respects… he had changed more than I did.

The thought made the alcohol churn in my stomach; the thought of that being the Kerres I had once loved made me want to throw up. I just wanted him to remain my crimson-haired protector in my mind forever.

Not a Crimstone.

The implications of it made my head hurt, it made me want to curl up into Elish's closet and hide from the world, but I wasn't a kid anymore, I couldn't run from reality. So when the apartment doors opened I immediately rose to greet him.

Elish's face was the unreadable mask of control and calm, but I only glanced at it for a second before my vision took in the young man cowering beside him, looking from side to side like he was being dazzled by strobe lights.

"Luca, bathe the boy and feed him, throw these rags out while you're at it." With a rough push Elish directed Jem towards the calm Luca, holding in his surprise better than I.

"Another stray?" Luca said cautiously. He gave me a glance and I could already tell he was assuming that this was what I was upset about. "Should I chain him?"

"No, this one will not fight." Without a second glance Elish turned away from him and turned his attention to me.

To my surprise he narrowed his eyes. I felt the room grow colder around the two of us. "Wipe those tears of joy from your face, you pathetic weak worm."

I watched his eyes and I watched his aura... both dark, foreboding entities that told me more truths than his poisoned words ever could.

"He's... he's alive?" My voice broke the heavy atmosphere in the room, like a drum beat in a silent auditorium. I felt my knees weaken; I shook my head at him in disbelief. "No, that's not possible." Nausea rose to my throat, I stumbled back, only the couch stopping me from falling over.

"Your boyfriend is very much alive, and a full-blown Crimstone whose devastation over you has turned to a hatred of you that rivals Silas's. Now get out of my sight, those tears on your face are making me sick."

Elish's cold words hit me hard, but not his dead and dismissive tone, it was the meaning behind them. He thought I was happy, he thought I was relieved and whatever he was feeling from it, whether it was jealousy, disappointment or disgust was coming out in the shape of a sharp tongue just waiting to lance me alive.

Kerres.

You fucking asshole.

I wasn't relieved, fuck, what was wrong with me? I wasn't... I was mad, I was pissed off. My blood was filling with acid as every second passed by, sinking into my brain and dissolving it into a puddle of useless mush. He wasn't my loving red-haired boy, he was a terrorist masquerading as a man trying to unbrainwash his boyfriend.

I had never thought I would see his face again; I thought that red hair, those kind chocolate-brown eyes, and his friendly smile were lost in the tides of time, that I'd only ever have a couple pictures and my childhood memories to replay in my head when I thought of him.

Good memories. Not tainted by the last month we had together when I had scrubbed away the soft exterior he had once had, leaving him bleeding and raw, only a disfigured scar to remain.

Now I didn't even have that, I had a traitor, a terrorist...

My sweet baby-faced boy.

'They killed Jade, they gave me a chimera in return.'

"I said get out of my sight, Cicaro."

And what have the Crimstones given me back?

"Jade!" Elish cut through the swamp in my head. I looked up at him and saw two blazing violet eyes glaring at me. He looked a thousand feet tall, an imposing deity with an overbearing aura that mine could never hold a candle to. He was a powerful Adonis of grace and elegance who could bring me to my knees with just one look.

And for that, as his eyes pierced me, I felt my resolve pop like a balloon full of acid. I broke my gaze away from him and held my hand over my mouth in a pathetic attempt to try and stop the tears that were springing to my eyes. Then my other hand dropped, spilling the glass of liquor I had been holding, soundlessly onto the carpet.

The room disappeared around me, and all that remained was his cold aura and my own, this chimera who had claimed me as his, and to whom I felt bound to for our eternal lives. He was my beacon now, and with a pull of guilt my heart went to him for comfort.

"You think you know me inside and out?" I whispered looking down as the vodka and lemon made a damp stain on the carpet. "And yet you have no idea how I feel? You don't know me at all do you, *Master*?" I picked up the glass and turned it around in my hand, I smiled sadly and choked back the tears. "You don't know what this means."

"It means I should've left you to your fate in that brothel, you're more trouble than you're worth, slumrat."

"Shut the fuck up!" I screamed, feeling the last shreds of whatever spider string was preventing me from dissolving into insanity. I clenched the glass, wanting so badly to throw it at him but he was glaring at me in such a way I knew he would catch it before it had a chance to even get vodka on his collar. "For someone so hyperintelligent you're a moron when it comes to me and in all respects YOU!" I threw the glass onto the ground and took a heated step towards him. "Do you know what it's like to know he hated who I had become so much that he'd fake his death? He was my boyfriend, my protector, Elish. He was my guardian, and now the sight of me made him so sick he sold me off to be brainwashed. Do you know how that feels?" The tears ran freely down my face. "You dismissed and abandoned me because I fell in love with you, he didn't love me because of what I turned into after you did that. No one fucking likes me or what I've become and now the man who had been taking care of me since I was nine would rather me be a brainless robot than be the person, no, the *chimera* I am now. So fuck you, Elish, you're so far off the mark with this one it's ridiculous. Piss off."

"You're fooling yourself," Elish growled. "Your gutter rat boyfriend is alive, come to reclaim his bottom feeder, it's a perfect love story." Elish narrowed his eyes. "What a hero, you must be so proud."

"You're such an idiot." His words deflated me again. I sunk down, my hand going back to my face, my only defence against his words. I took a step to go to my old bedroom but my legs wobbled and a wave of dizziness came over me. I opened my mouth to talk again, but all that came out of my mouth was a sob. I grabbed the back of the couch and started to cry.

Why does his crying always strip every shred of anger from me?– Is it because he rarely cries? Or is it because whenever he does it was over something I did that I will later regret?

Elish watched his cicaro bend over the couch with his back to him, his shoulders shaking with an unimaginable grief, a grief that Elish knew, in the very pit of his heart, wasn't aimed in the direction he had thought.

Perhaps he is sad over the ramifications of Kerres's resurrection... perhaps I am wrong.

No, how could that be so? Elish had had his spiders watching the slums before Jade had become his; they were two magnets to each other, they were inseparable and dependent.

Elish felt the corner of his mouth twitch. Had this been along the lines of the same error he'd had to face after he'd dropped Jade off in Moros? The one where he had assumed Jade would be fine and would fit back into his lifestyle like a well-used glove?

Elish rarely made errors, it was only with the boy that he'd had to admit more than a few times that he'd been wrong in his assumptions. Though it was a popular belief Morosians were anything but predictable, this young chimera had turned out to be no exception. Elish had to admit to himself that when it came to Jade Shadow Dekker he had to throw the book of 'chimera reading' out and go with his own experiences with the teenager.

I do hate it when he cries…

Elish took a step towards Jade, and put a hand on his shoulder. The boy sniffed and looked over, as if not believing what he had felt. When he saw it was Elish's hand, to Elish's shock, Jade turned around and collapsed into his arms.

"Get rid of him, please, Elish, make him disappear!" Elish couldn't believe the words that were coming out of his mouth. "Don't make me have to see him, please don't. I can't see him like that. Get rid of him before he ruins what good memories of him I have, please?"

He really had been being genuine… this isn't what I had expected that all. Why was I so sure he would be happy? I have received the complete opposite reaction to that which my calculations had predicted. That boy never ceases to amaze me… no, frustrate, he never ceases to frustrate me.

Elish put his hand on the boy's head and stroked back his hair. "I will take care of it, quietly and discreetly. I would forget you even know; it will not make a difference by the week's end."

Jade cried quietly in his robes. Elish had to hold him up, the boy was such a wreck.

"Are you going to kill him?" Jade croaked.

"Do you want me to?"

The boy was quiet, and Elish knew the answer before it even left the boy's lips. "No."

Elish's mouth frowned, but he pushed aside his own thoughts regarding Kerres and Jade's former relationship and attempted to understand the boy. He might be a chimera, with a penchant for darkness and an aversion to mercy, but Kerres had once been all he had.

"Then I will not." *That does not mean my brothers won't. I will skirt around Kerres's fate for this stunt he has pulled on us and give the boy the reassurance he needs. Though the end will be the same. Kerres will die, if not because of what he has done now, then he will die because I hate that Jade still shows attachment towards him.*

The boy is mine, and I will not let him share his heart with another man.

"Why do you all hate me?" Elish's attention turned as he heard the boy whimper. It sounded like he was in physical pain. "I hate myself so much for driving him to become so desperate he thought this was the only option. Fuck, I hate myself so much. What's wrong with me?"

"You're a chimera, you're incompatible with most ordinary people," Elish responded with an almost caring tone to his voice. It always took effort to not say some things in a taunting manner. "The only person's opinion that should matter to you is mine, and I say you have no reason to hate yourself. You're old enough now to quit with this ridiculous self-loathing, you're an empath and a chimera. No matter if I would've claimed you or not, the bloodthirst inside of you wouldn't have waned with age. If I was not here to temper that hand you would've done a lot worse." Elish shook his head as he drew the boy back, wiping Jade's nose with his own sleeve. "Most chimeras come to us on their own at seventeen to nineteen, or make themselves known some way or another. Can you guess how?"

"They murder people?" Jade mumbled.

Elish nodded. "You say that satirically but you're right. Did Sanguine tell you how he came to us?"

Jade shook his head.

"Well, once his pointed teeth grew in, his family tried to crucify him as an abomination, a half-demon. They chased him away from their settlement. Nero brought him feral and wild at nineteen. He was… fun to deal with, but he adjusted. Silas trained him and later he went back to the settlement and crucified those who had hurt him. Now Jack was an interesting one too –"

"You're trying to distract me from Kerres right now." Jade's brow furrowed. "You're giving me a shiny object to chase after, stories you know I like hearing."

Elish smirked, he nudged Jade's chin before wiping Jade's tears with his sleeve. "It's better than your whining, now clean yourself up. Quin is coming, so is Ellis and the vagabond in my apartment will emerge soon. I don't want either of them to see you like this, it will stick in their mind and reflect badly on me."

I looked up at him helplessly. "You invited over the two chimeras that despise me and you brought home some dirty stray animal? You are angry at me."

I liked how I was able to make him smile, even if most of the time it was a bordering on mocking smirk. He pulled my shoulder towards our private bathroom. "Ellis has her own personal vendetta against the Crimstones, she would be quite angry if I begrudged her the opportunity for revenge. Quin is coming for different reasons, and unless you wish for a new friend to gallivant with, you will play along to whatever manipulations I wish to feed him."

I turned around and gave him an unimpressed look. "You're a one pet owner. I will make good on my word with what will happen if we get a new cicaro in the house."

"If times were more boring I may have just done it for entertainment, but right now I am much too busy to torment you. We will be going with our original plan to solder him to Joaquin, now clean up and make yourself look presentable. You're seventeen, and you're a chimera. You've had time to cry which I've been patient with, and now you can take half an hour to absorb the rest during a hot shower. Once you emerge, what do I expect from you?"

I thought for a second and his cold yet calming words from many months ago came to me. "Stay stoic, stay calm, stay collected, no matter what happens. I am a chimera and they're all watching me."

"*Always* watching you, your every move, even more so because you're my cicaro and in their line of vision more than other chimeras at your age." Elish nodded. He walked into the bedroom with me and as I showered I heard him gather his own clothes. Like me he had clothes he wore when we were expecting company, his flowing and fancy designed robes, white slacks, all of his usual chimera clothing. When we got home at night he usually changed into a button-down and trousers, and if I had behaved myself during the day I got to wear jeans and a t-shirt or cargo pants. It was always a relief to get out of the restricting and tight leather he made me wear. I was envious of Luca's sengil uniform, black trousers, white shirt, and a black vest, though sometimes his vest or shirt changed to different colours if the routine-loving sengil was feeling adventurous. Compared to my usual clothing he wore the equivalent of marshmallows and cotton balls.

I buffed myself dry and changed into the pet clothing Luca had laid out for me while I was showering. Then when I decided I looked presentable I went into the bedroom to put on my cufflinks and collar.

But as my eyes scanned the made bed and the grey-coloured room, I couldn't spot the leather collar I had sworn I'd put on the bed. It was gone, but where?

I was about to go and complain to Elish, suspecting him of using me as some further manipulation when he walked back into the bedroom.

Looking like his elegant self, his hair neatly brushed back except for small bits that fell down his shoulders, he called me over. I noticed he was holding something black in his hand.

It was a new collar. This one was a lot fancier than the one on my neck now, with two rows of silver studs instead of only one, and green gems embedded in every third stud.

"You'll not be needing the other collar anymore." Elish put the collar over my neck, and lightly brushed back the strands of the hair at the nape so he could fasten it. When he belted it he stood back and gave me a long look.

This collar was lighter than the last one; automatically I raised a hand and felt along the edges. It was an incredibly soft leather, like it had been broken in for years but it was brand new and smelling like shaving cream almost. I turned around and looked at myself in the mirror.

Elish appeared behind me, and he put a hand on my shoulders. I looked at him through the mirror and for a brief moment admired the two of us standing as a solid unit. A former slumrat, dressed in leather pants with laces up the sides and black loafers, with a leather vest with the same style of laces drawn together over my chest, crisscrossing against my pale skin. With my leather cuffs on my wrists and ankles and my new collar on my neck I looked every bit a cicaro.

"Do you notice this collar is lighter?" my master, draped in white and grey, said in the mirror. He ran a hand over the silver studs, the other hand still resting on my shoulder.

I nodded and saw a shine of approval in his eyes, deep purple, matching the earrings in his ears. Three piercings in each ear, one white, one black, and one purple, all precious gems with a value I didn't even want to guess.

"That is because this one isn't a shock collar. I have decided you have outgrown it. You've earned the privilege by obeying me and proving yourself, though if you let this privilege get to your head, I will not hesitate to demote you back to that gaudy leather bind, am I understood, Cicaro?" Elish said the words carefully and coldly, like he was sculpting each syllable from gold. I took each in and treasured them, knowing I would never forget a single word.

"Thank you, Master," I said looking into the mirror. "I won't disappoint you, and I'll do anything you want me to do to help bring down Kerres and the Crimstones. Kerres died in Garrett Park, and no matter if his physical form is still here… he isn't him anymore."

I saw Elish stare back at me, not a single breath out of place or a flicker of a nod; he only ran his hand along the collar; yellow and purple eyes locked in the reflection of the full-length mirror.

"It is an easy thing to say right now, Cicaro, just hope you never have to prove your words to me. Because I will expect you to hold yourself to them." To my surprise he put a hand up to my ear and stroked the lobes. "I'll be piercing your ears tonight as well; we have a tradition in this family, and since you're a chimera you have to maintain that. Two more on each side, in our family you get to choose which colour the third will be, but you will not have a choice. It will be a purple ruby like –"

There was a knock on the apartment door. Elish turned his head, before sliding his hand off my shoulder. "Well, here we go, pay attention and remember yourself, Cicaro."

I watched him turn away from me, and with a sweep of his robes he disappeared out into the main area of the apartment. With a deep sigh and a gathering of my strength I followed him, pushing down every numb feeling for Kerres I had. Like Elish had told me, I'd had my time to process it and now it was time to go back to my life. I had to be stronger than this.

I was a chimera, Elish's chimera, I had to be. Though if my body would obey the stern warning in my mind, I didn't know.

CHAPTER 36

JOAQUIN DEKKER LOOKED UPON ME LIKE THE PARASITE he was so sure I was, his turquoise eyes sweeping me up and down while he held a stemmed glass of red wine. He looked just as aloof and stuck up when I had seen him during Elish's meetings, and dressed in such a way as well; a black blazer with a blue tie, slacks, and a blue kerchief in his breast pocket. To top it off his black crinkly hair was neatly styled, parted in the middle with a flair of his bangs covering the left side of his forehead. If I would've gotten him as a pet I would've eaten him alive; the prospect almost made my mouth water.

Behind him Ellis was on her phone, giving me nothing more than a passing glance of disinterest, more interested in the conversation she was having with someone back in the precinct. She was talking in a hushed and quick voice, hovering around the sliding glass door like she was waiting for the conversation to shift where she had to go somewhere private.

"You look well, did you manage to kick that heroin habit then?" Quin asked airily, taking a small drink before taking a seat on a cream-coloured chair in the sitting room, a small area in the apartment partially closed off by two bookshelves. He smoothed out the wrinkles in his slacks and adjusted the white cuffs of his shirt as well.

"Months ago," I said without a single hint of bite in my tone, Elish's words echoing through my head. "And you? I heard you're applying for a teaching position at the college?"

Quin sniffed and shook his head. "Chimeras don't need to apply for anything, I am merely waiting for an opening to come about."

I nodded back soberly. "Odd, I didn't think chimeras had to wait for openings either, no matter, can I get you anything else?"

Quin gave me a withering look but I only stared at him back, not a single muscle movement out of place. He devoured my flesh under his smouldering gaze before his odd blue-green eyes flicked past me.

To my amazement I saw his pupils dilate. "You? What are you doing here?"

I looked behind me and I immediately felt a hidden thrill rush through my body, it looked like either Elish had already pulled some strings, or the two magnets had attracted each other without our interference.

Jem was behind me, dressed in a crimson red button-down and a leather vest with his coppery hair freshly styled and primped, looking like a completely different (and attractive) person. He still looked terrified though; those soft and innocent blue eyes had a glint of primal fear embedded in their sapphire gems and an aura about him that told me he was about to piss his pants. I could relate, if it had been two years ago I would've been terrified to behold this sight myself. Elish, Ellis, and Quin were all terrifying chimeras in their own right, and the tension from my ex-boyfriend's shenanigans were only tightening the already taut strings. The room seemed like a ticking time bomb with over a half dozen fuses just dangling over the flames.

The vagabond's eyes went from Quin's to mine, then to back to Quin's, his mouth opening and stuttering as he held the chilled wine bottle in a white knuckle grip. I saw Jem swallow the boulder in his throat before he managed to eke out a response.

"Hello, sir… I am… I um…"

Or a partial response.

I watched with amusement as Joaquin's brow slowly started to crease before he gave me an accusing glare, like I was obviously the sole cause of everything wrong in the world. "Why do you have him? Why is he here?"

I smirked and put a hand on Jem's shoulder. I felt him cringe and even give a small whimper. There was no mistaking that this kid was terrified of all of us. I wished I could pick him apart to gauge my next move, but I had an idea as to what Elish would want me to do next. We hadn't planned on anything, or at least he hadn't told me we were supposed to do anything, but this opportunity had fallen on my lap wrapped in a copper-haired bow. Even if my master was planning something else I just couldn't let this present slip between my fingertips.

So with that in my head, I adopted my most primal of states. "My master gave him to me." I lowered my voice, and fixed my eyes on Quin's. "A little chew toy for when he's too busy to appease my... thirst. For some reason fear just tickles the inner transgressions of my mind."

"What?" Jem choked. I grabbed the wine bottle from him just as he stumbled to the side; he put a hand on the bookshelf to steady himself. "I'm... I'm just a merchant, not a pet, I'm sorry for the hassle... I'll just be leaving now."

I tightened my grip and growled into his ear. "You're not going anywhere, *Cicaro*."

The boy whimpered and froze solid, but a moment later I felt Quin grab my shoulder and yank me back. "Get away from him, you fucking slumrat!" Quin snapped before I was pushed away from the boy.

"He is not yours to protect, Joaquin," I sniffed, running my hand down my black hair. I gave them both a cocky grin and sauntered up to Jem with a dangerous smile on my face. "Perhaps once I tire of him and start shipping him off to Elish's brothers you can have a turn of what's left."

"To hell with that!" Quin snarled, getting more and more upset.

"Is there a problem?" my master's cold voice sounded from the living room. I saw him walk towards the sitting area with a tea mug in his hand.

Jem cowered like a puppy in the presence of a tiger; he slunk back, looking around for a dark place to hide himself. He was the picture of fear to the point where the kid was practically catatonic, I could hear his heartbeat thrashing in his chest from a mile away. It was all sickeningly fascinating.

"I can tolerate this obsession you have for that pet, but you're giving him flesh to devour now?" Quin snapped, his brow was creased and his turquoise eyes smouldering gemstones that if given the chance would set the room aflame.

"Elish gave him to me, to do as I wish." I crossed my arms defiantly, though my only point in saying that was so Elish would take my hints and play along. "Your brother is trying to deny me my dinner."

Quin looked at me fuming, before he fixed his glaring eyes on Elish, but he didn't speak. It looked like he wanted to but he didn't; he only stood tall, his once crisp black blazer wrinkled under his constantly folding and unfolding arms, even his blue tie was crooked.

"What happens during my pet's personal time is no one's concern but my own, if the young boy's presence upsets you, Joaquin, I can have him tied to Jade's room now rather than later. Jem, go with Luca," Elish replied coldly.

"What?" Quin exclaimed, just as Jem's eyes widened, giving us all terrified looks.

"I'm not a pet." Jem's meek voice was a thin wheeze. "I just want to go back to my parking lot… I was born to the… my chip… just scan my chip and it will tell you."

Elish gave him a disinterested look. I took this opportunity to put a hand on the kid's shoulder as Quin looked at us with scathing hatred. Behind Jem, and unbeknownst to the terrified boy, I licked my lips in the most vile manner I could. Quin gritted his teeth.

Elish smiled thinly. "Jem, as you must know from even the most basic school curriculum, chimeras can declare ownership over every and any human. You will not be returning to your home in the parking lot, you are now my, Elish Dekker's, Cicaro."

The auburn-haired boy looked green; I saw his hand start to tremble. He gave a slight nod and said meekly, "Okay."

That was it? Jeez, this kid gave up so easily; I thrashed and bit for several months and got beaten into the ground before Elish drew submission out of me. No wonder my master had no need for him, like he had told me a long time ago, he preferred pets with a little bit more bite to them.

Joaquin continued to smoulder, it wasn't until I took my first step with Jem towards my bedroom that he finally was broken of whatever hypothetical pride he had been holding onto.

"I'll buy him," Quin said in a low and dangerous tone. "I need a new serventmaid anyway, fine, how much do you want for him Elish?"

"He isn't for sale." Elish's tone was still winter frost. "Do you think I would let such an attractive creature go? My pet hand-selected him."

Joaquin looked like a tomato about to burst; he stalked over and grabbed Jem from me. "Fine, I'll give you an ocelot kitten."

"I have no need for an ocelot kitten." Though behind us in the living room I heard Luca's heart given an excited jolt, before it fizzled with disappointment. In truth I wanted an ocelot kitten too. I had seen Joaquin with his ocelot during a few meetings and he was always entertaining.

"What do you want then?" Quin said impatiently, at this point he was seething mad and Jem was stricken with full-body paralysis. Out of the corner of my eye I could also see Ellis looking at the scene with the look only a woman who had been seeing similar exchanges happen for the past eighty years and had gotten quite tired of it, could have.

"Want? Nothing at this moment, but perhaps the knowledge that you do owe me a favour, two perhaps, since we are dealing with flesh and blood. Two favours, Joaquin," Elish said casually, before he gave me a nod to step away from Jem. I did as he was asked and took my place beside him.

Quin grabbed the boy's shoulder in a protective hold, and I knew for sure in that moment our plan couldn't have worked better. "Fine, two favours, take your blood price, brother, it seems this feral teenager hasn't blunted your edge. Now can we get down to the reason why we're here? I've almost had enough of being around your cockroach."

Elish didn't move, instead he crossed his arms and blocked Quin's path from the living room. "You can apologize to my cicaro first; he is a chimera and far from a cockroach. Apologize to him."

I squared my shoulders and smiled at Quin, enjoying seeing the 'stick up his ass' chimera squirm under Elish's thumb, knowing he was walking a thin line with his blond brother, Quin gave me a sneering look and said with acid on his tongue, "My apologies, Jade."

I bowed with a smile and when I raised my head I said back, my own tone dripping in honey. "Apology accepted, Joaquin."

"About fucking time, if this soap opera is over with I want to get down to business. Quin put your pet away, he's not hearing what's about to be discussed." Ellis's disgruntled voice sounded from the living room, and at that note we all took our seats. A very scared and shell-shocked Jem was led away to the dark safety of Luca's bedroom. I was sure the sengil would be a calming influence on him, a lot more calming than Elish or I would've been.

Ellis roughly threw down a stack of papers onto Elish's coffee table, in a way that reminded me of when she put down the folders of missing people in Skyfall when I had been brought in for questioning. She was a woman of no bullshit that was for sure, I was looking forward to seeing how she interacted with her brothers. Every one of them seemed to have their own sync when they interacted with each other, some seemed to be subs, others seemed to be dominant, and some were kind of in between. I, for one, didn't see myself as a submissive-type like Lycos, Drake, and, from what I'd seen, Teaguae and Grant, but I was submissive to Elish and low on the totem pole. Elish was, of course, submissive to no one, except Silas and he was plotting on killing Silas so that shed light on how he felt about bowing down to someone.

"I should knock out Teaguae's teeth for this one, he didn't verify Kerres's story or even look at his body before he reported it; he just saw the dyed hair. Someone tipped off Shay –" I recognized that name as being one of the main news reporters in Skyfall. "– about the apartment renter's body being found and he just ran with it, and after it was reported everyone took it as fact. It was an obvious Crimstone plant making those claims and it wouldn't surprise me if it was Milos himself."

I stared at Ellis, my teacup halfway to my mouth, I was sitting beside Elish looking over at the folder he was holding. "Milos is alive? I strangled him."

"Not quite, but you did permanently mark him. I suppose you should stick to biting, young one." Ellis handed me a folder. I took it and saw right away the photo attached to the upper left hand corner. It was of Milos, and it looked like the screen cap from a video. I could see a large red and inflamed lesion around his neck, an inch thick in some places.

"You almost decapitated him, well done," Elish praised beside me, putting a finger down on the paper so he could see the photo better. "If your handcuffs didn't break, perhaps you would've been able to do it."

"I didn't kill him though," I muttered, even though inside I was beaming at the compliment. "I'll remedy that; can I face him when we bring him to Stadium?"

"I'm planning on making you face all of them," Elish said with a hard edge to his voice, and I wondered if he meant Kerres as well.

"Good, film it." I gave him a small forced smile and checked over Milos's file before closing it. "Do we have any idea where their base is?"

Ellis seemed surprised at the fact I was engaged in this. I guess she, like most of my family, assumed I would be heartbroken. There were parts of my heart very sore, but I wouldn't show it in front of them.

They were all watching me.

"We think they're in the borderlands, but where they are isn't important, it's where Kerres and Milos are. Jem's report says they were together and seemed quite cordial towards each other," Ellis said. The last part threatened to stab my heart, but I steeled myself. I had left Kerres begging me to go to their base, begging me to go to the Crimstones. For all I knew he was the one who got Milos out of the apartment before the thiens came.

"Kerres could be back in their base by now but I suspect not." Elish tented his fingers and tapped them together. "I can assume if he is still in Skyfall your people will be doing everything they can to find him?"

Ellis nodded. "It won't be long before they make another move and we'll be ready for that. I want Milos alive, that's my only request in this. You can kill Kerres, he hasn't been involved in this long enough to be valuable to me."

They're all watching you... I swallowed down that remark.

"I will decide Kerres's fate, and once he is out of the picture and Milos captured, my involvement in this will cease. My concern is for my cicaro's safety; Milos and Kerres have already shown they have every intention of hurting Jade." Elish put the file folder down. "Which brings me to my next request, I want thiens guarding my skyscraper, double the usual, and I want Ares and Siris guarding my cicaro."

I gagged on my tea. "What? Them? They hate me! I hate them, I *killed* them, they raped and tried to kill me. We do not get along."

Elish didn't bat an eye. "You don't need to get along with them, or even speak with them, they'll only be accompanying us when we're out. Ellis, can you do this?"

I was relieved when the female chimera pursed her lips to the side and shook her head. "No, I need to agree with Jade on this one, Elish. Your boyfriend has a mouth on him and Ares and Siris have a short fuse when it comes to snippy subordinates. I'd rather send Sanguine or Jack."

I perked up and grinned. "I like Sanguine, I get along with him great."

"I know," Elish and Ellis said at the same time, both in very flat and insipid tone. Elish continued, "So the master isn't awake yet then? He has no need for our needle-mouthed brother?"

There was a small pull of her lip, but besides that no other expression crossed her face. "No, not yet, soon though. Jack says his heart is beating. Once he wakes he will swiftly take care of this Crimstone business. No matter what his feelings regarding you and Jade's pairing he will not take kindly to a terrorist trying to kidnap one of his creations. You have that going for you."

"There is no *pairing*."

I looked over as I heard Quin, who had been a fly on the wall during this meeting, groan incredulously, Ellis too rolled her eyes, which unfortunately was the last straw for me. I stifled a laugh.

"Do you have something to say, Cicaro?" I flinched at the frost behind his words, and I remembered myself and my place. I had to be stoic, calm and in control. They were not my friends, even if the prospect of ganging up on Elish was tempting.

"No, Master, just remembering the look on Joaquin's face when I licked his new pet's neck, I wish you could've seen it."

There was a pause from Elish, but in the silence I could see the heat rising to Quin's ears, his turquoise eyes glared at me, partially covered by his crinkly black hair.

"Which reminds me, I will be taking my pet and leaving. Is there anything else you need me for, brother? Do you have all the marketing notes on your laptop now?" Quin said crisply. "I'll be needing your report and sign off by Monday for the biannual budget."

"I have everything, my thanks for the files, Quin." Elish rose and so did I. I stayed by the couch as he reached a hand out to shake Quin's. "I will draw up Jemini's papers by Monday; if you wish I have a shock collar that just came available, though I doubt that boy will give you trouble." Elish looked towards Luca's bedroom. "Luca, the boy."

As Quin was getting ready to leave, the bedroom door opened and Luca came out with an apprehensive look on his face. "Master Elish... he, um, he's hiding under my bed and he refuses to get out."

Elish stared at him for a moment, a plain and almost pained stare, but a moment later he, as he always did, saw this as a teaching opportunity. Which is why he turned to Quin and said with a cold smile, "Well, Quin, he's your problem now, go retrieve him."

Joaquin paled slightly, he scratched the back of his head before his brow creased. "Well, alright then, Luca get me a broom stick."

"For fuck sakes…" I heard Ellis whisper under her breath.

Suddenly, there was a rumble behind us, like the low rolling thunder after a lightning strike; immediately we all turned around to look out the skyscraper window.

I couldn't believe what I saw.

A plume of black smoke rose up, with orange veins showing fire that became dimmer as it rose to the sky. I heard Ellis swear, but it was drowned out by a second explosion only a block away. I saw debris rise up into the air before crashing back down to the ground.

"That's… oh fuck, Elish, that's coming from the precinct, Eve and Garren are in there." Ellis immediately got on her phone. I saw a tremble coming to her hand, her steeled countenance quickly dissolving, but who could blame her, those two were her kids.

Elish's eyes narrowed, but he retained the cold resolve that had made him him for almost ninety years. "There is no need to guess what those were, another bombing. Jade get my phone, on the coffee table."

I nodded and reached for the phone but as I did it rang. I clicked the green *accept call* button and handed it to Elish. Not knowing what else to do with myself as the other chimera leaders did what had to be done I watched the black smoke rise into the air. Polluting the crystal blue sky, not just with its ugly black plumes, but with the dark omen I knew it was sending to us.

Was Kerres there right now? Watching the blast, hoping he had killed a chimera or at least the offspring of one? Why did he blow up the precinct and not Elish's skyscraper? I suppose the answer to that was that the Crimstones wanted to bring down the entire chimera kingdom, not just Elish. I might be a priority to Kerres and he might be looking for information on me, but I doubt I was in the main scope of Milos and the others.

This didn't make me feel better, it just made the hole in my gut worse. Even if I wasn't their target I had still helped shake the hive; the

Crimstones hadn't done anything in years before Kerres tried to offer me up to them.

I went up to the window, my stomach dropping to my feet. I knew the Crimstones had been doing this for a while now, but I still felt responsible for this. This wouldn't be getting me any brownie points with the chimeras, especially if someone within the family died.

My mind snapped back when I heard screaming on the other end of Elish's phone. I looked over and saw Elish's stoic face staring forward as the person on the other line talked to him in a way I had never heard before.

"We will be right there," Elish said placidly, before putting the phone into his pocket. Ellis was talking hurriedly and Quin was as well, but it didn't matter, and with what Elish said next I knew why.

"That was King Silas. He's awake and he wants to meet with all of us."

Royal blue and turquoise eyes focused on him, and at the same time I saw Ellis and Quin's faces change, within a fraction of a second, from angry and desperate to completely taken aback. I knew the look on my own face wasn't any different.

Ellis, still holding the phone up to her ear talked hurriedly. "I... I need to go. Go to the safe house in Moros and take your brother and the little ones, call me when you get there not before." Ellis hung up her phone. "Silas? Really? Where is he? Jack told me he had him in his skyscraper."

Elish grabbed his jacket and put it on. "He didn't say, but he, of course, is angry that we let this happen. I don't want to keep him waiting, come, we're going."

I turned around and grabbed my leather jacket. I got one sleeve on before a crisp voice stopped me in my tracks. "Not you."

"Why not!" I exclaimed. "Silas said all of us. I'm a chimera; I'm part of this family."

With a rough pull Elish took the jacket from me and tossed it onto the side table beside the hallway. "You're not a part of this family and you won't be until you've earned it; you're my cicaro and you're staying to watch over Jem and Luca."

I gave him a heated look but his calm but dangerous face stopped me from saying anything too disobedient, instead I took a step back and shook my head. "Fine, I'll babysit. I killed Ares and Siris, plus over a dozen Morosians and I saved Sanguine from the Crimstones, but yeah, I'll babysit the pet and the sengil."

Elish buttoned up his jacket and nodded towards Quin and Ellis. "Ellis we'll drop you off at the precinct, I doubt Silas needs you. Quin give Garrett a call, we'll be picking him up, the rest can get there on their own."

When Elish was at the door, and the other two in the hallway still busy on their phones I managed to grab Elish's sleeve.

"Come home soon," I said quietly.

Elish gave me an annoyed look, and I knew he was busy and I knew his mind was elsewhere but I still needed to make that connection.

"You're in charge of Luca and Jem. No one leaves this apartment, am I understood?"

There was nothing else for me to do but nod. "Yes, Master," I said quietly. I pursed my lips wanting to tell him to be careful, be safe, but the chimera code he had been teaching me told me I couldn't, and before my brain could force the words to my lips he was gone.

The chimeras were gone.

They were gone, leaving me alone with my own thoughts, and Luca behind me looking at the billows of smoke rising up from the north. There would be chaos there, noise, yelling, and dozens of thiens trying to keep the public calm, but right here, in this skyscraper, there was only deafening and maddening silence.

I felt useless, like I should be doing something, but what? I might be a chimera, I might've ruled the slums as the Shadow Killer but now the real chimeras were off doing the men's work. I was at home like a housewife minding the sengil and the pet who was cowering under the bed.

I wished he would've let me go, but there was a million reasons in Elish's head to keep me safe here: so Silas wouldn't notice me or blame me, so the Crimstones or Kerres wouldn't see me, so Elish could keep me in his protective hold until my brain was matured and I could survive the surgery that would bind me to him for all eternity.

Until then I was a Ming vase to be kept safe from harm... I suppose I should have been flattered that he wanted me beside him that badly, but I was a chimera, a tiger kept in a zoo.

In the slums I was a prince…

Only a sigh made my feelings audible and before Luca could comment on my mood I grabbed my jacket and some cigarettes and went onto the patio of the skyscraper. I didn't know why but I felt closer to Elish that way, even if it was only several feet from the spot I was currently in. I just hoped he didn't come back pissed off and blaming me for all of this.

Shit, Silas was awake?

What if he didn't come back at all?

I swallowed the thought and sat down on a patio chair. I lit a cigarette and watched the daylight burn off the smoke that rose steadily into the air. I wouldn't be surprised if they saw this smoke in the borderlands. So many things must be burning right now.

Every minute ticked by like its only purpose was to be as slow as possible, but after a while I found my rhythm of one cigarette after the other, inhaling the tangy tobacco until I was hitting the filter, then almost immediately lighting another one. I wished for something stronger, purely for my nerves but Elish would know and if I gave him one reason to get pissed off at me he would eat me alive.

The smoke was still coming, but to my relief it wasn't as thick and choking as it had been in the beginning. I knew they had a couple fire trucks up and running, pre-Fallocaust refurbished ones, ones that had always only stayed in Skyland or on occasion Eros, never in Moros where if a building caught fire it was just tough luck.

How long had it been now? I should be keeping track, but what was the use? Time would only drive me crazy right now, at least I knew Elish would eventually come back. Surely Silas would have better things to do than –

I jumped a mile high, my heart thrashed into my chest as the sliding glass door opened quickly and slammed with a deafening bang against the glass, rattling every bone in my body and dropping my cigarette to the floor. I whirled around to start to cuss out Luca when in an instant, the words stuck to my throat.

It wasn't Luca…

Oh shit… oh my fucking god.

It wasn't Luca

Elish got out of the car, his revolver snugly in his coat pocket and a knife never far from reach. He had grown even more impatient with Silas's controlling of him in the past year and had decided it would be easier to have a weapon on him, even if he didn't plan on using it unless Silas tried to confine him, or kill him for that matter.

Jack's skyscraper was about ten-storeys, made of dark grey brick with gleaming chrome windows. It was always a blemish on the horizon, a tower of darkness more suited for one of the novels Jack wrote than the cityscape of Skyfall.

Every brother got to choose their own skyscraper and at least this one was far from the eye, almost on the outskirts of Skyland. Which was what Silas had wanted for Jack, since every so often a chimera did die in the greywastes and it was best for the Grim to slip out unnoticed if needed be.

They had dropped Ellis off at the precinct, half a block away from where the bombs had gone off, one on the left wing of the building next door and one across the street; it had been a relief to everyone to hear they hadn't managed to get bombs inside the building. That would mean a dangerous breach in security, or even worse, a traitor amongst the ranks. But from the looks of it they had been planted in an apartment building and a warehouse. There were casualties, and lots of them from the screaming and the blood, but none of them were chimeras or half-chimeras and in the end that was all that mattered.

Elish waited for Quin and Garrett, and when he felt his younger brothers' presence beside him he walked into Jack's skyscraper.

This was different than the welcoming lobby of Garrett's, or the regal feel of Elish's own. Jack's lobby wasn't a lobby at all; most of the area had been walled-off completely and all that was in front of the chimeras was a long mirrored hallway with grey and black marble floors leading to a single elevator. The thien bodyguards, as per Elish's gothic brother's request, were behind those walls behind shrouded two way mirrors, always watching but never seen. To be a bodyguard of Jack Dekker you had to be nothing more than a wraith skulking in the shadows. His brother enjoyed being alone and his only company was his timid sengil he endearingly called Juni and a black cat whose name did vary since he had to replace them every fifteen to twenty years.

The elevator closed behind them and they rose silently to the tenth floor; no one spoke and the ones that wanted to speak knew better.

When the two metal doors opened they were immediately greeted by Juni, a tall black-haired boy with a soft innocent face and a quiet personality. Like Luca and all sengils he was a wallflower, disappearing into the shadows when he wasn't needed, a personality trait that complimented Jack's own; though Elish's brother enjoyed isolation he liked the company of at least one person he could share conversation with. He was one to enjoy not being bothered, not so much being alone.

"Good afternoon, Master Elish, Master Garrett, and Master Joaquin. Jack is in his study right now, can I make you something to drink?" Juni bowed, he was dressed in a butler-type suit, all the way down to a cummerbund and coattails.

"Where is King Silas?" Elish walked past the sengil, ignoring his offer, and started looking around the apartment. It was dark-themed apartment adorned in vintage age furniture and paintings; everything either resembled or was from the Victorian era and had usually been taken straight out of a ransacked museum or the basements of untouched mansions.

"The king? Master Elish, he's in his usual –" Juni was cut off by the carved out wooden door of Jack's study opening; the sengil turned to him and bowed before making himself scarce.

Dressed in a black frock coat that touched his knees and long black netted gloves Jack gave all three of them a pointed-toothed smile. His silver-grey bangs were brushed to the side, framing two black onyx eyes that stole every shred of light in the room. He was a handsome chimera; his face was well-defined and his chin strong, and though most chimeras had inherited thin lips from Silas, his were full and usually painted one dark colour or another. He was one of the most unique-looking chimeras of all of them, like his fellow Chimera D brother Sanguine, a fact that was only accentuated by his odd sense of fashion.

"Now this is unusual, who died now? I didn't get a notification." Jack pulled on the end of his black gloves and nodded towards Juni. "Get them some bloodwine. Elish, would you prefer tea?"

Elish's eyes swept the room; the empty, dark apartment made his senses even more aware. He tuned his hearing to try and pick out the familiar heartbeat of his master but there was only silence.

"Where is King Silas?" Elish said quietly.

Jack raised an eyebrow and looked behind him. "Right where I left him I hope; he's breathing now so I would wager a day or so before he —"

Elish didn't hear the last part. He stalked past Jack into his study, a room full of bookshelves, knickknacks from museums, and a spiral staircase leading to a small library. All of this was brightened by a giant skylight that filled the room with natural light.

On a long daybed lay the king wrapped in silk, and in that bundle a small heartbeat could be heard.

When Elish walked towards the king, a haunting realization came over him.

He was still dead.

Elish outstretched a hand and put it to King Silas's face. His head was mended now, only a faint red road zig-zagging his scalp which was quickly closing. The king's face was still cold, his eyes still closed and his body, wrapped in grey silks, as still as a summer day.

Quin's heart could be heard behind Elish; he watched Elish brush his hand almost caringly over the king's face. "Elish? What's going on?"

Elish retracted his hand, before he brought out his cell phone and checked the call history.

Unknown Number.

"It was not King Silas who called me." Elish's cold and dangerous voice echoed through the walls of the room, making every chimera and sengil around him freeze and listen. "We were tricked."

"But... why?" Garrett whispered.

Elish stared at his phone, the caller ID taunted him, sneered at him, and laughed at him through the screen. He tried to go over the voice on the other end of the phone but his mind was still telling him it had sounded like King Silas, but he had been so distracted by everything and the king had been screaming at him.

Had it been?

Jade had picked up the phone and pressed the button to receive the call; something he had done many times before. *If I had —*

The boy.

"Jade..." Elish whispered, he looked up at the afternoon sky, shining down on them through the dome skylight.

In that moment an odd noise filled the study, a high pitch beeping noise, a long tone without a break. Immediately, Elish brought out Jade's tracker.

Heart: N/A
Blood Pres: N/A
Health: N/A
Rad Lvl: N/A
Overall Hlth: NULL

Elish stared at the tracker, before with a single snarl he crushed the plastic device into his hand and threw it against the wall.

Everything was a blur to Elish as he stalked out of Jack's apartment and out to the awaiting car. Then Jack stopped him and directed him to his own garage. Yes, that was right, Jack had that stupid sports car Silas had given him, the black one; it would be faster.

He had to be fast.

Garrett had hurriedly told Elish with a hand on his shoulder that he wasn't fit to drive; in response Elish almost smashed his face on the concrete of the undercover garage but his mind was going in a thousand different directions, there was no room for primal anger. Jade was at stake here, and he couldn't lower himself to such a display.

He relented and before his car door even closed, Jack was pulling out of the dimly lit garage, tearing up the streets of Skyland. Every car in Skyland knew the small black sports car and they pulled over for him the way they would for an ambulance. Traffic lights didn't matter, pedestrians didn't matter. They had to be quick.

Elish refused himself thought. He capped the frayed wires of his mind one by one and concentrated on getting to Olympus as quickly as possible. Nothing could be decided until he knew the circumstances, so there was no use speculating; men had gone mad speculating about events that might not even come to pass.

And Elish grabbed onto this thought with all his might and branded it into his emotions with a white hot knife. Daring the soft area he reserved only for Jade to force him to feel differently, his mind was a machine, a computer void of emotions he didn't wish to feel, and there would be no outbursts of anger or sadness on its lonely watch.

So why is my heart racing? And my hands clenched and clammy? Elish folded his hands over his lap, hoping that Jack's eyes wouldn't wander from the road.

When Jack stopped in front of Olympus, Elish was already opening the door. There had been no billows of smoke, no secondary explosion; everything seemed quite and in its place.

"Has anyone entered this building?" Elish barked at the two thiens holding their assault rifles, as still as statues with not a rattled look on their faces.

"No, sir."

Then what... how? What was going on? Without another word he pressed for the elevator, and as he waited he was joined by Joaquin and Garrett. Jack would be taking the car back to his tower. He was never supposed to leave King Silas alone while he was regenerating; this was a favour from him Elish would have to one day repay.

A thick and heavy atmosphere descended on them as the elevator took them up to Elish's floor, and with every floor Elish felt a knot inside of his chest. There was no telling what he would find; for all he knew Jem was a plant and he had killed Jade, but there was no way his Shadow would be outmatched by that small weak wraith, nor Luca who knew where the guns were.

Elish's answer was given to him as soon as the elevator doors opened.

"Oh shit," Garrett whispered.

The hallway was covered in blood, leading to the locked flight of stairs that would lead them to the roof. Without a word Elish ran down the hallway and into the open doors of the apartment.

Blood, blood and madness, like a tornado had come through his apartment. Everything had been tipped over, broken and ransacked, but it was also empty.

"Jade? Jade!" Elish called. He took several steps inside the living room, his eyes going to all different directions until they fell to a heap on the floor; a blond-haired young man dressed in a vest and trousers, unmoving and still. Before Elish went to him he scanned the kitchen and the wide open doors of the bedrooms, but there was nothing but the heartbeats of his brothers.

Elish bent over him and grabbed the sengil's chin, he shook it and felt a small distant prick of relief as his hand touched warm skin. "Luca?"

The sengil was still and when Elish moved his head to the side he saw why. The boy's head had been bludgeoned, and his arm broken so badly he could see the bone protruding from the skin. The sengil had fought, and hard.

"Quin, get Lyle, Luca is alive but not for long." Elish rose and tried to survey the area but his mind was jamming, something that had never happened to him since his youth. He prided himself in knowing his own mind inside and out, a trick that had taken decades to perfect, but now his emotions were rising to the surface and what would happen after that he didn't know.

Elish found himself still and he realized with a sickening jolt of emotion that he didn't want to go into their bedroom. He didn't want to find his cicaro's body, he could not see him dead.

"Elish? He's gone, he isn't in any of the bedrooms," Garrett whispered behind him.

His eyes closed, allowing himself a brief moment of relief, but as he opened them another inner well of fear gripped him. "The stairwell, there was blood leading there, they may have chased him to it, perhaps he fell down the stairs? I do not know, either way the boy is dead."

"Elish…"

"The boy is dead!" Elish whirled around and snapped. Garrett visibly cringed but didn't say anything else.

Elish felt the heat rise up his collar; he didn't know what to do, or what he could do. He hadn't been in this situation in years, he hadn't fled from a reality like this since he was forty. Now he stayed away from the bedrooms and the stairwells like they were plague, rather staying in suspended animation with the small prospect…

Then Elish's eyes fell to a pool of blood, cold against the grey and black marble, it had shreds of flesh in it and a piece of black. Without a single breath leaving Elish, he dipped his hand into the pool and rested it on top of the small black square.

It was… Jade's tracking chip, it had been broken in half and smashed;

it had been disabled.

He wasn't dead, they had kidnapped him.

"We need to go to the stairwell; if the guards say no one left they still might be in the building." Garrett was already at the door, Lyle appearing a moment later. Elish followed his brother without a word and left Quin and Lyle to the scene inside the apartment, one which would explain itself.

The brothers rushed up the stairs two by two, the smell of fresh blood and dirt encasing the stairwell like a tomb, doing nothing to quench the festering feeling inside Elish's gut. Too many questions and not enough answers to go around, all he could do was push his feelings down and refuse them entry to his heart.

They should be trapped at the roof... shouldn't they?
Unless...

Elish didn't speak it, because he knew his brother was thinking the same thing. They had similar thoughts those two, always coming to the same conclusion, usually at the same time.

They took Jade alive, if there is any good news to be had over this trickery, it is that they took him alive. He might not be alive for long, but it was a far cry from thinking they had shot Jade in the head where he stood.

Garrett pushed the door open and ran out into the deceptively calm day, with Elish not far behind; it didn't take the two brothers long to realize their rushing had been in vain.

The Falconer was gone.

"Shale," Garrett finally spoke their mutual theory out loud. "Artemis had taught him how to fly. They stole the bloody plane."

Elish walked over to the empty Falconer pad and saw where the blood trail ended. He scanned the blue horizon and the grey mountains in the distance as if hoping to spot the plane but it was nowhere to be seen. The Falconer was fast, it had been refurbished to be fast; they were probably at their destination in the borderlands by now.

"They stole a military plane, we'll have Kessler and the Legion to aid us now," Elish replied in an unemotional tone. He reached down and took some of the blood onto his fingers and raised it to his lips to taste it, only to make sure it was indeed Jade's blood, and it was. "We'll have the

Legion tear apart the borderlands, including Irontowers. If they could cull the abominations inside it would make a suitable base." He turned around and made his way back towards the stairwell.

Then Garrett grabbed his arm. "Brother… are you alright?"

"I am fine." Elish answered calmly, Jade's blood reaching the inner areas of his mind, and making the cold iceberg that was his heart warm at the reminder of his boy's unique taste. "Get Kessler, tell him everything, and double the thiens at the door and at Lyle's hospital doors."

Garrett nodded, before saying in a quiet tone, "I don't want to go back to Skytowers. Put your brother up for the night?"

Garrett would be fine staying alone, but he wanted to be near his brother and in that moment Elish didn't begrudge the company. Elish nodded and they made their way to Lyle's hospital wing.

"You're lucky you came when you did, they bashed him good, Elish," Lyle said with a grim purse of his lips. He was standing beside Luca's bed. The boy's head was wrapped in a clean white bandage that was already leaking through, and his arm was in the process of being casted by Nels. "They wanted to kill him with that blow; they weren't fucking around that was for sure. Garrett, I got some flesh samples from underneath the boy's fingernails, you can test them if you want to know who did this to them. That sengil fought hard to prevent them from taking Jade."

Elish looked down at the boy, remembering all the chimeras, sengils, and cicaros he had seen lying in the same hospital bed. For some odd reason Luca laying there out cold reminded him of Lycos, so many years ago, when Elish had brought him here with the small newborn Reaver.

"How long do you think he will be out for?" Elish asked. He glanced down to watch Garrett take the small vial full of bloody skin fragments. "He's the only one who can give us a report on what happened."

"Depending on the swelling on his brain; it could be a week, Elish. He might be up sooner but he'll be very groggy–"

"Oh fuck!" Quin suddenly exclaimed. Everyone turned to him as Quin held a hand up to his head. His face paled and he looked at Elish with a grim realization. "Elish… Jem, Jem was hiding under the bed. Did they take him? Fucking hell, I didn't even think of him!"

In the flurry of activity and information coming into Elish's mind he had completely forgotten about the young boy hiding under the bed. Had the Crimstones taken him? The boy was a timid, weak thing, it would be a surprise if he had come to Luca and Jade's rescue. No doubt he would cower under the bed like a mouse, useless to everyone.

"Lyle, call me tonight or if Luca's condition changes."

"Of course."

Once again the three brothers swept out the door, but the mood was different now. At every passing moment Elish's drive to find Kerres and Milos grew, from a small guarded flicker of hope to a flame that refused to die. The boy was alive, he was a chimera and he was strong. If there was any time for Elish to have faith in him, now was that time.

Elish threw open the door. Garrett was behind him, on his phone with Kessler.

When Quin rushed ahead of him, Elish grabbed his shoulder and wrenched him back. "No, I'm going in."

"Please, Elish, you'll be harsh with him. If he's in there he's terrified," Quin pleaded quietly.

Elish's first instinct was to forbid his brother, then grab the stupid boy from where he hid and shake him like a ragdoll until he spoke, but as these thoughts speared his usual calm demeanor he remembered that this was what he had wanted for Quin. Elish had wanted him to show small signs of attachment towards the boy. If their auras matched as Jade had said, perhaps Quin should be the one to coax him from his hiding place. Elish was in no mood to deal with whining or weakness, and perhaps he wouldn't handle it well if the boy didn't immediately give him what he wanted.

Quin crept into the room and Elish stayed in the doorway watching his brother, with Garrett behind both of them speaking quickly on the remote phone. Elish had put his phone on silent; it was all he could do to not throw it against the wall.

"Jem?" Quin whispered. His voice was quiet with a caring tone that in any other circumstances would've had Jade giving him a smug 'told you so' look. "It's Quin, are you under there?"

The silence in the room was tense, and growing tenser as the moments passed.

"Yeah," a soft-spoken voice said quietly. "Are they gone?"

Of course they are gone, you snivelling idiot, what happened? Elish clenched his hands, before flicking the light switch on.

"Yes, come out… you must tell us what happened." Quin reached a hand in. "No harm will come to you."

"I… I want to talk to Elish."

Quin turned around and gave his brother a puzzled look. Elish had no expression to give him back but inside he was feeling the same confusion.

Elish walked up to the bed as Jem crawled out. He looked at Elish and immediately cowered down, almost hiding behind Quin who seemed to have made himself a protective barrier, as though he half-expected Elish to throttle Jem.

Jem wouldn't make eye contact. "I know you think I was hiding, and maybe I was, but there were six of them, Mr. Dekker, and I'm not stupid; they would've killed me like they killed Luca."

"Luca is not dead," Elish said coolly.

Jem winced from the tone but nodded, before he continued, "I stayed hidden and watched them, so instead of being a useless hero I could be a useful coward."

Interesting… though Elish had no words for the boy cowering under the bed, there was no mistaking the truth behind his words.

"I want you to know… that Jade went with them to protect Luca and me. They had a machine gun to Luca's head, they had already beat him into submission. I think they broke in while Jade was outside smoking. He's not seriously injured they just gouged out the chip implanted in him. I… their names, besides Kerres and Milos, one was called Shale, another one was Tate, and one Armando. Their base they called the Rock, and they told Jade they were going to correct his altering."

Correct his altering… they're going to brainwash him.

"The Rock? It sounds like Ellis was right in her suspicions, they are in the borderlands." Quin put a hand on Jem's back. "Do you know how they got in?"

The boy shook his head. "The bedroom door was closed; it only opened in the scuffle when Luca was fighting with them. There was a lot of shouting, then everything went quiet. I thought they had killed Luca - he passed out as soon as they injected Jade. They drugged him to keep him quiet."

That was wise... my cicaro would've fought them until there was no breath left in him, once they got him out of the apartment and away from Luca.

He had gone with them to protect Luca, my sengil, and his friend. There was an endearing quality in that that made Elish proud of Jade, though all in all he would have traded the loyal sengil in a second. But in the same breath, there would have been no way he would've let it get to that point anyway, so perhaps that was another useless thing to think.

"Quin... take him home, if he remembers anything more call me," Elish said. He brought out his phone and saw the twenty missed calls. The bombing earlier today was a thousand miles from his mind, and something so unimportant it was like it had happened fifty years ago. "Garrett... what is Kessler doing about this?"

"I'll get him on the phone. Elish, why don't you call Ellis? They're going to need to clear things up to the public before they start talking."

One day later

Elish let Apollo fix his tie, but as soon as Apollo took his hands off him Elish started to walk away from his brother's preening. Elish made his way towards the black curtain where he could hear the news reporters and bulletin writers chatting nervously amongst themselves.

But Apollo could only be shaken off for so long; a moment later he picked something off of Elish's suit and said quietly behind him, "I'm sure as soon as they see that expression on your face they will deliver that boy with a bow on his head."

If only it could be that easy. Elish turned around and nodded towards his brothers: Apollo, Artemis, Teaguae, Kessler, and Garrett of course. They would stand behind him in quiet support as Elish addressed the media, and more importantly, bribed the parasites into snitching on their comrades, coworkers or family members.

Whatever had to be done would be done... and as every second slowly dragged on Elish only became more determined to enlist the help of whoever he could to bring Jade home safely. Too much time had passed already and he hated how helpless he felt. Though it was a king's nature to sit on his throne and order people around, Elish had never been that type when it came to someone close to him. He felt frustrated and useless if he wasn't out there doing things himself.

Setting those emotions aside Elish walked onto the stage, dressed in an onyx black suit and a purple tie.

The small crowd hushed but the fenced off area where the public was looking in erupted in steady buzzing. Thiens kept a close watch on all of them, holding large guns and wearing combat helmets, watched over by Ellis who was standing with her daughter Eve and son Garren. Those three had just finished their own address regarding the bombings and there were a lot of rumours to quell.

Elish stood in front of the pedestal, and as soon as he heard his brothers behind him he squared his shoulders and spoke into the microphone.

"You are all familiar with the terrorist organization called the Crimstones run by Milos Remi, and now also run by a former Morosian named Kerres. His image will appear on screen and his information, which will also be handed out and will be in each day's bulletin until further notice." Elish paused for a second, hearing the faint buzzing around him from dozens of electronic devices, all recording images and sound; it always made the inside of his ears itch. "There have been many rumours spread about what happened yesterday, but the truth is this: My personal cicaro, and a chimera of seventeen years, Jade Shadow Dekker, was kidnapped and my sengil Luca left for dead. Jade was kidnapped by the Crimstones, and during their escape a Falconer jet was stolen.

"As mentioned before, one of the people responsible was a man named Kerres from the Moros District and also a Tate Couli. I am announcing a one hundred thousand dollar reward for Jade Dekker's safe return, and twenty thousand dollars for every proven Crimstone member turned into the precinct. I am also announcing this reward for any Moros resident. Tate, Kerres, and Jade were both long-term residents of Moros, and there is no question that someone in Moros has information that would be useful to the Dekker family. Any resident that helps us with the return of Jade will get an upgrade on status and will become eligible for residence in the Eros district." This was Elish's ace, on top of bribing the cockroaches with money he would offer them something of even greater value: a chance to move up from being a slumrat.

As Elish had predicted the news reporters were abuzz, and the people cordoned off behind the metal fence were talking loudly amongst themselves. This kind of reward had never been offered before, and perhaps never would be again.

"Any questions can be addressed to Commissioner Dekker. Good day."

There, that was over with. Elish held out his hand to Garrett, and he handed him a cigarette and then a lighter. Without another word to his brothers Elish went back to his empty house, Garrett following closely behind.

CHAPTER 37

I TRIED TO RAISE MY HEAD, BUT IT WAS A LEAD WEIGHT, like an anchor was tied to my neck and pulling me down, down through the chair, down below to the brimstones of hell. It was no use, my body was weighed down with the drugs and my mind was nothing but a foggy mess.

I could barely sit up straight, and each day I was brought into this room it became harder and harder to support my own weight. Once again I had grown accustomed to darkness and now the unnatural bluelamp lights stung my eyes.

There were lights on me, and a cold breeze that swept in through cracks in the brick; it complimented the musty damp smell of old buildings, and from that smell, I knew we were in the West End beside what used to be a large park.

The abandoned part of Skyfall west of the stadium, where no one in their right mind would go, where buildings fell and were devoured by scavers and radrats. It would be perfect for this terrorist organization; it was like Moros but worse, there had been no attempt at restoration or preservation of the buildings. No one lived here, no one human anyway.

I saw Milos's ember illuminate the ugly red scar on his neck and parts of his war-ravaged face. The same cigarettes that had burned me multiple times already, in a vain attempt to get me to open my mouth and talk. My body by now was covered in burns, bruises, and lesions, though I felt none of them. I was in chimera mode; I was the Shadow Killer and I would not speak.

And when they realized I wouldn't utter a word, they made me scream instead.

My collarbone was bruised and I suspected it was broken, my wrists were sore and blackened and my legs wobbly from being kicked and stomped on, but not a word left my lips nor would it.

How did I end up here? And how long had I been locked in that dark room? I had been brought out into these four brick walls multiple times to be drilled by Milos, only to be thrown back when the Crimstone leader grew frustrated with me.

I couldn't believe my eyes when I saw Milos in the sliding glass door, and behind him my Kerres and four others beating on Luca. What should've been a breathtaking moment when I saw my boyfriend alive brought nothing but a soured hatred that made me immediately charge at him.

Milos had grabbed me, struck me behind my head and then drew my hands behind my back; it took two of them to pin me down and one machine gun to Luca's head to get me to go with them.

It had happened too quickly; they had wanted to get out of there as quickly as possible before Elish came home. I tried to delay them, but it was no use, they had timed everything and stuck to a schedule based on how long it would take Elish to get to Jack's skyscraper and back.

They worked as a flawless unit, each one waiting for Milos's orders, even Kerres.

Because he wasn't my Kerres anymore.

The surgical scar on the back of his head said more than his cold emotionless eyes ever could. Kerres barely gave me a second glance; the Crimstone soldier didn't act like he knew me or wanted to be near me. Kerres was gone, he had died in that park, what person was in his body now I didn't know.

My heart didn't hurt for him, only for my family back in Skyfall. Elish would know by now and he would be outraged I was sure. Had Luca survived? I saw him breathing hard and leaning against the back of the couch before they drugged me and I passed out cold. Blood was leaking down my shoulders and neck from them gouging out Elish's tracking chip. Jem had stayed hidden like the coward he was; he better have helped Luca after they took me.

Obedient, soft-spoken Luca; he had given me his jacket and hugged me goodbye with a tear trailing down his cheek, before becoming lost in the trickles of dripping blood. That was all I got for not putting up a fang and nail fight against them. I had gotten to say goodbye to the sengil on his request.

Milos looked behind me when the door opened; he nodded to the shadow behind him before taking another inhale of his cigarette.

"The little chimera slut still hasn't said a word." Milos blew the smoke out and onto my face, I kept my eyes focused on the metal rim of a window covered in pressboard. "I'm starting to think his mouth is too tired from sucking Elish's cock."

Yeah, keep talking shit Milos... I didn't waver my gaze, my eyes didn't even squint even though the cigarette smoke was burning them.

"It doesn't matter, Richard is ready for him and Vecht says the cameras are charged. Do you want to do this now or rough him up a bit more?" Kerres said behind me, in a voice that still burned the edges of my heart. I had never thought I would hear his voice anymore, but in a way, I still hadn't. His voice had never had the tones it had now.

Milos nodded and rose, becoming a towering figure clad in camo and shrouded in the thick cigarette smoke that filled the room. He walked past me and I steeled my body as he extinguished the cigarette on my hand. "No, I want some scream to him." Milos grabbed my collar and yanked me to my feet before he walked me out into the dirty brick hallway. It stretched out until it branched off into two different hallways, the walls nothing but ribbons of peeled paint, revealing stained drywall underneath and the ceiling nothing but a mess of wires and plastic fasteners.

I tried to breathe but it was laboured, they had wrapped a tight muzzle around me, making me look more like Hannibal Lecter than a chimera. It was made of black plastic that sweated from the breath of my nose, and it was there to keep me from biting. They knew my strengths, anyone who watched the Shadow Killer on the Sky News Network did.

On top of having a muzzle, my hands were also bound with handcuffs made out of dog prong collars. They dug into the nerves of my wrists every time I moved them, the same went for my stomach and my legs. Essentially every movement I made was painful, but I didn't let it show on my face. I wasn't weak, and I would not let these people believe for one second there was a chink in my armour.

The tense atmosphere devoured me alive, but I refused to wonder just where they were taking me. Either I was going to get my head cut open or I was going to be paraded in front of a camera that would go straight to Ellis and the thiens and eventually Elish.

If I got brainwashed… I would be okay, right? Because Elish could come and find me, do the immortal trick thing and my brain would go back to normal, back to its default.

That was a pathetically small silver lining on this situation. Elish would have me as a brainless monster for two years until I could have the operation. He would've probably moved on by then, gotten himself a new pet to entertain him.

My eyes squinted as Kerres shoved a door open, and I saw I was in an open room, covered with sheets and flags, well-lit and obviously where my video was going to be filmed.

My ex-boyfriend grabbed my collar and threw me down onto the ground. I heard a group of people laugh around him.

"Look at him, fucking hell Milos your lobotomy surgery never ceases to amaze me," a deep voice sneered. "I was impressed when you managed to teach Shale to mimic Silas's voice and now this? Brilliant." I glanced up in time to see a middle-aged man with a shaved head and a pissed look pick me up, only to deliver a hard blow right to my face.

I felt my teeth crack as my body hit the sheet-covered floor. I groaned and rolled to my side, spitting up shards of tooth along with the blood that was gushing into my mouth.

Like the descending of the autumn fogs a haze slowly crept to my mind, and the room became a contorted rotation of colours, spinning back and forth, hammering senses into me I could no longer comprehend.

Then I heard Milos beside me and the sound of something scraping against brick.

"I've never done it on a chimera before. He's going to make a great solider, one of many, this I know."

Fuck all of you… I opened and closed my eyes hard to try and get my bearings, but a moment later there was another punch to my jaw, throwing out any sense I had managed to gather back into me. I groaned again and tried to get up, only to fall down to the cold floor, feeling more shards of my teeth start to prick me as they swam around in the lake of blood in my mouth.

"Kerres, you asshole…" I groaned and spat the blood.

They laughed, but I didn't hear Kerres laugh. I drew up my aura abilities to see which one he was, and saw the muddled seafoam green right beside me; it seemed dark and stagnant now, but I could still see the old Kerres in it.

Then I saw his knees bend, and a hand rest lightly on my forehead. For a moment my heart jolted at the familiar touch, before recoiling back inside in an act I could only describe as self-preservation.

"Don't worry," Kerres said in a thin whisper. I was shocked to hear a flicker of warmth to it. "We'll fix you soon, J. Then you'll be mine again, just mine."

"Ker… you have to let me go, I don't belong here." I looked at his face, scanning it for any sense that he was still Kerres. "I know you're in there somewhere."

He was… he had to be, it might be over between the two of us… but I knew, brainwashed or not, he was in there – I saw it in his aura, I saw it in him.

But he only shook his head. "You belong with me, and only me." Kerres petted my head, before he glanced up and nodded. "He's ready, let's show Elish and the chimeras just what we can do."

Skyfall

You should've never been far from me.

Now for all I know your flickering spirit could be out of my reach, in a place where no demanding, yelling or chimera science can bring you back.

I am a man who has grown used to having my commands obeyed with a wave of my hand and here I stand with the prospect that you could be beyond even my abilities.

I can see now, with new eyes, what King Silas went through when he lost Sky. I have never felt this nervousness in my gut and I still struggle to accept it.

Oh, how far has this immortal being fallen from grace.

Or perhaps I just carried you into the sky, only to drop you down to the greys of the world.

"We have the Legion looking under every rock and inside every building, Uncle Elish," Caligula said, pointing out a group of trucks stationed on the outskirts of Irontowers, blue and black specks noticeable on the roads below the skyscrapers of the abandoned cities. They were legionary in uniform, combing the area. "Dad says they'll be done looking by tomorrow, and after that we'll move on to some smaller villages in the borderlands. Anywhere that sounds like it could be called the Rock we're looking."

Kessler's teenage son, a chimera he had been given to raise with his husband, was flying a second Falconer, so Elish could see with his own eyes just what was being done to find Jade and the Crimstones' base.

It had been three days now since Jade had been kidnapped and to Elish's anger not a word had been heard from the terrorists. That wasn't like the Crimstones who revelled in releasing bloody videos of interrogations, threats, and sometimes even executions. Elish had expected at the very least a ransom, but it had been quiet.

Kessler had been willing to give him legionaries to take apart the borderlands, and Ellis had given him thiens to check Skyfall, but still nothing of the Crimstones or Jade had shown up. It was as if the boy and Elish's Falconer had disappeared into thin air.

"Good, take the plane over to the West End, the thiens are too stingy with that area for my comfort, I'd rather an aerial view," Elish said quietly, looking down at the cityscape below him. Underneath his feet were skyscrapers, some with sides completely missing and others nothing but a mountain of gravel and steel on the ground. A city of nothing but decay and desolation, there would've been no way the Crimstones could've gotten electricity or running water here. No Ieon charger would be able to hold the power of their cameras, lights and equipment, but still that forced the question of where then? Where would they be?

Jade... Jade... where are you? Why did you have to be a hero?

The answer to that was simple, Jade was a chimera and Luca was a sengil, he would've never forgiven himself for sacrificing Luca for his own safety. That was not how a chimera worked or a Morosian. Elish knew this, but still he wished things had turned out differently.

The emptiness that Elish felt without Jade couldn't be ignored, though he had tried to force his brain to believe otherwise. No matter how much he tried to control every emotion that came forth from him, he had failed again and again over the last three days. There was no denying the guttural wrench in his heart knowing that Jade wasn't with him and was in danger. It made Elish unable to sleep without an aid, or eat properly. It was even affecting his decision making to the point where he didn't know if half the things he was demanding were right.

He felt powerless, and if there was one thing Elish Dekker couldn't stand to feel it was powerless.

Elish had to have control over everything, whether it be Jade or all of Skyfall; the only decisions he had ever trusted were his own, and now he wasn't even sure if they were right. His only thoughts were to get Jade back to the safety of his arms, to lay him on his lap and stroke back the boy's long bangs. Nothing else mattered; Elish would kill a thousand innocent people and raze all of Skyfall if it meant that Jade was safe.

Two years ago Elish would've looked down his nose at any brother who coveted a pet in this way, and now look at him. If he didn't have a million things on his mind it would've made him sick, but he had no time for self-loathing. Once Jade was returned he could despise the weak state he had found himself in, but until then there was only one thing that mattered.

The boy.

Skyfall's horizon came into view, tall buildings touching the setting sky; it looked beautiful but as the Falconer flew over the miles and miles of skyscrapers, empty stretches of districts unnamed and long since abandoned, the city seemed a vast threat, where tens of thousands of people could hide and not be seen.

Jade was a small needle in a large haystack and all Elish could do was wait. He was a man of endless patience, who could bide his time for decades waiting for a seed to grow, but now every hour seemed to take a day to pass. He had to have the boy back and punish the people who took him. It wasn't just about getting Jade back, it was about showing the world that no one stole from Elish Dekker, or the Dekker family for that matter.

Elish had that on his side, and for that he was thankful. Some of the chimeras might not like Jade and they might have hated the way Elish treated him, but when it boiled down to it, a group of terrorists had stolen a chimera, and when someone wronged a member of the family it affected everyone. During these times the Dekker family banded together, pushed old rivalries and feelings aside and became one unstoppable, deadly unit.

Stadium appeared below them, with grey roads leading to it like tentacles attached to a monster, now glowing as the sun set and the streets became dark. His night vision wouldn't permeate this darkness, but at least the green-hued night vision and heat censor of the Falconer could do more than their chimera eyesight ever could.

Then Elish's phone rang, as it had done dozens and dozens of times since Jade's kidnapping and the precinct bombing. It was Garrett though; Elish pressed the green button and put the phone to his ear.

"Elish, get Clig to drop you off… we just got the blue screen."

Caligula gave him a glance. His hearing was matched by none other beside his brother Reaver; he had heard Garrett.

"Alright." Elish hung up the phone and said nothing else.

The blue screen… which meant that they had thirty minutes to shut down the television signal in every single persons home in Skyfall and the factory towns. The Crimstones had done this before, when they wanted to show the Dekker family what they were doing live. They hacked into the TV signals from their base and ran their feed live, though there was no hacking this time. Elish had told Teaguae to take down the firewall which had prevented them from breaking into the system, in hopes that one of his computer literate brothers or their workers would be able to trace the signal.

Though Elish knew Garrett would already be on it, he called Teag and then called his tech loving sengil Kori to make sure that everything that could be done to track them was being done. The family had been waiting for this moment, and though Elish was dreading what he was going to see on this screen, it was a lot better than waiting.

Caligula dropped Elish off, before taking the plane back to his father.

As the first raindrops hit the black tar roof of the skyscraper he nodded to the thien now keeping permanent watch of the door leading inside the skyscraper and went down to his apartment.

Garrett was sitting on the couch with the television on to the news; he looked pale and distraught. Elish's good-natured brother had more emotion to him than most of the other chimeras combined.

Garrett had been trying to take care of his oldest brother as well as Elish would allow him too, even if it was only coaxing him with Valium to sleep and urging him to eat, two things Elish had not been in the mood to do.

When Garrett saw him, his face crumpled, he put his hands over the top of his head. "I'm going to be sick, I can't stand this, Elish."

He isn't even his cicaro and he's acting more distraught on the outside than I am, though his emotions didn't die like mine. Perhaps die isn't the right word, I think they're locked in a steel cage deep inside of me, where I refuse to let them out.

Elish got himself some tea from the pot Garrett had waiting for him.

"A resolution is better than waiting, brother," Elish responded in his usual calm and cold manner. He sat down with his tea and stared at the news station, flashing Jade's picture on the screen with a reward of one hundred thousand dollars for his safe return, a reward no one had ever seen before.

The boy's image made Elish's chest stir, it was a photo taken only a week ago, when he had remembered that the photo Elish had had on his file was when he was only thirteen. He had a half-smile on his face, and the same lively glint in his golden eyes. His black hair was freshly trimmed and his bangs broke up the perfection of his thin pale face. The boy was beautiful, in every way that could be imagined.

Garrett looked up at Elish, his face green and his eyes heavy. "I know you don't want it, but I just want Silas to wake up so he can help us. He'll put aside his dislike for you and Jade's relationship to get him back. Silas always has shit figured out, a lot more than I ever did." The president of Skytech wiped his face with his hands; he was visibly sweating.

Elish didn't respond, he had nothing to say to that. It was like trading one evil for another, though only one was the more immediate threat. He could handle Silas, because Silas wouldn't hide his advances like the

Crimstones. Perhaps it would be better if Silas woke; Jack had said it would be any day now. Sometimes Silas's slower regeneration was a gift, other times a curse.

Garrett let out a groan, Elish looked over and saw the blue screen on the television appear again. He walked over to the television set, setting his tea mug on a side table and crossing his arms around his chest.

Elish's hands clenched together when the image flickered, before focusing on an unmoving Jade on the ground, a heap of black and blue, chained and bound like an animal, with a muzzle over his mouth to dehumanize him even more. For a moment Elish thought he was dead, before none other than Kerres leaned over and dealt him a hard smack to the face.

Jade had blood all over his face, pooling underneath his head and staining the sheet he was laying on.

Elish felt a small flicker of relief as the boy's yellow eyes opened and looked around dazed.

What about his head? Show me his fucking head... Elish's jaw tightened, he had to see if they had cut Jade's head open yet.

"Put him on the chair, get him to his feet." Milos's voice could be heard in the background. A moment later Kerres, covered from head to toe in old camo, grabbed Jade by the collar he was still wearing and viciously yanked him to his feet. He then slammed him down onto a metal chair and grabbed Jade's chin to make him look at the camera. Milos said a few more meaningless words, half-drowned out by the buzzing and laughing of the people around them. The room seemed to be full of people, though like cowards most were out of sight.

"Recognize him, scumbag? I got *my* boyfriend back, *my* property," Kerres sneered. "I'll let you take a good look at him, drink him in, fuck him with your mind one last time. He's mine now. I won, understand that, chimera? You took my boyfriend from me, I took him back; he's where he belongs and no longer under your control." Kerres patted the side of Jade's face, before he ripped off the muzzle and shook Jade's chin, making his head rattle and his eyes open wider.

Jade's eyes found the camera; he stared at Elish like he knew he was looking at him. There was not a single bit of submission or fear on his face, just unemotional stoicism.

Elish had never been more proud of him.

"This is where we tell you what we want, right? Ransom money, a prisoner, you know the drill. Well, guess what, Elish? I don't want shit from you, because I already got it. I got Jade back and no amount of money is going to make me give him up. So fuck you, fuck you, Elish, fuck you, Silas, and fuck every chimera in existence. The Crimstones will take Skyfall and will take the world –"

Suddenly, with a flash of teeth, Jade, only a moment ago seeming like he was half-conscious and in a daze, whipped his head to the side and sank his teeth into the side of Kerres's face. Garrett gasped as a spurt of blood erupted from the side of Kerres's head as Jade ripped his ear off, before jumping on top of him, and tumbling out of the shot of the camera.

There was an outbreak of panicked yelling and barked orders, then the camera was toppled over, falling to the ground with a thunk, but it continued to run. Elish saw Milos grab Jade and slam him down onto the ground. The boy's snarls and growls could be heard as he clutched in his jaws a large chunk of flesh, before a punch to the side of the head made him drop it.

Ignoring Garrett's panicked swearing, Elish watched as Milos pinned Jade down, before yelling something at a person nearby, a moment later he was handed something.

Pliers.

Elish's hands tensed and he felt his chest grow cold, but still he didn't move. He watched as someone pushed the handle of a whip into Jade's mouth before Milos reached in and pulled out Jade's left canine, but not just the implant; the entire blood-streaked root and tooth was pinched between the metal pliers.

Garrett cried out, muffled by his hand over his mouth. Elish's gaze still did not waver; not even when Milos pulled out the second canine, then the two at the bottom, Jade's screams echoing off of the walls and blending with the excited noises of the room they were in.

When he got off Jade, the boy choked on his own blood and spat it, speckles of it getting on the camera lens. He opened his mouth to breath, revealing the four large gaps now in his mouth.

"I defanged your pet, Elish, does that make you mad?" Milos's voice could be heard, then a swirl of movement as he picked up the camera. It focused on Jade, whose chest was rising and falling rapidly, the pool of blood around him growing larger and larger.

Elish didn't move. Garrett was sniffing now, swearing under his breath. Still though Elish's purple eyes never left the television, nor did they even blink. He was as still as a statue, an unmoving sculpture on a pedestal, watching helplessly at the scene unfolding before him. There was nothing he could do; the prince of Skyfall, an immortal bred to be intelligent, bred to be perfection, had been reduced to this.

"I'm not done yet, you realize that right?" The camera panned again as it switched owners, and when it focused on the scarred face of Milos, Elish realized he was holding an old drill in his hand.

The Crimstone leader smiled at the camera, before pressing down on the trigger to make the drill spin, he did this several times before he kicked Jade onto his stomach.

With one hand on the boy's head, he turned on the drill.

And with a shrill ear-piercing scream from Jade, Milos started to drill into his skull.

Whether the camera feed got cut first, or it was the TV being smashed by the side table he had just set his teacup on, Elish didn't know. The only thing he did know was, moments later, as sparks flew around him and he raised the table to deliver the television another blow, Garrett grabbed him and held him back.

"Let me go!" Elish snarled. He whirled around and took a swing at Garrett but his quick brother ducked and put his hands up, his eyes red and his face pale and twisted in agony. He looked pleadingly at his brother, an anguished expression on Elish's face that Garrett hadn't seen in years.

"Please, Elish, calm down. You can't lose it, not now! We need you, Jade needs you!" Garrett pleaded, as two tears ran down his face. "Teag, Teag will call soon, he'll have a location, right? Please, Elish, remember yourself. I know it's hard to see him hurt but you're no use to him like this."

Remember myself? The person he was referring to was who I was before Jade, before that stupid boy burrowed into my insides like a parasite. Before he injected me with these emotions I have never felt before. Thrown me off my feet and made me realize I don't know myself as much as I thought.

The same boy who is getting his head drilled open as we speak.

Elish's eyes were fixed on nothing, smoke filling the apartment from the now unplugged television, with the screen smashed in and wire components smoking inside.

The smoke brought Elish back to the reality around him. He scanned the apartment before opening the sliding glass door to let the smoke out. Garrett followed him, and rested a hand on Elish's shoulder. It was a small comfort, a meaningless gesture, but for Garrett to do that to the brother he knew as the most unemotional one of them all, it meant something.

Elish looked at the dark sky, and the rain falling around them, hitting the railing of the patio to make their own soft songs. He wondered if he listened hard enough, if he could hear Jade's screaming. Screaming as they drilled into his brain, peeling back the scalp to alter his own personality and thoughts.

He was mine to protect.

"I am helpless," Elish said quietly, and though Garrett was the only person he could ever show this side of him to, it still made him feel uneasy and vulnerable, yet another emotion he had dismissed years ago. "I have a thousand trained soldiers at my fingertips, army generals, thien chiefs. I have twenty chimeras searching for him… and here I am, without a thing to do but watch them openly taunt me, and torture him in front of my eyes."

Garrett squeezed his shoulder. "You're the thinker, not a soldier, Elish. You're more useful keeping track of these people and planning ahead, not tearing up buildings. Think of it this way, if you were down there or in the borderlands that's all the good you would be. Here you can think. That's what our master made you for, to think like he does and you know you both are bloody brilliant."

Elish heard Garrett's words, but what good they did was lost in the overwhelming feeling of hatred and helplessness that had claimed and overthrown his steeled emotions, drawing up each one with a steel hook before cutting them down. Though his brother was trying to help, there was nothing he could do. Jade was being altered at this minute and no amount of consoling would prevent that from being Elish's reality.

At this very moment, right now, they are brainwashing him. How can I just be standing here? My frustrations are overwhelming, I feel like I am about to explode into myself. How can I stand in this apartment, knowing what is happening to him?

I am his master, his protector... I was supposed to take care of him and keep him safe from harm, whether it was from the Crimstones or King Silas. I have done a lot to keep that boy as my cicaro and look where it has brought both of us. How did I let this happen?

I am better than this.

Elish turned from the sliding glass door. He opened his mouth to tell Luca to clean up the mess and grab another sengil to help dispose of the television but he stopped himself. Luca was still unable to talk, only waking up for brief moments to mumble incoherently.

Then his phone rang and before it could even get a second ring in, Elish held it up to his ear.

"Teaguae, anything?" Elish didn't mince words.

"Elish we have something, the signal got relayed off a station west near Cypress, it's a bounce but it's the best we could've hoped for. I already have Caligula and Tiberius notified, they're flooding the area as we speak," Teaguae said hurriedly, it sounded like he was running. "Sage and Kori are going over every bit of video to see if they can recognize anything. When the video was playing Kessler dropped a couple shells on Irontowers just to see if we could hear them but there was nothing. We know for sure they're not in that city but Cypress... they just might be there, Elish."

Elish allowed himself a brief moment to close his eyes with relief, before with a deep breath he felt his chimera self come back. The brief moments of emotion was gone with the small flames of hope that they were on the right path.

"Good, get Ellis to send some thiens over as well. I want the entire place picked apart, make sure you use the heat readers as well... if they have power they have to be drawing the power from somewhere." Elish glanced at Garrett who was now on his phone as well. "Their generators should be giving them away... there is no way they can survive in the borderlands for that long without something stronger than an Ieon."

"I agree with you, we'll keep in touch, either myself or Sage. Just stay where you are so we can pick you up or drop him off when we find him." Elish heard a plane in the background; he quickly said goodbye to

Teaguae and hung up the phone.

He paced around, before the idle thoughts started to drive him mad. To distract himself he called downstairs to his maintenance man and ordered another television. A bigger one, with new game systems. Jade had been whining for a Nintendo GameCube, so he ordered one of those as well.

"Actually, just find me any electronic video games, find the Pokémon ones, and the newest Game Boy they made. I want all of those things in my apartment before the week's out, am I understood?" Elish didn't even know why he was doing this now, but he felt like if he planned for Jade to be back by then, perhaps it meant he would be home.

"I'll get into contact with some people, Master Elish. It will be costly but we can get through that list."

Good... the boy will have to return now. He has all these time-sucking video games, there is no way he couldn't. He wouldn't defy me by not returning to accept his gifts, that stupid Morosian slumrat would not dare.

...

I really do despise these emotions at times. Elish put the phone back in his pocket. When he turned around his brow furrowed as he saw Garrett giving him a sad smile.

"Stop looking at me like that," Elish hissed. He walked towards the skyscraper window and looked out onto the now dark horizon, only the twinkling little candles of the Skyland lights could be seen.

"If you're ever needlessly cruel to him after this, I will skin you alive, you realize this, don't you?" Garrett rattled around in the kitchen before bringing Elish a glass of wine, and holding one for himself.

"I will not have a reason to be, over the last several months he was the perfect pet," Elish responded quietly. He swirled the bloodwine around in the glass before he took a long drink. "He was still a little shit, still a sarcastic idiot... but... he seemed content. I never thought he would actually enjoy being my cicaro."

"Or that you would enjoy having someone who just didn't stand there and obey orders?"

"Yes, it is a rarity we get people like that. Who knew it would be something we both desired."

"I guess a chimera is good for that; they have that thirst for equality amongst the ranks."

Elish looked down at his wine glass and shook his head. "No, it had nothing to do with him being a chimera. It was being a Morosian, someone separate from Skyland who didn't even know they were supposed to obey chimeras, or care for that matter." He paused, and almost stopped himself from saying what was on his tongue next but in that moment he decided to take the risk of being scorned.

"His personality and the way he spoke to me and acted towards me fascinated me no end. And not just disobedience… it was everything. I had never met someone before who made me want to laugh; sometimes I had to bite my tongue to keep myself from chuckling at the moronic things that would come out of his mouth."

Elish looked out the window, though once he saw his own expression and the emotion that was apparent in his eyes he turned away with mild disgust. He wondered how he could despise what that boy had done to him, yet hunger for more. Jade was like a drug in that way, Elish had tasted him, mind, body, and soul, and now the thought of never tasting him again drove him to the fringes of madness.

Garrett handed him a cigarette and lit one himself, Elish blew the smoke out of his mouth and saw it was silver. He hadn't had one of these since he had dropped Jade off in Moros, and during that time he had chain-smoked them to the point where even Luca was giving him concerned looks.

At least when he had done that he knew where the boy was. He had checked the tracker so often he just kept it in his hand when he was in his apartment, constantly watching what Jade was doing, and what his body was doing. It had almost become an obsession for Elish until he had finally become fed up with himself and banned even the mention of the boy's name.

Now Elish had nothing, no information, only the knowledge that the boy was being hurt and a faint hope that the Legion would find the Crimstones' hiding place.

"I never thought it would be them we would be protecting Jade from, but if the boy managed to win over our cold chimera of a brother, I can see how it would be hard for that little red-haired chap to let go," Garrett said. "It is that chimera attraction, for some reason we're engineered to be drawn to one another, sometimes as family, sometimes as pets, sometimes as more."

"We're supposed to be together, whether we like it or not," Elish responded. He inhaled from the opiate cigarette and blew the smoke onto the window, creating a faint mist. "Even the ones born to the districts, the borderlands or wherever else... they'll always find their way to their family."

"And Jade will come home." He could see the small smile on Garrett's face in the reflection of the window. "He's strong, did you see him rip the ear off of that boy? It was incredible."

"I saw it." Right before they pulled his teeth out with pliers; Elish wished the boy would've just behaved, but that would not be in his nature. If the Shadow behaved, he wouldn't have come as far as he did.

That night Elish barely slept. Every time he nodded off he woke up with a start, half-expecting to feel the boy curled up beside him. When he found Jade's side of the bed cold, Elish got up and paced around the living room, until he grew angry at himself and force himself back to sleep. Elish had never needed that much sleep, but the accumulating nights of insomnia were starting to wear on him, and he knew he needed all of his wits about him for when they did find the boy

By morning there was still no word.

"We have everyone looking, Elish," Kessler said. Elish could hear engines and higher-ups barking orders as the Legion leader talked into the phone. "The sewers down here are intact. We have men and deacdogs checking everything out but our heat readers aren't showing anything bigger than a scorprion. Ellis's thiens arrived a few hours ago though so we're going to expand to Suicide Bay."

"Send all the forces, even if it brings up nothing I want to check it off the list," Elish said, feeling his hopes start to wane. It had been almost twelve hours since the video feed was cut off and he had gotten the call from Teaguae. Perhaps the bounced signal was nothing, maybe this had all been a wild goose chase.

Giving me hope where there was none to be found, would fate mock me so? Of course it would.

"They have everyone there right now, the place sounds like a hive," Elish said to Garrett who was sitting at the dining room table eating a breakfast sandwich. Elish's sat cold and untouched.

"Good, they'll find those fuckers." Garrett dabbed the corner of his mouth with a towel and pushed Elish's plate towards him. "Now eat. My god, I've had to become your nanny."

Only Elish's favourite brother could get away with talking to him in that way.

There was a knock on the door, but before Elish could open it Lyle let himself in; he had a strained expression on his face.

"Luca's awake, come now, he's flipping out and he says he has to talk to you." Before Lyle could even see Elish's response he had disappeared into the hallway.

Elish and Garrett exchanged glances before the both of them started after Lyle, barely catching the elevator as the doctor rapidly pressed the button for his floor.

"Is he stable?" Elish demanded, the last time he had seen Luca he was mumbling and talking nonsense, his injury worse than Lyle had previously thought.

"Emotionally stable? No, he's a damn wreck, but mentally he's all there. I think, ah, I don't know, Elish, but he demanded to speak with you now, and the boy has never demanded a thing in his life." Lyle shook his head, the former sengil still dressed in a lab coat with a stethoscope slung over his neck.

As soon as the door opened Luca could be heard, he was talking rapidly to Nels, in a tone Elish had never heard from him before, making him step up his pace ahead of the other two. He looked around and spotted Luca in the far corner of the room, his face flushed and upset and his large green eyes lit up and glassy.

"Master!" When Luca spotted him his pupils got large, his head still wrapped and his arm secured in a white cast. As he shut his eyes tight and opened them, as if to make sure Elish was indeed there, his eyes started to well. "Please, tell me you looked, please, tell me Jade's back, you found him didn't you? Please, Master! Tell me they're lying!" Luca's voice was desperate. As soon as Elish was in grabbing distance he sat up in the hospital bed and grabbed the cloth of Elish's sleeve, he jerked it towards him desperately. "Tell me! Tell me they don't still have him?"

Elish put his hand on Luca's and shook his head, he answered back in a calm tone. "No, we haven't found him; we don't know where they took him."

The blond sengil looked at him in horror. "You didn't... Master, you didn't check... I, fuck, why didn't you force me to wake up! Master, I put my jacket over Jade after they ripped out his chip. I had the Mp3 player in it, the one with the tracker. Where is that receiver remote? It's on Jade, you can find him!"

Garrett swore, and so did Lyle, but Elish could only stare, a cold adrenaline rushing through his veins and freezing the blood to ice. For a moment he couldn't move, it was as if the boy's words had turned his body to stone.

"Garrett... let's go."

Elish quickly walked out of the room, Garrett close behind, his mind giving him a thousand reasons not to hold out hope, and a thousand more that told him this was what he had been waiting for. They duelled for rights to his mind with sharp swords, but both were evenly matched. All Elish knew for sure right now was that he had to find that device, and until then even his mind was holding its breath.

So with tunnel vision, and his mind flashed frozen, not allowing another thought to enter his head, Elish exited the elevator, ignoring what Garrett was mumbling behind him, and pushing out every last useless emotion in his head.

He had to find that device, he had to know.

Had it really come down to that foolish electronic? The first way he had started to track Jade, by a single Mp3 player that he had taken from the bag of loot Jade had stolen. A small whim that pleased him when he had first decided to do it, to track the Morosian boy just out of curiosity and a need to make his presence known to him; if only to drink up the shocked expression on the boy's face. It had been a pure delight to knock Jade off his feet in such a way and back then Elish had enjoyed it immensely.

It was something to do out of pure amusement but now... now it could hold the key to finding his cicaro.

Luca... I will get you that damn kitten if your sleight of hand is the reason we get Jade back. To hells, I will buy you five.

The hallways passed quickly, Elish felt like he was floating on nothing as he entered his apartment and made a beeline for the credenza he had kept the tracker in. Then, with Garrett watching him intently, though smart enough to not say a word, Elish took out the remote with the small LCD map screen and turned it on.

He looked at it, and when he saw where the position was he felt dizzy. The next thing he knew he was leaning against the wall, his eyes fixed on the small red dot flashing on the screen.

Not in the borderlands, not in Cypress.

In the West End of Skyfall.

Less than an hour's drive.

CHAPTER 38

THE STRING OF DROOL DRIPPING FROM MY CHIN OOZED off me, before retracting sharply as a drop fell down onto the cracked concrete of the basement floor. Another one followed, this one with rosy highlights of the blood mixing in, each one was different, as it ran down different lesions and bruises on my face.

I blinked, but my eyes were raw, swollen and red. It was hard to do anything but stare down at the concrete. I couldn't even hold up my head anymore.

Where was I?

The dried blood behind my head pulled on the fine hairs of my neck as I tried to move, but it was nothing compared to the pain in my hands. I remembered how I had bit my lip clean through when they had nailed me to the crosshatched pieces of wood. Two large nails in my hands, and the pronged handcuffs now binding me to the wood. Naked but for my boxer pants and shivering cold, I stayed here in the dim lighting, my friends nothing but radrats, croaches, and the hanging shadows.

Sometimes I would moan and make noise, to hear my weak voice echoing off of the walls, but mostly I was quiet so as to not wake the dead.

My mind had surrounded me with corpses.

They hung from rafters, with grey frayed ropes tied tightly around their necks, making their rotting faces split from the pooled blood, to leak rancid rotting fluid from the concaves of their faces.

Sometimes they opened their eyes, but they never had good things to say.

Grabbing onto a small trickle of strength, I raised my head to the cracked door frame that held a metal door painted blue, beside it was a viewing window, and behind me a large blast hole in the wall. I did not know what was behind that blast but it brought a cold wind that stung my exposed back.

Who was I?

I had to have done something terrible.

My head dropped, but as soon as it did I cried out as the prongs dug into my neck. I hissed through my broken teeth and raised my head, in time to see a croach, the size of a beer can, crawling up the glass window beside the door, ticking around on a dozen legs as it looked around for food.

The blond-haired one appeared in the window and looked in. I stared back wondering if I could have some water to wash down the taste of blood in my mouth. My mouth was as rough and dry as the paper wings of the croach, and each slide against the insides of my cheeks were so coarse my tongue had started to peel.

The man walked in with a blank look on his face; he patted the side of my cheek and I looked up at him.

"What's your name, scum?" the man growled. He had a scar down his face, it was bleeding and the bandage had half come off.

"I don't know," my hoarse voice croaked back. "Water?"

A brush of his hand went up my face, and trailed down to my neck. A moment later I screamed as he pushed the prongs of the collar into my neck, before it cut off the breath in my throat reducing me to desperate coughs.

The man stared back at me, his brown eyes aflame, pieces of coal in snow, drowned out by a hatred I didn't understand. He stood back and behind him the hanging corpses rallied, their purple black faces, swollen and leaking, glaring at me through shining black eyes.

Shadow Killer.

Murderer.

Impure.

Whore.

In every direction these words assaulted me physically, making me slump lower and lower in my crucifixion. What had I done to deserve this? I must've been a bad person; I must deserve this treatment.

"I'm sorry," I whispered to them, though the decayed corpses held no forgiveness in their eyes. They only swayed in their places, back and forth on the rafters in their own dance with death, black spots falling off of them like rain, chunks of putrid flesh breaking down with every movement until they became nothing but stained skeletons.

The blond-haired one made me drink, an amber solution that stung my lips, but it was liquid and it was a relief against my dry mouth, so I drank.

"You are a Crimstone, you are a soldier, you are the chimera assassin," the man whispered, he tipped the glass back and made me drink all of it. "You were only born to obey the Crimstones and carry out their orders, is that right?"

I gasped and took in a shaky breath, unable to breathe through my blood-filled nose as my mouth drank down the liquid.

The man nodded his approval.

"You only obey us, you were created to obey us, you have no name, no history, no family, you are a tool, our weapon." The man took the Styrofoam cup and, without another word, he walked past the corpses and through the blue door.

When the man left, the corpse started to laugh to themselves, speaking to each other in low and taunting voices as they stole glances at me. I couldn't hear what they were saying, their words were only a low disruptive buzzing in my ears, but with the ways their swollen eyes stared at me I knew it wasn't good.

Everyone spoke, there was always that humming, that itched the inside my ears, followed by a burning heat.

Burning heat... every time he gave me that amber liquid my head burned for hours afterwards, and the pain inside my mouth, inside my broken and missing teeth, only got worse.

"It's scary in the dark, people can do whatever they want to do to you, and there is nothing you can do about it," one of the bodies whispered to me. I recognized his grey splotchy face; he had been the boyfriend of one of my former friends, in a life that I had lived millenniums ago. What had his name been? Like a sea of faces that slipped through my memories like water through my hands, it was all lost to me, every single one of them.

"I had never been afraid of the dark," I rasped, giving his face a longer look than before. He seemed solid, but in the same sense, I think I knew he wasn't there. "The darkness and the shadows have always been old friends of mine."

"And where are your friends now, shapeshifter?" an old woman croaked, with messy grey hair and wild eyes, she was hung up by her neck like the others, but her head had been caved in. "Demon-eyed jinn."

When my eyes strained to look at her, I saw the nail sticking out of my hand, flickering blue in my night vision, surrounded by glistening purple. "I have no friends."

"You're right… you don't." The woman grinned at me, and as yellowed teeth were exposed, more black drops fell soundlessly to the concrete floor. Her wild eyes rolled around in her head, before she started to shake it back and forth, raining bugs, blood, and bits of flesh onto the windowed room. They showered down on me like putrid raindrops.

I closed my eyes to the murmuring voices, my entire body fatigued to the point where only the prongs of the handcuffs and the nails in my wrists held me up. I had no strength. I let my body slump and fall into the darkness, into the dark void behind me that brought in the bodies and the insects.

As time was lost in the darkness, I stayed within my own memories and thoughts, until light came into my vision again.

I looked up and the thick-necked one, the soldier with the camo of greens, browns, and blacks, was looking at me with a smug sneer on his ugly face.

"It seems like you're coming along nicely, whore." He laughed and put the cigar he was holding out on my chest. I gasped and tried to clench my teeth but the shards only dug into my gums, cutting and slicing them to shreds. I spat the blood and took a deep breath through my nose. A moment later he pushed the glass of amber liquid to my lips and forced me to drink.

"I would like nothing more than for you to die, chimera slut, but having you be a bitch curled up at my feet is too alluring. What is your name?" the man snarled, crushing the cup into his hand and throwing it into a dark corner. The corpses where gone now, I didn't know where they had gone.

"I don't know," I whispered, running my ripped tongue along my teeth. "No name, I don't have a name."

The camo-dressed man grabbed my greasy hair and wrenched my face up. He grinned at me, for some reason looking proud of himself. He was still ugly, all of them were ugly, dark auras of sickening colours and a smell on them like they had smouldering tire fires inside of their guts. Nothing smelled right here, and I knew this wasn't where I was supposed to be, but where my home was was lost in the amber liquid and the permanent darkness.

Then a door slammed. "Milos… you're going to want to take…." before the voice could finish his sentence there was a loud scream that echoed off the hallway, followed by a guttural and sickening crack, like the sound of a skull breaking onto the pavement.

I looked up and saw the ugly-faced leader turn around to face the commotion. I saw a black-haired man in his fifties with eyes so wide the whites were showing; he was grabbing onto the door frame with white knuckles.

Milos threw the cigar away and ran out, the door slammed behind me and with its slamming echoing off of the walls I heard yet another gurgling scream.

A splash of blood appear on the grey, dirty walls outside.

Then a red-haired one ran in, his brown eyes wide with fear. I furrowed my brow at him in both recognition and confusion. He looked upset… I was sure I knew –

"Kerres?" I cried weakly before a scream came to my lips; he was pulling my hands off the crossed beams.

He covered my mouth before wrenching my other hand off. I fell forward and into his arms.

Something was different… his aura, I could feel him.

"Ker?"

"No, please be quiet!" Kerres's voice was full of fear. He steadied me by my waist before slinging one of my bleeding hands over his back. Dressed in dark camo clothing and his red hair damp over his face, he started to drag me to the blown-out wall behind me, into a darkness lined with illuminations of blue.

No… you're evil now… so why are you scared?

The low but pain-filled scream of a man came from behind us, before two men started laughing and exchanging silent taunts, voices I also recognized. I tried to turn my head to the side but the prongs along my neck dug into the already rubbed raw flesh. I had to see who they were, I recognized these people... the red-haired one.

Kerres... I remembered Kerres.

"Home?" I asked weakly, hearing my boots scrape against the dirty floor. I glanced down and saw them drag through bits of crumbled drywall and shards of split wood. Where we were or where we were going I didn't know, but it seemed like he was dragging me through holes in walls. Like a steam engine had blasted its way through an apartment building, the continuous holes in the walls seemed to stretch out all the way to the other end of the building.

"Yeah... yeah, we can go home, do you know where home is? Do you remember, J?"

His voice sounded so sullen and dead, but the fringes of it lit up parts of my brain that had become dormant over the last several days.

My feet dragged over a cut up piece of support beam. I stumbled, hearing my boot crunch against a fragile plastic tote lid. My eyes tried to take everything in, seeing if the images around me would help me recall where home was.

But it was useless, there was nothing around me I recognized. We were in an open room now, with old chairs stacked two men high, covered in dirt and cobwebs; tables were pushed against walls and sheets covered items unknown to me. The walls had the typical peeling paint and spider webs that dripped down like moss. Everything smelled so cold and damp, like we were the only things beside bugs and rats who had been here in decades, perhaps centuries.

Kerres pulled me towards a blown-out door, with an EXIT sign that hung from a single frayed electrical cord; it brought us to a hallway, even darker than the last.

Another scream behind us. Kerres moaned from fear and continued to half drag, half help me walk.

"J? Where's home? Do you know who I am? Remember Moros?"

Moros? I remember... tall grey buildings with many windows, black and without glass, peering down at me like the eyes of a thousand insects. I remember it was dark all the time, even when the sky was blue it was dreary and full of despair. Everyone walking around waiting to die, trapped in the inescapable class system. Moros was a cesspool, of early death, malnutrition, misery, and crime.

But there had been light…

My head ached as it desperately scanned the fuzzy images in my brain.

Suddenly, I saw him, crystal clear in my head, the cold visage, the calm elegance, long blond hair that had been cut short but still… still he was so beautiful to me.

Where was he? There was no small beacon in this darkness, only the decay and sadness, so many auras of desperation…

"Elish?" I said weakly. I sniffed and felt my broken teeth try to clench. "Elish?"

"No!" Kerres cried. He dropped me onto a table and leaned down to my eye level and to my surprise he smacked my face. "No, Jade, no! Fuck, you should be getting fixed by now. Not Elish. Me, J, Kerres! Moros is home, I'm your boyfriend! Not Elish!" Kerres grabbed my shoulders and shook them.

Another scream echoed off the walls, and I saw fear come to his face. After a quick glance towards the metal door he looked at me again. "Jade, Elish is evil, the chimeras are evil, all of them. They're bad, Jade, you need to let us make you good."

I looked back into his eyes; I tried to get my mind back but it felt like I was trying to gather a dozen bouncing balls while wearing oven mitts. "No, Ker, you're bad. Luca was harmless, we were unarmed… Crimstones… brainwashed you."

Kerres looked at me and shook his head in disbelief, refusing to believe my words.

"It comes and goes, doesn't it? What they do to your brain? Normal Kerres now, heartless fuck in ten minutes," I whispered. "Normal Jade now, crazy Jade in five minutes." I reached out and touched the back of his head feeling the zig-zagged scar.

I was surprised to see his face crumple at my touch. The next thing I knew he put his arms around me and started to cry. I couldn't hold him back, I couldn't even move my legs properly.

"I miss you so much, J."

My eyes closed, trying to steel myself to his words, my mind was a swimming mess, an ocean of random thoughts and impulses but if I got only a few moments of lucidity I had to take it. "You need to let go, if you want to stay alive. Ker, I'm not J, anymore, I'm Jade Dekker."

I felt him shake his head, before he whimpered, "You'll always be J, no matter what Elish did to you. I'll never stop trying to take you home."

"One day maybe you can come home with me." I didn't even know what I was saying, or if it was possible, but my heart was softening towards him again. Maybe he could train to be a sengil and we could see each other still. "I could talk to Eli-"

Suddenly, there was a low, menacing laugh, one without a doubt I recognized. Kerres recoiled and gasped in shock, before taking a quick step back.

In the doorway, a tall figure took in the scene before him. Two red-embered eyes were staring at us with a sardonic glee that showed on his face with a closed lip smile, though as Kerres screamed at him to stay back, the lips separated into a sharp-toothed grin.

"Mihi, my wonderful little shadow, where is he trying to take you? Far far from here?" Sanguine's throat erupted into a lethal and menacing growl. I saw on his belt, partially covered by a silver buttoned black waist coat, his dirks, and beside them a Magnum.

Sanguine... I remembered Sanguine... I felt my mind start to slip back into obscurity, but with every ounce of mental energy I had I tried to fight the haze that was claiming me again.

"Sanguine... he's sick, don't hurt him," I rasped. I leant forward, letting several blood droplets paint the dirty floor. "He's sick."

A small whimpering noise escaped from Kerres's lips; he took another step back and held out his hands in a submissive posture. "Get away from me! This place is surrounded by Crimstones, behind me, around me, above me. Let me take him or they'll cut you down where you stand and cut open your fucking brain!"

No, Kerres... shut up...

Sanguine only laughed before looking behind him, and out of the shadows our brother Jack appeared. He was dressed in a black tailcoat belted with a turquoise vest underneath, black netted gloves and his silver hair brushed to the side.

The Grim grinned at the scene playing out before him.

"Penguin, you found our little Jade Kitten, and who is this with him? Dinner?"

"Indeed, brother, a meal fit for our family." Sanguine took a step towards Kerres, and as his high-heeled leather boot clicked against the floor he started to growl again.

"Sanguine, no!" I tried to get up, but as soon as my feet hit the floor I stumbled.

In the same moment Kerres jerked to catch me, and, as the rapid movements of a prey brought forth a primal instinct in a predator, Sanguine and Jack arched their backs and pounced. Their auras, both a mixture of silvers, reds and blacks, shone in a brilliant ambiance that illuminated the entire room. It clashed with Kerres's sick and dying seafoam green and seemed to repel it, shooting its own raw energy off in all directions.

I could feel static come to my fingertips.

Silver and black, as powerful as a nebula, encompassing such a weak green flame it was as if a black hole was swallowing the smallest of flies.

My fly.

I screamed. I gathered up every bit of strength that I could, like the implosion before a nuclear blast. I reached my hands out and I released it.

Everything after that seemed to happen in slow motion.

Kerres was crouched down with a hand held over his face. Sanguine and Jack were both lunging towards him, their crimson red and black eyes shining with bloodthirst; mouths open to showcase their pointed white teeth just waiting to rip Kerres limb from limb. All of this in front of me, bathed in light three times brighter than the daylight outside. Their auras and mine were making everything glow in a haunting brilliance.

As soon as I touched their flesh an electric snap went through my fingers and into their bodies, sending a vibrating static through my weak frame with an intensity I had never been able to wield before. My hands clamped around their arms as the current rushed through me and in response to the intense electric charge the two chimeras screamed.

Sanguine and Jack's bodies shook, their eyes rolling back into their heads, and as gravity took them they both fell to the floor with a hard thud, smoking and twitching with only rattling desperate breaths breaking the thick electrical field around us.

Then, as time started to pass by normally, it all disappeared.

The brilliant and blinding light, mixed with the colours of their auras disappeared, and like someone had pulled the plug on my abilities the hallway went back to black, darker than before. Everything seemed darker now, my night vision… it was as if my brain couldn't handle all of my abilities anymore.

A strange feeling overcame me; I reached my hand up and touched my ear.

I blinked hard and looked down at my fingertips and saw that my ears had started to bleed.

Then footsteps… boot steps… coming closer…

"Kerres… run," I whispered. I looked down at him, still cowering and trembling from fear, strands of his hair sticking up from the dissipating current.

He stared at Sanguine and Jack with a mixture of shock and awe. He was a shaking mess, petrified and shell-shocked, but I didn't have time to comfort him.

"Kerres!" I gasped as the boot steps came closer. "They'll kill you! RUN!" I groaned as my vision started to shimmer and swirl, the wetness in my ears dripping down my neck.

My ex-boyfriend took one look at me and sobbed, before putting a quick hand to my face. He kissed my cheek. "I'll never stop fighting for you, I love you."

Then, with the echoing boot steps coming closer, one after another, Kerres ran.

Skyfall

Once more fate toys with me, and I fight my emotions to not let me feel hope. I have learned over the course of many years that fate is a vengeful beast. Though what is one to expect? Our family is a family that does not know time, or death, and as such we know no fear but the fear of those we love being carried away.

Immortals have gone mad seeing those they love die, whether it was from fate or just old age. I have seen it with my own eyes and had once sworn I would never surrender myself to such mortal emotions.

Then I met you.

Wet from the drizzling rain outside, Elish and Garrett's boots squeaked as they ran into the Eros apartment Elish had given to Jade for his birthday.

Elish made a beeline for the gun cabinet and fumbled with the keys. He started handing Garrett guns as Garrett talked on his cell phone.

"Yes, we're right outside Griffin Park right now, land there. We have some good weapons here we just need a quicker way to get there." Garrett took off his black blazer and grabbed a bulletproof vest. Elish was behind him discarding his robe and button-down, and dressing in all the pieces of armour he could find.

"I know, bloody all of them are out there, Elish ordered them to be out there, we just need the plane –" There was a pause, Garrett picked up a handgun holster and started belting it around his waist. "Yes, that's fine, make it quick." With a frantic anxiety about him, he hung up the phone and loosened his tie as he put the vest on. "We have legion soldiers on their way with the plane, landing in Griffin Park in twenty minutes."

"Good." Elish hadn't been saying much since he had gotten into his personal car and drove to Eros, where he could get weapons and armour without too many people knowing.

Elish zipped up his bulletproof vest and checked the tracker again.

The boy hadn't moved much but he had moved, even the small millimetre the red flashing blip had moved meant everything to him. It told him Jade perhaps still had Luca's jacket on him, or if not he was smart enough to keep the Mp3 player on his person. Otherwise, at least the person who was wearing the jacket or had the device in his possession would know where Jade was.

This was the break he had needed. Jade was so close to him he could smell his unique and fragrant scent. It filled Elish with a drive to step back into the heartless beast he had been and strip himself of the worry that had overtaken his once sterile and cold senses.

Though deep inside Elish couldn't extinguish the overwhelming sense of relief he felt, the feeling of guarded abatement that reduced the pressure on his brain, if only slightly.

Elish glanced up and gave his brother a look.

Garrett was looking at himself in the mirror. He was wearing Jade's leather bulletproof vest, over top of his shirtless chest.

Elish watched his brother stick out his chest and crane his neck as he looked at his own reflection.

"I swear I will rip out –"

Garrett jumped and turned around with an embarrassed smirk. "I do look rather sexy in this. I still have the body for it, don't I?"

"This is neither the time... nor place..." Elish growled, throwing him an assault rifle. "Now hurry up, and put that lined hat on your head, at least a portion of our skulls can be protected from their gunfire."

Garrett put on his hat and gave himself one last look before zipping up the leather vest. Elish had a derisive comment on his tongue but he let it slide. Garrett had been giddy over the good news they had gotten regarding the tracker, and it was in his nature to act like a fool when he was feeling that way. Elish had been far more reserved.

Elish put his own armour-rimmed hat on his head, and an ammo belt over his chest. He looked like one of Kessler's generals in that moment, not the robe-draped chimera he was used to being.

After securing his own jacket to hide the ammo, he belted up the assault rifle inside his duster and secured a knife and a handgun.

"Alright, let's go." Elish locked the gun cabinet and they both walked out towards the park.

Only an hour had passed since Luca had told him that valuable piece of information, and now time seemed even more of the essence than it had been before. Every minute that ticked by was another minute for Jade to fall deeper into his own psychosis, as the Crimstones unravelled his brain and poisoned it with their own suggestive thoughts. It could already be too late for all he knew, and if it was... Elish didn't know what he was going to do.

He would not allow himself those thoughts, the boy would be fine. It had been twenty-four hours since the video feed cut off; perhaps even with the incisions on his brain Lyle could cure him. If not Lyle then Sidonius, their doctor brother who had been performing risky surgeries for years now. Perish perhaps as well, there was no shortage of chimeras who knew the medical field, or ones who could unravel the science behind what had happened inside Jade's mind.

Everyone looked at Elish and Garrett as they walked into the park, and for good reason. Garrett was in a black trench coat with his bowler hat, black boots and a stern expression on his face. Elish was in his off grey overcoat, belted in the middle with his own armoured black bowler hat and white boots. Black and white brothers, ready for a battle the parasites of Eros had no idea was about to go on.

The drizzle rained down around them, turning the day into a murky, dreary mess. The smells of wet grass and pavement reached their noses to mix in with a cold breeze from the ocean.

Elish followed the paved walk that stretched through the park, to a small bench in the middle of the freshly mowed green grass. By that time they could hear the plane overhead, a different frequency than the Falconer, but one that was even faster. It started out as a large speck behind an apartment building before it came closer and closer into view, cutting through the steely grey sky.

Garrett looked up and blinked away a raindrop, before giving his brother a smile. "This is going to be fun. It's been so long since I had some excitement in my life, I'm almost hoping I get shot in the head. I haven't died in years; I've been meaning to repair my lungs."

If Jade was immortal I would feel a bit more inclined to enjoy this disruption in the everyday monotony of being an immortal, but the boy could die; he could be dead now. Though I can't expect my brother to appreciate that fact. Or maybe he does and he's just trying to lighten up this dark cloud I can see surrounding me. Garrett has never liked seeing us upset, it bothers him for some reason, such a caring creature he is. Reno will be good for him.

Though if Jade dies, he will not be getting Reno. Why should he have him if my cicaro is dead? Elish felt tempted to tell Garrett that just to be cruel, since his brother's laid-back attitude was starting to grate on his already fractioned nerves, but he refrained.

A cold wind blew from the plane landing. Elish and Garrett walked towards it, but when the sliding door opened they were greeted by a familiar face.

"Hop in!" Siris grinned, winking at the both of them. "Let's kick some ass, bruddah!"

Elish glared at him, his violet eyes turned to see Ares in the cockpit smiling the same cocksure grin his identical twin brother had.

"What are you two doing here?" Having the two chimeras there who had such a past with Jade filled Elish's mouth with burning. He stepped onto the plane and slammed the door hard.

Siris sat on the arm of the co-pilot's seat and lit a Blueleaf blue-embered cigarette, before passing it to his twin brother; their own purple eyes glistening with violence and bloodlust, a shine Elish had seen in their faces when they were only a year old, another success of Perish and Silas's engineering.

Unwanted in this situation or not though, they had their value. The two brutes were a force to be reckoned with. Two tanks that seeped physical energy and a distinct thirst to kill, devour, and protect their family at all costs. They were the chimeras' bodyguards for a reason and Jade was a chimera.

"Ah, bro, we can't let you go into that pit to rescue our little bunny-wunny. He's a Morosian like us and we need to stick together, you know how it goes, Elish. Anyway, you two suits need our help." Siris threw the pack of cigarettes to Garrett, and the distinct feeling of the plane lifting up off of the ground could be felt by all four of them.

Elish grabbed himself a cigarette and leaned against the wall of the plane. He used to silently judge Garrett for his chain-smoking and binge drinking but now Elish was smoking more than he was. "You two know how it goes, you follow my orders and if you see Jade –"

"We love our little brosy, we won't hurt him." Siris waved a dismissive hand, knowing what Elish was warning them of. "You gotta respect a guy who can rip someone's ear off like that, and how he acted in Stadium with us? I've been fucking to that memory since it happened."

Ares gave a whistle. "When he fucking clawed your face? I almost came in my pants!"

"Indeed." Elish's face darkened, wishing he had an excuse to dismiss the two imbeciles but any chimera help he could get going into the Crimstone den was welcome. Kessler's army wouldn't be able to reach the area for at least another hour or two, and even at that point it would only be a dozen or so legionary. Half of the army was in the borderlands right now, looking for the boy who had been right under Elish's nose the entire time.

Though as the plane started to pass over the western corners of Moros, Elish decided that this development was for the best. If the Legion stormed into the West End, they would bring with them heavy machinery, noise, and destruction. The Crimstones would hear them before the Legion could find Jade and with a Falconer at their disposal they might flee with him and disappear into the greywastes. The Falconer had been freshly refuelled and they could get far before the tank got tapped dry.

"Brudder, where are we parking this boat?" Ares asked, glancing behind him; they had just passed Stadium and were heading towards the grey coastline.

Elish thought for a moment, the plane was one of the most silent ones they had, but it was day still and it would be visible to the naked eye. "The tracker is saying they're near Kitsilano, park anywhere in Stanley, we'll walk the rest of the way." It's too bad they couldn't have brought along Sanguine or Drake, they had noses like bloodhounds and surely they would be able to smell where humans had been recently. At least they all had their hearing to aid them; there was little chance of the Crimstones being able to get the jump on them with four sets of ears.

The tall ghosts of buildings could be seen as the brute twin lowered the plane; as it descended onto an expanse of dead, greywaste-quality ground Elish checked the tracker. Still beeping in a building a half-block from the coast; it hadn't moved more than a fraction of an inch since he had checked it.

When I am through with this I am going to put so many tracking chips inside that boy he will be half-bionic, Elish said to himself. *Deep inside his flesh, in the marrow of his bones where no man will be able to cut it out of him. Though it will be pointless because he will never be off his leash.*

The plane touched down and shut off. Then with amused and mischievous glances, the twins went to the back of the plane. They both opened up identical wood crates and pulled out matching rocket launchers.

The twins held them up in the air laughing, before clinking them together like they were beer glasses.

Then with the sound of metal on metal the plane door opened. Everyone jumped down onto the flat ground, nothing but compacted grey dirt and rock surrounding them, broken up only by the occasional twiggy bush or black tree.

The abandoned park stretched out for miles behind them, but Ares had dropped them off right by the road, where the buildings started and the park ended; tall buildings that touched the sky, all in a row, with apartments inside that once sold at high prices for their million dollar views.

Elish had seen photos of what this park had once been; endless green, Native American totem poles and, further on, a crystal blue ocean. Deeper inside the park were dried up river beds, brick bridges still standing, and beautiful stonework that led to the churning, salmon-stocked oceans beyond.

Now just grey, colour was far away, enclosed in Skyland, like a cardinal caged. No other area of the world got to see the green blades of grass sweep across the flat parks with gentle breeze, or the violets rise out from black dirt, it was all trapped in Skyland.

Elish wished he had gotten to see everything through Jade's eyes or Reaver's eyes when he eventually came here. He had been born into royalty, raised on fruit, sugary cakes, and fresh baked bread.

Even so, no matter what, death still followed him, and though you can ease a flower from a two hundred-year-old seed, it was never the same as walking amongst a forest made by nature.

Mother Nature was dead, only the Father of the Fallocaust remained.

"Elish? Which building?" Garrett's voice snapped Elish out of his reverie.

Elish looked around before checking the tracker, then his eyes swept up the streets and to the tall apartment buildings.

The same old ruins, with mould-stained balconies that stretched around every broken floor, showing off their insides like a decayed man with lacerations across his body. Every building looked the same, but only one of them harboured a priceless treasure inside.

Elish took a breath, hoping that the connection he felt with Jade would tell him for sure which one. They were all crammed so close together, shoulder to shoulder like the humans before the bombs, how could he know the boy wasn't underground?

"The one with the flat roof." Elish looked up at the building and pointed, before he scanned each floor for any electronic light, but it was an empty shell, a wraith in the wind.

They are underground... I know it.

"Keep your guns out. Ares, Siris, have those rocket launchers ready, we're going through the garage," Elish said under his breath, in the soft rumbled tones that only chimera ears could pick up.

They walked towards the building, which had several pillars holding up an entrance to an underground garage. In front of it a gate lay strewn, nothing more than a rusted twist several feet away, creating a perfect rust shadow underneath it.

"Quietly now."

The four of them hopped over a railing, sticking close to the stained wall, before they descended into the dark parking lot.

"Someone's here, Ares, Sir-" There was a thunderous crack as a bullet flew past Garrett's head, immediately Elish pressed his back against the wall. As his eyes scanned the area where the bullet had come from, Ares and Siris were already bounding ahead with their assault rifles out.

With hoots and hollers the twins opened fire, and as the echoes of gunfire ricocheted off the walls, they were met with screaming.

Elish and Garrett, now with their own guns in their hands, joined the twins, seeing heads poking up from abandoned cars to shoot off a couple of rounds before ducking back in like whack-a-moles. Elish aimed for one that he saw, and as a bullet grazed his leg he picked him off with a single round to the head.

I still have it... Elish said to himself, before turning and aiming for the Crimstone behind him; but before he could squeeze the trigger Garrett picked him off. Every chimera was trained by either Kessler or Nero in riflery and infantry, and the fact that it was dark down here did the Crimstones no favours.

Elish's head snapped to the side, attracted by movement; he saw a man dressed in the Crimstone camo jump out from behind an old pickup truck, before making a mad dash towards what looked like an empty area of the garage.

Ares raised his assault rifle and shot the man in the back.

With a short scream the man stumbled, before to their surprise they heard the unoiled hinges of a door and a second later the sound of the man falling down a flight of stairs.

"That's our entrance, follow us," Ares called, twirling his assault rifle with a large thumb, before spinning it up into the air, catching it and pointed it towards the door.

The door was discreet, almost hidden in a small alcove surrounded by three graffiti-covered concrete walls, but it was there – it was the entrance to the base.

Elish breathed out another cautious sigh, feeling small pricks of appreciation towards the imbecile brutes. The twin hadn't even broken a sweat, to these two this was one huge video game; life in general seemed to be that way for them.

Garrett did one last sweep of the area, but Elish was running on emotion now, the thought that Jade could be underneath his feet was making his heart clench. His mind was alternating with thoughts of holding Jade until his bones broke and beating the living shit out of him for existing in the first place.

Elish followed Ares and both of them ran down the stairs, Siris and Garrett keeping up their flanks; when they reached the bottom floor it opened up into a small room with two doors branching out.

Ares pointed to an extinguished cigarette butt on a dirty plastic table, and said under his breath, "Smell that? It's fresh." Elish nodded and held his gun to his chest, listening for any electronics but there were no cameras watching them; there didn't seem to be any outside electrical source in this building. Elish hadn't expected that.

When Garrett and Siris's footsteps matched the tone of theirs, Elish and Ares looked through both doors and after checking out the second one, which held a rat-chewed couch and an old vending machine, they proceeded down to a row of what looked like apartments and maintenance rooms.

The smell was damp, but there was a linger of tobacco and a sweat smell that stuck to the peeling drywall; they had been here recently.

"Elish... holy fuck."

Elish looked behind him at Siris, who was peeking through an open door and into a small storage area; he let out a whistle and shook his head in disbelief.

"Keep your damn voice down!" Elish hissed. He walked over and pushed the door completely open and looked inside.

"Oh shit…" Garrett whispered behind him.

A few feet from where Elish was standing they could see what used to be a Crimstone. He had been completely disembowelled; his intestines slopped over his stomach and back, with a single string of long intestine wrapped around his neck. He had been strangled with them.

"Jade?" Garrett whispered.

Elish stared down at the body, before looking at the tracker; the tracker wasn't accurate enough to show him the exact position but there was no doubt they were in the right place.

"I don't know, Jade usually goes for the throat, but he did disembowel that boy in Moros, did he not? The one you found in his lair?" Hope filled Elish. He turned from the grisly scene and started to walk back down the hallway, covered in ripped up carpet with dusted drywall and filth pressed into the edges. "Check the other apartments; his hearing is as good as ours now. If he hears any of us he'll come…"

Elish stopped again and smelled; he turned around and looked at Garrett who was smelling too.

"Burnt corpses?" Garrett whispered.

Elish nodded. He turned around and held his assault rifle tight against him. When he reached the end of the hallway he listened for any signs of life.

The smell got stronger, but there were no noises to be heard. He pushed the door open with his gun and burst in.

His nose wrinkled when he saw them, and as the pungent and distinct smell of burning flesh filled his nostrils, a sick wave of nausea overcame him. There could be no other blatant trade mark.

"Elish…" Garrett whispered to him, once again he knew they were sharing the same thoughts.

"This is Sanguine's work."

"Jade!" Elish suddenly called. Garrett hissed behind him and tried to grab Elish's shoulder but he pushed him off. Elish ran into the next room, trying to ignore the charred and mutilated bodies around him, some of them still smoking inside their carbonized skin. "Jade? Jade?"

"Elish Sebastian... for fuck sakes, shut up!" Garrett snapped, but Elish was too far away now.

Elish continued to ignore him as he ran down the hallways, checking the tracker, wishing he had put some sort of beep tracking on it so he could know when he was close.

The boy has to be close, he has to be... Sanguine was his companion... he wouldn't hurt him... but why would he come here without telling me? That sengil knows better... he would grab at the chance to get in my good books. Like the other submissive-type chimeras they thirsted for praise from their dominant brothers.

All of the bodies Elish found were dead, their camo clothing peeling away from their blackened skin, showing off splits of red cooking flesh and melting bubbles of fat. The rooms were unscorched though; Sanguine had personally incinerated each one.

Elish turned as he heard the faint rustling of clothing, and a moment later a low moan. Without thinking Elish burst into the room it was coming from.

Yes, this was all Sanguine's work.

Tate, one of Jade's former friends, had been crucified. He had been nailed against the wall of a small room with a viewing window; his hands holding two nails in each palm and several more sticking out of his feet.

The former friend's head rose, he looked at Elish and as he beheld the chimera standing in front of him he tried to spit, but it only ran down his face. Like the others Tate had been badly burned, his short hair nothing but a charred burn mark, and his fingers scorched to the point where they were just nubs.

"Pathetic; he was your friend," Elish growled. He went to walk past him into a blasted out wall when Tate's choked breath could be heard.

"Kerres has him, you'll never get him back," Tate said quietly; for a betrayer and a coward his tones still held bite. "And even if you do, his mind's gone, rather him be a fucking robot than the piece of shit that came back to Moros."

Elish's hands clenched, he turned around and stood behind Tate. The back of his head had been burned raw to the scalp, so deep Elish could see the white of his skull.

"Where is he?" Elish said coldly. "Tell me and I speed your death."

He could see the small smile appear on Tate's burnt face. "He was nothing but a babbling, hallucinating idiot. If you think you won, think again. I might die but the Crimstones are far from here and will continue their campaign. You? You'll be stuck with nothing but a mindless vege-" Tate's head snapped to the left as Elish dealt him a full forced punch to the jaw, one that held such a power over it his jaw ripped from his skull and hung loosely, only attached by flesh and sinew.

The second blow ripped it almost entirely off of Tate's face; it slung down on only a shred of flesh before it fell to the ground with an echoing thud, blood dripping down between the upper row of teeth.

Tate groaned, his throat releasing nothing but a high-pitched wheezing sound as the blood ran down his neck. Elish let him linger for a moment before he brought out the gun holstered to his belt.

The chimera raised it, pushed it into Tate's eye and pulled the trigger; a rain of blood and brain splatter disappearing into the blown-out wall behind them.

Elish cleaned his gun and put it back into its holder, before walking through the blown-out wall, and deeper into the building.

As his ears slowly stopped ringing from the sound of the gun blast, he was puzzled to hear a strange noise. He stopped and listened, putting all of his abilities into his hearing to figure out exactly what the odd noise was.

His brow furrowed as he realized it was music, a soothing soft melody…

Elish recognized it right away.

Requiem for a Dream. A song they all knew and had learned at young ages on the violin – chimera music.

They were close.

Jade was close.

CHAPTER 39

"SANGUINE? JADE?" ELISH YELLED. A CHURNING PANIC flared inside him, and in that moment he lost himself entirely. Drawn by panic and a fear for the boy's safety he ran towards the soft violin music, his once steady, unwavering heartbeat a desperate pounding in his chest. The music only amplified the waves of anxiety, crashing forth and breaking every barrier he had resurrected, filling him with a sort of madness.

What has happened to me...?

It didn't matter; he no longer cared to chastise himself for what he was feeling. All that mattered was getting the boy home safely; he could deal with his own internal consequences once this had been resolved. There were more important things at hand right now.

Elish opened every door, running inside and listening but all he could hear was his pounding heart. With a desperate growl through grinding teeth, he checked every apartment he found.

"Sanguine?" Elish slammed a hand against mouldy concrete, his breath catching in his chest and his anxiety rising with every long draw of the violin bow.

He jumped through a blown-out section of wall, and looked around what had once been a kitchen, before stepping through the next hole in the gyprock.

It looked like someone or something had just barrelled itself through; the doors looked rarely used. These people had just blasted holes through each wall, even the supporting ones. It made everything seem like a maze, one hole after another leading into identical apartments with identical layouts; it was confusing and taxing to the brain.

Elish stopped to listen, trying to force his own heart and his own breathing to return to normal, but his ears strained for the violin.

The music... it's coming from the walls, through the holes. With his brothers far behind him Elish followed the sound of the violin.

Then it became louder, so loud he knew it was close, he turned around and looked through an open door, into what looked like a large auditorium, with high enough ceilings that the acoustics would carry the tune long and far.

He was in there.

Before Elish could set foot in the large hall, a blur of black shot from a darkened corner, cowering in between two stacks of chairs; a moment later another black silhouette let out a growl and pursued it.

Taking a step back Elish watched with curiosity as the figure ran towards the door, but his curiosity quickly turned to anger when he realized who it was.

"Kerres!" Elish growled.

Caught off-guard Kerres skidded to a stop; his brown eyes widened with shock before with a cry he pivoted and tried to dash behind Elish, but, of course, he was too slow. Elish grabbed his shoulder and slammed him down onto the ground.

"Where is he?" Elish snarled.

Kerres whimpered; he put up his hands in defence and started stumbling his words. "I tried to get him away... I tried!"

Then the second shadow spoke, he recognized the voice immediately.

"Hey, that's mine!" Drake protested. He slowed down his pace, but when he realized it was Elish he stood up straight and put his hands behind his back.

Elish shot him a withering look, he pressed a boot against Kerres's neck, but the crimson-haired boy made no move to flee. "Where's Jade? Where's this damn music coming from? Who has him?"

Drake looked towards where the music could be heard. "Jack is so talented. Sanguine and Master have Jade. Jade's dying; they're staying with him as he dies. I am sad about that; I enjoyed Jade."

Elish's eyes widened, he took a step towards the auditorium before he paused. "Tie up Kerres, and leave, Drake. Find Garrett, Ares, and Siris and leave the building. If you see any other Crimstones kill them." Without another word he pressed on.

Sure enough, as he stepped into the large room he saw a dim blue light shining through a cracked door partially hidden behind a stack of plastic and metal chairs, bathing the auditorium in a haunting cold glow. Behind him Kerres was crying and begging, then Elish heard the sounds of chains rattling and skin being beaten.

"Jade?" Elish whispered, the taunting music filling his ears with its haunting tune.

He looked to his left and saw the image in the corner, an arm swaying back and forth as he played; only illuminated by his own night vision.

There was the player. He had silver strands of hair falling over black eyes, his face as pale as the moon itself, to the point where he almost seemed to glow in the backdrop of curling paint and specks of black mould.

"Jack? Is he still alive?" Elish said quietly to the Grim; a man whose job had been to collected the corpses of chimeras, immortal or not.

Jack only smiled at him, his arm still coaxing the beautiful tune out of the tight strings of the violin. He closed his eyes as if lost in the music, and knowing he would get nothing else out of him Elish quietly walked towards the open door. Like a doorway to the heavens it glowed and slew the permanent blackness that had stayed in this building since the Fallocaust.

"Sanguine?" Elish whispered. He pushed the door open slowly, and as it opened his eyes fell to the scene below him.

A figure with a cloak over his head, with the boy, nothing but white skin and red blood, cradled in his arms. The man in the cloak was shrouded and bent over the boy, a pale hand stroking Jade's thin and bruised skin in a deceptively caring manner.

Elish's heart froze inside of his chest, his breathing stopped and the room around him seemed to disappear as he realized who was holding his cicaro.

King Silas looked up at him, his burning green eyes a deep turquoise in the bluelamp, with blond hair falling over his forehead in soft silken strands. He smiled at Elish, before leaning down and gently kissing Jade's face.

"My love, my beautiful... I have been waiting for you," his haunting voice whispered, as cold as the light of the lamp beside him.

Silas was awake; he had come to collect Jade, bringing his sengil and his Grim with him. But how did the king know where he was?

Foolish question... Silas knew everything, he was an unpredictable shapeshifter. As soon as Elish had been caught up in his own emotion the king had leapt several paces in front of him. Elish had been a mere hour or so late but it might as well have been a month.

Elish looked down at the boy, a small pitiful wraith in the clenches of the Ghost King.

Like Tate he had been crucified, black holes that wept blood were in the middle of his wrists; and his neck, though still holding his collar, had been shredded like it had been wrapped in barbed wire. And those were only the injuries he could see; the boy was covered in Silas's black cloak, and what was hidden underneath Elish didn't know.

But he was here... he was here. Elish's heart ached for him.

"Jade?" Elish took a step towards him, but with a glance by Silas to an unknown figure behind him Elish felt a hand grab his shoulder. Elish jerked his head and saw the glowing red eyes of Sanguine, shrouded in the dark shadows of the room.

"Is he alive?" Elish whispered, trying to listen for the boy's heartbeat but his ears could only hear his own hammering thuds. Instead he scanned Jade's face for any signs of life.

When Elish saw the blood dripping down his ears he froze, a move that did not go unnoticed by the king.

"His mind was unable to handle electrocuting Jack and Sanguine's brains. A unique talent; you didn't tell me he had discovered his absorption abilities," Silas whispered. He dragged a finger across Jade's lips, before sliding it down to his prickly chin. "Such is the tragic, short life of an empath."

Elish's mind flared with anger, though it was a mask to hide the anxiety and fear that was ripping him apart piece by piece.

Jade needs that surgery and he needs it now... if it's not already too late. He electrocuted the demon chimeras? His abilities when he was testing them with me were shoddy at best. What was he thinking... Jade...

Jade, I told you you were not allowed to use that parlour trick of yours anymore.

"His death... what emotions it brings out of you, gelus vir," Silas whispered, his burning eyes glaring up at Elish like a monster in the shadows. "This boy has certainly cut your wings. Just listen to that heart... the emotions radiate off of you with such a vigour I swear I am an aura reader myself."

Unhand him... you dirty, vile creature, you have no right to hold him, to touch him... he is mine, he belongs to me! Elish's stomach soured as he saw a smile come to Silas's lips, a sardonic grin full of derisive thoughts. What plans did he have for the boy? Elish didn't know, all he knew was that none of them were good.

Elish had to get Jade away from him... disappear into the greywastes, hide in Aras, something, something to keep him safe. The impulse and urge inside of Elish was unimaginable; it held him in such a tight grip he felt like he could no longer breathe until the boy was back in his protection.

"Is he alive?" Elish whispered back, afraid that if he spoke at a normal volume his voice would give away the fear he was feeling. The predator could sense fear and like all beasts, alpha males didn't back down from the chance to assert dominance.

Silas tipped the boy's chin up, before flattening his hand to stroke Jade's cheek. "Alive? He breathes... but that is it. His mind is a ruin, a hollow shell, a shadow of what he once was. You will have no more use of him; the family will have no more use of him."

Silas scanned Elish's face, and drank in the look of agony on his firstborn's countenance. Every minute he saw these reactions from Elish was as good as a climax; he had thirsted for this for years. There was no better drug than seeing the pain on Elish's face.

"Let me hold him..." Elish whispered.

Silas smirked. "No."

"LET ME HOLD HIM!" Elish's booming voice cracked the heavy silence of the room; his eyes flared with unbridled rage. He took a step towards Jade, and fell to his knees in front of him. When Silas didn't stop him Elish stretched out a hand and put it against the boy's cheek. He could feel the blood run through it, but the boy was cold.

"Cicaro?" *Once he had demanded I call him that when I only referred to him as Jade, once he had thirsted for me to imprison him again. Now he was gone... he was gone.* "Jade? Jade? Open your eyes, Cicaro."

Like the black hole his aura was, Silas drew in every moment of Elish's pain, unwrapping him and devouring him, feasting on Elish's insides as his emotions poured out of him. But Elish didn't care... for once in his life, he didn't care if his pride was dissolving, or if Silas was watching every moment of it.

"Cicaro?"

His heart stirred inside his chest as Jade's eyes opened, unfocused and dim. The boy looked around, before his chest gave a start, making him open his mouth wide as he struggled to take in a breath. Half of his teeth had been broken, and his mouth was cut open and shredded, a mess of dead flesh and unhealed wounds. With that and the dried blood stuck inside the rims of his ears, he was in a devastatingly bad state.

Drake was right, he was dying... the boy was dying.

Elish slowly stroked Jade's prickly facial hair and cheeks, cold and clammy under his touch. "Jade? Your master is here."

Jade turned to him, his eyes fluttering in all directions, unable to focus on anything.

He was gone.

The boy's mind had left him.

"Sanguine... leave us alone for a moment." Elish's voice came out a strangled rasp, a slightly higher octave than normal.

Sanguine didn't move, he didn't take orders from Elish anymore, and as Elish's ears craned to listen for any movement he heard the heartbeats of many others. Garrett and the twins were behind him as well.

To his surprise Silas looked past Elish and nodded towards Sanguine. "Leave us; all of you wait outside the building. I want no ears to hear this exchange."

There was a slam of the door, but Elish didn't look up, he was patting Jade's face in a sullen attempt to get any reaction out of the boy.

He wished for nothing more than the cicaro to rise up and start swearing at him, throwing tantrums, raving, and pacing around angrily. To do something... something that would show Elish the boy was still in there somewhere.

Even if you are but a small speck lost in a sea of catatonia, I will dive into the depths as far as Marianas Trench and I will find you.

I will find you.

"Such a sad sight, you really are pathetic, Elias," Silas whispered. He shoved the boy into Elish's lap and shifted himself onto his knees. "To think this slumrat has drawn out such emotions from you. Nothing but a whimpering mess in front of your king. I used to respect you."

Elish held the boy tight and as Jade's yellow eyes darted off in all directions Elish stroked back his black hair. He wished he had their book to read him, and wondered if there was enough of Jade's mind left for him to comprehend the words.

If there is any shred of you left, Cicaro… and even if there isn't, I will bring you home anyway.

Silas continued to devour Elish's pain; the both of them had always been men who could sit with each other for hours without a word needing to be said. In Elish's youth they used to do that, go on walks in the park, play chess, or even read books together.

Once… long ago, when you were still the evil king I know you as today, but there was still a redeeming light inside of you. Now, as Jade had told me, it was all a colourless void of darkness, one that no man could go near without feeling its sharp, tainted essence.

Are you anything more than a cesspool of jealousy and hate, Silas Dekker?

The thought brought darkness to Elish's brain but as the hopelessness threatened to overtake him and bring him into grief, he saw Jade's face and remembered something.

This boy has brought me to my knees, in a matter of two years he has torn out and reseeded emotions in me once lost.

Love has always been our Achilles' heel, which is why I systematically used it to control Garrett and Quin. Instead of hating what Jade had done to me I used it to my advantage to further my patient campaign against Silas.

I had seen what it had done to the Ghost King, I had heard it from the mouth of the king himself, and from Perish during his lucid moments. I knew things, I knew stories that no other chimera knew, and perhaps…

Just maybe.

I can find the hinges in his armour.

"Why do you do this, Silas?" Elish whispered after many minutes had passed.

Silas's eyes, still fixed on Elish's face, narrowed and as they did Elish, a man of sculpted ice and unmatchable elegance, met his gaze.

"Because it pleases me." Silas's response was gilded in steel. "I love to see you a broken shell, practically crying at my feet. No other thing fills me with such joy than to see you like this, all over that slum whore."

"Why?" Elish asked quietly, urging his words forward with the slightest of pressure. "Why do you want to see me like this?"

"I told you why."

Elish curled the boy's hair over his ears. "No, Silas, it is because you hate to see us happy. Why should we be happy when you're so miserable? Why should we have people we care about, when you have closed yourself tight like a steel trap?"

Elish watched as his king's expression changed, his lower lip tightened for the briefest of moments. At his king's silence Elish pressed on.

"That is why you must kill your competition, because whenever you feel threatened by one of them, one of these lesser beings, it enrages you… because it then brings up the question… why not me? Why do they love them, and they don't love me?"

"Watch yourself, Elish…" Silas's tone dropped to a low growl, and with that growl Elish saw the first lesion in his king's impenetrable wall. He had always known his master's tender spots and now, in the situation he had found himself in, he had to go against the loud warnings in his head and push through. Elish had no choice. Though the odds were stacked against him he had to try and reason with the Ghost King. Even if it meant throwing away the pride he had been building up since he had turned fifteen years old.

"And it makes you remember other things too, doesn't it? Because the reason why we can never achieve the privilege of being your one and only is because you were hurt too badly by the last one," Elish continued in a cold whisper. "You keep us at arm's length because of what Sky did to you, but at the same time you demand we keep ourselves devoted to you and only you."

Silas's mouth dropped open, his pupils retracted. No one had spoken to him like this in years and no one but Elish had that pull on the king to do it without immediate punishment. "S-shut up, Elish... I told all four of you to... to never mention his name."

Elish held Jade close to him, gripping the boy's back hard. He was doing this for him, it was for the boy. "How can we forget? You named our city after him, we celebrate his birthday every year, you ended the world for him, you died for him, lived for him... and in the end he only hurt you. Not only did he kill himself, he researched, planned and forced Perish to help him figure out how to permanently kill an immortal... all to get away from *you*."

Suddenly, Silas lunged at him. He grabbed Elish's shirt and yanked his face to his, the small area where their skin touched suddenly electrified. "Shut up, Elish! I said shut up! That's not what happened! That's not! Stop saying that."

Elish lay Jade on his lap, and adjusted himself so the boy stayed on him without having to hold him up. He then brought his hands to Silas's and held them.

An electric current passed between the two of them, making their hands vibrate together.

In a fit of rage Silas snapped his hands away from Elish's and hit him across the face with an agonizing yell, before grabbing his neck and making his touch burning hot.

"I will fucking burn you alive, over and over for all eternity if you mention him again!" Silas's voice was without control or restraint, his eyes wide and half-crazed. As smoke rose up from Elish's skin he clenched his teeth tightly together.

But Elish, calmly, even though his neck was screaming in pain, put his own hands over Silas's and cooled his skin. He rubbed Silas's soft hands with his and slowly eased Silas's grip from his neck.

"You don't need to be strong in front of me, love. It's Elias, I am not here to judge you," Elish whispered.

With an intake of breath Elish warmed his touch, trying to soothe his king, knowing that what he was going to say next would devastate him. The touch was a calming, small gesture, but it might prevent the king from tipping at the wrong angle. Like he was trying to cut down a tree, Elish had to make every cut in a specific area, or else Silas would fall in the wrong direction, and at this time that would be devastating. He had to play his cards carefully, or Silas's psyche would snap, and he might kill Jade right in front of him to show the world his hurt.

Silas Dekker had ended the world to show everyone how much his previous life had hurt him, with Sky leading the charge.

Elish chose his next words carefully and said in a stern but calm voice, "Silas… I know Sky hurt you, but we are not Sky. I am not Sky. You don't need to do this to me, to someone who has lived his entire life to please you. King Silas, my endearing feelings towards Jade don't mean I love my king less. You created me; you raised me in your image, why do you feel like you have to hurt me? Sky is dead, and you cannot punish me or the others for something that happened before we were even born."

He could hear Silas's breathing become rapid, and his small pinprick pupils, no longer holding taunting malice, widening under Elish's words. In front of Elish Silas's countenance crumbled with his face, his grip weakened and the remains of the burning touch dissipated.

Yes, that's right… fall, fall from your grace, Silas. Fall where I can catch you.

I know you, inside and out I know you, and I will rip you down and build you up as I please, and when my cicaro's life is at risk I will not hesitate to rip open festering wounds. It will be up to you whether I bind them or contaminate them more.

In a calmed whisper that didn't match the sinister thoughts in his head, Elish continued, "I'm sorry he hurt you, and I know your love for him was deep, and I know you miss him, but we're a family, and hurting us does not equate to hurting Sky. Silas, I know you were not born to be this man you are now, and I ask of you… instead of driving us to resent you, help us help you recover."

The king's lip tightened and his wide eyes filled with unshed tears. "I tried to recover… I tried, Elish. I tried to bring him back or at least a part of him, so I could have him again but Chimera X failed. I can never make a born immortal. He's gone forever, my Sky is gone forever and I am doomed to an eternity without him."

Elish put an arm over the back of Silas's head, and brought his forehead to his lips. He gave it a single kiss and, as if a floodgate had been unlocked, King Silas, the man who ended the world with a single pulse of sestic radiation, started to cry.

With Jade between them, Elish put an arm around Silas as he sobbed into his shoulder, kissing the side of his head and rubbing his back.

And because he couldn't see him, Elish allowed himself a fleeting smile, filled with pride in himself and his abilities. Once again he had played his king like a stringed instrument, slowly drawing out each sad and mournful noise.

And Silas's tears were indeed music to his ears.

Silas let out a mournful sob and buried himself into Elish's shoulder. "Why did Reaver have to die? I almost had him back; I almost had my Sky back, Elish. I had the formula right, I had it all right, for fuck sakes! I spent years making his personality, everything as suited for me as I could. He was mine."

"I'm sorry."

"I miss him, Eli," Silas sobbed. "I miss him so much it physically hurts. I loved him; we were supposed to be together forever."

"I know."

"Why did he hate me?"

Elish brushed Silas's golden-blond hair back, and shushed him. "I cannot answer that, but I can urge you to perhaps stop driving us to hate you, yes?"

King Silas sniffed; he pulled away with a look of anguish on his face. "I designed you to counsel me, to make sense of me, and I despise you for it now." He wiped his eyes and whimpered. Several minutes passed with only the sound of Elish stroking his hair, before finally the king spoke.

"Could we try again? Something, give me some hope, Eli. I just need a shred of hope."

So you can have a meltdown and kill another chimera like you murdered Lycos? Such a fool... oh, to see the look on your face when –

No not yet.

Elish leaned over and wiped Silas's tears with his thumb; he forced a smile to his lips. "I'll do everything I can. I will find someone to make you happy; it would be nice not to have to worry about you terrorizing us for a while."

Silas gave him a sad smile, his eyes red and puffy. "Only you could be so brutally honest with me. I suppose that is why I made you."

Elish noticed the king looking down; he glanced down too and saw Jade's still unfocused eyes looking around the room, his fingers twitching back and forth as the nerve pulses in his mind went haywire.

"Do you trust me, Elish?" Silas whispered.

With him? I would be a fool to trust my cicaro with such an insane monster. I bashed your head in with a driver the last time you asked me this, but now... but now –

Now Jade lies on my lap, his unfocused eyes taking in everything but seeing nothing. I can see his mind in its ruins, once a brilliant spectacle of life, full of sarcastic wit, biting disobedience, and endless intelligence. It has all gone from him now... cut away and stabbed by the instruments of the Crimstones.

What choice do I have?

"Yes, I do," Elish said, each turn of his tongue dripping more acid into his mouth.

Silas held out his arms, and though Elish's mind screamed at the thought, he handed Jade to Silas.

The king looked down at the boy, in a manner that for once didn't hold malice, jealousy, and hatred. He gazed down at the teenager as he should have from the beginning, as a chimera, a creation, and an extension of Silas's own mind and body.

"Put your hands on his head, love, cool him down."

Elish felt a cautious relief flood through him. He did as King Silas asked and watched as his king placed his hands down on Jade's head.

The boy's unfocused eyes shifted from one face to another, and Elish felt through his fingers a surge of blood rush into the boy's head.

He took a deep breath and surrendered his cicaro to the king; the only solace knowing that Silas couldn't make him worse. It would've only been a matter of time before Elish killed Jade himself, unable to handle seeing such a magnificent creature reduced to the vegetable in front of him.

Elish watched the long graceful fingers of Silas trace up the boy's skull like a small detector trying to locate its point, before, with a static charge and a pull on Elish's own senses, he felt the first pulse. A low murmuring electricity, an ability Elish could never even fathom having, filled the room, making the hair on the back of Elish's neck prickle. It was like a vortex, and all of it was focused into Silas's hands.

Elish looked down at the boy, cold in the bluelamp, a pale ghost trembling and shaking in the king's arms; his eyes were wide and his irises a green hue from the light. They rolled back, and, with another pulse of electricity, small purple droplets started to fall onto Jade's face.

Elish made his touch grow colder, feeling his cicaro's head become burning hot under Silas's touch.

Then the static grew again. Unable to breathe, Elish glanced up to the king. Silas had his teeth clenched together, a stream of blood running down his nose, mouth, eyes, and ears, pouring onto Jade. What he was doing would kill him, which is why Elish had only seen Silas do it a handful of times.

As the king destroyed his own body for the boy, Elish could feel every neuron, blood vessel, and crease in his own brain vibrate. Like a steadily beating drum whose rhythms were increasing in tempo, the vibrations came more rapidly, one after another until they were steadily assaulting everyone's senses. Elish found his own teeth clenching together, and a moment later the feeling went to his hands, which snapped around Jade's head like a steel trap.

Then he screamed... the boy screamed.

"ELISH!?"

Elish's hands jerked away, and in the same second so did Silas's. The two of them let out a gasp as they slumped back; Elish's back hitting the side of the small room. He caught Silas before he fell backwards.

Drained of all energy, and with the vibrating electricity still trying to leave his body, Elish pulled Silas to a sitting position. Jade was whimpering in a daze between them.

"Thank you," Elish gasped. He leaned his head onto Silas's shoulder and closed his eyes. "Thank you."

Silas's heavy breathing filled his ears; he managed to raise a hand and place it on Elish's shoulder. "You are still my golden boy, but still, for your brothers to see, you are still being punished for what you did to me. But the boy is yours no less, intact."

Elish nodded; he would take any punishment at this time, it was nothing he hadn't handled before.

"Yes, my king."

Suddenly, there was a rattling of the door knob. Elish glanced up at it and so did Silas.

"Someone didn't listen?" Silas murmured, but Elish narrowed his eyes.

"I left Jade's ex-partner tied up; perhaps Drake didn't secure him well enough." Elish was reaching across his back for the gun, when with a hard kick the door swung open, slamming up against the wall with a thunderous crack.

Milos stood in the door frame, smiling.

The leader of the Crimstones had a grin on him that was a mile wide. His mouth had been cut open from ear to ear; so with that smile came the view of all of his teeth. The leader had been tortured, sliced open, and burned; it was a wonder he was still alive.

The scar-faced terrorist beheld the sight in front of him, and as the chimera and the king looked up at him in shock, they saw something reflect underneath his ammo vest.

C4, several sticks of it, duct taped to the inside of his vest.

"So much concrete above us…" Milos whispered. "It will take a year to dig you out."

"No!" Elish hollered. He tried to push Jade off him, but Silas, whose eyes never left Milos's grinning face, shot to Elish.

To Elish's confusion Silas grabbed him, and as Elish saw Milos's finger press down on the detonator he felt King Silas push Jade in between them, wrapping his arms around Elish with the boy tight against their bodies. As a flash of light filled the chimera's eye sockets, followed by a deafening explosion, he managed to secure his arms around Silas as well.

Then there was light, and fire.

Why does it always end in flames… they all know how I feel about smoke and fire.

Darkness was around him, but the small white flame of his immortality did not claim him, instead it was the searing, unmerciful burning pain that ripped him from the frozen state of animation and pushed him back into the pits of hellfire that encased him.

Elish smelled burning flesh first and then smoke; each pungent smell was infused with heat that seared his nostrils and throat. When he opened his eyes he saw the raw peeling skin of King Silas, and his smoking clothes, some still smouldering with a blue flame.

With his ears ringing Elish pushed him away and looked around in a daze. The entire room was aflame, fire of all colours devouring the old building. Beams of wood were snapping and cracking in soundless percussions as they were reduced to charcoal, waning and bowing, waiting to release the thousands of tons of concrete looming over the top of their heads.

He's right, it will all fall upon us and it will take months to dig us out. I will heal and awaken to this dark tomb, with Jade's rotting body to remind me of my failure. I see why the walls were blasted out now; he was weakening the building's support. This was a death trap from the beginning. His last-ditch plan to entrap us and kill the boy he held hostage.

Elish's heart seemed to stop. Once again his only discomfort, fire, was surrounding him, licking its flamed tongues against his flesh, charring it to coal beneath his robes. He was in so much pain he didn't want to see how badly the explosion had wrecked his body.

Then a rumbling vibrated underneath his feet. Elish watched through the hole the explosion made as the roof of the auditorium started to cave in, raining fire-lit insulation and gyprock onto the floor with a vibration that seemed to block out every noise he should be hearing.

Suddenly, there was a shift of movement. Elish looked down and inside his heart clenched. In his shock he had forgotten the boy, and even the king lying scorched and dead against his body. All of what had happened before the blast seemed swallowed by the flames themselves.

"Jade?" His voice was lost inside the buzzing in his ears, but the boy heard him. He half-opened his eyes, his chest rising and falling rapidly. It appeared that he was trying to open his mouth to speak but he only inhaled the black smoke that encased them.

There was no more time to be idle. Elish rose and grabbed onto Jade's collar, and with another hand he reached down to grab King Silas's arm.

The king's skin peeled off of him as Elish did, shedding like snake skin onto his hands. Silas was dead, his arm almost completely blackened, smoking like a roast too long in the oven. There was nothing but cooked skin to grab onto. So instead, he grabbed onto the tie Silas had loosely around his neck and started dragging both of them out of the room, through the pulverized remains of what had once been Milos.

The auditorium and the room they were in were now one, a flaming inferno of smoke and fire, slithering up and consuming the roof with orange-red flames, reflecting its glow onto the still dark corners. From darkness to burning light, fire destroying a building that had once survived the apocalypse. It was almost like a quiet foreboding, a sinister message that told that no matter what, even centuries after, light could still destroy the cold and dark.

Elish grunted; his teeth clamped together as he drew up every last ounce of energy he had. Though both boys were light, his body was screaming in pain, especially his back, his neck, and head, the areas which had been directly facing the bomb. He knew he was gravely injured, but what consequences he would have to face from that would have to wait, he needed to get the boys to safety.

But not four steps after this solemn promise to himself, his knees buckled underneath him; as the fires continued to eat the support beams of the basement his energy drained. Elish took a gasp of air, scorching and burning his throat, and looked around for a cold place where he could spend a second to gather up every last ounce of energy.

As he looked into the dark corners, to the rows of stacked chairs and sheets now reflecting the flames behind him, he saw a crimson-haired man strung up by his neck, crying and screaming. Elish realized with both fear and confusion that the explosion had made him deaf; the sounds of the beams snapping around him had been felt through his body, not his ears. He had blown-out his eardrums.

Elish dropped Silas and Jade and walked towards the figure, his mouth still open as he writhed in unbridled fear, a fear that knew no pride, a fear that only a man who knew he was about to burn to death could feel.

When Kerres saw Elish, he started to plead with him, tears running down his face. Elish could read lips, not well but enough to manage. He was begging for his life in a rapid steady whine.

"Carry Jade." Elish made the sound with his lips. "Carry Jade and follow me, do you understand me?"

He could feel another crack of a breaking beam; this one was loud enough to be felt underneath his boots. He and Kerres looked towards the burning auditorium in time to see the entire roof collapse.

In response Elish quickly unhooked the chain that had been connected to a hinge in the wall, he pulled on it and glared down at Kerres. "Do you?"

With sweat beading down his face, and the flames dancing in his eyes, Kerres looked at Elish and nodded. That was all Elish needed to see; there was no time for interrogation, or to search his mind for deception; he pushed the Kerres ahead of him and picked up the heated remains of King Silas.

Kerres picked up Jade, but his eyes were fixed on Elish.

"Your back is blown off; I can see your spine and ribs." His lips moved.

Elish adjusted King Silas in his arms and let Kerres walk in front of him; not only did he need the boy to help him carry one of the two, he would know the quickest way out of here as well.

Jade's eyes were still open; they were one of the things that kept Elish from giving into the screaming pain of his body. The boy was alive, and even though his eyes were unfocused he was still with it enough to move; the blast had not claimed him.

Kerres led them through the blasted holes in the walls; past the apartments now smelling of smoke; past each raised groove of drywall and insulation which he stepped through with shaky feet, only occasionally looking behind him to make sure Elish was there.

Suddenly the vibrations under their feet got louder. Kerres looked behind him with his eyes wide and shell-shocked, and Elish did too.

Drywall and dust started to rain around them, falling onto their shoulders. Elish took one look around and pushed Kerres forward, his boots rattling and his knees shifting like there was an earthquake under their feet.

Then another crack and another one. Kerres kept looking behind him but Elish pushed on, drawing up every ounce of endurance he had, mining all of his adrenaline stores to flow fresh energy into his brain, but even his chimera engineering was giving into the horrific wounds he had endured. Elish was dying and he knew it.

"If I fall behind, run, get the boy to my brothers," Elish called, and right on cue his knee gave out in the middle of a bloodstained hallway.

Dust now surrounded them like a thick fog.

A war zone, they were in a war zone... "Just run, don't let him die here, you owe him that." Even if it does take a year to dig us out of here... Jade will be safe, and that was all that ever –

Kerres suddenly jumped backwards; he opened his mouth in a muted scream. The only possible explanation was that the exit was caved in. They were done for, all of them...

Then his saviour appeared; his saviour in a bowler hat.

Garrett's green eyes were wide with relief; he ran over and grabbed King Silas from him and handed him off to Ares. Siris was behind him as well; he mouthed something to Elish that Elish didn't catch, before turning around and taking Elish's arm. Siris drew it forward and supported Elish's body on his bowed back. Elish turned and before he could demand it, he saw Garrett take Jade from Kerres.

Garrett cradled the boy, and visibly flinched as he saw how badly burned Elish was.

"I can see your bloody spine, and your ears... my god," he mouthed, but Elish didn't care, not even when Kerres mouthed that the blast had made Elish deaf.

Garrett has the boy... Garrett has the boy... Elish felt a smouldering haze slowly envelope his mind like a cloak.

Then a familiar darkness, one he had been experiencing since he was young overcame him. With no noise, only the smell of burnt flesh and scorching smoke, he succumbed to it, embraced it, and welcomed the pain-free darkness it offered.

Garrett has the boy.

I can sleep.

CHAPTER 40

*I*N REALITY, TIME IS NOTHING BUT A WORD TO US, AN ISLE
in a crystal sea that brings us this way and that with ebbs and flows. Though our destination was never from point a to point b, or to be drifting with no air to our sails, a mercy to the tides. This was a mortal's burden. We are no longer passengers without a voice, we are islands watching as each ship passes us by to a destination unknown. We are nothing but stone figures to you, you are naught but passing images to us. Neither giving nor taking, just observing until eventually out of sight.

The cold ribbons seemed to glow with every mental movement, embedding themselves in flesh without solidity, to knit it back together with a silver needle and thread made from the thickest of spider webs. Repairing the body that the fates forgot, breathing life into charred lungs, blood to burnt flesh, and warmth to the cold, cadaverous skin.

Elish opened his eyes and saw the study around him through a thin sheet of white silk. He looked to the skylight and with that breathed in his first open mouth breath, smelling the familiar oak and must smell that Jack's books brought to the room.

He was no longer in pain; the burnt shell he had died in was repaired and new, and now he lay in the leather-cushioned daybed, where all the chimeras rested while recovering.

Elish rose and withdrew the silk wrapped around his face; he pushed it down his body and saw he was dressed in white robes and nightclothes.

He was alone. All those who may have died with him must have already been repaired and released back into the world.

"Jack?" He coughed as his words came out dry and raspy. He massaged his throat and felt the back of his neck bare. Running his hand up the nape he discovered his hair was even shorter than it had been when Silas had cut it. It had been burned off during the blaze.

Elish looked around the dark study, rows upon rows of books on bookshelves of thick polished wood, with a silver and black carpet lying in the center of the round room. The fireplace beside a lounge chair was flickering reflections which at that point in time made Elish cringe. The explosion and what burning came from it were still fresh in his mind.

How long have I been resurrecting for? Where's Jade?

As if a phantom came in to deliver his answers, Jack sauntered in with a smile and a small bow. He was dressed better than usual, which was saying a lot for him; a black surcoat with a ruffled collar and silver buttons the shapes of roses down the breast, his sleeves had the same ruffles which brushed against midnight blue trousers.

"Elish... so he was right. Today would be the day. How are you feeling?"

Elish saw that his brother was holding a grey envelope in his hand, emblazoned with Silas's red seal. The scorpion-cougar hybrid. The chimera mark.

Elish rose and tested his legs with his weight; he was stiff but able to walk. It couldn't have been more than a week then. To save him the embarrassment of falling over he steadied himself against the iron rung railing of the spiral stairs. "How long have I been out for? Where's Jade?"

Garrett has the boy... he would not let him go.

"Silas has your cicaro now."

Elish's eyes shot to Jack, his teeth clenched inside of his mouth. "How is he?"

Jack walked over. Behind him his sengil, Juni, was holding a tightly folded stack of clothing.

"Garrett had Sidonius and Perish perform the surgery on him, that is all I know," Jack explained. Elish turned and received the bundle of clothing. A tightness in his chest started to knot together his insides, as he wondered what all of this meant.

"And he survived it?"

Jack ignored him. As Elish tucked the clothing underneath his arm, his Grim Reaper brother handed him the grey envelope.

"All I am authorized to do is to dress you and give you your invitation. We are leaving within the hour, brother. I bathed you but a day ago, so change and we shall go to the car."

A flare of anger rushed through Elish, but he forced it down with a purse of his lips and ripped off the seal to the letter. Confusion claimed most of his emotions, but deep down were small strands of curiosity as to what was inside the envelope.

Silas is always planning something…

A disciplinary hearing has been arranged for
Elish Sebastian Dekker
April 2nd at 8 PM, Alegria.
Attendance mandatory, formal attire.

Silas S. Dekker

"So my punishment is going to be public?" Elish murmured to himself, remembering one of the last words Silas had said to him, but with that reminder came the solemn resolution that he would take whatever Silas could give to him. The boy was healed and safe, and since he wasn't dead beside him it meant he had survived the surgery.

"It seems so," Jack responded with a sympathetic grin. "Perhaps you will not have that boy for long? What a pity it would be if he killed him after all this trouble you went through to save him."

Elish's purple eyes glared into Jack's, but the Grim only smiled back. Then with a small bow, though his black slabs of coal never wavered from Elish's eyes, he turned to leave the room, his long coat tails swaying behind him.

"How long have I been out for, Anubis?" Elish said coldly.

Jack stopped. Elish saw a slight tightness in his shoulders from being called by his second middle name. It echoed a history between the two that both of them had tried to forget.

Jack turned around, his black lips pursing together. He paused and wavered for a moment before saying in a low tone, "Two weeks, Elish. You've been unconscious for two weeks. King Silas for nine days, and the boy hasn't regained proper consciousness from the surgery." With a vexed glare, and Juni's eyes shining in the shadows giving them both weighted looks, the Grim disappeared out of the study.

Elish swallowed down the pit so busily forming in his stomach and changed into the clothing that Jack had given him. He was annoyed at the fancy attire thrust upon him, but he dressed in it without complaint.

It was a black cape with purple designs traced along the fringes, and a black fitted button-down with silver buttons, crisp and newly pressed; the black and silver matched his pants perfectly creased in the middle and belted with a leather belt and silver buckle.

When Elish was dressed he put on the shoes beside the daybed, leather with new black laces and purple socks. What was going to happen tonight, as he emerged new to the world in his repaired body, he didn't know, but Silas wanted him looking nice for it.

He checked himself one last time in the mirror. An angry man with purple flames for eyes glared back at him with hair so short it barely touched his cheekbones.

Though he did look presentable. His eyebrows had been shaped and his skin scrubbed clean, Jack wasn't just a collector of bodies; he prided himself in making his brothers look their best when they emerged from their silken cocoons, as was the job of the harbinger of death and immortality.

With a sweep of his robes Elish left the room, and found Jack sipping bloodwine by the door; when he saw Elish he handed Juni the cup and clasped his hands together.

"Beautiful," he said simply with a satisfied smile.

Elish gave him nothing but a cold recognition as he pushed past him and out the engraved double doors. "I want this over with; when his games are concluded I'm taking my cicaro and leaving. Let him do what he will to me."

Whatever it may be, I will take the humiliation. There is nothing more he can take from me now. Not even my once long hair can be offered up as a sacrifice.

Jack followed behind him. Like a shadow whispering dark secrets that only made sense in the night, Jack trailed behind his brother; admiring for the brief moments he could see it, the silver and white beacon of light draped in misery and darkness.

But Elish had no room inside his overtaxed and troubled mind to give thought to how Silas had dressed him, even if the clothing and his look was alien to all of them.

They were used to seeing Elish a certain way, but that cage had been rattled almost two years ago when he had taken in the stray from Moros. Now it was as if his physical appearance was the last straw in the transformation of Elish Dekker. Though not at all a bad one, they had thoroughly enjoyed their cold, emotionless, and humourless brother being taken for his ride.

Immensely actually...

A black car with tinted windows was waiting for them as they entered into the overcast and drizzling day. April showers fell all around them, cloaking the quiet corners of Skyland in an eerie mist.

No one was out and no one saw them. Jack's tower had always been a place that the common elites avoided; even though they were uninvolved in chimera goings-on, it was a looming omen in the sky.

Elish breathed in the misty and cold air, taking a moment to enjoy the soothing feeling it had on his lungs. Not long ago his lungs had screamed for clean and crisp air, taking in nothing but toxic smoke and scorching embers. It was to be enjoyed and appreciated, even if only for a moment.

Elish entered the car and the door closed; soon they were on their way to Alegria.

As they always did, and with this moment being no different, Elish's thoughts turned to Jade. Immediately he felt his heart fill with apprehension, and a yearning inside of him to take the boy and once again leave Skyfall. It seemed like a mortal's age since he had held that boy in his arms. Not the empty shell without consciousness, but the boy he had once known. There had been so much stacked up against them, and it seemed that whenever Elish was sure he had gotten ahead something or someone was standing in their way, kicking them back down the mountain they had both been struggling to climb.

Everything was so much easier before I had him to worry about, my usual self would discard the increase in responsibility and move on with my life. I already had running Skyfall to concern myself with and keeping the king from uncovering the secrets hidden in the greywastes. But now I would forsake so many things for that one boy. Oh, how far I have fallen, though no matter how hard I am on myself I cannot, for one minute, view it as falling... if anything I just acquired someone to help lift into the sky.

The car stopped in front of Silas's skyscraper, and with not a word exchanged with Jack, Elish walked into the building.

Sanguine was standing beside the elevator, his hands clasped behind his back.

Dressed in a black tailcoat with a red bowtie and high heeled boots, the blood-eyed chimera smiled a large closed-mouth smile, and squinted his eyes at the two of them like the Cheshire cat he was.

Elish noticed he was holding in his hand a black rose, with petals that edged on the colour purple. As he walked towards the elevator, the sengil handed him the rose and bowed his head. "Floor Five, Master Elish."

Elish reached out with suspicion and took the rose, his eyes travelling to Sanguine's to search for deception, or some nefarious plot he was trying to keep to himself. The chimera's eyes showed everything, and at the same time... nothing.

"Is Jade here?" Elish dropped his voice.

It was no use; there never was a use in reality. As soon as Silas had awoken in his silks, his chimeras were his creatures again. An invisible barrier had been erected between them; Elish was blocked off from all further information, and what wasn't blocked had been filtered down to useless courtesies.

And to drive in that very point, Sanguine only smiled and took a step back, taking the liberty to press the button on the elevator door. Elish walked in with the rose in his hand, and took a deep breath to steel the emotions that only Jade could draw up in him.

When the door opened, it opened to darkness and a low buzzing in the back of his head that made the fine hairs inside of his ear prickle and itch. The only light inside was a small lamp, and beside it... a dark figure.

"Come, love."

What sort of disciplinary hearing is this? Elish walked down the softly illuminated hallway, seeing only darkness on either side of him and hearing the same low hum. He did as he was told and walked up the two steps onto the platform he realized King Silas was standing on.

Silas, as new and unblemished as Elish himself was now, was holding a blue-embered cigarette in his hand. He was sitting on a winged chair with a wooden side table beside him, holding on it a bluelamp, an ashtray, and a pair of pliers.

Is he going to rip my teeth out? Is that it? Or pry out Jade's remaining teeth like Milos had done to him? Elish bowed to his king and met Silas's gaze with his.

But he always does this in front of my brothers. When Joaquin had defied an order once, he castrated him in front of us and ripped out his fingernails. Does he really respect me so that he would do this with only us? Had the mental shapeshifter once again lived up to his title?

"How do you feel, gelus vir?" Silas whispered, twirling the cigarette in his hand with a small but sinister smile. Nothing but dark plans could be seen behind those green eyes, ones so intricate they were matched only by Elish's.

Perhaps as time went on, he started looking at my bringing up Sky in a different light...

Then there was a small flash of silver. Elish only stood up straighter when he saw King Silas reach behind the wooden table, and bring out the same driver Elish had smashed the king's skull in with.

Then the king rose. Elish stayed where he was, smelling the tangy scent of the smoke as Silas stalked a circle around him.

"In front of my creations, my subjects, you decided to betray my trust, and shame yourself in front of my family. When I ordered you to leave Jade here, you murdered me. What explanation do you have for this?" Silas demanded, slinging the driver behind one of his shoulders. His teeth firmly clenched the cigarette.

Elish stared forward, looking into the darkness around him. With the elevator closed there was no light but the cold glow of the bluelamp. The entire room, save for the odd buzzing, seemed completely empty.

"I knew you would kill him if I left," Elish answered simply.

Silas walked into his view; his eyes seemed to glow black under the faint light. He picked up the driver and pointed it at Elish's chest. "And why am I not allowed to kill my own creation if I see fit?"

"I saw you as not thinking clearly, caught up in the energy of the room and the bloodthirst that inflames the throat of every chimera. Jade is an empath, a valuable creation and an asset to our family. I saw it as an error for you to murder him and as your counsel I decided to risk punishment for my actions in the faint hope that once you recovered, and the energy of the night wore off, you would see you were in error," Elish responded in a firm but quiet voice, though in the dark room around them it seemed to echo off of the walls.

"Error?" Silas's own tone dropped. He shoved the driver into Elish's chest, his face twisted into anger. "You dare call my judgment an error?"

"I am your counsel, your prince; I am the only one who is allowed to do so," Elish answered, his purple eyes still facing forward.

"So all of this was merely for the benefit of the family? Not for your own personal feelings towards the boy?" A smirk started to form along the king's mouth.

"Yes."

Suddenly Elish's eyes snapped towards a corner of the room. A scream bounced off the walls, seemingly coming in all directions.

It was Jade.

"Jade?" Elish turned towards where he thought the scream was coming from, when Silas's voice snarled, "Stay where you stand, Elish." Behind him Elish heard a condescending laugh roll off of Silas's lips.

"You say no… but look at that heartbeat, look at that clench in your chest." In a flash, like the ghost he was, Silas's hot breath could be felt against Elish's neck, and a moment later, Elish felt the softest of kisses along the side. "I can taste your fear… golden boy."

Elish tried to stuff down his own emotions, but when another rattling scream reached his ears he felt his teeth grind together. "What are they doing to him? Release him at once!" Elish demanded. He tried to move away from Silas's lips but the king grabbed him. He put his mouth over the chimera's neck and gently sucked on it.

"The boy has caused so much trouble; look at what he has done to you. Never have I tasted such sweet ambrosia, dripping off you like honey. It makes me want to take you right here, my beautiful man so carved in ice," Silas purred. "Take a moment, love, and think to yourself. Do you wish to pursue this? He has dragged you from grace, ripped away your steeled pride and injected you with this unstable madness. Do you really want him in your life?"

Elish's heart constricted. He scanned the corners of the room for the boy, but all there was was darkness, not a single object to be seen; even his night vision lay every inch of it bare, like he was staring into a void.

"Yes," Elish said. He looked around frantically as Silas kissed his neck. "I do, there is no question, no decision. I made that decision long ago."

The wet lick of a cold tongue drew itself up Elish's neck to his ear; with a breath of warm air Silas whispered to him, "You are so thick with disease, Elish, and I devour every infected cell. Oh, how I love this side of you. That unbreakable, impenetrable wall is just melting into my hands."

A hot fire of both anger and frustration shot through Elish, and as he pushed Silas away a third scream sounded. That was the last straw for him. With a bellow of rage Elish yelled into the darkness. "BRING HIM TO ME!"

The king's cold, morbid laugh rang behind him; he leapt to his feet and put an arm around Elish's neck. With a cold snicker he hissed into his ear. "Why?"

Why? Why? What kind of question is that! Elish gritted his teeth as he heard Jade whimpering into the darkness. Elish couldn't understand why he couldn't see him, and how the buzzing noise was blocking his senses. Where was he?

"Why, Elish?" Silas's voice rose. He shifted himself in front of Elish and grabbed his face. "Why? Why?"

"Bring him!" Elish felt his breath growing short, like a wild animal who was caged in nothing but darkness. He whirled around and screamed into the void. "Bring him!" He dropped to his knees, feeling his chest heaving through an unseen fire, his mind a swimming mess, unable to comprehend what was happening inside of him, or the emotions he was feeling. All of it was alien to him, and nothing was going how he had expected.

I have never had emotions… and now that I do, it is wildfire around me. Uncontrollable, and doing nothing but destroying everything I touch.

"You heard Elish. Bring him."

Elish rose to his feet and saw the elevator door open at the end of the room, though oddly its light shone against nothing but a strip in front of him, like the walls had closed in on the large room.

Two silhouettes stepped out of the elevator, one leaning against the other.

But something was wrong with the one being supported... Elish focused his eyes to try and identify just what he was seeing. The person appeared to have a crown on his head.

As he came closer and the elevator doors closed so only the bluelamp shone on him, Elish realized it was no crown.

Jade had almost a dozen thin wire rods sticking out of his skull.

A cold shock rushed through Elish's body as he stared at the boy almost being dragged towards him. Sanguine had his arm around Jade's waist, and he was leaning to the left to accommodate most of his weight. The boy was only making automatic movements; even his eyes were barely blinking. Just small setting suns, with the rays not sunlight but dried streaks of blood running down his face.

"Jade?" Elish whispered. He reached out a hand to touch him but he was too far away and Elish's own legs were seemingly welded to the floor. He could only stare as the boy was led to Silas.

Jade looked up at him, with a mouth partially open and a disconnected look of fear on his face. Inside his mouth Elish saw silver; all of his shattered teeth had been replaced by silver and porcelain implants, which, with the thin rods jutting out almost six inches from his scalp, gave him an almost unworldly look. He was a metal angel who had found his way into the hellfires of Alegria.

"Isn't he dressed nicely?" Silas whispered as Sanguine disappeared back into the darkness.

Elish looked at the boy. Jade was wearing his cicaro pants but his leather boots were knee high with a three inch high heel, something more suitable for Sanguine than his cicaro. He was also dressed in a black button-down similar to Elish's and as Silas moved his hand across Jade's neck Elish saw he was in a similar cape too.

"Such beauty. I fixed his teeth, I stitched his hands, I repaired his mind... look at my creation, my steel kitten," Silas purred, admiring Jade standing crooked behind him. "He is such perfection now."

"What did you do to him?" Elish whispered. He reached out a hand to touch the boy's face but Silas stopped him with a glaring look.

Then with the same look Silas brought out the pliers and clamped one of the metal rods.

Jade screamed but remained still; his eyes welled with tears as Silas slowly drew out one of the metal rods, streaked with blood. When it disconnected from his head, Elish could see a thin wire coming out of the middle of it, the end of it holding a small silver tube that, from the sounds of it, held an electric charge inside.

"I decided to save the last part of his surgery so you could see, love." Silas dropped the steel rod down with a clang onto the wooden floor, before his gaze once again met Elish's. "One wrong move, and just like that... he's dead."

Silas pinched the next prong between the pliers, his eyes watching Elish's every movement, drinking in his fear once again. He gave out a cold laugh and to Elish's horror he started to push the metal prong deeper into Jade's head.

The boy screamed and at the same time Elish held out his hands and screamed, "Silas, no!"

"Why?" Silas's smooth and dangerous voice whispered, drawing out the next prong.

"Just be careful... be careful." Elish's voice raised another octave, to a tone he had never heard in himself. "Please... be careful with him."

Another prong dropped to the floor with its metal clang. Jade whimpered, a trail of drool and snot running down his face. Elish tried to read him for any sanity but every scan of his face brought out only the fear and pain the boy was feeling.

"Why should I not just kill him, Elish?"

Jade shrieked as Silas pinched the prong with the pliers and started pulling the thin metal rod up above his head. "Save you your pride."

Unable to control himself, his once steeled countenance and unbreakable pride a ruin on the floors, Elish's face twisted in agony. He was watching Silas kill the boy right in front of him. Elish completely caught in his spider web, unable to escape the Ghost King and his games. He felt like nothing but a fly waiting for the final venomous blow.

He was helpless...

How did I let it get to this?

Elish stretched out a hand and shook his head, watching as Jade's eyes rolled back into his skull. "Please, King Silas… don't, don't hurt him."

In the darkness a cold laugh echoed off of the walls, and like poison it sunk into Elish's skin and paralyzed him. With his hands outstretched he felt a burning behind his eyes that stung him like smoke. They were starting to well with unshed tears.

Another prong dropped, and faster than Silas should have, he pulled another one out.

"Why, Elish?"

Stop hurting him… stop hurting him… I swear… I swear I will take away everything you have ever loved and ever will if you kill him in front of me…

Another scream came from Jade's lips, and with that a rush of panic ripped through Elish's body like he had been struck by lightning. Acting on this rare display Silas only laughed, before taking the last prong and with a violent shove, pushing Jade's head down to the floor. Silas put a hand down the boy's pants and gave the most demonic, foreboding laugh Elish had ever heard.

The king looked up at Elish, his eyes green flames of a fire so evil Elish's chest rocked.

Then with a bellowed scream Elish pushed Silas off Jade, shoving him to the floor. Elish grabbed the boy into his arms and held him tight against his chest, tears running down his face.

With a muffled cry, a foreign tone to the once carved from ice chimera, he held him.

"Because I love him, I love him. Don't hurt him."

A small sob broke Elish's lips. "I love him."

His throat tightened and his chest trembled; he reached behind the boy's head and pulled out the last prong. It dropped onto the floor with the same clang though it was muffled by Elish's own hammering heart.

Elish held Jade and closed his eyes tight; he sniffed and took in the boy's aura, his scent, and his being, and said to him quietly, "I love you."

There was a pause, a heavy silence, then a small whimpered voice sounded, barely audible from Elish's robes.

"I love you too."

In an act that only sealed Elish's unprecedented state of mind, he let out a strangled laugh, before squeezing the boy tighter. Then with a sniff he kissed the boy's head and didn't let him go.

For what seemed like hours, but in reality had only been half a minute there was silence in the voided room, before, with the clicking of boots, Silas rose to his feet.

"Such a sweet display," the Ghost King said in an eerie calm voice. "And are you ready to receive your punishment, gelus vir?"

Elish felt the boy's warm blood dampening his hair, small trickles from the holes inside Jade's skull. Elish held him tight against his body, knowing that not even death would pry the boy from his grasp. This was where Jade would stay, no matter what Silas said next. Even if it ruined everything he had built within himself for almost ninety years, he would not let go of this boy.

"Yes," Elish whispered, knowing there was nothing more for him to say. He kept his eyes closed and braced himself for whatever horrors Silas had dreamed up for him.

"Your punishment for murdering me in front of your brothers, for defying me, is one I have found most suited for you," Silas growled. Elish heard a scrape of metal against wood which could only be the driver. He put both of his hands over Jade's head to protect him from the blow he knew could be coming.

"I sentence you, Elish Dekker, to misery, to an immortal lifetime of imprisonment, daily emotional agony –"

"Silas, no!" Elish screamed, but the king went on.

"A life that, I assure you, will become a living hell, that will devour every shred of pride you have and leave you as a shadow without dignity, self-respect, or prestige." A cold laugh echoed around the room, before he delivered the final blow.

"Or as they called it before the Fallocaust… marriage."

Elish froze, as if his swirling and tormented mind couldn't comprehend what he had just heard.

Elish raised his head and saw Silas looming over him, his arms crossed over his chest, with a grin on his face that seeped self-satisfaction.

"What?" Elish's tone dropped.

"Congratulations on your engagement, golden boy." Silas unfolded his arms before turning to the darkness of the room around them. "Turn on the lights, boys; let's get this done before he finds a way out of it."

Elish stared at Silas, but a moment later a blinding light flooded the room, then suddenly the buzzing in his ears was gone, replaced by the sound of over twenty chimeras. They were sitting around in banquet chairs, a thick black curtain separating both sides that quickly rose up to the ceiling. Everyone was there: Garrett, Joaquin, Perish, Kessler and his family, and over a dozen others, sitting in a room decorated for a wedding reception.

They sat, they laughed, and cheered, before each one started banging on the table in front of them, in a steady quickening rhythm, making their wine glasses rattle up and down, plates full of appetizers as well, and even the vases filled with purple and black roses.

It had been a set-up, all this time.

"You've got to be kidding me," Elish growled, but the sound of his dangerous tone only made Silas's smile widen. He raised his arms.

"On your feet, love. I will not marry you as you grovel at me like a common peasant, rise up."

"Elish?" Jade whimpered in his chest. Elish brought the boy away from his hold and looked down at his pale sweaty face.

"It's alright…" Elish couldn't hide the bitterness rising in his throat, mixed in with the humiliation, confusion, and the disappearing remnants of the consuming fear he had only felt moments ago. "It's –" Elish felt a growl rise in his throat, as every intense emotion he had just exhibited turned into blinding hatred and rage. He glared at King Silas and held onto the boy tight; it was all he could do to not kill Silas where he stood.

You fucking trickster… you fucking trickster, this is how you humiliate me? By this? This is your master plan? Killing the boy would be too easy wouldn't it? I swear on our immortal lives…

"Elish? Come now, it's not that bad, stand up, at least the bloody boy is alive, yes?" Garrett's cheery voice sounded behind him, mixed in with the chattering and busy atmosphere of his chimera brothers. Every one of them was ready to witness the conclusion to Silas's newest game. Elish didn't even want to accept the fact that they had also seen everything that had just gone on as well. Every tear, every plea; his brothers had seen everything.

"Elish…?" Garrett's voice could be heard again.

"Don't touch me," Elish whirled around and snapped; he went to walk away with the boy when he felt Jade's hand tighten around his chest.

"Elish?" he whispered.

With the room overflowing with talking, Silas off to the side talking to Sanguine, making plans for their union. Elish petted the boy's hair back and said again, possibly more to himself than to the cicaro, "It's alright."

"You're growling..." he whimpered. "I've never felt you so angry."

Elish felt his body around him and realized he was shaking with rage, a red haze creeping up along the rims of his eyes, threatening to overtake him with the same uncontrollable anger that made him kill Silas in the first place.

"It's alright..." Elish said again, it seemed to be the only thing he could say to the boy at the moment.

Jade looked up at him, his dim yellow eyes heavy like he had just woken up from a long sleep. He raised a weak hand and touched it against Elish's cheek.

Immediately the chimera felt his heart soften, a small weakness in the sculpted ice that had only grown harder with Silas's words. He looked down and met his eyes with Jade's.

"You don't have to do this," Jade whispered to him.

Elish stared down at him, wondering how foolish it was that the boy believed they had a choice; he opened his mouth to tell him just that when his memories took him.

So long ago, Silas had moved his first chess piece, had made his game known. The night in Stadium when Silas had arranged for Ares and Siris to kill Jade's mother. Jade had smashed the window and Elish had grabbed him before he had jumped out, knowing for sure the boy was about to jump to his death. Jump into the game Silas had set up.

I had whispered that to him, and though he thought I had meant he didn't need to avenge his mother's death, I had meant he didn't need to play Silas's game.

You don't have to do this...

I am playing into his game, like he wanted. I am getting angry, for I have every right to be angry, but that is what he wants... that is what he wants for me.

"Well, get up then, loves," Silas called. Everyone around them laughed and started banging on the table.

Elish looked down at the boy, and as Jade gazed back up at him he felt the hot anger start to drip away, until nothing but frustration and annoyance remained.

The boy was right... I don't have to do this. I don't have to play.

"Alright," Elish said quietly. He put his hand over Jade's and held it to his cheek, before he helped the boy rise to his feet.

CHAPTER 41

HE HELD ME UP; THOUGH I THINK I COULD HAVE stood on my own two feet it didn't seem like he was going to let me. He held onto me with hands as strong as steel traps, clutching me to him like I was his most valuable possession, fending off the beasts that surrounded him, daring one of them to come near me again.

My mind was eerily calm, and I think it was because for once in our time as master and pet, I had to be the one to set the precedent for how this was going to go. I had to show him I was going to be okay, even if inside I was pulling out my hair and screaming. Perhaps I was at the point mentally where my brain had shorted out, filled with too many emotions to the point where everything had shut down. My mind had blown a fuse, but in the blackout I felt inside of me, my other senses were now functioning better than they had in weeks.

I had to keep Elish calm, even though I was sure as soon as we got home he would kill me, if only for an outlet to unleash his humiliation.

I was getting married… to Elish.

My god, I could feel his anger radiating off him and sinking into the marrow of my bones; he was livid to a point where I didn't know how he was containing it. I had to get my master home, away from his family and safe into a quiet environment, into his environment.

Silas cleared his throat. I looked behind me, still being held by Elish, and saw that Silas was holding in his hand a small notebook. To his side was who I assumed was our ring bearer, Sanguine. He was holding two black roses, each with a silver ring tucked between the flower and the stem.

"Gentlemen... and Ellis." Silas smiled and spread his hands in a welcoming manner. I felt Sanguine's hand on my shoulder drawing me back. Elish loosened his grasp and let me take a step away from him, until we were standing facing each other like the people in the movies did.

"We are gathered here to see a very unique union... a marriage between Elish Sebastian Dekker to Jade Shadow Dekker. A master and a cicaro, which at this point –" Silas paused for a second and I could feel the grin on his face. "– is now dissolved."

We were no longer master and pet? I glanced up at Elish and felt my shoulders slump underneath the icy glare he was giving me. I felt like shouting that this wasn't my plan at all, but I just stood there and trembled.

"Now we will have equals, in all aspects, in all chains of command. Jade, you are no longer a cicaro; you are now an equal to Elish."

Oh fuck, he is going to kill me...

A hush filled the room, and I think at that moment every chimera who was watching us was thinking the exact same thing. That at any moment Elish was going to snap again and murder every single one of us. This would be too much for my chimera's unbreakable pride and dignity. I was nothing but shit on his shoe as he had told me on many occasions, a slumrat, a gutterwhore, I was the worst chimera of all of them and lower than even Drake.

Now I was equal to him? I wouldn't be surprised if he took me out into the greywastes and shot me in the back of the head.

"It brings me great pleasure to be the one to join this union; Elish is my first born chimera and my prince. He is your older brother, your counsel, and your rock as he is mine. I love him very much and it brings me great joy to punish him, I mean... *give him* this gift," Silas continued.

There was some nervous laughter behind us; all I could do was stare at Elish's chest as it rose up and down, his rapid heartbeat matching the quickened rhythm of my own. I couldn't look at him, though I knew his eyes were probably burning a hole in the back of my head.

"Elish Sebastian Dekker... do you take Jade Shadow Dekker as your lawfully wedded husband?" Silas's voice dropped to a smooth, slippery purr, full of derision and condescending glee. This was no inside joke between us; every chimera in this room knew what Silas was doing to Elish in this moment.

As Silas's words faded, a tension descended on us, so thick I could see it fill the room. It condensed the very essence of time around us until it became the consistency of molasses, slowing down the natural expense of time to what seemed like the millisecond.

"I do."

My chest unclenched at this, from relief or just surprise that he said it I didn't know. What was important was that he was still standing still, and he hadn't attacked me or Silas yet.

Around me I could also hear a collective sigh, though from the auras that touched the fringes of my own I knew there were a few of them that were hoping to see Elish snap.

"Excellent," Silas murmured before he said to me, "and you? Jade Shadow Dekker, do you take Elish as your lawfully wedded husband?"

I nodded, though I still couldn't look at him. "I do."

I heard Garrett whoop behind us, breaking the tension around the room which I knew was probably driving the most conflict-hating chimera crazy. Everyone chuckled and I heard Sanguine's boot steps. I looked over to him and saw him hand me a rose, and one to Elish too. A ring was nestled in the top of the stem.

I withdrew the ring, and looked at it; it was a silver band with three stones, one black, one purple, and one white.

"Elish? Put the ring on his finger, and say something nice, love." Silas's voice still didn't hide his enjoyment as he watched Elish's inner turmoil.

I felt him take my hand and gently slip the ring onto my finger, before he said to me in a quiet voice, "I have learned more about myself being around you for two years, than I have in the eighty-seven I have experienced without you."

I smiled shyly, though I still couldn't look at him, and slipped the ring onto his finger with trembling hands, my mind racing at what I was supposed to say.

"Jade? Or is your brain too scrambled to form a proper sentence?" Silas said acerbically behind me.

I tried to find the words, but every time I attempted to find a string to the racing thoughts they left me as quickly as I found them. I looked up at him, and as a weakness set into my legs and a hot dizziness flushed my system, I managed to say quietly,

"Thank you."

He caught me as I fell over, and the ground disappeared underneath me, and as darkness overtook my fleeting consciousness I heard Silas say with a low cold laugh.

"I now pronounce you… husband and husband, two equal partners. Enjoy eternity, golden boy. Kiss him."

As Elish held me I felt him take my chin into his hand and he raised it; then I felt his lips against mine.

I fell back into unconsciousness.

I came to, to the feeling of soft robes against my cheek, and the distinct smell of mint and nutmeg. I squinted my eyes and looked around, realizing with an insurmountable relief that we were back in Elish's apartment.

He was holding me and we were on the couch. I looked around wondering if this was the same dream that I had been having ever since the Crimstones took me, wondering if at any moment I could be plunged back into that cold isolation, that dark room with the swinging bodies.

But no… I was home?

How could I be so lucky to be home with him? In his arms, the ones that wrapped around me and held me to his chest like I was his prize and his prize only. There is no luck in the world that would grant me this solace.

My time with the Crimstones had been terrifying, painful, and humiliating, even the thought left me burying my head into his robes.

"Is the light too bright?" a quiet voice, that still held its cold tones, said to me.

I shook my head, and felt him brush my bangs away from my forehead. "Then why are you hiding from me?"

I took in his fragrant scent, and felt his shorter hair tickle against my ear. "If I open my eyes, I'll know this is just a dream."

Elish ran his long graceful fingers along my jawline, before gently drawing my face up.

I saw his purple eyes, staring down at mine; he looked tired and I realized he must not have woken up long before me.

He looked over every inch of my face, before drawing his hand over the back of my head. I winced as he found the healing scabs where Perish and Sid had performed their surgeries. A faint memory that was a thousand miles away from me, nothing but a small narration of which I barely had a visual image. I just knew it had happened, and that I had lay drugged and in a stupor in the hospital bed for over a week.

"You seem okay, I was worried..." Elish found my hands and looked at them, they were not bandaged anymore; he had unwrapped the bindings while I was asleep. "They seemed to do a fair job with you and your teeth as well. Do you remember anything?"

I ran my tongue over my pointed metal and porcelain teeth and shook my head.

Then I held up a hand, seven stitches on each side of my palms, which had had thick nails driven through them. Thankfully, they had missed my tendons. "The last three weeks have been a blur, I barely remember..." I let that hang, not wanting to foul his mood.

"When Silas married us?" Sure enough, Elish's tone dropped down to frigid waters, my heart skipped inside my chest. "Equality in the eyes of my family, I bet that makes you happy doesn't it, dear husband?"

The last two words sent a shockwave down my gut. "I know nothing changes," I said hurriedly, stumbling over my own words like I had just mentally tripped down a flight of stairs. "Don't... don't think so low of me that I'd assume we were equals. I'm not taking my collar off, you... you know me better than –"

"Shush... I know, Cicaro, I know. Don't get yourself worked up," Elish said quietly. "I am sure the union will only get brought up when you are throwing one of your classic tantrums and I will deal with it then."

I looked down at my hands and saw I was wearing my wedding ring now; I couldn't help the spark in my heart when I realized he was too.

We were silent for a moment, both of us looking at our matching wedding bands and enjoying being alone in the apartment together. Safe and in silence, away from judging eyes and the scathing presence that was Silas.

"How quickly did you get out of there after I passed out?" I asked, resting my head back onto his shoulder. I made my ring shine in the light of the fire. It had three small stones in it, one white, one black and one purple; Elish's colours, the same pattern of gemstones he had in his pierced ears.

"Rather quickly. Garrett was kind enough to distract Silas for a few moments as I took you and left, no one stopped me for obvious reasons," Elish responded, but a moment later I felt the mood change around him.

His voice grew colder. "So you are aware of it, he let Kerres go. He made a point to tell me that, after you had lost consciousness."

I raised my head but he pushed it back down onto his chest. "Why?"

"To anger me of course."

The emotions inside of me were mixed. I was happy he was still alive... but his last words to me haunted my memory. Would he still try and get me to go back to Moros? Or back to the remaining Crimstones?

I sighed and was silent for a long time.

But still something weighed on me...

There was something that I remembered, and I didn't think he knew I was conscious during it. It was when I was between Silas and Elish, everything that went on in that room between the two of them.

"Elish, can I ask you something? May I speak freely?" I asked quietly.

There were a few more moments of silence before he answered. "Yes."

"With everything that happened, when you talked to Silas about Sky... when Silas broke down and he did that thing with my head, and afterwards... he saved my life by pushing me between you two..." I saw parts of Silas I had never seen before. I had seen his heart as he exposed it to Elish and though he had forced Elish to marry me, it was nothing compared to what he could have done to us. Silas had... I hated to even think it, but he had shown love towards Elish. Though I could never outright ask him if Silas was as bad as I thought, I decided to ask him something else. "Are you still going through with your plan with Reaver? I know I don't know him like you do, but seeing that side of him come out... it's confusing, I guess. I had never seen him as anything but heartless, cruel, manipulative and well... evil."

Elish remained in his silence, only leaning over to pick up a mug of tea for me, and one for himself. "I praise you on your wording of that question. The notion of you thinking Silas is a good king in any respect would anger me, but the way you phrased it... I understand your confusion." Elish took a drink of his tea, slow and drawn-out. I knew he was thinking of his own way to word his next response.

"King Silas did a dangerous thing in that building, *maritus*. He showed me weakness, and not only did he show me weakness... he broke down in front of me, and in his pain he only gave me strength by repairing you." My body went cold as every frozen word left his lips; I saw a dark glint in his eye. "I was able to turn the tables on him with nothing more than a wild card pulled from my sleeve, and with that card I turned my Ghost into a snivelling mess, so broken down and defeated he turned to me for strength..."

I gaped at him, surprised at the cold words that were coming from his mouth. "But you sympathized with him, Master. I heard you... you seemed like you genuinely cared. That was all to manipulate him?" I couldn't even tell he was doing it; he was a master of his craft.

"I exposed my own emotions to him, yes, I had to sacrifice a part of myself to save you, but in return he bore me the most delicious and forbidden of fruit. We drank of each other but in the end... look at where we are? I am safe, as are you, and though he sits in his tower as smug as a cat with a bird in his mouth, I am here with someone he could never dream of having. Someone who is my complete opposite, in every way, from our light and dark appearance to the contents of our hearts, minds, and souls."

"What do you mean?" I asked cautiously.

"Hot and cold, light and dark, black and white... we are opposites Jade, no one can deny that, but together we form a rather unstoppable force." Elish moved himself on the couch and I shifted off him, watching as he rose to the towering figure he was. He walked towards the skyscraper with his tea in hand and I followed him.

"I meant what I said. I have learned more with you than I ever have being alone, and I realized in this time that together we do indeed complete each other, whether my pride wanted to admit it or not. When I am overcome by anger, or emotion, you cool me down, as I do you. Together we will temper each other and together, master and cicaro, we will put this plan into effect and usurp that Ghost King from his throne."

I stared in awe, and watched his reflection in the windows as he drew the tea up to his lips.

"That man will regret the day he showed me weakness, and with that missing scale in his armour I will drive my sword into him until he is nothing but a writhing dog waiting for the last strike. That day is coming, Jade, and with you by my side I will rule the world he destroyed." I saw a dangerous smile appear on his lips, and a dark energy that I had never tasted before.

Perhaps this is not as cut and dried as I thought... I watched Elish, smiling at the twinkling lights of Skyland, and the faint images of cars going up and down the roads. I saw for a moment in my mind the broken king that I realized Silas was, and the cold, hyperintelligent chimera that loomed over him. One with a thousand dark omens on his shoulder and Reaver the immortal killer tucked securely in his pocket...

For once I didn't see the Mad King as an all-powerful deity, gone crazy with power with only the thirst for pain in his heart. I saw the broken boy who begged Elish, as he collapsed into his arms sobbing, to resurrect his long dead boyfriend; I saw a man who was surrounded by family but who had a heart that still belonged to the man named Sky.

I saw Elish create that man, only to steal him away from the lonely king, to raise him instead as a weapon.

Yeah... this wasn't so cut and dried; this wasn't as simple as overthrowing a Mad King. Elish was the one driving him to this madness. Through seeds planted and strings pulled... I couldn't help but wonder if this could've all been fixed years ago if he would've just given him Chimera X. Then Silas would've had the partner that he wanted, right? Wouldn't that have cured his jealousy towards his fellow chimeras having lovers? He would've had Sky back, or at least someone genetically engineered to be like him.

My body went cold with a realization that made me nauseas. With all my might I pushed it down and tried to remember everything bad Silas had ever done to me, though I couldn't help but flood my head with explanations and justifications as to what had driven this immortal to those actions. It was the empath in me, this I knew. I saw things through Silas's eyes, and saw the internal pain of losing the one you loved.

Not just that, but one who had sought out a way to kill himself, all to get away from Silas. What a heart-breaking existence, to roam the world and surround yourself with creatures engineered to be devoted to you, only to yearn for the true love you lost.

– But what did it matter? I would follow Elish to the ends of the earth, no matter his cause, no matter his plans. I loved him with every breath I had in my chest, no matter what cruel intentions he had underneath that frozen smile.

Then in my mind I heard his sweet words, whispered into my ear as he held me and drew the last metal rod out of my head.

He had said he loved me… Elish loved me.

I took Elish's hand and held it, and he held mine back.

My eyes found his through the reflection of the window, and I raised my mug of tea. Then I turned to him and said with a small, almost shy, smile.

"Long live the king."

A half-smirk appeared on Elish's face; he raised his own mug and chinked it against mine.

"Long live the king, Cicaro," he said, before leaning down and kissing me.

THE END

A NOTE FROM QUIL

And so ends the first companion book in The Fallocaust Series. Nothing can ever be black and white can it? Every person has a reason for being who they are, and it seems in this world there is no such thing as just being evil. Everyone is good and evil; it just depends on your perspective and whose eyes you're looking through. In a way, this is what I want the companion books to be about; you get to see the other side. Perhaps one day we can see King Silas's side of the story. Though there is no 'official' plan yet, I do plan on letting the king explain himself one day.

Well, once again, thank you for taking the time to read my book. We will meet again for Book 2: The Ghost and the Darkness, as well as its companion book which has yet to be named but will be from the point of view of one of my favourite characters: Sanguine.

I would also like to take this moment to thank Jon who has been with me from the beginning, when Fallocaust was just an idea in my head inspired by a Rob Zombie song. Thank you for your continued support, and Jon… thanks for listening to me talk about Fallocaust for the past five years of our lives.

As always, if you want to view excerpts, hear updates, be my friend or just say hi, my Facebook is /quil.carter, my twitter is @Fallocaust and my main website is www.quilcarter.com.

And thank you, for allowing me to tell my boys' stories. I love them a lot, they're always in my head and I hope they will stick in yours too.

Sincerely,

Quil Carter

Printed in Great Britain
by Amazon